TELEKINETIC

TELEKINETIC

BOOK I OF THE ADVANCED SAGA

Love you guys! ♡

Rani Divine

RANI DIVINE

To order additional copies of this book, contact:

Xlibris LLC

1-888-795-4274

www.Xlibris.com

Orders@Xlibris.com

128185

CONTENTS

Dedicated to

Karen
for being my best friend and for always supporting me

AJ
for being there to guide me and teach me, always with a smile on your face

Tiffany
for always reading my first drafts and never saying they're terrible

Casey
for never tiring of listening to me talk about my writing
and never letting me give up

I love you all
This one's for you

The Future

The precise year is unknown. It was one of the many things that was forgotten after the Crash of the twenty-third century and will likely never be remembered. What is remembered is this:

War broke out in the late twenty-third century, nuclear explosions wiping out over half of the global population. Once the world's most powerful cities, New York, Washington DC, Hong Kong, Tokyo, Berlin, London, and Paris were turned to ash under the power of nuclear bombings.

The world as we once knew it was gone, and everything had changed. The majority of technological resources had been destroyed, and people were fighting to stay alive. People slept with P90s and MP5s at their sides, fully loaded and ready to kill anyone who woke them—they lived in constant fear both day and night, afraid of everyone, even the people they loved.

World governments still existed, but the majority of the people chose to ignore what was said to them by government officials. The war continued. Soldiers mindlessly obeyed the tyrants who governed the countries of the world, and people died for reasons only politicians knew.

In the midst of the fighting, somehow science managed to survive. A scientist named Marcus Admiri developed a drug that would prolong a human's life span, aging them only to an average of thirty years before halting it completely and unlocking new advancements of the human brain, allowing individuals to develop new and unheard-of powers, which Marcus called "gifts."

Marcus estimated that there would be an eighty-seven percent success rate if they gave the treatment to every person on the planet, and he announced his breakthrough on C532—five hundred and thirty two days after the final nuclear bomb was set off.

The world accepted his scientific breakthrough as the one thing that would finally bring them out of the darkness. Marcus was then joined by dozens of scientists and asked to develop enough of his treatment to give to the remaining people of the world—approximately two million.

The treatment was soon dispersed among the people of the world—men, women, and children alike. When the treatments were procured and injected into each human, fifteen percent died due to allergic reactions to the serum, forty percent received positive advancements in their abilities, and the rest remained purely human, their bodies simply disposing of the injected treatment. When all the abilities were catalogued, those who remained purely human suddenly realized their mistake—the newly dubbed "Advanced" were now much more powerful than they would ever be.

Marcus soon discovered that those who remained completely human would forever remain human. The treatment had been absorbed completely by the bloodstream, blocking any further attempts to create advancements in them.

Less than a year after the treatment was given to the public, concentration camps were set up outside of every remaining city, and the Advanced were forced inside. The humans did this on the grounds that the Advanced were no longer human, so they no longer had the rights of humans. In their eyes, the Advanced were nothing but animals. The docile, or "stable," Advanced were sent to the camps, and those whose advancements were deemed unsafe or "unstable" by the remaining governments of the world were sentenced to immediate death.

Some of the humans did not agree with what the governments had done to the Advanced, and still some Advanced hid among the ranks of the humans, disguised as those on whom the treatment had no effect. By C579, it was discovered that the Advanced were not able to bear children with each other but that it was still possible for them to pass along the advancements if they bore children with pure humans.

Soon after, the humans began to experiment on the Advanced, searching for one of two things: a cure for their advancements or a way to make themselves Advanced. These actions caused a split between the ranks of the humans. The group that broke off from the humans called themselves the Purists, for they desired to remain human, while the main ranks remained the Humans, desiring more advancements than even the Advanced now held. Still the Advanced lay low, living in the camps under heavy guard from the Humans, waiting for their time to come. The Purists broke off from the Human cities, building their own camps in the vast emptiness left by the dead after the war.

By C600, the Arctic and Antarctic were completely abandoned, most cold regions following in their footsteps; Europe and Africa were controlled by the Purists; the Americas, along with Australia, were controlled by the Humans; and Asia was left to the nomadic Advanced, those whose gifts were too unstable for them to be left with the general public but whose abilities also prevented them from easily being destroyed. The remaining Advanced still lived in the camps outside the majority of the Human cities, biding their time.

Every few years, the Advanced asked the Humans to give them one thing: one continent on which they could live their lives in peace, away from all the humans.

But the Humans knew something that the Advanced did not. Due to the large amounts of crossbreeding, the Advanced now vastly outnumbered the Humans, and they feared the Advanced more than ever before.

Finally, the Advanced had enough of the Humans, and the war between the peoples of earth began once again.

The Advanced broke out of their camps. They overtook all major cities in the world and began to massacre the Humans. Anyone caught in the middle was destroyed—any Humans that sided with the Advanced were slaughtered by their own, and the same would happen to the few Advanced who sided with the Humans. Everywhere the Advanced went, they destroyed all forms of life in the name of the Superiors—those they had named their leaders, including the scientist, Marcus Admiri. They then began to build in secret a city at the center of the vast desert that was once Africa, and the city was called Admiri, after Marcus himself.

When the city was finally complete, the sheer size of it was enough to house half of the Advanced population, and they began their pilgrimage to Admiri. Within their ranks were those who could sense the others' abilities, and they used them to ensure that no human would ever enter the ranks of the Advanced.

Among those who made the pilgrimage were teleporters, Advanced with telekinetic and telepathic abilities, and those who could give or take advancements with a single thought. Some could run at the speed of light, others had grown wings and could fly, and still others developed a massive amount of strength or healing.

When Admiri was fully populated, two other cities were built—the second, in the previously unmanned Arctic, was called Mettirna; and the third, in the empty space that was once filled by the city of Washington DC, was called Athena, after the Greek goddess. The three cities held the majority of the population of the Advanced, with several small Advanced camps scattered across the continents; and whenever any Advanced was found outside these cities, they were killed by the Purists and experimented on by the Humans until they either died or went mad from torture.

In secret, the Advanced began to develop their own technology, a bioweapon that would specifically target humans, leaving the Advanced unharmed in its wake. The weapon was unsuccessful, but as of C1995, the scientists were on the verge of a breakthrough.

The war continued, with the Advanced standing strong in their cities and the Purists almost constantly laying siege to them. However, though the situation was dire, the teleporters and flyers soon discovered that the human population had greatly diminished; and even though the Advanced could not bear children, their numbers held strong, high above the number of humans.

In the year 2438, before the war, before the treatment, Karyn Willow gave birth to her first son, Jameson, named after his deceased father, who had died six months before his son was born. Three years later, in 2441, Miriam Kahrin gave birth to her first daughter and named her Reem, after her mother. Jameson was born in what was once Canada, and Reem in what was once India. The two children were raised on separate continents, and when the treatment was given to the public, both received it, and both were the only humans in their families on whom the treatment was successful. Their families both disowned them and sent them to the camps, where they were marked by branding an "X" onto the skin of their right wrists and catalogued. Reem was catalogued as a class two telekinetic and deemed safe to keep in the camps, and Jameson as a class five teleporter, the highest class of any advancement, and deemed unsafe and sentenced to death. But when Jameson was sentenced, a second ability manifested itself inside him—the ability to make anyone who heard his voice obey him—and he convinced the guards that he was a class one telepathic, nothing more, nothing less. When the cities were built, both Reem and Jameson went on the pilgrimage, Reem settling in Admiri and Jameson in a small camp outside Athena.

After the siege on the cities began, Reem and Jameson still fought for the rights and protection of all the Advanced. Jameson, being a teleporter, took many other Advanced outside the city walls for food and supplies and, while on one of these trips, discovered that his abilities were still growing. He now had the ability to both give and take abilities to and from other Advanced and humans. On many occasions, he tricked the humans into giving the Advanced free food, water, and supplies and had also turned many humans into Advanced, with any power they could dream of.

Reem, on the other hand, discovered that though she had been branded a class two, she was now a class five, the highest level of telekinesis ever found in an Advanced. She was able to use her ability to aid her people in the war, able to fire off an entire clip of bullets straight up into the air, and guide each one to a different target using only her mind. The leaders of the Advanced placed her far back in the ranks and had her use a sniper rifle to take out the most skilled of all Humans and Purists. Though Reem was taught as a child that the front lines were the place of greatest honor in any battle, every Advanced in the world knew of the special abilities of Reem Kahrin, and she was a great aid to her people.

It is now C2200, and Reem Kahrin still resides in Admiri. The people of Admiri refer to her as their savior and think of her as the one who will save the Advanced from the siege of Admiri. Tomorrow Reem is to be sent to the city of Athena. A message was received stating that the city may soon fall, and the Superiors called for the best of the best to be sent to their aid in the hope that the city would remain an Advanced stronghold.

Three teleporters were sent to Admiri, and tomorrow, the best of the best will be sent back with them. Reem Kahrin has been paired with Jameson Willow, the best teleporter in the land, as the Superiors believed that the best should be sent with the best.

Reem was to be sent with the one thing the Advanced had fighting for them: the bioweapon.

Reem rose and dressed for battle though she knew that she had never and most likely never would see the front lines of any battle. She packed what few things she needed for the journey: ammunition, various weapons the Superiors had suggested she bring along, and, of course, the bioweapon. She hoped against hope that she wouldn't have to use it, but she knew that it could very well be a possibility, which was why the Superiors had assigned to her the greatest teleporter in all of the Advanced cities. He would be her way out, her guardian. Many people didn't think that she would need such a thing, but she was aware that teleporting was one gift that she would never master and that it was a gift that she may very well need. He would arrive within moments, and they would be on their way; however, the trip wouldn't be as quick as many would assume. She was, after all, the beacon of hope throughout all Advanced cities.

Her long brown hair fell past her shoulders, halfway down her back. She pulled it back into a bun so it wouldn't be in the way on the mission. She looked up into the mirror and her piercing dark brown eyes stared back. She caught the slight silver reflection that was contained in them, glinting in the sunlight. She'd never known why her eyes were the strange combination of brown and silver, but it seemed that anyone who looked into them couldn't help but listen to whatever she had to say.

She turned away from the mirror, collecting her thoughts.

Soon the Superiors would have her and her guard walk through the village, gaining support and spreading hope through all the villagers before their journey. This process was very tedious, but Reem had always known that it aided her people greatly. She lived and breathed for them. She would die for them in a heartbeat. As she readied herself and completed packing her backpack, there was a soft knock on the metal door that enclosed her in the small room she had come to call home.

"Enter," she said, not turning to face the door.

"Ma'am, Jameson Willow, teleporter, to see you," said Peter, her bodyguard.

"Let him in, Peter." She turned to face the door while throwing her pack over her shoulder.

The man who entered the room was in and of himself a beacon of hope for their people. He was well known as the great teleporter, the man who could make humans bow to him, and the man who could make a human Advanced. Many humans even desired for him to give them advancements, though the Superiors would never allow that.

He was dressed in the same battle garb as she: desert camouflage; dark heavy boots; and a backpack over his left shoulder. His shaggy hair was uneven and unkempt, like he never cared for it and cut it with a razor blade, but its dark chocolate color made up for his mistakes in hair care, and his face looked as though it was covered in a few days' unshaven stubble.

At first, she saw him as not unlike any of her men—tired of the war and bitter about the losses—but when his face finally turned upward and he looked her in the eye, she lost all sense of time and space. For in those deep green eyes she saw more than she had ever seen in any of her men: she saw love. She had never known an Advanced to love, for it was well known that they could not bear offspring, and so the Superiors deemed it unnecessary. But in his eyes, she saw a love of his people, a love for his family, a deep love that she never would have suspected to be there. His deep green eyes held hers for what seemed like ages, and when he finally spoke, his deep, husky voice was exactly the voice she would have pegged him with—at least she got one thing right.

"So you're the almighty Reem Kahrin?" he asked mockingly.

"It would seem that way, yes," she replied. "And you are the almighty Jameson Willow, class seven teleporter."

"I would not say almighty, but Jameson I am, and by the Superiors' orders, I am yours to command," he responded, dipping his head slightly.

"Then we should be on our way. Our people would like to see us off."

"Again, only by the Superiors' orders."

"The people desire to see their warriors off to battle, and they shall. As you said, you are under orders of the Superiors to do whatever I command you, and we will both walk out among our people and give them hope." At that, he laughed mockingly in her face, causing her to respond bitterly, "You do not believe in giving the people hope?"

"I didn't believe them when they told me you would preach to me about hope."

"I only speak what I know to be true."

"Same difference. Let's go." He turned and walked back out the door, expecting her to follow, and so she did, pushing the strap of her pack farther up on her shoulder as she walked out the door.

The city was beautiful in the early-morning light; the Superiors had built it to be so. Every building in the center was a skyscraper—holding thousands upon thousands of Advanced within their walls. As you moved closer to the edge of the city, the smaller the buildings got. It was deemed safest by the Superiors to house the brunt of the people in the center, where they would be safe. The Superiors had thought of everything when it came to the building of the city. It was perfect. And to Reem, it was home.

Once they finished their walk around the homes of the city, the three travelers and their assigned teleporters met in the very center of the city—the home of the Superiors. The Superiors saw them off, giving them each a sip of wine to represent the blood of the Advanced that had been shed in the city and the blood that would be paid for their deaths.

The teleporters then discussed with the Superiors what routes they would be taking—Jameson's being the fastest, as he could teleport the farthest without exhausting himself. Once the routes were approved, the Superiors left them alone, and the three travelers joined them.

Reem approached Jameson warily, and he smiled a crooked smile at her. "You've never teleported before, have you?" he asked.

"No. Never," she responded as he walked around her.

"Don't worry. It's not hard. Just take a deep breath and—" He reached out, grabbed her shoulder, and teleported all in the same second. When they landed in a previously determined "safe zone," she gasped and jumped away from him.

"What was that?" she demanded.

"We teleported." He smiled. "Sorry, ma'am, I couldn't resist seeing your reaction when I did that."

"Never do that again," she ordered.

"Yes, ma'am." He dipped his head slightly.

"How many more teleports?"

"Five."

"So many?"

"The others make the trip in seven, and they rest for two nights. Which would you prefer?"

"Okay, I see your point. Let's keep moving. I don't like being out of the city."

"Yes, ma'am."

"Don't call me that."

"Then what should I call you?"

"Call me Reem."

"Ready, Reem?" he asked, placing his hand gently on her shoulder.

"Yes," she said a mere second before he teleported them.

Killer

"What the hell was that?" Jameson shouted as soon as they landed in the safe zone.

"How far out are we?" Reem asked.

"Answer my question!"

"That weapon's power will reach us unless we are over two hundred miles out. How far out are we?"

He grabbed her by her shirt and teleported again, this time to a farther-out safe zone, several hundred miles away from the city. As they landed, he asked again, "What was that? Tell me." He held firmly to her shoulders and shook her violently.

"You're not cleared for that information. I'm sorry, Jameson. I can't." She freed herself, unmoving from his side.

"Tell me! I have the right to know what you've done to my home!" He pointed his finger at her, being sure not to touch her.

"You have to be cleared before I can tell you anything. I'm sorry." She turned and faced the city, barely visible in the distance. It looked so peaceful, but she knew what was really happening there.

"Tell me, Reem," he said, walking up to her and gently placing his hand on her shoulder.

"I can't." She turned toward him and automatically wrapped her arms around him, burying her face in his chest. "I'm sorry."

They took their time setting up camp, neither of them speaking a word. Something about that weapon had affected her, and tears frequented her eyes as they put up a small tent and started the fire. At the moment, Reem was searching for some sort of food inside her bag, while Jameson continued his work on the fire. It wasn't much of a camp, but it would suffice.

"I'm sorry. I don't know what's gotten into me," Reem said, finally breaking the silence.

He turned toward her and nodded. He continued his work on the fire, trying to build it up enough to keep them warm. It would be dark soon.

"Please talk to me," she said.

He acted as though he hadn't heard her and rose to search the area for more wood.

"The weapon," she began, "is a genetically based bioweapon, intended to only kill pure humans."

"Intended to?" he asked, finally answering her.

"The weapon wasn't ready to be used. It wasn't perfected."

"What do you mean?"

"It kills every humanoid within two hundred miles of ground zero."

He dumped more wood on the fire. "Why would the Superiors authorize the creation of anything that would cause so much damage?" he thought aloud, sitting down next to Reem at the fire.

"It was basically a doomsday device. Had it been perfected, it would have been the most beneficial weapon we have."

"But how could they approve it when it wasn't finished?" He clenched his hands into fists.

"It was the only way they saw to end the war in our favor. So many Advanced in the city were already dead, and the rest likely would be within the week. We were losing. The Superiors have only settled the score in their eyes."

"You condone their actions?" he asked, an angry fire filling his eyes as he turned to face her.

"No, I don't. I'm only telling you what they were thinking. I did not want to use the weapon. If it were up to me, I wouldn't have brought it to the city with me. I had no choice."

"We always have a choice." He rose from his seat and went back to collecting wood for the fire.

"I'm sorry I didn't inform you of the weapon's power before I set it off. I know you feel that you could've saved many of them," she said, tears welling up in her eyes when she realized that it was true. "I was given a direct order. I had to obey." She blinked away her tears as she spoke. "I'm sorry. I don't know how I can ever face our people again." As she spoke, she realized that this was much more difficult for him than she had at first realized. He paced along the opposite side of the fire from her, face held low in shame.

"Despite the rumors, I am not the coldhearted warrior that our people say I am. When I joined the Advanced military, I joined only because the Superiors asked that any Advanced with gifts that could aid in the fight join them. I joined to help save our people from the Humans and the Pure.

"When I was given the order, I denied it. But had I not gone through with it, the Superiors would have sent another to make sure that it was done, and I would be sentenced to imprisonment in Admiri. Either way all the people in the city would have died, but this way I remain fully able to protect our people when we return. That is all that I ever wanted to do."

She paused for several long minutes before speaking again, "All I ask is that you think no less of me than you did two days ago. I am still the same person."

"You are as much a murderer as they are," he said, his voice deeply filled with anger. "Don't you tell me that you didn't want to use the weapon. Had you told me about all of this up front, we could have destroyed it and allowed the people of Athena to live." He fell to his knees in front of the fire, his face contorted with pain and anger.

"What would you have done were you in my position?"

"I would have saved them."

"How? My gifts are not suited for saving lives. They can't stop people from dying. How would you have saved them?"

After several long minutes of silence, she knew that she had made her point. He saw her side. "I'm so sorry, Jameson. I never wanted to be a killer . . ." Her voice drifted off as she spoke, and she lay her head in her hands.

They both fell fast asleep, dreaming of the events of the day—the good, the bad, and the conflict that had risen between them.

When Reem woke, the sky was still black, and the fire was almost burned out. The wind had picked up, and she shivered in the cold of the night. She walked to the woodpile Jameson had made and carefully took several pieces from the pile and placed them on the fire.

Wrapping her coat closer to her body, she searched for warmth but received none. She was chilled to the bone, her whole body shaking with each gust of wind. She began to use her gifts to shield herself and the fire from the harsh wind and realized that Jameson was nowhere in sight.

"Jameson?" she called out but heard no reply. She checked the tent—empty. Searched the immediate area around the camp—nothing. He was gone. She called for him again and again to no avail—he had simply vanished.

Jameson sat alone in the forest, far enough away from the camp that it would be unlikely for Reem to find him, but close enough that he would still hear her if anything happened.

He'd left her. He couldn't explain why; he'd just left her there. He would go back for her, of course. The Superiors had demanded that he keep her safe, and though he felt abandoned by them, it was best that he do what he was told.

He just couldn't stand to look at her any longer. She looked so beautiful, so peaceful, as she slept, and he hated himself for thinking it. She was a killer. She may have attempted to pass the blame onto the Superiors, but she was as much a murderer as they. He never wanted to face her again, but the Superiors demanded it of him.

Before she'd demanded that he teleport her out of the city, he'd been considering how to get the people out safely, but now there were no people left to save.

Why would anyone create a device that would kill so many in so little time?

It didn't look deadly, the small vial that she had opened on the table before he'd teleported out. Apparently its effects spread as quickly as a wildfire. A silent weapon that would kill so many in so little time—and it spread farther than any weapon he'd ever encountered. Two hundred miles away from the center of the city, there would be no life—no Humans, no Purists, no Advanced. Nothing.

He couldn't believe that she had done this.

To see her at work was a beautiful thing. When they'd arrived in Athena, she said a few words to those who were there to greet her and got straight to work. He'd watched her as she meditated on top of the tallest building in the city, searching with her mind for all of the Humans and Purists around the city. She'd fired her weapon straight up in the air five times, closed her eyes, hit all five of her targets, and repeated the process. The only trouble was that they'd arrived too late to really be of any help. The work was draining for her, and she could only fire off a single clip before having to rest.

He saw how much she hated having this restraint, saw how it pained her to see the Humans and Purists breaking into the city, and saw how much she hated ordering him to teleport her out. He saw it all but could do nothing to stop what was about to happen. He'd done as he was told and teleported her out as soon as she'd left the vial on the table.

Now as he sat in the woods, he thought that there must have been more that he could have done for the people. He could have gotten a few of them out before Reem had set off her bioweapon. But he knew deep in his heart that there was nothing he could have done. The city had been breached. Even if he had gotten more of them out, it was doubtful that they would have all made it far enough out to be safe from the weapon.

He blamed Reem, yes, but he also blamed himself. But most of all, he blamed the Superiors for giving up hope on the people of the city and on Reem.

He hated to admit it to himself, but he believed her. She seemed genuinely sorry about what the Superiors had forced her to do, and she had made the best decision. She challenged him to say what he would have done that would have changed things, but deep down in his heart, he knew she'd chosen correctly. There was no way to save the people of Athena.

He knew it, but he hated to admit it.

The sun would be up soon. He would return as soon as it did, and then he and Reem would continue their journey.

⁂

Reem had been alone for hours in the freezing wind. She didn't know where Jameson had gone, but she had a clue as to why. He'd seemed very upset during the night and likely couldn't bring himself to stay with her any longer. If she were him, she would have left too.

Once the fire had built up, she decided that as soon as the sun rose she would head for Admiri. If he didn't show up by then, he likely wouldn't. It was safe to assume that she would be on her own for the duration of her journey home.

She packed up the tent and what few supplies they had into her bag and sat back down in front of the fire, going back to shielding both herself and the fire from the cold wind. It took the majority of her concentration, and she hated to use her gifts for her own benefit only, but at the moment, it was use her gifts or freeze to death in the forest.

⁂

The sun slowly rose over the edge of the horizon, and she knew it was time to be on her way. So she rose, dumped sand on the fire, collected what few things she had, and started walking into the woods away from camp.

"Where are you going?" a voice asked from behind her when she was only a few yards in.

She turned, and to her surprise, there stood Jameson leaning against a tree, his head tilted down and his eyes looking up at her through his eyelashes. "Back to Admiri," she responded, turning and walking away from him as she spoke.

"You don't know the way, Reem," he said, his voice condescending.

"I'm not an idiot, Jameson." She turned again, this time walking up to him and putting her finger to his face. "The fastest way to Admiri is to head to the coast, and that is where I am going."

"And what will you do when you get there?" he asked, unflinching.

"I will charter a boat to take me across the ocean."

"Would this be a Purist's boat or a Human's?" He moved closer to her, putting his face in the small empty space that was between them.

"You're the one who left me, Jameson. If you wish to complete your mission, you will take me back to Admiri yourself," she said, unmoving, though her face became flushed with heat.

"I know that. And I never said you were stupid." He placed his right foot between both of hers, and she stepped away from him, clearly uncomfortable having him so close.

"If you were trying to abandon me, you've done a terrible job of it."

"I never intended to abandon you. The Superiors ordered me to take you to Athena and back, and I fully intend to obey." He moved away from her and leaned back against the trunk of a large tree.

"Then why did you leave me?"

"I had my reasons."

"Oh, I'm sure you did. If you really do intend to take me back to Admiri, I suggest you get to it. The Superiors will be concerned if we arrive late."

"A few hours won't make a difference. Besides, I can have you home in less than a day if necessary." He moved from his place against the tree and approached her again, placing his hands on her shoulders. "Don't worry. Your people can survive a few more hours without you."

"Take me home."

"I think we should move two safe zones closer and then rest again. I know I said that I can have you home in less than a day, and I can, but it would be safer if we rest."

"Then we should be on our way." She reached out her hand and placed it on his chest, coaxing.

"You have all of your things on you?"

"Yes."

He teleported them to the next safe zone, where a group of Advanced travelers waited for the next shuttle into Athena, oblivious to the fact that the city had been deserted and that the people were all gone. They stared unbelievingly at Reem, until she clenched her hand around his shirt, her face pleading with him to teleport again. When they landed, they found themselves in the most unsafe zone she had seen in years—the middle of a Human camp. Jameson motioned for her to remain silent as he led her away from the center of the camp, toward the outer edges. Her face again pleaded with him to teleport again, but being one of the foremost leaders on stealing from Human camps, Jameson led her on.

When they reached an empty house on the very edge of the camp, Jameson led her inside, a smile forming on his face.

"What are you doing?" she whispered.

"It's the safest place, really. They'd never suspect you to be hiding among them. We don't have to stay for long, just a few hours. Don't worry about it." He smiled at her and winked.

The house was small, twenty feet long by thirteen wide, she estimated. To the left of the cloth door sat a small table and two chairs, and to the right sat a small bed. The walls were made of cement, with chunks cut out as though it were shot with a high-powered weapon. It didn't look safe to her.

Jameson walked to the bed and sat down. "Come on, sit down." He patted the bed next to him.

"This is not a good idea," she replied, sitting next to him, though obviously not relaxed in any sense of the word.

"Stay here. I'm going to go find some food."

✦

He'd left her—again. This time he'd told her he was going, of course, but he'd still abandoned her just like before. He was overly confident. They shouldn't have stayed in the Human camp—it wasn't safe. The Humans had ways of testing to find out whether the treatment was effective in you at all. To make matters worse, neither she nor Jameson had the mark of the Humans or of the Purists. The Humans all bore the mark of Adam—a ring cut open on one side, open for all to see. The Purists bore the mark of Infinatum—the sun, rimmed in black to represent the dark forces around them.

The people in this camp were Human, bearing the mark of Adam, which could be construed as a good thing or a bad thing. Good because if she was captured, they would likely keep her alive, bad because of what they would do to her after they captured her. This was not a good idea.

Jameson was far too sure of himself and had gone out and stolen food for them to eat two hours ago and had gone out again moments before to find a source of heat. If teleporting over such distances didn't land you hours later than when you started, this wouldn't be such a problem. The sun would be going down soon, and it was already getting cold.

She hadn't been able to sit still since they'd arrived. What if the worst were to happen? Jameson had kindly offered to give her his gift of teleportation, but she did not accept. It was unnatural, his gift of giving. She preferred to keep only what powers the treatment had given her. When she'd told him that, he'd even offered to take the gift back when they arrived in Admiri, but she still felt it was cheating.

Now she sat alone on the bed in the concrete house, shivering in the cold. It felt like she'd been alone for hours, though she knew that it had only been mere minutes. What if something had gone wrong? What if Jameson didn't return?

"Calm down, Reem," Jameson said, breaking her chain of thought as he moved the cloth aside and stepped in the door.

"Where have you been?" She stood as he walked to the table and leaned against its edge.

"If you weren't so afraid of looking outside, you would have seen me. I never left sight of the door." He smiled cockily.

"Did you find anything?" she asked, wrapping her arms around her body for warmth.

"Nothing. And we can't start a fire, since there's no place for the smoke to vent. Most of the Humans' technology is stored in their underground camps, so there's really nothing left on the surface." He sighed heavily and shrugged his shoulders.

"The price we pay for our gifts," she whispered as she walked to the table and took a seat next to him. Jameson walked to her and rubbed her shoulders gently.

"All because of a treatment that was supposed to make life easier." She looked up at him as he spoke, and he realized that he'd crossed a line without even thinking about it. "Uh . . . you should pack your things," he said, removing his hands from her shoulders. "We might have to leave in a hurry."

"My things are packed," she replied, walking back to the bed and motioning to the bag that lay beside it on the floor. She lay on her side, facing him, and shivered.

"You're cold."

She rolled her eyes and wrapped her arms closer around her body, pulling her coat as close as she could.

He sat on the bed next to her, stroking her arm gently. "I'm sorry," he said.

"It's fine. Goes with the territory." She gave a weak smile and closed her eyes, searching for sleep.

As he watched her, she shivered again and wrapped her arms even tighter around herself, sleeping—but not so peacefully. He could feel her gift trying to warm her body with friction, but she wasn't making much headway. He knew he had to do something for her.

So he gave himself a new gift. A gift that would radiate heat throughout his body. He lay down next to her and wrapped his arms around her. She opened her eyes and stared at him groggily. "Go back to sleep," he told her, "I'll keep watch."

"Thank you," she whispered, moving her body closer to him and laying her head against his chest.

When she woke, the sun wasn't yet up, but the cold was unable to reach her. The room was pitch black, and even her dark-adjusted eyes could see nothing. She could feel Jameson's body against hers, feel the heat radiating from him, and finally realized what had happened. He'd given himself a gift to keep them warm, and her gifts had kept the heat inside the room while she'd slept.

Why he'd gone to such extremes, she could only guess. She supposed it was to make up for leaving her behind in the woods the previous night. This was his way of asking forgiveness.

"Reem? Are you awake?" Jameson whispered to her, his voice barely audible.

"Yes," she whispered back, only slightly louder than him.

That was when she heard them.

Voices.

Outside the room.

Humans.

They were whispering—so many voices that she couldn't tell what any of them were saying. "What's going on?" she asked.

"They've found us," he whispered back, his voice remaining calm.

"Can you teleport?"

"Where did you leave your bag?"

"Right here. We can't leave without it. It still has another vial of the weapon inside."

"Okay. Stay here." He stood and reached for the bag, the bedsprings squealing loudly in protest. A Human walked in just as his foot hit the ground, and the man yelled something and rushed him just as he stumbled back onto the bed.

"Ready?" he asked as he took her hand.

"Yes."

The Humans rushed through the door, Reem's power holding them at bay while Jameson teleported to the next safe zone.

"I thought you said they'd never find us!" Reem laughed at him when they landed.

"I said they shouldn't, not that they wouldn't." He smiled back.

She gazed around their landing site: African desert as far as the eye could see. The sun greeted them over the horizon, and her smile grew questioning. "Africa?" she asked as she turned to look at him once again.

"Yes. Africa," he replied as he collapsed onto the ground in front of her.

She dropped to her knees to help him. "What's wrong?" she asked, removing the weight of her bag from his shoulders and checking his pulse.

"I think . . . we may have to . . . stay here for a while," he replied, his breathing shallow and ragged.

"You're exhausted. Did you use your powers all night?"

"Yes," he responded, closing his eyes and clenching his fists as he tried to move.

She removed her coat and wrapped it into a ball. "Here, rest," she said as she placed it under his head.

"Thank you," he replied as she took hold of his hand. "Admiri is no more than a day's walk away. Go. I'll catch up to you in the city."

"You teleported too far?"

"Yes."

"Why?"

"I don't know. Just go, Reem."

"No. I'll stay with you."

"Thank you . . . ," he said as he leaned his head back and lost consciousness.

She unpacked her things and set up a makeshift camp while she let her mind wander. Why would he have teleported so far from the start point? He should have known that doing so would exhaust his body—plus he'd been using his gifts the entire night. He would be immobile for a day at least. His antics were nonsensical at best. But even though she hated to admit it, the two of them worked well together. Their abilities offset and enhanced each other's. The Superiors would likely assign him to her for any other missions where she would have to leave Admiri.

She'd been noticing a change in herself lately. She hadn't told anyone, of course, because that would mean subjecting herself to a countless number of tests to find if the treatment was still in her system. She was gaining another gift—telepathy. She didn't know why it had waited until now to manifest itself inside her, but it could have been due to the dramatic growth in her telekinetic powers—which she had also kept secret from the Superiors.

Apparently in her the treatment was a gift that kept on giving—a fact that Jameson himself had also encountered. He had originally been classed as level one—the lowest of any gift class—but found himself gaining more and more as he aged. Many people now referred to him as a class seven, even though the scale only went up to five.

She had had no desire for any other gifts. It was hard enough having one gift that made people call her a savior, and now she could also work as a spy. But for some reason, the majority of the time she couldn't read Jameson's mind. It seemed he'd somehow known about her gift and given himself one to shield his thoughts from her. She hoped that he didn't know, but she could guess that he did.

He was awake. She could feel his mind spinning as he lay there, though she couldn't make out the words. She'd decided that for his sake she would not inform the Superiors of this incident and advise Jameson to do the same. If he wanted to keep his place in the Advanced army, he would need better training. He was still as stubborn as a new recruit, but his skills were necessary ones. She'd been considering asking the Superiors if she could train him herself. It would be a good experience for her though she didn't want to spend any more time with him than necessary. But she was a good trainer, and she knew that he would be a good student for her. He would challenge her—that much was certain.

She looked across the small camp at him, where he pretended to sleep, and tried once again to read his thoughts . . .

"My god, she's beautiful," he thought. *"Just look at her. But the feelings will go away. They have to. There is no reason for love now, and the Superiors have all but banned . . ."*

She closed her mind to his thoughts, unwilling to hear the rest. How could this be? He hated her as much as she hated him, didn't he? He certainly acted like he did.

How could this have happened? How could someone so . . . how could someone like him fall in love with her—one of many who vowed to the Superiors to dedicate her life to the war, to never love, and to follow their orders above all else? She'd saved lives by killing others, and he'd saved them by removing them from harm's way. She was a warrior in every sense of the word, and he . . . he was . . . annoyingly cocky.

Love and attraction were a thing of the past, a thing that only Purists did. Even Humans had given them up in sight of their goal.

"What are you thinking about?" Jameson asked her.

She turned toward him and shook her head.

"What's wrong? You look stressed."

"It's nothing," she replied hastily.

"Oh it's something, alright," he joked. "Tell me."

A million thoughts passed through her mind when he uttered those two words. Should she tell him? How would he take it? He would know her secret, but he likely already knew . . .

"You love me?" she asked, turning toward him once again.

He coughed and blushed. "How could I forget . . . ," he whispered.

"Forget what?" she asked.

"Your gift. You read minds." He nodded his head toward her.

"Why do you think that?" she kept her voice even, unwilling to give up the secret.

"Because you just asked if I love you, when you obviously thought that I hate you as much as you hate me." He laughed, seemingly uncaring that she knew about his feelings. "But listen, I know you haven't told anyone yet, or I would have known before I met you. I won't say anything if you don't want me to. I swear."

"Thank you," she replied, sitting down several feet in front of him.

"And yes, I am in love with you," he added.

She started to speak, but he cut her off. "Let me finish. I've taken the very same oath you have. Love is a thing of the past, but it happens. My feelings will change, so don't worry. Which I can tell you already are."

"How did you know about my gift?" she asked, staring him straight in the eye.

"My gifts tell me what your gifts are. I knew when I first met you that you had two powers, and it only took a few seconds more to know exactly what they were and how strong they are. I guessed that it was a secret, your second power, so I didn't say anything."

"I won't tell the Superiors."

"About your gift?"

"No. About your feelings, about teleporting too far, nothing. They would not approve."

"And you know better than most what they will and will not approve of, don't you?" He winked.

"I suppose I do." She smiled slightly.

They both laughed, and she decided that no matter Jameson's feelings, she would request to the Superiors that he become her apprentice. She may find him obnoxious much of the time, but he had the makings of a great leader.

"Get your rest, Jameson. We need to get back to Admiri as soon as possible. It's not safe out here after dark."

"Oh, don't worry, I should be ready to teleport by then," he said sarcastically.

"Good."

"What are you going to tell the Superiors?" he asked.

"I haven't decided yet. You rest, and I'll think. Deal?"

When he started to reply she said, "Sleep, Jameson. That's an order."

He laughed hysterically before adding, "Yes, sir. I mean, ma'am." And he closed his eyes for rest.

"How are you feeling?" she asked several hours later when he woke. It was starting to get dark out, and it seemed they would be spending the night in the desert.

"Better." He sat up. "Much better." He smiled at her as she sat a few feet away.

"Good. We don't want to be out here much longer." She looked to the horizon where Admiri could be seen as a speck in the distance. "It's not safe."

"It'll be at least a few hours before I can teleport. Sorry."

"It's fine, Jameson. My gifts will protect us."

"As long as you've got that gun, they will," he said, motioning toward the pistol she'd strapped to her calf.

She shivered again and ran her hands along her arms, trying to warm them.

"Are you always cold?" he asked her, jokingly.

"Only when I'm away from the cities. The people fuel my power—being so alone, I always feel cold." She stared once again toward the city she called home.

"Come here." He patted the ground next to him.

"Is that a good idea?" She tilted her head to the side, a reminder that she knew his thoughts when he wasn't guarding them.

"Just for warmth. Don't freak out, Reem. Come here," he insisted, and she scooted across the distance that had separated them. He took the jacket she'd let him use as a pillow and put it back over her shoulders before rubbing her arms gently, transferring heat from his body to hers.

"Don't." She turned to face him, and found his face only inches away from hers, staring deeply into her eyes.

"Don't what?" he asked, wrapping his arms around her and kissing her neck.

"Don't. Stop!" she shouted, her voice echoing around them as she jumped up and stepped away from him.

"I'm sorry . . . ," he said when he'd gotten over the shock. "I shouldn't have done that."

"No. You shouldn't have done that. I am your commanding officer. Remember that," she responded coldly.

"Then as my commanding officer, what are your orders?" he said, his voice matching hers as he closed his eyes and clenched his fists in an attempt to rein in his anger.

"If you have the strength, teleport us out of here. If not, lie back down and act dead. It's best they don't see you here," she said as she walked to her bag and began to strap more pistols and knives to her calves, thighs, and arms.

"What's going on?" he said, opening his eyes and staring at her as she continued pulling weaponry out of her bag.

"They are coming. Lie back down. They must not see you!" she ordered, pointing off in the distance toward a cloud of smoke.

"Humans?" he asked.

"No. Purists. They will kill you if they see you."

"I don't have the strength to—"

"I know. My gifts will protect us as long as I have this gun, remember?" She winked before throwing him both a pistol and a knife. "Just in case."

The horses galloped ever closer, and she fired her first weapon five times straight at them, killing the five that made up the front line.

"Good shot," Jameson said as he lay back down on his side.

"Thank you," she responded as she repeated the process, killing five more riders. "Rest, Jameson. I will not let them reach you." She nodded at him and threw two knives in quick succession, hitting two of the leaders squarely between the eyes.

"How many?" he asked.

"Twenty-seven more, by my count," she replied, firing eight more shots and killing eight more riders. "Make that nineteen."

The riders started firing on their position, and she shielded the area, causing them to get caught in midair in front of her. She took four knives from their sheaths and threw them in quick succession, killing four more. "They're almost here," she said as she picked up her machine gun from the ground by her feet and firing it at the Purists who rode toward her, not needing her power at this distance—she had a killer aim.

Jameson sat back up and watched as she fell to her knees with exhaustion, still firing her weapon at the oncoming Purists, still shielding the camp from their bullets. When the clip was empty, only one rider remained, yet he plowed onward. She took her last knife from her calf and threw it, hitting him square between the eyes before she collapsed completely with exhaustion.

"Reem!" Jameson cried out, trying to force his legs to stand. "Reem! Answer me! Reem!" he shouted as she moaned and fell silent.

He got to his knees and crawled to her side, immediately checking for a pulse. *Thump-thump. Thump. Thump . . . thump. Thump . . . . thump. Thump-thump. Thump-thump.*

She was alive, though completely unconscious.

When she woke, she could feel the cold sand against her side, feel someone's arms wrapped around her, feel someone stroking her hair, but she couldn't will her eyes to open.

"Take your time," a familiar male voice said as she tried to move. "It'll be a while before you can move. You exhausted yourself." He rolled her onto her back and sat her up.

She slowly opened her eyes and blinked, Jameson's smiling face being the first thing she saw amid the blackness of the night. "Welcome back," he said. "Before you ask, I still can't teleport. They sent another round after us shortly after you collapsed, and I had to give myself your gift in order to save us. Almost exhausted myself again."

"Thank you . . . ," she whispered, closing her eyes once again.

"Don't thank me, thank your gift," he said jokingly.

She smiled and sat up. "Whoa . . . don't go too fast there, Reem," Jameson warned her.

"I know you were trying to prolong the amount of time we spent together, Jameson. I'm not an idiot. Exhaustion effects of that magnitude wear off in a matter of hours for me."

"How do you feel?" he asked her.

"Light-headed. Cold. Thirsty." She motioned to her canteen, and he handed it to her.

"Well, congratulations young lady, you're going to be fine," he joked again.

She laughed and nearly choked on the water before slapping his arm and shaking her head. "Don't do that," she warned playfully.

"We should get some rest. I'm sure I'll be able to teleport us out first thing in the morning." He lay down beside her as he spoke, spreading his arms wide.

"Which reminds me, I've decided to ask the Superiors if I can take you on as an apprentice," she said as she lay down as well, on top of his right arm.

"I thought you couldn't wait to be rid of me." He cocked his head to the side as she turned to face him.

"You have the makings of a great warrior, you just need training. And I think I can train you well."

He'd never had anyone say that he could actually be a great warrior before, and to have Reem be the one to say it made it that much more honorable. Of course, it was all up to the Superiors, but if she'd decided on this course of action, it must be one that she knew they would accept. "If you say so," he said, coiling his arm around her and pulling her on top of his body. "Best to keep warm," he said when she started to protest.

"Fine." She lay her head on his chest and let herself fall back to sleep.

Superior

Reem woke to the sound of Jameson's snoring in her ear, and she propped herself up and smacked his arm. "Wake up!" she yelled.

His eyes popped open and he groggily sat up and smiled at her. "What was that for?"

"You were snoring as loud as the Superiors!"

"That bad?" He winced.

"I'm sure all the Purists in the area are aware of our presence now." She winked. "Can you teleport?"

"Yeah, I'm good to go. Pack your stuff and we'll take off." He yawned.

She walked through all the dead bodies and collected her knives, cleaning them as she went. She then placed them all in sheaths inside her bag and followed them with her pistols and machine gun. She pulled the zipper shut, hoisted the bag onto her shoulders and turned back toward him. "Let's go."

He stood and walked to her, taking her hand in his. "Ready?" he asked.

"Of course," she replied.

He lifted her hand to his lips and kissed it gently, staring straight into her eyes as he teleported them back into her quarters in Admiri. "Welcome home," he told her, releasing her hand and gesturing around him.

They walked out of the door, and applause broke out among the dozens who saw her. "They have returned!" someone shouted in the distance. Soon all of Admiri would know that their savior, Reem Kahrin, had returned to them. She held out her hands and bowed to the masses, causing their cheering to erupt into a noise filled with joy.

"Reem Kahrin," came a thunderous voice from the distance—the Superiors were summoning her.

"Jameson, stay here," she told him as she used her gift to slowly lift herself off the ground. "*I will call to you if things go wrong,*" she whispered into his mind.

"But—" he protested, and she lifted her hand to silence him.

She floated gracefully through the air and landed on the balcony outside the Great Superior's chambers. He stepped out to greet her, and she bowed in reverence. "Superior," she said, "I have come, as you asked."

"You have used the weapon?" he asked her.

"Yes, sir, just as you asked. It is done."

"Then perhaps you can explain this."

She lifted her head to see of what he spoke, and a young woman was brought before her.

"Who is this?" Reem asked the Superior.

"Tell her your name," he addressed the woman.

"I am Faith Rommun. I was there, in Athena, when people started dying. I was underground in the safe house with nine others."

"How is this possible?" Reem asked.

"It seems that the weapon does not penetrate the soil. She found the rest of her people dead and came here to inform me."

"What happened to my people?" Faith asked her.

"I . . ." Reem shook her head in shock.

"Send them in," the Superior ordered one of the guards who'd accompanied the young woman.

"Who?" Reem asked him.

"Reem Kahrin, you are under arrest for the attempted slaughter of all of the people of Athena. We have convened and found you guilty. Your punishment shall be the same fate of the Athenians. You will be taken to the city's looking point and shot before the people for all to see," the Superior replied as ten more guards came in the door.

"No. No, Superior. You ordered the weapon's use. You ordered it yourself! You wanted the weapon tested full scale in Athena. You ordered me to slaughter them!" Reem cried out.

⁂

He sat exactly where she'd told him to—on the balcony of her quarters. He'd been waiting mere minutes when the message he somehow knew he would receive was delivered.

"Jameson. Help me," Reem's voice carried through his mind.

He teleported to the Great Superior's quarters and saw her struggling with someone on the balcony. "What are they doing?" he whispered to himself before teleporting between her and her attacker. He swung his fist, connected with the guard's jaw, and saw the man tumble backward into the Superior.

"Jameson," the Superior said.

"Sir?" he questioned, standing between his guards and Reem, who had wrapped her left arm around his waist and was peering up over his shoulder toward the guard.

"Step aside, young man. She has been found guilty of treason."

"It is you who has committed treason. Reem Kahrin has done nothing wrong."

"Stand aside," the Superior shouted, the loud bass of his voice shaking the building.

"I can't do that," Jameson said as he teleported both himself and Reem to the outer edge of the city, where the incident would have been least heard. "Are you alright?" he asked her.

"No," she whispered as she fell to her knees.

He dropped to his knees beside her and bowed his head in reverence. This once mighty warrior had been taken from the fight, and she would likely never see it again. She was considered to have committed treason and would be found and killed if they didn't leave soon. "Reem," he whispered in her ear. "Reem, we must go. We'll take what supplies we need and leave this place."

"And go where?" she cried, wrapping her arms around his neck.

"I know somewhere we can stay for a while. It's safe. The Superiors know nothing of its existence. But we must go now." He put his hands on her shoulders and pushed her gently away from him so that he could look her in the eyes. "Reem, look at me," he said when she refused to look anywhere but at the dust-covered ground. When she slowly lifted her head and looked into his eyes, he whispered, "We're going to be fine. We'll find a way to come back and clear your name. But the time isn't now. We need to hurry. Do you understand?" When she slowly nodded, he picked her up off the ground and carried her to a nearby building. "Stay here," he said as he set her down. "Not as many people here know my face. I'll be back in fifteen minutes, and we'll go." He kissed her forehead and walked away, struggling to do so as he had sworn never to leave her side of his own free will.

Tears rolled slowly down her cheek as he walked away from her, but she did as he asked, sitting down by a pile of scrap wood, trying her best to hide from any passersby.

❧⬩✦⬩☙

He gathered everything he thought they might need—short term, anyway. He packed a bag with stolen food, two canteens, warm clothing, and weaponry before going back to Reem's quarters and picking up her bag as well. He then found a few things in her closet that would help her to blend in with the people where they were going and grabbed his own pack from the ground in her quarters before teleporting back to the exact spot where he'd left her.

She jumped up from her hiding place alongside the house and threw her arms around his neck again. "I thought you'd left me."

He wrapped his free arm around her waist and whispered, "Never," in her ear before teleporting them both to his safe zone.

When they arrived, she took her arms off him and looked around. The space around her was completely dark, and when she reached for Jameson he was gone. "Jameson?" she whispered, though it sounded loud in the open space.

"Over here," he replied from a few feet behind her as he lit a small torch with a gift he'd apparently given himself. It was a dark cave, and she couldn't see an opening anywhere. Fire flowed freely from his fingertips as he continued lighting preset torches until the whole space was alight with the glow of fire.

"Where are we?" she asked as he set down all of the supplies he'd brought with them.

"We're underneath a Purist settlement outside of Admiri. I stayed here many times when I was on my own—found it by accident. Even they don't know it's here, as far as I know." He walked up behind her and wrapped his arms around her waist as she observed her surroundings. "What do you think?" he asked.

"First Humans, now Purists. What am I going to do with you?" She laughed, leaning her head backward on his shoulder, causing him to hold her tighter against him.

"You didn't answer my question," he whispered in her ear.

"It's perfect." She smiled as she closed her eyes.

"Only because you're here," he said as he kissed her neck.

She opened her eyes and pried herself free of his arms. "How big is this place?" she asked, shaking her head slowly as she walked toward an opening in the small cave. "Where am I supposed to sleep?"

"I wouldn't recommend wandering too far from here. There is a Purist camp above us, after all," he reminded her. "The main chamber would be the safest place, but if you'd like privacy, you can use one of the side chambers." He pointed to the east, where two small holes appeared in the light. "There's one torch in each, and they're about the same size, so . . ."

"Thank you, Jameson," she said. "I would be dead now if not for you."

"You never have to thank me," he replied.

"I do. You didn't have to do that. You risked your own life to save mine, you deserve more than my thanks." She walked back to him and wrapped her arms around him once again.

He rubbed her back gently, and kissed the top of her head. "Which room would you like?" he asked.

"Why don't you show me around first?"

"Follow me." He released her and took only her hand, pulling her toward the eastern wall of the chamber. "These are where I keep the supplies, usually. We can stock up a great deal in here, but you can use one as a bedroom and we'd still have plenty of space." He showed her inside, lighting the torches so she could see everything. He then led her to the Southern wall, where there was one small hole. "That's the washroom. There's a hot spring that came up inside a few years back. Makes getting water a whole lot easier. The hole is plenty big enough for even a large man to fit through—it just doesn't look like it." He winked as he lit the torch inside. "The halls you were considering going down I haven't had time to explore, though I do occasionally hear voices coming from the northern tunnel. I think they're coming from above."

"Is that it?" she asked, turning to face him again.

He nodded, "I know it's not much, but we should be safe here for a while, at least. Time enough to find a way to clear your name." He gave a weak smile before leaning against the wall and sliding down to the ground. He patted the spot next to him, and she smiled and sat.

"It's perfect. Thank you." She leaned her head on his shoulder and closed her eyes, allowing her tears to once again flow down her face. She watched as they dripped to the floor, dampening Jameson's sleeve and turning the ground almost black. In time, her tears lulled her to sleep in the quiet of the caves, and she slept soundly on his shoulder.

"Sleep well, my love," he whispered as she slept.

***

Reem woke to find herself lying on the ground where she last remembered sitting with Jameson, but he was nowhere in sight. "Jameson?" she called.

"In here," came his reply from one of the storage rooms.

She stood and walked to the openings and peered inside the first. Seeing nothing but supplies, she turned and peered inside the next. "Why do I always lose you when I fall asleep?" she asked.

"Because you're a sound sleeper," he replied and winked.

"What are you doing?" she asked, stepping inside the room to find him unpacking a bag of her things and putting them beside the small bed he'd set up. "Those are mine," she said.

"You've got a sharp eye," he said, turning to wink at her again.

"Where'd you get my things?"

"Your chambers. I went there while I was collecting supplies. Hope you don't mind."

"Not at all," she said as she walked up to him and looked at what he'd brought her. "You didn't have to do this," she said, seeing all of her favorite things— including her pistol—laid out on a small rock ledge beside where he'd set up a small cot.

"This will be your room," he said, stroking her arm gently.

"Then where will you sleep?" she questioned.

"In the main chamber, unless you'd like me to be somewhere else." "*I belong with you,*" he thought.

"I heard that."

"I know," he whispered, smiling slightly.

"Jameson, there's something you should know," she began.

"I already know. Peter warned me before we left Admiri. The first time."

"What did he tell you?"

"That you were spoken for. That one of the Superiors had you revise your oath so that you could be with him."

She closed her eyes and bit her lip, breathing deeply. When her eyes opened, they were filled only with anger and hatred. "It wasn't my choice."

"Yet you let it happen," he replied, looking away from her.

"It was not my choice. I was given by the Great Superior. I was under orders. You know the law. What was I supposed to do?"

"Do you love him?"

"No. I never have, and I never will." She put her hand on his cheek and he turned to face her. "Believe me, Jameson. I do not love him."

She wrapped her arms around his neck and pulled his lips to hers. He trembled with pleasure and parted his lips slightly against hers before she pulled away and looked him in the eyes. "Got it?" she asked.

He smiled and pulled her into an embrace, lifting her off the ground and twirling her around in a circle. "Got it," he whispered into her ear as he set her down, smiling.

"Good," she replied, her smile matching his as they began to laugh hysterically.

He fell onto the bed and pulled her down with him. She climbed on top of him and kissed him passionately before he rolled her underneath his body and stood back on his feet. "Want to see the surface?" he asked her, his index finger pointing toward the ceiling.

"Is it safe?" she questioned, getting up and stepping outside her bedroom.

He followed her out, took her hand, and teleported them to the surface. "Of course it is. The Purists have gone to Admiri. During the night they're here, but during the day only the servants remain. Nothing to worry about at all." He winked and led her through the settlement.

"Where are we, exactly?"

"I don't really know. I never really paid much attention to locations and titles, just surroundings. I suppose we could ask one of the locals when they get back, but . . ." He smiled at her as her jaw dropped open at the thought.

"You never cease to amaze me," she said as they continued to walk, hand in hand, along the dusty streets lined with cement homes and shops.

"Really?" he said, turning to stand in front of her and running his fingers through her hair.

"Yes. I know it shocks you, but it's true," she replied sarcastically.

He leaned down to kiss her, but a startled gasp from behind him interrupted his thought. He turned, putting himself between Reem and whoever made the sound. To his surprise, a short elderly woman stood before him, staring him straight in the eye.

"Who are you?" she asked in a small voice.

"We're Humans," Jameson answered her.

"I think you're in the wrong place then. This is a Purist camp," she replied.

"We've fallen in love, and that is against the Humans' code. We've come to see if you would allow us to join you."

"We don't have any room for more people here. You'd better go. There's another camp to the east, they might have space there," she said.

"Oh. We're quite sorry. You're sure there's no space for us here? We really haven't the energy to travel more today."

"Listen, boy. I know what you are. I've seen your mark. You don't belong here. I'm giving you a chance to leave—I suggest you take it."

"Thank you. I appreciate it. Your thoughtfulness will not go unrewarded," he said, dipping his head as he teleported them back to their underground home.

When they landed, Reem burst up with laughter and fell to her knees. "She didn't see your mark, Jameson. She was bluffing. I can't believe you just told her you're Advanced!" Her laughter grew, and she fell to the ground, clutching her side.

"I should have had you speak to her. I keep forgetting that you can read minds." He chuckled and sat on the ground next to her, beaming as she entwined her fingers with his.

"Then how come you still don't let me read your mind?" she questioned.

"Because I don't always want you to know what I'm thinking." He reached her hand up to his lips and kissed it. "And I don't think you do, either."

"You're probably right," she whispered, squinting her eyes slightly as she spoke.

He lay down on the ground next to her, and they talked for hours about everything from their middle names to the chemical makeup of the bioweapon that she'd used in Athena.

"What time is it?" she asked, sitting up when she realized that she had no idea how long they'd been talking.

"Eleven o'clock." *"I have no idea."*

"You're a lot of help!" She turned back to him and slapped his arm, laughing.

"Why does it matter?" he asked, pulling her back down to the ground beside him.

"Because I'm tired, and I want to know if I'm tired because it's late or because you're boring," she joked.

"I'll go check." He teleported outside, leaving her alone in the main chamber.

She stood and walked to her bedroom, searching through the things he'd brought her for something that she could comfortably sleep in. She found the item she'd been searching for just as he teleported back into the chamber and announced, "I was right! It's almost eleven!"

She heard his feet shuffle around when he didn't see her in the immediate area, and she smiled, knowing this would probably be the last place he looked. "Reem?" he called.

"In here. Hang on, I'll be right there," she said as she changed into her loose-fitting cotton top and jeans. She then walked back out into the main chamber and found him lounging on the floor—again. "You really like the floor, don't you?" she asked as she leaned against the wall across from him.

"It's nice down here," he replied, turning to look at her, and doing a double take when he realized she'd changed her clothes. "You know, I've only seen you in your uniform before now," he said as she crossed her legs and slid down to the ground.

"And I've still only seen you in uniform," she replied.

"I can fix that," he said, jumping to his feet, grabbing his backpack, and heading into the storage room. When he returned, he wore only a pair of cotton pants, and her eyes widened at the sight.

"That what you normally sleep in?" she asked, laughing as he flexed his muscles and relaxed back into his spot on the floor.

"Aw, come on, you know you like it," he said seriously before laughing along with her.

She crawled to where he lay on the floor and settled in next to him, laying her head on his chest. "Well, I don't know about that, but I do like you quite a bit," she said, tracing his abdomen with her index finger.

"That tickles," he said, shivering.

They lay there for a moment before she swung her body on top of his and kissed his lips gently. "I'm going to bed. You're welcome to join me if you'd like," she said as she hopped up and walked quickly into the bedroom he'd set up for her. "Good night," she said as she snuffed the torch and lay down on the bed.

"Good night," he whispered, unbelieving of what he'd just heard.

Scars

Jameson woke to the feeling of the cold stone of the main chamber's floor against his back, and Reem running her fingers through his hair. He moaned and rolled to his side, making her laugh. "Good morning, sleepyhead," she whispered in his ear before kissing his cheek and walking away.

He opened his eyes slowly and smiled. It wasn't all just a dream after all. She was here with him. He sat up and looked around. She'd left? He rose and walked to the washroom, lighting the inside torch as he reached the opening in the cave wall.

"Oh," he said, eyes widening when he saw Reem standing waist deep in the water, her bare back now visible in the firelight. "Um. Sorry." He turned and leaned against the outside wall, once again very unbelieving that this wasn't all a dream his mind had conjured up.

"Oh, it's fine," she said as she dived into the water.

A few moments later, she exited the room, the towel he'd packed for her wrapped around her still-wet body as she walked to her bedroom. "Your turn." She smiled as she walked away from him.

He let out a heavy sigh and leaned his head against the wall, closing his eyes.

"What's wrong?" she asked when she returned, wearing her battle uniform once again, her long hair tied back into a bun behind her head.

She walked to his side and ran her fingers up his still-bare arm. "Talk to me."

"It's nothing," he said, opening his eyes once again and meeting hers.

"Tell me," she whispered into his mind. *"Or I'll find out the hard way."* She winked.

"You know you wouldn't do that. Besides, you don't even know what to look for."

"There it is," her mind whispered into his as she found the moment she'd been looking for in his memory. She closed her eyes as she replayed the memory in her own mind as well as his.

"Your thought patterns are so complex," she said, still watching the memory of only a few moments ago. She saw it all from his eyes: walking to the washroom, lighting the torch, seeing her. He blocked her from seeing his thoughts at that moment. "You saw my scars, didn't you?" She opened her eyes when he closed off his mind from her probing. When his eyes finally met hers, he saw that her eyes had darkened with anger once again. "You weren't supposed to see those," she whispered as she turned away from him and walked back to her bedroom.

She sat on the bed and put her head in her hands, trying to find the words to tell him what had happened to her. Tears filled her eyes, and she wiped them away with the back of her hand, remembering to never shed a tear because of that man.

Jameson walked to the gap in the cave wall peered inside. Seeing her like this was hurting him as much as her, but he needed to know. The scars he'd seen were long and angular, like she'd been beaten with a whip, and interspersed between those scars were smaller, shallower slice marks as if someone had taken a knife to her when the whip didn't have the desired effect. To make matters worse, some of the marks looked as if they'd been inflicted only weeks before.

She turned and looked at him. "I want to say it's not what you think, but that would be a lie," she said as she pulled her knees toward her chest and wrapped her arms around them.

"What happened?" he asked, walking inside and sitting down beside her on the bed. Everyone knew she'd never been in a battle where she wasn't standing on a roof, firing her weapon into the distance. There was only one other way he knew of that someone could get scars like those.

"What do you think happened?" She refused to meet his eyes, preferring instead to stare at the mattress.

"Who did this to you?" he asked, scooting closer to her and taking her hand in his. *"Did he do this to you?"*

"There was nothing I could do to stop him."

He closed his eyes, leaned back his head and transferred a new gift to her. She gasped when she felt a new kind of power surging through her veins, healing the scars that covered her back. She trembled and let go of his hand as she felt his thoughts drift into her mind. *"They are gone. If you wish it, I will take the gift back. It's your choice."*

"So?" he asked, taking her hand back in his.

"Why would you do that?" she responded, turning toward him.

"Because I don't want your scars to hold you back from anything, and I don't think you did either. Now they're gone."

"Thank you." *"I think I'll keep it, if you don't mind."*

She leaned her head on his shoulder, and he kissed the top of her head. "You never have to thank me," he whispered.

She took a deep breath and lifted her head. "What are we going to do today?" she asked.

"Whatever you'd like," he replied. "We can go back to the surface for supplies—or just to get out—or we can stay down here and eat MREs." He nudged her with his shoulder and she smiled.

"Supplies it is," she said, standing up and walking to her weaponry bag. "Just in case," she said as he was about to ask. "Can't be too careful." She strapped a pistol to her thigh and her four knives to her shins, followed by extra clips in her side pants pocket. "All set?" she asked when she'd finished.

"In a moment." He stood and wrapped his arms around her waist, closing his eyes and kissing her lips gently.

She stood to her tiptoes and coiled her arms around his neck, kissing him back. *"Take your time. We've got all day."*

He laughed into her mouth and teleported them up to the surface a short distance outside the Purist camp. She turned around and faced away from him— his arms still wrapped around her waist. "Let me do the talking this time," she said as he released all but her hand and led her toward the camp.

"Deal." He laughed.

They walked through the camp slowly, hand in hand, searching for anything that might help them, when a recognizable startled gasp stopped them in their tracks.

"Sarah," Reem said as she saw the old woman walking toward them once again. "We mean you no harm."

"How do you know my name, animal?" the woman replied.

"Because you told me," Reem whispered into her mind.

"I did no such thing," Sarah responded. "You animals do not belong here. Go back to your city."

"If I go back there, they will kill me."

"Then I suggest you go elsewhere. If you're still here when the fighters return, you'll both be dead for that mark on your wrists," Sarah said as she turned and started to walk away.

"Sarah, please. We are in hiding. We need only some supplies so that we can live in peace away from both our kind and yours." *"Please, help us."*

"Why should I? You are only animals."

"And you feed your animals every evening, do you not?"

"That's true . . ."

"Please, Sarah, help us. We have no desire to harm you."

"You know my name. I don't know yours."

"I am Reem Kahrin, telepath, and this is Jameson Willow, teleporter. Our gifts can do you no harm."

"Yet you come here armed," Sarah gestured to the gun on Reem's thigh.

"Only for our safety. I do not wish to use this weapon."

"Follow me. I've got plenty of leftover rations. I'd hate to see you two starve to death on my doorstep." Sarah led them away from the path and into her home, a small three-room cement building, similar to the one Reem and Jameson had spent a night in not long ago.

"Thank you, Sarah," Jameson said as they entered.

"Don't thank me, young man," she said sternly as she walked to the back of the house and picked up a large pot. "Leftovers from this week. It's not much, but it should feed the two of you for a few days more at least. Take it and leave," she said, handing the pot to Jameson.

"Thank you," he responded, taking the pot from her hands.

"I told you not to thank me. Now get out of here. The fighters will be back soon."

"Sarah, your kindness will not go unrewarded," Reem told her as she placed her hand on Jameson's shoulder, signaling that she was ready.

"Go. Now," Sarah replied.

Jameson teleported back into the main chamber of the cave still holding onto the pot of food with Reem standing behind him, her hand on his shoulder just as they had been when they left, and he turned toward her. "You *are* better at doing the talking, aren't you?" he said, smiling.

"Comes with being able to find people's weaknesses. She already knew we were together, but she didn't know we couldn't go back, and she didn't know that we didn't have any food. Once I told her that, I knew she'd open right up." She smiled back, taking the pot of food from his hands and setting it on the ground.

"You are . . . so beautiful," he said, placing his hands on either side of her face as she stood and faced him again. "You've changed my life. Completely."

Her smile faded as she put her hands on his wrists. "I don't know why you let me," she said.

"If you really don't know, then take a look for yourself," he said as he opened his mind to her. *"Everything I am is yours."*

She closed her eyes as she searched through his thoughts and memories for a reason, searching for a clue as to why he would have left his home for her. She saw the moment they met, when he scanned her gifts and gave himself one that would protect his thoughts from her; saw the moment he teleported her from the city; saw him watch her as she fought atop the building in Athena. She watched as his anger with her grew into pure hatred when she left the vial on the table and ordered him to teleport them out, heard his thoughts when he left her in the woods, heard his thoughts when they faced off outside the camp, saw the change in his heart when he saw her walk away from him. So it was true. He was in love with her. She wasn't sure she really believed it until now, seeing it in his mind.

He hit her with something she hadn't expected. He thought of their first kiss, and the thoughts that ran through his mind as she'd wrapped her arms around him. He replayed the memory in his mind, playing it also inside hers. She felt his emotion, his pure love for her as he'd picked her up and twirled her around. *"Got it?"* he whispered in his mind, knowing that she was listening.

Before she could open her eyes and speak to him, his lips were on hers and his arms around her. She wrapped one arm around his neck and the other around his back, pulling him closer to her as she kissed him. *"Got it."*

He slowly released her and pulled away gently. "Keep going." He tapped the side of his head. "There's more."

She dove deep into his thoughts, into his memories, seeing more than what he'd already told her—starting with the moment she'd left him on the balcony of her chambers. She saw how much it hurt him to see her leave his side, how he'd somehow known that something awful was going to happen. She saw how he'd almost gone to her side even before she'd called to him. She relived the memory of being teleported out of the Superiors chambers and saw how it had pained him to leave her side for those few minutes while he collected supplies. She saw how he'd picked only the things he thought she would need the most, saw him teleport back where he'd left her, felt the relief when she rushed to him.

Once again he replayed a memory for her, a memory of his past, the first time he set foot in the city of Admiri—the day it was completed. He'd been teleporting people inside from one of the camps—fifteen of them. This was the first day they'd met. She'd been among the first inside the city and was arguing with a man when Jameson had teleported directly in front of her—between her and the man. She'd completely forgotten about this . . . it was so long ago . . . the man she'd been arguing with had rushed her, and Jameson had knocked him to the ground before he could reach her, and teleported away. She'd never really seen the teleporter's face, and she had no reason to suspect that it was him. *"You only had one gift then, but I could feel it growing as I stood in front of you—I can feel it growing now. There's something special about you, Reem."*

"You . . . that was you?" she whispered.

"Yes," he replied as she opened her eyes to look at him again.

"Why didn't you tell me?"

"I had to be sure . . . I didn't know if you even remembered me—or even knew that it was me."

"Why did you stop him?"

"He was going to hurt you. I saw it in his eyes. And you . . . your gift was swelling inside you, ready to strike back. Had your gift continued to swell, I doubt that you would still be alive. I've never seen power like that in anyone before."

"Then why didn't you come back?"

"I had a mission. I tried to find you when it was over, but I never knew your name . . ."

"My name is Reem Kahrin, and my people have abandoned me."

"And my name is Jameson Willow, I have abandoned my people for you."

"I don't deserve it."

"I don't know why you think that," he answered, pulling her into an embrace.

Before she could say anything more, her stomach rumbled, and they both laughed. "Hungry?" he asked her, smiling brightly.

"Just a little." She smiled back at him as she pulled away.

They both sat on the floor and dug into the pot of stew with their hands. It may not have tasted like much, but they never would have known—they were too hungry for it to matter. When she'd eaten her fill—almost a quarter of the contents—she lay down on the ground and stared up at the ceiling. "It's a strange feeling," she said.

"What is?"

"Not being able to see the sky," she answered, turning her head toward where he sat.

"I can fix that." He smiled, reaching over and taking her hand in his before teleporting them both of them onto the surface.

"Where are we now?" she asked, once again staring upward—though this time staring as clouds rolled across the sky of the open desert.

"Somewhere away from everything else."

"It's beautiful." She smiled, still staring as the clouds moved lazily across the sky.

"I don't know if I'd say that," Jameson replied, rubbing her hand with his thumb.

"Why's that?"

"Your beauty is greater than any I've ever seen." He lay down next to her as she released his hand and ran her fingers through his hair. "Thank you," he said.

"For what?" She turned toward him questioningly.

"For trusting me."

"Why wouldn't I?"

"Isn't it obvious?" he asked, thinking about the night he'd left her in the woods.

"You were upset. I understood that even then."

"You're too understanding." He smiled, taking her hand back in his.

"Why do you think that?" she asked.

"How does it feel—not fighting all the time?" he asked in return, changing the subject.

"Different." She turned her head back to the sky, closed her eyes and felt the waning sun warm her face.

"Do you miss it?"

"I don't miss having to kill, but I do miss helping my people. I'm not sure I'll ever really be able to stop thinking like a warrior."

"What will you fight for, now that you can't fight for them?"

"I don't know." She shook her head as she turned to face him once again. "Maybe I'll just be a warrior without a fight."

"There's always something worth fighting for," he replied, stroking her cheek with his free hand.

"What are you fighting for?"

"You." He leaned toward her and kissed her lips gently, opening his eyes only when she pulled away.

"You sure I'm worth fighting for?" She smiled slightly, looking into his eyes as she spoke, her cheeks flushing with color.

"Positive."

Her smile grew as she rolled herself on top of him and kissed him passionately. *"I do believe I've fallen in love with you, Jameson Willow,"* she whispered into his mind as he teleported them back to the main chamber of the cave. He ran his fingers from her waist to her neck and turned, moving her body under his as they kissed. His lips suddenly stopped moving against hers, and he pulled away, standing back to his feet. "I'm sorry," he said, slowly walking away from her, toward the previously unexplored area of the cave.

"What's wrong?" she asked, her breathing heavy as she sat up and watched him pace along the large gap in the wall of the chamber.

Arguments

"I'm sorry, I just, I don't want to move too fast," he said as he continued to pace along the side of the chamber. "Please understand," he continued before she could speak. "I am in love with you, but . . . I don't want to hurt this. If something were to happen, I wouldn't . . . I don't want you to regret being with me. I—"

"Jameson. Stop. Please," she said, taking her hair out of the bun.

"No, Reem. Listen to yourself. Five days ago, you never would have been caught dead with me unless we were on a mission, and now you tell me you're in love with me? How do you expect me to react?"

"I expected you to be happier than this." She shrugged.

"Well, I guess you aren't as good at reading minds as I thought you were."

"You're the one who said I didn't want to know what you were thinking!" she said as she jumped to her feet. "Now you want me to read your mind all the time?"

"That's not what I said at all."

"Then please, enlighten me." She crossed her arms and tilted her head to the side.

"Decide what you want, Reem. That's what I'm saying. What am I to you? Am I your apprentice, or am I your lover?"

"I . . ." She placed her hands on top of her head and grunted, staring at him with eyes that burned.

"You don't know, do you?" he said, finally coming to a halt a few feet in front of her. *"Do you?"*

"Do I have to?"

"Yes. I need to know what I am to you, Reem. I don't want to be your apprentice for five hours a day and your lover for the rest. It's too complicated."

"Why? Why can't you be both? You need the training. You were ecstatic when I told you I wanted to train you, and even more so when I kiss you. Why would you only want one of those things?"

"Reem, I only want to know what I am to you. Just tell me that."

"You are . . . everything to me. Without you, I would be dead right now. What more do you want?"

"That doesn't tell me anything. Do you really love me, or are you merely grateful that I saved your life in Admiri?" His brow furrowed as he made the connection in his head.

"How could you even think that?" She approached him, holding her arms out as if to embrace him, but he turned away from her.

"How could I think that? It makes perfect sense! First, you're shocked to find out that I'm in love with you, and then I save your life and you start to believe that you're in love with me, when in reality you're only grateful that I saved you. Tell me how that would not make sense to you."

"No. No, you're right. Of course I don't love you. Why would I? You're nothing to me but a fool who gave up his life because he thinks he loves me. You're right. It makes perfect sense," she said, removing a knife from its sheath on her thigh with her mind and pointing it at him, dangling it in the air in front of his face.

He was speechless. They hadn't had an argument like this since they'd arrived here, and he had been hoping that it wouldn't happen. Her breathing got heavier as she stood there, only feet away from him, waiting for him to say something—anything.

When he said nothing, she walked up to him, took the knife in one hand, and slapped his face as hard as she could with the other, using her gifts to make it sting. "How's that for your answer?" she asked him as he moved his hand to his face, shocked. "Maybe I would have been better off in Admiri," she said, her whisper loud in the silence of the cave as she quickly walked back into her bedroom.

"Reem . . . Reem, please. Come back," Jameson pleaded as she walked away from him. "Reem!" he shouted when she ignored him.

"Jameson, take me back to Admiri," she said finally, reappearing in the doorway to the room.

"Reem . . . don't say that. Please," he said as he approached her slowly.

"What did you expect me to say?" Her head tilted to the side.

"If you ask it of me, I will take you back. But I beg you to reconsider the fact that they will kill you. Don't forget that. You will not belong among them until your name is cleared." He stood in front of her and took her hand in his. "Consider that."

"Jameson, take me back."

"To Admiri?" he questioned, staring her straight in the eye.

"To Athena. I need to know something. Take me back there."

"Are you sure that's a good idea?" His eyes narrowed.

"Yes. There's something I need to know." *"I'm not asking."*

Jameson disappeared, and reappeared again with a backpack slung over his shoulders. "Yes ma'am," he said, taking her hand and bringing it to his lips as he teleported them onto the surface.

She smiled and scanned the area of their landing: a small cement building containing one small table, four mismatched chairs, and a small bed. "Have I been here before?" she asked him.

"Why yes, I believe you have."

"How did you go so far?"

"I wasn't exhausted this time, remember? This is about the farthest I would feel comfortable teleporting with fragile cargo." He winked.

"Fragile?" She raised her eyebrows.

"What would you have me do?"

"Well, we could stay the night. We know what to expect here, after all."

"I still want an answer to my question." He cocked his head toward her.

"Which one?" she asked, meeting his eyes.

"What am I to you?"

She thought for a few moments about how to answer his question—all the while staring into his questioning eyes. He waited patiently, not wanting to rush an answer from her, but still needing an answer before they went any farther.

Losing patience, he looked up from her eyes, toward the curtain that served as the door to the room. As he stared into the distance, he found her arms wrapping themselves around his body and her lips pressing against his. He closed his eyes and embraced her, his lips now moving against hers. She pulled away slowly and kissed his neck. *"Does that answer your question?"*

"I love you, Reem."

"I know."

She met his lips with hers once again, her arms pulling his body closer to her as they kissed.

As they slowly pulled away from each other, he ran his fingers through her hair and down her spine, and she shivered with the feel of it. She pulled her body as close to his as she could and buried her face in his chest. *"Never let go,"* she whispered into his mind.

"Never," he replied as he kissed her forehead.

She hugged him tighter and then released him slowly, turning her head and looking straight into his eyes. "I am in love with you. Do you believe that?" she asked.

He smiled and nodded. "We'll need to find something for you to wear before we go into Athena. It's very likely that everyone in the cities has heard of what happened in Admiri, and if what the Superiors said is true, there are many people still alive in Athena."

"We can stick to the shadows. I don't want to hide."

"We will stick to the shadows," he said as he stroked her hair. "But I do not trust that alone to keep you safe."

"I won't hide from my own people."

"And what are you doing right now? You have to hide from our people. They will kill you if they find you."

"What do you want me to do?"

"I'll find you something. Stay here," he said, kissing her forehead before he walked toward the door.

"Be safe," she said as he walked outside.

He walked among the people of the settlement, searching for something that would hide her face from the people of Athena. If she were to be found at any time without him, they would kill her before he could get to her—he was sure of it. He searched through some of the people's homes, throughout the streets, anywhere he could think of before he finally found what he was looking for. Two matching hooded cloaks hung from a rod inside a small building several houses down from the one he'd left Reem in. He walked inside and took them before anyone saw him, put one of them on, and carried the other with him as he walked back to meet her.

Inside the small, one-room home, Reem paced slowly as she waited for him. What would he find that would be able to hide her from her people? She could think of nothing that would sufficiently hide her face. She'd been too deep in thought to see the cloaked man walk in and lean against the wall.

"You overthink everything," he said, startling her.

"Who are you?" she asked, turning to face him while putting her hand on the butt of her gun, ready to fire.

"You mean to tell me you don't even recognize me?" He laughed as he removed his hood.

"Jameson, I almost shot you!" She laughed in return, running up and slapping his arm playfully.

"You know you wouldn't have done that." He kissed her forehead and handed her a second cloak. "I found you one too."

"Thank you."

"How many times do I have to tell you not to thank me?" he asked. "I only want you to be safe on our journey into the lion's den." He winked.

"And how many times must I thank you before you stop saying that?" Her eyebrows rose.

"At least once more," he replied, dipping his head. "One more hour and I'll have the strength to teleport on to the next safe zone. Though I must warn you that the safe zone was created by the Superiors. If they suspect that you might use it, they will have heavy guard posted there."

She nodded her head as he spoke, lost in thought. "What do you suggest?"

"I suggest that we wait out the night here, and tomorrow we teleport past the next safe zone to avoid any such mishaps. There should be nothing out there but trees and wildlife—I inspected the area myself before our first journey there."

"Then we shall do as you suggest." She nodded slowly.

"And what now, Ms. Kahrin?" he asked.

"Now we wait," she replied, smiling as she unstrapped all of her weapons from her body and set them on the table.

She turned and walked to the bed, sitting down on the edge and facing away from him. "We should be safe for the night, shouldn't we?" she asked.

"Should, yes. I can't make any promises, but I don't think there will be a repeat of our previous stay—it's not as cold tonight," he replied, sitting next to her and rubbing her shoulders gently.

"How did this happen to me?" she whispered, obviously lost in thought.

"You never deserved to be an outcast."

"Then why am I?" She turned to face him.

"You placed your trust in the ones whom we all blindly give our trust, and they've broken it. The Great Superior must have been planning this for years, or it would never have worked. He needed someone to take the blame if any survivors were found, and that person was you. None of this is your fault, Reem. You never deserved to live on the run."

Her face grew hard as she took in his words. She never deserved this life. She deserved the life of a famed warrior. She deserved her old life. But now . . . now she would take a life with him over a life of killing any day. Now she knew that she could never go back to her old life, though she still desired to be among her people. She knew that she was destined to go with Jameson, no matter where he went.

"I don't know what I would do without you." She shook her head and smiled as she realized just how much she cared for the man who sat beside her.

"I will always love you. I will go with you wherever you go—or I'll take you there myself." He winked at her as she laughed.

She fell on her back with laughter—a sound that brought a smile to his face. She was so beautiful, lying there next to him. She reached her arm up and placed her hand on his shoulder, pulling him down onto the bed next to her as she continued to laugh.

She turned onto her side and kissed his lips, running her fingers through his hair. He grunted as he once again moved her body underneath his as they kissed passionately. Her breathing was heavy as he kissed her neck.

"Reem . . . ," he whispered into her neck.

"Yes?" she asked, her breathing still heavy.

"Don't take this the wrong way," he said, teleporting himself across the room from her, once again leaving her hanging.

"What's wrong this time?" She sat up as she spoke, obviously confused.

"We're in a Human camp," he replied as he ran his fingers through his hair.

"I see your point."

"If we're trying to blend in for the night, that's not the way to go about it."

"Good point." She nodded as she tried to slow her breathing. "Good, good point."

"Maybe we should talk about something else," he said as he leaned against the wall. "Why are we going to Athena?"

"I want to know how many people survived. I need to see it for myself. I want to know if all of them could have been saved."

"Is that such a good idea?"

"I don't know, but I need answers. I need to know why the Great Superior chose me to take the fall for him."

"What if you don't like the answer?"

"I just need to know." She shrugged.

"Then I'll help you find your answers."

"You don't have to. I know you're not exactly in favor of this whole thing. Just teleport me in and let me find my answers."

"I told you. I'll go wherever you go. I promise you I will keep you safe no matter where you are."

"Come here," she said, patting the empty space next to herself.

"Are you sure that's a good idea?" He leaned forward slightly.

"Please," she whispered.

He walked to the bed and lay down next to her, wrapping his arms around her as she buried her face in his chest. "Sleep well, my love. Tomorrow will be a long day," he whispered into her ear.

Travelers

She woke with a start as she realized that Jameson was no longer beside her. Her eyes opened widely and she sat up, confused. "Jameson?" she asked as she sat up.

"How many times do I have to tell you to relax?" he replied, chuckling. He sat at the table, strapping a few weapons to his legs as he chewed a piece of bread he'd evidently stolen.

"What time is it?" she asked as she threw her legs off the side of the bed and ran her fingers through her hair.

"Relax." He winked. "You have time. I found some bread and meat a few doors down. Help yourself." He pointed to the small plate beside a pot that sat in the center of the table.

She stood and walked to the table, taking a piece of bread and biting into it. "What time is it?" she repeated.

"Eight o'clock. I suggest we leave by ten. If we stop to rest after we reach the woods, I should be able to teleport us straight to Athena after that."

"So soon?" she asked as she set down her bread and began to strap her holsters and sheaths to her legs and sides once more. "I thought it would take longer than that."

"The Superiors had me take a slower route the last time. They wanted to be sure you were safe—or at least that's what they told me."

"How far can you teleport?"

"By myself, a quarter of the way around the world. With a passenger, I'd only trust myself to go half that—at least the width of the continent. I don't like to take any chances, especially with precious cargo." He winked once again.

"That's farther than any recorded. Why haven't I heard of that before?"

"Because I'm not cut out for all the fame. I specifically asked the Superiors not to share the extent of my gifts with anyone outside of the Seven."

"Well, it seems you're more full of surprises than I expected. And it's more like the Five now—two of them died in Athena," she said before picking up her bread and eating once again. He smiled at her, laughing when she smiled back—her mouth still full of food.

He walked to her and stood behind her, wrapping his arms around her waist. "I have a plan."

"For?" she asked as she lay her head back against his shoulder.

"When we are traveling, I will refer to you as my sister, Anna. With the cloaks, it should help with blending in with the locals, and if we need to speak to anyone, we shouldn't have any problems." He tightened his hold on her waist. "I wouldn't want anything to happen to you," he whispered.

"And what will I call you? Your name is as well known as mine," she asked, closing her eyes putting her arms over his.

"You may call me whatever you like," he whispered into her neck.

She thought for a moment, turning around in his arms and scrutinizing his face. "Simon. My brother, Simon," she said finally. "That fits you, I think."

"Simon . . . I like it," he replied, smiling.

"Good," she replied as she pushed up to her tiptoes and pecked him on the cheek.

He smiled and tightened his arms around her for a moment, running his fingers through her hair. "I love you," he whispered.

"I love you too."

He lifted her off the ground and twirled her around before finally releasing her and leaning back against the table. "You have no idea what that means to me." He shook his head slowly.

"Oh, I think I understand better than you think I do." She winked before sitting next to him and tapping her temple with her index finger.

"I suppose you do have a better understanding than most. You have an unfair advantage. Which reminds me, if anyone asks, you are a telepath. Nothing more. Nothing less."

"Are you sure that's such a good idea?" Her head tilted to the side.

"It's better than everyone knowing who you really are, isn't it?"

"True. Alright, my name is Anna and I'm a class one telepath. That sound good?"

"Yes, except that you're no class one. If there are any Sensors, they will know that you are class three. You'd better stick with the truth for now."

"I can do that," she said, nodding slowly. "What's our last name?"

"I haven't decided on that yet. Preferably something that won't draw attention to us in any way—just in case."

"Johnson?" she suggested.

"That could work. Anna and Simon Johnson, the telepath and teleporter. I can lie easily enough about my own powers, plus I can shield them from the Sensors, so we shouldn't have a problem there. But once we're inside Athena, you'd better let me do the talking."

"Shouldn't I be the one doing the talking?"

"No. I don't think that's smart. If anyone were to recognize your voice from the speech you made when we first arrived there, things could go badly. I don't think many people there know my voice that well."

"Alright. If anything looks like it's going badly from my perspective, I'll let you know." *"I'm good at that."*

"Indeed you are. You seem to be perfecting the use of your gift quite nicely."

"Being able to use it without fear is helping. I could never use my gift in the city—I didn't want the Superiors to discover it."

"I would not ask you to tell anyone that you are a telepath, except that everyone knows of the almighty powers of Reem Kahrin."

"Will any of them remember you?"

"I don't know. But I suppose you can tell me that. With our gifts such as they are, we shouldn't have any problem sneaking around the city without drawing attention to ourselves."

"One can only hope."

"If anything goes wrong, I will get you out of the city unharmed. At the very least, I can give you a gift that will make you go unnoticed by the majority of the people."

"I don't want any of your gifts."

"You've already taken one, remember?"

"Which is also one that will help me if the Superiors do catch us."

"They can't kill a healer." He nodded. "Though technically it's quite difficult to kill a class five telekinetic as well." He winked.

"They know I wouldn't resist them. If the judgment were fair, at least."

"I do not believe that I can live without you anymore." He took her hand in his as he spoke.

"I would rather die than be forced to live apart from you." She stood and walked to his side, bending down to kiss his forehead gently.

He stood in front of her and cupped his hand around her neck, rubbing her cheek lightly with his thumb before leaning in and kissing her lips. Her arms wound around his body, pulling him closer to her as they kissed, and he ran his fingers through her hair. "You know I'll always love you," he whispered into her mouth.

As they pulled away from each other, she turned around in his arms and faced away from him. He kept his arms tightly around her waist and whispered in her ear, "We'll need to be more careful when we're in the city. I don't think that's something a brother would do to a sister." He smiled when she laughed.

"No. No, it's not, is it?"

"As I said, we'll have to be more careful."

"Indeed." She traced the mark on his wrist with her thumb as she spoke. "How old were you when you were given the treatment?"

"Too young . . . I was the only one in my family on whom the treatment worked. Somehow even my family didn't trust me after my gifts developed. I was one of the first put in the camps," he replied.

"I was the only one in my family as well. At first they called me special, but when they discovered the damage my gifts could do, they threw me into the camps as well." She leaned her head back on his shoulder and turned her head to kiss his neck softly.

"It seems we have more in common than I thought," he whispered back.

"So it seems."

"You should eat. I don't know if the people at the next camp will have anything." He released her slowly, and she turned around to face him once more.

"How long will we be there for?" she asked.

"Not long, but I think we should do some reconnaissance around there too. They might have some useful information on Athena."

"No—they'll think it strange that anyone hadn't heard what happened."

"Not if I tell them that I just broke you out of a Human camp where you were being used in experiments. It would be obvious that I have been out of the loop for the duration of that time."

"How long have you been thinking about all of this?" She smiled, picking up her bread and taking another bite.

"I don't want anything to happen to you."

"Did you ever consider that you might be the one who needs to relax?" She winked. "I'll be fine. As long as I'm with you."

"Finish your bread. We'll leave when you're ready."

"Why so serious?"

"Because I have your safety to keep in mind. I don't know why you aren't taking this as seriously as I am."

"I'm not taking this seriously? Have you seen how many weapons I have on me whenever we leave the cave? I am deadly serious about all of this. I don't want to be taken back to the Superiors. I do not want to die this day. Or any other day for that matter. Understand this: I may not always seem serious, but I have scanned every mind that has walked past that door, checking to see if they know who we are. I have jammed the majority of the weapons in this camp, and I will do exactly as you ask me to when we leave here. I do not want to die. Nor do I wish to live without you." She took his hand in hers. "Please. Understand that."

"You jammed all of their weapons?" he asked, unbelieving.

"Yes. I've done it before. It takes a lot of concentration. The Superiors preferred to fight fairly, so they asked me not to use that trick unless I needed to," she replied plainly. "There's a lot that my gift can do. A lot that people don't know. Or at least choose not to think about." She looked away from him, toward the pot of stew that still sat in the center of the table.

"Your gift is virtually unstoppable, isn't it?"

"It takes a great deal of concentration in order to control it. If I ever lose that concentration, my gifts could destroy everything. If I had started out a class five, it could have killed me." She lowered her head, afraid to see the look on his face.

"I can help, you know. If you want me to."

"No, Jameson. This is my burden to bear."

"I don't want you to be in pain."

"I've gotten used to it. This is something that I need to do. I need to learn control over my gifts."

"But I can give you that control, Reem."

"And someday . . ." She looked into his eyes. "Someday I might want or need it. But not now."

He stared into her eyes, those beautiful brown eyes, and leaned in to kiss her forehead. "Eat. You need your strength. We'll leave when you're ready."

"Thank you, J—Simon." She smiled as she picked up a piece of meat from the plate.

"Eat it." He nodded, standing up and walking toward the door.

"Where are you going?" she said before putting the food into her mouth.

"Nowhere. Just checking outside," he replied absentmindedly.

"What's wrong, Jameson?" She stood and walked to his side, placing her hand on his shoulder. "Tell me," she whispered.

"Why won't you let me help you?" he asked, turning around to face her. "I want to help you."

"Because I . . . I don't understand your gift. How is it that you can give me any gift you like or take gifts away from those whom you dislike? I've never met anyone with your power before."

"My gift helps those who need help. I don't use it in immoral ways. I don't take gifts away from people just because I think they're a threat, I don't give people gifts just because they want them. Do you understand that?"

"It's just that your gifts frighten me. I can't explain it." She placed her palm on his cheek as she spoke. "I'm sorry."

"Let me help you, Reem. Please. I don't want to see you in pain, struggling to maintain control of the power that lives inside you. Please," he pleaded.

"What would you do?"

"Make you stronger. I won't take away your gift. I'll only give you the ability to control it. That's all."

She thought for a moment, her eyes dropping to the floor and her hand dropping to her side before he reached out and took it in his. "Please, Reem. Let me help," he said, placing his hand under her chin and tilting her face up so that they were eye to eye. "Please."

"Okay," she said finally.

"Are you sure?" he asked.

"Yes. I'm sure."

He closed his eyes, keeping her hand in his, and sent a jolt of power from his fingertips into her palm. She could feel power pulsing through her veins, feel the control that he had given her, feel her other gifts come more fully under her control, and feel the energy transferring from his hand to hers. When he opened his eyes, he saw that her eyes had closed and that her hands appeared welded to his. He could feel the power he'd given her flowing through her veins, and feel her attempts to bring all of her gifts under complete control.

When her eyes finally opened and she looked into his, the silver glint in her eyes was filled with a power that he'd never seen in her before. "Better?" he asked.

"Much. Much better," she replied, pulling him closer with her gifts and kissing his lips. Her arms wound around his body, but it was only a formality. The power that pulsed through her veins had rendered him immobile other than his arms that wrapped around her waist and his lips that moved against hers.

He groaned, and she released her hold slightly. She ran her hand from the base of his neck down his spine, and he shivered before lifting her off her feet and carrying her to the bed where he lay down gently, with her body on top of his.

Suddenly she jumped off him and walked quickly to the door. "Someone's outside," she whispered softly as he stood to his feet.

"Who?" he whispered back.

"I don't know. They're waiting for someone . . . Jordan . . . I don't know why."

"We should get going. Are you ready?" he asked, walking up to her and reaching for her hand.

"Yes."

He walked back to the table, grabbed a cloak, threw it to her, and put his own cloak on before returning to her side and holding out his hand once more. "Let's go," he said.

She put the hood over her head so that it covered her face, and she placed her hand in his. He teleported them into the edge of the next safe zone, right on the edge of the Advanced camp, and tightened his grip on her hand. "We're brother and sister. Remember that. And I've just saved your life, so there's no reason why I shouldn't hold your hand. Stay by my side. Please," he whispered into her ear before he led her to through the camp in search of someone who could help them. One hour and they would leave.

As they walked, she tugged on his cloak sleeve. *"There, the man standing near the heater in the tent. He seems willing to talk."*

Jameson nodded slowly and led her into the tent, angling their bodies so that his blocked hers for the most part. "Keep your head down," he whispered so quietly that she could only hear it through the power of her telepathy.

They walked up to the man, and Jameson held out his hands as though he needed warmth from the heater. The man was short, with slightly balding dark hair that he'd pulled back into a ponytail. His dark skin made him seem evil in the darkness of the tent, and his dark clothing only aided in that. When they reached his side, he lifted his head slightly and stared in their direction.

"Sir." Jameson nodded in welcome.

"Who are you? I've never seen you around here before," the man replied, his voice deep and throaty.

"I am Simon Johnson, and this is my sister Anna. We've come in search of shelter on our way to Athena."

"Athena? Haven't you heard?"

"Heard what?" Jameson asked, his voice thick with tension.

"Athena's been deserted. There's no one there now. I'm sorry to have to break it to you, but Athena's gone."

"Gone?" Jameson asked, seemingly unbelieving.

"Where have you been? Everyone knows about that."

"I've been . . . out of touch. My sister and I were being kept in a Human camp. We didn't get out until a few days ago . . . How much has happened since we were taken?"

"When were you taken?"

"I'm honestly not sure." He shook his head. "At least a month ago, perhaps?"

"Then you've missed quite a bit. Come on, have a seat and we'll talk," the man said, motioning with his hand toward a set of chairs that sat along the edge of the tent.

"Thank you, sir."

"It's Charlie."

"Charlie then." Jameson nodded.

The three of them took their seats, Charlie and Jameson sitting two seats apart, and Reem taking her seat next to Jameson, never letting go of his hand. "So you two are brother and sister?" Charlie asked.

"Yes, sir. We've always been very close. We were the only two in our family on whom the treatment was successful. It's brought us closer together."

"What are your gifts?"

"I am a teleporter, and Anna is—"

"A telepath. I'm a telepath. You needn't always speak for me, Simon," Reem cut in.

"Of course," Jameson replied, nodding.

"Telepath? What class?" Charlie asked curiously.

"Class three. What are your gifts, Charlie?" she asked.

"I'm a hunter. I can find anything if I put my mind to it. Not as much fun as telepathy, if you ask me." He chuckled.

"It's not as glamorous as it sounds. It can be quite intrusive if I don't keep it in check."

"Hunting isn't all it's cracked up to be either. Sometimes I can't find my mark, and the more that happens, the less the Superiors ask me to work with them."

"I'm sorry to hear that," she replied.

"It's not your problem. Are you two from Athena?"

"Yes, sir," Jameson replied. "We haven't seen it for some time though."

"Oh dear," Charlie said, rubbing his face with his hand. "I hate to be the bearer of bad news."

"What's happened?" Reem questioned softly.

Athena

"I really hate to have to tell you this. You seem like such nice people," Charlie began, leaning back in his chair and running his fingers through his hair. "Athena has been evacuated. For the most part, anyways. There's still a group in place that are working on clearing the area and getting it ready for repopulation. But the thing is, Athena isn't safe anymore. The Superiors sent out a warning not to send any more transports, saying that Reem Kahrin herself set off a weapon that killed everything within several hundred miles of the city. I don't know what she did or how she did it, but she's made the area into a mess, to say the least. They say that the area is filled with dead bodies, and that the survivors were few."

"How many?" Reem butted in, jolting him out of his story.

"How many what?" Charlie asked.

"How many survivors? The city was filled with my friends. My family. How many survived?" she asked, her voice full of panic.

"Not many, I'm afraid. I'm not sure on the exact numbers, but it was less than three hundred. I'm so sorry." He hung his head in reverence as she lifted her hands to her face.

"So few? But Athena was the second-largest Advanced city," Jameson said, bringing Reem's hand to his face and kissing it gently.

"I'm so sorry." Charlie leaned over and placed his hand on Jameson's shoulder in an attempt to comfort him. "I can't even begin to imagine what you're going through right now."

"We needed to know," Reem replied as she stood and walked back to the opening of the tent.

"You should know that there's no way you'll get back into Athena. The Superiors have cornered it off. No one in, no one out—except for the dead, that is. The team that's there will be removing the bodies for at least a month, I hear. I'm sorry, but there's no way you're getting in there."

"I understand . . . I'll take my sister to Mettirna."

"Admiri is closer, son. Maybe you should take her there. She looks like she needs to see a healer," Charlie whispered.

"Admiri is under siege at all times. I will not put my sister in unnecessary danger."

"In that case, there're camps set up all the way between here and Mettirna. I'll show you a map of the area, and you can be on your way as soon as you're ready."

"Thank you so much, Charlie. The sooner I can get my sister to a city, the better. I don't like keeping her out in the open—not after . . ." Jameson shook his head, and Charlie nodded in response.

"I understand," he replied, his voice a whisper. "I'll go get you those maps, and then you can be on your way. I wouldn't advise keeping her here much longer. She doesn't look to be doing so well."

Jameson nodded and they both stood on their feet, Charlie walking toward the exit, Jameson walking to Reem and placing his hand on her shoulder.

"We should go. It's not safe," she whispered into his mind.

"Do they suspect?" he whispered back.

"Charlie suspects something. He doesn't know who we are, but he didn't buy our story—not completely anyway."

"Whenever you're ready we will leave."

"I'm ready now. I don't trust them. He's speaking with the camp leaders— they want to see us."

"Why?"

"I'm not sure . . . they . . . they want to know who we are." She turned toward him. "We should go. Now," she said.

"Where to?"

"Athena. I still need my answers. It won't take long. On the way back, we can stay in the woods for a while. We should be fine there."

"Athena it is," he replied.

Charlie and four newcomers walked in the tent just as Jameson teleported Reem and himself to the edge of the city. "Welcome to Athena," he whispered as he scanned the area for anyone that may have seen them teleport in.

"No one saw us. There's no one in the area."

"Where can you find your answers?"

"The tower. I need to find that vial."

"The tower it is." He teleported them just outside the tower and waited for her to give him the all clear.

"It's safe. No one's inside," she whispered.

He teleported inside, to the last room they'd been in before the Athenians had been destroyed. She left his side for a moment, searching the room for the small vial she'd left her so short a time ago. The city was virtually untouched. Everything seemed exactly as they'd left it—only there was no one to be seen. "Where's the team Charlie said was here?" Jameson asked.

"I don't sense anyone in the immediate area. I believe they're somewhere on the outskirts . . . yes . . . that's where they are. They're burning the bodies of the dead Superiors . . . they've no idea we've come."

"Good. Get what we've come for and we'll be on our way."

"It's not that simple, Jameson. I need answers."

"Charlie lied to us?"

"No, as far as he knew he was telling the truth. But I want to know the truth from the mouth of someone who really knows. Someone on that team has the answers I'm looking for. If we can get closer, I can search their minds for the information I need."

"It's not safe," he whispered, taking her hand and turning her to face him.

"I'll be fine, Jameson. As long as you're by my side." She smiled before going back to her search.

"Have you found anything?" he whispered.

"It's gone. I left it right here. They must have taken it."

"Then we'll have a chat with someone on that team and go. I don't feel right staying here. Something is very off."

"We need to have a look around. Can you give us a gift that would make us invisible to their eyes?"

"Gift giving drains my energy even faster than teleporting. I would rather be safe than sorry."

Her face turned down as she considered the fact. "We still need to have that look around. If anything should go wrong, you can still teleport us to safety. That's something at least."

"I don't want you out there. What if something happens?"

"Nothing will happen to me. Not with the powers you've given me. Trust me, I'll be fine." She walked past him toward the door, decidedly heading down into the city.

"Reem, wait," he said, grabbing her arm and stopping her before she could exit. "Just wait."

"Jameson, I've already explained this to you. I need answers."

"I understand that. I'm only asking that you wait until dark. By then, I'll have the power to teleport us past the safe zone and into the safety of the woods. Plus the people here will likely rest after nightfall. Please, Reem. Just wait. Only a few more hours."

"Only a few more hours?" she asked.

"We only have to wait until dark. I won't let you leave here until then."

"Fine. But only until dark."

"And once you get the answers you're looking for, we leave. Deal?"

"Deal," she replied.

"It's almost time," Jameson said, moving away from the window and sitting next to her on the floor on the side of the room.

"Good. The team seems to be settling down for the evening. The leader appears to be the most well informed of the lot of them," Reem replied.

"And I assume you know which one he is?"

"He's taking first watch while his men sleep. He'll be the only one awake." She smiled.

"So how are we going to do this?" he asked, taking her hand in his.

"You're going to teleport to the camp, grab the leader, and teleport him back here so I can ask him my questions."

"What if something happens to you while I'm away?"

"Jameson, you'll be gone a total of fifteen seconds; I'll be fine. Besides, there's no one in the area." She smiled sweetly at him.

"Okay. But I don't want this man to see your face. Then he'll know who we are. We need to maintain that we are brother and sister—Simon and Anna."

"I'll keep my hood over my face the entire time."

"Good," he said, standing to his feet and releasing her hand. "I'll be back in fifteen seconds." He winked.

"You'd better," she replied.

"One more thing: what's his gift?"

"It's an unusual gift—not many Advanced were given such simplicity in their gifts. He's smart. Incredibly so, with heightened senses and intelligence beyond belief. He's the only one who might be able to figure out who we are."

"He's that smart?"

"Yes, I'm afraid so. Now go. The sooner I get my answers the sooner we can leave." She stood to her feet beside him and kissed his cheek lightly.

He turned toward her and kissed her forehead before teleporting himself near the camp.

Everything was dark. He was glad he'd allowed his eyes time to adjust to the darkness before teleporting—if he hadn't he wouldn't have been able to see his hand if he held it right in front of his face.

He could see the camp. He'd teleported himself between a rock and a hard place—literally. A rock that had been catapulted into the city during the war stood only inches in front of his face, and he leaned back against the wall of a building near the camp. He could see they'd built a small fire in the middle of the city's courtyard, and the majority of the men were fast asleep.

As far as Jameson could see, only one man was awake: a tall, well-built man seated near the fire, cleaning his weapon. Surely this could not be the man that Reem intended for him to bring to her. He was young, no older than his mid-twenties, with golden eyes and long sandy hair tied back in a ponytail.

One teleport. That's all it would take to get to him. But Jameson didn't want to teleport into a trap. He stood there and watched, waiting to see if the men were really asleep or if they were simply waiting for him to try something.

He was peering around the area, making sure that they hadn't somehow surrounded him before he'd even teleported when he realized that the man was walking toward his exact position as if he'd seen him standing there all along. "Jameson Willow. That is your name, isn't it?" the man asked when he stood a few feet away.

"You know my name. I don't know yours," Jameson replied, still unbelieving that the man could see him, but remembering that he could get out at any time.

"Seth. Seth Green. Where is she, Jameson?" The man stepped closer, obviously able to see him. "Where is the savior?" His eyes burned with an intensity that Jameson had never before seen in any man.

"Savior?" he asked.

"Where is Reem Kahrin? I know you have her with you."

"She's safe. You will never lay a hand on her."

"I do not wish to. Whatever has been said to you about me is a lie. I am not who the Superiors believe me to be. Please, take me to her. I must see the savior."

"How can I trust you?"

"Truthfully, you cannot. But I'm sure she'll contact you soon and tell you that she needs information that I carry."

"Jameson . . . ," her voice whispered.

"And how would she do that? As I said, she's safe. Far away from here," he said, ignoring her voice.

"You and I both know that the savior is a telepath."

"Jameson," her voice whispered once again. *"Bring him to me—I will be fine."*

"But . . . ," he started to reply.

"Bring him."

"Do we?" He tilted his head to one side, trying not to tip his hand.

"Please, Jameson. I need to see her."

"Bring him, Jameson."

Jameson reluctantly reached out and placed his hand on Seth's shoulder. "My sister wishes to see you," he said before teleporting the both of them back to where Reem waited, standing in the corner of the room, her hood pulled down to cover her face.

"Thank you, Jameson," Seth said as he turned to face her. "Savior," he said, dropping to one knee in front of her.

"Who do you think that I am?" she asked, masking her voice slightly.

"You are Reem Kahrin. The savior. I have been waiting for you."

"I am not the one you speak of. My name is Anna, and I am a telepath. I am here only to receive the answers to my questions," she replied as Jameson moved to stand beside her.

"And yet you travel with the best teleporter in the world, Jameson Willow. He has already told me his name, savior. And every Advanced knows that Reem Kahrin is with Jameson Willow."

"Then what is it that you wish to tell me, Seth Green?" she said, turning her head toward Jameson slightly and lifting her hood so that Seth could see her face.

"You are not alone, savior. You still have supporters."

"Stand." She paused. "What do you mean?"

"My men and I, we would follow you to our deaths. And we are not the only ones," he replied, standing to his feet.

"I do not understand."

"He wants you to lead them in battle against the Superiors," Jameson whispered.

"Do you?" she asked Seth.

"I would not have worded it as such, but in a way, yes. We are taking over Athena in the name of freedom, and if you were to join us, I know we would have the advantage over the Superiors."

"Explain."

"The Superiors sent me and my men here to clean out the city, removing all evidence of the vial and of the deaths. We've burned the bodies of all that died in the immediate area, and the vial has been destroyed. We are taking the city tonight, in your name, if you wish it."

"Your timing could not be worse, Seth. I am here only for answers. I will not lead a battle against those to whom I have pledged my allegiance."

"Perhaps you will once you receive the answers that you desire. I'm sure that you can find them at your own will." He tapped the side of his head, an invitation for her to find her answers.

"Are you sure you want that? I'll be able to see every thought you've ever had, every lie you've ever told, everything," she replied. "I do not wish to know your secrets, Seth. But I will not let a stone go unturned. Understood?"

"I am at your mercy."

"Clear your mind," she said, approaching him and placing her hands on his shoulders. "I will find my answers." Jameson took a step toward them, and she turned her head toward him. "It's alright, Jameson. He's not going to hurt me."

"I don't trust him."

"Trust me then," she replied, turning her head back toward Seth and closing her eyes, searching for her answers.

Seth's eyes rolled back in his head as she searched, his head falling forward as though he'd fallen asleep. "There were no survivors," Reem began, stating her findings so that Jameson could hear as well. "The Superiors lied. They sent Seth here to make it look like there were survivors, to make it look like I had attempted to kill everyone of my own accord. He found . . . the vial. There, on the table where I left it. He took it and destroyed it, just like the Superiors had ordered him. But . . . he . . . he didn't finish his work here. He won't. He realized . . . his men believed me to be their savior, believed that the Superiors had lied to them. They mutinied. Seth has been working with them ever since, and he's taken their side. He's discovered that over one-third of the Advanced population would follow me, and . . . the Superiors do not plan to repopulate Athena. He decided that it is the perfect location for my followers to take their stand, to fight against the Superiors. He's . . . started rebuilding the city from the outside in, and they've almost finished the outer wall. The damage is severe, but they believe that if they get enough time, they will be able to complete their task and rebuild the city. They wish to start immediately, bringing in new recruits to help them . . . they want you, Jameson. They want you to teleport them here. They know you're the fastest, and they know you're the best man for the job. He believes that this is the best course of action. The Superiors believe that he and his men are in Mettirna, in seclusion. The Superiors are easily fooled by an Advanced as smart as Seth Green.

"Only one thing stands in their way. The vial. The Superiors have more of them, and they would not hesitate to use them in the case of an uprising in Athena. The vials must be destroyed. It's the only way that their plan will work. It's the only way. But they need our help." Her eyes opened, and she removed her hands from his shoulders and turned to face Jameson. "Without us, they have nothing."

Seth's body still stood there, shoulders sagging and head fallen as though he were in a trance. Jameson's eyes glanced to him and back to Reem, confusion flooding his mind.

"He's fine, Jameson. I went through a lot of information in a short amount of time. Give him a moment," she said as she took Jameson's hand in hers.

"The Superiors are not who we vowed to protect. We vowed to protect the people, and protect the people we will. But his idea still has several flaws, if you ask me."

"I am aware of that," Seth said, lifting his head toward the sky and rolling his neck, stretching.

"You can't hide from the Superiors forever. They will find you eventually."

"I know. We are planning to fake our own deaths. And the deaths of many more who wish to rally to our side and rebuild Athena to its former glory," he responded, walking to the table where Reem had left the vial and leaning against it.

"How far have you gotten in your rebuilding efforts?" Jameson asked.

"We've almost finished the outer wall and a few of the smaller homes on the edge of the city. There really isn't all that much damage, it'll just take some time to get the larger centers up and running again. But with the savior on our side, we shouldn't have any problems."

"Now is not the best time for her to show herself. It's only been a few days. You'll need to wait before Reem can show herself again."

"He's right. If you really need me so badly, then wait until we're sure I'm safe and we're sure they think we're dead. Wait until the rumors die down. A few months and we can begin," Reem chimed in, still holding on to Jameson's hand.

"I cannot wait that long, savior. We must begin now."

"You must begin now. I must wait. Now is not my time—it's yours."

"I am nothing without you. I cannot bring the people to see my side without proof that the savior sides with me. I need you. Both of you."

"You only need a token of mine to prove that I side with you. I must be sure that the Superiors will not bring your operation down before it starts. If I am with you when that happens, all efforts will be thwarted," she replied, reaching into her cloak and producing a small object from one of its pockets. "I believe this should do the trick," she said, releasing Jameson's hand and walking to stand in front of Seth. "Take it."

"What is this?" he asked.

"Something that they will believe came from me. I was never seen in public without it. I had it on me when Jameson and I disappeared from the Superiors' chambers—the people will know that. They will believe in it," she replied, walking back to Jameson's side as Seth opened the small box.

Inside was a small leather band, given to Reem in her initiation ceremony by the Great Superior. "He told you to mark the band once every time you missed your mark," Seth remembered.

"Yes."

Seth took the band from the box and examined it. "Not a scratch," he said, his fingers feeling along the smooth leather.

"Not one."

"You never missed," he said, lifting his head to look her in the eye.

"The people know that, and they will know that the band is mine. The Great Superior gave one to every recruit at their initiation, and as far as I know, mine is the only one that remained without a mark."

"Thank you, savior."

"My name is Reem." She smiled slightly.

"Thank you, Reem," he corrected, still smiling. "When will you return?" he asked, sensing Jameson was about to tell him it was time for them to leave.

"When it is safe," Jameson responded before Reem could open her mouth.

"Is there any way that I can contact you—in case of emergency?" Seth asked him.

"I'm afraid not. I'll stop in by myself to check on you from time to time, but I will not put Reem in harm's way." He took Reem's hand in his and kissed it lightly. "We should be on our way," he told her.

"I know," she replied. "I'm ready."

"I look forward to the day you return to Athena. That day will be remembered in all of eternity, I swear it."

"I look forward to it as well," Reem replied.

She turned to Jameson and nodded, and he teleported them away, leaving Seth standing alone in the room, holding Reem's leather wristband in his hands.

Connections

Jameson teleported them into a small clearing that he'd found before taking Reem to Athena the first time. "Well, that was interesting," he said as they arrived.

"You didn't see it coming, did you?" She smiled as she faced him.

"I take it you did?" he replied.

"Our people call me their savior. It wasn't probable to assume that so many would up and decide that they were wrong. People don't do that, you know." She winked.

"I didn't think you liked to be thought of as their savior," he responded.

"I don't. But I do know that the hearts of the Advanced are not easily swayed. If they believe I am their savior and the Superiors tell them that I am not, they will not likely follow the Superiors. It's completely logical that they would follow me. I've known that for quite some time. I wondered if that was the reason they desired to be rid of me—to be rid of the notion that I could be the savior of the Advanced. I am in their hearts, and I doubt that can be changed so easily."

"Well, you certainly have my heart." He leaned in and kissed her lips lightly before pulling her into an embrace.

"And you mine," she whispered as she wrapped her arms around him.

They stood there a moment, holding each other tightly as the seconds passed. A light breeze blew past them, rustling the leaves in the trees as he loosened his grip slightly and ran his fingers through her hair. "We should be getting back," he said. "I don't want to be out here any longer than we need to be."

"How far can you teleport us?" she asked, still leaning her head against his chest.

"I can take us to a place I know of—just outside the Human camp we've been staying in. If we can stay there for a few hours, I can get us back to the cave in one straight jump," he replied.

"What's this place you know of?" she asked as she pulled away from him and looked into his eyes.

"You'll see." He smiled and teleported. "What do you think?" he asked as they arrived.

She turned around and gazed out upon their landing site. They stood on the side of a small mountain, looking down over the Human camp—the firelight of the settlement clearly visible in the night.

"We'll be safe here for a while. The Humans don't leave their camps after dark," he said.

"I wasn't afraid," she replied.

"I'm merely easing my own mind by telling you." He released her and took her hand in his, leading her away from the edge of the cliff and toward a more protected area not far away. "We can rest here," he said. He sat down against a rock wall and patted the ground next to him.

She sat next to him and leaned her head on his shoulder, looking up at the stars. "I used to watch the stars from my balcony every night," she told him.

"Why?" he asked.

"I always slept more peacefully if I watched the stars before I went to sleep."

"Do you miss them?"

"You're what helps me sleep now," she replied.

"Then sleep, my love," he whispered before kissing the top of her head. He watched as she smiled and as she closed her eyes.

❧❧❧

When Reem woke, she was lying on her back on the bed Jameson had set up for her inside the cave beneath the Purist camp. She sat up and lit the torch with the lighter Jameson had left and looked around. Everything inside was exactly as she'd left it, besides all of her weapons being neatly stacked beside her bed—Jameson must have removed them while she slept.

She stood and exited the room, searching for him. When she didn't find him in the main chamber or the storage room, she decided that he must have gone to the surface to search for more supplies. She walked back to her bedroom, found a cotton shirt and a pair of jeans, and crawled into the washroom.

The room was dark—Jameson hadn't lit the torch before he'd left—but the water was warm as always. She stripped off her uniform and dove into the water. She swam to the opposite side of the cavern, trying to keep her bearings as she went.

When she reached the far wall, she leaned against it and let the water do its magic, working out the kinks in her back with its warmth. She heard splashing from a short way away, but she assumed it was one of the many water currents kicking back against the wall of the cave, and she continued her relaxation efforts.

Her arms floated out in front of her, her legs kicking to keep her afloat in the water. She slid her hands over the surface of the water, her fingers suddenly coming into contact with what felt like flesh. Her gasp was loud in the mostly empty room, and a loud splash sounded a short distance in front of her.

"Reem?" Jameson's voice echoed.

"Jameson?" she replied, her heart pumping a mile a minute.

"I . . . Uh . . . I'm sorry. I'll go," he said slowly.

"Where are you?" she asked. She reached out her hand once more to find him.

"Here," he replied, placing his hand in hers.

She traced her other hand from his wrist to his shoulder and entwined her right hand with his. "Don't go," she whispered, tracing her hand across his bare chest and moving her body closer to his. She ran her fingers through his hair as she leaned in and kissed his lips.

"Reem . . . ," he whispered into her mouth.

"Yes?" she breathed.

"I'm sorry," he whispered as he pulled away slightly and vanished from in front of her.

"Jameson?" she asked, loudly enough that he could hear her from the storage room where she knew he had gone.

"I'm sorry, Reem," he replied.

She swam back to where she'd left her towel and clothing and stepped out of the water. She quickly dried off and started dressing. "What's wrong?" she asked as she crawled into the main chamber.

Jameson sat against the wall next to the storage room, dressed in jeans and a white cotton shirt, his eyes closed as though he were deep in thought. She walked to where he sat and kneeled on the floor next to him, putting her hand under his chin and turning his head so that he faced her. "What's wrong, Jameson?" she asked when he opened his eyes. *"Tell me."*

"It shouldn't matter, really," he started. "My parents always told me to treat women with respect, to love them purely. But my parents were human—things are different for Advanced. It shouldn't matter to me that we aren't . . . married." He turned his head away from her and faced the floor.

"Human ideals are at the very heart of the Advanced. It's perfectly understandable," she responded. "Jameson, we have a Purist camp above us."

He turned to look at her once again, his brow furrowing.

"A Purist camp, dear Jameson, is the only place left in the world where two people can be joined in marriage," she said.

"What are you saying?" he asked, tilting his head to one side.

"I'm saying we get married." She smiled.

"And what about Sarah?—she knows we're Advanced."

"I don't think Sarah will be telling on us anytime soon."

"Reem, think about this. Is this even what you want? The Purists take the ritual very seriously. We'll each be fitted with a Lock that will bind us together for the rest of our lives. It's one of the last known pieces of technology that the Purists continue to use. It will not allow for us to be separated."

She tilted her head to the side and closed her eyes, reading his memories about those who had been fitted with Locks. A husband and wife would be joined in a ceremony called the Connection, where the Locks—metal bands about an inch wide—would be fitted to their wrists. The Locks contained certain chemicals and sensors that bound them to each other, and if the two Locks were separated for a large amount of time, a toxin would be released into both people's systems. Jameson had seen how fast the toxin could work when the Humans captured his friend Jonathon and took him to one of their camps. He and his wife had been fitted with the Locks several years before, and when the rescue mission failed, Allison—Jonathon's wife—was killed in less than a week.

She opened her eyes and looked deep into his green eyes, waiting for the real reason he was being so skeptical.

"Keep searching, if you don't have your answers," he whispered.

"I still won't know if it's the truth that I'm reading in your mind."

"I don't have that gift anymore. I saw no use for it."

"And how would I know if that were the truth?" She winked.

"You'll just have to take my word for it." He smiled slightly.

She sat there for a moment, deep in thought, before finally standing up. "Jameson, I'll let you decide what you want to do on your own." She walked away from him, into her bedroom.

He sat right where she'd left him—unmoving. He didn't know why, but it seemed like marrying her wasn't the right thing to do. He knew that he wanted to be with her and that something was still standing in his way, but he couldn't name that something, couldn't shake the feeling that something was horribly wrong.

"You still think you owe them your allegiance. Because you vowed it to them," she whispered into his mind.

"I thought you said you weren't going to try and influence me." He chuckled.

"Sorry."

She waited a few more minutes then walked back out of her bedroom and stood in front of him once more. "You've also vowed your love to me," she told him.

"I'm sorry, Reem. I just need a moment."

She slid back down onto the floor next to him and took his hand in hers. "Take your time," she whispered, lifting his hand to her lips and kissing it gently before releasing it altogether. "What's the range on the Locks?" she asked.

"It's set differently for each couple. The most I've ever seen was ten miles."

"And how long would we have to be apart before the toxin would be released?"

"Several hours at the least. Long enough that a husband could go out and procure food for his wife without both of them dying. Why are you asking me this?"

"Because I didn't look for it in your memory before, and I thought it would be good to know." She smiled, already seeing the decision he'd made in his mind.

He smiled back as he took both of her hands in his and looked her in the eye. "Stand up," he whispered, and she obeyed. He rose to his knee, keeping both of her hands in his. "Marry me," he said. Then whispered into her mind, *"If you don't, I won't show you the way out of the cave."*

She laughed, considering his offer. "Though I'm certain that I could find my way out by myself, it would be much easier if I said that I'll marry you." She winked as he stood and wrapped his arms around her waist, kissing her passionately as he teleported to their usual spot right outside the camp. "Let's see if the Purists are willing," he said as he released all but her hand. He led her to the center of the camp, where the priests would be.

"You're nervous," she said in his mind.

"Shouldn't I be?" he replied.

"That depends on what you're nervous about."

"What if they find out we are Advanced?"

"Then teleport us away. Just that simple. My healing power has erased my mark, would you like me to erase yours?"

He stopped next to Sarah's home and held out his wrist for Reem, the Advanced mark scarred deeply in his skin. She ran her fingers over the mark, then brought his wrist to her lips and kissed it gently, her healing power completely removing the scar.

"What are you doing here?" a familiar voice asked as they began to walk again. "I told you not to come back. If they find out what you are, you'll be dead."

"Hello, Sarah," Reem said, smiling as she turned to face the woman. "We've missed you."

Jameson smiled and dipped his head slightly, agreeing.

"You shouldn't be here," Sarah responded.

Reem opened her mouth to respond, but Sarah cut her off. "Hurry up, come inside." She motioned with her hands toward her home and ushered the both of them inside—seconds before a group of Purist soldiers walked past.

"Thank you, Sarah, but we need to see the priests," Jameson said softly after the soldiers had passed.

"The priests? They'd be the first to kill you."

"We need to see them, nonetheless," he replied.

"Why? Why do you two want so badly to die?"

"We don't, Sarah," Reem began. "We want to be Connected."

"Connected? Two Advanced want to be Connected?" Sarah threw her hands up in the air, unbelieving.

"Sarah, we are in love," Jameson said before Reem could even open her mouth to respond.

"But we may need your help," Reem added. "You are the only one here who we've actually met, and they may want to speak to you about the two of us."

"No. No. No. N-O. No," Sarah replied, turning and walking into the adjoining room. "I won't go through with this. If they find out what you are, they'll kill me before they even lay a finger on you."

"We won't let that happen. If Reem sees that something may go wrong, we'll leave and never return. I promise," Jameson said, following her.

"This isn't a good idea."

"We want this, Sarah. Please, help us," Reem whispered into her mind.

"Don't do that!"

"Reem, stop. She doesn't want to help us. We'll just go on our own," Jameson said calmly, walking back to Reem and taking her hand in his as they headed for the door.

"Wait," Sarah whispered. "Wait. I'll go with you," she said as she ran to the door, blocking their path. "At least if they find out what you are, I might be able to convince them that you're not a threat."

Reem and Jameson smiled in unison and thanked her.

Ceremony

They walked through the camp, angling toward the center, Sarah leading the way followed closely by Jameson and Reem. They hadn't spoken a word since they'd left Sarah's home after her insistence that they let her do all of the talking. She still wasn't fond of the idea of the two of them being joined in the Connection ceremony, but she seemed willing enough to help them convince the priests that they were ready to be Connected.

"How much farther?" Reem whispered, unease sweeping over her with their slow pace.

"Not long now. This camp is one of the largest around. Did you know that?" Sarah replied.

"Certainly not as large as Admiri though," Jameson added quietly.

"No, certainly not, but we will get there soon. At the moment, we are at about half the size of Admiri. If people keep moving here at their current rate, this camp will be as large as the city in a few months."

"I didn't realize that the Purists camped together so frequently. I had heard stories that they preferred living in solidarity," Jameson replied.

"It's true, many of us do prefer solidarity as you put it, but many more of us found that life is simpler when you have others around to watch your back. We are being attacked almost as often as you are now. The Humans are gaining strength."

"So why don't you do what the Advanced did?" he asked.

"We are not like Advanced. We do not believe so strongly in war against our own kind. We believe that reconciliation may still be reached between Human and Purist."

"I find that difficult to believe," Reem said. "Humans are almost impossible to reason with."

"There are many things we disagree about, but Humans and Purists share one thing in common—the Advanced are killing us in the thousands. I don't know why the killing can't just stop. The world could be brought to peace if only the leaders of our peoples would let it. Someone wants this war to continue that's what I think."

"What do you mean?" Jameson asked.

"I mean this war could be over in only a moment if our leaders would get together and come to terms, but there is a form of hostility between Humans and Advanced that will not allow that to happen. As we speak, the Purists are attempting to bring peace between ourselves and the Advanced. Maybe this Connection ceremony will aid in that."

"Doubtful," Jameson whispered.

"What did he say?" Sarah asked as she turned and looked Reem in the eye.

"The Advanced would not appreciate your helping us," Reem answered, her eyes falling.

"Why's that? What did you two do?" Sarah questioned.

"Technically," Jameson began, "we didn't do anything wrong. I'm sure you've heard about what happened in Athena." He waited for her to nod before continuing, "The Advanced Superiors ordered Reem to kill everyone in the city, and when we returned to Admiri, they accused her of treason. They sentenced her to death. Fortunately, I was able to remove her from the city before they did so, and I brought her to—"

"You took her to the caves under the camp, didn't you?" Sarah asked, cutting him off.

"I was not aware that the people here knew about the cave system," Jameson responded.

"Of course we know about them. Why else would we choose this place to make our camp? The caves are our safety measures, just in case the Advanced do attack. We know that they never leave the city, but should they decide to, we can all evacuate into the cave system beneath the camp. Though with all the migration, we won't have nearly enough space down there."

"I suppose that makes sense as a backup plan," Reem chimed in quietly.

"We're almost there," Sarah said, effectively ending the conversation as she turned and began walking at a much quicker pace toward the priests' quarters.

They rounded a corner and saw the building for the first time. The building was made of cement, just like everything else in the camp, but it was obviously more important—five soldiers armed to the teeth stood in front of the door, guarding it from anyone and everyone. They were the only soldiers they'd seen in the camp other than the team that had passed by Sarah's home moments before they left.

"The priests are inside. You must go before them alone. If they desire to speak with me, I will be here," she said. "I would not advise that you tell them who you are."

"Thank you, Sarah," Jameson said as he squeezed Reem's hand and led her to the doors.

Sarah nodded her reply and leaned against the wall adjacent to the priests' quarters.

"Who wishes to see the priests?" the guard questioned Jameson.

"We are Simon Johnson and Anna Trilla. We wish to take part in the Connection ceremony," Jameson responded.

The guard looked toward Sarah, and then nodded to a man who stood just inside the door before he stepped away from the entryway. "You may enter," he told them.

"Thank you," Reem said.

They stepped inside, and a young man greeted them. "How may we serve you?" he asked, dipping his head as they entered.

"We wish to take part in the Connection ceremony," Jameson told him, still holding firmly onto Reem's hand.

"You will need a witness. Unless you wish for only the priests and myself to know of your Connection," he informed them.

"Either way is fine. We have a friend waiting outside, but she didn't seem to want to join us."

"What is your friend's name?"

"Sarah Marksonna," Reem answered.

"Marksonna . . . I know this name. Is she Connected with someone?"

"I . . . don't know. We haven't known her for that long. We've only recently moved to the camp," Jameson told him.

"I see. Perhaps I should have her escorted inside."

"As you wish," Reem said.

The young man turned to the guard and told him to find Sarah and bring her inside before turning back to Reem and Jameson. "You will need to go to the preparation rooms." He motioned to a young woman who stood a few feet behind him. "Anna, if you would please go with Terrun, and Simon, you may come with me."

Jameson gave Reem a long look, and she nodded her approval before he let go of her hand and followed the young man down one of the many halls.

"Follow me," Terrun instructed Reem as she walked slowly down a different hall.

"I'm sorry. I don't know much about the ceremony. What exactly am I preparing for?" Reem asked as she followed.

"You must prepare your body, mind, and spirit. I will show you how." The girl smiled.

"Thank you," Reem replied as the woman motioned for her to enter a brightly lit room that smelled of sweet flowers and candles.

"Sit." She motioned to a chair that sat in the center of the room.

Terrun began running a brush through Reem's long dark hair as she sat. "I can do that myself, if you'd like," Reem told her.

"No, no, the bride and groom must be decorated by a priestsman and priestsmaid before they can take part in the ceremony. It is no inconvenience, I assure you."

Reem sat in silence as Terrun ran the brush through her hair and pinned it up behind her head. "Take off your clothes," she told her.

"Why?"

"I must dress you in more suitable attire." When Reem looked even more confused, she added, "A gown."

"Oh," Reem said, standing and beginning to remove her clothing.

Terrun left her for a moment, and when she returned, she held folds and folds of lace and silk: a gown for Reem to wear for the ceremony. She helped Reem dress herself before sitting her back down on the chair and applying powder to her face.

"Why do I have to wear all of this for the ceremony?" Reem asked Terrun as she applied shadow to her eyes.

"Because the priests say it should be as it was in the days of old. They believe that a woman must look her best on the day of her Connection."

"I'm not used to so much being like it was in the old days."

"You make a beautiful bride," Terrun smiled and stepped back, making sure that Reem's face was perfect.

"Thank you, Terrun."

"You are very welcome. Would you like to see?" Her smile grew.

Reem nodded excitedly, and Terrun took her hand and walked her to an adjoining room, one which had a full-size mirror, complete with dozens of cracks that distorted her reflection, affixed to one of its walls. "What do you think?" Terrun asked.

Reem looked at her reflection, and for a moment she didn't recognize the woman in the mirror. Her long dark hair had been pinned back on one side, and on the other it flowed in graceful curls down her side. Her gown was flowing silk, falling over her body and enhancing her curves. The gown was white, strapless, and laced up the back. Terrun had applied powder to her face, hiding the few scars that her healing power hadn't yet erased, and her lips were full and inviting. She turned toward Terrun and smiled brightly. "I've never seen myself like this before."

"You look beautiful," Terrun replied.

"Thank you. Thank you so much." She turned back to the mirror and looked at her reflection once more, amazed at the transformation from warrior to bride.

"Your body is prepared. It is time to prepare your mind and spirit. Come with me," Terrun said, smiling as she led the way out of the room and back down the hall to yet another room. This one was filled with the calming sounds and smells of ocean waves rippling against the shore. Reem walked inside after Terrun and sat in a chair in the center of the room. "The Connection ceremony is not something to be taken lightly, Anna," she began, sitting in a chair opposite her. "You must be certain that this is what you want, for once the ceremony is completed, you cannot go back."

"I am aware of that," Reem replied.

"Remember, Anna, the ceremony is not something that should be done for someone else. It should be done because the two who are to be joined are in a state of mind consistent with that of a Connected couple and desire to move their relationship to the next level in Purist society."

"I know. Simon and I talked it out, and this is what we want to do."

"I can see that you love him. You are willing to fight to stay with him, yes?"

"I would destroy anything that stands in my way, yes."

"Then I believe you have already prepared yourself. Wait here, I will see if Caleb is finished preparing your groom." She stood.

"Are you and Caleb Connected?" Reem asked curiously, seeing the gleam in her eye when she spoke his name.

"We are to be Connected within the month." She smiled brightly.

"Congratulations." Reem smiled back.

"I will return shortly." The woman turned away and walked out the door, leaving Reem alone with the sounds of the ocean waves all around her.

Reem was practically in a trance when Terrun finally returned. "They are ready," she said as she entered the room.

"So soon?" Reem stood to her feet and placed her hands over her stomach, suddenly nervous at the thought of the ceremony taking place.

"Don't be nervous, Anna. Simon is your one true love, and you belong together. This ceremony will only show that to the world." Terrun walked to her side and took her by the hand. "Be brave. I know it's a frightening prospect—I'll be going through with it sooner than I think."

Reem just stood there, one hand over her fluttering stomach and the other in Terrun's. She swallowed hard and looked Terrun in the eyes, obviously unsure.

"You'll be fine," Terrun assured her.

Terrun led her out of the room and back down the hall, this time into a much larger room—a room where the priests waited to join her and Jameson in the Connection ceremony.

In the center of the room, there was a small table on which sat the four bracelets that would be affixed to Reem and Jameson's arms during the ceremony. A large circle of priests stood around the table, some moving to make space for Reem to stand next to Jameson in the center. The Priest on the end nearest her gave her an encouraging smile, and Terrun nudged her gently to get her into the center where Jameson waited, hand outstretched to take hers. She stood next to him and took his hand, still not brave enough to look him in the eye.

The priests didn't speak a word; they only began to chant in a language that Reem had never heard before, but Jameson's mind said was Old Latin.

Reem finally lifted her head and looked up at Jameson, who was staring at her, smiling. *"I love you,"* was all she could hear in his mind. She saw Sarah standing behind the row of priests, cowering as though she didn't belong there.

As they stood there listening to the priests chant, the row suddenly opened and an elderly man walked to the center and began to speak. He had them repeat the traditional wedding vows, and put oil on their foreheads before picking up one of the bracelets. "Anna Trilla," he began before spouting off something in Latin. She smiled, and he affixed the bracelet to her wrist before picking up another and repeating the process on Jameson's wrist. "Simon Johnson," he said before speaking in Latin once more. He then took Reem's other wrist and silently affixed the second bracelet before placing the last on Jameson's wrist. "You have been Connected, Simon and Anna Johnson. Go and live in peace, bride and groom," he said finally before leaving the circle of priests.

Once again, the priests began to chant as one by one they came and kissed each of the bracelets before following the old man down a dark hall in the back of the chamber. Soon, the only ones left in the room were Reem, Jameson, Sarah, Terrun, and Caleb.

Reem slowly looked around the room, amazed at how quickly the ceremony had gone by. Jameson squeezed her wrist and she turned around to look him in the eye. She smiled brightly as he wrapped his arms around her and kissed her passionately.

Sarah cleared her throat loudly, and Jameson slowly released Reem. She blushed, and Jameson smiled at her.

"Shouldn't we be on our way?" Sarah asked them, obviously not wanting to stay in the temple any longer than necessary.

"Of course," Jameson said, finally turning from Reem to face Sarah.

"Come on, then," Sarah told them as she pushed passed Terrun and Caleb toward the exit.

"Thank you so much, Terrun," Reem said as they followed her out the door.

Terrun smiled as Caleb took her hand, and waved as the three walked out the door.

Sarah led them at a much faster pace back to her home on the edge of the camp. In the still-light hour of the day, no one walked the streets, no one saw their Locks, and no one would have noticed if Jameson had teleported them back to the caves, but Sarah insisted that they come back to her home.

When they arrived, Sarah led them back through to where she'd left a fire burning. A small pot of stew hung over the fire, boiling. She walked to it and used a towel to protect her hand as she removed the pot from the heat. "Take this with you." She handed the pot to Jameson, forcing him to release Reem's hand.

"Thank you, Sarah," Reem said. "We should be on our way now."

"I know, I know. Go, live in peace," she said in mockery of the Priest waving her hand at them.

Reem dipped her head slightly as she placed her hand on Jameson's shoulder and he teleported them back down into the caves. When they arrived, he set the pot down on the ground and turned back to Reem.

She smiled seductively as she put her hand on his chest and pushed him backward into the wall. She kissed his lips as she unbuttoned his jacket and pushed it off his shoulders. He threw the jacket to the ground before wrapping his arms around her waist and pulling her closer to him. She stepped back slightly and unlaced the back of her dress before pushing it off and stepping back into his arms where she helped him remove his shirt.

She locked her arms around his neck as he lifted her off the ground and carried her to the bedroom. He fell back onto the bed, her body on top of his as they kissed.

※≈✿≈※

When Jameson woke, Reem's naked body lay beside his, her fingers drawing patterns on his chest. He looked down at her face, which was smiling up at him, and he smiled back. He wrapped his arms around her. "Reem Willow . . . I like it."

"Me too," she whispered back as she wrapped her arms around his neck and kissed his lips.

She sat up when her stomach rumbled loudly, and she smiled down at Jameson.

"I'll make some breakfast." He laughed.

Moments later, they sat together on the floor of the main chamber, leaning back against the wall, both wearing their uniforms, neither speaking a word. They'd each eaten two helpings of Sarah's stew before they collapsed on the floor where they now sat.

"Does it feel strange to you?" Reem asked, effectively breaking the long silence.

"What?" he asked, stroking her arm with his fingertips.

"Knowing that we're the first Advanced to be Connected in so long. Knowing that with all the laws that the Superiors are putting in place, it will soon be illegal for people to love anyone," she replied, turning to look him in the eye.

"I'm only happy that you're mine, forever, and that nothing can change that." He smiled at her.

"Good answer," she whispered as she leaned in to kiss his lips gently.

He pulled away from her slowly and kissed her forehead. "I love you," he whispered.

Sarah

Jameson and Reem spent the entire day there on the floor of the chamber, talking about the pros and cons of the new uprising that was appearing in Athena. They talked about Sarah and her strange behavior while they were at the temple, and they talked about the young couple, Terrun and Caleb. They discussed how the small Purist group had been growing exponentially and the possibility that they might actually be working to gain peace between themselves and the Advanced. And they talked about themselves, about the fact that now that they were Connected; it would make things even more difficult for them.

When Reem yawned and leaned her head on Jameson's shoulder, he teleported the both of them onto the bed and cradled her in his arms for a few moments before kissing her lips lightly and laying her down. She smiled as she fell fast asleep, and he lay down next to her and wrapped his arms around her.

As he closed his eyes and started to dream, suddenly Reem shot up out of his arms, breathing heavily.

"What is it?" Jameson asked. "What's wrong?" When she didn't respond, Jameson sat up next to her and placed his hand on her shoulder. "Reem? What is it?"

She turned her head and looked him in the eye. "We have to get back to Athena. Now."

"Why? What happened?" Jameson asked, holding her back from getting up and packing all of her things.

"The ambassadors the Purists sent to Admiri . . . they've returned. The Superiors told them that for peace to be reached between them, they had to bring me to them—dead or alive." Her eyes widened as she listened to the people's thoughts. "We have to get as far away from the Purists as we possibly can."

"Pack your things." He teleported away, leaving her to pack her belongings.

He arrived in Sarah's home not one second after he teleported and found her sitting in a rocking chair beside the fire. "What are you doing here?" she asked him.

"Has news reached you yet?"

"They're looking for you—both of you."

"Will we be safe if we stay in the caves?"

"The safest place for you is somewhere far away from the Purists. They want you both dead."

"Where can we go? If both the Purists and Advanced want us dead, where else is there for us? Going to the Humans would be suicide!" he shouted.

"Keep your voice down!" she whispered as she rose from the chair. "Come with me." She led him away from the fire and down into an underground bunker beneath her home.

"What is this?" he asked her as they walked down the steps.

"Keep your voice down. No one knows of this place." She picked up a candle and started to walk back up the steps to light it when Jameson lit it with his gift. "Thank you," she said, furrowing her eyebrows.

"At the risk of sounding redundant, what is this?" he said, his voice quiet enough for her not to say anything about it.

"This is my secret." She turned away from him briefly, and when she turned back, his eyes widened as he took in the sight of the once-elderly woman.

"How is this possible?" he asked, approaching her carefully as his eyes looked at her curly brown hair and young face.

"I am not Purist. I am Advanced," she said.

"What is your gift? How didn't I sense it?"

"My gift blocks yours from seeing it. I am a shapeshifter. As far as you knew, I was completely human because that was what I wished to be."

"Who are you?" he breathed.

"My name is Suri." She paused, her eyes falling to the ground. "Suri Kahrin."

"What?"

"My gift protected me from anyone finding out that I was Advanced, and when I saw what my parents did to my sister, I decided not to tell anyone. When the Purists came out of the ashes, I decided that this would be the best place to hide." Her eyes met his. "Reem is my sister."

He turned away from her, anger filling his eyes.

"I am sorry I didn't tell you the truth from the beginning—I'm even more sorry that I didn't tell Reem. But I don't want to see either of you hurt. Please, you must go." He turned back and placed his hand on her shoulder. "No, no, Jameson, please!" she said as he teleported both of them back down to where Reem waited in the main chamber of the cave.

Reem had been pacing, unsure of where Jameson had gone. She'd already packed everything into both of their backpacks and was only waiting for him to return. "Jameson. Who is this?" she asked as they arrived.

"Reem," Suri said, stepping away from them. "I'm so sorry."

"Reem, this is Sarah. Or rather, Suri," Jameson said, gesturing to where Suri stood.

"Suri?" Reem said, stepping back against the wall, shocked. "Sarah?" Confusion washed across her face as she watched the young woman who stood across from her.

"Yes," Suri replied, unable to look her sister in the eye.

Jameson quietly stepped back, walking toward the storage room. "Jameson, take me to Athena. Now," Reem ordered.

"Reem, I think you should talk to her," he replied as he walked into the room.

"Jameson!" she shouted at him.

"I'm so sorry, Reem. I should have told you," Suri whispered.

"Yes, Suri. You should have." She glared angrily.

"I didn't want to be put in the camps!"

"So why didn't you tell me when we met? What stopped you then?"

"I thought they would find out who you were and then find out about me, and then we'd all be dead."

"You still could have told me!"

"Reem, I couldn't. I'm Advanced! If the Purists had found out, they would have killed me! You know that."

Reem walked away then, toward the storage room where Jameson had gone. She peered inside and whispered, "Jameson, I want to go. Please."

"Reem—"

"No, Jameson. I want to go. Now. Please."

Suri walked up behind Reem while she was still occupied with Jameson and took her hand. "Reem, look," she said, holding out her wrist for her sister to see.

Reem turned toward her and looked down at her wrist; a wrist that bore the mark of the Advanced, the telltale "X" that revealed Suri was in fact Advanced. Reem looked back at her sister and watched as her faced aged in the span of seven seconds, aging her from a thirty-year-old Advanced to an eighty-year-old Purist, her wrist now bearing the mark of the Purists.

Suri released Reem's hand and took a step back, changing back into the young woman. "I'm sorry I didn't tell you. I know I should have."

"Suri," Reem replied, her eyes filling with tears. She stepped forward and wrapped her arms around Suri as tears flowed down her face. "I thought I'd never see you again," she whispered.

"Me either." Suri laughed as she released her sister and turned to face Jameson. "You need to get her out of here," she told him.

"You're coming with us," Reem said, holding a hand out to Jameson, silencing him before he could speak.

"I belong here," Suri replied.

"You belong with me." Reem took her hand again and dragged her to Jameson. "Let's go, Jameson."

"I'm not sure," he replied.

"I belong here. I am a Purist!" Suri said.

"No—you're Advanced. You showed me that yourself. I won't leave you here by yourself."

"I've been by myself for years," she said.

"I won't leave without you. I can't," Reem replied.

"Suri, would you give us a moment?" Jameson asked calmly.

"Of course." She walked out of the room and walked to where Reem had been pacing, waiting for Jameson to talk sense into her sister.

"Reem, think about what you're asking her to do. She's lived with these people for years. You can't ask her to leave everything behind."

"I'm not leaving without her. I won't go. I can't," she told him.

"Alright, fine. If you can convince her to come with us, I will take her. But only if you can convince her. I'll give you fifteen minutes—I don't want you here any longer than that."

"Thank you, Jameson." She reached up and kissed his lips lightly.

She walked away from him and approached her sister. "Suri, please hear me out," she started before Suri could speak. "I can't leave here without you. You're my sister—now that I know that, I can't leave. I won't."

"This is my home. I've lived here for years—I don't want to leave it."

"We're family. We can't abandon each other."

"I can't abandon my home, Reem."

"Please, I can't stay here. I have to go back to Athena."

"In case you haven't heard, Athena is deserted."

"I will be safe there. As will you if you join us."

"Tell me why you're going to Athena, and then I'll tell you if I'll come or not." Suri placed her hands on her hips.

"There's an uprising among the Advanced. A man named Seth is there waiting for us to return. He wishes us to help him in recruiting people to our cause."

"Against what?"

"The Superiors. Seth believes that I could lead over one-third of the Advanced people against them."

"You can't go there now, Reem. It can't be safe for you to be there! What if the Superiors catch on to you and send someone to kill you? What then?"

"Jameson will keep me safe," Reem replied.

"And what if he can't?"

"Suri, you know he can't leave my side. We're Connected!" She lifted her wrist to show Suri the Lock that had been fastened there.

"You shouldn't go back to Athena."

"Honestly, I agree with her, Reem," Jameson said, poking his head out of the storage room.

"Jameson, stay out of this," Reem told him.

"Calm down," Suri said, holding a hand out to Reem, eyes pleading for her to lower her voice.

"I don't think Athena is the safest place for you right now, Reem. I honestly don't," Jameson said. "Please listen to me. I will teleport you somewhere safe, but not Athena. Not yet."

"Why?" Reem asked.

"Because I don't want you in harm's way."

"Listen to him, Reem," Suri said. "It's not safe."

"We will do as we told Seth," Jameson added.

"Where will we go?" Reem asked him, ignoring Suri.

"I know of a place," Suri whispered. "But I cannot go there with you."

"Why not?" Reem turned and faced her sister.

"Because I think you should be alone. You have just been Connected, sister. Do not make the mistake of thinking that I don't know what that means." She winked at her sister.

Reem blushed and shifted her eyes to the ground.

"Where?" Jameson asked her.

"There is a small camp of people, where there are no Purists, Humans, or Advanced. They live as equals. It is the only one left that the Humans have not destroyed, and it is that way because no one knows of them."

"Where is it?" he asked her.

"In the mountains. I will show you a map if you will take me back to my house."

"Suri, I can't just leave you here," Reem said, lifting her eyes to look at her sister.

"I will meet you in Athena, Reem. I promise," Suri told her before turning back to Jameson. "Take me back to my home. I will show you where to go." She walked to Reem and hugged her tightly. "Be safe," she said.

"And you," Reem whispered as Jameson teleported away with her sister.

A few minutes later, Jameson reappeared beside her, alone. "Where are we going?" she asked.

"I can get us there by morning."

She walked to the backpacks she'd prepared and threw one over her shoulder before handing him the second. "Then let's get going," she said.

He smiled as he put his backpack on and walked up to her. "Ready?"

"Of course." She smiled back as he teleported them away.

Their landing site was cold—very cold. Snow was falling all around them and stood a foot tall on the ground at their feet.

Frozen

The cold seeped in all around them and Reem pulled herself closer to Jameson, searching for warmth. "I'm sorry," he said, holding her as close as possible. "I didn't know it would be like this. I can't teleport very far now."

"Is there any place warm around?" she asked, shivering.

"Suri would know, but we can't very well go back and find out."

"Maybe we can find another cave," she replied, gesturing away from them, toward a nearby hilly region.

They walked as fast as they could into the hills, looking for a place where the cold wind wouldn't reach them. The wind bit at their legs and arms, snow sticking to their skin and hair, their bodies becoming cold enough that the snow stayed frozen when it touched them. After searching the majority of the region, Reem gave up hope. The cold seemed to be seeping into her brain, stopping her from thinking clearly, from thinking about anything other than warmth. Finally Jameson squeezed her hand and guided her to a ledge, sitting down in the snow and pulling her down next to him. It wasn't completely sheltered, but at least it blocked out some of the wind.

They sat there in silence for what felt like days, shivering in the cold, shaking violently when the wind picked up even more, and the snow began to fall with such force that they would soon be buried in it if they didn't find shelter.

"This isn't working!" Reem whispered harshly into Jameson's ear.

"I don't know where to go."

"How far can you teleport?"

"A few miles, maybe."

"That's something, at least." Her whole body shook as the wind picked up and knocked her back against the rock wall.

"If I teleport even a few miles, it will take longer before I get us to the settlement."

"I can't feel my legs . . ."

He took her hand in his and teleported as far away as he could in the direction of the settlement. Their landing site was cold—colder than before, if that was possible. They'd landed near a lake, one Jameson hadn't remembered seeing on Suri's map.

"Where are we?" Reem asked him, shivering as she pulled herself closer to him.

"I don't remember this place from the map."

"Where can we go?" She shivered.

"I'm sorry."

They walked away from the frozen lake, searching for shelter. They walked as far and long as their feet would take them, always angling in the direction Jameson thought to be the settlement Suri had sent them to. Reem's feet ached with the cold, her hands and arms numb from the harsh winds that kicked at them from every angle.

"I need to st-t-top," Reem said as loudly as she could muster.

"W-w-where?" Jameson asked, gesturing to the vast emptiness that surrounded them.

"C-c-can't you t-t-teleport y-yet?" She shivered.

"N-not yet, n-n-no," he replied. "I'm s-s-sorry."

"I need to s-st-t-top," she said again as she fell to the ground, her body sinking beneath the snow banks.

"Reem!" Jameson shouted, dropping to the ground beside her, checking her body for a pulse.

He placed his ear over her chest, listening for her faint heartbeat. He took off his jacket and wrapped it around her before shouting his frustration into the sky.

She would die here if he didn't get her out soon.

He couldn't teleport—he'd already tried—so he picked up her limp form and carried her toward the settlement. They would be able to save her—or at least, he hoped they would. He couldn't bear to live without her.

His feet ached with the strain of holding both himself and Reem upright while continuing to walk. He didn't know how much longer he could go on. He'd been walking for what seemed like hours, but because of the constant strain on his body, he was still unable to teleport.

He fell to his knees, holding Reem's still form in his arms. He couldn't give up—he wouldn't give up. He had to get her somewhere warm. He could feel the healing he'd given her, trying to keep her alive. He could feel the weak pulse that passed through her veins, feel the life in her—feel it fade with each passing moment.

He didn't feel the tears as they started pouring from his eyes—he was too cold for that—but he knew they were there. His vision was blurred, his eyes stung, and he couldn't see a thing. Snow fell all around him, strong gusts of wind threatening to knock Reem's body from his aching arms. He stood back to his feet and took another step before falling to the ground.

The last thing he remembered was falling onto his back, Reem's limp body lying over his before he passed out, joining her in the space between life and death.

⚜

Reem woke to the sound of voices beside her, but she found that she couldn't open her eyes. She was lying in a bed somewhere, but Jameson wasn't beside her. Pain flashed through her body—too great for her to do anything but lie there. Where was Jameson?

She tried to lift her arm and found it immobile. Finally she willed her eyes to open, and even more pain flashed its way through her veins. She screamed at the top of her lungs.

"Miss, miss, calm down," a soothing feminine voice whispered from somewhere off to her left, but Reem didn't stop screaming.

Pain seared through her arms, her legs, her face, like a thousand razor blades being dragged across her body. What were they doing to her? Was this her punishment from the Superiors?

"Miss, my name is Mila. The pain you're feeling is your body's reaction to the heat in the room. Please, calm down." The young woman placed a cool cloth on Reem's forehead, and she relaxed slightly, closing her mouth to stop from screaming in pain when the cloth was removed.

"Where? Where is he?" was all Reem managed to get out before she groaned in pain.

"The . . . the man? The man you were with? He's here." Her voice sounded strained, and even with the amount of pain searing through Reem's body she could tell something was wrong.

"What happened?" she said through clenched teeth.

"He tried to save you. He covered your body with his, trying to keep you alive."

"Where is he?" The pain seared even harder through her body as warmth flooded around her.

"He's here," Mila replied hesitantly.

"I want to see him!" she screamed, reaching up and grabbing Mila by the collar. "Where is he?"

"Miss, please calm down. You need to relax. It'll be a while before you're fully mobile." Mila gently moved Reem back down onto the bed and dabbed at her forehead with a cold cloth one more. "Please, rest."

"Where is Jameson?" Reem asked, trying to remain calm.

"He's here. Quiet now, miss. Things may get worse before they get better. I'm sorry, but you need to stay here."

Reem felt her healing gift as it finally started to work its magic, pulsing through her veins, warming her body from the inside out. She closed her eyes and concentrated as the healing ran its course, her pulse steadying and her breathing becoming more stable.

She opened her eyes and sat up, staring at Mila who now stood next to her bed. "Where is Jameson?" she asked.

"How?" Mila whispered under her breath.

"Tell me. Where is he?" Reem ordered.

Mila backed against the wall, amazed at how soon Reem had healed. She lifted her arm and pointed toward a room adjacent to the one they were in.

Reem turned her head toward the room and heard people shuffling around busily. She listened with her mind, searching for Jameson's voice.

There.

She felt something.

She got up and ran as fast as her feet would take her into the other room, where she knew Jameson would be. The two other men in the room grew silent upon her entrance and stepped away from her.

Jameson lay on a bed identical to hers, completely unconscious. She ran to his side and took his hand, her fingers feeling for his weak pulse.

His chest rose and fell lightly though he remained unconscious.

"Jameson it's me. I'm here," she whispered to his unconscious form.

"Miss, please. You shouldn't be here," one of the men said in a deep-yet-gentle voice as he placed a hand on Reem's shoulder. "He's not well."

"I'm aware of that—do you think I'm blind?" she answered, refusing to turn and face the man. "Jameson, I'm sorry, I can't heal you yet. A few more hours though and I'll have the energy. You're not leaving me," she told him.

"He can't hear you, miss," the man told her calmly as the second man left to speak to Mila.

"What's wrong with him?" she asked.

"He's unresponsive. He has been for quite some time. To be quite frank, we didn't even think you would wake so soon."

"What happened?" She turned to face him, seeing his bright blue eyes staring back at her intently.

He ran his fingers through his short dirty blonde hair and sighed. "When we found you, you were both unconscious. It seems that you were trying to locate our settlement, but the snow proved quite . . . well, let's just say that you never made it. When he passed out, we lost track of where you were. We only found you a few hours ago, still unconscious in the snow. You shouldn't be alive, much less awake right now."

"Who are you?" she asked.

"Nicholas Swan. I'm a doctor here in the settlement."

"You mean we made it to the settlement?"

"If this is where you were intending to go, you've made it."

"Did you hear that, Jameson? We made it. We'll be safe here," she whispered, smiling as she kissed his hand.

"Who are you?" Nicholas asked.

"My name is Reem, and this is my husband, Jameson. We were sent here by my sister, Suri Kahrin. Though I suppose she goes by Sarah these days."

"Suri? We haven't heard from her since the beginning of the Purist movement in Africa."

"She's my sister." Reem smiled up at him.

"Why would she send you here?"

"It's the only place left where we're safe." She paused. "We won't be staying long though."

"We'll find you a place to stay." He nodded. "I assumed that neither of you have gifts, judging by the links, but judging by your quick recovery, I'd say you're a healer."

"We were told that there was no difference here."

"But if you had gifts that could aid the community it any way, we would appreciate it if you would tell us so that we may all benefit."

"Oh—of course. Well, I am a telepath and a healer, and Jameson is a teleporter."

"I must say it surprised me to see two Connected Advanced. The Superiors outlawed—"

"We fell in love," she cut him off. "It was never up to the Superiors whether two people would fall in love or not. Going through the Connection ceremony seemed like the right thing to do."

"I see. Can you not simply heal him?" he asked, furrowing his brow.

"My gifts strained themselves enough trying to heal me—I don't have the energy to heal him too. I may be able to heal him slightly, but not enough for it to matter."

"It can't do any harm, can it?"

"I'm just afraid that I'll overwork myself, and I know he would tell me to never do that."

"He's not awake to argue with you." Nicholas winked.

"Why are you so insistent?" She raised an eyebrow.

"I'm sorry." He smiled. "I've never met a healer before. In many ways, you are what I long to be. I'm a doctor, but there are so many things that I can't heal." He sat across from her on the bed, checking Jameson's pulse. "His heartbeat is getting stronger—that's a good sign. I don't know how much longer it'll be before he's awake though."

"Thank you," she whispered. "Watch."

She placed her hand on Jameson's forehead, sending the healing gift through her palm. He jerked slightly and Nicholas held him down as gently as possible.

Jameson's eyes snapped open for a second and his breathing heightened, his chest rising and falling quickly, his eyes darting about before snapping shut a second later.

"Jameson," Reem whispered, "Jameson, I'm here. It's fine. Keep still. I know it hurts."

"Jameson, my name is Nicholas Swan. I'm going to inject you with something that will help with the pain. Please don't struggle—that will only make this worse." Nicholas picked up a syringe from the table beside the bed and cleaned the injection site before inserting the needle and injecting its contents into his bloodstream.

Reem removed her hand from Jameson's head, her breathing labored as though she lacked energy. "I'm sorry, Jameson. A few more hours and I can heal you. I'm so sorry," she whispered as she leaned down and pressed her lips to his forehead.

He groaned lightly, clenching his fists against the pain that now seared through his veins.

Nicholas picked up a cold cloth and placed it on Jameson's forehead. "You did the best you could. At least he's stable now."

"I hate seeing him in pain." Tears welled up in her eyes as she saw the grimace growing on Jameson's face.

"Reem, if you hadn't healed him, he wouldn't have lasted much longer. You did the right thing." Nicholas placed his hand on her shoulder.

Tears slipped down her cheeks as she watched Jameson's fists clench and unclench, his teeth grinding together as he tried not to scream. She knew he was trying to be brave, not to let her know how much pain he was in, but she could feel the searing sensation that was coursing through his veins.

Nicholas walked to Reem's side and placed both of his hands on her shoulders, turning her to look him in the eye. "Reem, listen to me," he said, "I don't think you should stay here anymore. It's going to be a while before he's well again, and you need to rest. Don't pretend I didn't see how taxing that was on your system."

She turned her face away from him, back toward Jameson's. "I won't leave him," she whispered.

Nicholas stood and gestured to the man who had walked out before, motioning for him to remove Reem from the room.

When the man came in to take her away, she rooted herself to the bed with her telekinesis. "No. No, I'm not leaving him, Nicholas. I can't leave him," she whispered, not wanting Jameson to overhear.

Jameson's body shook as he struggled with the pain, and the man continued to try and pry Reem off of the bed. Jameson suddenly bolted out of bed, his eyes wide with pain and his nostrils flaring as he took Reem's hand and teleported away.

"They're Advanced?" the man asked Nicholas, who only placed his hand over his eyes and shook his head.

"How else would they have survived?"

⊱⊰⊱⊰

When Jameson and Reem landed, he collapsed on site. They'd landed very close to their start point—only a few meters outside of the building where they'd been taken. Reem cradled Jameson's head in her lap as Nicholas, Mila, and the other man came rushing to her side and carried him back inside to the bed.

She followed them closely, still not wanting to leave his side. She listened to their thoughts as they carried him, believing that Jameson must have had a reason for fearing them so much, but their motives were pure. They sincerely wanted to help him, and so she let them take him back to his bed and only stood by and watched as they injected him with something to boost his ability to thwart the burning pain that seared through his veins.

She moved to sit next to him, and the others made no move to stop her—they knew what could happen if they tried that again.

"How is he?" Reem asked, directing her question at Nicholas.

"He's in pain. There's not much that we can do for him but try and keep him comfortable." He sat beside her on the bed, placing his hand on her forearm. "He suffered more of the effects of the cold than you did."

"How long were we out there?"

"Quite some time, I'm afraid," the other man replied. "I'm Terrence."

"Terrence, perhaps you and Mila should check on the other patients. I'll be fine here on my own," Nicholas said, turning to look at the man.

"Of course, sir," Mila replied, taking Terrence by the elbow and pulling him out of the room alongside her.

"With your help, I'm sure we can save him—we have only to wait until you're strong enough to do so. Until then, we'll try and keep him as comfortable as possible."

"What if he doesn't make it?" she whispered.

"He's going to be fine—I'm sure of it." He placed a comforting hand on her shoulder and stood next to her, watching Jameson's chest as it slowly rose and fell.

Reem picked up the cold cloth from the side table and dabbed it on Jameson's forehead gently. "How long would it traditionally take you to heal him—without my help?" she asked.

"Months, at the very least—though he'd be lucky if he survived at all, honestly."

"It was that bad?"

"I'm afraid so." He walked around the bed and sat across from Reem, picking up Jameson's hand and checking his pulse. "His pulse is much stronger now though. You've done a great deal of good for him, Reem, but he's not out of the woods yet."

She picked up Jameson's other hand and kissed it gently before setting it back down on the bed next to his chest. "What now?"

"Now you need to rest. As you said yourself, if don't have the energy, you can't heal him. You can sleep in the other room if you'd like." He gestured to the room she'd woken up in.

"I don't want to leave him alone."

"I'll be with him the entire time. You're a telepath, yes? Read my mind if you don't believe me."

She did as he said, reaching out with her mind to read his thoughts. He was concentrating on Jameson's still form, deciding what the best form of medication would be, as though he knew she was listening—which he did. She searched his mind for any reason he might have to fear them, to kill them in their sleep, and found none.

"You're not lying to me," she told him.

"I know." He turned to wink at her. "Get some rest, I'll keep him stable. If anything major occurs, I'll wake you—I promise."

She waited a moment, continuing to stare at Jameson's unmoving body before slowly nodding and turning back to Nicholas. She nodded again and stood, walking back to the bed where she'd first woken and lay down, falling asleep as soon as her head touched the pillow.

"Reem. He's awake," Nicholas whispered, shaking her shoulder lightly.

"How long have I been asleep?" she asked, keeping her eyes closed.

"About eight hours. How much energy do you have?"

"Not enough, but I can help if he needs it." She yawned and sat up, running her fingers through her hair as she did so. "How is he?"

"He's still in a lot of pain though he's trying not to show it." *"He wants to see you."*

She stood and walked back to Jameson's side, ignoring the rest of the thoughts in Nicholas's head. "Jameson," she said as she sat next to him, smiling when his eyes met hers. "How are you feeling?"

"I'm fine," he replied, his voice barely a whisper.

"Don't lie to me." She tapped the side of her head.

"Then why ask?" he breathed, forcing a smile.

"I'm working on my bedside manner." She winked.

His smile widened, and he groaned slightly.

"Here," she said, placing her hand on his forehead and sending her healing gift through her fingertips into his body, healing him as best as she could. "How's that?" she asked when she'd finished.

"Better." He took her hand from his forehead and kissed it.

Nicholas walked in the room and stepped up to where Jameson lay, taking his wrist and checking his pulse once more before injecting him with yet another shot. "This'll help you heal faster," he said before picking up another syringe and injecting the contents into Jameson's arm. "And this will help with the pain." He put the empty syringes back on the table. "How do you feel?"

"Much better," Jameson replied. "Thank you."

"It'll be a while before I let you go. I want to be sure that we don't have any repeats of the earlier incident. You don't mind, do you?"

"No, I don't mind. So long as my wife doesn't have to leave. I would die if she did—literally." He lifted up his wrist, the metal bracelet sliding down slightly as he did so.

"Reem may stay as long as she likes. In fact, as long as you are planning on staying in the settlement for a time, Reem could be of a great deal of help here."

"I would be happy to help—as soon as Jameson is well," Reem told him.

"Your help is greatly appreciated."

"May we have a moment?" she asked.

"Of course. I'll be back when I've finished my rounds."

"Thank you." Reem smiled at him as he walked out the door.

"What's wrong?" Jameson asked.

"Nothing, really. I just didn't want him looking over my shoulder."

"What is it?" He furrowed his brow and reached up his hand, stroking her hair lightly.

"He thinks of me more highly than I'd like."

"Does he? He's only just met you."

"All it took was me using my gifts to heal you." She shrugged. "You find it so hard to believe?"

"No, I understand his feelings perfectly. I would kill for you. You know that."

She blushed lightly as he traced her lips with his thumb. "I love you," she whispered into his hand.

She leaned down and pressed her lips to his lightly, running her fingers through her hair for just a moment before sitting back up and smiling at him. "How are you feeling?" she asked.

"I'll be fine, as long as you're with me." He smiled.

"I'll be right here, always," she whispered, smiling brighter as he linked his fingers with hers.

Jameson groaned quietly, and she put her hand back on his forehead, trying to finish healing him. "Reem, Reem, stop. You don't have the energy. I'm fine, really."

She continued to heal him, expelling her energy into his body when Nicholas walked back into the room.

"Reem! You don't have the energy to heal him yet," he said, running up and removing her hand from Jameson's forehead only seconds before she fell to her side with exhaustion.

"Thank you," Jameson whispered as Nicholas lifted her off the bed and carried her out of the room.

When Nicholas reappeared, Jameson sat up and leaned against the wall behind him. "She tries to do more than her body will allow. She always has, really," he told the doctor.

"I noticed. How are you feeling?" he asked as he leaned against the wall across from him.

"Better, but I still can't feel much of my legs."

"That's amazing. You shouldn't even be anywhere near able to sit up yet, honestly. Her gift is quite amazing."

"Thank you. I developed it for her."

Nicholas furrowed his brow, uncomprehending.

"Did she not tell you about my gifts?"

"She only said you were a teleporter," he replied.

"I can give or take any gift that I can think of or feel. Along with my teleportation gift, it made my life among the Advanced very taxing."

"They must have wanted you to do many things for them."

"As a matter of fact, they did. The fact that we have limitations according to the amount of energy we have at the time was my only relief." He smiled back.

"How long have you two been together?"

"We've only been Connected for a few days, but we've been together for longer than that—almost a month now, I believe."

"A month? And you're already Connected?" Nicholas asked, shocked at the prospect of two people being Connected so soon.

"Yes. A month."

"How did you meet?"

"We have the Superiors to thank for that, oddly enough. They threw us together to aid Athena—shortly before its destruction."

"And how did you end up out here?"

"That, is a very long story."

Nicholas nodded, sensing Jameson's want of privacy. "How long will you be staying?"

"Do you always ask your patients this many questions?"

"Oh. I'm sorry. I'm interrogating you, aren't I?" He smiled, his skin turning slightly red.

Jameson smiled and nodded.

"I'm very sorry. I'll go check on Reem."

"She exhausted herself. Her breathing is normal, and her pulse is steady."

"How do you know that?"

"My gifts allow me to sense the gifts of others. I'm used to sensing her vital signs. It's almost second nature to me now."

"Of course. You are Connected, after all." He smiled.

"Why do you care for her so much, Nicholas? You've only just met her."

"Why did you fall in love with her so quickly?"

Jameson nodded slowly. "Oh. Yes. I know what you mean. It seems she has the ability to get inside people's heads very quickly. It's not a gift per se, but it is something that she seems to be uncanny at."

"You're very right. And I'm sorry, I don't mean to intrude. I know you are Connected, but I cannot help but feel how I do about her—she's a healer. The first I've ever met, actually."

"I understand. But if you don't mind, she doesn't appreciate all of the staring and attention you give to her. And don't forget that she can read your mind." He winked.

"She read my mind, didn't she? That's how you know how I'm feeling."

"Yes, she did. She doesn't mean to intrude either. It's just hard for her not to listen when someone is thinking about her. I'm sure you can understand that."

"Of course." He stood and started to pace. "I should have guarded my thoughts more carefully."

"It doesn't really help any. If she wants to know what you think about her, she'll find it."

Kiss, Kiss, Bang, Bang

Reem woke with Nicholas sitting next to her again, this time checking her pulse and being careful not to wake her. She could hear his thoughts, concentrating on the task at hand, though she knew what he was really thinking. She could hear the thoughts he was trying to block from her, hear everything his mind thought about her. She kept her eyes shut, not wanting him to know that she was awake. When she finally opened her eyes and looked into his, she realized that he'd known all along.

"Morning," he said. "How are you feeling?"

"How is he?" She nodded her head toward Jameson's room as she sat up.

He pushed her back down gently. "Sorry, Reem. I'm under orders to keep you in here for a while."

"Orders from who?"

"Who do you think?" He nodded toward Jameson's room, smiling. "He doesn't want you to hurt yourself trying to help him."

"I don't care."

"He told me to tell you that he'll take away your healing power if you try to see him before you're rested."

"He would, wouldn't he?" she said to herself, shaking her head slightly.

"Yes, I think he would," he answered her.

She smiled up at him. "Would you bring me some water?"

"Of course." He walked out of the room, returning within seconds with a small mug in his hands.

He handed it to her and helped her to sit up, placing another pillow under her back.

"Thank you," she whispered.

"Now, stay here. I'm going to go check on Jameson." He walked away, leaving her alone with her thoughts—though she could still hear Jameson's and Nicholas's as well.

Not wanting to pry, she closed her eyes again and tried to fall asleep—without much luck.

She lay there with her eyes closed, monitoring Jameson's vitals just as she knew he was monitoring hers. She listened to the rhythm of his heart, the steadiness of his breathing, the low bass note of his voice as he spoke with Nicholas.

Her thoughts went to Nicholas. It hadn't taken him very long to decide that he was smitten with her, and she'd known it right from the start. She'd known the effect telling him she was a healer would have on him, but she saw no reason not to tell him. She could help them here, and she wanted to. She never wanted to keep her gifts all to herself; she wanted to help people.

As her thoughts continued to delve deeper into the happenings of the past few days, she found herself drifting off once more into a deep sleep as she heard Jameson's thought in her mind: *"Sleep, my love. Sleep."*

And sleep she did.

***

"So, can you talk with her, using only your mind?" Nicholas asked, fascinated.

"Yes, I can. I can only hear what she wants me to know, but she frequently talks to me." Jameson smiled.

"Is she talking to you now?"

"No, now she's sleeping."

"Really? It seemed like she would be awake for quite a while."

"Yes. She's sleeping." His smile brightened. "So tell me, Nicholas, why are you so fascinated with the two of us?" he asked seriously, his smile fading.

"I don't really know. I was given the treatment when I was a very young child in the Human camps, but I was one of many who didn't receive any gifts. All my life—before I found the settlement—I thought that something was wrong with me, that that was the reason I didn't have anything special like the rest of my family. When I found this place, those feelings slowly started to go away. Though I still feel similarly whenever we get new Advanced members in the settlement. So really, I don't know why you fascinate me so much." He paused. "I suppose it's because I want to be like you."

"Nicholas, I can give you what you want," Jameson replied slowly.

"You what?" His eyes widened.

"I can make you Advanced. I can give you any gift you want—anything you can dream of."

"You would do that? Why?"

"Because Reem seems to think that you're a nice enough guy, even though she gets a little nervous when, you know." He shrugged. "If she thinks you're that nice, then I don't have a problem with it."

"Here in the settlement we believe that there is no difference between Advanced, Human, and Purist. We are all the same."

"Nicholas, if you want this badly enough, I'm sure the people here would think no less of you. I can give you the same gift that I gave Reem: healing. I'm sure no one would think less of you for wanting to be better at what you do—for wanting to heal."

"They would think nothing of it. But it feels like letting them down. I just don't think I could go through with it—at least as long as I was staying here."

"So come with us," Jameson said, shrugging.

"You would be okay with that?"

"I don't believe that she would have a problem taking you to Athena with us."

"I'll think about it." He nodded slowly.

"Perfect." He smiled once more.

"You should be getting some rest too. I'll be back soon."

Jameson nodded at him as he walked out the door, smiling as he heard Reem's waking heartbeat. *"I thought I told you to sleep,"* he thought.

"I tried."

"Good."

"How are you feeling?"

"I'm fine, Reem, honestly. My legs are still a little numb, but I'll be completely back to normal before you know it."

"I'll be able to finish healing you soon."

"Get your strength back. Please—for me."

"I hate seeing you in pain."

"I'm fine, I swear. Nicholas is giving me medication on the hour—and yes, it's helping."

"Are you sure, Jameson? You're still in pain, I can tell."

"It's not that bad. Don't worry yourself. Just get some rest. Please, for me."

"Jameson, I—"

"No, Reem. Just rest. Remember what Nicholas told you."

"You'll take away my healing gift if I come see you, I know."

"Just rest, my love. For me, please?"

She sighed slightly, and he chuckled at how well the sound transferred from her mind to his without ever leaving her lips. He thought of the curve of her lips, the way he felt when her lips pressed against his when she whispered, *"Can I at least come give you the real thing before I go back to resting?"*

He smiled, and she got up and walked to the door, not waiting for his response. "So?" she asked.

He held out his arms, and she walked up and sat on the bed next to him, leaning her back against the wall as she settled in to the crook of his arm. He cupped his hand under her chin and turned her face to meet his eyes, meeting her lips with his.

98

She pulled back slowly and leaned her head against his shoulder. "You don't mind, do you?"

"Sleep, my love," he whispered, kissing her forehead.

When Nicholas returned to check on Jameson, he was surprised to find Reem nestled into his arms, sleeping soundly.

Jameson lifted his head and smiled to him, shrugging slightly, not wanting to wake her.

Nicholas tapped his own inner elbow, mouthing that it was time for Jameson's next shot before he walked in and prepped the syringe. Jameson held out his arm, and Nicholas swabbed it gently before inserting the needle and injecting its contents into his bloodstream.

Reem's eyes flickered open, and she yawned. "How long have I been out?" she asked.

"Only a little under an hour," Jameson told her, stroking her hair with his free hand as Nicholas cleaned the small amount of blood off his other arm.

Reem stretched and slid her legs off the side of the bed, gently edging out of Jameson's arms. "How do you feel?"

"I think the shots are helping," Jameson said, motioning to the arm that Nicholas still held.

"I'm glad to be of assistance," Nicholas replied, releasing his arm and taking a few steps back. "You need to get some rest now though, sir. If you'd like, I can give you a sedative."

"Give it to him, Nicholas. He'll say he doesn't need it, but I can tell he does," Reem said, standing up and looking directly into Jameson's eyes.

"As you wish." Nicholas smiled, plopping two small pills into a water glass and handing it to Jameson. "Drink this, please."

Jameson looked up and Reem who winked at him. "Do as he says. You need the rest more than I do," she said.

He drank the glass of water quickly, ignoring the bitter taste as best he could before setting the glass back down on the side table. Within moments he'd fallen asleep, and Reem turned to Nicholas.

"Where can we stay while we're here?" she asked.

"Well, as long as he's still here, you'll stay in the hospital."

"And after he's well?"

"Come with me, I have a place you can stay." He walked out the door and motioned for her to follow.

They walked through the small hospital, passing several patients with doctors buzzing around them. "Are you the head doctor here, Nicholas?" she asked, still following him as he wove through the halls.

"Yes, as a matter of fact, I am. For the most part, I concentrate on the most dire patients, but I have several other young doctors who work under me that can take over if need be."

"And Jameson is . . . ?"

"One of the patients who requires more attention than most, I'm afraid. What with the medication I've been giving him and the fact that he's relatively unstable for the early stage of his recovery—no matter what the boost was from your healing gift."

"What medication do you have him on?"

"It's something that we developed here. It heals the frostbite patients in half the time that the leading Purist and Human medicine does, with almost no side effects."

She smiled as they finally exited the building and walked out into the cold evening light. "I could've sworn it was earlier than this."

"Yes, I know our lighting leads to confusion as to what time it is in the outside world." He stopped along the side of a building.

"Where are we going?" she asked.

"We're already here." He gestured to the building they stood in front of, and she cocked her head to the side, confused. He linked his arm with hers and led her to the entryway of the building, walking her to the fifth door on the left. He released her arm and motioned for her to go inside.

She entered the brightly lit room and smiled. To her left sat a small table with two matching chairs, and to her right sat a small fire pit with a large skylight above it to vent the smoke. Ahead of her was another door, and she walked to it and peered inside, seeing a small bed and a bedside table.

She turned back to where Nicholas stood, just inside the door, and smiled brightly. "It's perfect," she said.

"You and Jameson can stay here for as long as you like. It's the hospital quarters, so as long as you're willing to help out around the hospital, it's yours." He smiled back.

"Thank you."

"I've already had the things that we found on your persons sent here. They're in the bedroom closet. I'll have some people drop off your cooking supplies this evening, and if you need anything else after you move in, don't hesitate to ask."

"Thank you, Nicholas."

"It's the least I could do."

She closed her eyes for a moment, trying not to listen to the thoughts that plagued Nicholas's mind. "Nicholas, don't forget that I can hear what you're thinking," she said, opening her eyes.

He turned his eyes away from her, trying to mask the thoughts that still worked their way through his mind. "I'm sorry. I didn't mean to cause any harm."

"I know you didn't." She paused. "We should probably get back to Jameson."

"He won't be awake for a while."

"But I'd like to be there when he wakes up—no matter when that is. Please, take me back."

He dipped his head slightly and gestured for her to lead the way back out of the building. Once they were outside, he once again took the lead, guiding her back down the street to the hospital and back through the long winding halls filled with patients and doctors. He walked her to Jameson's door and peered inside at the sleeping man. Reem was about to turn to walk inside when he took her by the arm and quickly pulled her to him, kissing her lips.

She pushed him away, slapping his face with as much force as she could muster. "I warned you, Nicholas."

"I'm sorry," he said, looking toward the ground, ashamed. "I shouldn't have done that."

"No, no you shouldn't have." She pointed to Jameson. "He is my husband— you know that."

"I'm sorry, Reem," he said, walking away from her and back down the hallway, ducking into a patient's room to avoid her glare.

Interrogation

Jameson woke to see Reem pacing beside his bed, obviously too deep in thought to notice that he'd woken. He watched her for a moment, trying to decipher what was going on behind her beautifully worried eyes. "What's wrong?" he asked.

She jumped, startled at his question. "You're awake," she said.

"Yes, I'm awake." He smiled. "Tell me, Reem."

She stopped pacing and sat on the edge of his bed. "It's Nicholas," she said.

"What happened?" His eyebrows rose slightly.

"After he gave you the sedative, we went to the hospital quarters—he was showing me where you and I can stay while we're in the settlement—and while we were there, I heard his thoughts and realized that it would probably be better if we weren't alone together. I asked him to bring me back here, and so he did, but when we got here he . . ." She stopped, unable to finish.

"He what? Reem, what did he do to you?"

"He didn't hurt me. He just—he kissed me."

"He kissed you?"

"Yes. He grabbed me and held me to him and kissed me."

"And what did you do?"

"It all happened too fast for me to stop it, but I did slap him—harder than I slapped you before."

"I didn't think that was all you had in you." He laughed lightly.

"Please, Jameson. Don't joke about this."

As Jameson opened his mouth to reply, Nicholas appeared in the doorway. *"Don't say anything to him. He's embarrassed enough as it is,"* Reem warned, whispering the thought into Jameson's mind as her eyes glared into his.

"Nicholas." Jameson nodded as the man entered, holding a syringe.

"Jameson." He nodded back. "I have more medication for you, if you need it. How are you feeling?"

"Better than before, but isn't that what I say every time you ask?"

"Yes, I believe it is." He smiled a nervous smile. "Do you need more medicine, or has Reem already healed you?" Reem's glare worsened, and Nicholas took the hint. "You still won't let her heal you, will you?" He laughed lightly.

"No." Jameson chuckled along with him.

"May I?"

Jameson nodded and held out his arm for Nicholas to swab and inject the contents of the syringe. When he finished, he placed a small bandage over the injection site and smiled. "There. I'll be back in an hour to check on you again." Nicholas exited quickly, never meeting Reem's eyes again though he could feel her eyes on him as he left.

"Why wasn't I allowed to say anything?" Jameson asked.

"Because he feels bad enough as it is."

"Well, with the stare you gave him, I can understand that." He chuckled.

"Will you stop laughing about this?"

"Come here." He held out his arms, and she sat down beside him, letting him curl his arms around her body.

"I love you," she whispered as she kissed his neck lightly.

"I love you too," he told her.

"I'm sorry. I should've seen it coming. I just didn't think he'd actually act on any of his feelings. He thinks so highly of you—he doesn't want to hurt you. He's seriously considering your offer to make him Advanced. I wish I would've seen it coming; I could've stopped it before it started."

"Reem, it's fine. You made your intentions clear, and he seems to have understood that completely." He stroked her arm gently.

"He can't stop thinking about what happened."

"Reem, it's fine, really. Once I'm out of the hospital, you won't see him so much, and then we won't even have to worry about it."

"Jameson, I'm going to be helping him here. I'm going to see him every day."

"If he knows what's good for him, he'll leave you alone."

She closed her eyes and leaned her head against his chest, trying not to think about everything she'd gotten herself into after spending such a short time in the settlement.

"How are you feeling, really?" she asked.

"I'm fine, Reem. If you don't believe me, search my mind. I can almost feel my legs."

"I have enough energy now. I can heal you."

"No, I don't want you to drain your energy for me. I'll be fine."

"I want to help you. Please, let me help you."

"I'm fine. By tomorrow, we'll be staying in a real home, and I'll walk there myself."

"We could be there tonight if you'd let me help you."

Jameson sighed audibly, rolling his eyes though he knew she couldn't see them. "Alright."

"What?" She moved her head from his chest and looked him in the eye.

"I said alright. If it means that much to you, go ahead."

"Really?" Her brow furrowed.

"Yes, Reem—before I change my mind, preferably." He laughed.

She smiled, placing her hand on his forehead once again and sending her healing gift through her palm and into his bloodstream. She could feel it working inside him, feel the healing flowing through his body as she willed feeling into his legs, willed him to be able to stand.

He groaned slightly, and she lifted her hand from his head to look him in the eye. "How's that?"

He looked back at her, smiling brightly as he threw his legs off the side of the bed and stood, taking her hand and kissing it lightly. "Much better."

"I told you I could have you home tonight." She smiled, standing and wrapping her arms around his neck as she kissed him passionately.

She released him slowly and linked her fingers with his. "How about I show you our home?"

"Perfect." He smiled as she led him through the narrow passageways of the hospital.

As they walked together down the hallway, Nicholas appeared in front of them. "I take it you let her heal you?" He smiled.

"Yes, he did. And now we're going home," Reem answered, not meeting his eyes though she could still hear every word he thought.

"Good, good. If you need anything, I'll be in the hospital." He paused. "Reem, when you're feeling more rested, we could use your help with a few of our patients if you're still up for it."

"Thank you, Nicholas," Jameson said when she didn't reply.

Reem pulled him along beside her as she continued down the hall and out the door.

She led as soon as they exited the hospital, walking down the street a short distance in the darkness before entering the same building she and Nicholas had entered earlier. She led Jameson to their room and sat on a chair by the table. "Welcome home," she told him.

He smiled and walked up behind her, rubbing her shoulders gently. "And to you," he whispered in her ear before kissing her neck.

She smiled brightly as he walked around the chair and picked her up, carrying her to the bedroom and laying her on the bed. "I shouldn't have let you heal me," he whispered as he lay down next to her.

"And why not?"

"Because now you need rest." He slowly ran his fingers through her hair as he spoke. "And there are things I'd much rather be doing than sleeping."

She laughed and rolled her body on top of his, kissing his lips.

He moved her onto her side, pinning her arms to her sides as he pulled away from her. "As I said—rest." He smiled slightly.

Nicholas paced around his empty home, trying to decide what to do. His feelings for Reem were growing stronger every second he saw her—he couldn't help it. Like Jameson had said, something about her was drawing him in, calling to him. He couldn't help but fall in love with her.

He knew the kiss was a mistake—especially since Jameson could have been awake by then—but he couldn't not kiss her. He had to kiss her. He had to know what it would feel like to have his arms around her, had to know how it would feel to press his lips against hers.

He'd been surprised that Jameson hadn't brought it up the last time they'd seen each other. Why wouldn't he be upset that another man had kissed his wife? Had Reem not told him? Had she asked that he not bring it up? The suspense was killing him—he had to know what Jameson was thinking.

He hadn't meant to do anything that would ruin the new friendship he'd found in Reem's husband—they'd already become close in the short time they'd spent together in the hospital. He was still considering Jameson's offer to give him the gift of healing, but now he wasn't so sure that they would take him back to Athena with them when they left. It didn't seem likely that Jameson would allow him to spend so much time with Reem—especially after what he'd done.

Of course, she hadn't kissed him back. She'd slapped him harder than he thought anyone ought to be able to, in fact. She hadn't really spoken to him since it happened. Yes, she'd said that she and Jameson were going home, but she'd never looked him in the eye, never even truly acknowledged his presence.

He didn't want to admit how much it stung that she wouldn't look him in the eye, but it was true. He couldn't help how it felt—like a knife being wrenched through his heart.

The kiss never should have happened—he knew that. But he just couldn't help himself.

He continued pacing, trying to decide what to do. Should he talk to Jameson, clear things up with him before anything truly awful happened between them?

He ran his fingers through his hair and sat down at the table—the first time he'd sat down in what seemed like days.

All he wanted was for her to love him back—but he knew that wasn't possible. She was married to the very man who he'd become so close to in such a short time.

He leaned his head on the table and fell fast asleep.

Jameson woke early and started a fire, not wanting Reem to think he'd done nothing all morning. Some of the hospital staff dropped off the food Nicholas had promised, and so he began making their favorite morning meal: Suri's recipe for beef stew. She'd given him the recipe while she showed him how to get to the settlement; she was sure Reem would love it.

He'd just finished preparing all of the ingredients and put the pot over the fire when Reem appeared in the bedroom doorway wearing her favorite jeans and cotton sweater.

"Good morning." He smiled at her.

"What are you doing up so early?" she replied.

"Making breakfast. What else?" He winked.

She smiled and walked up to him, wrapping her arms around his waist and leaning her face against his chest as his arms coiled around her. "I didn't know you could cook."

"I can't. Unless I have a recipe," he said. "Say, Suri's beef stew?"

She pulled away slightly and looked him in the eye. "She gave it to you?"

"She said she thought you'd like it."

"I miss her," she whispered.

"I know." He pulled her back to him.

They stood there for a moment, holding each other and waiting for Suri's stew to finish cooking.

"Good morning," Nicholas's cheery voice echoed from the entryway.

Jameson turned his head to look at Nicholas while Reem released her hold and walked to the fire to stir the stew.

"Sorry to barge in like this," Nicholas said. "Just thought I'd pop in and make sure Reem's healing gift did the job."

"I'm fine, thank you," Jameson replied. "We're both fine. Reem and I are going to take a look around the settlement today, and tomorrow she'll help you out at the hospital."

"If you'd like an escort around the settlement, that can be arranged easily enough. I'll have one of my staff show you around."

"Oh, I'm sure we'll be fine. Reem has an uncanny sense of direction." Jameson smiled.

"I'm sure." Nicholas smiled back. "Well, I'll be off. Enjoy your day."

Jameson nodded his farewell as Nicholas turned and exited the room, leaving as suddenly as he'd come.

"If you're trying to make him feel better about this, you could try actually speaking to him," Jameson said, still facing the doorway.

"I know," Reem replied bitterly.

"So why don't you?" He turned back toward her, raising his eyebrows as he spoke.

"Because I don't know what to say. I'll have to talk to him tomorrow, in any case." She stood from beside the fire and walked toward him.

"If you'd like, I can have a word with him before you do." He placed his hands on her shoulders.

"No, no, I'll deal with it myself."

He smiled condescendingly. "Alright. How's the stew coming?"

"It'll be done within the hour. And then we can go have a look around the settlement."

"Good."

They both walked to the table and sat as they discussed the settlement. Jameson discussed the offer he'd given Nicholas with her—though she already knew—and they determined that even after all that had happened they couldn't just leave him in the settlement. If he wanted to go to Athena, there was nothing they could do to stop him. They decided that no matter what, if he truly wanted to go with them, they would take him.

Jameson stood when he'd finished his stew and walked behind her, rubbing her shoulders lightly while she continued eating the last of her food. "Almost ready to go?" he asked.

"One more bite," she said as she scooped up a spoonful and put it in her mouth.

When she finished chewing, she got up off the chair and took his hand in hers. "Let's go," she said cheerily. He smiled back at her as they walked out of their new home, hand in hand.

As soon as they exited the building, they could see why no one outside of the people in the settlement knew about it. All around them were high mountains covered in snow—snow that wasn't falling anywhere in the settlement, even though they could see it all around the outside.

"Maybe we could use a guide," Reem said, awed by the high snowcapped mountains.

"Perhaps," he replied. "Should I see if Nicholas's offer to find us a guide is still available?"

"It might be nice to have someone who can tell us how they got that"—she pointed up to the sky—"to work."

"Stay here. I'll go find Nicholas," Jameson told her before turning and walking back in the direction of the hospital.

He rounded the corner into the hospital and wove his way through the halls, searching for Nicholas.

When he finally found him, he was seated on one of his patient's beds, listening to them describe how they were feeling. Jameson stopped in the doorway and waited until they were finished before he walked in to speak to Nicholas.

"Nicholas, can I talk to you for a moment?" he said after Nicholas gave the patient a sedative.

"Oh. Jameson. Of course," he replied, gesturing for him to follow as he walked out of the room. "Let's go somewhere more private," he suggested.

Jameson followed him down the hall, past three more patients' rooms until they reached the first empty room. Nicholas gestured for Jameson to enter, and he followed after him.

"What did you want to talk about?" Nicholas asked as he leaned against the wall and looked Jameson in the eye.

"Two things, actually. First off, Reem told me what happened yesterday," he said.

"Oh. Right. Look, I'm really sorry about that," he said. "But I just couldn't help myself. Like you said, she just got in my mind."

"She asked me not to speak to you about it, but I thought it best that I ignore her in this case."

"Jameson, listen, I didn't mean to overstep any boundaries, really, I didn't. I don't know what came over me. I just—" He shook his head and shrugged.

"You couldn't help but fall in love with her?"

"No. I couldn't."

"Nicholas, I'm not going to say anything else about it. Reem doesn't even want me to talk to you about this, and she's planning on talking to you about it herself when she comes in to help you. I can tell you're already upset enough about this. Just remember that I know, and that I'm not normally as nice about things like this as I'm being right now."

Nicholas nodded slowly. "It won't happen again, I swear. And I really hope this doesn't do anything to our friendship."

"We'll see." He paused. "We'd like someone to show us around. We have a few questions that we'd like answered—about the settlement, of course."

"Right, right. Well, I can get one of the staff to take you, but I'm afraid the majority of them don't know much about the goings-on in the settlement beyond the hospital walls."

"So who would you recommend that we get?"

"I can take you, if you'd like. I know it might be a bit awkward, but out of everyone in the hospital, I probably know the most about the settlement."

"So long as you don't do anything that gives me reason to kill you." He winked.

"I'll behave myself, I promise." He smiled nervously.

"When can you leave?"

"I have one more patient to check up on."

"Meet us in front of the hospital when you're finished?"

"Of course." Nicholas nodded as Jameson exited the room and started down the long hallway.

He could see Reem from the doorway of the hospital; she was walking toward him with a scowl on her face. He smiled as she approached, knowing that she'd been listening in on the entire conversation.

She stopped in front of him and crossed her arms. "Well?" she asked.

"Well what?" Jameson replied.

"What was that?"

"What was what?"

"You know what I'm talking about."

"Fine, fine." He smiled. "Where would you like me to start?"

"I told you not to say anything to him."

"Reem, it's my right as your husband to talk to the man who kissed you against your will. I only told him that I knew—I left the rest up to you."

"But why is he taking us around the settlement?"

"Because he knows the most about the settlement, and he offered. Do you have a problem with it?"

She paused. "Why are you so good at answering my questions?" She smiled brightly.

"Because I love you," he answered, wrapping his arms around her waist and kissing her forehead.

Nicholas appeared a few moments later, walking out of the hospital door and facing them. "Ready to go?" he asked, favoring looking at Jameson over looking straight at Reem.

"Of course," Jameson replied, smiling at Nicholas's obvious struggle.

"How do they do that?" Reem asked, pointing up at the sky.

"The dome, you mean? Here in the settlement, we actually use technology to startling amounts. We've found that the frigid temperatures here make it impossible to survive the winter, so our scientists developed the dome. It keeps the internal temperature of the settlement at sixty-eight degrees Fahrenheit year-round," Nicholas answered, gesturing to them to start walking while he spoke. "It also gives the appearance to anyone on the outside that the city is nothing but a frozen lake."

"This building, as you know, is the hospital staff housing," Nicholas added as they passed the building Reem and Jameson were living in. "I hope that you've found it satisfactory. I'm in charge of keeping everything up to par in the hospital as well as the staff housing, though I have other people do the majority of the work."

"How does one man have so many responsibilities?" Jameson asked. "Shouldn't things be more equally spread in a settlement as large as this?"

"You would think so, but in fact there aren't many people in the settlement who have the experience to run the hospital or the tact to keep the staff housing in prime condition. As I said, I pass off a lot of the responsibilities onto people that work under me—I just have the title." He smiled.

"In Athena, the title was what everyone always wanted," Jameson added. "I never understood the principle, personally." He lifted Reem's hand, their fingers still linked together, and kissed it lightly while they walked.

"I honestly don't understand the principle either. I do my fair share of the work. I just hold the title so the people under me actually get the work done," Nicholas answered, trying not to stare at the couple who walked beside him.

"Do you have specific leaders here, or is it like the republics of the histories?" Reem asked, lost in thought as far as Nicholas could tell.

"We have three main leaders who decide the important things, like who is in charge of what and who goes to the Human and Purist colonies to gain information on the outside world, but the majority of minor decisions are made by a vote of all those to whom in pertains.

"Most of us refer to the leaders as the elders, though we haven't really chosen a specific name for them. When the settlement was started, the people took a vote as to who should lead us: one Advanced, one who follows closer to the principles of the Pure, and one Human. All things considered, they are very fair. If someone ever had a problem with one of them—something that could jeopardize the integrity of the settlement—they can go to the elders and straighten it up, and if the Elder refuses to change his ways, the people have a right to vote on whether or not he be forced to step down or not. So far the system works for us, though we've only been here for a little over two decades."

"So it's similar to the Purist form of government?" Jameson asked.

"Somewhat, yes. But our leaders are not our priests, they are our equals."

"I would think that would work much better than the Advanced system of government," Reem said, breaking her long silence.

"Yes, I believe it does. No offense to you or anything, but the Superiors decide everything for you. In our government, we decide what we want to do and say, and we decide who we want to love."

"I like that," she said. "It seems fitting that you all be able to decide everything for yourselves."

"Our thoughts exactly."

"Have you been here since the settlement was started?" Jameson asked.

"Suri actually introduced me to it several years ago. We met in a Human camp. She told me about this place, and I've been here ever since."

"Where are we now?" Reem questioned.

"We're near the center of the settlement. The elders have their housing here, along with the majority of the decision makers of the settlement. We all voted and decided that this would be the safest place to house them. It's also the site of our evacuation center."

"Evacuation center?" She tilted her head to the side.

"Yes, it's similar to one that we found in a Purist camp. We've dug a series of caves underneath the settlement where the entire population can go if another people group were to discover us here."

"We were staying in that Purist camp—before we came here. We were even staying in the caves," Jameson told him.

"Really? Perhaps you'd like to see the evacuation center for yourselves then. It's quite spectacular. We've set up all sorts of technology that would aid us in surviving over a century underground."

"That's a brilliant idea, the caves. They even have a few in Athena, from what I'm told," Reem added.

"Are they extensive?"

"No," Jameson started. "They're quite small, actually. Only enough space for the Superiors and their personal guard."

"Well, that defeats the purpose, doesn't it?"

"Yes, I believe it does," Jameson said solemnly.

Nicholas led them around the entire settlement, showing them the elders' chambers, which were viewable by any who wished to see them, the entire science facility, and the dome integrity center. By the end of the day, they still hadn't seen everything that the settlement had to offer, but Reem's feet were saying that it was time to stop.

"Would you like to try some local cuisine? One of our newcomers was a famed chef for one of your Superiors before she faked her death and came here. She's set up a small eatery near the hospital staff housing," Nicholas told them as they neared their home.

"What do you think?" Jameson asked as they stopped in front of the building.

"Let's try it. Nicholas can tell us more about the settlement while we eat," she answered. "You will be joining us, won't you, Nicholas?" She turned to face him.

"Of course," Nicholas answered, nodding nervously. "Right this way." He motioned away from the building and led them to a relatively new-looking house where he opened the door and gestured for them to enter.

Inside they were greeted by a woman in her thirties, with short light-blonde hair and pale blue eyes. She led them to one of four tables in the house and told them that she would bring them their food shortly—without asking them what they wanted to eat.

"Tina serves only two things so far, since it's made with what few foods we can obtain easily," Nicholas explained as they sat. "She'll bring us a plate of each."

Reem and Jameson both smiled the same crooked smile they'd been smiling all day as they'd walked around the settlement bombarding Nicholas with questions.

"Is there anything else you'd like to know about the settlement, or is it my turn to ask you questions?" Nicholas asked them, looking back and forth between them.

They glanced back at each other, presumably sharing some conversation in their minds before turning back to him. "Your turn," Reem said.

Hiding

"Where are you both from?" Nicholas asked.

"Reem is from Admiri, and I from a camp outside Athena," Jameson answered quickly.

"And how did you end up in a Purist camp and now here?" His eyes were wild with confusion.

"It's a long story," Reem said.

"But one we're willing to tell if you'd like to hear it," Jameson added.

"I'd love to hear it." Nicholas's smile was brighter than they'd ever seen as he waited for one of them to start their story.

Reem nodded slightly to Jameson, and he began, starting the tale with their meeting in her quarters in Admiri and pausing when he reached the death of the Athenians. "When we returned to Admiri, the Superiors accused her of treason and sentenced her to death," he continued. "By this point I was already deeply in love with her, so obviously when I found out, I took her from the city. We went to the Purist camp, where we stayed in the caves. I assume you've heard about the Purist alliance with the Advanced?" he asked.

"Of course. We were in the Purist camp when the ambassadors returned."

"They were looking for me," Reem told him flatly. "Dead or alive, the Superiors want me back."

"So you came here." Nicholas nodded slowly.

"Yes," Jameson said.

"Suri told us to come here. She said we'd be safe until the time was right to return to Athena," Reem added.

"What's so special about Athena then?" Nicholas asked.

"There's a group of Advanced there—rebelling against the Superiors. They want me to come and lead them once they get going," Reem told him.

"So we will be spending a few months here with you in the settlement, but then we intend to go back to Athena," Jameson said, ending their story.

"Who are you to them, Reem?" Nicholas asked, his eyebrows rising as he stared into her eyes.

"They call me their savior, though I do not claim to be. I am merely a class five telekinetic."

"That's all that they know her to be," Jameson added. "They don't know that she developed a second gift—telepathy—or that I've given her the healing gift. And we'd like to keep it that way."

"You developed a second gift?"

"I don't know why and I don't know how, but I did. Jameson did so as well."

They all paused while Tina brought back two platters of food, neither of which Reem and Jameson recognized.

"You are Reem Kahrin," she said after she'd set the platters on the table, her eyes never leaving Reem's face.

"Yes," Reem answered. "I am."

"What are you doing here then?"

"Running," Jameson said, seeing what this conversation was doing to Reem.

Tina nodded to him and walked away, back to the kitchen. Jameson turned back to Nicholas, his eyes serious.

"I'll be right back," Reem said suddenly, getting up and walking to the door behind which Tina had disappeared.

Jameson nodded to her as she walked away, having heard her intentions whispered into his mind.

"How do you know Athena will be safe when you get there?" Nicholas asked him as soon as Reem had disappeared from sight.

"Having her leave the room doesn't mean she can't hear you, Nicholas. And we won't know it's safe until we get there, I'm afraid," Jameson answered.

"What if something happens when you get there?"

"She knows more about what's going on than I do. If something were to happen to her, I would die—literally—but there's not much I can do when her mind's been made up like this. She wants to go back, so I'll take her there."

"Are you sure that's such a good idea?"

"Nicholas, I know how you feel about her, but that doesn't mean that I feel any less about her. I love her more than you could ever know, and I won't be putting her in any danger. We're going to teleport outside Athena and determine if it's safe to continue on from there."

"I know, I know. I'm sorry. I just can't help but worry about her."

Jameson nodded slowly. "She's still willing to bring you back with us, you know."

"Really?" he asked.

"At first she wasn't sure, but after today, she wanted me to tell you she's fine with it."

"Thank you, Jameson." He nodded. "Thank you."

"You'll be coming with us then?" Reem asked, appearing from the kitchen and walking toward them.

Nicholas looked up at her, trying to forget about his feelings as he replied, "Yes. I believe so." He smiled slightly.

"We'll be looking forward to it." She nodded back as she sat down beside Jameson, and smiled as she kissed his cheek. "Did you tell him yet?" she asked.

Jameson shook his head, smiling. "I thought you might like to."

"Tell me what?" Nicholas asked, confusion sweeping over his face.

"There's something you should know—about yourself," Reem said, her smile growing.

"What is it? Jameson?" He looked back and forth between the two of them. "What is it?"

"You'd better tell him," Jameson told Reem. "Put him out of his misery." He winked.

"What is it?" Nicholas asked worriedly, his stomach dropping.

"You're not what you think you are. It's just that your gift is too simple for you to notice it right away and too small for anyone to find unless they were looking for it," Reem said.

"What?"

"Remember telling me that you always wanted to be Advanced?" Jameson asked.

"What's that got to do with anything?"

"You *are* Advanced, Nicholas," Reem told him.

"I'm . . . what?"

"You heard her," Jameson said. "You're Advanced. We didn't notice it until today, but you are."

"How's that possible? Wouldn't I have been put in the camps when I was a child?"

"Not necessarily. There were many Advanced who hid or who simply went unnoticed until the war broke out. You just so happen to have a gift that went unnoticed—even by you," Reem said.

"Then what's my gift?" he asked.

"You have the ability to hide yourself and everyone around you. It went unnoticed because you've been using it—unknowingly, of course," she answered. "I know it's nothing glamorous, but it is something that we could use in Athena."

"Is that the only reason you want me to come with you—because I can hide you?"

"No, no, Nicholas that's not it. If you want to come to Athena, there's nothing we can do to stop you. We've only decided that as long as you still desire you go, you can come with us," Jameson said. "If you wish to stay, then stay. If you wish to come, we'll gladly take you with us. We do need someone with your gifts, and from what I can tell, you don't seem like one who wouldn't want to help those around him."

"I'll go with you then." He nodded slowly.

"Good." Reem smiled. "We'll be glad to have you with us."

"So long as you keep your hands to yourself." Jameson winked.

"Oh. Of course." Nicholas smiled back. "Of course."

"Don't you want to know how it works?" Reem asked.

"Please," he replied. "I don't even really know what I do."

Reem looked at Jameson, gesturing for him to explain.

"Nicholas, your gift is so simple, that it works without you even thinking about it. You're using it right now actually. You've been hiding your gifts from everyone even before we got here."

"We didn't notice it until you let your guard down. I would've realized earlier, but even you didn't know you had a gift," Reem added.

"How would I not know that I have a gift?"

"At first we thought you might've been lying to us, but Reem searched your mind," Jameson answered.

"You had no idea," she said.

"I'm sorry. This is a lot to take in at once," Nicholas said, running his fingers through his hair and looking up at the ceiling while he let out a slow breath. "I don't even know what to say. I wish I'd known sooner. Maybe I could've done something with my life."

"You did do something, Nicholas. You're a doctor, remember?" Reem said softly.

"But I could've been more than that."

"Nicholas, listen to me," Jameson said. "You are Advanced. That means you won't die of natural causes. You have as much time as you need to make your life into whatever you want it to be."

"You're right—I know you are. It's just going to take a while for me to absorb all of this."

"Take your time," Reem said as she picked up a fork and scooped up a bite of food. "We should eat before this gets cold," she told them before putting the bite in her mouth.

The rest of the evening was spent with small talk and large bites of Tina's cuisine. The three of them talked about their plans for the next few months: how Nicholas was going to step down from his position at the hospital, what work Reem would be doing with him, and how Jameson would spend his time without his wife. The distance across the settlement was too great for Jameson to be able to go very far from the hospital, so they decided that the next day they would go to the elders and find somewhere he could help.

"I'm sure we can find something for you to do—something that's not that far away from the hospital. We have several positions that are still open," Nicholas told him.

"Good." Jameson nodded.

"I think it's time to get home," Reem said as she took Jameson's hand in hers.

"Of course." He nodded. "Teleport or walk?"

"Teleport—my feet would prefer it." She smiled. "I'll see you at the hospital in the morning, Nicholas."

"I look forward to it." He smiled back at her as Jameson teleported them back to their home, leaving him alone at the table.

Nicholas stayed at the table for a few more minutes, thinking about all that had occurred. He still couldn't stop thinking about Reem, couldn't stop thinking about the kiss, couldn't stop thinking about the fact that she was still fine with him joining them in Athena. It didn't make sense that Jameson would approve of Nicholas working with his wife after what had happened. Jameson should have been angrier about it, but for some reason he wasn't—and after today, Reem didn't seem to be either.

In any case, he would be spending a lot more time with Reem in the days to come, and he wasn't sure if that was a good thing or not. Yes, he wanted to spend more time with her, but he didn't know if he could handle it. Through the day, all he could think about was the kiss, and he knew that Reem was listening in on his thoughts. Every time he thought about her, she would ask a question that would distract him—every single time.

And then there was the fact that they'd told him he was already Advanced. How could that be possible? It shouldn't be. If he were Advanced, he should have already known it by now. He was a child when he'd taken the treatment; he should have noticed by now.

Was it possible that he really was Advanced?

Knifed

Jameson woke with Reem's body lying on beside his, her face buried in his chest and her arms around his neck. He ran his fingers up her bare spine and kissed her forehead gently. "Reem, wake up," he whispered.

She groaned and tightened her arms around his neck. "No," she whispered back.

Jameson chuckled and moved her arms as gently as he could. "You don't want to be late for your first day at work."

"Yes, I do." She wrapped her arms back around his neck, pulling herself up to look him in the eye. "I don't want to go anywhere today," she whispered. "I just want to stay here with you."

"You just don't want to have to see Nicholas without me there to stand between the two of you." He laughed lightly. "You did say you would be there today," he whispered.

She groaned. "You're right." She rolled off him and sat up, running her fingers through her hair. "You're right, you're right, you're right," she said as she swung her legs off the side of the bed and started to stand.

Jameson grabbed her arm and pulled her back down beside himself, pulling her face to his and kissing her lips passionately. "You'd better get going," he whispered as he released her.

"You're walking me down there," she said matter-of-factly.

He smiled back at her and nodded before standing to his feet and walking to the closet to stand beside her. "Of course I am," he whispered in her ear. "Of course I am."

They dressed as quickly as they could—Jameson in his usual jeans and white shirt, and Reem in her old uniform—before they finished off the rest of Suri's stew and walked out the door. They walked together hand in hand down the street until they reached the hospital, pausing in the doorway.

"Do you need me to come inside with you, or can I go find something better to occupy my time until the two of you come with me to see the elders?" Jameson asked jokingly as they stood together in the doorway.

"I'll be fine from here, thank you. You'll be here when we're finished?" she asked, her eyebrows rising slightly.

"Yes, of course I will." He leaned toward her and kissed her lips gently. "I love you," he whispered in her ear.

"I love you too," she whispered back as he kissed her hand and turned, walking away from her for the first time since they'd reached the settlement.

She walked into the hospital, searching for Nicholas.

He was with a patient, so she waited in the doorway, leaning against the frame until he finished and turned to see her standing there.

"Reem—you're here," he said.

"You didn't think I'd come?" she asked him, standing up away from the doorframe.

"No. Well, yes, I thought you'd come, but I didn't know—"

"You didn't know if Jameson would be coming too?" Her eyebrows rose.

"I suppose that . . . works." He nodded, the corners of his mouth turning up ever so slightly.

"Thought it might." She winked. "Which would you rather do first: put me to work here or talk about the other day? I'll leave it up to you." She crossed her arms over her chest and stood in the center of the doorway, cornering him in the patient's room.

"I suppose it might be best if we talked first," he said finally, gesturing for her to walk down the hallway. "There's an empty room a few doors down."

She moved out of the way, motioning for him to lead, before she followed him into the empty room.

"I'll let you start," she told him.

"I'm not sure what to say, exactly," he replied nervously.

"Fine then, I'll start," she said. "If you ever do anything like that again, I won't hesitate to do much more damage to you than before. Understood?"

"Yes, yes, of course." He nodded. "I don't know what came over me. I'm so sorry." His eyes turned to the ground.

"I understand that—believe me, I'm being very understanding—but that still doesn't mean that I forgive you. I'm having a hard enough time with the fact that Jameson wants you to come with us to Athena."

"Thank you—for letting me come with you. I belong there, with my people," he whispered, his eyes never leaving the ground.

"Nicholas, look at me," she ordered.

He looked up, still not wanting to meet her eyes.

"You love the people of the settlement, you love the way of life here. Are you sure you want to give all of that up just to be with more Advanced?"

"Yes." He nodded, shifting his eyes to the doorway. "It's time we get to work. I have several patients who need your attention," he said, walking past her and into the hallway. "Follow me."

She did as he asked, following him down the hall past several patients' rooms.

"This is the critical condition center—the CCC—where we keep the patients who need our care the most. I believe you will be of most assistance here," he said, gesturing for her to enter a room.

They walked into a patient's room, seeing a young man lying on a bed, covered with blood that seeped from a wound in his leg.

"What happened to him?" Reem asked as she approached him.

"There was an accident on the last survival mission—the trips we take to gain food and supplies from Humans and Purists. There were seven wounded, he is one of five who are still alive," he read off a chart that hung in the doorway. "You work with him, I'll be next door," he said as he exited.

She walked to the patient's bedside, slightly nervous as her hand gently touched his leg, sending the healing power through her fingers and into his body.

His face relaxed as his leg began to heal, and the healing power charged through his veins. He sat up and opened his eyes to look at her, standing at the edge of his bed, barely touching his leg with her healing fingertips.

His bright golden eyes stared into hers for what seemed like a century. They pierced into her soul, searching.

"Hello," he said finally, his voice light and young—younger than he looked. When she nodded her response, he reached out and took her hand. "Thank you," he whispered.

"You're welcome," she replied, still stunned by the power of his eyes.

"I didn't mean to frighten you. I'm sorry." He turned his eyes to the ground, trying not to look her in the eye. "I forget sometimes."

"Forget what?"

"My eyes. They frighten people sometimes. I didn't do it on purpose, I promise."

"It's fine. What's your name?"

"Mikah," he said as he lifted his face to look at her.

"How do you feel, Mikah?" she asked, her eyebrows rising slightly as she spoke.

"Much better." He smiled. "You healed me?"

"Yes." She smiled back. "Yes, I did. Are you going to be okay here by yourself? I need to go check on some other patients."

He nodded his response, leaning back on the bed and resting his head on the pillow as she turned and walked out of the room.

She walked into the next room and found Nicholas sitting next to a middle-aged woman, wrapping strips of cloth around her waist in an attempt to stop the blood flow that poured onto the floor.

"Reem, help me," he told her.

She stood frozen in the doorway as she watched blood pour from the woman's body. Her eyes widened when she took in the amount of blood that pooled on the floor, and she took a step back toward the hall.

"Reem! Now!" Nicholas demanded.

She nodded slowly and ran to his side, placing her hand on the woman's midsection and sending the healing power into her as quickly as she could. Nicholas slowly relaxed the pressure he'd been putting on the woman's bleeding body and nodded to Reem. "It's working," he said.

Reem continued to pass her healing gift into the girl, trying to completely stop the blood from flowing out of her midsection. She closed her eyes and concentrated, trying to feel for the wounds and heal them one by one. "She has a bullet in her abdomen," she said flatly. "We'll have to get it out before I can finish healing her. Can you get it yourself?" She opened her eyes and looked into his, only inches away from her own. "I'll slow the bleeding, you find the bullet."

He nodded and ripped the woman's shirt off her body in preparation of removing the bullet. He picked up a syringe from the side table and injected the woman with its contents before surgically removing the bullet that had penetrated her torso. Reem closed her eyes as he scooped out the small projectile and dropped it in a small container he'd set on the side table.

"Reem," he said. "You need to finish up here. There are still others that need your help."

Her eyes snapped back open and she shot the healing power through her fingertips into the woman's torso, healing her as fast as she could, trying to prevent her from losing even more blood.

When she finished, she met Nicholas's eyes once again. "What's next?" she asked.

"Follow me." He smiled. "We've got plenty of work for you."

She followed as he stood and exited the room, washing his hands in a small bowl of water before walking into another patient's room. Inside were two people—a linked couple—both suffering from large gashes in their legs and arms. Both were awake—the first time one of the patients had been awake when she'd entered the room.

"They both refused sedation," Nicholas whispered in her ear before he walked to the man and began to look over his wounds.

Reem walked to the woman and ordered her to lie back on the bed, placing her hand on the woman's forehead and feeling for her wounds as she sent her healing gift through her fingertips. The woman gasped as she felt the power rushing through her veins, healing her one gash at a time.

She was almost finished, when Nicholas yelled, "Reem! He's crashing!"

"I'm almost finished," she replied.

The woman slapped Reem's arm from her forehead, looking her straight in the eye, pleading for her to save her husband. Reem nodded to the woman and ran to Nicholas's side, trying to send the healing power through her fingertips before she'd even reached the dying man. She reached out and touched the man's arm, trying to bring his heart rate back to normal as she tried to stitch his wounds back together.

"How is he?" the woman demanded, standing to her feet and approaching them.

"She's the best we have, I promise you," Nicholas replied.

"Almost finished," Reem whispered, closing her eyes and concentrating on healing. "Almost there . . . His heart rate is normal. He won't be awake for a while though, I'm afraid."

"But he's alive?" the woman asked, trying to move to stand beside her husband.

"Ma'am, I need you to lie back down until we've finished with your husband," Nicholas told her. "You can't help him right now. I'm sorry." When she started to reply, he raised his voice. "Sit. Down!"

She did as he said, walking back to her bed and sitting down slowly, ready to jump back up if anything happened.

Nicholas placed his hand on Reem's shoulder comfortingly. "You're doing fine, Reem. How much energy do you have left?"

"Enough," she answered, opening her eyes slowly and removing her hand from the man's forehead. "He's fine." She nodded, turning around and facing the woman once again. "He's fine," she repeated.

She walked back to the woman and sat next to her. "May I?" she asked, holding out her hand.

The woman nodded slowly, never taking her eyes off her husband who lay still on his bed, his chest rising and falling slowly with his breath.

Reem put her hand on the woman's knee and sent her healing gift through her body, stitching up her wounds with her mind.

When she finished, she patted the woman's knee lightly and smiled at her, looking her straight in the eye. "Go to him. He needs to hear your voice," Reem told her as she stood and followed Nicholas out into the hall to wash their hands once more and go to yet another patient's room to heal them.

Two hours later, Reem sat in her eighth patient's room. The patient was a middle-aged man who had been in the wrong place at the wrong time and ended up with four knives embedded in his body: one in his right arm, one in his chest, one in his abdomen, and the fourth in his left thigh.

Nicholas had removed the blades one at a time—starting with his arm—and Reem healed his wounds in the same order. She was running dangerously low on energy, but she couldn't bring herself to say no to helping the man. He'd been running through the street, trying to catch up to his son when he'd passed a target practice session near the school. He'd ended up with the four large blades in his body, and they'd brought him straight here.

Reem kept her hand on his forehead, trying to heal him as Nicholas slowly removed the blade from his chest. She healed it as quickly as she could, draining her energy more than she wanted to before Nicholas pulled out the fourth blade.

"Wait," Reem whispered, too quietly for Nicholas to hear. "Wait."

Nicholas removed the blade and she did the only thing she could—she tried to heal the man. She healed him from the inside out, stitching his wounds inside his body before starting to seal the skin around the wound.

"I'm sorry," she whispered, barely loud enough for Nicholas to hear, as she fell to her side, almost on top of the still-bleeding man.

***

"Reem?" Nicholas said, his mind filling with worry though he kept his hands on the man's abdomen and stitched his wounds the old-fashioned way, digging out his supplies from his medical bag.

As soon as he finished with the man, he picked Reem up off of the bed and carried her out of the patient's room and into a room of her own. He left her there for a few moments under the care of another doctor.

When he returned, she still hadn't woken, and Jameson would be arriving soon. Nicholas picked her up off the bed and carried her back through the halls. Jameson was already there at the exit when he arrived, his face filling with worry when he saw him carrying Reem.

"What happened?" he demanded, walking up and taking Reem from Nicholas's arms. "How could you have let this happen?"

"We were almost finished for the day when a last-minute patient came in— four knife wounds. I'm sorry—I didn't realize how little energy she had until it was too late."

"I'm taking her back home," Jameson said angrily as he turned away, carrying Reem back to the staff housing center.

"Tell her I'm sorry!" Nicholas yelled as Jameson walked away from him. He turned around and walked back inside the hospital, unwilling to leave the patients with a less-trained doctor.

Jameson walked into their home and laid Reem down on the bed before kissing her forehead. "Sleep, my love," he whispered in her ear as he lay down next to her and wrapped his arms around her waist.

***

Reem woke on her side with her arms wrapped around Jameson's body and her face buried in his chest. She moaned lightly, rolled onto her back and let out a deep breath. Jameson kept his arms around her and smiled brightly. "I wish you wouldn't overwork yourself so often," he said.

"I wish I didn't have to," she whispered, turning to face him.

He twined his fingers with hers and kissed her hand. "I hated having to carry you back here, Reem. I hated seeing him carry you out the door. Promise me you'll be more careful," he said, his eyes burning into hers.

"Is he okay?"

"Who?"

"The man. The one I was trying to heal. I don't remember what happened."

"I don't know, Reem. It wasn't high on my list of priorities at the time."

"Maybe it should've been." She turned away from him.

"Reem." He put his hand under her chin and turned her head to face him. "Listen to me. If you keep pushing yourself like this, you're going to die, and I cannot live without you. You know that. Please don't make me take you away from here." He smiled slightly.

"I can't just stand by while people are dying, Jameson."

"Just promise me you won't exhaust yourself to the point where I have to see Nicholas carrying you out of that hospital again, Reem. That's all I'm asking."

She looked into his pleading bright green eyes, tears pooling in her own. "I'm so sorry, Jameson," she whispered.

He pulled her back into his arms as she tried her best not to cry, burying his face in her neck.

"I'm so sorry," she said again.

"Don't," he whispered, kissing her forehead lightly. "Don't."

Visitor

They lay in bed for what seemed like hours, Jameson holding Reem tightly in his arms. When her eyes finally dried, she fell back asleep in his arms, still exhausted from the day before. Jameson rolled onto his back, pulling Reem close to himself as he closed his eyes and tightened his arms around her, falling asleep to the sound of her breathing.

She woke to the sound of Jameson's snoring in her ear. She reached her arm up and covered his mouth with her hand, laughing as she did so.

His eyes snapped open, and he rolled over on top of her, pinning her arms to her sides. "Snoring?" he asked, a smile turning up the corners of his mouth as he stared into her eyes.

"Yes. Loudly." She laughed again.

"Sorry." He laughed along with her, slowly running his fingers through her hair and sliding his hand down her neck to her shoulder.

She moved her arms from her sides and wrapped them around his neck, pulling his lips to hers for a moment before he pushed her away and turned her on her side so that her back lay against his chest. "You're still exhausted, Reem," he reminded her as he wrapped his arms tightly around her waist.

She leaned her head back against his chest and sighed loudly. "Why are you so nervous that I'm going to hurt myself?" she asked him.

"Reem." He closed his eyes and leaned his head against hers.

"Tell me," she whispered.

"Read my mind. It's easier when you can feel my emotions," he told her as he opened his mind.

She listened to his thoughts, watching the memory of Nicholas carrying her out of his room in the hospital the first time she'd exhausted herself. She watched his feelings turn from nervous to angry the moment Nicholas touched her, felt how hard he tried to move, tried to go to her. She watched the more recent memory of Nicholas carrying her out of the hospital; once again felt the anger that built up inside him when he saw her unconscious in his arms.

"I don't ever want to have to see that again," he whispered.

She opened her mouth to reply, but another memory stopped her from doing so. She felt the fear that ran through him when he saw her fall to her side beside him in the hospital, felt how he wished he could give himself a healing power to bring her back to him.

"You're so reckless . . . I love that about you, Reem, but I don't want to see you get hurt."

Once again she opened her mouth to reply, and once again he stopped her by replaying a memory in her mind. She watched through his eyes as he carried her back into their home and lay down beside her, waiting for her to wake. She watched as he stroked her hair lightly, waiting patiently for her eyes to open and look into his.

"One more," he whispered in her ear.

She watched in his mind's eye as he carried her through the snow, searching for the settlement, and still unable to teleport. She watched as he stumbled, as he crashed to the ground on his knees and screamed out his anger at the sky. She watched as his numb fingers released their hold on her body, letting her fall to the ground; watched as Jameson covered her body with his in an attempt to keep her warm.

Her eyes snapped open as she watched his memory—the memory of her heartbeat stopping.

She turned around in Jameson's arms and looked him in the eye. "What happened?"

"Watch."

"No, Jameson. Tell me."

"I felt you die in my arms. I gave you the last of my energy—I restarted your heart." He pulled her closer to him.

"That could have killed you," she whispered.

"I didn't care."

She pulled her lips to his and kissed him. "I'm sorry," she whispered in his ear.

He pulled her away slightly and looked deeply into her eyes. "I've felt your heart stop once. I don't want to feel that again, Reem. Promise me."

"I promise." She closed her eyes, trying to hold back tears when Jameson pulled her back into his arms and kissed her forehead.

"Nicholas is on his way," she whispered. "He wants to know how I'm doing."

"Of course he does," Jameson said bitterly.

"What do you want to do?"

"You stay here. I'll go talk to him." He released his hold on her and sat up. "I'll be back when he's gone." He ran his fingers through her long hair and kissed her hand before he stood and walked out of the room.

Nicholas debated with himself for hours on whether or not he should go check on Reem. He knew Jameson would be monitoring her vitals constantly, but he still had a hard time believing that she would be better off without a doctor at her side—or at least that's what he told himself.

Now he was standing a few feet away from the door, afraid to go inside. He knew Jameson would likely be waiting there, knew that Reem had probably already noticed that he was standing outside their door. He took a tentative step forward, toward the door, stopping to collect his thoughts before he took the final step into the doorway.

Jameson sat on the ground beside the fire, keeping it going. He wore a pair of jeans and a white T-shirt, spotted with soot and ash from the fire. He turned his face to look at Nicholas, who still stood in the doorway. "She's fine, Nicholas," he said. "She's resting."

"I just came to—"

"I know. She told me."

"I'm sorry I let this happen, Jameson. I really am." He took a step into the room.

"I know." He nodded.

"May I see her?"

"No. As I said, she's resting." He motioned toward the table. "Have a seat."

Nicholas nodded and walked to the table, sitting down slowly as Jameson walked toward him. "Are you sure she's okay?" he asked nervously.

"I am monitoring her as we speak."

Nicholas ran his fingers through his hair, letting out a deep breath as he did so.

Jameson placed his hand on Nicholas's shoulder. "Why did you come here?" he asked.

"I don't know. It's like something was calling me here, pulling me to see her."

"Nicholas, if you would please remember that the woman you are in love with is my wife, things would be a lot easier for the both of us."

"I'm sorry, Jameson. I just, I can't get her out of my head, off my mind. It's like she's always there, taunting me."

"Then why do you insist on coming with us to Athena?" He removed his hand from Nicholas's shoulder and walked to the bedroom doorway, leaning against the wall facing Nicholas.

"I want to be with my people."

"With your people or with my wife?"

"With my people."

"I'll ask Reem to find out for me."

"Jameson, I swear to you, I only want to be in Athena. If you do not take me with you, I will go there myself."

Jameson nodded slowly. "I know you would. But I need you to think. Why do you really want to go to Athena?"

"I want to be with my—"

"Nicholas. I need you to think harder before you answer. Now. Think."

Nicholas's eyes slowly slid shut as he thought, considering all of the options. "I want to be with more Advanced, Jameson. Yes, I want to be with Reem too, but that's not the main reason for my wanting to go to Athena."

"Are you sure?" Jameson tilted his head up to the ceiling, staring at the ventilation hole for the fire.

"Yes, I'm sure. I want to be with Advanced."

"Which Advanced?"

"Not the ones who think Reem is a traitor. Anyone can see that she loves her people—she would never do anything to hurt them. Not of her own will, that is."

"So you will be staying with us when we reach Athena then."

"If you'll let me, yes."

Jameson nodded slowly. "I won't be leaving you behind any time soon."

"Thank you, Jameson. You won't regret it. I can help you, you know. Once I learn how to use my gift to the best of my ability."

"I know. And I appreciate it immensely." He looked down from the vent to look Nicholas in the eye. "But if I ever see you touching my wife again, it will be the last time you see her."

"I understand. I'll be careful. I promise. I'll assign one of the other doctors to work with her at the hospital, if you'd like."

"I'll ask her what she'd like."

"Are you sure I can't see her? When she passed out, I—"

"She's fine. How many times do I have to tell you that? I don't want her to see anyone right now."

"Please, Jameson. I want to see her. I need to."

"No, Nicholas." He fell to his knees, closing his eyes and clutching his head as though he was in pain.

Nicholas ran to his side and knelt beside him. "What's happening?" he asked.

Jameson's eyes snapped open, and he stared at Nicholas. "Reem, would like to talk to you," he breathed, the corners of his mouth turning up slightly.

"She did this to you?" Nicholas asked, his eyebrows furrowing. When Jameson nodded, he added, "What's she going to do to me?"

"That depends on what you say to her." Jameson motioned toward the bedroom doorway, gesturing for Nicholas to go inside.

Reem was wrapped tightly in a blanket, sitting up and leaning against the wall behind the bed. "How is he?" she asked as Nicholas walked in and sat next to her.

"Who? Jameson?" he asked, looking her in the eye.

"The man. From the hospital."

"Oh, of course. He's doing well. He has seven stitches in his abdomen, but they're healing quite nicely. He should be up and about in a matter of days—all thanks to you."

"I'm glad to hear he's doing well." She smiled.

Nicholas nodded. "I have something I need to ask you."

"You want to know if I still want to work with you, since Jameson doesn't want you near me." Her smile brightened.

"Yes." His eyes moved to stare at the ground by his feet.

"It's up to you. I would like to continue working with you—you do know my limits better than anyone else in the settlement."

"You really think Jameson is going to let you keep working with me?" He looked back up at her, staring into her silver-flecked eyes.

"I think it's time you leave, Nicholas," she whispered.

"Oh. I'm sorry. I didn't mean to—" he said when he realized she'd been reading his thoughts.

"Nicholas. Please leave," Jameson said, his voice coming from a few feet behind where he sat.

Nicholas nodded and stood, walking out of the room before either of the couple could say anything.

"What was he thinking?" Jameson asked as Nicholas started back down the hall.

"It's probably best that you not know," she whispered, moving the blanket so that he could join her.

"Probably right." He sighed as he sat beside her and took her hand in his. "How are you feeling?"

"I wish you wouldn't make me stay here for so long," she said, turning her head to face him.

"I have my reasons." He smiled as he wrapped his arms around her and kissed her passionately.

She pulled back and helped him pull his shirt off over his head before she moved back into his arms, kissing his neck. Jameson laughed lightly and ran his fingers through her hair, starting at her forehead and ending at the small of her back. She shivered and slid her fingers into his hair, pulling his face to hers and kissing his mouth.

"What did you tell him? About the two of you working together?" Jameson asked as he spooned Suri's stew into a bowl for Reem, who sat on the ground by the fire and leaned against the wall.

"I told him that it would be up to him whether or not we continue to work together. I don't mind working with him, but I know he has trouble keeping his mind on the task. I thought it would be best to let him decide," she answered, taking the bowl and spoon from Jameson.

"What do you think he'll decide?" He put a bite from his own bowl in his mouth as he sat down next to her.

"I think he'd like to continue working with me, yes. But I also think that he'd rather be somewhere he didn't have to think about the fact that you're the one who gets to kiss me whenever you want." She winked before putting a bite of stew in her mouth.

"You mean like this?" He leaned in and kissed her lips gently.

She laughed. "Yes, just like that."

"I wish I didn't have to worry about him doing that when you're together."

"He won't do anything—and if he tries, I'll stop it before it starts." She placed her hand on Jameson's cheek. "Don't worry. If he decides to continue working with me, I'll be more careful—about everything. I promise."

The corners of his mouth turned up slightly. "I love you, Reem."

"I love you." She smiled. "When are we going to see the elders? We still need to find something for you to do while I'm at the hospital."

"I suppose we'll go today, if you're feeling up to it." He winked.

"Today will be fine. Nicholas is still sitting right outside the staff housing, hoping we'll come out and run into him if we go to the elders. He seems to think he'll be able to help you."

"Maybe he will. We'll have to wait and see."

Forced Exit

Nicholas paced outside the staff housing building, waiting to see if Reem and Jameson would come outside. He knew they would likely be going to see the elders today, and he wanted to help them. Or, more accurately, he wanted to talk to Reem again while Jameson spoke to the elders.

He continued to pace, wishing that he knew what to do. He loved her, and it was wrong for him to feel that way. He didn't want to love her—in fact, he'd been in love with someone else before she'd come along—but he couldn't help but fall deeper in love every time he looked into Reem's eyes.

Jameson had said there was something about her eyes. Those piercing silver-flecked eyes that seemed to be able to see into his soul. He both hated and loved how she stared at him when she was focusing on his thoughts. He guessed that Jameson felt the same, judging by the way he looked back at her when she did that. Her eyes reminded him of Suri's when she changed her shape.

Suri had been his first love. He'd asked her to join with him in the Connection ceremony of the Purists, but she'd denied him. He'd thought she loved him as much as he loved her—his heart still jumped every time he heard her name. His love for Suri made more sense. They'd spent every moment of every day together while she was in the settlement. He'd fallen for her slowly, but his love still blazed inside him like a wildfire.

It made more sense than his love for Reem. She was much like Suri, but somehow his love for her blazed even higher than his love for Suri. He hoped that Suri would keep her promise: that she would meet up with them in Athena. It was the only way he knew to get over her sister.

How could this have happened to him? First he fell in love with Suri, the young attractive woman who'd helped found the settlement, and now Reem, her Connected sister. There was something about Reem though—something he couldn't place. He loved them both, and now he wasn't sure which he loved more. How could he decide between them? It just wasn't—

"You're overthinking it, you know," a voice whispered into his mind. Reem's voice.

His mind stopped. He was only able to focus on the voice he'd just heard inside his head. She'd never done that to him before. He'd known she could communicate with her mind—he'd seen the obvious signs of unspoken conversation between herself and Jameson—but he never thought that the voice she used would be exactly like the voice he always heard her using, the voice that would make him stop dead in his tracks.

"What am I overthinking?" he whispered aloud, hoping she was still listening.

"Everything." She laughed lightly.

"Why are you doing this to me, Reem?" He leaned against the wall and put his head in his hands.

"Something wrong, Nicholas?"

He jumped forward at the sound of Jameson's voice. What would he say if he knew his wife was talking to him with her mind?

He looked up and saw Jameson standing in front of him, and Reem two steps behind, staring up at the sky she found so fascinating. "No. Nothing's wrong," he replied, unable to take his eyes off Reem to look Jameson in the eye.

"Nicholas, please," Jameson said.

Nicholas closed his eyes and opened them to meet Jameson's. "I'm sorry," he said. "Very sorry."

Jameson nodded slowly. "We're going to see the elders. You can come along if you'd like." His eyes burned into Nicholas's, warning him not to make the wrong move.

"I could use the exercise." He smiled slightly.

Jameson nodded again before walking to Reem and taking her hand. She lowered her eyes to meet his and smiled as he lifted her hand to his lips and kissed it. "Shall we?" he asked.

"Of course." She turned and started walking toward the center of the settlement, with Jameson following beside her and Nicholas at his side, trying not to look like he was intently watching them.

When they reached the building of the elders, Jameson walked inside, leaving Reem and Nicholas standing outside: Reem leaning against the wall and staring at the sky, and Nicholas doing his best not to stare at her.

"Jameson thinks you're going to try something again," Reem said, her eyes never leaving the simulated clouds that floated past in the sky.

"What?" Nicholas asked, his eyebrows furrowing.

"He thinks you're going to try something. With me," she replied, moving her eyes to meet his.

"He thinks that?" He turned away for a moment then turned back. "And what would you do if I did?" he asked, his eyes staring into hers.

"You won't," she replied coolly.

"How do you know that?" He took a step forward, standing directly in front of her so she couldn't move without touching him.

"Because I can read your thoughts. And because I can do this." She pushed him away, knocking him to the ground a few feet in front of her without ever laying a finger on him.

Nicholas groaned, rising to his knees slowly. "Good reason." He laughed. "Very good reason."

"I thought so." She laughed along with him, walking up and helping him get to his feet.

He dusted off his jeans as they walked back to the elders' building and leaned against the wall. "What did you mean—when you said I overthink everything?" he asked.

"You don't understand why you're in love with me, and you didn't know you were Advanced. You didn't even know that Jameson thinks there's no possible way we could leave you here—that he thinks we need your help and thought that since before you even knew you were Advanced."

"So if you're so smart, then why am I in love with you?" He turned to face her, crossing his arms over his chest and staring into her eyes.

"Because I remind you of my sister. You know it too—you just don't want to admit it. Just like you didn't want to admit to yourself that you are Advanced. You wanted it so bad that you made yourself believe that you didn't have it," she answered, staring back at him.

"I don't even know what to say to that." He shook his head.

"Of course you don't. You've overthought all possible answers already." She winked.

"Did not."

"I can read your mind, remember?" She turned away and looked back at the sky. "She loved you too, you know," she said seriously.

"She what?" he asked, his voice turning completely serious yet unbelieving.

"She loved you." Reem turned back to face him. "My sister. She was in love with you. That's why she didn't come back with us."

"What did she say?"

"She told me to find you, to bring you back to Athena if I could. She wanted to see you, but she can't come back to the settlement—I don't know why. She told me you wanted to be Advanced, asked me to get Jameson to make your wish come true." She smiled.

"She said that? Suri?"

"Not out loud, no."

"I have to get to Athena." He started to walk away when Reem stopped him with her gift, holding him still in the center of the street.

"Nicholas, she isn't there. There's no point in you leaving before we do, and trust me, we'll be leaving before too long."

"What do you mean by that?" he asked.

"Jameson will be walking through those doors in a moment." She pointed to the door. "And when he does, he's going to say that we have to leave. The elders don't want us here."

"They cannot forbid you from staying. Not without a majority vote," he told her, his voice completely serious as he stared into her silver-flecked eyes.

"They have it, Nicholas. We'll be leaving in three days, and you're coming with us. I will not disappoint my sister." She released her hold on him and walked back to the door, putting her in front of it at the same time Jameson walked through.

"They don't want us here," he said.

"I know." She nodded, wrapping her arms around his neck.

"They want us out in three days."

"Why don't they want you here?" Nicholas asked, walking up and standing behind them.

"Both the Purists and the Advanced are looking for her," Jameson answered, his voice grave.

"They have good reason. I don't want to put any of your people in danger," Reem added, turning around in Jameson's arms so that she could face Nicholas.

"Where will you take her?" Nicholas asked Jameson.

"I don't know." He shook his head. "Coming here was Suri's idea."

"We will go to Athena," Reem said, ignoring Jameson.

"I won't take you there, Reem. Not yet."

"Yes, you will because it is the only place left that we can go to. We don't have a choice. It's time," she said.

Jameson nodded reluctantly. "I know."

"When will you leave?" Nicholas asked.

"You mean 'we,' don't you?" Jameson asked.

"Yes, yes, of course." He nodded. "When will we leave?"

"When they make us," Reem replied, her brow furrowing as she read his thoughts. "Jameson, go start packing. I'll meet you there in a moment."

Jameson turned her around in her arms, listening as she explained everything to him in his mind's eye. When she finished, he nodded slowly and leaned down to kiss her lips for a moment before he teleported away.

"You're coming with us, Nicholas. I won't leave you here," she said as she turned around to face him.

"It's you I can't stop thinking about, Reem. *You.*" He ran his fingers through his hair and turned to his right. "What would she say to that?" He turned back to her and stared into her eyes.

"She would tell you to think long and hard about the permanent accessory on my wrists and then come back to her when you're ready." She held up her wrists for him to see, never letting her eyes leave his. "I know my sister, Nicholas. Don't forget that."

Nicholas let out a heavy sigh, still staring into her silver-flecked eyes. He leaned forward and ran his fingers through her hair slowly.

"Nicholas. Don't," Reem warned.

He leaned in closer and barely brushed his lips against hers before she knocked him to the ground in front of her with her gift. "I said don't," she said again as she stepped over his prone body and started walking back toward the hospital staff housing building.

As she walked, she yanked his body up off the ground and left him in a standing position, watching her walk away.

"You're coming with us," she whispered into his mind.

"I know. Do I have a choice?" he replied aloud, knowing she could hear.

※☼☼☼

Jameson stood in the center of the room, holding Reem's hand firmly in his as they listened to the sound of the approaching guards—coming to forcibly remove them from the settlement.

Reem and Jameson had packed their things two days ago, and just like they'd planned, they'd waited until the very last minute before they would leave. They each wore a backpack, and Jameson held a small bag of supplies in his free hand.

Even now, Nicholas was waiting for them in the hospital. He'd packed his things at the same time as they and had been waiting in the hospital, training another staff member to take over his duties in the short time he had left before Reem and Jameson would come for him.

Jameson turned to Reem, who was monitoring the distance between the guards and themselves. She looked into his eyes and nodded ever so slightly. He brought her hand to his lips and kissed it, teleporting away just as the guards walked in the door.

"Already?" Nicholas asked when he saw them appear out of thin air into the corner of a patient's room. "Give me a moment." He picked up his backpack and threw it over his shoulder before walking back to where Jameson and Reem had appeared.

Jameson held his arm out to him, gesturing for him to come closer so that he could teleport them away. Nicholas froze for a moment, and Reem pulled him to Jameson's side using her gift.

"Don't worry," she told him. "It's perfectly safe."

Jameson put his hand on Nicholas's shoulder and teleported the three of them out of the room, as far away as he could go with the amount of energy he had.

They landed for only a moment before Jameson teleported a second time, taking them far enough away from the settlement that if the people there decided to look for them, they wouldn't be able to find them.

They landed on the outskirts of the ruins of Old London, rain pouring down on them from the moment they arrived. London was one of the first cities to be taken over by the Advanced, but when the Humans made their stand, the city was almost completely destroyed. Now it was home only to the plants that grew up over the ruins, covering them with green vines that made the old city look even more desolate, and the animals who found that the ruins were still tall enough for them to make their homes inside. They scanned the area, seeing nothing beyond a few feet in front of them due to the heavy fog that always seemed settled on Old London.

Nicholas stepped away from Jameson, who still held firmly to Reem's hand. They were all soaked in a matter of seconds, shivering as the cold wind picked up around them.

"Well, this is familiar," Reem shouted over the sound of the wind and rain.

"We should try and find shelter. I can't teleport across the ocean yet," Jameson shouted back.

Reem and Nicholas both nodded their responses as Jameson led them deeper into the city to find a building still intact enough to house three humans for the night.

The going was rough, the ground covered in wet, slippery plants and the wind throwing rain and hail into their eyes. They walked over countless demolished buildings and vehicles, stopping only to check inside some of the small houses for shelter—and finding none. They'd almost reached the center of the city and had yet to find anything that could be used as a shelter from the pouring rain and harsh winds. None of them spoke a word, and even Reem's mind was silent as they trudged onward, searching for a building large and dry enough to house the three of them for the night.

Jameson still refused to let go of Reem's hand, always sensing danger when they were out in the open and preferring to know that he could teleport her away at any time. If they hadn't taken Nicholas with them, he could have teleported all the way across the ocean, but he couldn't risk taking two people across before he'd rested, and at this rate it would take even longer for him to find rest—and for them to reach Athena. They continued to walk through the old city, both Reem and Jameson helping Nicholas to scale the higher pieces of wreckage as they went.

As the sun began to dip below the horizon of, Nicholas spotted what might be their best hope for a shelter, the sun barely dipping below it in the distance. It was the only bridge they'd seen that was still somewhat intact though it didn't reach all the way across the street. The center of the bridge had collapsed, and now half of the bridge lay on top of the cars in the street, but one half of the bridge still stood, suspended by two large trucks that had been under it when it collapsed. The space under the bridge was wide enough that the center was dry, and the space was big enough for the three of them to rest and attempt to dry off.

Slowly and carefully, they made their way to the bridge, being careful to avoid the sharp edges of the demolished cars and deep pitfalls among the wreckage. They reached the bridge mostly intact, but still soaking wet, with their hands and arms burning from the cold and their faces stinging from the harsh winds and rain. The trio threw their backpacks on the ground and collapsed in the dry space made by the bridge. Reem shivered violently, and Jameson wrapped his arms around her to keep her warm while Nicholas sat up and tried to think of a way to keep warm in the harsh conditions.

Reem quickly fell fast asleep, and Jameson still held her tightly to his body, listening to the steady beating of her heart while he watched Nicholas pace.

"What's wrong, Nicholas?" he asked.

"How long until we can leave?" Nicholas asked in response.

"I don't know," he replied. "She needs more rest than me now."

Nicholas furrowed his brow, confused. "You said we would leave in a few hours."

"She's exhausted too, Nicholas. She blocked many of the harsher winds during our journey, and using her gift for such an extensive time is very draining to her. I won't leave until she's ready."

"Wouldn't it be safer for her to rest in a place where she's not going to be killed by the water pouring from the skies?"

"I do not know what lies in wait for us on the other side of the ocean, nor does she. Her gifts cannot see that far away. I won't teleport her into an even more dangerous situation than this one without her being rested enough to fend for herself if something were to happen to me."

"You're right, you're right." He sat back down and put his head in his hands. "I just hadn't expected that we'd be in this kind of a situation. I thought it would all be smooth sailing." He paused and lifted his head out of his hands. "I guess I thought wrong."

"You should rest, Nicholas. I'll keep watch."

Nicholas nodded to him and lay down on the hard road surface, using his soaking backpack as a pillow as he closed his eyes and searched for sleep.

Nicholas woke to find Jameson asleep across from him and Reem nowhere in sight. The rain had died off during the night, and the wind had gone with it, but the air was still frigid and icy. He could hear the sounds of excess water dripping off the edges of the bridge, see where they fell into small puddles on the ground near his feet. He sat up and rubbed his eyes, fighting off the sleep that threatened to overtake him once more as he stood and walked out from under the bridge, facing the rising sun.

In the center of the wreckage of what had once been a building stood Reem, her arms spread wide at her sides, her head tilted upward toward the sky. He slowly walked toward her before he realized exactly what she was doing. Strewn on the ground all around her were knives, sharp pieces of wreckage she'd taken from cars and broken buildings, and large wooden rods. With her mind, she lifted them all off the ground and began to fight off a million unseen warriors, stabbing at the air around her.

She somersaulted, grabbing a wooden rod out of the air and beginning to fight off the other weapons that she had suspended in midair. He could just make out her closed eyes, moving rapidly beneath their lids, as she fought off every invisible assailant that haunted her. She threw kicks into the air, stabbing at her enemies with grace and brilliance as she vaulted and launched herself this way and that, destroying pieces of the broken building and shattering the windows that remained.

Nicholas watched her from a distance, taking in how beautifully she fought off every possible type of attack from every possible angle, all done with her mind. He watched her defeat enemy after enemy, watched the weapons as they fell to the ground at her feet, watched as she twisted her body this way and that to destroy an invisible assailant who hid behind a concrete wall.

She continued for several long minutes, practicing her skills with ease, knowing that no Human or Purist could possibly defeat her. Her only weakness, Nicholas realized, would be in fighting off other Advanced who would have greater skills in arts like these than the Humans or Purists.

It was then that she suddenly stopped, landing squarely in the center of the tiny clearing she'd made herself at the beginning of her exercise. She dropped her arms to her sides and lifted all her weapons off the ground, packing them away into the bag that lay by her feet using only her mind. Each knife went into its own sheath, each piece of debris back in its rightful place among the wreckage.

Only when she'd finished packing everything away did she open her eyes and turn to face Nicholas, who still stood a few feet away from the bridge.

"Do you know how to fight, Nicholas?" she asked, her hand motioning for him to join her among the wreckage.

He took a few steps forward before answering. "Not very well, I'm afraid. My training was only basic." He shrugged. "But I've never had the need to fight anyone."

She smiled as he neared her position. "You will need to learn then." She handed him a wooden rod she'd been using in her exercise.

"Can't I be taught when we reach Athena?" he questioned as he took the rod from her hand.

"You could, yes—but not in a place such as this. Not with so much open space and so many places to hide." She winked before picking up another rod from the ground near her feet.

"What do I do?" he asked, seeing that she meant to teach him.

"Defend yourself," she answered, throwing the rod forward in her arms to hit his abdomen before she jumped quickly away, vaulting herself onto the higher ground offered by a broken building. "Fight me," she ordered, smiling at his stunned face.

He thought for a moment, and she took that moment to attack again, launching herself off the high ground and landing her hands on the ground behind him, kicking both of her feet into his back and knocking him to the ground. "Fight me!" she ordered again as she landed on her feet a few meters ahead of where he'd landed.

He jumped up and thrust his rod at her as she jumped forward and knocked it from his grasp, her fist connecting with his abdomen. He buckled over in pain, and she threw her elbow into his back, knocking him to the ground once more.

"That's two points for me, zero for you. First one to fifty wins," she told him.

"Fifty?" he asked as he stood straight and tried to regain his breath.

"Yes, Nicholas. Fifty. Now fight me!" she shouted as she launched herself again, this time thrusting the rod into the ground as she threw herself over it and landed both of her feet on Nicholas's chest. "Three to zero. You know how to fight, Nicholas. I can see it in you." She paused. "Fight!" she yelled at the top of her lungs.

He smiled slightly as he stood back to his feet and twisted around as he took a step forward, thrusting his rod at her. She put her hands out, caught the rod squarely, and yanked it from his hands before thrusting it back into his abdomen. "Four," she whispered in his ear as she handed his rod to him and walked back to her own, plucking it from the ground and turning to face him.

He took his fighting stance, holding the rod in both of his hands and crouching slightly, making himself a smaller target for her to hit.

"The rod is an extension of your body. Use it as such," she said, vaulting toward him and once again knocking him to the ground. "Five," she told him before walking back and taking her fighting stance. "It can be used for you or against you. Make sure it is working for you," she told him. "My rod is an extension of my body, and your rod is an extension of my own. I can use it to my advantage." She thrust her rod forward, locking it with his and twisting, knocking Nicholas to the ground and taking his rod from his hands. "Six."

Jameson woke to the sounds of grunting and yelling and knew immediately what was going on. He stood to his feet and walked out from under the bridge just as Reem yelled, "Forty-five," and helped Nicholas back onto his feet. He smiled as he watched Nicholas trying to fight off Reem's perfect fighting skills and almost laughed when he saw how quickly Reem got to forty-six points, knocking Nicholas to the ground by thrusting her wooden rod into the space between his legs and twisting it around him.

"Good morning sleepyhead," she whispered in his mind as she continued to attempt to teach Nicholas how to fight without a real weapon.

Jameson smiled as he walked closer to where Nicholas and Reem sparred, his smile growing even brighter when he saw the amount of blood on Nicholas's body compared to Reem's. He had a gash on his forehead that looked like it had been healed by Reem, but the bloody evidence was still there, along with several cuts on his forearms and chest, while Reem didn't even have a scratch. Nicholas's breathing was ragged as he attempted to fight off Reem, who didn't look as though she'd even broken a sweat. He was covered in mud and sweat, and, standing next to Reem, he looked like he'd just come out of the center of a tornado.

"Forty-seven!" Reem yelled at Nicholas after she knocked him to the ground once again.

"How many points do you have, Nicholas?" Jameson asked, startling the young man into turning away from Reem just long enough for her to knock him back off his feet.

"Forty-eight," she said to Nicholas before turning to Jameson. "He has one," she told him as she turned back around and went back into her fighting stance.

"You picked a fight with the wrong woman, Nicholas." Jameson laughed as the man got back to his feet and went into his fighting stance, waiting for Reem to make the first move.

"I take it you've fought her, Jameson?" Nicholas asked, not taking his eyes off Reem.

"Yes, though it was simply hand-to-hand combat training." He winked at Reem, thinking of their first night after being Connected.

She smiled back before launching herself once more, this time taking the time to allow Nicholas to fight back. She thrust the rod this way and that, easily being deflected by Nicholas, who should have seen it coming when she suddenly dropped her rod and ran behind him, kicking his knees so that he fell to the ground before she put her knee in his back and pulled his rod up to his neck, easily pulling it from his hands. "Forty-nine," she whispered in his ear. "One more and I win." She stood up off him and walked to the hood of a demolished car, sitting down slowly. "I'll give you a moment to catch your breath."

"Care to help me out, Jameson?" Nicholas asked.

"What do you think, Reem? Want to take us on two-to-one?" Jameson asked her, his smile growing as he considered how easily she would defeat both of them.

"As you wish," she replied, reading Jameson's thoughts.

Jameson picked up a rod off the ground and took a stance next to Nicholas, who was still trying to catch his breath.

"Ready?" Reem asked them, not waiting for an answer before she launched herself into the air, landing directly between them and thrust her rod to the side, connecting with Nicholas's head at the same time that she threw her right leg into the crook of Jameson's neck.

Nicholas moved to intercept her at the same time that she pole-vaulted herself up and over his head, sending her fist flying into his rib cage before she took the rod from his hands and thrust it into the ground, using her momentum to propel herself off the ground, spinning around and kicking both Jameson and Nicholas squarely on their foreheads before she landed both feet safely on the ground in front of them.

Jameson then decided that it was time to use his gifts to his advantage. As Reem moved to land another kick on Nicholas's side, Jameson teleported behind her and put his rod over her neck, pulling her into his chest.

"Well, if that's how it's going to be," she started as she turned around to face him and threw her knee into his crotch, shocking him into falling to his knees and releasing the rod, "then that's how it's going to be," she finished as she took his rod and knocked him to the ground. "You're out." She threw his rod back to him. "Your turn," she said as she turned to face Nicholas, whose eyes were wide as he watched her. She took a rod from the ground and approached him slowly, waiting for him to make the first move.

He threw his rod toward her at the same time that he threw his right leg up in the air to kick her side. She dodged to the left and took his rod from the ground, spinning both rods so that she held one under each arm as she took her fighting stance once more.

Jameson got up off the ground and walked up behind her, knowing that she knew he was there. He watched her as she faced off with Nicholas, his face filled with fear as he tried to determine where she would strike.

Nicholas did the only thing he could: he attempted to vault himself up and over Reem's head. Unfortunately, before he could land safely, Reem moved to intercept him and knocked him to the ground, pointing her rod into his neck. "Fifty," she said triumphantly.

Spar

Jameson walked to where Reem stood, still holding her rod to Nicholas's neck, and wrapped his arms around her waist, pulling her off him. He kissed her neck, and she leaned her head back on his shoulder. "Good fighting, my love," he whispered in her ear.

"Thank you," she replied, throwing her rod off to the side as Nicholas rose to his feet. "You did fairly well, considering."

"Considering what?" Nicholas asked.

"Considering that I've never had any formal training," Jameson answered, releasing his hold on Reem but keeping her hand held firmly in his.

"I can still train you, Jameson. But it seems you know more than you let on," she replied. "You could even beat Nicholas in a fight." She winked at Nicholas, and all three of them started laughing.

"That's not hard to do," Nicholas admitted.

"You only need more training," Reem replied. "If you wish, we can stay here another night. I could continue with both of your training before we move on."

Nicholas turned his eyes to Jameson, whose expression said he didn't care either way. "What do you think, Nicholas?" he asked. "Would you like my wife to train you for another few hours?"

When he didn't answer, Reem turned to Jameson. "We'll stay," she told him.

Jameson smiled back at her and turned around, leading back to the bridge. "We'll eat first, and then you can go back to teaching," he said.

Nicholas followed them back to the bridge and sat down next to his pack as Reem dug through the bag of supplies and threw him a small loaf of bread. He caught it and immediately began eating, trying to gain some strength from the food.

Jameson sat next to Reem, smiling brightly as she handed him a piece of bread. They sat together in silence as they ate, though it seemed to Nicholas that they were having a conversation inside their minds.

"Where will we be going—the next time we teleport?" Nicholas asked as he finished his loaf of bread and stood to his feet.

"Near Old Montreal. There's an abandoned castle-like structure near there that we can stay at for a while," Jameson answered.

"And we should be able to practice sparring there too. It'll be good to spar with different surroundings after today," Reem added.

"Speaking of which, we should probably get started," Jameson said, smiling brightly.

"Already?" Nicholas asked, collapsing back down onto the ground.

"A war would not wait for you to finish resting, Nicholas," Reem said. She stood and walked back out to the scrap yard.

Jameson laughed and helped Nicholas to his feet, walking back with him to where Reem now stood, contemplating over the weaponry in her bag.

"Have you had any weapons training, Nicholas?" she asked when they arrived.

"None," he answered.

"We'll work on that when we reach Athena then. They'll have places where we can work with you on target practice. What would you prefer for now?" She turned to face him.

Nicholas walked to where she stood and picked up a rod from her feet.

"Rods it is." She nodded to him, picking up her own rod from the ground and throwing one to Jameson. "I'll take on both of you at the same time, but I don't want you fighting on the same side. This is free for all. First one to fifty points wins." She placed the end of her rod on the ground between the three of them. "Rods in for restart," she explained.

They followed her lead, taking their stances and placing one end of their rods onto the ground in the center of the circle they created.

"Remember, this is free for all, so there's no taking sides," she reminded them. "Fight!" she yelled, standing to her full height and twirling her rod so that she held it high above her head for a moment before she twisted her body to the side and rammed it into Jameson side. "Points are based on hits. One hit is one point."

Jameson swirled back to her in defense, thrusting his rod in her direction and missing by mere centimeters as she dodged and thrust her rod into Nicholas's abdomen.

"Fight, Nicholas!" she ordered.

Nicholas bent his knees, crouching to make himself a smaller target before launching himself at Jameson, striking his opponent squarely in the chest before rebounding and striking out for Reem, who dodged his blow easily.

Once again, Reem placed her rod in the center of the circle. But this time, she used it along with her momentum to swing her body up and roundhouse kick both men, knocking them to the ground before she landed safely on her feet, unscathed. "Restart." She plucked her rod from the earth and took her fighting stance while Nicholas and Jameson got back on their feet and took their own stances. They all placed one end of their rods into the center before Reem shouted, "Fight!"

All hell broke loose.

Nicholas swung his rod and connected with Jameson's scalp before Reem punched Nicholas's rib cage so hard he couldn't breathe for a few moments.

Jameson teleported behind Nicholas and kicked his knees out from under him before hitting the side of his head with his rod and turning back to Reem who had just started her jump and landed a kick to Jameson's chest before he could even think about moving out of the way.

Nicholas got to his feet and scored a point on Reem who was still midflight after kicking Jameson to the ground.

"Good job, Nicholas," she told him as he helped her up off the ground. "Restart."

The three of them once again took their stances, placing the ends of their rods in the center.

"Points?" Reem asked.

"Four," Jameson answered quickly.

"Two," Said Nicholas.

"I have fifteen." She smiled. "Fight!"

Once again Reem made the first move, swirling her rod around to connect with both Jameson's and Nicholas's rod, knocking them from their hands before she twirled and made a second swing, knocking both men's legs out from under them.

"Learn to anticipate your opponent's moves. Let the rod be an extension of your body," she reminded them as they got up off the ground and took their stances one more.

"That makes seventeen for me," she reminded.

Jameson was about to attempt a kick when Nicholas landed a blow directly on his chest and turned around to find Reem in midair, knocking him to the ground in front of Jameson. Reem and Jameson fought, both equally blocking each other's moves while Nicholas lay on the ground at their feet, unable to move without being crushed by one or both of their feet.

Reem hit a glancing blow to Jameson's shoulder as he feigned a move to the right and hit her side squarely with his rod, knocking her to the ground beside Nicholas.

"Good, good," Reem said as she got to her feet. "Restart."

They stood in their circle, all taking their appropriate stances and placing the ends of their rods in the center once again before Reem called out for them to begin.

This time it was Nicholas who made the first move, launching himself up off the ground and kicking Jameson to the side before Reem deflected his blow and knocked him into a pile of debris with her rod.

"Anticipate!" she shouted.

Jameson threw a punch in her direction which landed in thin air only seconds after she dodged and threw a punch of her own onto his chin and hit his rib cage with her rod. He moved to defend himself when Nicholas started his attack on

Reem, yelling as he fell from the sky, trying to land a kick to her scalp and instead getting only air and a rough landing as she brought him down from the sky with her gift and hit him with her rod.

"Use your gifts. Fight!" she told them.

Jameson teleported behind Nicholas as he was getting up off the ground and connected with a blow to his scalp before teleporting back to Reem and connecting with a blow to her abdomen. She read his thoughts and deflected every blow after that as he teleported all around her, trying to find her weakness.

Finally, Nicholas got up off the ground and connected with a kick to Jameson's forehead while the man was still attempting to fight Reem. He then attempted to punch Reem and thrust his rod in her direction, both of which she easily deflected before twirling around and bringing her own rod down on top of him, bringing him to his knees in front of her before she used her rod to knock him to the ground beside Jameson.

"Good, Nicholas. You're getting better," she said. "Points?"

"Twenty-one," Jameson told her.

"Same," Nicholas said.

"Forty-three," she told them. "Don't worry, you're both doing fine. Restart."

Again, they all took their stances; and again, they all placed the ends of their rods into the center.

"This will be the last restart. That means you can leave the circle whenever you wish, which means that Nicholas's gift will come into play now. Don't forget to use your gifts and anticipate. When I reach fifty, I'll drop out, placing my rod in the center of the circle. After I'm out, you two continue facing off, and I'll give you pointers while you're going. Understood?" She waited for them both to nod. "Then fight!" she yelled, throwing her body up and over them both, landing securely on top of a large piece of what was once a building.

Nicholas and Jameson both watched her as she landed and stared at her for a moment before turning back to each other, ready to fight.

Jameson thrust his rod into the ground and used his momentum to throw his body in a circle, connecting first with Nicholas's head, and then with his back as he fell flat on the ground. He then teleported up beside Reem, attempted to land a blow to her side, and was knocked off the precipice by her heel to his abdomen.

While they fought, Nicholas ran behind the piece of scrap metal where Reem stood and attempted to hide himself using his gift. Reem found him easily and landed a blow to his side.

Jameson teleported between them and knocked both of them to the ground before connecting with two more successful hits on Nicholas with his rod. Reem then twined her leg around Jameson's and knocked him to the ground before she rose to her feet and backed away from them.

"Forty-eight." She vaulted herself to another piece of debris, waiting for them to come to her.

144

Nicholas and Jameson rose at the same time and began to fight. Jameson teleported to his left and right successively, landing blows to Nicholas's sides and legs frequently while Nicholas only connected with four successful hits.

"Anticipate, Nicholas!" Reem reminded him as she watched them spar.

Jameson then teleported to her side and landed a blow to her side before she could react and knock him to his knees. "Forty-nine," she whispered as Nicholas appeared beside them, ready to fight. He thrust his rod at Jameson who snatched it out of the air and used it to disable Nicholas for a moment while Reem vaulted herself back to the circle, knowing that her next hit would mean she was done.

Nicholas grabbed his rod from Jameson and struck his side firmly before twisting around and landing a kick to Jameson's midsection and running back to meet Reem at the circle. He thrust his rod into her side and twirled around for another blow when she struck his back firmly and threw her rod down in the center of the circle.

"Fifty," she announced.

She stood back and watched as Jameson teleported in front of Nicholas and began parrying and thrusting his rod to and fro as Nicholas matched his moves perfectly.

"Don't let your enemy anticipate."

Jameson started teleporting around Nicholas, making himself unpredictable as he connected several hits on his foe while Nicholas swung his rod and fists to no avail.

"Nicholas, make a move," Reem yelled.

Nicholas nodded to her and moved out of Jameson's reach just as he teleported behind him and attempted to thrust his rod into his side. Nicholas then rammed his fist into Jameson's rib cage and spun, thrusting his rod between his opponent's feet and knocking him to the ground.

"Points?" Reem asked.

"Forty-three," Jameson answered, getting up and connecting with a blow from his fist to Nicholas's chin.

"Thirty-six," Nicholas said after he recovered and sent his rod into Jameson's shoulder.

"Don't let him beat you, Nicholas!" Reem shouted.

Jameson threw his rod into Nicholas's side once again before turning and knocking his legs out from under him. As Nicholas's body fell to the ground, Jameson sent his rod into his opponent's rib cage before teleporting a few feet back, waiting for Nicholas to make the next move.

"Good, Jameson," Reem said. "Nicholas, use your gifts."

Nicholas rose from the ground and rushed to Jameson, knocking him to the ground in a single blow before connecting three more times with his fists to Jameson's chin, rib cage, and abdomen.

"Forty," he said, stepping back and allowing Jameson to make the next move.

"Good! Now, Jameson, fight him like you mean it. Either one of you can win this battle. Nicholas, watch your back—Jameson has fewer hits than you before he wins. Both of you, anticipate, but don't be anticipated. Use your rods as extensions of your bodies, but remember that your opponent's rod can be used to your advantage." She paused. "Fight!"

Jameson teleported behind Nicholas and thrust his fist into Nicholas's rib cage at the same time that Nicholas propelled his rod behind him, scoring one point for each of them, before Nicholas turned around and faced Jameson, taking his stance and holding his rod in both hands.

Jameson followed suit, taking his stance and holding out his rod, ready to fight. He made the first move, thrusting to the right while pivoting forward on his right leg to punch Nicholas with his left fist. Nicholas easily blocked his rod but fell to the ground when Jameson's fist connected with his abdomen.

Nicholas moved before Jameson could teleport away, thrusting his rod forward and hitting Jameson squarely on the chin before he spun around and sent his rod into Jameson's stomach, causing him to buckle forward in pain as Nicholas knocked his legs out from under him and punched his rib cage.

"Forty-five!" he shouted.

"Don't get cocky either of you!" Reem shouted back. "Fight!"

Jameson got back to his feet and teleported behind Nicholas once again, this time leaving his rod behind and roundhouse kicking Nicholas as soon as he landed before reeling back and punching his abdomen.

"Fifty!" he announced triumphantly.

"Good," Reem said as she approached the two of them and helped Nicholas back to his feet. "You're both doing very well. But you need to remember to feel your surroundings, to remember that the rod is a part of your body and should be used as such. You need to remember that when you're fighting more than one opponent, you can't just stop fighting one of them and focus on the other. Your enemy doesn't work that way. They will attack you in groups, and they will be relentless. Remember that and you may actually get somewhere in a real battle." She paused. "So what do you think, boys—one more spar?" She smiled.

Jameson smiled back as he spoke. "Reem, I think we should take a break." He walked up to her and wrapped his arms around her waist.

"And why's that?" she asked, still smiling brightly as he moved his hand to run his fingers through her hair.

Jameson leaned forward and kissed her lips, wrapping his arms even tighter around her waist as she wound her arms around his neck and kissed him back.

Nicholas cleared his throat loudly and turned away from them, causing Reem to laugh and pull slightly away from Jameson. "Sorry, Nicholas," she said.

"I'm not," Jameson said as he pulled her back toward him and kissed her again.

Newcomer

Nicholas walked away from them, not wanting to watch as the woman he loved kissed her husband. The whole time they'd been sparring, he'd only scored a few points off Reem. He couldn't bring himself to cause her any physical pain. He'd tried his best to fight her, but he knew that even if he tried, he couldn't hurt her—not with how he felt about her. But Jameson, Jameson he could punch and kick and thrust a rod into a hundred times over if it would make Reem think any higher of him. He knew there was nothing he could do to win her over—she was Connected to Jameson, a permanent situation—but he couldn't help himself. He wanted her to think highly of him. He needed her to.

So he walked away. He couldn't watch them—his heart would be torn in two if he did. He walked back to the bridge and sat down under its shadow, putting his head in his hands. He listened to the sounds of the remaining drops of water as they fell off the bridge into the large puddles all along the ground at his sides.

He turned back to Jameson and Reem, who still stood in the circle, Reem burying her face in Jameson's chest as he gently stroked her back. Nicholas closed his eyes for a moment, imagining that he was the one holding Reem in his arms, that it was his chest her face was buried in, that it was him who was stroking her hair and kissing her forehead.

"Nicholas. Stop. Please," Reem's voice whispered in his head. *"Don't do this to yourself."*

"I'm in love with you," he thought.

"I already have my love," she whispered, her voice sounding as though she would cry.

When Nicholas opened his eyes again, he saw Jameson wiping a tear from her cheek and kissing her forehead. He whispered something in her ear before she wrapped her arms around him again, pulling herself closer to him as she buried her face in his chest once more.

Once again, Nicholas closed his eyes, this time leaning his head back and focusing every bone in his body on not screaming his frustrations to the world.

Instead, he lay on his side and listened to the sound of the rain as it slowly drizzled down onto the ground outside the bridge.

"It's raining," Jameson said.

"Yes, yes, it is." Reem laughed at him. "Which is the perfect time for sparring!" she added loudly, pulling away from him and spinning around, tilting her head to the sky to let the rain fall on her face.

Jameson smiled back at her. "Are you sure Nicholas is up for more sparring right now?" He nodded to the bridge where Nicholas lay on his side.

"I'll go see," she said as she started walking toward the bridge.

"Are you sure that's such a good idea?" he asked her.

She kept walking, knowing that she had the best possible way of getting Nicholas to join them for a sparring session. She walked under the bridge and dropped to her knees beside where Nicholas lay on the ground and said, "If you come join us, I'll pit you against Jameson and outlaw the use of gifts."

He smiled and opened his eyes, knowing that she'd read the idea from his own mind only moments ago. He looked up at her and smiled brighter, nodding slowly as he rose to his feet beside her. "Deal," he said.

She smiled back at him as they started walking back to where Jameson waited in the mud-filled circle, soaking wet. By the time they reached him, the rain was pouring down so hard that visibility was low, yet Reem still smiled at the both of them.

"We're upping the stakes," she said.

Nicholas and Jameson only stared at her as she picked up two rods off the ground and walked to the bag she'd left on the ground. She took two knives from the bag and tied one to the end of each rod, making sure that it was secure enough not to fall off during the sparring session.

"Reem, are you sure this is such a good idea?" Jameson yelled over the sound of the pouring rain as she stood and handed him a rod.

"Yes," she replied. "You will be fighting to the death—figuratively speaking, of course." She handed Nicholas his rod and stepped back so that she could face both of them. "Like last time, the fighting may take place anywhere in the field, but there will be no use of your gifts—we'll just pretend that you exhausted them. Don't worry about getting cut or cutting your opponent, that's what my gifts are for. Place the sharp end of your rod in the center of the circle upon restart. I'll heal you after every two rounds or as necessary." She paused. "Got it?"

Nicholas and Jameson warily turned from Reem to face each other, both unsure about her new sparring rules.

"The rain affects your visibility, but remember that you can use that to your advantage. Remember, your rod is an extension of your body. Anticipate, but don't be predictable! Please don't actually kill each other—that could be a bit difficult for me to heal." She looked back and forth between the two of them. "I will give you pointers individually during the battle, so be listening for me. Ready?" she asked.

Jameson took his stance and placed his knife in the center of the circle, waiting for Nicholas to follow suit.

"Nicholas, don't be afraid," she whispered into his mind. *"You can do this."*

Slowly, Nicholas took his stance in front of Jameson, with Reem standing between them in the center of the circle. "Remember, don't use your gifts," she reminded before shouting for them to begin and stepping nimbly out of their way.

"Nicholas, fight him!" she yelled when neither of them made the first move.

Finally, Jameson started moving. He took two steps to his right, which Nicholas countered with two steps to his own right. They continued to walk around in a circle, testing each other's defenses briefly with twitches of the wrist and spins on their feet.

"Fight!" Reem yelled again, getting bored watching them walk around in circles.

"Go for his feet. He's leaving them unguarded," she whispered to Nicholas before telling Jameson, *"He's not watching his back. Vault over him and you could have a kill in less than five seconds."*

Jameson did as she recommended, pole-vaulting over the top of Nicholas's head only seconds before Nicholas struck for his feet. Jameson landed directly behind him and brought up his rod, slicing Nicholas's back and leg before pulling up on the man's shoulder and placing his knife to his neck.

"That's a kill," he shouted.

"Good, Jameson. Nicholas, watch your back. Restart!" Reem shouted back, her voice strained as the rain poured down around them and the wind picked up, spraying the small drops of water into their eyes and making it sting.

Jameson returned to the circle and placed his knife in the center, taking his stance and readying himself for the next round while Nicholas did the same.

"Fight!" Reem shouted as she squatted atop her newly acquired position on what used to be a building but was now only a large pile of rubble.

Nicholas moved first, jabbing his rod toward Jameson's leg and spinning around to connect the blunt end of his rod with Jameson's forehead, knocking him to the ground before he had time to react. Nicholas stood over him and bent down to press his knife to his neck when Jameson suddenly did the only thing he could. He shoved both legs up into the sky and knocked Nicholas backward onto the ground. Jameson then stood and took his fighting stance, ready for Nicholas to make the next move.

Nicholas rose and took his own fighting stance, quickly making his most vital move, thrusting his rod into the ground and pole-vaulting himself so that he landed directly behind Jameson and held his knife to his neck before the man even had time to process the maneuver.

"One," he shouted, triumphant at his first score.

Jameson knocked the rod out of his way and turned around, ready to restart.

"Restart!" Reem shouted, smiling as she watched them.

Nicholas followed Jameson's lead, taking his stance and readying for restart, placing his knife in the center near Jameson's only seconds before Reem shouted to begin.

This time, it was Jameson who made the first move, hooking Nicholas's rod with his own and throwing it out of his reach before using his own rod to push himself off the ground and roundhouse kick Nicholas in the chest and abdomen. Jameson landed to his feet with his rod pointed down at his opponent's chest.

Nicholas countered by swatting Jameson's rod away from his chest and crawling for his own rod when Jameson countered by kicking his midsection and toppling him back down to the ground, his face now covered in mud and his eyes blurred from the muck that filled them. Jameson used this to his advantage and plucked Nicholas's rod from the ground and threw it even farther away before using his own rod to slice open Nicholas arm and point his knife to his neck.

"Two," Jameson said.

Nicholas nodded slowly, acknowledging his win before Jameson removed the knife from his neck and took his fighting stance.

"Nicholas, don't let him do that to you again! Your rod is an extension of your body. Do not let him remove it from you!" Reem shouted, standing to her full height as she scolded him. "Restart!"

Jameson smiled as he watched Nicholas rise slowly and hobble over to where his rod lay in the mud, picking it up gingerly before turning back and taking his stance in front of Jameson. "Let's do this," Nicholas said.

"Fight!" Reem shouted.

Again, Nicholas made the first move, this time attempting to copy what Jameson had done to him only moments before, hooking his rod to Jameson's and yanking it to the right before he realized that Jameson had already grounded one end of his rod and was in midair, about to strike him with both feet once again.

Jameson's feet connected with Nicholas's face and neck, knocking him backward. Nicholas thrust his rod into the space between Jameson's feet and twisted only seconds before his landing, causing both men to fall in the mud on the ground, groaning in pain.

"Anticipate!" Reem shouted, "Fight!"

Jameson jumped back to his feet and leapt atop Nicholas's prone body, punching his face before jumping back and waiting for him to make the next move. Nicholas countered by rolling to his side and nimbly getting to his feet, throwing his rod through the air and landing it squarely between Jameson's legs before he ran and kicked his chest with enough force to knock him to the ground. He picked up his rod from beside Jameson's prone body and stepped back, waiting for him to move.

Jameson once again jumped back to his feet, this time rushing to Nicholas before the man had any time to brace himself, and jammed his fingers into the cut on his back. Nicholas cried out in pain, and Jameson used the distraction to knock him to the ground and thrust his own knife to Nicholas's throat.

"That's three," he whispered in Nicholas ear.

The rain started to slow to a drizzle, barely pouring down on them as the sun peeked out from behind the clouds.

"Break!" Reem shouted as she leapt from her perch and landed beside them in the circle.

"What for?" Jameson asked innocently, smiling brightly as she playfully slapped his arm.

"He needs healing." She laughed as Jameson stood and backed away. "How do you feel?" she asked Nicholas.

"I feel like I should've known better." He laughed.

She smiled and shook her head, closing her eyes as she placed her hand on his forehead and healed him. "Now how do you feel?" she asked, opening her eyes once again.

"I still should've known better." He smiled.

"Probably right," she replied as she stood and helped him get to his feet. "How are you, Jameson?" she asked as she turned toward her husband.

"Nothing I can't handle," he replied.

She scowled and walked up to him, pressing her hand against his cheek and feeling with her mind for any injuries. When she finished healing him, she put her hand on the back of his neck and jerked his head down to kiss her lips briefly before she walked back up to her perch.

"Restart!" she ordered.

Three hours and seventeen restarts later, Nicholas held Jameson in a headlock, attempting to reach his rod so that he could end the sparring session as Jameson attempted to punch his stomach hard enough to make him release his hold.

Finally, Jameson reached down and grabbed Nicholas knee, pulling it upward and causing the both of them to fall backward onto the mud and Nicholas to release his hold just enough for Jameson to wriggle out and punch his opponent in the face. He stood and looked around for the rod—one had been thrown so far out of sight that neither wanted to look for it, so they'd been sparring with one rod placed directly in the center of the circle.

He began to run for it when suddenly Reem cried out in agony.

Both the men looked up to the top of the building where they saw the last thing they'd expected to see—a young woman with the rod they'd misplaced jammed into Reem's abdomen.

Jameson teleported up to the top of the building and back to the circle with the woman in tow. He left her in Nicholas's capable hands and teleported back up to where Reem was still crying out in pain, her face contorted as she pulled the knife out and threw it to the ground. Jameson picked her up in his arms, causing her to cry out once more before he teleported her back to the bridge where the bag of supplies waited. He pulled off her shirt and began tending to her wound.

The dark-skinned woman kept her eyes to the ground, not struggling as Nicholas held her arms behind her back and tied her wrists together with the rope that used to bind a knife to one of the rods and dragged her back to the bridge. Nicholas stopped when he saw that Jameson had removed Reem's shirt and pushed the woman to her knees several meters outside the shadow of the bridge, holding the knife to her throat while he waited to hear from Jameson.

Reem's groans finally slowed in intensity as her healing power began to work its magic. She ground her teeth as Jameson held the wound together while her gift started to stitch the pieces back together. The woman gasped as she watched the bloody hole in Reem's abdomen slowly heal itself, watched the blood flow come to a halt as the newly healed skin began to cover the wound.

Reem's breathing slowed as the healing completed, and she smiled up at Jameson. "Thank you," she whispered.

"Who is she?" Jameson asked.

She closed her eyes as she searched the young woman's mind for the information she needed. "Her name is Aniis. She lives in the wreckage of Old London," she whispered.

"Why did she stab you?"

"She thinks it's not safe for any more people to be here. Purist groups come through Old London frequently. She thought they would find her if we were here when they pass through. She thinks it's safer to be alone." Reem opened her eyes and stared into Jameson's. "She's . . . different. Like the people of the settlement. She doesn't see people as Human, Advanced, or Purist. She sees everyone as equal. But she doesn't know about the settlement, doesn't like . . . people. She only wanted to be alone."

"What should we do with her?" he asked, holding her down as she tried to get up off the ground.

"I'd like to talk to her." Her eyes stared into his, pleadingly. "Jameson, please. I'm fine."

"Are you sure?" His worried eyes stared back into hers before flashing briefly down at the blood that still sat stagnantly on her abdomen.

"Yes. I'm fine." She smiled. "Help me up."

He smiled back at her and helped her stand to her feet. Jameson cleaned the blood off her body with her old shirt, dunking it in a puddle of clear water on the side of the bridge before wiping the wet cloth across her bare skin. She found a clean shirt in her backpack and put it on before walking back to Jameson and wrapping her arms around his neck and gently kissing his lips. "I love you," she whispered.

"I love you too." He wrapped his arms around her waist.

She moved her arms from his neck and looked him in the eye. "Shall we?"

He smiled and nodded, releasing his hold on her waist and taking her hand in his. He gestured for her to lead the way, and they walked out from under the bridge and approached the woman whom Nicholas still held at knifepoint.

Aniis

Reem walked to the woman and squatted by her side, motioning for Nicholas to remove the blade from her neck as she did so. The girl flinched away from the comforting hand Reem attempted to place on her shoulder, and her eyes refused to meet anyone's. She stared at the ground, at the water that swirled around her knees and the mud that was smeared on her dark green pants.

Her white shirt was covered in mud and sweat mixed with blood from Reem's body, and the sight was enough to make both Nicholas and Jameson sick to their stomachs. They watched as Reem placed her hand under the girl's chin and tilted her head up, trying to look her in the eye though she continued to stare at the muddy ground beneath her knees.

"Aniis, my name is Reem," she began, moving her hand away from her chin to motion to the others, "and these are Jameson and Nicholas. We mean you no harm." She tilted her head to the side.

When Aniis continued to stare at the ground, unmoving and unspeaking, Reem continued, "Listen to me, Aniis. We are going to Athena, the city that once belonged to the Advanced. We are making it into a safe haven for all who would join us. I know you don't want to stay here, that you want to be somewhere safe. We can take you with us, Aniis. We'll be there in a few days, and if you decide to leave Athena, I can have my husband return you here in the same amount of time."

"If you stay here, they will find us. They are coming," the girl said finally, still not meeting Reem's eyes with her own.

"I know, Aniis. My husband, Jameson, is a teleporter. He can take us far away from here—far enough away that they will never find us."

"You can't stay here." She struggled, trying to free herself from Nicholas's grip. "You must go!" she shrieked, turning her face to look Reem in the eye. "Please! Go!"

The woman's dark eyes matched her tanned skin, blacker than any Reem had ever seen in her life. She gasped slightly at the sight but kept her position as she spoke. "We will. My husband will teleport us away soon, I promise. You can come with us, Aniis. You don't have to live in fear anymore. Come to Athena with us," she said.

"They will kill me!" Her eyes filled with panic. "Please, go!"

"Oh, I see," Reem said, suddenly realizing what Aniis was trying to say. "We'll go."

"Go now!" Aniis screamed at the top of her lungs.

"Nicholas, untie her. Let her go," Reem ordered, standing up and stepping away from the girl.

When Nicholas didn't move, Reem whispered in his mind, *"Nicholas, please. Untie her. There's more going on here than you know."*

He furrowed his brow as he stared into her eyes, still not understanding what she was trying to tell him. Finally, she moved beside him and untied Aniis's bonds herself, slicing them with her knife.

Aniis quickly stood to her feet and faced Reem, her black eyes seemingly staring into her soul as she spoke. "They are coming."

"Who is coming?" Nicholas asked, stepping between her and Reem.

Aniis shifted her eyes to meet his, and he stepped backward in shock, nearly stepping over Reem as he did so.

"Nicholas, let me handle this," Reem warned, stepping around him to face Aniis once more. "We need time to gather our things."

"No. You must go now. They are coming," she replied, keeping her eyes trained on Nicholas.

"He doesn't know anything," Reem told her, stepping closer to her.

"He does. He knows."

"No. He doesn't know anything, Aniis. Trust me. I can hear everything he is thinking, remember?" She tapped the side of her head. "He doesn't know anything."

Aniis shifted her gaze off Nicholas, and he stumbled to the ground. She turned her head to look at Jameson, who shifted his eyes to Reem before they could meet the blackness of her eyes.

"Don't look at her, Jameson," Reem whispered in his mind. *"Look at me. Don't look away. She's testing you."*

He nodded ever so slightly and kept his eyes glued to hers. *"Won't she do the same to you?"* he whispered back.

"She can't," she replied.

Aniis continued to stare at Jameson's eyes while he stared at his wife's. "Look at me!" she screamed at the top of her lungs.

"He doesn't know anything either, Aniis. I can hear his thoughts," Reem spoke calmly. "Please, look at me, Aniis."

"They are coming for one of you. Which one will it be?" She tilted her head to the sky ever so slightly, keeping her eyes trained on Jameson's. "The boy, the man, or the woman?" she whispered, her voice deep and scratchy.

"Look at me, Aniis," Reem repeated.

"I thought she wasn't Advanced," Jameson thought.

"She doesn't want to be," Reem replied, *"Don't look at her. Remember that."* Her eyes flicked to Jameson's before returning to the woman who slowly approached him.

"What is the boy's name?" Aniis asked, turning her head to face Reem and shifting her eyes to look at Nicholas who still lay motionless on the ground behind her.

"Nicholas," Reem answered.

"And this one?" She turned her head to look at Jameson once more, lifting her hand to gently stroke his cheek. "What is his name?"

"Jameson." *"Don't look at her."*

"And you are Reem, yes?"

"Yes." She paused. "Please, Aniis. Look at me."

"They must know something." She traced her fingers down Jameson's neck and chest, her hand stopping when she felt his heartbeat.

"They do not."

"Then why does this one not look at me?" She stood on the tips of her toes and leaned forward to whisper in his ear, "Look at me, Jameson."

Jameson's eyes wavered slightly, and Reem whispered in his mind, *"Don't look at her. Look at me. Don't listen to her. Remember my voice? I am your wife. Listen to me. Look at me."* His eyes once again moved to meet hers as Aniis gently kissed his neck.

"Aniis. Look at me!" Reem shouted.

The woman's head snapped around to look Reem in the eye, and her dark eyes burned with anger.

Aniis watched as the silver flecks in Reem's eyes arranged themselves in a circle around her pupils, brightening to the point where they shone straight out of her eyes. Aniis screamed as the bright light began to burn through her, shrieked as she fell to her knees, still staring Reem in the eye, unable to look away.

"Reem, what are you doing?" Jameson asked, still staring at her eyes but feeling no effect from their brightness.

"Don't look at her, Jameson," she replied.

Aniis shrieked again as Reem stepped toward her, staring down at her with eyes that shone brighter than the sun.

"Jameson, I'll be right back. Help Nicholas," Reem whispered into his mind before she grabbed Aniis by the collar and flew away with the force of her gifts, leaving his sight in a matter of seconds.

"Reem!" Jameson called after her, but to no avail. As soon as they were gone, he ran to Nicholas side and knelt beside him. "Nicholas, Nicholas, wake up," he said, feeling for the man's pulse.

Nicholas suddenly sat up from the ground, his breathing heavy. "What happened?" he asked.

"I don't really know."

"Where's Reem?"

"I don't know." He paused. "Are you alright?"

Nicholas ran his fingers through his hair as he slowly stood to his feet. "Yeah, I'm fine."

"Good." Jameson stood next to him. "We should pack our things. I have a feeling that when she gets back, she's going to want to leave right away."

Nicholas nodded his response and ran back to the circle where they'd been sparring only moments ago, taking the knives off the rods and packing all Reem's weapons into her backpack while Jameson packed everything from under the bridge.

⚜

Reem propelled both herself and Aniis to the edge of the city, far enough away that Aniis wouldn't be able to reach Nicholas and Jameson before her, but not so far that the toxin in the bracelets would be released into her and Jameson's blood systems.

They landed in unison, and she released her hold on Aniis's collar.

"How did you do that?" the girl asked, dropping to the ground in pain.

"I told you, leave them alone." The silver in her eyes continued to shine down on Aniis's shriveling figure.

"They will come for you, Reem. You know that," Aniis whispered, her voice low and groveling.

"They won't find us."

"But I know where you're going." She turned her head to look at Reem, making sure never to let their eyes meet as she smiled wickedly.

"You can forget," Reem replied, kicking the girl and kneeling at her side, holding her neck into the ground. "And I can make sure you don't remember. Look at me."

"Please," she whispered, closing her eyes and struggling to break free from Reem's grasp.

"Look at me!" Reem shouted at her.

Aniis slowly opened her eyes and looked into Reem's shining silver eyes, screaming when the light shone into her now light blue eyes.

Reem delved into Aniis's memories and erased everything from the moment they met, using her eyes to keep the girl distracted. When she finished, she released Aniis and stood beside her, turning her head away.

Aniis stopped screaming, her breathing becoming very heavy and labored. "What's going on?" she asked, her voice barely a whisper.

"Leave this place. Now," Reem replied before she lifted her feet off the ground with her mind and propelled herself back to the bridge where she'd left Nicholas and Jameson.

⚜

Nicholas ran back under the bridge where Jameson continued packing Reem's belongings inside her backpack. He dropped his pack to the ground and knelt beside him, helping to pack things up, starting with the medical supplies.

"Where did she go?" Nicholas whispered under his breath.

"She said nothing," Jameson snapped, not looking up as he clipped the backpack closed.

"She tells you everything!" Nicholas replied harshly, cramming the last of the medical supplies into a bag and zipping it closed.

"She said nothing," Jameson repeated, standing and throwing the pack over his shoulders.

Nicholas picked his bag up off the ground along with Reem's weapons bag and followed Jameson out from underneath the bridge. "What happened, Jameson? I don't remember a thing."

"You looked into her eyes, didn't you?" Jameson asked, staring off in the direction that Reem disappeared.

"I think so, yeah," he replied as he sat the bags down and ran his fingers through his thick hair.

"What did you see?"

"I saw," he shook his head, "darkness. Emptiness. Nothingness."

"What did she do to you?"

"I'm not sure, but whatever it was, it hurt like hell." He paused. "Looking into her eyes was like looking straight into the pit of hell." He closed his eyes, deep in thought. "I thought I'd died," he whispered, barely loud enough to hear.

"I wouldn't have let her kill you, Nicholas," Reem's voice came from behind them, startling them both. Jameson turned around quickly and ran to embrace her while Nicholas continued to stare at the horizon.

"What happened?" Jameson whispered in her ear, holding her tightly to his chest while she coiled her arms around his waist.

"She was going to kill you. I'm sorry I didn't tell you more before I left," she replied, pulling away slightly so that she could look him in the eye. "I would never have gone far enough away for that," she told him as he stared at the silver flecks that rearranged themselves inside her pupils.

"I know," he replied, pulling her close to him and kissing her lips.

She smiled as they pulled away from each other, running her fingers through his hair slowly. "I'm sorry, I'd love to stay here a while longer"—she winked—"but we really need to go. She wasn't lying about someone coming."

He nodded and released her, turning to face Nicholas, who continued to stare off into the horizon. "Are you ready?" he asked.

Nicholas turned around quickly, keeping his eyes low to the ground in case Reem was still in Jameson's arms. "Yeah. I've got everything." He shrugged with both arms, holding Reem's weapons bag in one hand and the medical supplies in the other.

Jameson handed Reem her pack, and she put it over her shoulders. "Then it's time to go," she told them as she took Jameson's hand.

Together, Reem and Jameson stepped closer to Nicholas, and Jameson placed his hand on his shoulder. "Let's go," he said, teleporting them away in the same second.

Castling

They landed in the center of a courtyard, cobblestones beneath their feet and clear blue sky above their heads.

"Welcome to Canada," Jameson announced, releasing Reem's hand and walking across the cobblestone yard to two large wooden doors that opened into what was once a castle but was now only the dead remains.

Nicholas lifted his head and viewed the area—the grass that now grew between the stones on the ground, the vines that covered the once-vast stone walls that surrounded him on all four sides, the heavy wooden doors that Jameson carefully pried open and stepped into, and the tall trees that were barely visible over the edges of the shattered tops of the stone walls. It looked as though a great battle had taken place here long ago, and the remains of the castle were all that was left to tell of it. He lowered his head and met Reem's smiling eyes, smiling back at her instantly.

"What do you think?" she asked.

"Where are we?" he asked.

"This was once the site of where the Advanced first made their stand against humans," she said proudly. "It was all started in the cells belowground, and when people in the other camps heard of their success, the idea of rebellion spread. This site is a historical landmark for the Advanced."

"Why did they leave?" He furrowed his brow.

"Humans made a stand of their own, and the war was started. They abandoned it shortly after that. Jameson used to come here when he was sent on missions by himself. It's a good place for an Advanced to find himself."

"I can see why." He nodded slowly. "How long will we be staying here?"

"As long as we can. Jameson still doesn't want to go to Athena yet." She paused, seeing the concern on his face. "No Human has been seen here since after the beginning of the war, and the Advanced rarely come here either."

"Why don't the Humans come back—or the Purists, for that matter?"

"I don't know about the Purists, but the Humans aren't concerned with finding somewhere out of the way to make their camps. They camp in plain sight, laying siege to the Advanced cities by day and conducting experiments on their prisoners by night. We always know where they take the unlucky ones, but we can never see them again."

"Can't the teleporters get them out?"

"You have to have a location in mind," Jameson shouted from behind the large wooden doors. "If you don't, then you'd just disintegrate."

Nicholas was speechless as he considered all the Advanced that were taken as prisoners of the Humans, how many Advanced had been experimented on and left to die in an underground cave system like the one Reem and Jameson had told him about at the Purist camp.

"Don't worry, Nicholas, we won't let them take you," Reem joked, laughing as she walked passed him to join Jameson behind the doors. "You coming?" she yelled as she walked through.

Nicholas quickly followed her, running to the doors and pausing a moment before he walked into the old castle. "Wow." His eyes took in the fire-lit stone entryway and the vines that covered the walls from years of being allowed to grow free. To his right stood the remains of a staircase, leading to what used to be the upper levels of the castle. Now all that remained above the staircase were a hole and fallen stones that plugged the majority of the space made from whatever had hit it.

"Beautiful, isn't it?" Reem asked, her voice coming from a hall to his left.

He turned and followed the sound of her footsteps, walking as quickly as he could while he took in the sights of the once mighty building. He rounded a corner into a small room and found the exact thing he was hoping he wouldn't see. Reem stood against the wall with Jameson standing in front of her, kissing her lips. Her hands wound through his hair, while his hands rested on her waist.

Nicholas stopped in his tracks, turning and looking away before his heart could propel him into attacking the man who kissed the woman he was in love with. He leaned against the wall of the entryway, trying to steady his breathing.

He tried not to listen as Reem laughed lightly when Jameson kissed her neck, tried to ignore the sound of his lips pressing against her skin, tried to think about anything other than the fact that the woman he was in love with was the one woman he couldn't be with. He closed his eyes and leaned his head against the wall, sighing as quietly as possible in the echoing hallway.

The next thing he knew, Reem was tapping his shoulder lightly. "Hey, we found a couple of bedrooms down the hall, and I cleaned off the beds so we can use them. Jameson went to a nearby Human camp to get some supplies." She turned and walked away when his eyes didn't open, and he continued slowly inhaling and exhaling, concentrating on anything but her.

She walked through the room and down another short hallway to one of the bedrooms they'd found, lying on the bed and closing her eyes, trying not to listen to Nicholas's screaming thoughts while she waited for Jameson to return.

She was too busy distracting herself to notice when Nicholas entered the room, and she opened her eyes only when he sat down next to her.

"I'm sorry," he whispered under his breath, knowing that she could hear him.

Her eyes flicked to him, though he'd turned his head so she couldn't look him in the eye. "For what?" she asked as she sat up.

"You don't have to ask me, Reem. I know you know," he responded, his voice calm and even.

"Nicholas, talk to me," she whispered.

"Reem, you're the one person I shouldn't be talking to about this," he replied, laughing bitterly as he turned to look her in the eye.

"Do you have something better to talk about?" she asked, her eyebrows rising.

"What happened—back in Old London after I fell?"

She sat up and tilted her head to the side. "What do you remember?"

"After I fell, nothing," he replied.

"I stopped her," she said, quickly looking away.

"How?" he asked, placing his hand on her shoulder and turning her to face him, removing his hand when she looked him in the eye.

"I don't know," she replied. "I think I developed another gift—maybe. Jameson said the silver in my eyes realigned to something like rims around the pupils of my eyes." She shrugged. "I don't know what happened, Nicholas. I only know that when I saw what she was thinking—what she was trying to do—I did everything in my power to stop her."

"That's why you didn't say anything?" His eyebrows furrowed.

"I honestly don't know how I stopped her, I swear."

"What was she trying to do?"

"She came dangerously close to succeeding with you, Nicholas. She was trying to kill you. Her gifts don't work like normal gifts—that's why I didn't see them sooner. She knew the Purists were coming to the city, but she didn't want them to find us. She wanted us and them dead, and her gifts would have helped her get there." She paused, trying to remember everything that she heard in the young woman's mind. "Her gift—her eyes—can kill with a single look. Somehow, I knew she wouldn't be able to kill me, and I think she knew it too. She almost killed you, Nicholas."

"Does Jameson have any idea how you stopped her?"

"No."

"Wow."

"You've been saying that a lot since we got here." She laughed. "Now it's your turn. Talk to me."

He shook his head, not wanting to talk to her about the fact that he couldn't stop thinking about her—a fact she already knew, no doubt—and the fact that he didn't want to stop thinking about her.

"Pretend I'm someone else if it helps."

"It's you. You know that." He turned his head.

"Why are you here, Nicholas?" she asked.

"What do you mean?"

"You could have stayed out there—there are plenty of other rooms in this building. Why did you come in here?"

"You know the answer to that," he whispered, staring off into the short hall outside the room.

"Out loud, Nicholas," she ordered.

"I love you, Reem," he said, turning to look her in the eye. "I love you more than I've loved anyone else in my life. I can't stop thinking about you, and frankly, I don't want to. I don't want to be without you, Reem." He paused, lowering his voice to a whisper. "I love you more than he ever could."

She stood to her feet and leaned her back against the wall, hands clenching over her stomach as she considered everything that he said, never looking him in the eye.

"Nicholas, I . . ." She paused. "I don't know that that's true."

"It is true." He stood and walked up to her, standing less than a foot away from where she leaned against the wall. "I love you." He smiled slightly.

"I know you do—that's not what I meant," she replied, still refusing to look him in the eye.

"You really think he loves you more than I do?" he asked, reaching out his hand to touch her cheek lightly.

"Stop, Nicholas," she warned.

"No," he whispered as he leaned forward and kissed her lips gently.

She froze for a moment, unsure of what to do as her eyes stared into his closed eyelids and his lips moved to separate hers. She put her hands on his chest and pushed him as hard as she could; using her gifts when she realized that he wouldn't be moved so easily. She pushed him a few feet away and slapped his face as hard as she could. His unconscious body fell to the ground in front of her, and she leaned back against the wall and closed her eyes, wiping away the tears that had formed in her eyes.

When Jameson returned, he found her leaning against the wall with Nicholas unconscious on the ground in front of her. He ran to her side and gathered her up into his arms, carrying her into another bedroom. He set her down on the bed and let her cry into his shoulder, kissing her forehead and massaging her back.

"I figured it out," she whispered into his mind.

"Shh," he replied, holding her tighter when he heard noises coming from the bedroom where he'd left Nicholas's unconscious form.

"Jameson, it's important," she said between sobs.

"What happened?"

"He—"

"I kissed her," Nicholas voice cut her off, coming from down the hall.

"You can feel it too, can't you, Jameson—like some sort of power is growing inside me."

"What?" Jameson asked, his hands balling into fists.

"Jameson, listen to me," she whispered, pulling away from him and wiping the tears from her eyes. "I figured it out," she repeated.

"Stay here," he told her. He stood and took a few steps away before she stopped him in his tracks.

"I'm pregnant, Jameson."

Hunter

Jameson slowly turned around to face her, his eyes blank as he stared into hers. She clutched her stomach, taking quick glances between her belly and his eyes.

"How is that even possible?" he asked, his eyes widening when he realized she wasn't joking.

"I don't know!" She stood up and walked to his side, taking his hand and placing it on her stomach. "Do you feel it?" she asked.

He closed his eyes and searched for signs of life, his eyes snapping back open when he felt the light, fluttering life force inside his wife's body—separate from her own. He lifted his eyes from her stomach to look her in the eye. "How is that even possible?" he asked again.

"Does it matter?" she asked, smiling at the amazed look on his face.

A smile grew on his face before he wrapped his arms around her and lifted her off the ground, spinning her around in a circle. "No, it doesn't matter," he answered as he set her back down on the ground.

She laughed lightly and kissed his lips for a moment before pulling away and looking him in the eye. "We're going to have a baby," she whispered, smiling brightly into his eyes.

"We're going to have a baby," he repeated, still unbelieving of the tiny life inside Reem's body.

Just then, Nicholas appeared in the doorway.

"Not now, Nicholas," Jameson snapped, turning away from Reem briefly before turning back to look her in the eye.

"What's going on?" Nicholas asked, his brow furrowing in confusion.

Jameson turned away from Reem, standing almost in front of her as he spoke. "Nicholas, do not make the mistake of believing that I did not hear what you did to my wife. I will deal with you momentarily, but I have more pressing matters to attend to with my wife," he said as calmly as possible.

"What pressing matters?"

Reem peered around Jameson's shoulder, shaking her head lightly.

"Nicholas. Go. Away."

"What's wrong? Tell me."

"I'm pregnant, Nicholas," Reem said as she stepped out from behind Jameson and took his hand in hers. "We would appreciate it if you would leave us alone for the time being."

Nicholas reeled back his fist to punch Jameson in the face, his fist stopping midpunch mere inches from Jameson's face, having been stopped by Reem's gift.

"May I?" Jameson asked, turning to look Reem in the eye.

She shrugged and nodded lightly, stepping out of the way before Jameson threw his fist into Nicholas's jaw.

David and Mitchal Sanders waited outside the Great Superior's quarters, having been calling there hours ago. David paced along the wall, impatiently waiting for someone to tell them why they had been called here while Mitchal sat on the floor, meditating.

"How can you just sit there like that?" David asked, his deep voice echoing through the long hall.

Mitchal opened his eyes to look at his brother. "I am not like you, brother. How have you not seen that by now?" he asked, laughing lightly as his brother continued to pace, ready to pull his black hair out by the roots if no one showed up within the minute.

"I just don't see how you can be so calm about all of this," David said, stopping in front of his brother and squatting down so that they could be eye to eye. "How do you do it?"

Mitchal looked into his twin brother's brown eyes, thinking a moment before he responded. "David, as a tracker, you tend to be more anxious about everything—especially when it comes to the Superiors. I am only a—a human lie detector for lack of better words—and I have never had an assignment that I could possibly fail at. You, dear brother, have never had such an assignment." He paused. "Though, honestly, the reason as to why the both of us would be asked here at the same time is beyond me." He closed his eyes once more, trying to go back to meditating.

"There! Right there! How can that not drive you insane?" David said a little louder than he intended, his voice echoing even louder through the building.

"I am meditating," Mitchal answered calmly.

"How can you be meditating at a time like this?" David asked, standing and beginning to pace.

"Because I have been taught to meditate when stress threatens to invade my life." Mitchal opened his eyes to look at his brother. "Why can you not accept that we are as different as night and day?" He laughed.

David huffed in response, knowing that his brother was right. He continued to pace, walking along the side of the wall while his brother meditated.

<hr/>

Nicholas woke remembering that he should never have gotten on Jameson's bad side. He hadn't expected Reem to step aside and allow her husband to strike him—after all, she hadn't let him before. He'd thought that maybe she really did like him, but because she was already connected to Jameson, there was nothing she could do. It turned out he was wrong.

Once she'd stepped aside, Jameson had knocked him to the ground faster than he could think of what to do. He was bleeding from at least three cuts on his head before Reem finally stepped in and stopped Jameson from killing him. Shortly after, he'd passed out; and now he found himself lying on a bed somewhere in the castle, though he didn't really know where.

He tried to get up and found that he couldn't move—at all. He groaned lightly, and that was when Reem appeared in the doorway.

"I'm sorry, Nicholas," she whispered. "I should never have let it go that far."

"What's going on?"

"I want you to stay in this room, okay? I don't think you and Jameson should be around each other for a while. It's better that way," she said, walking away before he could ask another question.

As she left, he felt the power holding him down dissipate, and he was suddenly able to move again. He rolled to his side, throwing his feet off the edge of the bed as he sat up, waiting for his head to stop spinning before he stood and walked slowly to the doorway.

He reached out his hand to the empty doorway and found that she'd moved her barrier there. He was trapped.

<hr/>

"David, please. Sit. Your pacing is making it difficult for me to meditate," Mitchal said, never opening his eyes.

David did as his brother asked, sitting down beside him and crossing his arms over his chest. "I still don't see how you do it."

Mitchal was about to respond when the doors to the Great Superior's chambers opened and out walked one of the guards. "Mitchal and David Sanders," he said. "The Great Superior will see you now."

David rose quickly and helped Mitchal to do the same before stepping up to the guard and whispering nervously, "Do you know why we're here?" He glanced quickly between the door and the guard that stood in front of it.

"He will see you now, sir," was all the answer he gave, gesturing for them to step through.

"Calm down, brother," Mitchal whispered harshly as he walked through the doors.

Inside, the floor was paved of marble and led to the Great Superior's throne, though he was nowhere in sight. Red and purple cloths hung from the ceiling, enhancing the fact that this chamber was meant for royalty.

Mitchal turned to the right, toward the source of light of the room, and saw the Great Superior standing on a balcony, facing away from them toward the city.

Beside Mitchal, David walked in while turning around in circles, making sure that nothing was going to ambush him once he walked inside. He knocked a few cloths off their perches on the ceiling and began to check over the rest of the room while Mitchal walked out to the balcony, leaving his brother to his worries. He stopped several feet behind the Great Superior and dropped to one knee, bowing his head as he spoke.

"Superior. You sent for me, and I have come," he said.

The Superior turned around to face the man who knelt before him. "Rise, my son," he said as he walked past, his flowing black robe catching momentarily on Mitchal's leg sheath as he did so. He moved his robe aside and walked to his throne, sitting down gracefully.

David knelt as the Superior sat. "Superior," he said, "you sent for me."

"Come, stand before me with your brother," the Superior said, his voice low and raspy.

David and Mitchal both walked forward to stand before the throne, stopping when they were still several feet away.

"Forgive me, Superior," David began, breaking the silence, "but what task is there that would require the gifts of both myself and my brother?"

Mitchal turned his head to look at his brother, shocked that he would be so bold before the commander. "Guard your tongue when you stand before the Great One, brother."

"Do not scold him, Mitchal." The Superior laughed. "I am well aware of his inability to hold his tongue."

"I am sorry, my lord," David replied, throwing a sour glance in Mitchal's direction.

"I require the unique services that both of you provide," he began. "David, I need you to locate the traitor. When you locate her, Mitchal will then try her and kill her when she is found guilty."

"Should she not be tried publically?" Mitchal asked.

"I have reason to believe that if she is brought to any of our cities, an uprising will occur. I need you to handle this personally." He paused. "Find her. Before the Purists do."

"Of course, my lord," Mitchal replied, bowing his head.

"Yes, Superior. It will be done," David said, not wanting to be outdone by his brother.

"Then go and complete your task," the Great Superior commanded.

Both men bowed in reverence and exited his quarters, walking quickly as they considered the importance of the task that had been given to them.

⁂

Nicholas paced along the wall, still unbelieving that Reem had confined him to this room—he didn't even know for sure where inside the castle he was. He'd looked outside the doorway at least ten times already, but he hadn't been able to see anything. It seemed Jameson had removed all the torches from this area.

He couldn't believe she was pregnant. He didn't want to believe it. The woman he loved was pregnant with another man's child. How was he supposed to take that?

As far as he knew, it wasn't even possible for an Advanced female to be impregnated by another Advanced. This shouldn't be happening.

He continued to pace, his memories of the few moments when Jameson was gone passing through his mind over and over as he walked. He remembered what it felt like to press his lips against hers for those brief moments. As he thought of it, he knew how he'd even been able to kiss her—he'd caught her off guard. He hadn't even been thinking about kissing her until a mere second before he did it. He'd known that kissing her was wrong, that she would be angry with him, but how could she not have loved that feeling as much as he did? He couldn't bring himself to believe that she didn't love him.

He remembered the looks on their faces as he'd first walked into their room last night. They'd looked so happy until he'd made himself and his intensions known. Truth be told, he'd only been looking to pick a fight with Jameson; and when Reem had told him that she was pregnant, he couldn't hold it in any longer. Reem had known that when he'd walked in—she'd made it clear that she was always monitoring his thoughts.

He hadn't thought she would allow her husband to fight with him.

⁂

"Are you sure you want to go through with this?" Mitchal asked David as they walked to the traitor's old home among the people of Admiri.

"We were given orders, Mitchal. Of course I want to do this. The better we do on our tasks for the Great Superior, the more we will be asked to do, and the more important we will be to our people. Do you not want to be seen as great among our people?" he replied.

"Who wouldn't want to be where Reem Kahrin was before the events in Athena?"

"Then what are you on about?" David asked, stopping as they reached the door to her home.

"After I try her, you will be the one who may have to kill her. Are you telling me that you're okay with that?" His eyebrows rose.

David turned to walk inside without answering, and Mitchal grabbed his arm to hold him back. "Answer me, David. Are you willing to kill for them—kill the one so many say is the savior for the Advanced?"

"If the Great Superior commands it, then his will be done," David replied. He twisted free of his brother's grasp and walked inside. "I will find her, and when she is found guilty, I will kill her."

<hr />

"How is our child?" Jameson asked, walking into the bedroom where Reem lay on her side.

She smiled as he sat beside her on the edge of the bed, running his fingers through her hair. "He is well," she replied as she reached her hand up to touch Jameson's face lightly.

"He?" His brow furrowed.

"Better than calling him an it." She shrugged, laughing.

"Do you know what you want to name him yet?"

"No. Not yet." She winked. "Do you have any ideas?"

"None." He shrugged.

She scooted over and patted the bed beside her, inviting him to lie beside her. "How about Samuel—if it's a boy?" she asked as he lay down and wrapped his arms around her.

"My father's name," he replied, whispering in her ear. "And Miriam if it is a girl?"

"After my mother?" She pulled away from him slightly so that she could look him in the eye.

"Of course." He smiled back, pulling her back into his chest gently.

"I like it," she whispered, burying her head in his chest.

<hr />

Nicholas could hear the others talking, but he didn't know where the sound was coming from. He tried again to look outside the door, but he couldn't see anything beyond what was illuminated by the torch above his bed.

As he listened to the sound of their voices, he couldn't help but think how wonderful it would be to have her in his arms. It would make him the happiest man in the world. He stepped away from the doorway and pulled his hair from his head, screaming as loud as he could.

A few moments later, Jameson appeared in the doorway. "Do you need something, or are you merely trying to keep me away from my wife?" he asked.

"I want to see her, Jameson," Nicholas replied, avoiding looking him in the eye.

"No."

"Let me see her!" he shouted, running up to the empty doorframe and sending his fist slamming into the invisible wall that stood in its place. He screamed again and jumped back in pain, clutching his fist with his other hand.

"I told you it would be better if I saw him," Reem's voice came from somewhere in the darkness.

"Reem? Please," Nicholas whispered, barely loud enough for anyone to hear.

"Nicholas, are you alright?" she asked, staying in the darkness beyond the doorway.

"Let me see her," Nicholas demanded, staring Jameson straight in the eye.

"I'm sorry, Nicholas, but I agree with Jameson. It's best that you not see me for a while."

"Even if I've broken my hand on your invisible wall?"

"Stay there, Reem. I'll check on him," Jameson said as he walked through the doorway, completely unhindered.

"No, no, let me see her," he pleaded as Jameson took his hand and checked for breakage.

"She is my wife—remember that," he replied, feeling his hand gently and checking over all the joints a second time. "You'll be fine." He walked back through the doorway.

"I'm sorry, Nicholas," Reem said as Jameson disappeared from the doorway and presumably joined her in the darkness.

Quietly, Nicholas walked back to the door and put his hand on the invisible wall that Reem put up to prevent him from leaving, feeling comfort in the fact that it was her gifts that kept him here. It made her feel so much closer to where he was even though he didn't know where he was. He pressed his face against the barrier and quietly sobbed.

⁂

They walked through the traitor's old home, looking through her things and getting a hold on what David would be tracking. It looked as though they weren't the first to rummage through her things, though it seemed that they hadn't been gone through in quite some time.

"Do you have what you need yet?" Mitchal asked, leaning against the wall while he watched his brother go through Reem's old belongings. From the looks of things, she hadn't returned to this place since the day she'd been accused by the Superiors.

"Almost. I can feel where she is, but she's very far away. We may need a teleporter," David replied, picking up a dress from her closet and lifting it to his nose. "She was a beautiful woman, wasn't she?" he asked, deep in thought.

"They say she was the most beautiful woman among all of the Advanced. They say she was to be our savior," Mitchal replied, closing his eyes and going into meditation.

"The prophecies were wrong. Everyone was wrong."

"Then who will bring the Humans to their knees? Many of the people have lost hope since she was named a traitor. They think there is no hope in this war."

"There is always hope, brother. Do you still think that the traitor is our savior?" David joked.

"I only know that we are tasked to find her and try her—and the sooner, the better," Mitchal replied, never opening his eyes.

Gifts

Reem could feel Nicholas's tears running down the wall she'd erected in his doorway as though they were running down her own hands, and she struggled to hold back tears of her own. She hated to do this to him, but Jameson was right. They couldn't spend so much time together if he was ever going to be able to get over her. She was hoping that going to Athena would help him, that knowing Suri would be there soon would make things easier, but Jameson wanted to stay at the castle for another few weeks at least. He didn't want to take her to Athena so soon, especially now that they knew she was pregnant.

She sat on the edge of the bed, trying to hold back the tears that threatened to run down her face, while Jameson checked the perimeter of the castle. She battled with herself about whether or not she should allow Nicholas to leave his room or whether she should go and see him, but she knew if she did either one, Jameson would be furious.

She could hear Nicholas's thoughts, feel how much he desired to see her. If he could only see her, he would have no reason to cry; and by leaning against her barrier, he was as close to her as he possibly could be under the circumstances. She tried not to listen as he screamed once again, tried to ignore him as he called her name, tried to block out his thoughts as he yelled for Jameson to let her come to him.

She wanted to see him, yes, but she didn't want to make this harder for him. He needed to remember that she was married to Jameson and that it couldn't be reversed.

Nicholas screamed again, and she couldn't hold back her tears any longer. She closed her eyes as they slowly made their way down her face, wishing that she hadn't cried over him another time—for Jameson's sake at the very least.

"Go see him. I can't take another second of his screaming," Jameson said, walking through the bedroom doorway.

She opened her eyes and looked at him, ashamed of the tears that had pooled in her eyes. "We should have left him behind," she whispered.

"Don't say that." He bent down in front of her and placed his hands on her shoulders so he could look her in the eye. "We needed him to come with us. Your sister needed him to come with us."

She stood and wrapped her arms around his neck, burying her face in his neck while his arms wound around her waist. "Go to him, Reem. Remind him of his love for Suri," he whispered in her ear.

She pulled away and wiped the tears from her eyes with the back of her hand before she looked into his eyes. "He doesn't think he loves her anymore."

"Then remind him that he does," he told her. "I'll come with you. I'll be just out of his line of sight if you need me."

"Okay." She nodded lightly. "Okay." She pressed her lips to his for a moment before pulling away and walking down the dark hallway toward the sound of Nicholas's screaming.

She stopped in front of the doorway, knocking on the stone wall when he didn't notice her appearance. "Nicholas," she whispered, turning to her right to see where Jameson had stopped. "Nicholas, I'm here," she said, slightly louder than before.

His eyes snapped up to look her in the eye, shocked that she was actually standing there.

"Nicholas, you need to stop."

"Just let me out. I'll—I'll control myself, I swear. I won't be around you unless Jameson is there too. I won't let myself go overboard with my thoughts, anything. Please, Reem. Don't do this to me. I need to see you," he said, his voice rushed.

She turned to Jameson again, and she listened to his thoughts. *"Tell him, Reem."*

She nodded and turned back to Nicholas. "I don't know, Nicholas. You need to remember who you really love. You love my sister. And she loves you—why are you fixating on me?"

"I love you, Reem, why don't you see that?" he asked, pressing both of his hands against the barrier in an attempt to break through while his eyes stared into hers.

"No, you don't. You love Suri," she said softly. "You only think you love me because it's been so long since you've seen her."

"I love *you*!" he shouted.

"Will you please stop saying that?" Jameson asked.

"I'm sorry, Jameson," Nicholas whispered. "I'm sorry; I'll keep my feelings to myself. I will."

"I need to speak with Jameson for a moment." Reem pointed to her right where Jameson stood outside of Nicholas's line of sight. When she saw the nervous look on his face, she added, "Don't worry. I'll be right back."

He closed his eyes as she walked away into the darkness where Nicholas could only imagine Jameson's arms wrapping around her perfect body, his lips pressing against hers as her fingers wound through his hair.

"Nicholas, calm down." She sighed. "I'm right here, you can see me."

He opened his eyes again and saw her standing halfway between the darkness and the light, and though he could still see Jameson's hands on her waist, it comforted him to know that she didn't leave his line of sight.

He couldn't hear them as they whispered a few words between each other, but when she returned to the center of his line of sight, she wasn't the only one standing in front of him. Jameson stood directly behind her, his arms around her waist and her arms over his.

Nicholas took a step back away from the barrier that stood between him and the couple. Reem smiled brightly, the strain of holding up the barrier gone from her face as she watched him.

"There are conditions," Jameson reminded him. "You are not to tell my wife that you are in love with her, you are not to speak with her unless I am present, and you are not to touch her except in specific circumstances. You will not be left alone with her, but you will be completing your training with her, as I have to complete mine as well." He paused to kiss the side of Reem's head and pull her body closer to his. "Understood?" he asked, turning serious once more.

"Perfectly," Nicholas answered.

"Good," they said.

"Jameson, the lights?" Reem asked, still smiling.

"Of course," he replied, reaching out his hand and producing fire from his fingertips to light the seven torches that lined the hall.

Nicholas walked out of the room, breathing a sigh of relief when he was able to do so. "Thank you," he whispered.

"Get some rest, Nicholas," Reem said before pulling herself free from Jameson's arms and walking away.

"Do as the lady said," Jameson said before following Reem down the hall toward their bedroom.

"Okay," Nicholas whispered, loud enough for only him to hear though he knew Reem was likely listening in.

✦◦✦◦✦

"She's very far away. We need a teleporter to get us close, and then we'll go in alone," David informed a messenger.

The messenger nodded before running off to give the message to the Superiors.

"Where is she?" Mitchal asked, still leaning against the wall in the traitors home while David rummaged through her things.

"She's too far away for me to get an exact lock, but once we get across the ocean, I should be able to sense her clearly," he replied, taking a seat on the balcony.

Mitchal opened his eyes and saw his brother looking out over Admiri and walked to the balcony to join him. "She had the best view of the city—other than from the Great Superiors chambers, of course."

David nodded, tiring of talking much quicker than Mitchal thought that he would. "David, what's wrong?" Mitchal asked.

"Nothing," he replied.

"You know I can tell when you're lying, brother."

"You know that I am both stronger and faster than you."

"But I could take him far enough away from here that you couldn't get your hands on him." A female voice laughed from behind them, startling them both.

"Who are you?" Mitchal asked calmly as he turned to face her.

What he saw was nothing like what he expected. The seductively feminine voice came from a young woman with a short cropped hair as red as blood and skin as pale as the moon. She dressed all in black and carried an air of dominance around her. Her dark eyes were hauntingly beautiful, and when she looked into his eyes, he had a feeling he wouldn't be able to look away before she did. "My name's Maria. People call me Em." She paused, taking a black backpack off her shoulder and setting it on the floor. "I'm your teleporter."

"So soon?" David asked, standing up and turning to face her.

"Twins? Well, that could get confusing. Or kinky." She laughed again. "Which one of you is David and which one's Mitchal?"

"I am Mitchal." Mitchal held out his hand for her to shake, and she shook it slowly, allowing her fingers to rest a moment in his palm when he released her hand.

"Which makes you David," she said, reaching out her hand to shake his as well.

"I am," he replied. "How fast can you get us across the ocean?"

"Straight down to business. I like that." She smiled, and Mitchal was completely entranced. "I can get you to the edge of the continent by the end of the day, but we'll have to wait there another twenty-four hours before I can get two passengers across the ocean," she said, staring straight into David's eyes.

"Then we should be on our way," Mitchal told her.

"You're in a hurry now, brother?" David laughed, walking to the door and picking up his pack from the ground before throwing an identical pack to Mitchal.

"Well, come here, boys," Maria said, taking David by the hand after he'd put his pack over his shoulders and pulling him to where Mitchal still stood leaning against the wall. "Ready?" she asked.

Both brothers nodded decidedly, and she teleported.

Reem fell backward onto the bed, tired beyond belief; and Jameson lay down beside her, running his fingers through her hair. "How's Samuel?" he asked.

"He's fine. He's happy," she replied, smiling brightly.

"Good," Jameson replied, rolling so that she was underneath him and he could look her in the eye. "You have no idea how happy I am." He leaned down and kissed her lips passionately.

He pulled away and stood to his feet, looking out the doorway toward where they'd left Nicholas only a few moments ago.

"What's wrong?" Reem asked, sitting up on the bed.

"Something doesn't feel right." He paused, turning to face her once more. "What will you be teaching Nicholas tomorrow?"

"I'm not sure yet." She stood and walked to his side. "When I started my training, my mentor started by teaching me about my gifts."

"Then perhaps we should start with that," Jameson replied, wrapping his arms around her back. "I think we may need his gifts sooner than we thought."

"Why do you say that?" she asked, pulling away from him and looking him in the eye.

"I don't know, but something isn't right," he replied.

"Then we'll start his gift training first thing in the morning. If it gets too difficult for him, we'll work on his sparring some more." She smiled slightly. "How does that sound?"

"Perfect." He kissed her forehead gently before releasing her. "What is he doing?"

"He's nervous about his training, and he's not sure if it's wise for him to stay here with us instead of moving on to Athena," she replied.

"I don't want you in Athena yet."

"He's not thinking about asking you to take him."

"He doesn't know the way." Jameson laughed.

"I have no doubt that he could find his way there on his own," she told him.

"He won't leave without you, Reem. He thinks he loves you, and he'll do whatever it takes to keep you safe—just as I do." He rubbed her back with his hands.

"I know," she replied, reaching up to kiss his lips.

David paced along the side of the camp while Mitchal and Maria attempted to build a fire—he never was much good at waiting around for a teleporter to be able to take him somewhere.

"You're going to wear a hole in the earth if you keep pacing like that," Mitchal joked as they got the fire started. He sat down, crossing his legs as he did so and starting to meditate beside the heat of the fire.

"Your meditation has made you soft. If I didn't know any better I'd doubt that you'd even be able to try the traitor in your current state of mind," David replied, continuing to pace in spite of his brother.

Maria laughed as she sat down next to Mitchal. "Calm down, boys. By this time tomorrow, we'll be across the ocean and off to find your precious traitor."

"How could a traitor like Kahrin be precious to anyone, teleporter?" David asked, still bitterly pacing along the side of the camp and fuming at his brother's words.

"Well, she's precious to Willow at least." She paused. "Why else would he have taken her away from the Superiors before she could be put on trial?"

"Our quarrel is not with Willow. Leave him out of this," Mitchal commented, closing his eyes as he meditated.

"Touchy touchy. As I said, you two need to calm down. Get some sleep." She laughed, laying down beside the fire and using her pack as a pillow. "I know I will."

Soon Maria's light snoring was the only sound in the camp other than Mitchal's steady breathing and David's heavy footsteps.

"As she said, brother, you need to get some rest," Mitchal said, whispering so he wouldn't wake Maria from her deep sleep. "Your gifts are under strain with this constant use—you won't be able to find her until we cross the ocean, remember?"

"Keep your thoughts to yourself, Mitchal. They are not welcome here," David replied, kicking stones from under his feet as he paced.

"There is no reason to think that this mission won't go off as well as any other."

"I am not worried, brother," David spat.

"I am ashamed of you, brother. You forget my gifts after so many years." He laughed quietly.

David stopped pacing and stared Mitchal squarely in the eye. "If I was worried, Mitchal, I would not speak to you of it."

"Get some rest, David," Mitchal ordered as he lay down in front of the fire. "You need it."

***

Reem sat in the center of the courtyard, her legs crossed as she taught Nicholas and Jameson the art of meditating. Nicholas was trying his best, though his best wasn't very good, and Jameson wasn't fond of meditation in the first place, so it seemed her lesson wasn't of much use. She closed her eyes and allowed her breathing and heart rate to slow to a point where neither Jameson nor Nicholas could sense her presence. She could feel her child within her meditate with her as she went into her trance, waiting for her students to follow. Suddenly, her child pulled her into a vision—the future.

She took a sharp breath as she watched a tall man with dark hair walk up to Jameson and demand to know where he'd hidden her, watched helplessly as the same man went to Nicholas and shot his leg, interrogating him.

She saw a woman—a teleporter—walk up to Jameson. They knew each other. Somehow, they'd met before. She watched as she took Jameson's hand and teleported away, jumping out of her trance with a start as they did so.

Jameson and Nicholas both sat in front her, staring at her with worried expressions. Jameson reached for her hand as Nicholas backed away, not wanting to intrude.

"What's wrong?" Jameson asked.

Reem then realized that she must have frightened them as much as her vision had frightened her. "I saw something," she whispered between breaths.

"What do you mean? What happened?" he asked, furrowing his brow as he spoke.

"I don't know." Her eyes moved to the hand that he held, and she placed her other hand on her belly. "The baby," she whispered.

"Is he okay?"

"I—yes. He showed me something. The future?" Her eyes flicked up to meet his, her worried look matching the one that had appeared on his face. "Promise me you'll never leave me."

"I won't, Reem," he replied. He took both of her hands in his.

She threw her arms around his neck and pulled herself close to him for a moment before releasing him and looking him in the eye. "Promise me, Jameson."

"I promise," he said, running his fingers through her hair. "What's going on, Reem? Talk to me."

"He—the baby—he showed me the future, I think. I don't know how."

"What did you see?"

"I saw, someone interrogating you—both of you. And, a teleporter. You knew her. They're coming, Jameson. They're coming for me."

"Who? Who is it?" He placed both of his hands on her shoulders and looked into her eyes.

"I don't know."

"Teach me how to hide you. If I can learn that, no one will be able to find you," Nicholas said, speaking up for the first time.

"I don't know if I can train you that quickly, Nicholas. It's difficult to learn how to use your gifts efficiently," Reem replied, her eyes unmoving from Jameson's.

"Teach me, Reem. I can do it. I know I can."

"I don't want you in Athena. Not yet," Jameson added.

"Jameson, if I were to go, no harm would come to me. You know that. Seth has kept it secret, and when we arrive, he will be ready to protect us—to protect our child. You know that," she said.

"Please, Reem," Nicholas pleaded.

"If anything goes wrong, I can get us out of here before they reach us," Jameson told her, his eyes piercing into hers.

She nodded quickly, looking away from Jameson to see where Nicholas now stood beside the doorway. "Are you sure you're up for this? I don't know how soon they'll be here."

"Teach me," He replied.

Jameson moved away from Reem and sat back down on the ground across from her while she motioned for Nicholas to sit beside them. After he did so, she began.

"Jameson, would a hunting gift impair you too much?" she asked.

"Consider it done." He closed his eyes and concentrated on his gift.

"Nicholas, Jameson will try to locate you within the castle. I want you to try to hide yourself. I'll come with you."

"Won't he be able to find you though?" Nicholas asked, tilting his head to the side slightly.

"That's why you'll be attempting to hide both of us," Reem answered. "I know it will be difficult for you, but I'll help you." She turned back to Jameson who had opened his eyes and was staring intently at her. "Jameson, I know you're not comfortable having Nicholas and I alone together, but that should only motivate you more to try and find us." She winked. "I don't know how else to train him."

"It's fine," Jameson answered. "I want you able to hide from the hunters."

"Thank you," she replied. "Nicholas, do you understand?"

"Yes." He nodded slowly. "I'm not sure how good I'll be, but we can try."

"You'll get there, don't worry. I have no doubt that you will be able to hide the both of us from the hunters." Reem smiled.

He nodded again, his lips curving into a half smile as she stood and offered him her hand. He shook his head and stood on his own, not wanting to upset Jameson further.

"Ready, Jameson?" Reem asked, taking his hand in hers.

Jameson smiled and turned toward her, wrapping his arms around her back and kissing her lips lightly. "Ready," he whispered.

She smiled brightly as he released her, and she walked to Nicholas. "Let's go."

Beaches

Maria woke to find Mitchal lying beside her and David placing more wood on the fire even though the sun was already hot enough to make her skin burn. She sat up and stared at him, unable to form the words to tell him that the fire was unnecessary in her current state of mind. She let her head clear before she picked up her backpack and dug through it for something to eat. "What time is it?" she asked David without looking up to acknowledge his presence.

"Ten o'clock by now," he replied, obviously even more unhappy than before.

"Now what's wrong?" she asked.

"Nothing you need concern yourself with, teleporter," he spat.

"My name is Maria."

"I will call you what I will, teleporter," he replied as he stood and started pacing again.

Maria ignored him and walked to Mitchal's side, kicking his back lightly. "Wake up. I can't deal with your brother on my own." She laughed as she squatted beside him.

She was finally starting to be able to tell the two of them apart. David was always on the move, pacing if nothing else. He was jumpy, nervous, his eyes filled with anger and remorse, and his hair as unkempt as possible from all the times he ran his fingers through it and tried to pull it out from the roots. Mitchal was his polar opposite. His presence was calming—even for David to some extent—and his personality was cool, collected, exactly how you would expect a man who meditated whenever he didn't have anything better to do. Unlike David, his eyes were kind and lined from laughter, and his hair was always neatly combed back into a ponytail.

Mitchal rolled onto his back and opened his eyes, jumping slightly when the first thing he saw was Maria's bright red hair only a few feet from his face. "Morning," was all he managed to say, making her laugh even more.

"Sleep well?" she asked.

"Yeah. You?" he replied, sitting up beside her and glancing toward his brother who continued to pace around the edge of their camp.

"Fine, thanks," she replied, placing her hand lightly on his shoulder and sliding it gently down his back. "By the way, your brother is insane." She winked as he turned to face her, finding her face mere inches from his.

"Yeah, I know." The corners of his mouth turned up slightly. "He's always been that way." His eyes flicked from her eyes to her lips and back again as he spoke.

"He doesn't like me." She squinted slightly, sliding her hand back up to his shoulder before she stood to her feet and walked back to her pack.

"What's wrong now, brother?" Mitchal asked loudly as he stood and walked toward him.

"What makes you think that something was wrong?" David replied sarcastically.

"David," Mitchal said, placing his hand on his brother's shoulder and forcing him to stop pacing.

David looked Mitchal in the eye, his eyes piercing into his brothers. "I can't find her anymore. She's just gone." he whispered harshly, not wanting Maria to overhear his confession.

"Even the best of the concealers cannot hide from you. You know that," he whispered back.

"Not this time—I feel no presence from her, and unless she dropped off the face of the planet, that can only mean that the Purists got to her first. They would rather kill her than bring her back alive."

"Willow would never have let them get to her. Can you find him?"

"We've no guarantee that she is with him."

"She's with him. Trust me."

"So where am I taking you?" Maria asked loudly as she walked up behind them with her pack already over her shoulders and both of their packs in her hands.

"Canada," David replied. "We go to Canada."

"We can head out in a couple of hours. Thought we'd go for a hike in the meantime." She tossed each of them a backpack.

"Sounds perfect," Mitchal said. "It's just the thing to keep David from pacing." He laughed as he turned from Maria to face his brother once more.

"And it will give Mitchal something other than meditating to do," David countered.

"Boys, boys, boys, calm down." She smiled as she walked between them, swinging her hips as she walked away.

"Don't think I haven't seen how you look at her, Mitchal," David whispered as he turned to follow her.

"You—what?" Mitchal replied, waiting a moment before he followed as well.

"Does he know where we are?" Nicholas whispered as he crouched next to Reem behind a fallen pillar in the castle.

"He can't find us. Good, Nicholas," she whispered back, smiling as she turned to face him.

"What if he finds us?"

"Don't lose your concentration. Don't discount yourself yet. You're just as skilled as any beginner," she whispered.

Nicholas nodded as he attempted to focus his gifts on hiding the both of them from Jameson who had been hunting them for the past hour and a half.

Jameson stood in the center of the courtyard, trying to locate either Reem or Nicholas and not succeeding in the slightest. Somehow, he doubted that Nicholas was actually able to hide both himself and Reem on his first day—let alone first hour—of training, but he didn't want to call him out on it. Reem likely knew already and somehow was blocking herself from Jameson being able to find her. He closed his eyes as he used his newly acquired gift to locate them, scanning the area as well as he could and once again coming up empty.

There.

He ran through the large wooden doors toward where he'd felt Nicholas's presence on the upper level of the castle. As he neared the area, Nicholas hid his presence once more—he'd obviously been distracted for a moment. Jameson smiled and ducked behind a pillar as he saw Nicholas crouching behind a similar—but broken—pillar with Reem by his side.

"Nicholas, we're exposed here," Reem whispered as quietly as she could, though she knew Jameson could still hear her.

"Follow me," Nicholas replied as he tried to walk away as stealthily as possible.

Jameson stepped out from behind the pillar and teleported directly behind Reem, wrapping his arms around her waist to stop her from following Nicholas and kissing her neck lightly. *"Found you,"* he thought.

She smiled brightly and tried as hard as she could not to laugh as Nicholas continued to walk away, thinking that she was following him.

"I need to talk to you," he whispered in her ear.

She nodded and turned around in his arms to face him. "What is it?" she whispered back.

"I can sense Nicholas right now—but not you."

"He has more gifts than we thought," she replied, moving her hands to her belly for a moment. "He knows we don't want anyone to find us, so he's hiding me."

"How is that possible?" He smiled slightly.

"How is any of this possible?" She smiled back, wrapping her arms around his neck.

"Doesn't matter," he whispered before pressing his lips to hers once more.

"Reem?" Nicholas voice was louder than he intended as he turned around to find that Reem was no longer following him. The next sound he heard was laughter coming from where he'd been only moments go. He stood to his full height and retraced his steps, following the sound of the laughter that he knew was coming from Reem. He found her laughing in Jameson's arms next to a pillar he'd passed several minutes ago. "When? How? What?" was all he managed to say, unable to form a complete question.

Reem laughed again as she turned to face him, her eyes bright as she looked at him. "Jameson wanted to talk to me, and we wanted to see how far you would go before you noticed I wasn't with you," she said.

"Uh. Not that far. Just down the hall a little way," Nicholas replied.

"Sounded like you were farther away than that." Jameson laughed, pulling Reem closer to himself.

"Oh stop, Jameson. He did well for his first session," Reem chided. "Jameson found you while we were hiding behind the fallen pillar." She pointed behind her to the spot where they'd been hiding only minutes ago.

"Oh," was all Nicholas managed to say.

"Don't worry, Nicholas. You'll get better." She paused. "Let's take a break, eat some lunch. We'll get back to training afterward."

"Meet us in the courtyard in a few minutes," Jameson said as he teleported away with Reem in tow.

As they walked along the ocean, Mitchal let his thoughts wander, wishing that he could be meditating now instead of hiking with his brother and Maria, the strange and beautiful teleporter. He listened intently as the waves washed up on the shore and drew back into the ocean to join with their brothers. If only he and his brother got along as well as the waves and the oceans from whence they came. He brought up the rear as they walked, David leading the way and Maria walking only a few feet behind him. Mitchal couldn't help but steal short glances at her every few minutes.

In any case, in an hour or less, she would be able to teleport them across the ocean and who knew what David had planned for her then. Knowing David, he would likely tell her to leave and that they would go it alone from there on out. He wished that he could meditate right now. He needed it. He couldn't concentrate with her walking in front of him and his brother being unusually grumpy about anything and everything. He was used to having his meditation to keep him from going insane when spending prolonged periods of time with David, but when on a mission, that entire idea went out the window.

His eyes followed the patterns that David's and Maria's footsteps had left in the sand and dared to follow the path straight to Maria's long toned legs, moving up to shapely hips and a thin toned waist. He stopped there, pointing his eyes quickly back to the ground as he chided himself for staring at the woman. Such a thing would be frowned upon by the Superiors. Besides, they were from completely different walks of life. She took whoever needed transportation wherever the Superiors desired them to go, and he, he tried people and often falsely convicted them at the Superiors' request. How could anyone as beautiful and witty as Maria even look upon someone as low as him?

In any case, he had taken the oath, and he planned to keep it.

He slowed as he noticed his footsteps catching up to hers, never looking away from those footsteps that marked themselves in the sand near his feet.

She came to a halt, waiting for him to catch up. "You're awfully quiet," she commented.

"I'm just thinking," he replied softly, still staring at David's footprints, which were now the only set that stood on the ground in front of him.

"What about?" she asked—he guessed she was smiling from the tone of her voice.

"Many things."

"Like what?" He could imagine her perfectly formed eyebrows rising slightly as she spoke.

"This would be a wonderful place for meditation. The sound of the waves and the feel of the breeze would be very relaxing," he replied.

"I've never been that good at meditation myself."

"Have you really tried?" he asked, finally allowing himself to look up into her eyes.

"Well, no. Not really anyway. I guess I don't have the patience for it." Her smile brightened.

"And I haven't the patience for your talking," David chimed in from a few feet ahead of them. "When can we leave?"

"We might be able to make it there now, but I don't know if I'd chance it just yet. Give me another half hour, and I can be sure that we'll land on a beach in Canada instead of the ocean near the beach in Canada." Maria laughed lightly, her voice sounding beautifully melodic in Mitchal's ears.

"We go now then," David announced, turning around and walking back toward them.

Jameson stood beside the large doors that led into the castle from the courtyard, watching as Reem and Nicholas practiced sparring with knives. He'd originally been opposed to the idea of Nicholas fighting his pregnant wife, but when he'd seen how badly Nicholas really was at hand-to-hand combat, he knew Reem would be fine. Nicholas hadn't even been able to touch her, much less get his blade near enough to her skin to make a mark. He didn't know if Nicholas was actually that bad at hand-to-hand or if he was only afraid of hurting Reem or the child, but in any case, the spectacle was amusing to watch.

Reem moved with a particular grace and agility, while Nicholas was jumpy and almost robotic in his movements. Reem tried to teach him to let loose, to let go of everything and live in the moment during hand-to-hand. But for some reason, it wasn't coming so easily.

Occasionally, Reem would turn to Jameson in the middle of her session with Nicholas and smile brightly at him, batting her eyelashes in a way that always made him want to take her in his arms and kiss her—her smile would only brighten when she read his thoughts. He loved watching her attempt to train Nicholas, even though the young man was still completely in love with her. It gave him a chance to see the Reem that he'd never known—the Reem that lived in Admiri and trained under the Great Superior himself. He wished he could have seen her when she was called the savior of the people.

His people—the people of Athena—rejected him from the get-go, saying that he was an abomination who had somehow found a loophole and gotten himself more than one gift during the treatment session. He'd never really had a home after his parents left him in the camps, so he never knew what it was like to be needed by his people—a fact he was reminded of every time Reem spoke of her past life in Admiri. He wished that he could go back in time and change the events that had occurred just so that he could see her smiling face as she spoke to her people from her balcony, but at the same time, that would mean changing the fact that she'd ever fallen in love with him. She was everything to him—and somehow, in the midst of it all, she would be the first Advanced to bear a child with another Advanced. It shouldn't be possible, but it was happening right in front of his eyes.

He loved her with all his heart, and he knew that she loved him back.

"I do. More than you know," she whispered into his mind.

"I think it's time for a break," she announced to Nicholas after knocking him flat on his back for the hundredth time since they started their sparring session.

"Finally," Nicholas replied, collapsing to the ground with a heavy sigh.

Meditate

Mitchal walked through the water on the beach, laughing at how close Maria had been to where she had intended to land her teleport. They'd landed on the beach, yes, but closer to the deep end of the ocean than the dry white sands of the beach. David hadn't been too thrilled about their landing site. He'd even knocked both Maria and Mitchal into the water when he realized that he was standing waist deep in the salty ocean waves. Now they trudged onward through the water, wincing when the ocean breeze whipped against their cold skin.

"Is he always this angry?" Maria whispered as David reached the beach ahead of them and started pacing.

"I'm afraid so, yes. He'll be better once we complete our task," Mitchal replied, keeping his eyes glued to the beach ahead of him rather than staring at Maria.

"You know, for twins, you two don't act that much alike." She laughed.

"We used to be more similar before David started taking tasks from the Superiors and I started my training with a thinker."

"You trained with a thinker?"

He nodded slowly, his eyes flicking from her to the beach and back again. "David and myself both had the opportunity to be trained by him, but I was the only one who took it. David decided that it would be better for his state of mind if he started working for the Superiors before he completed any training." He paused. "He was right to do that though. David is the best hunter in the world. Completely unchallenged."

"Wow." She turned toward David, watching as he continued to pace.

"What about you? Who did you train under?" Mitchal asked as they finally reached the beach, several meters away from where David paced.

"I didn't. I taught myself everything I needed to know," she replied, lowering her gaze.

Mitchal's eyebrows came together as he recognized her lie. "Really?" he asked.

"There were a few other teleporters that taught me a few tricks of the trade, but nothing formal."

"I would think you would have trained with someone, especially since you're working for the Superiors on a task of such high importance," he baited.

"I'm just good at what I do." She looked up to meet his eyes—eyes that stared into hers, trying to determine why she had lied—and smiled brightly. "It's freezing." She walked away from him toward the trees that lined the beach, her hips swaying with each movement of her long legs.

"How could anyone miss that?" David whispered as he approached his brother.

"Miss what?" Mitchal asked, tearing his eyes away from Maria to look at his brother.

"The way you look at her. Remember, she is only a means to an end. She will take us to the traitor and return us to Admiri. That is all she is good for."

"I've taken the oath, same as you. I will not break it," Mitchal announced, placing his hand on David's shoulder for a moment before walking up the beach to help Maria collect firewood.

"I'll be watching you, brother," David told him.

"You always are," Mitchal whispered, barely loud enough for David to hear.

"What was that about?" Maria asked as Mitchal approached her, a bundle of firewood in her arms.

"Nothing." Mitchal smiled and took the bundle from her. "I'll go put these on the beach. I think David's found a good place for camp." He motioned back to where he'd come from, where David continued to pace.

She laughed and went back to her task. "Of course he has." She smiled.

⁂

"What are we working on today?" Nicholas asked as Reem and Jameson walked out of their bedroom, her hand securely held in his.

"Meditation," Reem replied. "We'll start in a basement where you won't have many distractions and then hopefully move to the courtyard after that."

"Hopefully?"

"It takes time, Nicholas. We'll wait and find out how well you do in the quieter room first." She smiled as they led the way down to the basement level—the only level so far that was completely intact.

Jameson lit torches as they walked down the uneven steps down into a long, tall room twelve feet tall and seventy feet wide, large enough to house the entire population of the castle comfortably. As they reached the bottom of the staircase, Nicholas couldn't help but look up to the top of the pillars where they met with the ceiling, holding it from falling on top of them. He almost tripped on the uneven cobblestones that made up the floor as he walked, and he brought his eyes back to eye level to watch as Jameson lit the rest of the preset torches to bring the room up in both heat and visibility. He stared at the patterns made on the walls by the flickering flames and drew in a deep breath of the smoke that billowed lightly from their burning oil.

Reem sat gently on the floor in the center of the long room, crossing her legs and placing her hands palm up on her knees. "Sit, Nicholas," she said as Jameson walked passed her and leaned against the wall behind her, watching intently.

"Jameson will watch for today." She smiled, glancing backward to Jameson and winking before turning to Nicholas.

Nicholas walked slowly toward her and sat down a few feet away from her. "Now what?"

"Make yourself comfortable. You can't meditate if you aren't completely relaxed." She rolled her neck, cracking it twice before she started on her hands, nodding for him to do whatever he needed to be comfortable.

He crossed his legs and cracked his knuckles, nodding back that he was already comfortable. "Now what?" he asked again.

"Close your eyes. Let your mind go. Feel for your gifts. They are like a fifth appendage, and when you become experienced enough in meditation, you will be able to feel it and use it to your advantage. Relax. Breathe in"—she took a deep breath—"and out," she whispered as she exhaled. "Concentrate on your breathing and heart rates. Focus. Breathe. Relax," she whispered. "The rest is up to you and your gifts. Let them find you. Focus. Breathe. Relax," she breathed, settling into meditation as her eyes rolled back inside her head.

Nicholas sat very still, his eyes barely open so that he could still see both Reem and Jameson as he attempted to meditate. He didn't understand why Jameson wouldn't be joining them in this session of their training—he'd thought that they would both be participating in all of Reem's training, not picking and choosing which parts they wanted to learn. He watched as Jameson moved and squatted behind Reem, brushing her hair back behind her ears gently before kissing her neck. Nicholas closed his eyes completely so that he wouldn't be tempted to do anything and tried once again to meditate. He concentrated on his breathing, his pulse, anything other than the fact that the last thing he'd seen was Jameson kissing Reem's neck.

Mitchal sat in front of the fire, meditating, while he listened to David's heavy footfalls that circled the fire in front of him.

"I don't see why you like her," David commented to Mitchal while Maria slept, leaning against a tree on the edge of the woods.

"Why does it matter?" Mitchal asked, opening his eyes to watch his brother pace.

"If you're going to break your oath, shouldn't it be over someone better than her—better than a teleporter?" David asked, trying to get his mind off whatever was plaguing him.

"As I said before, brother, I will not break my oath. Besides, I'll likely never see her again after this task. It's rare that the Superiors order me to leave Admiri." He closed his eyes again, finished discussing the issue.

"I know you better than you think. You like her," David said, stopping in front of Mitchal and squatting so that he could look him in the eye. "Why?"

"Honestly, I don't know." He opened his eyes once more. "Honestly."

"Nothing is worth breaking your oath."

"How many times must I tell you that I will not break my oath, David?" He stood to his feet at the same time as his brother, looking him directly in the eyes. "I. Will. Not. Break. My. Oath," he said.

David laughed lightly. "I know you, Mitchal."

Mitchal took a deep breath before replying, his voice even and cool. "Believe me, David. I will keep my oath to the best of my abilities. There is nothing I want more than to be able to aid my people, and you know as well as I that if I break my oath, I will no longer be able to do that. Please, do not bait me further." Mitchal sat back down and closed his eyes, meditating once again as David began to pace.

"You meditate too much."

"You pace too much."

"You argue too much," Maria yelled from her position against the tree.

Mitchal's eyes snapped back open when he heard her voice, and his eyes flicked to hers as she stood and walked gracefully toward the fire, sitting down beside him. "Sleep well?" he asked.

"Most definitely." She winked. "Argue well?"

"Always do." He smiled slightly. "When are we leaving?"

"I'll be able to teleport the distance soon. Thought I might go for another walk." She smiled back, placing her hand on his shoulder and gently sliding it down his back—just like she had before. "Care to join?" she asked, sliding her hand back up to his shoulder.

"I'll catch up with you in a moment," he answered, his smile brightening as she stood and offered him her hand. He took it, standing quickly and gesturing for her to walk.

"Don't take too long." She winked before walking away from him, her hips swaying with the movement of her legs.

"Do you really think that's a wise decision, brother?" David asked spitefully.

"She's lying to us about something, David. I am only going to find out what it is," Mitchal replied, staring him in the eye. "I will not break my oath." He turned and walked away toward Maria.

He quickly caught up with her, slowing down when he reached her side. "Has David given you your orders for when we reach the target area?" he asked.

"Honestly, I've been avoiding him." She nudged his side with her elbow as she laughed.

"I'm sure he'll fill you in before we leave."

"You don't know what my orders are?" she questioned.

"David's in charge, remember?" He smiled as he turned to face her. "I can guess what they'll be, but I don't know for sure." He shrugged.

"What do you think then?" She casually linked her arm with his as they walked.

"Most likely, he'll have you teleport us close to the location of the traitor and then send you back to Admiri while we get the work done. He doesn't like to take the fast way back." He unlinked their arms.

"My orders are to stay with you," she replied, shocked.

"If David doesn't want you with us, he'd rather kill you than let you tag along somewhere."

"I'm not leaving, Mitchal. I will obey my orders to the letter," she told him as she stopped and crossed her arms over her chest.

"And what were your orders, Maria? The orders the Superiors gave you, that is," he asked as he turned around to face her.

"To take you to the traitor and bring both of you and her back to Admiri."

Mitchal knew she was lying, but he needed to know more. He needed to know why she would lie about something as simple as her orders from the Superiors. It didn't make sense that she would be lying to him. "He won't allow you to accompany us any farther than the next landing point, Maria. I know that."

"I'm going. I don't care what he says. I'm going."

"No, you're not." He shook his head. "David's going to burn down the forest." He laughed as he watched his brother, who was attempting to add more wood to the fire. "Enjoy your walk." He walked past Maria to help David with the fire.

Maria huffed as he passed and started walking once again, letting her mind wander as she did so. He'd been baiting her the whole time—she knew it. She was trying her best not to reveal herself, but she had a feeling he was already on to her.

"Nicholas, I know you're not meditating. You're supposed to be letting the room go, remember?" Reem chuckled, opening her eyes to look at his still form while Jameson sat beside her and linked his fingers with hers.

Nicholas sighed, opening his eyes to meet hers. "What am I doing wrong?"

"Try not to concentrate on Jameson or I—that will only distract you from your goal," she replied, closing her eyes. "Concentrate on your gifts, on connecting with them. Think of them like an extra appendage. They work just like an arm or a leg, just with a little more concentration."

"Why aren't you meditating?" Nicholas asked Jameson.

"My gifts don't require that I meditate in order to use them," he answered, glancing to Reem.

"His gifts work more like my pistol—point and shoot—whereas ours work more on the level of a nuclear bomb—it takes a lot to make it work," she clarified. "He knows how to meditate. It's just that he doesn't need to."

"So why not meditate just to relax?" Nicholas asked.

"I don't enjoy it as much as my wife." Jameson turned back to Nicholas to look him in the eye. "I feel that there are better ways for me to spend my time."

"No more questions, Nicholas," Reem said as Nicholas opened his mouth to speak. "Meditate."

⁂

Marcus Admiri, otherwise known as the Great Superior of the Advanced, sat on his throne thinking over the proceedings of the previous days.

The rumors of a rebellion had reached his ears long ago, but he hadn't considered it to be a real issue until three days ago when the so-called leader of the rebellion was finally named—Seth, the man whose gift allowed him to know and understand everything on earth. No one knew for sure if Seth really was the leader of the rebellion, or if Seth was his actual name, but Marcus knew that he was not a man to be trifled with. Seth had few who had seen his face and even fewer he confided in. He knew everything about the Superiors—about Marcus— but thus far, he hadn't told a soul, or at least not one that Marcus had heard.

He didn't know what had taken the man so long to start the rebellion, but he had to assume that it had something to do with Kahrin. She had been close to discovering Marcus's secret, and he'd had no choice but to remove her from her high seat among the people of the Advanced. Their savior was now a traitor, a killer. She had killed thousands of their own for the simple purpose of testing a new bioweapon that Marcus had previously deemed unsafe. Of course, he still had a vial of the bioweapon in his possession, and he had to believe that she did too—but she would never use it. That was the difference between them. She would never kill one of her own to better herself, but Marcus would kill them all in a heartbeat. He knew more about her than she liked to think.

His first attempt to get her off his tail was his gifting her to one of the under-Superiors—Lance—who had always fancied her. It had worked for a time, but she was more persistent than he had at first thought. When the Athenians had called for aid, he saw it as the perfect opportunity to take both her and them out of the picture.

He had planned everything perfectly, thinking through all of the possibilities—except of course for Willow. He had never thought that Jameson would fall in love with her.

Now he had even more problems than he had before all of this started. At least when Reem was in the city, he could keep her under his watchful eye at all times. With her out of the city, he thought it would be easier to be rid of her for good, but he'd been dreadfully wrong. A rebellion was starting, and he knew without a shadow of a doubt that Reem was somehow tied to the whole thing.

Sending David and Mitchal was his last option. He had no other way to find her, no other way to end this rebellion. He'd known when he'd chosen David that he was headstrong, but he hadn't expected them to leave without the teleporter that he'd arranged for them—though it was possible that Jameson had relocated Reem to somewhere closer to the city, but Jameson was no fool.

Marcus had known all along when they were underneath the Purist camp, and he'd known that the only way to flush them out would be to send the Purists down into the tunnels. So he told the Purists that if they found Reem, he would forge an alliance with them, but not before. Of course the first place they looked would be the cave systems underneath the camp. He'd thought that the Purists would have discovered them there sooner, but it appeared that they had more help than he had known.

After they left the camp, they'd fallen off his radar, and he knew that would be the last time he knew for sure of her location without the help of a hunter. David was the best of the best, and soon Reem would be dead by his hand. Marcus almost wished that he could be present at the time of her trial and death, but he knew the people would suspect him if he left the city now.

Marcus stroked his facial hair with his thumb as he thought, getting lost in his mind's fabrication of the look on Reem's face when she saw David and Mitchal. There was nowhere they could hide from a hunter, and they knew it. There would be no point in running. David prided himself in knowing that he'd never lost a target, and he wasn't about to start with the most important target of his career.

He stood and walked to the balcony, looking out of the city in the dwindling evening sunlight. He watched as people hustled down the streets toward their homes, as they lit the street torches, packed up fruit and stores from the marketplace for the night. He had the best view of Admiri from this balcony, and he enjoyed it. He loved being the leader of these great people.

They had no need of major technologies, no need for the things of the past. Some would say that when the Advanced came to power, power was destroyed, but only Marcus and Marcus alone knew the real reason for their lack of technologies. It had been his executive decision to destroy all technology, and he kept his real reasons a secret from all of the fools whose minds he controlled—the people of Admiri.

They were like puppets in his hands.

Traitor

Mitchal had been completely right. As soon as Maria returned to the camp, David informed her that once they reached the target site, she would be returning to Admiri. She fought it, but David wouldn't take no for an answer, and now the three of them were only waiting for Maria to be able to teleport. David had finally settled into a seated position shortly after Maria had returned, and now she took up his habit of pacing while Mitchal meditated.

"Will you please sit down, Maria?" Mitchal asked, not opening his eyes.

"You meditate too much, Mitchal." David chuckled. "Are you ready yet, teleporter?" he asked, turning his attention from his brother to Maria who continued pacing.

"My orders are to take you both there and bring you both back."

"Your orders are overruled, teleporter. You will leave as soon as you get us to our destination," David replied, standing up and walking to her side, grabbing her wrist and pulling her close to him, their faces only inches apart. "Take us to the traitor and then go about your business. I do not want to see you again after this mission, and I will see to it that the Superiors remove you from the task force," David whispered harshly in her ear. "Now."

She wrenched her wrist out of his grasp and sent her other fist toward his face. "No."

He caught her fist midair and twisted her arm behind her back, kicking her knees and dropping her to the ground. "You will do as I say, teleporter."

Mitchal got to his feet and walked to his brother's side, placing his hand firmly on David's shoulder. "David. Let her go."

"I will not disobey orders because you have your own agenda with the traitor," Maria spat, trying to wrench herself free from David's firm grasp.

"Don't fight him, Maria," Mitchal advised before turning back to his brother and leaning in to whisper in his ear. "David, if you order her to stay exactly where she teleports us, we have no problem. She won't be in your way, and she'll be fully capable of fulfilling her orders."

David turned to look Mitchal in the eye. "We will have no more need of her assistance."

"I for one do not wish to walk the entire way back to Admiri. If you wish, you can hike back on your own while Maria and myself return to Admiri."

David released Maria and moved to punch his brother's face when Mitchal jumped to the side and pulled a knife, holding it close to David's throat as he spoke. "Do not try that again, brother," he whispered. "Remember that I am not as undertrained as teleporters." He moved the knife and pushed David to the side before taking Maria's hand and helping her get to her feet.

"I didn't need your help," she whispered. "But thank you."

"He would have killed you if I hadn't," Mitchal stated plainly before turning back to his brother. "Ready yet, David? You seemed to be in such a hurry a moment ago." He smiled as his brother fumed in front of him.

David picked up his backpack and threw Mitchal's to him before walking back to Maria's side and placing his hand on her shoulder. "Teleport," he told her as Mitchal followed suit.

"I'm not leaving you," she told them.

"Fine. Teleport," David spat as she teleported.

Reem woke with a start, sitting up in bed. Her breathing was heavy, and her heart beat erratically while she remembered the events of her vision. She was alone in the basement where she'd been training Nicholas in the art of meditation. She had suddenly felt as though she wasn't alone and was being dragged up the stairs by a strong man. She remembered feeling pain when he pulled her hair, remembered being angry with Jameson for leaving her. She'd seen him, standing in the courtyard just like last time. She'd seen him teleport away with that woman, seen two men approaching her before she ran down into the dark basement. She remembered seeing Nicholas on his knees in front of another man who pointed a gun at his head—remembered his pleading eyes staring into hers where she hid. The vision was blurry, frequently changing back and forth in time. She didn't understand.

Then the memory hit her. She remembered being brought back into the courtyard and questioned by two men—twins, black hair, brown eyes. She remembered one of them turning to Nicholas and shooting him squarely between the eyes when she wouldn't answer his question, remembered Jameson finally reappearing behind one of the men, and remembered him thinking to her that he was sorry. So sorry. Something hit her from behind.

That was when her vision had ended—when she had woken up.

She felt Jameson's hand on the small of her back, gently massaging her spine as he whispered in her ear, "What's wrong?"

She felt his lips on her neck, his fingers running through her hair, but she couldn't will her lips to speak—even if she had, she couldn't confront him about something that she didn't even know he would do. Her vision had told her that he would leave her, but that didn't mean it would happen.

"Just a dream," she whispered finally, turning to face him and kiss his lips gently. "Go back to sleep. I'm going to get some water." She slowly moved her feet off the edge of the bed and slid them to the ground.

"Don't take too long." He chuckled, taking her hand and kissing it gently before she stood, put on her clothes, and left the room.

As she walked through the almost pitch-black halls of the castle, she couldn't help but remember being dragged through this very spot in her vision. She walked to the storage room where they kept the water stores and dipped a ladle into the water before bringing it to her lips. She drank it dry, set the ladle down beside the table, and walked back out of the room. She walked through the twists and turns of the castle halls slowly, going in the opposite direction from the bedroom where Jameson waited for her.

When she reached the courtyard, she could just make out the sun coming over the horizon and could see enough of the space around her to know that it was not empty. She moved to the side of the doorway and allowed a moment for her eyes to adjust to the lighting, searching for the presence that she could feel in her mind.

There. A man—no, two. They were sitting inside the courtyard near the crumbling wall, waiting. She could read their thoughts and knew that they were here looking for her.

She slowly turned and walked back down the hallway, going as fast as possible to the bedroom. She found Jameson sitting up on the bed, his face confused when he saw her run through the doorway.

"They're here," she whispered. "One of them is a hunter, and they have a teleporter with them."

"I'll get Nicholas out of bed," he said. "Hurry." He got out of bed and put his pants on before running out of the room and across the hall to wake Nicholas.

She moved to the closet and started strapping her weapons to her legs as Jameson walked back into the room with Nicholas in tow.

"What's going on?" Nicholas asked louder than they would have wanted. Reem and Jameson both hushed him, and his eyes widened when he saw the seriousness on their faces. "Seriously," he whispered, "what's going on?

"The Superiors' hunter has arrived," Jameson told him as he fastened his pistol to his leg and started on his sheaths. "We can't run—they have a teleporter with them. The only thing we can do is fight them off."

"How do you expect me to fight someone?" Nicholas asked, worry forming lines on his face.

"Nicholas," Reem said, "we can't do this without you."

"I'll deal with the teleporter, which leaves the other two to the both of you," Jameson whispered, buttoning up his uniform shirt and throwing another one to Nicholas along with two holsters and three sheaths. "Put those on."

Nicholas did as he was told, silently considering his options. "I don't know about this."

"You'll be fine," Jameson told him.

"I mean, I don't think Reem should be out there," he said, staring Jameson straight in the eye.

"We don't have a choice. You can't take both of them, and until I take down the teleporter, it'll be twice as hard," Jameson replied.

"I'll be fine," Reem said, walking around the bed to stand by Jameson's side. "Trust me."

"I'm sorry, Reem, but I don't want you out there. As it is, I won't be able to stay with you during the fight. I don't know where I'll be if the teleporter takes me away." Jameson reached his hand up to stroke her cheek lightly. "I don't want you to get hurt—or the baby."

"We'll be fine. He wants to help," she whispered, taking his hand. "Don't worry."

He shook his head. "Don't let him. He'll overwork himself, and then so will you." He paused. "Be careful, Reem. Please. For me."

"I promise." She paused, looking down to the ground before continuing. "I had another vision."

"Why didn't you tell me?" His brow furrowed.

Her eyes looked into his, and she replayed her vision in his mind, lingering on the look on his face when he whispered in her mind, *"I'm sorry. So sorry."* Tears pooled in her eyes as the vision ended, and his eyes widened.

"I won't let that happen," he told her. "I promise you, I will not let that happen."

"Who is she, Jameson?"

He closed his eyes, searching for the right words before finally speaking. "Her name is Maria. We went on a few tasks together a few years ago."

She replayed the image of Maria's hand sliding up Jameson's chest to his neck as he looked at Reem from across the courtyard.

"She told me she loved me. Before we stopped working together."

"Why didn't you tell me about her?"

"I didn't think of her like that. She was a colleague, nothing more. I was ordered to work with her." He paused. "I asked the Superiors not to assign us to the same tasks after that incident."

"Then why are you going to leave with her?"

"Because I need to get her out of the way so that you and Nicholas can take down the two men—it's the best plan we have, and you know it," he replied, placing both of his hands on her shoulders as he looked her in the eye. "I swear to you, Reem, I will not let that happen."

"Um. Guys? You know I'm still here, right?" Nicholas asked.

"Sorry, Nicholas. Family discussion," Reem said as she turned to look him in the eye.

"No, it's fine. I—uh—I just didn't know if I should be listening."

"It's fine. I'm sure you didn't understand much of it anyway." She smiled.

"True." He smiled back. "So how are we doing this?"

⁂

Maria did as she was told, waiting in the woods outside the castle while the boys sat inside the courtyard, barely visible in the dim morning light. She knew she wouldn't be able to wait much longer before she teleported inside. She couldn't let them start their attack until she'd contacted the savior.

She waited as long as she could—until she saw David stop pacing and crouch down at his brothers' side—and teleported just past the large double doors that led into the castle. She didn't know her way around, so she followed the only thing she could—the smell of smoke from an oil torch. She hurried along the halls until she found two lit torches in the center of a long hall with three doors on each side. She looked through the first, the second, and the third before she found a room that looked lived in—but empty. She hurried past it, stopping at the last door and peering inside to see two men—and the savior.

"Maria," Jameson said as she walked in the door. He teleported to stand between her and Reem.

"I'm not here to hurt you. I'm here to warn you," she said, putting both of her hands on top of her head. "I'm not carrying any weapons—pat me down if you want." She winked at Nicholas.

"Do it, Nicholas," Jameson ordered.

Nicholas did as he was asked, checking her over for any weapons before turning back to Jameson and shrugging his shoulders. "Nothing."

"Told you," she said, smiling and tilting her head to the side.

"What are you doing here, Maria?" Jameson asked.

"How many times do I have to ask you to call me Em?" she asked. "My orders are to speak to the savior and the savior alone."

Reem stepped out halfway from behind Jameson to look her in the eye.

Maria dropped to her knees and dipped her head. "Savior," she said, "I have been sent by the Prophet, Seth."

"Seth? Why?" Reem asked.

"The Superiors have sent two men here to kill you. I was told to inform you and help you in any way I can before returning you safely to Athena."

"I will not take her to Athena. Not yet," Jameson said.

"That's not up to you, Jameson. If the savior does not wish to return, then I will remain with you as your guard until such time that you decide to return," Maria told them.

"I will return when it's time," Reem replied. "Stand. Tell me what you've come to say."

Maria stood. "Of course, ma'am. The hunter—David—he's never lost a hunt before, and he's not keen on starting. They sent his brother with him to put you on trial." She paused. "The brother—Mitchal—is like a lie detector. He knows when you're telling the truth and when you're not. He won't kill you if you're not guilty, but David will."

"Thank you, Maria," Reem said. *"I don't trust her,"* she whispered in Jameson's mind. *"Her thoughts are scattered."*

"I don't either," he thought back. *"The plan stays the same."*

Reem nodded slightly and relayed the information to Nicholas who nodded back.

"They're coming," Reem said. "Now."

"How do you . . . ?" Maria asked.

"It's none of your concern," Jameson said. "It's time to get to work." He stepped up to Maria and placed his hand on her shoulder, teleporting her away within the second.

"Nicholas, put out the torches. Hide in one of the other rooms until they pass by. Take down the first one you see and leave the second for me. I'll be here," Reem ordered, packing her belongings back inside her backpack and throwing it inside the closet before going to Jameson's things and repeating the process. "Make sure your things aren't lying around," she added as he left the room.

She put out the torch in her bedroom and knelt on the floor in the corner while she waited for Nicholas to complete his tasks. She watched the light die down little by little as Nicholas put out the torches and settled into a room of his own to wait for the hunter and his brother.

Nicholas waited while his eyes adjusted, listening for the sounds of footsteps that he knew would soon be approaching. He tried his best to slow his breathing so that he could hear sounds other than those that emanated from his own body. His heartbeat was loud in his own ears as he crouched inside the doorway, listening to the hollow sounds of the castle halls.

Reem continually crossed his mind, the look on her face when Jameson teleported away with Maria in tow. Something was about to happen, and he had a feeling that Reem knew what it was. The child inside her was allowing her slight glimpses into the future, and he was sure that she wasn't sharing all of the information with them.

He quieted his mind, concentrating only on his heartbeat and breathing. He felt his gifts, felt them slowly coming under his control as he heard the sounds of footsteps slowly approaching. He used his gifts to shield himself from the hunter and searched for Reem with his mind in order to shield her as well. His eyes snapped open when he realized she wasn't in her bedroom.

"He doesn't know about you. He thinks there are only two of us—myself and Jameson. Until Jameson gets back, you need to pretend to be him, and that you're exhausted. Can you do that?" Reem's voice whispered into his mind. *"Jameson will be back soon, and then we'll have the upper hand."*

Her voice calmed his mind and quieted his thoughts for the time being, his heart rate slowing to a quieter pace and his breathing slowing to the point where he could hear the hunter breathing near the entrance of the castle. He closed his eyes and felt for their life signs with his gifts, finding two identical signals—twins. The hunter and his brother. He felt them walking down the hall and knew the precise moment to jump out of the doorway and tackle the first man he saw.

The man fought back—harder than Reem or Jameson had ever fought him during their sparring sessions. Nicholas quickly fell to the ground, howling in pain when a bullet pierced his right calf.

The next thing he knew, he was being dragged down the hall by one of the men, slowly approaching the courtyard with Reem nowhere in sight. He hoped against hope that they hadn't found her yet. They wouldn't know their way around the castle, so Reem could easily hide from them as long as he could keep her hidden from the hunter. He hoped she hadn't tried to fight them off without Jameson to protect her—from the hunter and from herself. He couldn't live with himself knowing that he'd left her fighting alone when he'd been shot all of one time.

It was only a bullet. Only a bullet.

He lost consciousness.

Reem had sat by and watched while the brothers had taken down Nicholas, assuming that he was Jameson in the darkness. She'd known that using Nicholas as a distraction would be the only way she could run, and she couldn't bring herself to put her baby in danger—no matter how much she wanted to help him.

She'd done the only thing she could. She'd stood in the hallway near the door to the basement, and as soon as Nicholas had jumped out onto the brothers, she made her way down to hide in the vast darkness. Now she crouched behind a pillar, waiting, hoping that the brothers wouldn't find her. Not yet. Not without Jameson by her side.

She used her training in meditation to slow her heart rate and breathing level to a point where no one would be able to sense her life signs, and she used her child's gifts to hide herself from the hunter for the time being. She refused to allow herself to think the thoughts that continually crept through her mind—thoughts of Nicholas being shot, of Jameson being taken away by Maria and never returning to her side, thoughts of dying alone at the hand of the hunter and his brother.

She wouldn't let that happen. She couldn't. Not with so much at stake.

Glimmer

"What are you doing?" Maria whispered harshly as they landed in the woods outside the castle.

"Preventing you from harming my wife," Jameson told her as he wrenched both of her wrists behind her back. He began to tie a rope around her wrists when she jerked herself free of his grasp and looked him in the eye.

"What?" she asked, her brow furrowing as confusion crossed her face.

"I don't trust you, Maria," he replied.

"No . . . she's your wife?" she asked unbelievingly. "You told me that you would never break your oath. Not even if it meant saving your life!" she whispered harshly, knowing that her loud tone could alert the brothers to their presence outside the castle boundary.

"No, Maria, I told you that I would never break my oath for you. For *you*," he clarified, staring her straight in the eye. "I love her."

Her eyes dropped to her feet as she took in his words. "I was sent here by Seth, Jameson. I was not sent here to sweep you off your feet if that's what you're thinking."

"That's not what I'm worried about," he replied. "I don't trust you."

"Then let me prove to you that I'm not here to kill you—or your wife," she said, looking up into his eyes.

"And how do you propose to do that," he asked, once again taking hold of her wrist firmly, "without leaving this spot?"

"You have to trust me," she replied, staring him down with eyes that burned.

"Then it's not going to happen," he said, his eyes soft as he stared into her hard gaze.

"Bite me." She teleported—taking Jameson with her.

<hr />

Reem hid in the shadows, pretending that she couldn't hear the sound of her own breathing over the shuffle of approaching footsteps. She closed her eyes and tried to slow her heartbeat, tried to quiet her breathing, but her body would have none of it. The adrenaline that coursed through her veins was making it impossible to think rationally, impossible to calm herself.

The footsteps shuffled quickly down the stairwell into the basement. She could feel the presence of one man as he walked past her, and she inhaled a sharp gasp when she realized that he was alone. She quieted herself again, realizing her mistake as she crouched in the darkness.

She searched the man's mind—Mitchal? Not the hunter?

She read his thoughts, found the memory of being given orders by the Great Superior, felt his internal struggle, his hope that he would not be forced to kill the woman that he for so long considered to be his savior.

While she continued to read his thoughts, she forgot to pay attention to his location, and he suddenly took hold of her arm and dragged her to her feet beside him. She struggled to break free of his grasp, but his arm held tightly to her as he turned her around and pressed her chest into the wall while he tied her wrists behind her back with practiced ease.

"Mitchal, please, let me go," she pleaded as he pushed her through the room and up the stairs. "You don't understand. I did not do what the Superiors claim—I am not a traitor!" she whispered harshly, hoping that the man wouldn't take her to his brother.

"I'm sorry. I have no choice," he whispered gently in her ear as he led her back to the courtyard where his brother waited with Nicholas on the ground at his feet.

"We always have a choice," she whispered back before he threw her to her knees beside Nicholas's unconscious form.

"Traitor," David acknowledged, a wicked smile growing on his face when he recognized the look of pain on her face at seeing the man on the ground beside where she knelt.

"I am no traitor," she replied, spitting on his feet.

Without a word, he drew his weapon from its holster and pointed it level with her eyes. "Do not speak unless spoken to, woman."

"Oh, I'm sorry." She smiled. "Were you talking to your brother then?"

He drew back his weapon and brought it down across her face, knocking her to the ground beside Nicholas. She got up on her own, blood seeping into her teeth from a wound on the corner of her mouth as she smiled at him once again. "I am not so weak as you think me." She slowly stood to her feet to look him in the eye. "Let. Him. Go," she demanded, using her gifts to take Mitchal's weapon from its holster and point it at David the same moment she unbound her arms.

"Our quarrel is not with him, David," Mitchal whispered, walking toward Nicholas and kneeling to cut his bonds.

"I would not advise that," David replied, pointing his weapon at Reem to match the one that she continued to train between his eyes.

"Let him go or I will fire," she warned.

"As I said, brother, our quarrel is not with him." Mitchal cut Nicholas's bonds and dragged his unconscious body into the forest. "He is free to leave as soon as he wakes," he said as he returned to stand at his brother's side. "Please, put the weapons down."

Reem quickly moved the weapon back to its previous location in Mitchal's holster while David continued to train his weapon on her.

"Let me do what I was sent here for," Mitchal whispered as he stepped between Reem and David to look her in the eye. "Tell me, Kahrin, did you murder the people of Athena?" he asked.

⁂

Jameson and Maria landed just outside the courtyard, looking in at Reem as she was interrogated by the hunter's brother.

"Why are we here, Maria?" Jameson asked, unable to take his eyes off the woman who continued to defend herself in the mock trial.

"Saving your wife," she replied.

As Jameson watched, David walked to Reem and kicked the back of her knees, knocking her to the ground. He found that her eyes looked straight at him as he stared at the scene before him. He knew she wouldn't fight back. She needed him to do the fighting for her—whatever they did to her, it was in the name of the Superiors, and she still felt tied to them in some way. *"I'm sorry, Reem. So sorry,"* he thought, chiding himself for thinking the two words that he knew she didn't want to hear. He felt Maria's hand slide up his chest seconds before she teleported him away.

⁂

Nicholas woke to find that he'd been untied and left in the forest, blood still seeping from the wound on his calf. He stood to his feet to get his bearings and found that he was only a few feet away from the castle courtyard. He walked to the edge of the courtyard and saw Reem kneeling in the center with two men, one standing in front of her and the other crouching behind her to whisper in her ear. He could see the shimmering tears that ran down her cheeks as she listened to what he told her, and Nicholas couldn't help but wonder what it could possibly be when suddenly, he realized that she was looking him straight in the eye, her eyes starting to shimmer as the silver flecks in her eyes once again rearranged themselves.

"Don't look at me, Nicholas," she warned.

He did as she asked, looking away quickly before he heard the sounds of weapons being drawn and voices yelling as someone else appeared inside the courtyard. He lifted his eyes to see what had occurred and saw Jameson crouching beside Reem as Maria teleported away with one of the brothers and the other turned to point his weapon at Reem.

Nicholas watched as Reem slowly stood to her feet, her glimmering eyes shining into his. "Look at me," she ordered, and the man dropped his weapon as he looked into her eyes. It was all Nicholas could do to look away from her as the hunter fell to his knees, suddenly small as she approached him. The next thing Nicholas knew, the light that shone from Reem's eyes was gone, and the man fell to a heap in front of her while Jameson covered her eyes.

He limped into the courtyard and approached them slowly, unsure of what had actually happened. "What's going on?" he asked. "How did you do that?"

Jameson turned to look him in the eye, the look on his face warning him to stay back for the time being. He whispered something in her ear, but Nicholas couldn't hear what it was.

※❀❀❀※

"Reem, stop. You've made your point," Jameson whispered in her ear, still covering her glimmering eyes with his hand. "Please, Reem."

"You left," she said.

"I know, I know, I'm sorry," he replied. "Look at me, Reem."

"You don't want that, Jameson," she replied, shivering as he wrapped his arm around her waist and pulled her back toward his chest.

"I don't know how you're doing this, but you need to stop," he whispered. "Please."

"Help me," she whispered, closing her eyes beneath his fingers as she tried to stop her gifts from attacking the man on the ground in front of her.

"Here," he said, sending more control from his fingertips into her body.

Her body sagged, and he gently laid her down on the ground, cradling her head in his lap as she attempted to pull her gifts back under her control. Her hand found his, and their fingers linked together as she opened her eyes slowly, the silver flecks once again rearranging into their original pattern inside her eyes.

"I'm sorry," she whispered.

"You have nothing to be sorry for," he replied, leaning down to kiss her forehead gently.

"Is she okay?" Nicholas asked as he approached them.

"I'm fine, Nicholas," she said, just loud enough for him to hear as she turned to look at him.

"How did you do that?" he asked her as he knelt beside them.

"I don't know." She shook her head. "Is he?" She turned back to Jameson, her eyes filled with worry about the hunter who still lay in a heap on the ground a few feet away from them.

"Nicholas?" Jameson said, nodding to the man.

***

"How did you think I wouldn't know?" Mitchal asked her, leaning against a tree while Maria took up David's job of pacing back and forth across the span of the small clearing they'd found.

"The Prophet gave me specific instructions on how to get passed your gift. I thought I'd practiced enough to make it work," she replied, not looking up to meet his eyes.

"It's not so simple." He smiled. "I've never known anyone to get passed it. In fact, I would have told my brother that Kahrin is innocent, but you stopped me before I could."

"She didn't do what they claim? You know that?" she asked as she stopped to stare into his dark piercing eyes.

"She's telling the truth, I know that much. She won't say anything to incriminate whoever is responsible though," he replied, his smile fading.

"Why wouldn't she? She has no reason to protect them," she said, thinking out loud.

"Maybe she's not protecting them. It seems to me that her personality is what's preventing her from coming out and saying who is responsible." He paused. "She seems very . . . I don't know the word . . ." He shook his head.

"Mitchal, I need to tell you something."

"You realize I most likely already know whatever it is you want to say, don't you?" he asked, his smile reappearing on his face.

"I know." She walked up to him and pressed her lips firmly against his, closing her eyes as she kissed him. His hands remained at his sides, and his lips were unmoving as she kissed him, his eyes opened widely as she stepped back again and looked him in the eye. "Surprised or unsurprised?" she asked.

He continued to stare at her, and she smiled brightly. "I'll take that as surprised."

"Come on." She walked up to him again and took his hand in hers. "We should get back to the others. My orders are to get the savior back to Athena safely." She paused. "You're not going to try and kill her again, are you?"

"No," he replied, glancing down at their entwined fingers. "No, I'm not." He shook his head slowly before placing his other hand on the back of her neck and pulling her toward him to kiss her lips. He released her and smiled brightly as her eyes stared into his. "Let's go."

She nodded and smiled before teleporting back to the courtyard.

Mitchal released her hand and ran as they landed, rushing to David's side. He dropped to his knees beside his brother, glancing up at Nicholas briefly before returning his full attention to his brother and moving his hands to check his pulse.

"He's alive," Nicholas told him. "I don't know why he's unconscious, but in any case, he should wake up within a few hours at most."

Maria walked to where Jameson sat on the ground, still cradling Reem's head in his lap, and squatted beside them. "Savior, are you alright?" she asked.

"Why is he here?" Reem nodded to where Mitchal knelt beside his brother.

"He's with me." She paused, glancing up at him before returning her eyes to Reem's. "He knows you're innocent, savior. He wants to come to Athena with us."

Reem nodded her response before returning her gaze to Jameson's. "Help me up," she said.

He smiled and helped her get to her feet, wrapping his arms around her as she stood. "I'm sorry I hurt you," he whispered in her ear.

"I know," she replied, wrapping her arms around his waist.

"How's our baby?" he asked.

"Happy and healthy as ever." She pulled away slightly, and he placed his hands on her stomach.

"Good." He looked into her eyes once again. "You have no idea how much it hurt me to see you like that . . ."

"I think I have more of an idea than you think," she replied, tapping the side of her head.

He smiled, pulling her close to him again as he kissed her forehead lightly.

She pulled away from him again, looking into his eyes before turning around and walking to where Nicholas and Mitchal hovered over David's unconscious form. "How is he?" she asked.

Nicholas turned and looked her in the eye. "Better question, how are you?" he asked her.

"I'm fine," she replied.

"You sure? Want me to give you a once-over just to be sure?" He winked before hugging her lightly and pulling away to look her in the eye again. "And the little one?" He smiled slightly as he felt her healing power start to course through his veins, and the bullet hole began to heal.

"He's fine too," she answered. "Now back to my original question. How is he?"

"He's physically fine as far as I can tell," he whispered, trying not to let Mitchal overhear. "I don't know why he's unconscious, really."

"That would be my fault," she replied. "My new gift. I think I took away his gift. It could take a while before he wakes up. His body needs to get used to being . . . human . . . again."

"How many gifts is that then?" he joked.

"Four." She laughed. "Only four—and one of them was from Jameson."

"You get four, and I get one that I didn't even know about until a few days ago." He rolled his eyes.

"Savior, may I speak with you?" Maria asked, walking up and standing next to Nicholas.

"Of course," she answered.

Maria smiled and nodded, gesturing toward the outer edge of the courtyard.

Reem followed her as she walked, stopping near the outer wall. "What is it?" Reem asked.

"I'm concerned that the brothers might not be the only two that the Superiors sent to kill you. I think we should leave as soon as possible."

"I'm not going to Athena until my husband is comfortable with it," Reem said before turning to walk away.

"Wait, Reem, please." She paused as Reem turned around to face her. "He doesn't trust me."

"Neither do I," Reem said as she turned and walked back to where Jameson waited for her beside Nicholas and the brothers. She took her husband's hand and kissed it gently.

"What did Maria want?" he asked.

"She'll talk to you about it. She wants to leave here as soon as possible," she said.

"I'll go talk with her," he whispered as he released her hand and walked to Maria, leaning against the courtyard wall. "Maria." He crossed his arms as he stopped in front of her.

"Jameson."

"What are you suggesting?" he asked.

"We should leave for Athena."

"Not yet. It's not safe."

"It's not safe anywhere! The only place where she'll be at least a little more protected is Athena. The Prophet has the place locked down tight—there's no way anyone would get to her there," she whispered harshly, not wanting to raise her voice with the others so close by.

"Not yet," Jameson replied calmly.

"Why? Give me one good reason."

"She's pregnant."

"That's not possible." She shook her head.

"You heard me."

"The Superiors told us—"

"There's more that they lied about. Trust me, Reem knows. That's why they framed her."

"How does she know?" Her eyebrows furrowed.

"She's telepathic."

"How many gifts does she have?" Maria asked, shocked.

"Four, but one of them was a gift from my husband," Reem whispered in her mind.

"Whoa." She looked passed Jameson to Reem, who waved her fingers and smiled. "How?" She looked back to Jameson.

"She's very good at what she does." He smiled. "That said, I still don't want her in Athena yet. I don't think it's safe."

"Okay, how about this, we go to Athena, we look around at the security that the Prophet set up for her arrival, and you decide what you think then."

"I'll talk it over with Reem. We won't leave until tomorrow," he replied, smiling as Reem wrapped her arms around his waist and peered over his shoulder. "What do you think?" he asked her.

"It's up to you," she replied, kissing his cheek lightly before sliding around him so that his arm rested on her shoulders.

"Then let's go to Athena—at least for a day or two." He winked before glancing back to Maria who smiled brightly.

Sedative

Mitchal sat next to David's bed, waiting for him to wake. He couldn't believe what had happened. Who would his brother be without his gifts, without the possibility of doing tasks for the Superiors? Jameson had been willing to give David his gift back, but Mitchal highly doubted David would agree to his terms.

He stared into his brother's unmoving eyes, waiting for any sign of life. He was beginning to worry that Nicholas hadn't been truthful about his brother's condition when Nicholas himself walked into the room and sat at David's side.

"How is he?" Mitchal asked as Nicholas's hand moved to check David's pulse.

Before Nicholas could reply, David's eyes fluttered open, his face full of confusion as he took in the space around him: the castle bedroom, Nicholas standing over him and checking his pulse, and Mitchal sitting on the bed beside him, staring at him as though he were looking at a dead man who'd just risen from the grave.

"How are you feeling?" When David didn't respond, he added, "My name is Nicholas. I'm a doctor. I've been taking care of you for the past few hours." He paused. "I know everything must seem very different to you right now, but don't worry. We can still fix this."

"Why can't I feel my gifts?" David asked finally, his eyes glancing back and forth between Nicholas and Mitchal quickly.

"Kahrin. She's evidently developed a third gift that allows her to take gifts away from any Advanced. I don't know how," Mitchal answered.

"A third?" David's eyebrows furrowed.

"Telekinesis, telepathy, and her newfound ability to delete gifts. That makes three naturally formed gifts," Nicholas said before Mitchal could open his mouth to respond.

"That's not possible," David said as Reem walked into the room with Jameson in tow.

"It is possible, David. It's possible because the Superiors lied to us—to all of us," Reem said. "How do you feel?" Her eyebrows rose as she stared into his eyes.

"How could you allow this?" He turned to his brother, eyes conveying the shock in his voice.

"She's telling the truth," Mitchal answered.

"She's deceived you, brother." He stood and backed defensively against the wall, glancing furtively between the others. "What is this trickery?" he directed his question to Reem.

"It's not a trick, David," she said, carefully starting to approach him with Jameson close behind her, wary of his defensiveness.

"How could you let her trick you, Mitchal? She is a liar and a traitor to the Superiors—to the Advanced," he said, not taking his eyes off her as she slowly approached him.

"Savior, please, be careful," Maria pleaded as she stepped into the room.

"Don't tell me, brother, you broke your oath," David said accusingly as Maria started to approach and Mitchal took her by the hand to prevent her from doing so.

"Listen to me. The Superiors lied to us—to you—about all of this." Mitchal glanced to Jameson who shot a warning glance back at him before he continued. "There are things you don't understand. Let me explain, brother," he pleaded, acknowledging Jameson's angry stare.

"I will not turn against the Great One," David replied.

"Please, David," Mitchal whispered, stepping between Reem and his brother.

"'I will never break my oath'—isn't that what you said? You are dead to me—hypocrite."

"Brother—"

"I have no brother." He spat on his brother's face, and Mitchal lifted a hand to wipe the saliva from his face, dropping his eyes to the ground.

"So be it," he whispered before turning and walking out of the room with Maria following closely behind him.

"David, please—sit down. I don't know what effect this behavior will have on your system," Nicholas said, gesturing to the bed in the center of the room.

David nodded and sat, not knowing what else he could do.

"Stay with him, Nicholas," Reem whispered. "I'll go talk to Mitchal." She slowly followed Jameson out of the bedroom and into the hallway where Mitchal sat. He leaned against the wall, eyes closed and mind deep in meditation as Maria sat next to him massaging his hands.

"We need to talk," Reem whispered as she squatted next to them.

Mitchal's eyes opened to meet hers, his eyes pleading. "Please, don't hurt him. He's afraid and confused. Give him a day at least—please," he pleaded, tears running down his cheeks as he considered his brother's likely fate. "Please."

"I would love to give you more than that—believe me, I would—but we can't stay here much longer. We need to leave before more of the Superiors' men come looking for us," Reem replied, reaching out her hand to wipe the tears from his face.

"What would you have me do?" he asked, glancing quickly between her face and hands.

"As far as I can see, you have two options. We can take him with us, or we can drug him and leave him here. The only problem with the second option is that if he goes back to Admiri—back to the Superiors—they'll likely kill him." She paused, her eyes dropping to the ground at their feet. "We're leaving in two hours. Is that enough time for you to make your decision?" she asked, tilting her head to the side.

"Yes." He nodded. "I'll have my decision by then." He closed his eyes and sighed.

"I'm so sorry," Reem whispered before standing and taking Jameson's hand. Jameson motioned for her to walk with him, and they quickly disappeared down the hall toward the courtyard.

"What are you going to do?" Maria asked Mitchal as he stood and walked into one of the bedrooms. When she didn't hear an answer, she rose and followed him, sitting down beside him on the bed. "Mitchal, talk to me," she whispered.

"How can I possibly decide whether we leave my brother here with no memory or take him with us to Athena where they'll likely keep him in bonds?" he asked, turning to look her in the eye.

"Can't you talk to him? Maybe we take him with us, and in a couple of days, we decide what exactly to do. If he hasn't changed his mind about the savior by the day before we arrive in Athena, we decide whether to leave him or take him," she suggested.

"It's an idea, at least," he replied, shaking his head.

"I'm so sorry, Mitchal," she whispered, running her fingers through his unusually unkempt hair.

He turned to face her again, smiling when his eyes met hers. "I know," he whispered back, lifting his hand to stroke her cheek gently.

She nodded and leaned forward to kiss him before standing and starting to walk away. "I need to speak with the savior. You'll be okay without me for a few minutes, right?" She turned to wink at him as he nodded.

She walked down the hall, slowly making her way to the courtyard where she assumed Reem and Jameson had relocated. She stepped through the large doors into the vast space and paused for a moment when she saw them holding tightly to each other just inside the space.

"Maria," Jameson acknowledged, and Reem pulled away from him to look her in the eye.

"Sorry, I just needed to ask the savior a question," Maria whispered.

"I told you, call me Reem." She paused. "What is it?"

"I don't think you should let Mitchal make this decision on his own. I'm afraid of what it could do to him—deciding his brother's fate."

"I can't make this choice for him, and neither can you. It's up to him," Reem replied.

"Why are you pushing this?" Jameson asked curiously.

Maria shook her head before replying, "I just hate seeing him like this." She ran her fingers through her cropped hair, ready to pull it out by the roots.

"He'll get through it—and so will you. Don't worry." Reem paused. "You should be with him right now. He needs you."

Maria nodded and walked back down the passageway, deciding which of the many things she could say would be the most comforting for the man she'd grown to love over the span of only a few days.

⊱✿⊰

Mitchal sat alone in silence for the few moments after Maria had gone, sitting and thinking about his options. If they took David with them to Athena and he was uncooperative with the people there in any way, they would likely abuse him in order to obtain the information they desired from him, and he would die before he allowed anyone to torture his brother. The only other option would be to leave him here, drug him, erase his memory, and leave him. But he knew David better than to think that he would go to the Humans or the Purists instead of the Advanced. He would go to the Superiors, and they would kill him for failing to complete his task. Either way, it seemed his brother would end up either dead or dying, and it killed Mitchal to even think of it. It was hard enough dealing with David's attitude problems, but now he had to decide his fate, and it seemed that it was going to be harder than he thought.

But a choice had to be made.

Maria walked in the room, slowly dropping to her knees in front of him. "Hey," she whispered, wrapping her arms around his neck and pulling herself close to him.

"Hey," he whispered back, running his fingers through her hair.

She pulled away from him to look him in the eye. "I wanted you to know, whatever decision you make, I'll stand by you."

His eyes dropped to the ground, and he nodded slightly.

"Look at me, Mitchal." Slowly, his eyes moved back up to meet his as she whispered, "Whether you decide to leave your brother or bring him with us, I will stand by you."

"Thank you," he replied, dropping his eyes to the ground by her knees once again.

"I'm so sorry you have to make this decision."

"I've already decided." He paused. "He's coming with us."

"Good to know," Jameson said from the doorway, shocking the couple into turning to look at him. "Sorry." He smiled before walking toward the room where they'd left David.

He walked down the hall, turning into the doorway of David's room to see Reem leaning against the frame, staring into Nicholas's eyes as he once again checked David's pulse. Jameson walked up to her and took her hand, squeezing it gently and smiling when she turned to look at him.

"He's doing well," she whispered in his mind.

"Good," he thought. *"Mitchal's decided."*

"I know." She nodded.

"When are we leaving?"

"As soon as Nicholas is ready."

He nodded and turned to look at Nicholas seconds before the man injected David with the contents of a syringe.

"What was that?" David asked, jumping up to defend himself against Nicholas.

"Something for your heart," he replied, putting his hands up in defense.

"Then why didn't you tell me before you injected it?"

"Because you never would've let me give it to you."

"You're . . . right," David said, falling back to his seat before falling back down onto the bed, completely unconscious.

"What was that?" Jameson asked, his brows furrowing.

"Sedative. He's ready to go now." Nicholas smiled.

"Good, Nicholas. We just need Mitchal and Maria, and then we'll be ready," Reem replied, smiling back at him.

Jameson tugged on Reem's arm, and she followed him back down the hallway, stopping when they reached the room where they'd last seen Mitchal and Maria. "We're ready," Jameson announced to the couple as they stopped in the doorway.

"So are we," Maria replied, standing to her feet and helping Mitchal to do so after her.

"You and Jameson still need to decide on landing sites." Reem smiled.

"Shall we?" Maria asked, staring into Jameson's eyes.

Changing

"Shouldn't take more than one jump, right?" Maria asked as they walked to the courtyard ahead of the others.

"Two. I don't want to jump straight into the city. We'll teleport close, and I'll send Nicholas to check it out before we go in," Jameson replied.

"You still don't trust me?" Her eyebrows furrowed as she laughed.

"I don't trust anyone when it comes to the safety of my wife."

"Yet you're willing to let Nicholas decide if it's safe or not."

"True, but I have my reasons for that."

"Which are?"

"He's as in love with her as I am," he said as they stepped into the courtyard, turning to the right to lean against the wall while they waited for the others to arrive with David's unconscious form.

"That's complicated." She laughed again, turning to lean against the wall next to him. "So what makes you trust him?"

"He's been with us for a while—from a settlement in the mountains. He's knows nothing of betrayal. Unlike you." He winked.

"Right, because I have reason to betray the savior, don't I?" She shook her head unbelievingly.

"You have proven to me in the past that you cannot be trusted, Maria," he said, turning his head to look her in the eye.

"Isn't the fact that I saved your lives enough for you to trust me again?"

"With Reem's new gifts, it's not hard to fight off any Advanced, and Nicholas is better at fighting than he let on—he's only afraid that he'll let her down."

"You wouldn't have survived the two of them if it wasn't me who had teleported them here."

"For that matter, why did you teleport them here? Why not simply take them to Athena?"

"The Prophet insisted that I take them to you. He was afraid that they would find out and kill me—and I'm one of three teleporters we have on our side. We can't afford to lose any."

"Then we'd better get you back to your rebellion," Nicholas said as he walked through the doorway, helping Mitchal to carry his brother.

"Why didn't we just do this from down there?" Mitchal asked as they set David down on the ground.

"Because it's harder to teleport from underground, and I think it would be best if we save our strength, don't you?" Jameson replied.

"Right." Mitchal nodded, dropping to the ground beside David.

"Have you decided on a landing site yet?" Reem asked as she stepped through the doors and walked to Jameson's side, taking his hand.

"Not yet, no," he told her before kissing her hand and turning back to Maria. "Where is the least guarded area of the city?"

"The south side," she replied. "We haven't even come close to fully populating the city yet, but we're starting in the north and moving south. The Prophet decided it would be the best way to go, but that leaves the entire south side empty. He occasionally sends scouts to make sure the Superiors haven't sent anyone into the city to eradicate us." She smiled. "But we've never found anyone there."

"Especially if we teleport into a building, instead of out in the open," Reem added.

"Yes, my thoughts exactly," Maria replied.

"Have a building in mind, Maria?" Jameson asked.

"Yes, actually—I know, I have more than one thought, it must be a strange idea for you." She winked. "There's a building on the outer edge of the city that I think would work perfectly." She pulled a map out of her pocket and showed it to Jameson. "It's only one floor, and there aren't many walls on the inside for us to teleport around. The blueprints look like this." She flipped the map over, drawing him the floor plan of the building.

"Perfect." He smiled, taking the paper from her hands and looking over the map and floor plan.

"Thank you." She smiled back. "Whenever you're ready then."

"Just give me a moment, Maria."

"Take your time, slowpoke." She laughed, turning to walk to where Nicholas and Mitchal sat on the ground beside his brother.

"What's wrong?" Reem whispered in Jameson's ear.

"She's got this too planned out. It's not like her," he replied, his eyes piercing the spot where Maria now stood.

"She doesn't have any ulterior motives. I've already checked for that," she whispered back. "You're right though, something doesn't feel right."

"So what is it? Have you searched her entire mind?"

"Of course I have, Jameson. You know me better than that." She laughed lightly. "Maybe it has something to do with Seth—I don't know."

"Stay close. Just in case." He looked into her eyes, and she nodded.

"We're ready," she said, loud enough for the others to hear her.

"Good," Maria replied cheerily. "I'll take the twins, you take—"

"Yes, I know who I'm taking with me," Jameson cut her off, making her laugh.

Reem guided Jameson to where Nicholas stood next to David, and Maria took Mitchal's hand as she knelt beside his brother. "Ready?" she asked.

Jameson nodded and placed his hand on Nicholas shoulder, teleporting away seconds before Maria followed suit.

⚜

Jameson sat on the ground with Reem next to him, laying her head against his shoulder while she slept. Nicholas had left over an hour ago, and they'd been waiting for him to return before they went any farther into the city.

Reem had quickly fallen asleep next to him after they'd arrived. Maria and Mitchal were keeping an eye on David across the room from them, the couple holding hands as they whispered to each other. He'd attempted to have a conversation with them but quickly found it pointless, as they preferred to talk to each other rather than with him. Since then, he had nothing better to do than to sit and listen to the soft sounds of Reem's light snoring and the whispering of the couple—both of which were soothing enough to make it difficult for him to keep his eyes open.

He'd just given up on consciousness when Nicholas suddenly walked back through the door, his breathing heavy as he hunched over and tried to catch his breath.

"Nicholas," Jameson acknowledged.

Nicholas held up a hand to signal that he needed a moment. "It seems safe. They could use some of the technologies of the settlement to make it better though." He paused. "I spoke to Seth—don't worry, I didn't say anything about any of you—and he assured me that everything is perfectly arranged for Reem's arrival. I believe him, Jameson."

"We'll go in first thing in the morning," Jameson replied, motioning to Reem's unconscious form.

"Right." He nodded before dropping down to the ground a few feet away, still breathing heavily. "How's David?" he asked, turning his head to face Mitchal.

"Still out like a light," Mitchal replied.

"I'll check on him in a moment."

"Take your time." Maria laughed, waking Reem.

Reem lifted her head slightly, yawning as she did so. "Oh. Nicholas," she whispered, starting to stand before Jameson wrapped his arms around her.

"Stay," he whispered in her ear. "You haven't gotten a decent night's sleep in days."

"Athena, the city, we . . . need to go . . . ," she mumbled, allowing him to pull her back down onto the ground, laying her head in his lap.

"Sleep, Reem," he whispered again as her eyes started to close. He shot an angry glare at Maria, and she lifted her hands in defense.

"Sorry," she whispered.

Jameson smiled and shook his head, running his fingers through Reem's hair while she slept.

Nicholas finally rose and walked to David's side, checking his pulse and shining a light into his eyes. "He should wake up in a few hours," he whispered. "Should I inject him again so he stays asleep until shortly before we leave?"

"Just in case," Jameson whispered back.

Nicholas nodded and walked to his medical kit, removing another syringe of sedative before walking back to David and injecting him slowly. "He'll be out until morning."

Jameson nodded slowly, acknowledging Nicholas's remark before leaning his head back against the wall and falling toward sleep once again.

<hr />

Reem woke to the sound of singing filling her ears, and her eyes opened as the voices rose to a crescendo. She sat up and turned to look at Jameson in the glow of the firelight, confusion filling her eyes as she looked into his. "What's going on?" she asked.

"It's the day of the Changing," Maria replied before Jameson could open his mouth to reply. "Seth thought we should celebrate it the same as the others."

"I'd forgotten about the Changing," Reem said, astonished. "Jameson, come outside and dance with me." She smiled, taking his hand and pulling him to his feet.

He smiled back as she led him outside into the empty streets of the city, wrapping his arms around her back and twirling her as he used to do with his Advanced sisters at the ceremonies. Soon they were joined by Mitchal and Maria, dancing as the rebels sang along with the drums and strings that were played.

The rebels sang of Marcus Admiri, of his great victory in creating the treatment that gave them their advancements. Today, so many years ago, the first Advanced man was created. The first treatment was given, and everything was set into motion.

The song continued long past the time the couples grew tired and fell to the ground, laughing and smiling as Nicholas walked out of the room with confusion written all over his face.

Reem then told the stories of the Changing, the stories of old that were traditionally told by the Superiors themselves. The way she spoke was dramatic and smooth, told in the fashion of the best storytellers. She smiled at the faces of the others who stared at her as though they saw something amazing in her eyes as she spoke. When she finished, she lay back on the ground and stared up at the stars with Jameson at her side, running his fingers through her hair.

Maria and Mitchal went back inside to attempt to sleep through the singing of the rebels, while Reem and Jameson stayed outside in the dim starlight, counting the constellations as they remembered their first nights in the caves, nights when there were no stars.

Soon their laughter was joined by the sound of Nicholas snoring as he fell asleep on the ground just outside the building, and they smiled at each other at the thought of never having to fall asleep to the sound of Nicholas snoring after they moved into Athena.

"You should get some sleep," Jameson whispered finally, turning to his side to stare at her face in the glow of the moon.

"I can't. Not with the singing of the Changing. It's too beautiful."

"It's sad," he said, realizing that the songs had reached the ending chapters, the chapters of the war with the Humans.

"I wonder if they'll add something about the beginning of the rebellion," Reem mused.

"They should," he replied. "This will be the beginning of a new world."

Siblings

Seth stood in the underground room below the city, holding Reem's wristband as he considered all of the ways that Maria's mission could have gone sour. He rubbed on the leather strip between his thumb and forefinger as he thought.

"Sir, there's someone here to see you," one of his officers said from the staircase to the ground level.

"Send them down," he replied, not turning to watch as a he heard the sounds of footsteps walking down the staircase.

"Hello, Seth," a female voice said—a voice he recognized.

"Reem Kahrin," he whispered as he turned to face the staircase where Reem stood with Jameson by her side. "It's good to see you again—especially so soon. I hadn't expected you to return with Maria."

"It's Willow, actually, and we haven't decided if we're staying yet," Jameson answered, moving to stand closer to Reem's side.

"Willow, of course." Seth smiled.

"Yes." Reem smiled back at him. "It's good to see you as well, Seth."

He walked closer to them, stopping a few feet away so that he could look Reem in the eye. "Why wouldn't you stay?" he asked, his smile fading.

Reem turned to face Jameson who replied, "I won't have her here unless I'm sure it's completely safe. There are things even you don't know, Seth."

"I'm sure there are—and I don't expect you to tell me—not yet anyway." He smiled again.

"We shall see," Reem replied. "I have an apprentice with me, one I intend to finish training before the end of the month. Is there a place we can use to train?"

"Yes, we have many places you can use, but may I request that you put it off until tomorrow? I would like to show you all that we've done. Perhaps then you can decide whether you will stay or go."

"We shall see," Jameson said, copying Reem.

"Show me." Reem nodded, gesturing for Seth to walk up the stairs ahead of her.

When they reached the top of the steps, a crowd of people had formed, waiting to see if the rumors were true that the savior had arrived.

"You have heard right, my friends," Seth said, speaking to the crowds. "For here before you stands Reem Kahrin, the savior." He turned to face Reem, dipping his head.

The crowd fell silent as Seth turned to lead Reem and Jameson through the city, and Reem found herself letting her mind wander as he informed Jameson of all the security precautions they'd set up for her arrival.

As they walked through the now crowded streets of Athena, Reem's mind went back to their arrival in the city all those weeks ago—it was strange to think that it had only been weeks since she'd come to Athena to aid them in the war—and to the destruction of the people. She found herself imagining what it would have been like if they had been successful in the first place, what it would have been like if the city had never fallen, if she had not been forced to use the bioweapon. Thoughts of her actions that day still plagued her mind when she slept, and even with Jameson's comforting thoughts, she found herself continuing to lose sleep over the deaths of so many by her hand—a hand that, even now, hovered over the second vial of the bioweapon stored in her hip pocket.

Jameson held firmly to her other hand as they walked through the city, unwilling to put much distance between them as he took in the sheer mass of the crowds that had formed to see his wife. He would never allow any of them to harm her, and the best way he knew to keep her safe was to keep her beside him. As she had said all those weeks ago when they were on their way back to Admiri, his gifts were defensive in nature, and hers were the offensive. He didn't have the ability to protect her from danger, only to hide her from it.

They walked through the city at a slow pace, Seth leading the way to the center of their camp on the northern side of Athena. He informed Jameson of the places where they'd set up guard towers, each with four Advanced rebels to look out over the outskirts of their camp for newcomers or invaders. They'd reached fifteen thousand people not long ago, and more were on their way from Admiri and Mettirna. It seemed that more than Seth had first assumed were keen on escaping the rule of the Superiors for the more lenient rule of the one they called their savior.

As they walked, people stopped and stared at Reem, amazed that they were now so close to the woman who had saved each of their lives at one point or another. In her day, Reem had been to all of the cities, fighting on the side of the Advanced—the Superiors—and she had never lost a battle. She was the best warrior that the Superiors had, and Jameson assumed that this was what had led to her being called their savior in the first place. Before the destruction of Athena, people never spoke against the Superiors—not even in private. But now that Reem had been called a traitor, now that the one they called their savior was sentenced to death, they found themselves willing to risk everything to start anew, ready to follow Reem wherever she went.

Reem stood close by Jameson as Seth led them through the city of people, knowing that he preferred it that way, and found herself afraid not only for her own life but for that of her child among so many unfamiliar faces.

"Seth, may I ask you something?" Reem asked as they walked—the first she'd spoken since they left the underground chambers.

"Of course." He turned to smile at her.

"Has there been a young woman—a shape-shifter—here since you started your rebellion?" she asked, and Jameson turned to look at her knowingly.

"Hmm . . . A shape-shifter, you say?" Seth replied, stroking his chin as he thought. "None that I can think of. Someone in particular you seek?"

"Just an old friend."

"She'll be here, don't worry," Jameson thought.

"I'm afraid for her, Jameson. What if something happened? I promised Nicholas that she would be here," she replied.

"She'll be here," he replied aloud.

"Where is she from? Perhaps she'll be arriving with our new recruits this evening," Seth added.

"She's from a small settlement near Admiri," Jameson told him, not wanting to reveal the place that Suri had come to know as home over the past years. "Where are your recruits arriving from?"

"Mettirna, I'm afraid. We haven't had many come from Admiri as of yet, but we've had to work harder to keep our movements secret from the Great Superior within those walls. It seems the Superiors of Mettirna aren't as controlling, I suppose you could say, as those of Admiri."

"I'm aware of that, yes." Reem nodded. "Without Marcus's watchful eye over them at all hours of the day, they found that being more laid back suited both themselves and their people."

"Come, let me show you the place we've set up for you," Seth announced as they reached the central spire of the city—the most heavily guarded area of the entire settlement as far as Jameson could tell. Seth walked up the steps into the central tower with Jameson and Reem close behind and showed them down the main hall to the largest room in the tower—the place once reserved for the highest Superior of Athena. "We all agreed that this would be the best place for our leader to live," Seth said as he showed them into the chambers.

"I don't know, Seth. I never wanted this," Reem said softly as they walked through the rooms.

"This is the safest place in the city. Trust me," Seth urged.

"I can't live in a place reserved for leaders when I do not feel fit to lead." She shook her head.

"Jameson, talk to her. I'll leave you alone for a moment—my men and I have a raid to plan," Seth said as he walked back down the stairs to the exit.

"What do you think?" she asked when Seth had gone.

"I think it's up to you now. I can keep you safe here—Seth can keep you safe. What do you think?" Jameson asked in response, turning to stand in front of her and look into her eyes.

"I think it's a beautiful city, a wonderful place to raise our child. But I'm not fit to lead these people, Jameson. I'm not who they think I am."

"Yes, you are—and saying that only makes it more true." He paused. "Tell me, what is the first thing you would do if you were their leader?"

She shrugged. "I would make an alliance with the Purists and with the settlement in the mountains. There's no need for us to fight with either of them," she replied, her eyes dropping to the ground at her feet. "But would that be the best decision for these people? Would they agree with me that peace is what we need most?"

"I think they would, yes. We do need peace, Reem. The world has been at war for too long—the people are weary of it," he told her, placing his hands on either side of her face so that she would look into his eyes.

"I don't know about this, Jameson." She shook her head.

"Reem, you're the one the people have chosen to lead them. You know that." He smiled as he looked into her eyes.

"No, the warrior Reem Kahrin is who they chose. I'm Reem Willow, the mother. I am not who they chose anymore," she replied, tears forming in her eyes for the life she lost.

"You are *Reem*, and that's all that matters to them." He stared at her, his bright green eyes piercing into hers as he spoke.

"You really want to do this, Jameson?" she asked, unable to look away from his eyes.

"It's what you want, Reem. I know you well enough to know that." He smiled, running his fingers through her hair.

She smiled slightly as he slid his hand to her stomach.

"What does he think?"

"He doesn't care. He's happy now." Her smile brightened as she listened to the thoughts of her unborn child.

"Then do what makes you happy, Reem. I'm not going anywhere, except with you."

"I would follow you anywhere, both of you," Nicholas added, startling both of them.

"As will I," a female voice whispered from one of the side chambers.

All three turned toward the voice as Suri stepped from the doorway, smiling brightly as she stared into her sister's eyes. "All is not lost," she said.

"Suri," Reem whispered, letting go of Jameson's hand for the first time since they'd entered the settlement to run to her sister's side and embrace her. "I thought you hadn't come. Seth said there weren't any—"

"They don't know I'm here yet," Suri replied, cutting her off. "Had I known exactly when you were getting here, I would have met you in the outskirts."

"How?" Reem asked.

"The beauty of being a shape-shifter, sister, is that I can take any form I like for any length of time without anyone noticing me." She smiled, pulling away from Reem so that she could look her in the eye. "You will make a wonderful leader, Reem."

"I'm not so sure." Reem's eyes fell to the ground once more.

"I am," Nicholas replied, walking forward until he stood a few feet away from them.

"Nicholas," Suri whispered, surprise edging her voice slightly, "it's good to see you again." She released her sister and stepped up to him, gazing fondly into his eyes.

"Suri." His eyes stared back into hers, and Reem smiled as she read the thoughts that filled his mind.

"Told you," she whispered just loud enough for them to overhear as Jameson walked back up to her and wrapped his arms around her waist.

"Family reunion?" He laughed, kissing the side of her head lightly.

<hr/>

"Sir, rumor has it that the traitor has joined the rebellion," the guard said, dipping his head as he reentered Marcus's chambers.

"That's not possible. I sent my best men," Marcus replied.

"The reports say that the people of Mettirna are amassing to leave for the rebellion now that their savior has joined in the fight," he replied.

"Do not speak of such nonsense. Leave me," Marcus commanded before the guard dipped his head and left as quickly as his feet would take him.

Marcus stood from his throne and walked to the balcony, watching as the people swept up the remains of the décor from the nights celebration.

Surprisingly, he'd actually enjoyed himself last night. He'd spent the majority of his time with three young women, so he had plenty to keep himself busy with. The trio had left his chambers late this morning, and now he felt more alone than usual—which was a strange feeling for him.

Could it be possible that Reem had actually survived? That David had failed? He still hadn't heard word from the twins nor had he heard anything from the scouts he'd sent to locate them. It was very strange for him, being out of the loop. But he couldn't bring himself to believe that the rumors were true—that Reem Kahrin had joined the rebellion. If that were true, then he had much larger issues than he had at first thought. For if she had joined with the rebels, it was unlikely that so many people would remain faithful to him. Many of them referred to her as their savior, even now. He knew that soon a war would begin if he didn't rid himself of Reem Kahrin for good.

"Guard!" he yelled as he turned and walked back to his throne, sitting down as the guard walked through the giant double doors.

"Sir?" the guard said, dipping his head.

"Have you located any teleporters yet?"

"Not yet, sir. I'm sorry, we will try harder. I'm sure there are teleporters in the city willing to do whatever you ask of them."

"Don't bother. Call for Brittany—she'll be able to complete this mission successfully."

"Yes, sir," the guard said, keeping his eyes on the ground as he quickly exited the room to complete his orders.

Within the hour, the guard returned. "Brittany to see you, sir."

"Let her in," Marcus said from his position atop his throne.

The guard dipped his head once again and exited. When he returned, a middle-aged woman stood by his side, eyes as white as snow and hair dark as the night sky. "You sent for me, Superior," she said, her voice even and cool as she knelt to the ground.

"Brittany Green, it's good to see you again," he replied.

⁂

When Seth returned, he was surprised to find the inquisitive young man he'd met the day before, along with another young woman, alongside Reem and Jameson. He walked into the chambers slowly, his eyes darting back and forth between the two couples as he put the pieces together.

Reem and Jameson stood together on the balcony, looking out over what little of the city was populated by the rebellion, while the two others leaned against the far wall of the chamber, whispering to each other.

Seth walked up to the young man and laughed. "I suppose I should've known that you were checking the security for Reem's arrival. I've never heard of anyone so paranoid joining a rebellion."

"I'm sorry for the deception," Nicholas replied, smiling.

"As am I," the young woman added, holding out her hand for Seth to shake. "I am Suri. I've been living among you for several days now."

Seth took her hand and shook it. "You are the shape-shifter Reem spoke of," he said.

"That would be me." Her smile brightened.

"If I may, what settlement are you from? Reem indicated that you were from somewhere near Admiri, but it was my understanding that there were no Advanced settlements other than the city itself on that continent," he asked, tilting his head to one side.

"I'm not from an Advanced settlement," she answered. "Originally, I am from India. But after the war broke out, I moved to a small settlement in the mountains of Europe."

"I was under the impression there were no settlements there either. I'm sorry, my sources must be incorrect," Seth said.

"We've kept it secret from most everyone," Nicholas replied. "It's a place where there is no difference between human and Advanced. We all lived as equals."

"I take it you're from this settlement as well?"

"Yes." He smiled. "Suri and I met there. I'm a doctor, and she was working as a nurse in our hospital."

"And how were you separated?" Seth paused. "I'm sorry, it's not often that I come across information that I don't already know. When it does happen, I like to find out as much about it as I can." He shrugged.

"It's not a problem." Suri smiled. "I left. It's as simple as that. I left, and when I ran into Reem in my camp, I sent her to the settlement, promising that I would meet her here when she promised to bring Nicholas. Luckily, I found a teleporter willing to drop me off a short distance from the city a few days ago, so it wasn't much of a problem."

"Pardon, camp?" Seth asked, his eyebrows furrowing slightly.

"I lived with the Purists not far away from Admiri. They were like family to me, but they didn't know about my gifts," she replied.

"Ahh . . . I see. I'm sorry, it must have been difficult for you to leave them," Seth replied.

"I'm with my real family now." She glanced to Reem and back again.

"Let me guess, sisters?" Seth asked. "But I thought she was the only one in her family on whom the treatment was successful . . ."

"She thought that, yes," Suri answered. "No one knew I was Advanced—other than myself, of course—until I moved to the settlement. I was young. I didn't want to be sent to the camps, even though I knew I would be with my sister there. But when the war broke out, I heard about the settlement—by chance, really—and I knew I belonged there."

"That must have been a difficult life for you." Seth paused. "I'm sorry, I sound like a therapist, don't I?" He laughed.

"It's fine, really," Suri replied, turning her head as Reem and Jameson moved from the balcony to join them.

"I see you've met my sister," Reem said as they stopped a few feet away.

"Indeed." Seth smiled. "Have you made your decision yet?"

"I have." She turned to Jameson, waiting for him to elaborate.

"We'll stay, but we may require more security than what you already have here," Jameson said. "We also want to meet all of the guards—we want to be sure that we can trust them." He casually placed his hand on Reem's stomach.

"Of course," Seth replied. "I can understand how that would be an issue—especially with the child on the way." He smiled brightly, winking when Reem's shocked eyes met his.

"I forgot how intuitive you are," she said.

"You're not," Suri exclaimed, her hand moving to her mouth as it dropped open.

"You didn't tell your own sister?" Seth laughed mockingly.

"I hadn't gotten around to it yet, no," Reem replied, glancing away from her sister to shoot Seth an annoyed glare before looking back into Suri's eyes. "I'm sorry. I don't know why I didn't tell you sooner."

Suri moved from against the wall and approached her sister, placing her hands delicately on Reem's stomach when Jameson moved his hands. "Do you know what it is yet?" she asked, forgetting about the general lack of technology throughout the world.

"No, we don't." Reem laughed, slapping her sister's hand lightly.

"The settlement has the technology for you to find out, you know." She looked up to glare into Reem's eyes.

"I'm not going anywhere, Suri," Reem whispered. "Besides, it's more fun to be surprised." She winked.

"More importantly, how is it even possible?" Seth asked, directing his question at Jameson.

"I don't know," Jameson answered.

"But I do know that it's not the first thing that the Superiors have lied to us about," Reem added, turning to smile slightly at Jameson while Suri continued to stare into her eyes in awe.

Jameson took Reem's hand in his. "My wife seems to have developed a third gift—naturally, that is," he said as he turned to look into Seth's wonder-filled eyes.

"What is it?" Seth asked while Nicholas pried Suri off Reem, laughing when she wouldn't go easily.

"It appears she has the ability to remove gifts from Advanced—permanently," Jameson answered.

"And if you were to use this gift on a human?" Seth asked.

"It would likely kill them. But Jameson is helping me to control my gifts better. The only downside is that I become exhausted easily—especially with the little one," Reem replied, placing her hands on her stomach and smiling.

"I would love to study its effects," Seth mused, stroking his chin.

"That could be arranged," Nicholas said. "We have someone with us on whom Reem used her gift a few days ago."

"Do you?" Seth asked, his eyes lighting.

"Yes," Nicholas replied. "I'll take you to him."

Nicholas guided Seth back to the building on the outskirts where they'd left David, Mitchal, and Maria that morning. When they reached the building, they found Maria outside guarding the door, while Mitchal spoke in a loud voice to his brother.

"Sit down, David!" he commanded, grabbing his brother by the shoulders and yelling to his face.

"Please, David, calm down," Maria added calmly from her position in the doorway.

"The man has a brother who's also with us," Nicholas said when he noticed the confusion on Seth's face.

"Do you have any siblings, Nicholas?" Seth asked as they stepped up to the doorway and cautiously peered inside to see Mitchal holding his brother on the ground.

"No, thankfully, I do not. You?" Nicholas replied.

"I do actually, though I don't know where she is. We never got along," Seth said.

"Does she have any gifts?" Nicholas asked.

"Yes, she naturally developed a gift similar to mine, one that allows her to think ahead of other people—see into the future, some would say—and another gift she received from someone like Jameson. She's a hunter, I suppose you could say."

"What's her name?"

"Brittany."

Approaching

Brittany knelt on one knee atop the outer wall on the outskirts of Admiri, watching as the sun dipped under the horizon, fading from shades of orange and yellow into deeper hues of purple and blue. She had her sniper rifle and her hunting blade both slung over her shoulder along with a small bag containing a single full canteen, enough food to feed her for two days, and a pair of night-vision goggles, along with various smaller weapons and spare ammunition.

She'd sat on the outskirts of the city for the majority of the day, waiting for the sun to dip below the horizon so that she could leave under the cover of night. It would take time for her to reach her final destination, but she always preferred leaving under the cover of darkness. As the sun dropped, she stood to her feet and started walking—she had a long way to go. She headed south, walking as quickly as she could, knowing it would take days.

She had always avoided accepting tasks from the Superiors that would force her to cross paths with her brother, but in this case, she made an exception. This task was the greatest one she had ever been asked to do, and she would not fail it. She'd only ever failed one of her tasks, and even that was due to a fluke and was easily erased from her history after one heated night with Marcus Admiri. She'd hated that night, but she knew that Marcus had always thought of her as a beautiful woman, and she knew it would be the only way to keep herself from being dropped from the short list of the Superiors task force.

As she walked across the African desert, she listened to the sounds of the nightlife around her, the sounds of the people of Admiri as they prepared for the long night ahead of them. At least tonight, there would be no celebrating in the streets. To some extent, Brittany wished that she'd been able to stay one more night in the city—at least it would be a night of peace compared to the last night she'd spent there, a night filled with horrid dancing and loud obnoxious singing.

She quickened her pace as she considered her mission and the fact that Marcus had chosen her above all the rest, her feet sure as she walked the distance.

Reem dropped to the floor in the middle of the large center chamber of the central spire of the city, closing her eyes as she dropped into a deep meditation. She'd placed her usual objects around in the circle of the room, her knives, a few unloaded pistols, and rods of various sizes; and one by one, she began lifting them off the ground with her mind, twirling the knives in small circles and whipping the rods around in large patterns with force enough to knock a man from his feet. She dropped her head back and pointed her face to the high ceiling of the room, lifting the objects high into the sky as she envisioned the room from her gifts' point of view. She allowed her gifts to take control, to do as they pleased with the objects she allowed them to carry; and in her mind's eye she watched as they fended off invisible attackers and blocked blows from foes unseen to the naked eye. She watched as her gifts played out one of many battle scenarios she'd learned in her years while working for the Superiors, allowing them to fight off the enemy as they pleased.

"Still sparring with yourself these days?" Mitchal asked, cutting off her concentration slightly.

She lowered the objects to the ground as slowly as possible, setting them gracefully on the cold stone floor before turning her head to face the man who'd spoken to her.

"I am merely allowing my gifts to remember what it is like to fight. I don't know when the time may come that I will need to defend myself," she replied, watching as Mitchal walked to one of the rods and picked it up off the ground, hitting it against the stone floor lightly as though he were testing its strength.

"In my training, we were taught that fighting is for the weak and that thinking is for the wise," he whispered, barely loud enough for her to hear. "But that never stopped me from learning how to fight." He smiled, looking up from the rod in his hands as Reem got back to her feet.

"I was taught the same—by my father. But I never was one to listen." She smiled back. "I taught myself how to fight. It only came more naturally to me after I received my gifts."

"I'd heard you were an excellent fighter in your day, that the Superiors had called on you for many tasks and that you'd never failed one."

"My band was unmarked." She nodded.

"Sparring with you must be quite the experience." His smile brightened.

"If it were not for Jameson, I would spar with you now." She paused, her smile fading. "But in a sense, he's right. I shouldn't be sparring. Not now anyway." She smiled again.

"He's very protective of you, isn't he?"

She nodded. "Honestly though, I'm okay with it. It makes me feel safe knowing that he's taken so many precautions." She turned and started picking the objects up off the floor, placing the knives back in their sheaths and the pistols back in their holsters before putting them in her backpack.

"So riddle me this. If you have this gift that allows you to move these things around like you just were, why not use it to put them all back in the bag?" Mitchal laughed as he started gathering the rods from the floor and leaning them against the curved wall.

"Because I do not want to exhaust myself and because I am not as lazy as some would assume," she replied, laughing musically.

He laughed along with her as he took a seat on the floor, leaning against the wall. "Now that we've arrived, what do you think of the city?" he asked as she sat next to him.

"Athena was always a beautiful city. Once it's fully populated again, it will be back to its full grandeur," she replied. "But I would love to be walking in the city streets rather than staying here all day."

"Then why don't you?" His brow furrowed.

"Jameson asked that I not leave until he's certain that it's safe for me to do so." She smiled slightly. "He means well."

"I'm sure he does."

"What about you? Why aren't you off with Maria?"

"She already has a place here—she's gone to do her appointed task of acquiring food as well as transporting several of the new recruits into the city. It seems that their numbers are growing rapidly now that you've arrived." He nudged her with his elbow. "My gifts, however, are not well suited for anything beyond politics."

"I'm sure Seth could use your help with the new recruits." She smiled.

"I thought I said not to let anyone in," Jameson joked as he walked into the chamber with Suri at his side.

"No, you said not to let anyone I don't know in," Reem replied, smiling as she turned from Mitchal to look him in the eye, holding out her hand for him to help her up.

He walked to her and took her hand, helping her get to her feet as Mitchal stood beside her. "Miss me?"

"No, of course not. I had Mitchal to keep me company." She winked, taking his hand in hers and kissing it lightly. "What news?" she asked.

"Seth's guards all seem trustworthy. Did you find anything off with any of them?" he asked in response.

"I didn't see any abnormalities, no." She shook her head. "Has Seth found any new guards?"

"A few, yes. It seems the majority of the people are willing to guard the building, but the majority of those have no idea what they're doing when it comes to protection detail. Seth says we can train them, but it would take a few months at least."

"So we either deal with the amount of guards here for the time being until we can train more or we leave and have Seth train them while we're gone."

"Right." He nodded.

"What of my brother?" Mitchal asked.

Jameson turned to Mitchal as he spoke. "Seth says he should still be able to take on gifts, but he's still not willing to agree to our terms. He hasn't been very forthcoming yet either, but we don't need him to be if Reem wants to help." He turned back to Reem and winked, smiling slightly.

"Are there any other telepaths in the city?" she asked, slowly turning back and forth between the men.

"None with abilities as great as yours," Jameson replied. "There are a few, but they need their subject to be completely focused in order to determine their memories. They can read their immediate thoughts, but nothing more than that. And it seems David is very good at not thinking about things that he doesn't want us to know. He's been thinking about all of his past tasks—nothing more, nothing less."

"I'll go see him tomorrow." She smiled sweetly, looking into Mitchal's eyes. "Don't worry. He won't be harmed as long as I can help it."

"Thank you," he replied, dropping his eyes to the ground. "Am I allowed to see him yet?"

"Of course," Jameson said. "He's being held in the underground portion of the city—we thought that that would be the safest place for the time being."

Mitchal nodded slowly. "I'll leave you alone then." He turned and walked away, and Reem leaned back against the wall as she watched him leave.

As soon as he was out of sight, she spoke. "He's a good man."

"So it would seem," Jameson replied, moving to stand directly in front of her as he took her hands in his. "He appreciates your help."

"I know," she replied, turning to look him in the eye. "Anything else you should be telling me?" Her eyebrows rose.

"Hmm . . . Well, you should know that I am completely in love with you." He winked, leaning in to kiss her neck as his hands moved to her waist.

"You know that's not what I meant." She laughed lightly, moving her hands to his chest to push him away slightly so she could look into his eyes. "Talk to me."

"Why do you make me say it when you can read it in my mind?" he asked.

"You know why."

He smiled slightly, his bright green eyes staring into hers. "Seth got word from Mettirna. They're sending a squad here for a threat assessment. He's concerned that if we kill them straight off, it would be like starting a war with the rest of the Advanced—I agree with him."

"Then what do you want to do?"

"I think it might be better if we stay out of sight." He dropped his voice to a whisper. "And we shouldn't tell anyone else about the baby unless we have to. You'll be safer if they don't know."

"Okay." She nodded. "Okay. What do you want me to do?"

"Stay here in the chambers. I'll have someone we trust with you at all times, at least when I can't be here, but I'll try and stay here as much as I can."

"You're in as much danger as I am, remember?" she whispered, wrapping her arms around his waist as she pulled herself into his chest. "I don't want anything happening to you either."

"I know," he whispered back. "Don't worry, I'll be fine." He kissed the top of her head lightly.

"Nicholas just told me—the Superiors of Mettirna sent a squad?" Suri said loudly as she entered the room, stopping several feet away from them and crossing her arms.

"Yes. Yes, they did," Jameson replied, turning to look her in the eye.

"When will they be here?" she asked.

"Approximately four weeks."

"Enough time for you to find a safer place for my sister."

"I'm not going anywhere, Suri. I'm not. I hate not knowing where I'm going to sleep every night," Reem replied, pulling away from Jameson to lean against the wall once more. "I don't want to run."

"What if they find out about you—about the baby?" Suri asked.

"They're not going to find out," Jameson said.

"What if they do?" She took a few steps toward them, stopping when she stood beside Jameson. "Then what? What will happen to my sister then, Jameson? What?"

"Do not speak to my husband like that," Reem commanded, moving to stand between the two.

"Don't tell me how to speak, sister," Suri replied bitterly. "I'm only concerned for your safety. If anything, you should be happy that I am here for you."

Reem was about to reply when she felt Jameson's restraining arm wrap around her waist, pulling her into him as he whispered in her ear, "Don't fight with your sister on my account."

She laughed lightly and leaned her head back on his shoulder. "Thank you," she whispered.

"Jameson, tell me you won't let anything happen to her," Suri pleaded.

"I won't," he replied. "I could never live with myself if I did." He shook his head slightly.

"Then take her away. Please."

"I won't make her leave."

"Then may I speak to her for a moment? Alone," she asked, raising her eyebrows.

"Of course." He kissed Reem's temple before releasing her and walking slowly out of the room onto the balcony.

"Thank you."

"What is it?" Reem asked.

"Why aren't you leaving—really?" Suri asked.

"I told you, I don't want to keep running."

"What's keeping you here? You'd be safer if you left—you know that, and yet somehow you've convinced yourself and Jameson that you're better off staying here. What's going on?" She placed her hands on Reem's shoulders as she stared into her eyes.

"I'm not going to repeat myself." Reem shrugged, shaking her head.

"Please, Reem. I know you better than that."

"I'm staying because I can't leave," she whispered, her eyes dropping to the ground.

"What do you mean?"

"I mean, I can't leave. That's all there is to it." She glanced back into Suri's eyes before looking back to the ground.

"What aren't you telling us, Reem?" Her eyebrows furrowed.

"It's nothing you need to concern yourself with, Suri." She turned and started to walk away when Suri took her by the hand and stopped her.

"Talk to me, Reem. Please."

Reem shook her head and walked away, joining Jameson on the balcony. She walked up behind him and wrapped her arms around his waist, smiling when he linked his fingers with hers and turned around to face her. "I think we should talk," she whispered.

"Okay," he replied, confusion sweeping across his face.

She took his hand and led him through the main chamber and into their bedroom, sitting down on the bed and gesturing for him to do the same. As he did so, she pulled her legs up onto the bed and turned to face him.

"I'm guessing this has something to do with Suri's questions," Jameson said.

She nodded slowly, still looking down onto the sheets rather than looking into his eyes. "I can't leave."

He furrowed his eyebrows before he spoke. "I know—it's fine. We'll stay, and we'll make sure that both you and the baby are safe," he replied.

"No, that's not what I mean." She paused, lifting her head to look into his eyes. "I mean, I can't leave." She paused again, looking back to the sheets. "The baby doesn't like teleporting, and he doesn't like when I walk too much. I didn't want to say anything, but after the last time we teleported, I knew I wouldn't be able to do it again. It was all I could do, not to let you see how much pain I was in." She cringed, her hair falling into her face.

"Why didn't you tell me?" he asked, lifting his hand to brush her hair back behind her ear. "I never would have teleported you here if I had known—"

"I know—and that's why I didn't say anything. I knew we needed to get here quickly, or else we'd have to make a different decision concerning David, and I didn't want to have to put Mitchal through that. Plus Maria was insistent

234

that we reach the city as soon as possible, and I thought she was right, and I didn't want to—"

"Reem. Stop." He put his hand under her chin to lift her face. "Look at me."

She lifted her eyes to look into his, the silver flecks shimmering in the light.

"I never would have teleported you here if you'd told me—I don't care if everyone else thinks that we need to get somewhere quickly. I don't want to hurt you or our child." His green eyes pierced into hers.

She nodded slightly, tears forming in her eyes as she absorbed his words. She continued to nod as Jameson wrapped his arms around her and ran his fingers through her hair. "I'm sorry," she whispered.

"Don't be," he replied.

⚜

Brittany walked as quickly as she could—not having stopped at all for the past eighteen hours. She'd already made it halfway to the coast where a boat was waiting to take her across to North America. The trip across the ocean would be the slowest she would travel on her entire journey, and she did not look forward to stopping to sit on a boat for three days.

Marcus had sent her to deal with the rebels, and deal with them she would. She'd been taught in the art of hiding her thoughts, so as long as the traitors' gifts hadn't progressed further than Marcus thought, she would be fine. Marcus had asked that Seth be brought back to Admiri—alive. It wasn't something she was accustomed to, but she knew she could do it, especially since Seth was her brother. He wouldn't try to kill her any more than she would try to teach him to speak Old French. They knew each other too well for anything like that. He knew that she would not hesitate to kill him, and she knew that his gifts grew by the day, that he would be one of the very few who could defend themselves well against an opponent such as her; but they both knew that if it came down to a fight, she would be the victor. She had twelve years over him after all. He wouldn't stand a chance against her superior skill.

She let her mind wander in fantasy of what it would be like to challenge her brother to a duel, what it would be like to see him fail, to slice his throat with her blade or fire a bullet into his skull. Better yet, she would kill him with her bare hands—it would be more satisfactory that way.

She continued to stare into the horizon toward the coast—toward her destination. The boat there was manned by Advanced, one of the very few that they had. Marcus had arranged for it to pick her up and take her across the ocean, landing her as close to Athena as possible. There she would leave its company and complete her mission before returning for it to take her and her brother back across the ocean to where Marcus awaited with open arms. He'd even given her a goodbye kiss before she left—one she'd lingered into for a moment, allowing him to think that she might actually be interested in him before she left to complete her task. No doubt when she returned, he would want more than a kiss. And like the faithful child she was, she would give him what he wanted, and she might even tell her brother so that he could feel that much worse about the past that had forever set them apart as learner and killer.

She would die before she left her post with the Superiors to join in his blasphemous rebellion.

His gift must have driven him insane.

Seth paced along the span of his quarters, knowing that he was missing something and knowing that it was his intelligence that was stopping him from seeing it. Something wasn't right, and he couldn't place it. He'd been pacing for hours now, and still he didn't know what it was that was driving sleep from his mind and forcing him to consider and reconsider everything that had happened over the past few days, searching for inconsistencies. Something was off—or something was missing. He wasn't sure which.

Something wasn't right.

Something was coming.

Or some*one*.

He wasn't sure which.

Visions

For the third night in a row since arriving in Athena, Reem woke with a start after having another vision from her child. This time she saw the squad arriving in the city, saw a woman arriving with them, a woman shrouded in mystery. Someone she couldn't see and couldn't place in the context of her vision. The woman didn't belong there. She wasn't supposed to be a part of her vision, but still somehow there she was, standing on the edge of the horizon, poised and ready to strike. Reem tried to see the woman's face, but she'd hidden it from sight. She was hiding from something—or someone. Reem couldn't tell why, but she knew that the figure didn't belong. Even the baby knew that the woman wasn't supposed to be a part of the vision, yet somehow she'd made her way into it. It wasn't possible, but still somehow there she was.

Reem sat up in bed, rubbing her neck as she considered all of the content in her vision. Something wasn't right. It wasn't what they thought it would be. Something had changed.

She felt Jameson's hand in her hair, felt his lips brushing against her shoulder lightly. "Another vision?" he whispered, kissing her neck.

She nodded and turned to kiss his lips. "Go back to sleep. I didn't mean to wake you."

"I was awake."

"Why?" she asked, moving to lean her back against the wall.

"Couldn't sleep." He shrugged. "I think Suri's right. It's not safe to have you here. But I don't know how we can move you anywhere for the time being." He leaned against the wall beside her.

"We'll have to find a way to make here safe." She took his hand in hers and laid her head on his shoulder. "I'm sorry this is so difficult."

"Don't be." He kissed her hand. "It's not your fault. The baby has the right to decide what it does and doesn't like." He laughed lightly. "I won't let anything happen to you, Reem. To either of you."

"I know," she replied.

"What did you see?" he asked finally, running his fingers through her hair gently.

"I'm not sure." She paused. "It had to do with the squad from Mettirna, but something was off. I'm not sure really, but it seemed like there was someone there who wasn't supposed to be. I don't know if the vision was incorrect or if I just can't see who she is, but something is definitely off with her."

"What did she look like? Someone we know?" he asked curiously.

"I don't know. She was . . . blurry. Out of focus. I don't know why, but I couldn't see her face no matter how hard I tried." Her hands moved to her face, massaging her temples as she thought. "I've never seen anything like that in my visions before." She shook her head.

"What do you think it means?"

"Maybe she won't actually be there—maybe I felt like she wasn't supposed to be there because she's not going to be. Maybe her image leaked in from another vision." She shrugged.

"Or maybe she's someone with a gift that prevents you from seeing her," he added. "We'll have to be more careful in any case."

"I don't know why, but she makes me feel afraid." She shivered. "Something is coming, and I don't think it's going to be good."

"I won't let anything happen to you, Reem," he whispered, wrapping his arm around her shoulders to pull her closer to him. "I promise."

They sat in silence for several minutes, Jameson holding her tightly against his side while she tried not to think about the woman who had haunted her dreams.

"What about the squad? What happens with them?" Jameson asked, breaking the silence.

"It's not what we thought. They're not coming to determine how much of a threat we are." She paused. "It's all tied to the woman somehow. In my vision, she was being accused by one of the squad members, and she was laughing. She'd shrouded herself in darkness, her laugh was evil and yet somehow beautiful. I wish I could've seen her face." She shook her head. "The people from Mettirna obviously knew who she was, but no one here did—or at least, no one in my vision did."

"So she will be here then. The squad was accusing someone, and if not her, then who?" he asked in response.

"There was someone standing behind her. They could have been accusing him, but I dismissed the thought after seeing her. I suppose it's possible that they were accusing him though."

"Who was it?"

"Seth," she replied, turning to look him in the eye.

Seth continued to pace, though now he walked on the edge of the city, taking his turn at the watchtower while he paced. He could still feel that something was wrong, that something bad was about to happen, but he couldn't place it. His intelligence continued to get the better of him the more that his gifts continued to grow.

Something was coming. That was all he knew.

He watched as the sun rose over the horizon, smiling when its warmth touched his face, the heat spreading through his body. He watched as the sun highlighted the incoming clouds, making the sky shine with bright reds and yellows.

A storm was on the horizon—the first since the beginning of the rebellion. He knew that storms were common in the region, especially after the bombings, but he worried that its brutality would cause many to leave the city for good. The storms would cause many to wish that they hadn't left their cities. Admiri was always bathed in warmth and Mettirna was protected on the inside from the harsh weather conditions of the Arctic.

Many would desire to leave, and perhaps many would leave. But many more would stay now that Reem had finally arrived. She was the whole reason for the rebellion, and without her, it would fall apart.

The entire rebellion revolved around the peoples preconceived notions that somehow Reem would be the one to end the war with the humans, and many of them assumed that she would bring peace through war—after all, that was how the Superiors always did things—but Reem had other ideas. She would bring peace by following her heart, by dissolving the animosity between themselves and the others of the planet—and she would likely start by forming an alliance with the Purists. Since her sister had lived among them for so long, it would be easier for her to make an alliance with them—they would already know that she could be trusted.

Reem always followed her heart no matter what she did. Even when speaking to her husband, she wouldn't allow him to do anything that went against her well-grounded principles.

She was both a lover and a fighter, and the people would love her no matter which path she finally chose. Likely, she would live in the limelight, bringing her child into the world under the threat of the Superiors unless she could put an end to it before the end of her nine months.

They had a lot of work to do.

"Sir, Reem Willow has sent for you," a messenger announced, snapping Seth out of his reverie. "I will take your post until a proper replacement arrives."

"Thank you." Seth smiled, patting him firmly on the shoulder before running down the many steps to the ground level and briskly walking toward Reem and Jameson's home.

He slowed when he reached the staircase that led into the building, taking the steps slowly until he reached the circular main chamber of the tower. He turned to his right and quickly made his way to the balcony on which Reem and Jameson stood, looking out over the city.

"You sent for me?" he asked as he stepped into the sunlight.

"Yes, I did," Reem replied, turning to smile at him. "We need to talk."

"Of course. Shall we go to the meeting room?" Seth asked.

When both Jameson and Reem nodded their response, Seth led the way back through the main chamber, walking almost straight across the room into the meeting place that once belonged to the Superiors of Athena. A grand wooden table inlayed with gold sat in the center of the standard rectangular room, surrounded by seven grandiose chairs—three on each side and one at the head for the Superior of the highest rank. The ceiling was made of glass, and the walls lined with unlit torches, light shining down into the room from its skylight. Jameson and Reem each took their seats on one of the sides of the table, and Jameson motioned for Seth to sit across from them.

Seth did as he was asked, his eyes filled with both confusion and curiosity as he spoke. "Am I to assume that something is wrong?" he asked.

"You know about my visions, correct?" Reem asked, ignoring his question. When he nodded, she continued, "I've had another one."

"And you saw me?" Seth guessed, the confusion leaving his face as he considered all of the many possibilities of what she could have seen in her vision.

"Yes, I did." She nodded.

"Go on," Seth urged.

"I saw the squad that was sent from Mettirna." She paused. "I saw one of them accusing either you or a woman of hiding something from us—fighting for the wrong side. I'd like to know your thoughts on the matter," she responded.

"Take your time if you wish," Jameson added. "We have all day."

Seth's right hand moved to his chin, massaging his dry skin as he thought. "Who was the woman?" he asked after a moment.

"I couldn't see her face," Reem replied. "That's why we're talking to you."

"A general description would suffice. I know everyone in the city—and I do mean everyone."

"If I had to guess, I would say that she took the treatment after she had already passed the age. She looked to be between thirty-five and forty years old, with long dark hair that covered her face. I couldn't see her eyes. She was about your height, maybe slightly taller." She paused. "That's all I saw."

"That description fits several of the women here."

"Now you see our dilemma," Jameson said.

"Why would the squad be accusing anyone of anything?" Seth asked.

"Because they're not coming to determine if we are a threat," Reem replied. "They're coming to forge an alliance."

Mitchal paced outside the entrance to the underground, waiting for the opportune moment to go down and speak with his brother. He'd come to this spot yesterday, but somehow, he couldn't bring himself to go inside. David would never think the same of him, not even if he could convince him to change his mind and join the rebellion. Mitchal would always be thought of as a betrayer, and he wasn't sure that he could live with that. Even if he could bring himself to go down to where they held his brother, he wasn't sure he would even know what to say. David likely wouldn't want anything to do with him, and honestly, Mitchal didn't blame him.

He continued pacing—something he rarely ever did, but something he found suited the situation. Finally, he sat on the hard earthen ground beside the entrance and closed his eyes in an attempt to meditate on his problem. He cleared his mind, concentrating only on his heartbeat as he felt his breath flowing in and out of his body.

After several hours, he at last stood to his feet and walked down into the underground portion of the city, following the fire lit path down into the central chamber and then to his left into a side room where they were keeping his brother. He paused outside the doorway, collecting his thoughts before slowly walking into the room.

Inside, David sat on a chair in the center of the small stone-walled room, his wrists and legs fastened securely to prevent him from leaving the city. The room was dimly lit by two small torches in the back, the firelight dancing across the walls.

"David," he whispered.

"I have nothing to say to you," David replied, staring at the ground beneath Mitchal's feet.

"David, please," Mitchal whispered, "I only came to make sure you're alright."

"Leave me, Mitchal."

"Brother—"

"I have no brother." He looked up into Mitchal's eyes, his eyes burning with anger. "When will you see that they will betray you just as you have me?" he asked. "They are not who you think they are. They will not allow you to stay here with everything that you've done in the past."

Mitchal shook his head slowly. "No."

"They will betray you." He paused, his voice rising in volume. "And when they do, you will come crawling back to me, begging me to forgive you, begging me to save you from them."

"No, David," Mitchal replied calmly as David fumed in front of him.

"You will see!" he shouted, his deep voice echoing through the halls. "They will betray you!"

Mitchal shook his head again before turning to walk out of the room. "I'm sorry, brother, there's nothing I can do for you."

"I have no brother!" David shouted, struggling to free himself from his bonds as Mitchal exited the room and left his sight. "You betrayed me!"

Mitchal walked back up the steps to the surface, hanging his head in shame as he continued to hear his brother's screams echoing out of the underground chamber. He dropped to his knees on the ground outside the entrance, tears streaming down his cheeks as David's screams rose in both volume and profanity.

⚜

Brittany pulled a map out of her uniform breast pocket and double-checked her location as she saw the coast on the edge of the horizon. She could see the sun high in the sky, hours from reaching the horizon. She would arrive sooner than she had at first thought, which meant that she would be arriving in Athena much sooner than planned.

She smiled as she walked, anticipating her arrival in Athena. It would be an interesting task, this one. She would have to hide from her brother until she'd completed the first part of her task, and then she would have to either convince him to accompany her back to Admiri or drug him and carry him back to the ship. The first would be the easier option, but the second was more appealing in many ways. She would love to see her brother in pain. On the other hand, carrying her brother across the desert of Africa didn't seem so appealing. The last she'd seen him he had been at least two hundred pounds—and that would not be so easy to carry.

She picked up her pace, not wanting to leave any later than necessary. At the dock, there would be a messenger who would go back to Marcus and let him know that she'd boarded safely—a detail she thought unnecessary, but Marcus thought needed to be done—and she preferred that he left during daylight hours.

Within hours, she arrived on the coast, and she walked up the dock to where the boat awaited her arrival. The boat was small, but it would do for travel on task for the Superiors. Marcus had gone through a great deal to procure even this vessel for her—and he was the Great Superior. She walked up to the boat and casually boarded without announcing herself, walking straight to the upper level to where the captain briefed his crew.

"Time to go," she announced as she walked through the doorway. "Where are my quarters?"

"Brittany Green, I take it," the captain said nervously, approaching her and shaking her hand nervously. "We'll leave as soon as it is safe to do so. There are a few Purists vessels blocking our path at the moment."

"No. We leave now," she commanded. "I can deal with the Purists." The corners of her mouth turned up slightly. "Always up for a challenge."

"Yes, ma'am." The captain nodded. "I'll dispatch the messenger, and we'll be on our way."

"Good. Now where are my quarters?"

Decision

"What were they supposedly accusing me of?" Seth asked after several minutes.

"Sabotage," Reem replied.

"I wouldn't do anything to sabotage the rebellion that I founded." He shook his head.

"Which is why I initially dismissed the possibility, but since we don't know who the woman is, we have to go with what we have—which is you, Seth." She leaned over the table, looking straight into his eyes as she spoke.

"It doesn't make any sense." He shook his head once more, whispering under his breath, "Why would she come here now of all times?"

"Who? Why would who come here, Seth?" Reem asked, hearing the thoughts in his mind along with the words coming from his mouth.

"I'm not sure, but it's possible that it's . . ."

"Your sister?" She tilted her head to the side, confusion forming on her face as she read his thoughts. "Why would you think that?"

"She works very closely with the Superiors. They send her on tasks all the time, many of which require her to kill for them." He paused. "She fits the description."

"But you don't know for sure that it's her?" Jameson asked.

"It's just a hunch, really. I've had no contact with her in . . . well, I don't remember the last time we spoke."

"She's a born killer," Reem added.

"Yes, she is. She would do anything that the Superiors asked of her—even killing me if they desired it. She has very strong ties with Marcus Admiri in particular," Seth said, leaning back in his chair as he remembered his sister's uncanny ability to kill.

"Then we'll be on the lookout—just in case she shows up," Jameson said.

"If it is my sister, then whatever her mission is, she will complete it—successfully, I mean."

"If she can do the things you say she can, then I don't want her anywhere near this tower," Jameson replied, getting to his feet. "I'll go inform the guards." He turned to Reem. "You'll be alright for a few minutes?"

"Of course." She smiled, standing to kiss his lips softly before he exited the room, leaving her and Seth alone. She sat back down directly across from Seth, who continued to rack his brain for any reason the Superiors would send his sister—other than killing Reem or himself, that is. "Jameson won't let her get near this building—I know that much. If it makes you feel better, you can stay here as well."

"No, no, I'll stay in my home. I'll be fine. Most likely, she's coming for you. But if she is coming for me, then she likely won't kill me."

"She'll take you back to Marcus." She nodded.

"Yes," he replied solemnly.

"Marcus is not a person to be trifled with." She leaned back in her chair, a mirror image of Seth.

"What reason did they have for removing you from Admiri?" Seth asked, changing the subject to avoid the coming questions pertaining to his sister.

"I discovered things about Marcus that he never intended anyone to know. He had no choice but to get rid of me. I thought that I had hidden my discovery well enough for him not to find out, but I guess I was wrong." She shrugged. "I should have seen it coming."

"If you don't mind my asking, what did you find out?" he asked, furrowing his brow slightly as he leaned forward over the table.

"If it comes down to it, then I may just tell you, Seth." She laughed lightly. "But that time hasn't come yet."

"Jameson knows, I assume?"

She nodded. "He knows everything."

⚜

Nicholas and Suri walked hand in hand up the steps into the central tower. They walked into the circular main chamber and were immediately greeted by Jameson who stood just inside the entrance.

"Reem said you were close." He smiled. "We're all in the meeting room." He gestured to the small room where Reem and Seth sat across from each other. They all walked inside and took their seats, Jameson next to Reem and Nicholas next to Seth with Suri at the head of the table, smiling that she was sitting in a chair where once only the highest-ranking Superior in Athena would sit.

"Glad you made it," Reem joked as they sat, linking her fingers with Jameson's.

"We were a bit tied up," Nicholas replied, smiling brightly into Suri's eyes.

"Why are we here?" Suri asked.

"Reem's had another vision," Seth answered. "We thought we could use another set of ears on the topic."

Suri nodded in response before turning to Reem. "What did you see?" she asked.

Reem once again told the tale of her vision, starting with the squad's arrival and ending with the strange woman whom they presumed for the time being was Seth's sister.

"So you think that she's coming to kill you?" Nicholas asked, his eyebrows furrowing.

"I'm not so sure," Seth answered before Reem could open her mouth. "I think that if the Superiors sent her, they would have something larger for her to do. Like you said, Reem, sabotage. The best way to do that wouldn't be to kill you. It would be to plant some sort of doubt throughout the city about your capabilities."

"I don't know. I think that the Superiors would rather just kill both her and you," Suri replied.

"That would make them martyrs," Nicholas said, joining sides with Seth.

"So you see our dilemma," Jameson said. "We want your opinion on the course of action we should take. Should we search the city for her or leave it and if she does arrive allow her to complete her task for the Superiors unhindered?"

"I say leave her to her task," Seth said. "It's doubtful that she'll be able to cause any real damage to the rebellion at this point."

"I agree with Seth," Nicholas added. "It wouldn't make sense for them to send her to kill you, and even if she does come to kill you, I doubt that she would be able to."

"I think we should search the city," Suri said. "If she is allowed to complete her task, it could ruin the rebellion. We can't take that risk."

"I agree," Jameson said. "I don't want her anywhere near Reem, and it would be better if we knew for sure if she is inside the city."

"If she finds out that we know about her, it could ruin everything," Seth replied. "She could decide to go on a killing rampage. I know my sister."

"I'm with Seth," Nicholas said. "He knows more about her than any of us— Reem excluded, of course. We should take his advice."

"That leaves us exactly where we were a few minutes ago." Reem laughed darkly. "We need to make a decision. Do we really need to bring more people in on this, or can we come to a solid conclusion?"

"You haven't told us your opinion yet, Reem," Suri replied.

"Actually, I have." Reem lifted her hand, Jameson's fingers linked with hers. "I agree with my husband, whatever his decision is."

"Of course," Nicholas said. "I expected as much."

"So we do have a decision then," Suri added. "It's two to three. We should search the city."

"I would prefer if we all agreed on whatever we decide to do," Reem replied. "Otherwise, we would have gone ahead with that without calling you two here."

"So what's the next step?" Nicholas asked. "How do you expect us all to agree on something?"

"I expect us to continue racking our brains to find more options," Reem answered, leaning over the table. "We've come up with two extremes, so what can we find that fits somewhere in the middle?"

"I still say we should wait and see what she does," Seth said, leaning back in his chair once again. "Let her make the first move."

"And if that first move gets my sister killed?" Suri asked, her palm slapping the table harshly.

"I highly doubt that the Superiors sent her to kill Reem," Seth answered. "The Superiors usually use her for things more delicate than killing. Most of her tasks deal with reconnaissance."

"But they frequently end with a great deal of bloodshed," Reem added, realizing that he wasn't telling the whole truth. "You can't try to protect her forever, Seth."

"Who said that I was?"

"I can read your mind, remember?" She smiled slightly.

"Okay, okay, so what do we do?" Nicholas asked before Seth could retaliate.

"We increase security and wait," Suri replied. "The increase in security would be expected with the arrival of Reem and Jameson, and we can keep a sharp eye out for anyone that looks like Seth's sister—what's her name?"

"Brittany," Seth replied. "That could work. That way, we don't alert her that we know about her presence, but we can still be on the lookout in case she does show up in an attempt to assassinate anyone."

"What do you think, Nicholas?" Reem asked.

"It could work. Suri and I could move over here just in case if you'd like," Nicholas replied. "I'm getting much better with my gifts, and I think I can keep you well hidden while we wait." He paused, turning to look Jameson in the eye. "But it's not up to me."

Jameson shook his head. "I don't want Reem in any danger."

"She's in danger no matter what we do," Seth chided.

"Which is why I wasn't going to bring her here this soon," Jameson replied, shooting an angry glare at Seth.

"And I told you that we can protect her," Seth responded quickly. "And we will."

"I'm not so sure." Jameson shook his head once more.

"Look, so far, it's the only option that the rest of us agree on," Suri said, cutting off the bitter conversation. "If you don't agree, then tell me what you think we should do."

"Honestly, I'd rather leave," Jameson answered. "However, that's no longer an option."

"What do you mean?" Nicholas asked, concern edging his voice as he glanced back and forth between Jameson and Reem.

"I can't teleport anymore, and I can't walk very far before I'm exhausted," Reem replied. "I'll be fine, but it just means that I can't leave the city."

"Then that leaves us with upping the security or searching the city," Seth said. "Which do you prefer, Jameson?"

"Either way, we're upping the security, and I want to meet every single one of the people guarding this building." Jameson paused, running his fingers through his hair slowly. "We wait. It's the best option—of the options available, that is."

"Then it seems we've reached a decision," Suri replied.

No sooner did she finish speaking when a voice called out from right outside the central tower. "He needs medical attention!" the man yelled.

As soon as Reem heard his voice, she was out of her chair and running toward the staircase. The four remained for a moment, glancing between one another with confusion marking their faces before they rose in unison and ran to follow Reem outside.

Jameson caught up with her first, teleporting to the staircase to stop her before she rushed into an unknown situation. He wrapped his arms around her as she tried to pass, holding her back from descending the long staircase toward the man who screamed in agony at the bottom while his friend cried that he needed a healer. "You don't know what's going on," he whispered in her ear.

"I know that he's hurt," she snapped. "And I know that I'm going to help him." He felt her gifts prying his arms off her body and watched helplessly as she descended the steps, releasing him when she was a few feet away from the bleeding man, who writhed on the stone ground. "I'm a healer," she told the man who continued to attempt to keep his friend alive.

"He doesn't have much of a pulse. I don't know how long it's been," the man replied, his bloody fingers running through his clean brown hair before he stepped away covered in his thick red liquid.

Jameson walked down the steps quickly, Seth close on his heels as they approached the duo, Jameson stopping when he reached Reem, and Seth when he reached the bloodied man who had brought his friend.

"How is he?" Seth asked loudly.

"He'll be fine," she replied. "Chances are he won't be awake for a while though."

"Thank you. I thought I'd lost him." He wiped his hands on his jeans, his eyes widening when he realized what he'd done.

"You did. I brought him back," Reem said, nodding as she stood to her feet and turned toward Seth and the other man.

"How?" The man's light blue eyes widened in shock. "Who are you?"

"I could be asking you the same thing," she replied, smiling slightly.

"Reem Kahrin, meet Angel Wing," Seth said, cutting Angel off from saying anything more.

"I know, my parents were cruel," Angel said almost as though he'd rehearsed it. "Kahrin, you said?" he asked.

"Willow actually," Reem scowled at Seth. "Kahrin is my maiden name."

"But you are the savior?" he asked, sudden understanding showing on his face.

"I prefer Reem," she replied. "But yes, I am."

"Then it is my honor." Angel dipped his head, dropping his eyes to the ground. "I had not expected you to arrive so soon."

"Nor did we," Jameson added as he walked up behind Reem and placed his hand on her shoulder protectively.

"And you must be Jameson Willow," Angel said, awestruck. "I only wish I had the power you do. My shortcomings could have killed my friend this day."

"Speaking of which, who is he?" Jameson asked. "It looked like he was tortured."

"His name is Brandon Syll, and he was," he replied solemnly.

"How?" Reem asked before Jameson could open his mouth to speak.

"We were sent to Admiri. Brandon is a messenger, and I was his transportation. Had we had anyone faster, we would have sent them. But at the time, it wasn't possible." He shook his head.

"Who sent you?" Jameson questioned.

"The Prophet, of course." Angel shrugged.

"Seth?" Reem turned to look into Seth's golden eyes. "Why would you do that?"

"I did not order them," Seth defended. "The majority of the plan was Brandon's idea. He thought it was time that we deliver a message of our own to the Superiors in Admiri, and he volunteered to go himself."

"Brandon is my best friend. When I realized that he was serious about this, I volunteered to take him there myself," Angel added.

Reem shook her head and turned to walk away. "That was not a good idea."

"You don't know his gifts, Reem," Seth countered. "He had the ability to instill fear or doubt into Marcus's mind merely by talking to him about his fears. We believe that Marcus will be a less formidable enemy now that Brandon has worked his magic."

"You don't know Marcus like I do." She scowled as she walked back up the steps toward Nicholas and Suri with Jameson right behind her.

Marcus sat on his throne, his mind swimming through all the possible outcomes of Brittany's task. If she failed as he now assumed David and Mitchal had, he would be forced to go to war with the rebels. Though really, even if she did return successfully, they would be at war sooner than anyone could imagine. He had received news about the peace treaty that would soon be signed between the rebels and the Advanced of Mettirna, and it sickened him to think of how soon the fools would betray him after the start of the rebellion. But no matter, for soon the rebellion would be dissolved—especially after Brittany completed her task. She would ruin them before they could even sign their blasphemous treaty.

He rose and walked to the washroom, splashing water on his face before looking into the mirror at his aged eyes and skin that started to wrinkle before his eyes. He reached out his hand and pulled a syringe filled with thick yellow liquid out from underneath the water basin, injecting it into his arm.

His eyes closed as he felt the liquid work its way through his bloodstream, opening his eyes to see his skin reverse in age and his eyes lighten in shade and depth. He felt the serum work through his muscles, strengthening him as it went.

Trust

Angel sat next to Brandon's bed, waiting for him to wake up before he would believe that his friend would really be fine. After what happened in Admiri, he was sure that Brandon was going to die, and even now he still had trouble believing he was still alive. When Angel had felt his heartbeat stop, he'd done the only thing he could—he teleported into Athena, running on pure adrenaline. He knew it wasn't a good idea, that the teleport itself could have killed them. But he also knew that if he didn't get his friend into the city soon enough, he would be dead anyways. After they'd landed on the steps, everything started moving in slow motion. He knew that he was shouting for someone to help them, and he knew that Brandon was still bleeding—which was a good sign—but he didn't remember where Reem had appeared from. For all he knew, they had arrived in the city at the same time he had; and for some reason, he couldn't bring himself to trust the woman who healed his friend—even if she was the one whom they called their savior. Something wasn't right. He stood and started pacing around the room, unable to sit still any longer.

"Angel, will you please stop?" Brandon whispered, groaning lightly.

"You're awake!" Angel exclaimed, walking back to the side of the bed and falling to his knees. "How do you feel?"

"Stop yelling."

"I'm not yelling," he replied, his voice at a more natural level.

"Now you're not." Brandon laughed, finally opening his eyes to look at Angel. "I'm fine."

"Are you sure? I can get a healer here if you need one," he asked.

"Age, I'm fine." He nodded. "Stop acting like you're my boyfriend."

"Hey!" Angel said, standing to his feet and holding his hands up defensively. "I wasn't."

"Yeah, you were." Brandon laughed as he sat up and scratched his head. His eyes turned dark and serious as he looked up at his friend. "Is that my blood?" He gestured toward Angel's bloodied clothing.

"Uh. Yeah. Yeah, it is," Angel replied, looking down at what used to be a white tee shirt and pair of blue jeans.

"Who healed me?" Brandon asked, changing the subject to avoid the awkward topic. "I should thank them."

"You wouldn't believe me if I told you," Angel replied, smiling as he shook his head.

"Try me."

"The woman who healed you"—he paused—"was Reem"—he paused again—"Kahrin."

"Don't joke with me, Angel. The savior is only telekinetic." Brandon shook his head as he stood.

"I'm serious, Brandon. It was Reem Kahrin." His eyebrows rose slightly.

Brandon took a deep breath, and looked his friend in the eye. "Take me to her then," he whispered nervously before looking down at his own blood-soaked clothing. "Or maybe we should go after we get cleaned up." The corners of his mouth turned up.

"Meet you outside in an hour," Angel replied, laughing at him before walking out the door.

⁂

Reem sat on the floor of her bedroom, her hands still sticky with Brandon's blood as she closed her eyes and attempted to meditate. Her breathing was heavy, her heart racing, and her eyes snapped open at her failure. She could hear Jameson's steady breathing as he tried to sleep on the bed that sat beside her.

"Still can't sleep?" she asked, hearing his thoughts racing in his mind.

"Still can't meditate?" he countered, laughing ever so slightly as his smiling face turned to gaze into her frustrated eyes.

"No, no, I can't," she replied, tears welling in her eyes. "And apparently, the baby would like me to cry about it." She laughed as the tears streamed down her face.

He sat up and slid to the side, gesturing for her to join him on the bed as he tried his best not to laugh at her in her misery. She stood and walked to the bed, sitting slowly beside him and slapping his leg lightly when she read his thoughts.

"Don't laugh at me!" she said seriously.

"I'm not, I'm not," he defended, moving his hands to her shoulders to massage her gently. "Here," he whispered in her ear.

"Thank you," she whispered back, moving her long hair out of the way of his hands before she felt his lips on her neck.

"What's wrong? You're tense," he whispered.

"Seth should've known better," she replied, sighing heavily.

"Ahh," He paused, moving to massage her back. "Seth's had a lot on his plate, Reem—you haven't even taken charge of the city yet. I'm sure he was only trying to make the people as safe as possible from the Superiors."

"Don't defend him, Jameson. I need you on my side," she replied fiercely.

"I am on your side, Reem," he whispered, kissing her neck again. "I always will be."

"Then why don't you see that by sending the messenger to Marcus, Seth has basically handed our heads to the Superiors on a silver platter? Marcus doesn't take well to fear and doubt—especially in himself. It will cause him to declare war on the rebellion before we're organized enough to fight him off. They'll all be slaughtered." She shook her head.

"You forget that I don't know him like you do. The first task I'd done for him was the task we met on." He stroked her arm lightly. "Don't worry, my love, I promised you that I wouldn't let them hurt you, and I fully intend on keeping that promise."

"And what about the others? Suri and Nicholas, Maria and Mitchal, David, Angel, Brandon, Seth, all of them—what about them?" she asked.

"They came here of their own will—David excluded, of course—and they know what they've gotten themselves into." He paused. "I will do what I can for them, but in the long run, you and our child are my main priorities," he said.

"I don't want them all to die in my name," she whispered, shaking her head as she stared at the blood on her hands.

"Then we'll just have to keep them all alive, won't we?" He wrapped his arms around her and took her hands in his, wiping the blood off with his sleeve.

"That's what I'm afraid of. It may not be as easy as it sounds."

"It doesn't sound easy, Reem," he stated the obvious.

"My point exactly." She leaned her head back on his shoulder and sighed.

"We'll figure it out," he whispered in her ear.

They sat alone in silence for several moments, surprised when they suddenly heard heavy footfalls leading to a knock on the door.

"Angel Wing and Brandon Syll to see you, ma'am," the guard said.

Reem nodded, speechless, as Jameson responded, "Take them to the meeting room. We'll be there in a moment."

"Yes, sir," the guard replied, his heavy footfalls fully audible as he walked back to the main entrance and led the men to the meeting room.

Reem groaned lightly as she pulled away from Jameson. "This could get old fast." She laughed.

"That it could." He smiled as they stood to their feet. "Ready?" he asked, standing in front of the door with his hand held out toward her.

"Of course," she replied, taking his hand and kissing it lightly before he led the way through the door and across the main chamber into the meeting room where the men waited.

Inside, the two best friends bickered near the far wall, apparently unnoticing that Reem and Jameson had entered as they stood in the skylights waning evening light. Jameson lit two of the four torches with his gift as Reem cleared her throat loudly, causing both men to become suddenly quiet and both of their heads to snap around so that they could look her in the eye.

"Sorry," they said in unison.

"Have a seat," Reem said, motioning to the chairs that lined the table.

"Of course," they said in unison once again, turning to cast confused looks into each other's eyes.

"You wanted to see me?" Reem laughed as she and Jameson took their seats next to each other at the table and waited for the two men to do the same.

"Yes, I wanted to thank you," Brandon replied as he sat roughly in the chair across from Reem. "I can't express how much I appreciate you saving my life."

"You're welcome." She smiled back. "But if you are to thank someone, it should be my husband—he is the one who gave me the gift of healing after all." She turned and winked at Jameson before turning back to Brandon.

"Then I owe you my gratitude as well," he told Jameson. "Angel here tells me that you do not approve of our trip to Admiri," he added after a few moments of empty silence.

"I do not," Reem replied. "You do not know Marcus Admiri like I do." She shook her head as her eyes pierced into his.

"I studied under him during my training," Brandon said.

"Do not defend our enemy, Brandon." She paused. "You know nothing of him."

"I know enough to know that my mission was successful in making him think twice before sending another operative into our ranks."

"He already has," Jameson said, speaking for the first time since they'd entered.

"What?" Angel asked. "Who?"

"That is not important," Jameson replied.

"When will they arrive?" Brandon asked, leaning over the table slightly.

"We don't know," Reem answered.

"Then we should remove you from the premises just in case," Angel said.

"I would like nothing more, but I'm afraid it's not possible," Jameson replied. "She cannot teleport without risking serious injury, and walking great distances has become increasingly difficult over the past few days."

"But you're a healer—surely, you can heal yourself of whatever this ailment is," Brandon added.

"I'm afraid it's not possible," Reem replied. "I'm going to have to remain in Athena."

"Are you sure that's the best option?" Angel asked. "There must be something else we could do."

"The decision has already been made," Jameson told them.

"Of course, I'm sorry." Angel dipped his head slightly as Brandon leaned back in his chair to look up at the glass ceiling above their heads.

"What would you have us do then?" he asked as he stared at the dwindling light in the sky.

"I would have you return to your homes and prepare yourself for whatever is coming," Reem replied. "Even I don't know what to expect."

✦✦◎✦✦

Brittany roared her battle cry as she sliced her blade through the last Purists' throat, slaughtering him aboard his own vessel. She'd told her captain that she could deal with any Purist threat they found, and she'd proven herself quite well. Eighteen Purists now lay dead on the deck of the large boat where she now stood, waiting for her own boat to return as she'd ordered them to. She watched as her boat bucked against the waves as it attempted to approach the anchored vessel she stood on, wiping blood from her blade onto the dead man that lay at her feet. She kissed her knife and carefully placed it back in its sheath, though she knew that she would likely need it before too long. Soon her task would be complete, and she would be on her way back home—home to Marcus's filthy arms.

As her boat neared the side of the Purists', she jumped gracefully from the deck of one to the deck of the other, signaling the captain to be on their way now that the enemy had been sufficiently dealt with. She walked up to the top deck as the captain emerged, his eyes wide with shock.

He chuckled. "You'd come in handy whenever we're making shipments across the ocean."

"Not my kind of work," she replied. "I'm in the killing business, but not so much that I would desire to be out to sea all the days of my life." She spat off the side of the railing.

"In any case, if it hadn't been for you, we would have been at least a day behind on our journey," he replied, trying not to think about her being in the "killing business."

"When will we be arriving at the shore?" she asked.

"We should be there within thirty-six hours," he replied. "Our boat is not as fast as she once was." He shook his head.

"Make it twenty-four," she ordered. "I need to get there sooner than possible." She turned and walked back down to the lower levels, not waiting to hear his response—he knew what the result would be if he didn't obey her.

✦✦◎✦✦

"You don't trust her," Brandon accused as they walked quickly back through the torch-lit city toward their homes.

"No, I don't," Angel replied. "Something's off."

"And what would that be?" he asked, dodging a passerby as they walked.

254

"I'm not sure, but I can feel it. Something just isn't right with those two." He shook his head.

"Perhaps it could be the fact that you always had a secret crush on the savior, and now all your dreams have been taken away from you." Brandon laughed, elbowing his friend jokingly.

"Now is not the time. I'm telling you, something's not right." He paused. "Couldn't you feel it when we were in there talking with them? They're hiding something from us—from all of us."

"I felt nothing, Age, nothing at all." He shook his head slightly. "I don't see how you can't trust the woman that you call your savior."

"I only call her Reem Kahrin."

"Though it's Willow now if I'm not mistaken." He laughed.

"Didn't you hear what they said? The Superiors sent another operative, and they'll be arriving any day now. Doesn't that make you the least bit worried about the people here?"

"Angel, calm down," Brandon said as they made their way up the steps to their homes. "I'm sure that they're nothing we can't handle."

"But didn't you get the sense that there's something they're not telling us about the operative too?"

"That, I did." He paused. "But I'm sure that it's nothing more than them trying to protect us from the fear that would come if we knew the truth about the matter."

"How do they even know that an operative was sent?" Angel asked inquisitively, his eyebrows furrowing slightly.

"Both of them have gifts beyond what we know—perhaps one has allowed them to know the simple truth that the Superiors have sent an operative."

"It's too convenient." He shook his head. "I don't like it."

"Shall we go back and ask them what they're lying to us about?" Brandon laughed lightly. "Would that make you feel better about this whole thing?"

"It might, yes." He paused. "We need to go back tomorrow to work with Jameson about the security of the tower anyway. We'll talk about it with them then."

"Ahh yes, we'll go to the savior and demand to be told what my teleporting friend here thinks she's hiding from us—that sounds like a good idea." Brandon laughed again. "I'm going to sleep. I'll meet you at the tower in the morning." He walked inside his quarters.

"Don't joke about this, Brandon," Angel said as he turned to walk into his own home.

Nicholas and Suri arrived at the tower shortly after Brandon and Angel had left, walking inside without an announcement from the guard and finding Reem and Jameson standing in the main chamber, Jameson leaning against the wall while Reem stood in front of him and ran her fingers through his hair.

"Good evening," Nicholas said in his best vampire voice, laughing when they turned to smile at him. "Something wrong?" he asked.

"No," Reem replied, smiling brightly at him. "We we're just meeting with Angel Wing and Brandon Syll—the ones who just got back from Admiri."

"What did they have to say?" Suri asked, walking up to her sister and embracing her gently.

"Brandon wanted to thank Reem for saving his life," Jameson answered.

"How thoughtful of him," she replied. "So what is it then?"

"I'm just concerned—that's all." Reem shook her head slowly.

"For?" Nicholas asked, his eyebrows furrowing as he stepped toward them.

"The people." She paused. "I don't want them all to die in my name."

"And I've explained that we'll do all that we can," Jameson added, "but you know her."

"Reem, you can't expect everyone to stay alive now that you're here," Suri said softly as she gazed into her sister's eyes.

"That doesn't mean I have to like the fact that they're dying while I'm here holed up in this tower like some sort of dictator," Reem replied.

"You're not a dictator—you're their leader. Our leader," Nicholas said. "Without you, this whole rebellion would fall apart."

Reem's head dropped as she took in his words, nodding slowly as she took in a breath and stared at the ground.

"You had a choice, you know. We could've left." Jameson smiled, placing his hand under her chin and tilting her head to look him in the eye.

"I know," she whispered, smiling slightly as she read the thoughts in his mind.

"We came to ask if you wanted us to stay here with you or not," Suri said, changing the subject. "You never did say earlier."

When Reem didn't reply, Jameson spoke. "We'd love you to stay. You can have one of the other bedrooms." He paused, taking Reem's hand to guide her as she continued to stare at the ground. "Follow me," he told them.

They followed him to a short hallway, walking down the small space to a doorway which he gestured for them to enter. "You can stay here. We'll be down the hall." He smiled.

"Thank you," Suri replied. "Let us know if you need anything."

"Of course," he replied, dipping his head before guiding Reem a few feet farther down the hallway into their own bedroom, sitting her down on the bed and kneeling to look her in the eye. "They were only trying to help, you know," he whispered, smiling softly as her anger-filled eyes glared into his.

"I know," she said finally, looking back to the ground.

"I know this is hard for you, Reem, but Nicholas isn't all that used to you snapping at him." He laughed lightly.

"I don't know what's wrong with me." She paused. "Why am I always like this?" She sighed loudly.

"Because your body is changing to make room for Samuel, and it's difficult to adjust."

"That's the easy answer." She laughed back.

"Well, that's all I've got." He chuckled. "I'm sorry you have to go through this." He paused. "You more than anyone know how much I hate seeing you in pain." He lifted his hand to brush the hair away from her face. "But you have no idea how beautiful you are when you're angry." He smiled.

"Am I?" she asked, smiling as she wrapped her arms around his neck.

He smiled back and moved to kiss her lips lightly before pulling away to look her in the eye once again. "Not as beautiful as you are when you're fighting for what you love—or as beautiful as you are right now."

Her smile brightened as her cheeks flushed, her eyes dropping back to the ground at her feet.

"Look at me, Reem," he whispered, waiting for her eyes to finally lift back up and look into his before he continued. "I know you don't want them to die for you, but you need to know that they have decided that they will. They made that choice. The best you can do for them now is to lead them to victory—to peace." He paused. "I know you will make a great leader, Reem, and I will follow you in whatever you do."

"You don't have to," she replied, shaking her head slightly.

"Don't have to what?" he asked, his eyebrows furrowing.

"You don't have to follow me."

"Yes, I do." He paused. "And I will."

"No, Jameson, I want you to help me lead them. I want you to stand beside me, not behind me," she whispered, her eyes serious as they looked into his.

"I—"

"You're as cut out for this as I am," she cut him off, reading the thoughts in his mind.

"I'll help you then," he whispered, the corners of his mouth turning up slightly. "I love you, Reem. So much."

"I know." She winked. "I love you too."

Marcus sat on his throne, waiting for the effects of his medication to wear off. His head throbbed under the pressure of the serum, his muscles burning from the sudden onslaught of tissue buildup. At this rate, it seemed as though he would have to stop using the serum within the next few treatments, his body's natural age aiding in the deterioration from the serum. If he didn't find a new treatment soon, he would be dead, and his kingdom would die with him.

He'd ordered the guards to leave him alone for the next twenty-four hours, all of which he would spend either writhing in pain or sitting in this chair, waiting for the ache of the serum and the burn in his heart to dissipate. He had to use the serum once a week these days, and soon it seemed he would have to up the dosage once again. It was time he got back to the lab instead of dealing with the rebellion. But he needed them gone before he could know for sure that his people would never find out his secret. If he quit fighting now they could suspect and even more could go to the rebellion—which was something he didn't dare risk.

A small part of him wished that he could go back in time and change everything, kill Reem before she could become the savior of the people, stop Jameson from ever coming into any form of power, or maybe never inventing the treatment in the first place. It seemed to him that the world was better before it. He'd single-handedly changed the world forever, hadn't he? And now he regretted it, just like Lana had told him he would.

Oh, Lana. He hadn't thought about that woman in years. She'd been his assistant in his lab all those years ago when he made the treatment. She'd been among the first to receive the treatment and among the first to die from its effects.

Negotiations

Nicholas woke to the sounds of running and yelling outside in the streets, and the next thing he knew, he was sitting up in bed and rubbing his eyes to clear his vision. "What's going on?" he asked, knowing Suri must have been awake longer than him.

"They're early," she whispered, her voice coming from across the room. "Get dressed—we should be with Reem."

He did as she said, getting out of bed and running to the closet to put on his clothes before joining her by the doorway. "All set." Together, they exited the room, walking down the hall to Reem and Jameson's bedroom where he knocked loudly. "You two awake in there?"

"Just a moment," Reem replied loudly.

It was then that they heard the shuffling that was going on inside the room, a soft clicking sound and ruffling of cloth before Jameson opened the door.

"They're here," Suri told him.

"We know. Go to the main chamber. We'll meet you there in a moment," he replied, gesturing for them to walk down the hall to the circular room.

Nicholas nodded and took Suri by the hand, dragging her down the hall before she could protest. "Don't start with him today, Suri," he advised. "It's best not to anger him when Reem's life could be on the line."

She nodded, unspeaking as they stepped into the large room, walking to the balcony where they could clearly see the majority of the city—including the site where the Mettirnian squad had arrived. People were gathered around a small clearing in the city, Seth and a group of guards forming the innermost circle near the Mettirnians. The squad was made up of five people—four men and one woman—all dressed in the same battle dress of the Advanced that the rebels wore. They stood defensively, their hands held up in a show that they were not here to harm anyone, the woman dropping to her knees and ordering the others to follow her lead. Soon they all knelt with their hands on their heads while Seth slowly approached them, his guards keeping their weapons poised and ready to kill as he did so.

"How long have they been here?" Suri wondered aloud as she watched the scene play out in front of her eyes.

"Not long," Reem answered, appearing behind them on the balcony. "Only a few hours at most." She shook her head.

"Why the fuss?" Nicholas asked.

"Seth still thinks that they're here to kill as many of us as possible, and with their early arrival, it means that his sister will be arriving any day now," Reem replied.

"I should be down there," Jameson whispered under his breath as he appeared behind Reem and took her hand.

"Then go," she replied, smiling as she looked into his eyes. "I'll be fine."

"No, it wouldn't feel right," he replied, lifting her hand and kissing it lightly. "I told you I'd stay with you, remember?"

"Jameson, go," she told him.

"I'd rather stay," he replied, the corners of his mouth turning up slightly. "Besides, Seth will bring their leader here when he knows it's safe."

"He will." She nodded.

"Can you tell what they're thinking?" Nicholas asked Reem. "I mean, can you tell what they're planning on doing here?"

"I told you before: they're not here to hurt us. They're here to form an alliance," Reem replied.

"Mettirna wants to align with us?" he asked.

"Yes, they do. I had a feeling they might." She paused, turning from Nicholas to Jameson. "They never did like Marcus Admiri." She winked, and he smiled.

⁂

"I'm unarmed, Seth," the woman said in a thick Old British accent as Seth approached her. "You know that. And I'm sure you know that we're not here to hurt you." She reached a single hand up to brush her short blonde hair back behind her ear, the guards lifting their weapons to her head as she did so. "Will you please tell them that?" she asked, cocking her head.

"Princess, it's good to see you again," Seth answered, holding out his hand to help her up.

She took his hand and pulled herself to her feet, brushing off her pants as Seth waved off the guards. "And you, Prophet. But I'm no princess." She threw her fist up to hit his jaw firmly. "That's for making me kneel." She winked one of her light green eyes.

He rubbed his chin with his hands, spitting blood to the side before turning back to her, smiling with blood-filled teeth. "Just a bit of fun."

"Well, stop having fun at my expense." She motioned for the men who accompanied her to stand. "Take me to your leader." She laughed.

"A moment please, princess," Seth said as she started to walk away. "I'll need to clear that with Willow first."

"Willow?" she asked, stopping and turning to face him. "Don't you mean Kahrin?"

"No, I mean Willow." He shrugged, smiling. "Should've seen it coming."

"Together at last." She laughed back. "You're right, we should've seen that coming." She took a few steps toward him, stopping when she stood a few feet away. "Go on then. Go talk to mummy and daddy and find out if you're allowed to play with the new girl in town," she mocked.

"Don't do that, princess." He shook his head, his smile brightening.

"Go, Seth. Hurry back," she ordered. "I have orders, you know."

"Of course, princess." He winked. "I'll return as soon as possible." He dipped his head before walking past her toward the central tower where Reem, Jameson, Suri, and Nicholas all stood on the balcony, watching his every move.

Suddenly, Jameson appeared by his side, placing his hand on Seth's shoulder before he teleported them both up to the circular chamber of the tower where the others waited, leaning against the wall in front of them.

"Good morning all," Seth said, using his best mock Old British accent.

"Now's not the time for fun and games, Seth," Reem chided. "How is the princess these days?"

"Snappy, but no worse for wear." He smiled, blood still in his teeth. "She wants to see you."

"Wait, wait, wait," Nicholas said. "Princess?"

"Yes, Nicholas," Reem replied. "She's the daughter of one of the Mettirna Superiors. Her name's Hera, and she hates being called a princess." She smiled.

"And as I said, she wants to see you," Seth added.

"Then why don't you go get cleaned up and bring our guest to the meeting room?" Reem replied, lifting her hand to inspect the damage to Seth's jaw.

"I'm fine, really," he replied. "Just need to get the blood off my face."

"Go on then. Princess has orders, remember?" Reem winked.

Seth laughed and shook his head, turning and walking away before anything else could be said.

"Are you sure this is such a good idea?" Jameson asked.

"Hera and I used to be good friends," Reem replied. "In fact, I think that's why they sent her in the first place. She hates leaving Mettirna, but for something this big, I don't think she'd mind a visit to warmer, more humid climates." She smiled. "I'll be fine."

"I'm not so sure," Jameson said. "But in any case, you'll have the three of us by your side—plus Seth if he feels up to it." He winked.

"Meeting room then?" Nicholas said, gesturing to the door which led into the glass-ceilinged room. The others nodded and walked slowly into the room, each taking their seats around the table, Suri at the head of the table with Nicholas to her left and Reem to her right and Jameson standing directly behind Reem.

A few moments later, Seth arrived with Hera right behind him, ordering her guards to stay out in the main chamber. They walked into the room together, and Hera smiled as she looked into Reem's bright eyes.

"It's good to see you again, my friend," Hera said, dipping her head slightly.

"And you," Reem replied, smiling back. "Please, have a seat."

Hera did as she was asked, moving a chair from one of the sides of the table to sit at the head opposite from Suri. "Reem . . . Willow, is it?" she asked.

"Yes," Reem replied, blushing slightly.

"I knew you were not meant to be alone."

"Thank you, Hera," Reem said as Seth sat next to Nicholas at the table.

"Let's get down to business," Seth said, not wasting time. "Why are you here, princess?"

"You know why I'm here, Seth," she snapped. "But I would like to be introduced first if you don't mind." She paused. "I am Hera Emmagun, daughter of Superior Emmagun of Mettirna," she said, directing her words to Suri, Nicholas, and Jameson. "If I had to guess, I would say you are Jameson Willow," she said as her eyes rested on Jameson. "But I do not know the others. Negotiations will not begin until I know with whom I am negotiating."

"Of course, Hera," Reem replied, gesturing first to Jameson. "This is my husband, and these are my sister, Suri, and our dear friend, Nicholas." She gestured to the others respectively. "You are among friends, I assure you."

"Now then, please inform us why you are here, princess," Seth said again. "If not because we don't know, then for posterities sake at least."

Hera dipped her head slightly toward Seth before lifting it again and speaking. "I have been sent by my father, Superior Emmagun, and the others of Mettirna to forge an alliance between the cities of Mettirna and Athena. I have a few regulations, but nothing that is not understandable. I believe we should be able to come to terms very quickly."

"And what are these regulations?" Seth asked.

"First, we want no part in the war. We grow tired of fighting. If the Superiors of Admiri decide to wage war against your city, we will not come to your aid," Hera replied. "Second, we require that you keep a representative from Mettirna here to oversee your actions through the coming days up until such time that the Superiors of Admiri decide to attack."

"Is that all?" Seth asked mockingly.

"You will have assurances that Mettirna will not attack you, even if we are ordered by the Superiors of Admiri. We have no desire you fight you," Hera said. "We only want peace."

"Which is what we are trying to achieve as well," Reem replied. "By this time tomorrow, we will have sent representatives to both the Humans and the Purists in an attempt to have peace between us all."

"And you really think that this action will bode well for you, Reem?" Hera laughed. "They would kill you before your representatives could even set foot in their settlements."

"The Purists have already made it clear that they are willing to forge an alliance with us—one in which they will come to our aid if the Superiors of Admiri attack," Suri snapped. "And once that alliance is made, the Humans will likely join in as well."

"I highly doubt that, dear," Hera replied. "The Purists are trying to make an alliance with the Superiors of Admiri as we speak."

"Not anymore," Suri replied. "I put an end to that."

"Do tell," Hera encouraged, leaning back in her chair to hear what Suri had to say.

"I lived among the Purists in Africa, and when they found out I was Advanced, I informed them that I was a spy placed there by Marcus himself. They no longer trust Admiri," she replied.

"I should've known that any sister of Reem's would be just as smart and witty as she." She smiled.

"So let me get this straight," Jameson said, speaking for the first time since Seth and Hera had entered. "You want us to make an alliance with you so that we can protect you even though you will not come to our aid if we are attacked by the Superiors?" he asked her.

Hera shook her head. "We don't expect anything in return from you, though we would love to have a representative of your own within our walls. We do not require that you come to our aid should we be attacked by the Superiors of Admiri."

"You still haven't said anything about the Humans or the Purists," Reem added. "What if one of them decided to attack us—however doubtful that may be—then what would you do?"

"That would be up to the representative left in the city. They would be given the right to decide for us what would be the best decision for our own people in the actions done by this rebellion," Hera replied.

"So what is the benefit for us?" Jameson asked.

"As I said, you would know that the Mettirnians will not attack you. You will have full assurance of that, I promise you," Hera replied. "What more do you want?"

"Who would be your representative?" Reem asked before Jameson could open his mouth to reply to Hera.

"Who would you like?" Hera asked in response. "Perhaps someone you know? You have several recruits within your walls that are from Mettirna. Perhaps one of them would be willing."

"Like Maria, perhaps?" Jameson asked. "We've grown quite fond of her, and she is a recruit from your city after all."

"No, she is unacceptable," Hera replied. "She's trigger-happy and emotional—not someone that we would choose to inform us as to the goings-on of your rebellion."

"Who would you suggest?" Seth asked.

"I was thinking along the lines of Angel Wing or Brandon Syll— both of whom are from my city," she said. "And as I understand it, you're already acquainted with both of them. In fact, we could use both of them as representatives—they work best as a team, I'm sure you know." She smiled.

Reem looked around among Seth, Suri, Nicholas, and Jameson, relaying her thoughts into their minds and theirs into hers as she did so. "I think we need a moment to discuss your proposition," she said finally. "Would you give us a moment, Hera?" She gestured toward the doors.

"Of course," Hera replied, standing. "Take your time. My guards and I will wait in the main chamber."

Reem nodded and smiled as Hera exited the room and closed the door behind her. "Opinions, everyone?" she asked.

"I think that their main goal is to assure peace between us and them, without having to offer themselves up to fight. They're as tired of fighting as everyone else is," Seth added.

"I still don't see the point," Suri said. "They're far enough away from us that they should know we won't be attacking them anytime soon. Besides, with the way they've been acting lately, no one wants them on their side. They're worthless as an ally."

"No, not quite," Reem replied. "Hera has contacts all over the world. If we can get her to be the representative, it will be to our advantage."

"She'll never stay," Seth said. "I doubt she volunteered to come here in the first place—her father probably told it was this or he'd ground her for life." He laughed.

"I'm sure we can find an arrangement in which she would stay behind to be the representative," Reem returned. "If Angel and Brandon are the representatives, then we have no advantage at all."

"And what is our advantage if she is our representative?" Nicholas asked.

"As I said, she has contacts in many places around the world," Reem replied. "It isn't very well known, but the only way that the Humans are united is in the war. They are separated by city or settlement, and they have no formal government. They are falling apart, but Hera has contacts within the settlements— she knows things that we can use in our attempt to forge our alliances."

"Similar to how I would forge an alliance with the Purists," Suri added.

"Yes, similarly," Reem nodded. "So what do you think, my friends? Forge the alliance or send them back where they came from?"

"I think we need this alliance," Seth replied. "Without it, I think many of the people in the rebellion would return to Mettirna with them. Whereas if we make the alliance, there is a chance that many more people would come to Athena."

"Seth's right. We need this—if not for what it will give us, then at least for the assurance that if we lose the fight, those who survive will have a place to go," Nicholas added. "We need to be considering all the options."

"Of course," Reem replied, dipping her head. "We do need to be considering all of the options. Which means we need to be considering what will happen if the rebellion fails."

"Which means that we need this alliance. But we need them to offer safe haven for us if we fail," Jameson said. "And they haven't offered that yet."

"Then we'll make that one of our requirements," Reem replied. "Are we agreed then? Do we accept their terms?"

Everyone nodded their responses, and Reem whispered into Hera's mind for her to reenter.

A few moments later, Hera opened the door slowly and walked inside. "I'm assuming you've come up with some new term that you'd like my people to accept?" she asked as she sat back down.

Reem smiled at her bluntness. "We'd like you to offer safe haven for those of us who may require it should our rebellion fail," she replied.

"Safe haven? For how many?" Hera asked in response. "Mettirna—"

"Has more space inside it than you would like people to think," Reem said, cutting her off. "More than twice the amount needed to house the entire rebellion."

"I am not at liberty to offer that space to you," Hera replied.

"But you do have it, and we are only asking that you offer it in the most dire of circumstances," Seth said. "Most of the people here would rather die than run to Mettirna, but if Reem orders it, many will go. We're only asking that you offer a haven for those that do."

The room fell silent as Hera considered their terms, leaning back in her chair and looking up at the sky through the glass ceiling. "I may be able to give you what you want," she said finally, lowering her head to look around at the five who sat around her. "But I do not know how my father will react to my agreeing to your terms. We did not think of this as something you would ask of us. If the Superiors of Admiri find out that we have given you safe haven, they will slaughter us."

"They will try, but they cannot survive for long outside Mettirna's walls, and they don't have many teleporters within their ranks," Reem replied.

"Then I'll see what I can do. Do you have any teleporters who can take me back to Mettirna?" Hera asked.

"I'll see what I can do," Seth replied, standing and exiting the room.

"He'll find someone, don't worry. Our fastest, hopefully," Reem said, smiling. "I'm sure your father will agree to our terms."

"I will do what I can when I see him. I assure you," Hera said, dipping her head. "I must go. I will return with news from my father." She stood and walked out of the room, closing the door behind her as she did so.

"Now we have only to wait," Reem said.

"That's the hard part," Nicholas replied, smiling.

✦✦✦

Brittany stepped off the boat, glad to be back on dry land sooner than the captain had predicted—she knew he would come through for her.

"Wait here fifteen days. If I have not returned by then, I will not return," she told the captain before she turned to walk away.

"I will wait twenty if I must," he shouted back.

She turned around to face him once more. "Fifteen. No more. No less," she shouted, her white eyes glaring into his.

"Twenty," he whispered under his breath, quiet enough that she couldn't hear him as he watched her walk away from him, her hips swaying with every motion of her legs.

She walked quickly, knowing that the captain's eyes were on her as she did so, entering the woods as quickly as she could to ensure that he would no longer be watching her. It would take her two days at most to reach Athena, and that was if she was travelling slowly. She couldn't afford to waste time here—she had her orders, and she fully intended to carry them out.

Her feet were sure as they stepped through the various plants and young trees around her, and she wove her way through the tall trees and the shrubs that blocked her path, forging a trail as she went, heading straight to the city of Athena.

Morning Sickness

Mitchal paced in the main chamber of the central tower, waiting for Reem to meet with him. He'd been waiting for over an hour now—it had taken him twenty minutes to even get in contact with Jameson—and he found himself acting more like his brother than he cared to think about.

He'd heard from Maria about the princess's arrival and departure and heard that they were looking for a representative to send to Mettirna when she returned for good. He knew that he was right for the part, but he didn't know if Reem would agree. She didn't trust him as much as he trusted her, but he knew that he would be the perfect man for the job. Maria was even interested in returning with him—she was taking the squad back to Mettirna as he waited, and he knew she was wanted to return to her home.

Finally, Jameson appeared in the chamber once again, this time with a smile on his face. "Turning into your brother?" He laughed lightly, holding his hands up in defense when Mitchal shot him a fierce glare. "Reem's awake now," he said. "She'll meet you in the meeting room in a moment if you'd like to go and have a seat." He gestured toward the meeting room across the chamber.

"Of course," Mitchal replied. "Thank you." He turned and walked quickly into the meeting room, taking a seat at the table as he waited.

Several minutes later, Reem stepped through the door with Jameson at her side. She had dark circles under her eyes and held her hands over her stomach as though she were sick.

"Reem," he said, standing when she entered. "Are you feeling alright?" he asked as she sat.

"Yes, I'm fine, Mitchal. Thank you," she replied wearily.

"I told you not to see anyone," Jameson whispered under his breath.

"Don't tell me what to do," she replied, elbowing his side firmly and causing him to buckle in pain. "What did you need to see me about, Mitchal?" she asked.

"Uh," he started, pausing. "I wanted to talk to you about the possibility of myself being the representative that you send to Mettirna."

"What makes you think you're cut out for that?" she asked, her shoulders hunching in on herself as she spoke.

"Are you sure you're alright?" he asked.

"I'm fine," she snapped. "Answer the question."

"Um. Well, I know politics very well, plus Maria and myself were considering moving to Mettirna anyway since it is her home, and I just think that I am the right person for the job," he told her, leaning back in his chair.

Suddenly, she started to cringe, her whole body shaking as her eyes conveyed the pain she felt. "I—I—I—"

"I'm sorry, Mitchal," Jameson said, pulling her chair out and picking her up into his arms. "We'll have to continue this discussion later. My wife's not feeling well." He rushed out of the room, carrying her back to their bedroom as quickly as he could.

Mitchal stood and followed him out the door, stopping when he reached the center of the main chamber, hearing Reem's whimpers of pain as Jameson carried her away.

Something wasn't right. The savior shouldn't be in pain—she was a healer.

⁂

Reem did everything in her power not to cry out in pain as Jameson set her gently down on the bed. She'd been feeling sick all night long, a sharp pain running through her body every few minutes for no reason that she could decipher.

"What can I get you, Reem?" Jameson asked. "What do you need?"

"I don't"—she paused to take a deep breath—"know." Her eyes revealed the truth of the pain she felt though she tried to hide it from Jameson. "I don't know!" she screamed.

"What about Nicholas?" he asked. "He's a doctor, maybe he'll be able to help?"

She opened her mouth to speak, but all that ushered from her lips was a shriek of pain. "Go," she whispered as soon as she could take a breath to speak. "Hurry."

He nodded and kissed her forehead lightly before teleporting from the room. A few seconds later, he returned with Nicholas in tow, stopping when he stood beside the bed Reem lay on.

"Jameson, what's going on?" Nicholas said as they landed. "Reem?" he said as soon as he saw her writhing in pain on the mattress. "What's wrong?"

"Help her!" Jameson ordered.

"Okay, okay," Nicholas whispered, trying to reassure himself as much as Reem. "What do you feel?" he asked her as he knelt by her side and felt her forehead with his palm.

"Shooting pains. In my—abdomen. Hard to—breathe. Help me," she whispered in his mind, unable to get enough breath in her lungs to speak.

"Focus on your breathing, Reem. I need my bag. I'll be right back," he whispered. "Jameson, if she can't breathe, you might have to do it for her. Do you understand?" he asked.

Jameson nodded. "Go, Nicholas," he snapped, pushing the man out of his way and kneeling beside Reem as he used his gifts to feel for her life signs.

Nicholas ran out of the central tower, back toward the small building that he and Suri had called home before moving into the tower with Reem and Jameson the night before. His feet took him as fast as they could, weaving through the crowds and pushing people out of his way as he thought of Reem writhing in pain and the child that must have been in even more pain inside her. He'd never heard of anything like this happening in the settlement, but then again, he'd never known an Advanced to be impregnated by another Advanced.

Soon he arrived in his home, ran to the closet where he'd kept his doctors equipment and fished it out of the many bags that had been thrown inside. He then took a moment to catch his breath before taking off running once again, back toward the central tower, this time with his bag in hand. As he ran, Suri appeared beside him, easily matching his pace.

"What's wrong?" she asked as she ran beside him. "Who's been hurt?"

"Reem," he said as best as he could as he tried to keep his breathing steady and his feet sure as he ran through the crowds in the city.

"Reem?" she replied. "Hurry."

Together, they ran, soon arriving back in the tower, running quickly back into Jameson and Reem's bedroom, where Jameson was pumping air into her lungs. "She can't breathe," he whispered when he paused.

"Keep doing what you're doing, Jameson," Nicholas ordered. "I think I know what she needs." He knelt beside the bed, directly beside where Jameson now knelt, and began fishing around inside his bag for a serum that had been developed in the settlement that he thought might do the trick. When he found it, he firmly injected it straight into her neck, the needle easily piercing through her skin. "It shouldn't take more than a few moments," he said. "How's the baby?"

"Alive for now," Jameson replied between breaths.

"Good, let's try and keep it that way," Nicholas said, taking Reem's arm and checking for her pulse. "Pulse is getting stronger," he whispered, his eyes glancing away from Reem to Suri who stared at him, her eyes tearing with fear as she looked into his eyes. "Okay, Jameson, let's see if she can breathe on her own," he said, placing his hand on Jameson's shoulder.

Jameson nodded in response and waited a few seconds, staring at Reem's limp body in front of him.

He waited.

And waited.

The seconds ticked by slowly, and suddenly, her lifeless eyes opened, a silver light shining onto the ceiling above her. Her lungs took in an abundance of air, her chest rising and falling with the breath that flowed through her body.

"Reem?" Jameson whispered.

"How do you feel?" Nicholas asked, cutting Jameson off.

Reem's eyes closed once again, the light fading quickly before she reopened them and turned to look at Nicholas. "What happened?" she asked.

"I don't know for sure," he replied. "But it looks like we stopped it. How's the little one?"

She closed her eyes again, communicating with the baby that grew in her belly. "He's afraid. He doesn't understand what's going on," she whispered, her eyes remaining closed as she spoke.

Jameson let out a heavy breath, one not even he knew that he'd been holding. He placed his hand on Reem's cheek and wiped a tear from under her left eye. "How are you?" he asked.

"Better now," she whispered back, still breathing heavily. "Just need to catch my breath." Her eyes opened once again, and she smiled at her sister before her eyes flicked back to Jameson's. "Thank you," she whispered.

"Don't thank me," he replied. He turned to Nicholas and stared into his eyes. "Thank you. You have no idea how much I owe you now."

"Don't mention it," Nicholas replied. "Anything to help the two of you."

"We may need a convincing lie to tell Mitchal." Reem laughed lightly.

"We'll think of something." Jameson laughed back, though there was little humor in his voice.

"We'll leave the two of you alone," Nicholas said. "Let me know if you need anything else. I'll have my bag on me now." He stood and walked to the door, taking Suri by the hand and dragging her out beside him.

"How are you feeling, Reem—really?" Jameson asked as soon as Nicholas closed the door behind him.

"I'm fine," she replied. "Really." She smiled at his concerned eyes.

"Are you sure?" he asked, brushing the hair away from her face with his hand.

"Yes, I'm sure." She lifted her hand to stroke his cheek. "I love you, Jameson."

"I love you." The corners of his mouth turned up slightly.

"What will you tell Mitchal?" she asked.

"I'll tell him that you're developing another gift and that it's very straining on the body," he replied. "It's believable, isn't it?" His smile brightened.

"Good idea," she whispered, her voice still strained.

"I can get Nicholas back in here if you need—"

"I'm fine, Jameson," she cut him off. "Really, I am. I just need to catch my breath."

"Try and get some sleep then," he replied. "I'll be right here if you need me."

She nodded, closing her eyes and drifting off into sleep before she could reply, her chest rising and falling rhythmically as her breathing steadied.

"Sleep well, my love," Jameson whispered as he stood and walked to the opposite side of the bed, lying down beside her, being careful not to wake her. He watched her as she slept, content to watch as she dreamt of things that he could only imagine.

～✦✧✦～

Jameson woke to the feel of Reem's gentle fingers running through his hair. His eyes snapped open to the dim morning light, seeing her eyes only inches from his, smiling brightly as she stared at him. "Good morning," she whispered, continuing to run her fingers through his hair. "Sleep well?"

He shook his head. "I wasn't supposed to be sleeping," he replied.

"It's alright, Jameson." She laughed lightly. "I only woke up a moment ago."

"How do you feel?" he asked, sitting up and allowing his head to clear.

"I'm fine," she replied, sitting up behind him and wrapping her arms around his waist. "You?"

"Are you sure?" he asked, ignoring her question.

"Stop it, Jameson. I'm fine," she said.

"Reem, you know I'm only trying to help." He sighed, resting his hands on hers. "I'm sorry."

"It's alright." She laughed. "We should get up soon." She moved her hands and ran her fingers through her hair, yawning quietly before she stood and opened the curtains to peek outside.

"What time is it?" he asked, blinking against the light.

"Nine o'clock, maybe?" she replied, shrugging her shoulders. "Nicholas wants to see me."

"He probably has a theory as to what happened yesterday," he said as he stood and walked to the closet.

"He does." She smiled brightly as she picked out a pair of jeans and a cotton shirt out of the closet and put them on while Jameson did the same. "Ready?" she asked as he fastened his belt.

He nodded, reaching out a hand for her to take before opening the door and leading her through. "Where's Nicholas?" he asked.

"In the main chamber, waiting for us," she replied as they walked down the hall.

"Reem, Jameson," Nicholas said as they walked into the circular chamber, "did you sleep well?"

"Much better yes," Reem replied, smiling. "You think you know what happened?" Her eyebrows rose slightly.

"I have a theory, yes," Nicholas replied. "As far as we know, there hasn't been an Advanced pregnancy like this before now, so it makes sense to think that there could be complications." He paused. "The good news is that the medication I gave you yesterday seems to have worked well—so far, at least. I should be able to continue administering the treatment whenever you need it, but I hope that I won't have to use it very often. I've never had a patient who needed it longer than a month, so I'm not sure what the long-term effects of it will be."

"Is there anything else we can do?" Jameson asked.

"There are a few other treatments we can try, but this is the one that's had the most success in the settlement," Nicholas answered. "But the others don't have any adverse long-term effects as far as we know."

"Maybe we should at least give them a try then," Reem said. "It can't hurt any, can it?"

"No, I don't think so." Nicholas smiled. "The only trouble is that they only work after the onslaught of the symptoms occur, whereas with the one I gave you, I can administer it daily—or every other day—as needed."

"Okay, well, what do you think would be our best option?" Jameson asked.

"Honestly, it's up to you," Nicholas replied. "If you want something that I can administer before the symptoms occur, then stick with what I gave you. It all depends on how well you can deal with the symptoms, I suppose."

"In that case, maybe we should stick with the one you gave her yesterday," Jameson said. "I don't want her in any more pain than she's already in."

"But the pregnancy is going to last longer than a month," Reem added.

"I don't know, Reem." He shook his head.

"Well, hey, you don't have to decide right now," Nicholas said, trying to lighten the mood. "In any case, you have a visitor." He gestured to the meeting room. "Mitchal got here an hour ago—wanted to see if you were okay."

"I'll go see him in a moment," Reem replied, before turning back to Jameson. "What did you think about his proposition—sending him and Maria to Mettirna as our representatives?"

"I think it's a good idea," Jameson said. "Maria's smarter than she'd have you think, and Mitchal seems to know what he's talking about."

"Then what do we do about his brother?" she asked.

"We've gotten all the information that we're going to get out of him—which honestly wasn't much, even with you searching his mind. I say we keep him here for now." He shrugged.

"You're thinking of sending Mitchal to Mettirna?" Nicholas asked.

"Considering it, yes," Reem replied. "I haven't made my final decision yet, but then again, I haven't had much time to think about it." She smiled. "I'll talk to Seth today hopefully."

"Let me know what you decide," he replied. "I have a few house calls to make, and Suri's offered to let me make her a nurse for the day." He smiled. "I'll see you both this afternoon, yes?"

"Yes, of course." She smiled back as she watched him leave the room. "So what do you think?" she asked Jameson. "Do you think he'd fit the part?"

"I think so, yes," Jameson replied. "But I'd like to know Seth's opinion before we make a decision."

She nodded and started walking toward the meeting room.

He followed her across the chamber to the meeting room, walking inside just behind her as she spoke to Mitchal. "Hello, it's good to see you again." She smiled, taking a seat across from him at the table while Jameson stood behind her.

"It's good to see you as well," Mitchal replied. "I take it you're feeling better today?"

"Yes, I am thank you," Reem replied. "Nicholas found a medication that sufficiently cured me for the evening."

"It's strange. I didn't know healers could get sicknesses," Mitchal mused, glancing curiously between the two of them as he spoke. "How is that possible?"

"There are things you're better off not knowing, Mitchal," Jameson replied. "Trust me."

"I don't believe that for a moment," Mitchal replied. "You know I can be trusted."

"I know," Reem said. "But Jameson's right. There are things that you are better off not knowing. If the Superiors of Admiri ever captured you, it's better that you don't know what's happening to me." She paused. "Do you understand?"

"Yes." He nodded. "There's something going on that the Superiors would kill for—something important." He stood to his feet. "You're right, I am better off not knowing. And I take it you haven't made a decision yet?" he asked.

"No, not yet I'm afraid," Reem replied. "I'm meeting with Seth this afternoon to discuss it, so I'll let you know tomorrow. Plus we need to run it by Hera after she returns—but I'm sure you'll be a fine choice in her eyes." She smiled. "I'll have an answer for you by tomorrow night."

"Thank you," he replied. "I'll see you tomorrow then." He smiled before turning and walking out of the room.

"Did he really change his mind that easily?" Jameson asked when Mitchal was far enough away not to hear them.

"He did, yes." She nodded. "Remember his gifts, Jameson. He knows we're telling him the truth—we believe that he's better off not knowing about what's going on."

He nodded. "An unusual gift, that one."

"It is." She smiled, tilting her head to look up at him as he stood behind her.

Brittany stood on the edge of the hill, looking out over the valley below—out onto the city of Athena that sprawled before her. She'd arrived on the valley's edge a few hours ago, but she knew that it wasn't yet time. The squad had left the city for now, but they would be returning soon, and that was when she would make her move—when the people were occupied with the coming of the princess from Mettirna. That was exactly the distraction she needed.

She sat down and leaned against a tree, pulling her weapon from her backpack, cleaning the pistol with her hands before pulling her knife from its sheath and polishing it. She meticulously cleaned all of her weapons, knowing that soon they would be needed—the cleaner the better, if you asked her.

Soon she began to hum with the rhythm of her polishing fingers, singing the song of Freedom that her mother had written two days before the Crash. Two days. That was all it took before her mother was taken from her. She and Seth had been the lucky ones. Her mother had sent them to the country a week before the Crash. She'd called the day she'd written the song; she'd wanted to sing them to sleep.

She caught herself and bit her tongue, chiding herself for taking the trip down memory lane—memories she'd rather forget. She took the knife that was in her hand and nicked the skin of her forearm with its sharp blade, punishment for remembering. Life was about now, not about then.

She let out a battle cry and threw the blade through the air, embedding it deeply into the trunk of a tree a few dozen feet away from where she sat.

Representative

Seth walked quickly from his post at the watchtower toward the central tower, remembering that Reem had wanted them all to meet again exactly twenty minutes ago. Soon he was walking up the steps, taking them two by two as he hurried up them and through the main chamber, into the meeting room where Reem and Jameson sat talking with Nicholas and Suri who sat across from them. "Sorry I'm late," he said, sitting down at the head of the table where Suri usually sat. "I was taking my turn at the watchtower and lost track of time." He smirked.

"It's alright," Suri answered. "We had family matters to attend to anyway."

Seth cocked his head to the side. "Is something going wrong with the pregnancy?" He turned from Suri to look into Reem's smiling eyes. "What happened?" he asked.

"The Advanced version of morning sickness," Nicholas answered before Reem could speak. "We were discussing what treatment to put Reem on for the duration of the pregnancy."

"Ahh," Seth replied, stroking his facial hair. "Well, I wouldn't know anything about medicinal problems, would I?" He smiled.

"In any case," Jameson said, "we have something we need to run by you, and then we need to decide on a representative from Mettirna."

"Well, first things first, I think Mitchal would make a superb representative." Seth smiled, proud of his intuition on the matter.

Reem smiled back. "You think he would be a good choice? With Maria at his side, of course."

"He's an excellent scholar, and he knows when people are lying to him. I think he could use that to our advantage," Seth answered. "Next problem." He smiled.

"Seth, it's not that simple." Reem laughed. "Democracy, remember?"

"Mitchal would make an excellent representative," Nicholas replied.

"I don't know him well enough, honestly," Suri said. "But if Nicholas speaks so highly of him, then I'm sure he'd be a good choice."

"Well then, I guess it is that simple." Reem smiled, a tinge of pain showing on her face as her hands moved to her waist. "I'm fine," she said before anyone could ask. "He's just moving."

"Are you sure you're alright?" Jameson asked, his eyes filled with concern as they stared into hers. "Positive?" he added before she could say she was fine.

"I promise. I'm fine." She smiled, taking his hand in hers. "Back to business then." She nodded. "Do we want to push for Hera to be their representative, or are we content with Angel and Brandon?" she asked, still holding her hand over her stomach.

"Reem, are you sure you're up for this?" Seth asked.

"I just need to occupy my mind." She paused. "Someone answer my question please."

"Personally, I'm content with Angel and his friend," Suri replied. "But I don't know much about politics." She shrugged.

Nicholas stood and walked to Reem's side, placing his hand on her stomach gently and checking her pulse with his other hand.

"What are you doing, Nicholas?" Reem asked. "I said I'm fine!"

"As your doctor, I'm going to have to ask you to calm down," he replied, looking into her angry eyes until her anger dissipated. "Stay here. I'll go get my things." He stood and walked out the door, heading straight to his bedroom.

"Reem, if you're not up for this, Jameson and I can work it all out," Seth said, concern edging his voice as he leaned over the table.

"No, I'm fine Seth," she replied. "Really."

"Reem, please," Jameson whispered in her ear. "Just . . . just do whatever Nicholas tell you. Please."

"I just need some pain killers or something. It's nothing."

Soon Nicholas returned with his doctor's bag in hand and knelt beside Reem once again. "How do you feel—really?" he asked as he placed his hand over her stomach once more.

"I'm fine."

"That's not what I asked." He shot her a sharp glare.

She took a deep breath. "I feel a sharp pain here." She placed her hand on the right side of her abdomen, and Nicholas moved his hand to inspect the area. "And I have a headache." She winced when his fingers pressed lightly onto her abdomen.

"The headache I can fix easily." Nicholas smiled. "But it looks like you may have a broken rib. How long have you had this pain?" he asked.

"A few weeks maybe?" she replied.

"Your gifts should have healed this right away," he thought out loud. "But I can treat it." He looked up at Jameson's worried glare. "Don't worry, she'll be fine," he said, smiling. "Why don't you go lay down and I'll get a bandage ready for you?" He stood and held out his hand to help her get to her feet.

Reem sighed and stood, deciding that for the moment it was better not to argue.

"I'll take her to our room," Jameson said. He took her by the arm and gently led her back to the bedroom.

"I'm not that delicate, Jameson," she snapped as they walked through the main chamber.

"From now on, I'm ignoring everything you say about your health." He sighed. "Why didn't you tell me about this sooner?"

"I didn't think it was a problem," she replied. "I thought maybe it was something that my gifts needed a little extra time to heal."

He thought for a moment before replying. "I have an idea."

"Go ahead," she said as she slowly sat down on the bed and leaned back against the wall.

"You're sure?" he asked.

"It's worth a try," she replied, wincing before she lay on her back, facing the ceiling.

"Alright." He took her hand in his and sent healing through his fingers into her palm.

Her breathing quickened as the healing pulsed through her veins, her hand clutching tighter to his. Her eyes closed as she focused the healing on her broken rib, feeling the power as it stitched the bone together bit by bit.

Nicholas stepped inside, holding a large bandage in one hand and a syringe filled with clear liquid in the other. "Feeling better, I take it?" He smiled as Reem's eyes opened.

"Much." She smiled back.

"I'd still like to take a look if you don't mind," he said as he walked to her side, Jameson moving aside to make room for him next to Reem.

"Go ahead," she replied, carefully lifting her shirt for him to inspect her rib cage.

His hand brushed over her ribs, pressing down lightly on the soft skin as he felt along her bones. "Looks like that did the trick," he whispered, moving his hand to her belly. "How is he?"

She closed her eyes again and took in a deep breath, feeling for the child inside her. "He's fine. Happy as ever." She smiled as her eyes opened.

"Good. He should be." Nicholas smiled back at her. "Let me know if you need anything." He paused, picking the syringe up from the bedside table where he'd set it down and holding it up for her to see. "This is the treatment that we decided on. If you're feeling anything similar to what you felt before, you or Jameson should be able to administer the treatment without me." He set it back down on the table.

"Thank you, Nicholas," Jameson replied.

"Hera, it's good to see you again," Reem said as the four members of the squad made their way up the steps into the central chamber of the tower.

"And you," Hera replied, smiling at her old friend.

"What news have you brought us?" Reem asked, motioning for Hera to walk with her into the meeting room.

"My father sends his regards," Hera replied as they entered the room, taking their seats among Suri, Nicholas, Seth, and Jameson who were already seated in their usual places around the table. "And he is willing to agree to your terms. We are willing to house as many of you as is necessary in the case of emergency."

"Good." Reem smiled. "We wouldn't want to make enemies of you when it's not necessary."

"Nor would we." Hera smiled back.

"We've chosen our representative to send to Mettirna," Seth added.

"Good." Hera turned to face him. "Who will be returning with us?"

"Mitchal and Maria—I believe you know them both," Seth replied.

"I do." Hera nodded. "A good choice, if I may say so."

"So we thought." Seth smiled. "And we have a request."

"Go on," Hera replied, her eyebrows rising slightly.

"We would like you to be the representative from Mettirna—if only for a short time," he replied. "We believe it would be best if we had someone more intimately familiar with the politics in Mettirna."

"I'm not sure, Seth." She shook her head.

"We're not asking that it be permanent," Reem added. "We're only asking that you stay for a few months at most."

"Only a few months?" Hera asked.

"No longer than four," Seth added. "At which point we'd be willing to accept Angel and Brandon as your representatives."

"I'll"—Hera paused, her eyes dropping to the table—"think about it."

"Thank you," Reem replied. "I appreciate it." Her head dipped slightly.

⚜

David woke to the sound of feet shuffling around in the chambers beyond the one in which he was being held. His eyes opened widely as his head tilted, trying to hear more as the scuffling continued. A few moments later, a dark-haired woman stepped into the doorway, her white eyes opened widely to view his shocked gaze as she lifted the gun in her right-hand level with his face.

"David Sanders?" she asked, unmoving from her offensive stance in the doorway, her gun still aimed between his eyes.

Unable to will his mouth to speak at the sight of her white eyes, David forced a hard nod before glancing quickly between his bonds and her white eyes. "A little help?" he spoke finally.

"Glad to find you in one piece," she replied, placing the weapon back in its holster and walking to his side. He tried not to stare into her eyes as she pulled a sharp blade from a sheath on her side and sliced his bonds. "We need to hurry," she said. "Get up."

He did as she said, standing quickly to his feet and following as she handed him a pistol and ran from the room, angling toward the exit. She went up the steps first, making sure the area was clear before she signaled him to climb up behind her. When he did, she once again started running—this time in the direction of the central tower.

"Where are we going?" he whispered when they stopped three buildings away from the tower.

"The tower," she replied.

"Why?"

"I must complete my task," she answered, continuing to stare straight ahead toward the tower and away from David's staring eyes. "You don't need the details."

"Yes, I do," he replied. "Seeing as I'm part of your task, I think I need the details."

"No, you don't." Her head turned toward him, and he imagined that her white eyes were piercing into his.

"Yes, I do," he replied. "For one thing, who are you?"

"My name is not to be uttered here," she told him, turning back toward the tower. "I am to find the Prophet and return with him to Admiri."

"Then I'll help you."

"I don't need your help."

"Then why get me out first?" he asked.

"If I had taken Seth and then gone to retrieve you, I would not have made it out of the city alive," she said flatly. "I am no fool, nor am I one to suffer fools." She turned back to him. "Go to the far edge of the city, the vacant edge, and wait for me in the farthest watchtower." She paused. "I will be there in less than two hours."

He opened his mouth to speak, and she thrust her elbow into his crotch, knocking him to his knees as he cringed in pain.

"Do as I tell you," she commanded. "Until we return to Admiri, you take your orders from me."

"Yes, ma'am," he replied, carefully standing to his feet before he turned to walk away.

Hera took the steps out of the tower two by two, quickly making her way down to her guards who waited on the bottom step. Soon she stood beside them, her breathing heavy with the sudden rush of activity. She'd told the others that she needed time to think and that she needed to inform Mitchal and Maria of their duties for their arrival in Mettirna. She ordered her guards to find the couple before she sat on the steps and dropped her head into her hands.

Suddenly, she felt a hand on her shoulder, and she turned her head to look at Reem who now sat beside her with Jameson standing behind her, holding her other hand. Reem placed her arm around Hera's shoulders and whispered, "I'm sorry to put you in this position."

"No, it's alright," she replied. "I just need time to think." She smiled slightly before dropping her head back into her hands. "I don't know if I can handle being away for more than a few days."

"Then stay for a few days," Reem replied. "You'll need to be ready for if you're forced to leave your city, Hera. You can't always count on your father to keep you safe."

"I know." She sighed. "I can stay, but no promises on how long. And I'll need to return to Mettirna once a month."

"Thank you, Hera." Reem smiled, pausing when she heard the thoughts in Hera's mind. "I'll leave you alone." She stood and walked back up the steps with Jameson at her side.

Hera lifted her head and watched as her guards came into view with Mitchal in tow. She smiled and stood, motioning for them to come inside before she turned and walked up the steps. "Reem!" she shouted, seeing Reem and Jameson about to enter the main chamber.

"Yes," Reem whispered in her mind, stopping and turning to look her in the eye. *"You can use the meeting room."*

"Thank you," Hera thought, tilting her head to the side at the strange sensation of someone else talking inside her mind.

She made her way inside, passing Jameson and Reem in the main chamber and smiling as Suri, Nicholas, and Seth exited the meeting room and joined Reem and Jameson. She walked inside and sat down at the head of the table while she waited for her guards to arrive with Mitchal.

"What did she say?" Seth asked Reem when Hera was out of earshot.

"Yes," Reem replied, smiling into Seth's inquisitive eyes. "She said she'd stay."

Seth let out a breath of air. "Good. We need all the help we can get."

"There's no guarantee that she'll stay for very long though," Reem added. "She'll stay as long as she feels comfortable doing so, and she'll train Angel and Brandon for when she decides to leave."

"Okay." Seth nodded.

Hera's guards entered—four men and one woman—with Mitchal in tow. They turned to enter the meeting room when Reem spoke up. "Wait," she said, stopping them all in their tracks.

The men all came to attention, and Mitchal turned to look her in the eye. "What's wrong?" he asked, his eyebrows furrowing.

"Brittany," Seth whispered, so quietly that no one but Reem could hear him. The woman who had entered with the guards stepped out from behind them, her dark hair covering the majority of her downturned face.

Hera then appeared from the meeting room and paused, staring at the woman. "You," she whispered, "you shouldn't be here."

"Guards, take her," Reem said, pointing to the woman.

"Do it," Hera added.

Seth stepped between Brittany and the guards, holding out his hands defensively as he turned to face them. "Please, don't do this," he pleaded.

"Step away, Seth," Reem replied. "Or I'll be forced to move you."

"Reem, please," he begged. "She's my sister."

"She's here for you, Seth," Reem said, taking a step closer to him with Jameson right behind her.

"No, no, that can't be," Seth replied, turning to look his sister in the eye. "You promised," he whispered. "You said you'd changed."

"I lied," Brittany replied, pulling a knife from a sheath on her side and wrapping her arm around Seth's neck with the blade grazing his skin.

Escape

"Seth!" Reem shouted as Brittany sliced through a thin layer of his skin.

"Stay back!" Brittany said. "I will not hesitate to kill him—and don't think I came here alone." She started to back away from them, taking Seth with her.

"Reem, let her take me," Seth thought, knowing she could hear him. *"Have Jameson teleport to the bottom of the steps while we're on the way out. Once we're outside, it won't be as hard to stop her."*

"Don't hurt him," Reem replied, holding up her hands defensively as she nodded ever so slightly to Seth. *"Jameson, once they're outside you teleport to the bottom of the steps and wait for them. Seth thinks that would be the best way to take her."*

"Tell Nicholas and Suri to stay put," Jameson thought back.

"I will," she thought, her eyes starting to shine silver light.

"That won't work on me," Brittany replied. "Stop it or I'll kill him."

"If you kill him, you lose your only leverage," Reem replied, her eyes now fully silver and shining toward Brittany's white eyes. "Look at me, Brittany."

"Stop!" Brittany yelled, placing her knife back in its sheath and pulling a pistol from her belt, firing it at Reem's forehead, the bullet stopping inches from her face.

"I'm afraid that won't work on me," Reem mocked. *"Don't look at my eyes,"* she whispered into the minds of the others, warning them of her power. "Now look at me!" she shouted.

Brittany kept her eyes on Jameson as she pointed her weapon at Seth's foot and fired a bullet into his arch. He cried out in pain, faltering slightly as she started dragging him out of the chamber. "The Superiors have healers in Admiri who can fix that in an instant," she whispered in his ear.

"Stop, Brittany," Reem replied, refusing to show how much she hated seeing him in pain.

"Let me go, and you have my word he won't be harmed," Brittany replied.

"You've broken your word before," Jameson said.

"Don't you even think about teleporting," she snapped back. Suddenly, she felt hands around her neck, squeezing hard enough to stop the flow of air.

"The last time we met, you tried choking me to death," Hera whispered, stepping between Reem and Brittany as she strangled the girl with her gifts. "It seems fitting that I do the same to you."

"Don't," Reem whispered back. "Hera, stop."

"Why should I?" Hera asked. "She tried to kill my father, Reem. Did you know that?"

"I know, Hera."

The anger on Brittany's face grew as she lifted the gun once more and fired it at Hera's shoulder. The bullet pierced through her body, stopping when it passed through her body and made its way toward Reem. Hera fell to her knees, crying out in pain as she clutched her shoulder, blood pouring out from between her fingers.

Brittany took in a lungful of air, her arms still holding firmly to Seth, though she hacked at the onslaught of oxygen to her system. "Don't try that again," she said.

Nicholas ran to Hera's side, putting pressure on the wound in an attempt to stop the bleeding.

"Don't touch her," Brittany warned, pointing her weapon at his forehead. "I won't hesitate to kill you."

"She can't, Nicholas," Reem replied, stepping between them and Brittany with Jameson following closely behind. "Go. I won't stop you," she said, gesturing toward the exit.

Brittany backed out the door, taking Seth with her as she awkwardly descended the stairs, holding her pistol up against his throat. "Don't follow me," she warned.

As soon as she was out of sight, Reem's now brown eyes looked into Jameson's. "Go," she whispered. "We'll be fine."

He nodded and did as he was told, teleporting outside and landing directly behind Brittany who continued descending the stairs with Seth in tow. "I told you not to follow me," she said as she turned to face him.

"I never was one for taking orders." He smiled, teleporting again. This time, he landed directly next to her and took Seth's arm before teleporting away with him in tow. A moment later, he returned, still smiling brightly into her anger filled-eyes. "Sorry about that." He laughed.

She yelled at the top of her lungs, her fist flying to connect with Jameson's chin before he could teleport behind her and trap both of her arms behind her back. "None of that now," he whispered in her ear. "You've got a date with a holding cell, and I'd hate for you to miss it."

She struggled to free herself of his grasp before Mitchal appeared beside them and tied her arms behind her back. Soon Hera's guards appeared by their side, and together, they escorted her down to the underground.

"You can't keep me here forever," she said as they tied her to a chair in what was once David's holding cell.

"Actually, I think we can," Jameson replied as he exited the room. "I'll be back later," he told the guards. "Make sure she doesn't try anything." He made his way up the steps quickly and teleported near the tower where Reem was tending to Seth and Hera. He took the steps two at a time, entering the central chamber and stopping in his tracks when he saw Reem writhing in pain on the ground. "Reem?" he whispered as he hurried to her side where Nicholas attempted to inject the medication into her forearm. "What happened?" he asked.

"I don't know," Nicholas replied. "A few seconds after you left, she just buckled over. Help me hold her arm still."

Jameson took her arm from Nicholas and watched as the man injected the medicine into her bloodstream. "Reem, it's okay, you're going to be fine," he whispered, seeing the pained look in her eyes as she stared back at him.

She opened her mouth to reply and cringed in pain once again. "What's happening to me?" she asked, a quiet cry of pain escaping from her lips.

"I don't know," Nicholas replied. "I'm doing everything I can." He paused, looking across the room at Seth and Hera who were both trying to stop the blood from pouring out of their own bodies.

"Go, Nicholas," Jameson whispered. "You said the medication would take a few minutes to work, right?"

Nicholas nodded and walked to Hera, whose injury was more severe of the two.

Jameson held firmly to Reem's hand as she clutched her stomach with her other and looked up into his eyes. "I don't think the baby likes it when you leave," she whispered, the pain leaving her face. "Our leash just got a little shorter."

The corners of his mouth turned up slightly as he looked into her gentle eyes. "Then we'll just have to stay as close as possible." He smiled, though in his heart he felt only fear. This baby was going to be the death of them.

❦

David had seen the guards walk Brittany down to the underground where he'd been kept not long ago, and he'd seen her go willingly. She didn't seem like the type who would go that easily, but he assumed she had a plan. In any case, he had now developed a plan of his own. He'd been waiting outside the opening to the underground for hours now, watching and waiting. He hadn't seen her come out of the cave, and since his gifts were taken from him, he had to assume that she was still down there. The events played to his advantage—he knew the layout of the underground, and he could guess which room they'd placed her in. He had only to wait until dark before he would go down and retrieve her.

He leaned back against the wall of the building adjacent to the entrance, trying to look inconspicuous as he watched the guards shuffling positions around the entrance and people walking past to their homes. The gun Brittany had given him was still tucked nicely into his belt and covered by his shirt, and his hand continually moved behind his back to make sure it hadn't been magically whisked away by one of the Advanced who walked all around him. It seemed strange that he could no longer call himself one of them. He was purely human now, and he didn't know if that would be changing anytime soon. When Reem Kahrin had visited him a few days ago, she'd used her gift on him again. Apparently, now it would be impossible for any giver to give him gifts. His body's chemistry would no longer accept the advancements.

He lifted his eyes to the sky and watched as the sun descended below the horizon and waited for his eyes to adjust to the relative darkness before he moved. He walked across the street to another building adjacent to the opening and waited while the remaining people in the streets hurried to their homes, none of them aware of the demon that lurked in a holding cell beneath them. David watched and waited until the last of them disappeared into their homes, leaving only himself and the guards for the underground standing in the street.

He slowly made his way up behind one of the guards, slicing his neck with a sharp blade he'd found in one of the homes, before he turned to the other guard and pointed his pistol at the man's forehead. "Downstairs," he said, motioning for the man to descend the steps. "Take your friend with you."

The man dropped his weapon and hauled the first guard to the opening, pushing him through before he himself descended. As soon as he reached the bottom, David poked his head down the hole and checked for more guards before he walked down. He again pointed his weapon at the guard and stepped closer to whisper in his ear. "You're going to go to your friends and tell them that the Savior has requested their presence on the surface. Don't forget that I can hear you." The guard stared back at him, unmoving and unspeaking. "Do it or I'll kill you now."

"You'll kill me either way," the man replied.

"As you wish." David reached out and snapped the man's neck. He then peeked around the bend to the holding cell where he knew they would be keeping her.

Two guards stood next to the cell, with Brittany inside tied to a chair. Neither of them saw him yet. He continued to watch as Brittany recognized his arrival, her body growing stiff and her eyes widening as she stared at his location. She lifted her hand and waved femininely, signaling that she had already freed herself from her bonds before she stood and walked to the gated doorway that stood between her and the outside world. "Hey, boys," she whispered. "Wanna come out and play?" She reached her arm through the gate and grabbed one of the men's pistols, pointing it between his eyes as they both turned to point their machine guns at her.

David then came out from behind the bend and shot both of the guards before either of them could say or do a thing. "Miss me?" he asked.

"I was fully prepared to free myself before you arrived—you simply made that task slightly easier." She paused, pointing to one of the guards. "Get the key. Let me out."

"Yes, ma'am," he replied. He walked over to the guard and retrieved the key from his belt. Lifting it in his hand, he smiled. "I have a few conditions."

"I am your superior," she said, her white eyes burning into his.

"Stop taking me for granted and let me help you complete your task," he replied. "I saw what happened outside, and I have a feeling that's what's going to happen if you try this on your own again."

"Fine," she spat. "Now get me out of here before one of them finds you down here."

"Yes, ma'am." He walked to the gate and unlocked it, waiting for her to exit before he turned to follow her back up the steps. "You take point."

"Of course I'll take point," she said blandly. She disarmed one of the dead men, strapping all of his weapons and extra ammunition to her own body before turning back to David. "Disarm him."

David did as he was told, following her lead and disarming the dead man before he followed her back to the surface.

⚜

Seth placed his hands on the banister of the balcony as he looked out over the outside of the city. After Reem had healed him, he'd come to the only place in the city that he knew of where he could be completely alone—the watchtower on the far side of the city. He kept a watchful eye on the darkened horizon as his thoughts took him to other places, settling on the underground where Brittany was being held.

He'd expressed his wishes not to have her captured, and he'd even expressed to Reem that he would rather have gone with her to Admiri than have her placed down there, but it wasn't up to him. Still, he couldn't bring himself to go down there and see her. He'd heard that she'd freed David, and he knew that he should have been looking into his location, but he couldn't bring himself to do anything but stare out at the horizon. He wished that Brittany hadn't come. She could have refused the order, and then everything would still be as it used to be.

He knew he could change her heart—he knew it. He just hadn't had the opportunity to do so. Brittany wasn't much of a listener, but he knew he could get to her.

He heard footsteps behind him on the stairs, but he ignored the light shuffle. Most likely Reem had sent someone to check on him. He smiled as he thought of how she worried for him and the others. She was already a mother in so many ways.

"Hello, brother," Brittany's familiar voice whispered in his ear, startling him into turning to look into Brittany's white eyes. He could still remember the day that had changed her eyes from violet to white—the day of the Crash.

"Brittany," he whispered under his breath.

"Surprised to see me?" she asked, turning to face the stairs as she leaned against the banister. "You shouldn't be. You know how crafty I can be."

"Rather, he should have known that I would've come back for you," David added, the sound coming from the staircase where Brittany continued to stare.

Seth's eyes turned toward David as he ascended the staircase, smiling brightly as he did so. "You're right. Both of you," Seth said.

"You know what I need, don't you?" Brittany asked as she turned to face him once more. "You're such a clever little brother, I was sure you'd figure it out."

"You need information that only I carry," Seth replied. "But I won't give you that information, Brittany. You know that."

"And you know that I won't take no for an answer and that I have no problem with hurting you." She whipped a knife out of its sheath and threw it toward him, nicking his ear before it lodged into the wall. "And you know my aim well enough to know that I could have taken your ear off."

Seth did not reply as he turned back to look out across the vast forest outside of the city, his eyes darting here and there as he searched for any form of threat that needed to be voiced to the city. He wouldn't stop doing his job until she decided that it was time for the three of them to leave.

Brittany reached out her hand and cupped it around his chin, turning his face so he would look her in the eye. "Don't you pretend that I won't complete my task simply because you're my brother. You know I don't think very highly of family, Seth. Remember what uncle did to us."

"How could I forget?" he whispered under his breath. "He was drunk, Brittany. I am your brother, and I've done nothing to betray your trust, nothing to make you angry with me."

"You started the rebellion!" she shouted. "Family is nothing anymore, Seth."

"The rebellion would have started whether I was there to institute it or not." He paused. "Are you going to take me to Admiri or not?"

"You're coming willingly?" she asked as she walked to where her knife was embedded in the wall. "I wouldn't want to leave a scar on that pretty face," she whispered, her hand moving to the handle and yanking it firmly from the wood.

"I'll go willingly."

"David, tie his hands—just in case," she ordered.

David did as he was asked, walking up to Seth and wrenching both of his arms behind his back firmly before he tied them in place.

"I have a boat waiting." She walked down the staircase ahead of them, checking the area to make sure that it was clear before they left with Seth in tow.

⚜

"I'm surprised that Seth stepped up earlier. I didn't think he had it in him." Suri laughed lightly as she joined Reem on the balcony.

"I knew he would," Reem replied. "Seth's not quite who he has people think he is."

"Of course you would say that. You've undoubtedly read his thoughts—and mine too if I'm not mistaken."

"I have." Reem smiled. "But I couldn't help it. It's like I'm hearing you say whatever you're thinking at the moment. It's hard not to hear."

"So then you know about Alexander."

"I do." She turned to look into Suri's eyes. "I'm sure Nicholas would be very understanding."

"I'm not so sure." She shook her head. "He's only ever been in love with two women, and both of them are standing on this balcony." She laughed, though the sound was hollow. "I don't know if I could do that to him."

Reem paused as though she were listening to something from down on the street, her eyes moving to the far edge of the city where the lit watchtower stood. Seconds passed, then minutes before anything was said.

"Are you alright?" Suri asked finally.

"Seth's gotten his wish," she replied. "Brittany is taking him to Admiri."

"We have to go after them," Suri replied, turning to walk away before Reem reached out and took her by the arm.

"No, he's asked that I let this happen," she said. "He wants to go with her. She's his sister—surely, you and I can understand that."

Suri nodded solemnly and turned back toward the city. "Down one council member then," she whispered.

"He'll be back," Reem replied.

Warriors

"Why are you doing this, Brittany?" Seth asked, stopping and leaning against a tree as he tried to catch his breath. They'd been walking for hours, Brittany ahead of him and David walking alongside him, and he couldn't take it anymore. His feet needed a break. "You know you don't have to."

"I know that, dear brother," she replied, stopping to turn and look him in the eye. "But I would do anything to see the look of losing what you love on your face just one more time." She smiled before she turned and started walking again. "We don't stop again until we reach the docks."

"Yes, ma'am," David replied, prodding Seth roughly with the barrel of his pistol. "Do as the lady says, Prophet."

"Why go back, David? Admiri would rather kill you than allow you to remain there considering the fact that you're no longer Advanced," Seth responded, narrowly avoiding falling on his face. "You know if you untied me, this would go a lot faster!" he yelled to his sister. "I'm not going anywhere, Brittany," he added.

"Untie him," Brittany yelled back. "But keep your eyes on him." She turned back to look at them.

David pulled a knife from his belt and cut Seth's bonds, putting the barrel of his gun back on Seth after he did so. "Don't try anything," he whispered. "My aim may not be as good as your sisters, but I won't miss at this range."

"I know," Seth replied. "And I wasn't joking—I know that's what you're thinking. Marcus will kill you when we arrive in Admiri."

David spat. "He has no reason to kill me."

"I have no reason to lie to you," Seth replied. "Remember what he does to those who fail their tasks? You failed yours."

"Stop talking!" Brittany yelled. "We have nothing to speak of."

"Yes, ma'am," David replied.

"On the contrary, sister, I have plenty to talk about," Seth said. "For instance"—he turned to David—"do you know how her eyes became so white? They used to be lavender." When David made no response, he continued, "I've never met anyone with eyes that color." He paused. "Were you alive during the first Advanced attack?"

David shook his head slightly before thrusting the tip of his gun in Seth's back once more, urging him to move faster.

"Brittany and I were still fairly young at the time," Seth continued, picking up his pace slightly. "We were close to the site of the first bombing—too close. When it happened, we were outside the city, standing on the mountains that now make up the crest of the valley."

"Seth, stop talking or I will put another bullet in you—and it won't be in your foot!" Brittany shouted.

"I'll tell you later," Seth whispered, recognizing the look of interest on David's face. "It's a fascinating story, really." He smiled, walking even faster in an attempt to catch up to Brittany.

"Sir, you have a visitor," the guard said, coming to attention as Marcus walked from the balcony into the main chamber.

"Who is it?" Marcus asked, his tone relaying his annoyance as he sat on his throne, crossing one leg over the other.

"A messenger from the docks, sir," the guard replied. "She says she's carrying information of vital importance."

"Bring her in," Marcus commanded.

"Yes, sir." The guard turned and hurried out from the room, returning a few moments later with a young dark-skinned woman at his side. "Sir, this is Tisha from the city near the docks."

"I come bearing news of Brittany Green," she said.

"Do not speak unless spoken to, woman," Marcus replied harshly. "Tell me what you are here to say."

"Ms. Green arrived at the boat on the Western shore a day ago—with both the Prophet and the hunter. She should be arriving in days," she replied nervously.

"That's all? This is the important news that couldn't wait?" Marcus yelled.

"No, sir," she said.

"Then tell me!" he shouted.

"Yes, sir." She dipped her head. "My sources tell me that Reem Kahrin has taken control of Athena and that they have for a fact made an alliance with Mettirna. They are also trying to gain the support of both the Humans and the Purists in the area, and they are close to striking a deal with the Purists." She paused, trying to catch her breath.

Marcus heaved a heavy breath, his anger clearly showing on his reddening face. "Is that everything, or have you conveniently forgotten to include something?" he asked.

"There is one more thing, sir," she replied, nervously looking up at his angry face. "My sources tell me that Reem Kahrin has been impregnated with Jameson Willow's child."

"Who are your sources?" Marcus asked.

"Hunters across the sea."

"Give their names to my guard. You will stay in here for the night, and then you will return to your city. Do you understand?"

"Yes, sir." She nodded nervously.

"Leave me," he ordered, nodding to the guard.

"Yes, sir," the guard replied, ushering the woman from the room.

A few moments later, the guard returned, this time with blood on his uniform. "Do we have it?" Marcus asked.

"I have the names, sir," the guard replied.

"And the woman?"

"Dead." He dipped his head.

"Send word—her sources are to be killed under suspicion of rebellion."

"Yes, sir." He turned and left the room, leaving Marcus alone.

Could it be true that the rebel was pregnant? It shouldn't have been possible—not yet anyway. He'd planned for ten more years before the first pregnancy, and this could only add to the strength in numbers of the rebellion. He closed his eyes and drew in a deep breath, taking his time in exhaling before he called his guard to return to the room.

"Yes, sir?" the man asked, being careful to keep his eyes fixed on the ground.

"Do you know of the young woman we have in a cell upstairs?" Marcus asked, lifting his eyes to look at his guard.

"The prisoner? Of course, sir," he replied.

"Bring her to me," Marcus said quietly.

"Yes, sir, right away." He turned to walk away.

"And, guard, tell no one that I've asked you to bring her to me," Marcus ordered.

The man paused in the doorway, turning to nod toward Marcus once more. "Yes, sir, of course."

⚜

Reem stood alone on the balcony, looking out over the people as they went about their daily duties, knowing that her job had just gotten that much harder. She had sent for the top soldiers from the Mettirnian and Admirian armies hours ago, and now she was only waiting for them to arrive. It was time that they started building their army.

Soon Jameson joined her, his hands massaging her shoulders gently. "How are you feeling this morning?" he asked.

"I'm fine, Jameson." She smiled as she turned to look him in the eye. "I just didn't think I would have to build an army of my own so soon after arriving."

"I know." He smiled gravely. "But it's a necessary act if we're to defend ourselves."

She nodded, her eyes glancing back to the main chamber where military men started to file inside, standing at attention. "How many?" she asked.

"Fifteen leaders with seven thousand followers," he replied. "How are you thinking we'll go about this?"

"I'll have each one take charge of their own squad, teaching them in their own ways. They'll select their own men and women based on who works the same way. I'm thinking we should strategize according to our gifts—that's something Marcus never did believe in." She smiled, her eyes meeting his. "He won't see it coming."

"There's a lot of things that Marcus won't see coming." He winked.

She sighed. "I wish I could tell what was going on with Seth and his sister—they're too far out, I already tried."

"We'll just have to believe that Seth would never give away any of our secrets," he replied. "He'll take care of himself."

"I know." She nodded. "I'd better get to the leaders." She glanced back toward the soldiers before returning her eyes to Jameson. "By the way, you're my military advisor."

He smiled. "But I'll help any way I can."

Thirteen men and two women lined up in a semicircle inside the main chamber, watching as Reem stepped off the balcony and into the room, her eyes glancing from one warrior to the next as she paced inside the large half circle. "In two days, I will have all our fighters report to the main plaza," she began. "You will each have your choice of warriors—and I would advise you to select them according to their gifts and fighting styles. I ask that you do not argue over them. You will all have time to train with them before the Admirians arrive. Remember, we will have the advantage." She paused. "We will organize according to your specialties, so select fighters that have similar gifts to your own. Understood?" When no one answered, she continued, "Good. Then be at the plaza at dawn—two days." She turned and walked back to the balcony, leaving them standing at attention, with Jameson just outside their circle.

Jameson stepped forward, taking Reem's place in the center. "I suggest that you start thinking about your decisions right away. You are dismissed."

One by one, the warriors saluted and walked back out of the tower, leaving one woman who continued to stand at attention. "Sir," she said, her deep thickly accented voice enough to be mistaken for a man's.

"Yes, soldier, speak your mind," Jameson replied.

"I'm concerned that we are not being used to our fullest potential," she answered, still standing at attention though her eyes turned to look into his.

"At ease." He paused. "Explain yourself."

"She believes that I am not as strong a leader as she'd once thought," Reem replied as she walked from the balcony to stand next to him, her eyes drilling into the woman's. "And you were not aware that I could read your mind," she told her.

"I'm sorry, ma'am," the woman answered. "But that is what I believe."

"And you are entitled to your opinion," Reem replied. "But you should know the mind of Marcus Admiri. I have weighed all of our options. I will use all of you as best I can according to your strengths, weaknesses, and gifts. If that is not good enough for you, then I suggest you leave for Mettirna."

"The only way I am leaving this fight is if I'm ripped apart and dragged from the walls of the city."

"Good," Reem replied. "Then what is it that you wish to say?"

"Nothing, ma'am," the woman replied. "I should never have doubted your abilities. Please accept my apology." She dipped her head.

"You have no need to apologize—as I said, you are entitled to your opinion."

"Thank you, ma'am." She saluted before turning and walking from the room.

"Who was she?" Jameson asked when she was well out of earshot.

"A friend of Hera's," Reem replied. "Her name is Leticia."

"You may want to consider keeping her at a distance—I don't think she appreciated you talking to her like that." He laughed lightly.

"She is one of our best warriors, and we need her if we are to win this fight."

"I know." He smiled. "What else do you have today?"

"I need to go to the border and meet the newcomers," she replied. "We've been getting hundreds of new recruits by the week, and I need to read them all before we let them inside the walls of the city."

"That could take days, Reem," he complained, his smile still on his face. "Couldn't we leave that up to some of the other telepaths?"

"Remember how David blocked them?" she asked. "What if Admiri has trained someone else to do the same? We can't take that risk." She stepped closer and wrapped her arms around his neck. "Besides, it won't take that long. I should be done by this time tomorrow." She smiled.

He laughed. "You're trying to bore me to death."

"No, we wouldn't want that." She winked. "But it's important that we know who is entering the rebellion."

"But I can think of things that are much more fun to do." He smiled brightly.

"Let's go." She laughed, taking hold of his hand. "The longer we put it off, the longer it'll take to get it done."

Kari

Mitchal quickly packed all of his belongings, fitting everything into the small backpack from whence it came. He hadn't been planning on joining the rebellion when he left Admiri, so his possessions were few, but he still couldn't bear to part with the small remnants of his past.

Soon he and Maria would be on their way to Mettirna, and he would once again say goodbye to the place he now called his home. He knew that his assignment in Mettirna was a long term one, but he also knew in his heart that if Admiri attacked, he would return to help them. He may not be a warrior, but he could fight with the best of them—give him a weapon and he would show you what he was made of.

He'd heard about Seth being taken away by the operative, known that Athena would likely need the Prophet even more now that the thoughts of war ran through everyone's minds. They could only hope that there wouldn't be a rebellion within the rebellion.

He finished packing his things and slid his arms through the straps of the pack, stepping out the door and slowly walking down the hall toward Maria's room. Inside, she continued to pack all of her things, her head lifting to meet his gaze as he walked in the room.

"Hey there." She smiled. "You're already packed?"

"Didn't have much to pack." He shrugged. "How long will you be?"

"Not long." She laughed.

"I'm sure you can't wait to return home." He smiled. "I would love to see my home again."

"Honestly, I'm not as excited as I thought I would be," she replied. "But if the savior has decided that we should go, then I'll do it." She paused. "I never really fit in there."

"Understandably." He winked, walking up behind her and wrapping his arms around her waist. "You'll always have me," he whispered in her ear.

Seth couldn't help but laugh at the look of sickness on his sister's face, and she shot him an angry glare. "Enjoy yourself while you can." She spat off the side of the boat. "Tomorrow, we will be on dry land again, and you will fear me."

"You know I've been afraid of you since we were kids." He laughed back.

"Quiet," she snapped, turning from the water to look him in the eye. "I've no desire to speak to you, Seth."

"You don't have to speak," he replied, his smile fading. "I'll just talk to myself."

"Speak another word and you will never be able to speak again," she said blandly.

"Point taken." The corners of his mouth turned up slightly.

"Ahh . . . siblings." David smiled as he walked across the deck toward them. "You really should learn to get along."

"Stay out of this." Brittany threw him an angry glare.

"I just wanted to tell you that the captain is pushing to get us to the docks by dawn—it seems the two of you are disrupting the crew." He laughed quietly.

"Good—the sooner we get to Admiri, the better." She turned back to the water, trying to focus on the horizon rather than the rocking of the boat.

"They have a healer onboard if you need it," David said.

"I'm fine," she snapped.

"You don't look it," he replied, stepping closer to her.

"I never asked for your concern, David," she whispered, her voice barely loud enough for him to hear. "Take my brother below and keep an eye on him."

"Yes, ma'am." He casually patted her hand with his before he walked to Seth and gestured for him to lead the way. "Time to go, Prophet."

"I have a name, you know."

"I know." David grabbed him by the collar and wrenched him to his feet, shoving him toward the lower deck. "Now go."

Seth did as he was told, slowly making his way below and into the room the captain had set aside for him, taking a seat on the edge of the bed while David stood in the doorway.

"Would you like for me to finish telling you about her eyes?" he asked.

"I don't need to know how her eyes turned from lavender to white," David replied, his eyes gazing into the distance as Seth continued to stare him down.

"But you do want to know." Seth smiled. "I saw the look you gave me—you want to know."

"Not from you," David whispered.

"You care for her, don't you?" he asked, his smile fading from his face. "You shouldn't."

"Bite your tongue, Prophet," David snapped. "You have no right to—"

"She's my sister," he replied. "I have every right."

"If she knew we were having this conversation, she would kill us both, and you know it."

"Believe it or not, I'm trying to save you, David. You will die either by the hand of my sister or by the hand of her lover—which would you prefer?" When David's eyebrow's furrowed, he continued, "You don't know, do you?"

"Know what?"

"She and Marcus Admiri, they've been together for years. She doesn't think I know." He shook his head.

"They have no reason to want me dead." His head shook as well.

"You're human now, David. They have every reason to want you dead—and don't think I was joking about her and Marcus."

"You lie." He turned and leaned his back against the doorjamb, keeping Seth out of his line of sight.

Kari woke to the sound of approaching footsteps, her nose and mouth coated with sand from the ground on which she lay. She lifted her head and gazed around at the desert that surrounded her. Several hundred feet away, she could see a group of people approaching on foot and horseback, headed straight toward her. She stood and walked toward them, hoping that they would be able to help her. A few moments later, she reached the caravan, stopping at the same time as they.

Men and women alike walked together, carrying what looked to be all of their belongings with them. A tall dark-skinned man on horseback leaded them, his hand lifting as he yelled, "Halt! We rest here—one hour." He swung off his horse and walked the few paces that stood between himself and Kari, his forehead wrinkled in confusion. "Who are you?" he asked.

"Help me," she whispered before falling to her knees, her legs unable to keep her upright.

The man rushed to her side, propping her up before turning back to the caravan. "Send for a healer," he told the nearest man. He then unclipped a canteen from his belt and lifted it to her lips, pouring the cool liquid into her mouth. "Drink," he whispered.

He heard shuffling behind him as the healer made his way through the crowds of resting people, shouting that he was a healer. His pale skin and light orange hair filled the leader's vision, and he stepped back to make room for the man.

The healer placed his hand on her forehead, closing his eyes as his power flowed from his fingertips into her body. A moment later, her eyes flickered open, and he helped her to a seated position. "How do you feel?" he asked.

She nodded, swallowing with a dry throat that wouldn't allow her to speak. The leader then took a knee beside her and offered her his canteen, noticing her bright green eyes and light blonde hair for the first time. "Drink," he told her again.

She took the canteen and drank it down, a smile growing on her face as she finished. "Thank you," she replied, her voice still slightly hoarse.

"Can you tell us your name?" the healer asked.

"Kari." She nodded, turning to face him.

"Alright, Kari, how are you feeling?"

"Much better." She smiled, turning from the healer to face the leader again. "Thank you."

"I'm Robert," the leader told her. "This is Edwin." He gestured toward the healer. "Are you Advanced?"

"Advanced?" Her eyebrows furrowed, confusion clear on her face.

"It's possible that she has some memory loss," Edwin whispered to Robert.

"I don't think so," she replied. "I remember everything . . . except the past few days."

"Where are you from?" Robert asked.

She shrugged. "I don't know. My mother never told me."

"And how long have you been here?" Edwin added.

"I don't know." She shook her head. "I'm sorry."

"Don't worry." Robert smiled. "I'm sure everything's alright. I'll be right back." He stood and walked back to his horse, signaling for the man on the horse next to him to dismount. "She doesn't remember anything," he told him. "I think we should take her with us."

"Is she Advanced?" the other man asked.

"We don't know—she doesn't remember anything."

"Then we should leave her here. We can't afford any more delays."

"She'll die if we leave her here, Ethan. I can't do that to her." He shook his head.

"Nothing good can come of this," Ethan whispered, "but the decision is yours."

"The savior will be able to help her when we reach Athena."

"Then find a place for her."

Robert nodded and turned back toward the girl, walking forward and looking down at her. "We'll take you with us if you'd like," he said. "Someone in Athena can help you."

"Really?" she asked, shock now prominent on her face. "I can come with you?"

"I'm sure we have an extra horse for you." He nodded. "I won't leave you here in your state."

"Thank you," Edwin and Kari said in unison.

"I have a horse you can use," Edwin continued. "It's not far away—do you think you can walk there yourself?"

She nodded, accepting his help as she stood. Edwin then escorted her into the throng of people, guiding her past horses with their riders, and carts pulled by both people and horses. Eventually, he showed her to where he'd left his horse, three other riderless horses standing beside his own.

"I've had her since I was a boy," he told Kari as he touched the horse's mane. "Seems a shame that I'll have to leave her behind."

"Then take her with you." Kari smiled back.

"You don't understand. We're crossing the ocean by ship, which means that anything that's not completely necessary will be left behind at the docks—and that includes all of the horses," he replied.

"Then I'm sure she'll be fine without you."

"As long as she's not taken by the Purists, she will be—when they travel across the ocean, they take horses as sustenance." He stared sadly into his horse's big brown eyes.

She stepped forward to stroke the horse's neck maternally. "She's a beautiful creature."

"That she is." Edwin smiled, turning to take the reins of one of the other horses. "This one will be yours for the duration of our journey," he told her. "You do know how to ride, don't you?"

She shook her head, her eyes once again full of confusion. "You want me to ride him?" she asked, stepping back in fear. "I can't . . . I don't . . . I don't know how," she whispered.

"It's alright," Edwin comforted. "We'll teach you. You'll be fine." He smiled.

"I don't know," she whispered back.

"Don't worry, I won't let anything happen to you." He held out his hand, beckoning for her to approach him and the horse whose reins he still held.

⁂

The plaza was filled with people, almost the entire population of Athena waiting to find out where they would be assigned. Reem had read every newcomer, and every single one was allowed into the city. Now the sheer mass of the warriors lined up in the plaza was more than she ever would have hoped. The leaders walked through the crowds, searching out the few that they had preselected for their squads and selecting any others whom they thought would be of use to them. As soon as all of the preselected warriors had left, she would reorganize everything, but that could take several more hours.

She stood on an upper balcony overlooking the plaza, watching as everyone hustled about, pretending like they knew what they were doing. She leaned against the railing, letting out a heavy sigh as she watched—this wasn't going to be easy.

Her head dropped to look down at her bulging stomach, her hands moving to gently cradle it. Nicholas had been checking up on her frequently, and apparently the little one was growing much faster than expected. She smiled as a pair of familiar hands joined hers on her waist, and she turned to smile up at Jameson's cheerful green eyes. "It's a madhouse down there." She laughed. "I wouldn't recommend joining them."

"I wasn't planning on it." He smiled back. "I just came to check on you."

"But you never need to have a reason to distract me." She took his hand in hers and brought it to her lips, kissing it as she smiled up into his eyes.

⚜

Kari carefully mounted the horse, the look of fear never once leaving her face. Her eyes were wide with fear and her hand unsure and shaking when Edwin handed her the reins. "It looks like you'll have to learn on the go," he told her. "Robert's eager to get to the docks—it seems there's a sandstorm on the way."

"You're sure I can do this?" she asked.

"Positive." He smiled. "She'll want to follow the others, so you shouldn't have any problems."

"As long as you're sure." She smiled timidly, trying to hide the panicked look on her face as he walked away and mounted his own horse.

"You'll be fine, Kari. Trust me."

She nodded as the horses in front of her started walking, her horse naturally following along. "Edwin," she said, "may I ask you something?"

"Of course." He smiled as he pulled his horse alongside hers. "Ask away."

"Why are you all going to this Athena place?" she asked, cringing as her horse picked up its pace.

"That's a long story," Edwin replied. "But in short, we're going there so that we can live under a better rule."

"Where are you all from?" she asked.

"Admiri—you remember it, don't you?"

"Yes, that's where I grew up." She smiled slightly.

"You must be Advanced if Admiri is where you grew up. Marcus will not allow humans inside those walls," he replied.

"Marcus?" Her brow furrowed.

"Marcus Admiri—the city is named after him, and he rules it." He paused. "How could you have lived in Admiri and not known about Marcus?"

She shrugged. "It's just where I grew up."

"You're quite the mystery." He laughed lightly.

"What do you mean?" she asked.

"Your memory, your life, everything. You're just a big question mark." He smiled gently at her saddened face. "Don't worry, there's someone in Athena who can help you."

"Are you sure? I mean, I don't want to be a nuisance."

"You won't be." He smiled.

"May I ask something else?"

"Go right ahead." He laughed.

"How many of you are there?" She turned to look at the seemingly endless span of travelers.

"A few hundred Advanced, plus several hundred Purists. It seems we aren't the only ones who want a change in lifestyle," he replied. "The leader in Athena has made it clear that all people are welcome within its walls, and we all wish to take advantage of that."

"What's a Purist?" she asked.

"They're humans who desire no advancements. Those with us only wish to be free."

Death

"Don't try anything," Brittany warned as she pushed Seth down the dock, catching his eyes staring out into sea—knowing him, he would try anything to get back to his precious rebellion.

"I'm not going anywhere," he replied. "Put the gun away."

"I have no reason to trust you," she snarled. "Move faster—we're falling behind."

"I will go as fast as I will go." He sighed, continuing on at his slow pace. "I'm in no hurry."

"Then move faster or I will shoot the fingers off your prophetic hands one by one," she warned, her voice low and serious.

"Moving faster it is." He picked up his pace, stepping off the dock and onto the sandy shore, humming a deceptively cheerful tune as he did so.

"Quiet!" she snapped. "I don't want to hear your singing the whole way to Admiri."

"Speaking of which, I'm sure you can't wait to be back in Marcus's arms—or should I say his bed?" he replied wittily, turning his head slightly so that he could wink at her slightly surprised face. "Is that why you're in such a hurry, sister?"

"My affairs should mean nothing to you," she replied, pushing him faster to catch up with David.

"Let me guess—he's just a means to an end for you."

"You shouldn't care about this, Seth."

"You think I wouldn't care about how my own sister spends her time?"

"Why would you?" she asked blandly.

"You are my sister," he said, his voice fading as they approached David who had stopped a few yards away.

"You have no reason to, nor do I desire for you to. Now stop talking," she ordered.

A moment later, they arrived at where David stood staring back at them. "Would you like me to take charge of the prisoner?" he asked.

Brittany nodded and started walking away, leaving David and Seth staring at her as she walked into the distance toward Admiri.

Seth gestured for David to lead the way, and seeing the angry look on his face, he began walking in an attempt to catch up to his sister. David pulled his pistol from its holster and carried it at his side as he walked slightly behind Seth. "You shouldn't goad her like that," he said. "She's angry enough as it is."

"I have to try," Seth whispered, his voice barely loud enough for David to hear. "I'll try not to anger her further," he added, his voice somewhat louder.

"I doubt she'll ever see your side, Seth," David replied. "That's just the way it is."

"I am aware of the odds," Seth whispered back.

"Quiet—she keeps glancing back here," David whispered.

Seth nodded and continued to walk, following his sister who walked several yards ahead of them. She looked completely at home as she walked across the desert sand, and Seth couldn't help but remember the days when the two of them would play on these very shores. They'd lived here for a short time before moving across the ocean to the sight of the Crash, but she'd never been the same after that event.

⚜

Jameson lay on his side of the bed, fully awake though he was completely exhausted. Reem hadn't been sleeping well the past few nights. Otherwise, he would have woken her by now. For once, she was sleeping soundly, and he couldn't bear depriving her of that. He felt her body turn to face him, and her hands both instinctively moving to link with his as she slept.

Suddenly, her eyes snapped open and her breathing picked up, her eyes slowly changing from brown to shining silver. He tightened his grip on her fingers and closed his eyes, waiting for her to wake. "Reem," he whispered. "Reem, wake up." Her hands clenched and unclenched around his, and he could feel her body start shaking. "Reem!" he shouted.

A moment later, her body stopped moving, and he slowly opened his eyes to see her brown eyes staring back at him. Her eyes were wide with fear, and tears streamed down her cheeks. "What happened?" she whispered.

Jameson moved closer to her, wrapping his arms around her waist. "It's okay, you're okay," he chanted softly in her ear as he cradled her. "I'm here."

Her hands shook as she tried to wipe the tears from her face, and she leaned into him.

"Did you have another vision?" he asked, running his fingers gently through her hair.

She nodded slowly, trying her best to stop shaking. "What did I do?"

"Your eyes," he replied hesitantly. "I don't know what else happened."

"I didn't—you're not—did I?" she whispered frantically.

"No, no, I'm fine," he breathed. "How's our baby?"

"Fine. A little shaken, but fine," she replied, her voice wavering slightly.

"What did you see?" he asked.

"Marcus—he's sending his army soon. Seth didn't make it to Admiri, and he's not happy about it," she said quickly, her body still quivering as she pulled herself closer to Jameson.

"Are you sure you're alright?" he whispered, nervously wrapping his arms tighter around her.

She nodded again, tears starting to stream down her face as she leaned her head against his chest. "I'm fine, really. Go back to sleep."

Hours later, they finally fell asleep, Jameson's arms still wrapped tightly around her. Reem woke before Jameson, glad that he was still asleep after last night. She'd kept him awake for hours—and hated herself for it—but she couldn't bring herself to tell him what she'd seen.

With her gifts, she carefully removed his arms from around her and rose to her feet, relieved that she hadn't woken him. She dressed quickly, doing everything in her power to let Jameson sleep. She could hear the soft rumblings of Nicholas and Suri talking in the main chamber—for once she was glad that they always woke before her. She exited the room and walked down the hall to find both Nicholas and Suri now on the balcony, both leaning against the banister as they watched the people below. She slowly approached them and leaned her back against the entryway.

"Good morning," Nicholas said. "Sleep well?"

Reem shook her head, and Suri moved closer to her and took her hands. "What's wrong?" she whispered. "Another vision?" When Reem made no move to respond, she added, "What did you see?"

"Jameson," Reem replied, her voice barely a whisper. "I saw Jameson die."

Kari couldn't help but smile at Edwin's constant snoring, amazed by the loud tempo at which his piglike squeals resounded. The group had stopped hours ago, and soon after, Edwin had fallen fast asleep—something that everyone in the area hated. It seemed that beating Edwin to sleep would be a competition in which everyone competed. She'd considered waking him for everyone else's sakes, but by now, she didn't see the point. In minutes, the sun would peek over the horizon, and they would be on their way once again.

It seemed Robert was in quite the hurry, but that could be a good thing considering the weariness of the group. Most everyone she'd met seemed weary, but kind nonetheless. Still, she couldn't help but wonder if they were like that simply because of the memory loss they assumed she had.

The only problem she had with their theory of memory loss was that there were really only a few hours of her life that she couldn't remember. She remembered growing up in a single-room home with her mother, and she remembered everything that her mother taught her from the moment she turned five. She remembered three times a week when food would be delivered to the one and only door—the door that was locked from the outside—and she remembered never seeing the face of the man who delivered it. She remembered her mother vividly— the only person she'd ever met or spoken to before recently—and she remembered the day that her mother never woke, the day she died. That day, three men invaded her home and took her mother's body, leaving Kari alone in the small home.

After that day, she'd done the only thing she could—she studied. Her mother had left thousands of books behind, the walls covered in shelves that were packed to the brim with them. She read and reread every book in an attempt to continue her mother's efforts to teach her. Her mother had always said that she only desired Kari's happiness and that the road to happiness began with learning. She now knew most everything, just not the things that seemed to matter out here.

Then not more than a day ago, a man had barged into her home and dragged her outside—she couldn't see his face, but the man she pictured was evil. She'd never left that room her entire life, and leaving seemed like an impossible feat. He'd taken her to another man—a man who'd hurt her.

And that was all she could remember. The next thing she knew, she woke on the dusty ground to the sound of marching feet and hooves.

Suddenly, she heard what sounded to her like a battle cry, and everyone hurriedly rose from the ground and prepared to leave. The sun then started rising over the horizon, and she realized that the cry must have come from Robert.

She crawled to Edwin and shook him awake before rising to her feet. Apparently, he didn't wake easily. He hurriedly got on his feet and helped her onto her horse as everyone started moving. He then gracefully mounted his own horse and took both his and Kari's horses reins, bringing them both to a full gallop until they reached the front of the group where Robert sat on his horse, guiding the caravan at a much faster pace than the day before.

"What's going on?" Edwin asked. "Why the rush?"

"The storm's getting closer," Robert replied. "We shouldn't have stayed so long."

"The horses couldn't have lasted to the docks," Edwin said. "We can't keep going at this pace—many of the people are on foot!"

"If we don't hurry, the storm will be upon us, and then we will lose more than I care to consider. I have no choice, Edwin. I'm sorry."

"You'll exhaust them to death, Robert."

"Get the slowest onto the carts and leave behind what can be left. You'll have to organize it while we move. Mount horses to all of the carts—that will make it easier on some of the people," Robert replied. "I'll have Ryan help you."

"I'm afraid that won't be enough."

"The elderly and children Purists should be on horse-drawn carts within the next thirty minutes. See to it." He turned to Ryan and repeated his orders before turning back to a still stunned Edwin. "Edwin, get it done. I need you with me."

"Yes, sir," Edwin replied. "Kari doesn't know how to ride—keep an eye on her for me."

"Of course." Robert nodded as Edwin slowed his horse's pace and wound his way through the crowds, fulfilling his orders.

"How are you getting along?" Robert asked as he pulled his horse up alongside Kari's.

"Decently." She smiled. "Thank you."

"Good." He smiled back. "And don't worry, we won't leave you behind if the storm hits."

"What do you mean?" she asked, her brow furrowing.

"During the sandstorms, the horses tend to spook easily. Edwin told me you don't know how to ride," he replied. "I won't let anything happen to you."

"Thank you." She nodded.

"Don't be nervous." He chuckled. "As long as we keep a good pace, we should be able to stay ahead of the storm."

⁂

"You saw what?" Suri asked, her voice raising an octave in her shock.

"I saw him die, Suri," Reem replied, her eyes dropping to the ground at her feet.

"How's that even possible?" Nicholas asked.

"I don't know, Nicholas, but everything else that I've seen has happened!" she whispered harshly, trying her best to cover the hysteria in her voice.

"I'm sure it won't happen, Reem," Suri said. "Could it be that it was just a dream?"

"No . . . no, I don't think so." She shook her head. "It was too real, too lifelike."

"We won't let it happen," Nicholas replied.

"What if it's not something that we can stop from happening?" Reem asked, tears forming in her eyes.

"We can, and we will," Suri replied. "We will not let this happen." She stepped closer to her sister, wrapping her arms around her waist.

Tears flowed down Reem's cheeks as she held tightly to Suri. "Nicholas, please don't tell him about this," she pleaded. "I know what you're thinking."

"How can I not?" he asked. "It's Jameson's life we're talking about here."

"I don't want him to worry," she replied.

"He's your husband," Suri said, pulling away so that she could look her in the eye. "You have to tell him."

"If you don't, I will," Nicholas added.

"I won't let you," Reem replied.

"I know you better than that." He laughed. "You won't stop me."

"I can't tell him," she whispered.

"It's alright, Reem," Suri replied, brushing Reem's hair away from her face. "Nicholas will tell him." She turned toward Nicholas and motioned for him to leave. "Do you know when the vision took place?"

Reem shook her head. "I just know that I was too late to save him."

Nicholas paced outside Jameson's door, knowing that his friend was likely still sleeping. He'd come thinking that he would simply wake Jameson and tell him the news, but it didn't seem so simple after he reached the door. After all, what was he supposed to say? "Hey Jameson, your wife had a vision, and you're going to die"? It just wasn't that simple.

He knew Reem was reading his mind at this very moment, knew she was waiting for him to knock on the door and wake her husband. He could feel her in his mind, sense her listening to his thoughts. Somehow, it made the whole thing that much more difficult.

"Don't worry, Nicholas. I'll tell him," Reem whispered in his mind.

"No, I'll tell him," he thought back. *"I know how hard this is for you."* He lifted his hand and knocked firmly on the door. "Jameson, wake up," he said when he heard his lazy groan.

"Give me a moment, Nicholas," Jameson replied as he shuffled out of bed.

Nicholas stepped back and leaned against the wall across from the door, trying to calm his nervously twitching fingers as he did so.

A few moments later, the door slowly opened and Jameson appeared, his eyes bloodshot and his hair disheveled. "What is it, Nicholas?" he asked.

"It's not an easy thing to say," Nicholas replied.

"Oh, take your time. It's not like you woke me from a deep sleep or anything," Jameson said bitterly as he leaned against the doorframe and ran his fingers through his hair. "Sorry. I'm just tired."

"No, you're right. I shouldn't have woken you before I had the courage to tell you."

"What is it?" Jameson asked, his bloodshot eyes narrowing. When Nicholas didn't respond, his eyes widened. "It's not Reem, is it?"

"Uh," Nicholas groaned, stepping forward and looking straight into his friend's bright green eyes. "It's her vision—the one she had last night."

"What about it?" Jameson asked, furrowing his eyebrows. "She saw the army arriving sooner than we had expected—that only puts us a bit off schedule."

"She saw something else too," Nicholas replied, his eyes dropping to the ground. "She was afraid to tell you about it."

"Where is she, Nicholas?"

"She's with Suri. Don't worry, she's fine," he replied. "I told her that I would tell you."

"What did she see?" he asked.

"She saw you, Jameson," Nicholas replied. "She saw you die."

Jameson turned from Nicholas and bolted down the hall toward the main chamber, only one thing on his mind—finding Reem.

"Jameson, wait!" Nicholas shouted as he followed the man into the main chamber.

There Jameson rushed to the balcony where he knew Reem would be—she and Suri always watched the people from the balcony this time of day. He arrived out of breath and gasping for air, finding Reem crying into her sister's shoulder. "Why didn't you tell me?" he asked, his voice still breathy and rushed as Nicholas appeared behind him.

Reem gasped and lifted her head, turning to look Jameson in the eye. "I couldn't," she whispered, tears streaming down her face. "I couldn't."

"It won't happen, Reem," he replied, stepping closer and taking her hand in his.

"I'll leave you alone," Suri whispered before she turned and walked off the balcony toward Nicholas inside the main chamber.

Reem's sad brown eyes turned away from Jameson, afraid to confront the problem at hand. Jameson cupped his other hand under her chin and turned her face toward his. "Look at me, Reem."

Her bloodshot eyes finally looked up at his, tears continuing to stream down her face. "I can't lose you, Jameson," she whispered.

"No, you can't," he replied. "You won't." He wrapped his arms around her, pulling her close to his body. "I won't let it happen."

"None of my visions have been wrong before," she said as she cried into his neck. "How do you know you can stop them from happening?"

"Because nothing and no one can take me away from you," he told her.

Her arms wrapped around his waist, developing a firm grip on his body. "I won't let it happen," she whispered fiercely. "I won't."

"It's not going to happen," he replied.

She nodded and buried her face in his chest, angry at herself for how often she cried. Her hormones were getting to be a nuisance.

He kissed the top of her head. "How's our baby?"

"As afraid for your life as I am," she whispered.

"I'm not leaving either of you," he said as he pushed her away and stared into her dark eyes. "Nothing can take me away from you."

She nodded slightly and attempted a smile, though tears continued to stream down her face.

"I will not let it happen."

"I believe you," she replied as she pulled herself back into his arms, though neither of them found her words convincing.

Seer

Robert held firmly to both his and Kari's horses reins as they galloped through the desert, leading the caravan. It had been estimated that it would take them another day and a half if they continued at their leisurely pace, and Robert knew that if they took anywhere near that long, the storm would be upon them, and they would suffer severe casualties.

Once they reached the docks, it would be up to the sea as to how many of them survived, and he could live with knowing that it wasn't his fault that he'd lost them. But if any were to die or be left behind before they reached the docks, their faces would haunt him forever. He was a seer after all, and he should be able to see what would happen to the group—unfortunately, his gifts didn't work like that. In fact, they only worked sporadically.

The people were all good-hearted, and Robert couldn't bear to see any of them left behind or killed by the storm. He'd personally met and recruited every one of them, and he knew that they were all completely devoted to this rebellion.

Kari, on the other hand, was a mystery wrapped in more mystery. She hadn't spoken more than a few words since Edwin had left, and honestly, Robert didn't know what to say to the girl. She'd obviously been through much more than she was letting on, but he had neither the time nor the words to find out what she was hiding.

"Do you think you can take the reins?" he asked.

"I don't know," she replied nervously, glancing back and forth between him and the reins in his hands. "Do you think I'm ready?"

"Anything goes wrong, I'll help you." He smiled. "You're doing fine."

"Okay." She smiled slightly as he handed her the reins. Her horse continued to run alongside his, and her nervous hands gripped the reins fiercely.

"It's okay, relax your grip." He laughed. "He'll want to stray occasionally, but just do what I told you. Keep him with me." He paused. "Be assertive. He'll listen to you."

She nodded, smiling at the wind in her hair as they rode.

"My god she's beautiful," he whispered under his breath, too quietly for anyone but himself to hear. He'd noticed her pure beauty the moment they'd met, but he knew he couldn't let his feelings for her get in the way of his mission. After all, beauty wasn't the most important thing in the world, especially in times such as these. He closed his eyes and sighed heavily before opening them once more to stare out at the empty desert before them, trying to distract himself from the beauty who rode beside him.

They needed to board the ships before the storm hit. They couldn't afford to lose so many to a storm—he couldn't afford to lose so many at all.

Soon Edwin appeared between Robert and Kari, both himself and his horse clearly exhausted from running between the people in an attempt to carry out Robert's orders. "It's done," he said.

"Thank you, Edwin," Robert replied. "Where's Ryan?"

"He's taking care of the last of it," Edwin replied. "Some weren't so willing to leave their personal items behind."

Robert nodded slowly as he considered what he'd asked the people to do. He'd told them they would be allowed a few personal items, and now he'd ordered them to leave their beloved things behind on the desert floor. After how difficult it was for him to leave his own home, he should have known how hard it would be for them.

"When will we reach the docks?" Edwin asked.

"Before nightfall," Robert replied. "At this pace, we should be able to beat the storm. But it's always possible that though we've outrun one storm, we'll run into another. It's impossible to know the future." He shook his head.

"Unless you're a seer," Edwin replied.

"The future is ever changing, Edwin," he said bitterly. "If I had the choice, I would never have gotten these gifts."

Edwin sighed. "I'm sorry—I know it's hard for you."

"What are 'gifts'?" Kari asked.

"You don't know?" Robert replied. "Curious."

"Don't mind him." Edwin laughed. "Gifts are the abilities that the Advanced developed after Admiri's treatment was administered—trust me, the fewer questions you ask, the less confusing it will be."

"What kind of abilities?" Her brow furrowed.

"Like my ability to heal you and Robert's ability to see into the future," Edwin replied. "There are others too, like telepathy, telekinesis, teleportation, and some that aren't so simply named." He laughed.

She smiled excitedly. "I think that part of my history book was missing."

"History books?" Edwin asked. "You had books?"

"Doesn't everyone?"

"No." He shook his head. "They're very rare actually. How many did you have?"

"Hundreds, maybe more." She shrugged. "My mother collected them and had me read them over and over when I was growing up. She said it was the best way to learn."

"That's amazing . . ."

"Gifts like what?" she repeated, smiling innocently.

He smiled brightly. "Well, some people developed the ability to tell when someone is lying to them or the ability to find someone across vast distances just by thinking about it. And there are even some who can duplicate themselves—they can create a whole army of themselves, and each one could fight individually. It's amazing, really, how many different gifts there are in the world. They haven't been catalogued, but it's been my dream to travel across the planet and discover what they all are."

"It sounds amazing."

"It's really not all that it's cracked up to be. Most of the people here are like you—they're human." His smile brightened. "They prefer it that way actually."

"I think it would be more fun to have gifts."

"Personally, if I could, I would switch what gifts I got. I'm not fond of blood—healing just wasn't the right gift for me." He laughed.

"Isn't there any way you can change your gifts?" She tilted her head to the side, her hands gripping tighter to the reigns when her horse began to steer slightly off course.

"Not really, no." He shook his head, watching as she steered her horse back on track with him and Robert. "I suppose you could see a taker followed by a giver, but that just seems like cheating to me." When he noticed the confused look on her face, he added, "Takers can take gifts from Advanced, and givers give them."

She nodded. "If you dislike your gifts so much, then why not find someone to help you switch?"

He smiled. "I just think that I must have been given these gifts for a reason, and I don't want to get rid of them without knowing what that could possibly be."

"I understand." She smiled back.

"I've never met anyone who didn't know about the Advanced," Robert mused. "How did it happen?"

"She lived in isolation in Admiri," Edwin replied, leaning closer to Robert. "I'll talk to you about it later—there are things you should know."

Robert nodded his response as Kari stared at them, confusion filling her face. "What's going on?" she asked.

"Nothing," Edwin replied. "Don't worry about it."

"What's it like to see the future?" she asked Robert. "I'm sure it's amazing—to be able to see what's going to happen to you. That must be very exciting."

"It's not like that, really," Robert replied, keeping his eyes on the desert in front of him. "I can't call up a vision whenever I want to, I can't choose how far into the future I'm going to see, and I can't do any of what you'd think I'd be able to." He sighed.

"Is that how you knew about the storm?"

"Yes, that's how I knew." He smiled slightly, amused by her curiosity. "I can usually determine when in the future the vision will take place, but the future is ever changing. Even if I see something in the future, there's no guarantee that it will happen."

"So it does work to your advantage then." Her smile brightened. "You shouldn't be so ashamed of what you can't do."

"I know." He turned to look into her eyes. "I can't help it, really. I've lost too many people because of mistakes I made with my visions."

"What do you mean?" Her brow furrowed, and her smile faded.

"It's a long story actually," he replied, attempting to avoid the conversation that he could see coming and angry that his words had caused her smile to fade. "I'd rather not talk about it right now."

"Sorry, I didn't mean to pry." She shrugged. "I'm just . . . I've never met anyone before you." She turned to look at the caravan behind them. "It's amazing the many personalities you all have."

"We're very proud of our diversity," Edwin smiled.

⚜

Seth had been able to hear them for quite some time, but he'd only now seen them in the distance. He'd first heard the sounds of hooves at least half an hour ago in the quiet of the desert, but now he could make out the dust on the horizon from their galloping.

He knew for a fact that it was the rebels that approached. There wasn't much hope in the sound of their approach, however, but it was at least comforting to know that they weren't the only three out here in the desert. The only problem was, if they were running, there must be something chasing them, and he wasn't too keen on finding out what that was.

"Who do you think they are?" David whispered as they walked.

"I know who they are," Seth replied, knowing at this point Brittany wouldn't care whether they spoke or not. She walked at least twenty feet in front of them, and she was completely focused on how long this group would delay her.

"Who?" David asked.

"Rebels." Seth smiled. "They're on their way to the docks—remember those passenger vessels? They're there for the rebels."

"How do you know?"

He laughed. "It wasn't hard to figure out." He shrugged. "Thing is, if they're running, something must be wrong. I'd bet you anything that something is chasing them."

His brow furrowed. "There's no other reason why they would be running?"

"It's the only thing that makes sense," Seth replied. "The man leading them wouldn't be running for any other reason. He's a seer."

"A seer?" He laughed mockingly.

"He sees into the future," Seth replied. "He's not very experienced with it yet, but he's getting better. That's why we chose him to lead them to Athena."

"What are they running from then?"

"How should I know?" He laughed. "I'm here with you."

"Tell her—she won't want any distractions from our journey to Admiri," David replied.

"I'm sure she already knows." He nodded to himself.

The Witch

"It's turned," Robert whispered under his breath, once again despising the gifts that cursed him.

"What?" Edwin asked. "I couldn't hear you."

"It's turned," he replied, loud enough for both Edwin and Ryan to hear. "But that's not the last of our problems." He shook his head nervously.

"What did you see?" Ryan asked, obviously used to dealing with Robert's gifts.

"The storm turned south. It shouldn't hit us," he replied. "Admiri's witch is headed directly toward us."

"The witch?" Ryan whispered. "Are you sure?"

"Of course I'm sure!" he snapped.

"Witch?" Kari asked, her voice confused yet curious at this new turn of events as she leaned to Edwin and whispered, "I thought witches weren't real."

"Robert has seen the witch of Admiri crossing paths with us," Edwin replied. "And technically speaking, they're not real, but that is what we call her." He smiled.

"Who is she?"

"She works for Marcus Admiri. Her gifts help her to do what Marcus orders her—which usually involves killing someone with whom Marcus is angry." He paused. "She's very dangerous. Some say she could kill a man simply by looking into his eyes."

"What does she look like?"

"I don't know." He laughed lightly. "There are few alive who have ever seen her face."

"And what will happen if we run into her?" she asked, chills running up and down her spine at the thought of meeting such a foe.

"I don't know," he replied.

She cocked her head to her right where Robert and Ryan continued to talk and asked loudly, "What will happen, Robert?"

"Leave him be," Ryan told her. "He's trying to find out."

She nodded, trying not to let the sudden onslaught of fear show on her face any more than it already was. What if the witch killed them all? "I'm sorry," she whispered under her breath.

"Ryan, shouldn't we allow them to rest?" Edwin asked, gesturing toward the caravan behind them. "They need a break—we've been at this pace for hours." His eyes pleaded slightly.

"Not until we know what will happen," Ryan replied. "We need to know the future if we are to determine what path to take in the present."

⁂

Robert's eyes rolled back in his head, his mind swimming with images of the past, present, and future. He searched for what he needed to know—what the witch would do when they crossed paths and whether or not they would make it to the docks unharmed. He'd already lost seventeen people ferrying them between Admiri and the docks, and he didn't know if he could stand to lose any more. They didn't deserve to die from heat and starvation in the desert—it wasn't right.

He saw as he started to take more people out of the city—too far into the future.

Finding visions of nearby events was much more difficult than finding far-off ones. The near future depended greatly on the current mood and events surrounding each individual person, an ever-changing set of circumstances.

There it was.

The witch stood in front of him, a cruel smile growing on her face as he dismounted his horse. By his side, Ryan, Edwin, and the nervous Kari remained on their horses, ready to defend him on a moment's notice.

Where were the others?

Wait. There—he sent them the long way around. Why hadn't he thought of that already?

The witch pulled a blade from a sheath on her side and brought it to the throat of the man who stood next to her—a man who'd previously gone unnoticed—the Prophet, Seth Green, brother of the witch. What was he doing out of Athena?

Robert's eyes snapped back open as his vision vanished from his mind, gone with the winds of change. The witch had changed her mind.

"What did you see?" Ryan asked, placing his hand on his friend's shoulder as they rode.

"It doesn't matter—she's changed her mind," Robert replied. "She has the Prophet with her." Before Ryan had time to respond, Robert continued, "Slow them down and choose someone to lead them north, away from the witch. A few miles and they should be able to turn back toward the docks." He paused. "See that it's done. I want you and Edwin with me."

"Yes, sir," Ryan replied before he shouted for the caravan to return to a slower pace. "The storm will no longer be an issue?" he asked.

"No. Now carry out your orders."

"Yes, sir." Ryan dipped his head before riding off in search of someone to lead the group.

"Robert, are you sure you want me with you?" Edwin asked. "I'm only a healer."

"No, I'm not," Robert replied. "But I'm hoping that if I limit my actions to those I saw in my vision, she will be limited to something similar to what I saw."

"What did you see?" he asked.

"It's not important now." He paused. "Kari's coming too."

"I don't want her near the witch," Edwin defended.

"She was in my vision, Edwin. She will be there," Robert snapped. "Don't argue with me."

"Of course, sir," he replied. "But if she is harmed, you will have only yourself to blame."

"I know," he whispered. "I know."

A few moments later, Ryan returned, having already carried out his orders. The four then came to a halt while the remainder of the caravan started veering to the north, all obviously confused and angered at this new turn of events.

"They'll be fine," Ryan told him. "You saw that much."

"Did I?" Robert asked. "I only remember seeing us meeting the witch five miles ahead."

"They will be fine, Robert," he replied. "I can feel at least that much."

"Your gifts have nothing to do with knowing if they'll survive or not." He laughed. "You're just strong."

"Just?" he scoffed.

⚜

Brittany began to speed her pace, suddenly eager to meet whoever had been marching toward them. The dust had slowed moments ago, but she knew that they would still be coming to meet her. She knew the man who led them, knew of his gifts, and knew that he had seen Seth with her. The rebel would of course want to save his Prophet.

Robert was his name, and he was a seer. He'd likely seen her, and that was what had caused them to slow. If she had to guess, she would say that he'd sent the people the long way around, not wanting her anywhere near his ward—not that she blamed him. If her orders weren't stopping her from it, she would kill every last rebel in a single thought. Unfortunately, Marcus had ordered that she not harm any of them—and she intended to obey her orders. If she were to disobey, she would no longer be his mistress, and that would not suit her current goals. She had Marcus right where she wanted him, and she intended to keep him there.

She smiled as she started to hear the light sound of galloping hooves—Robert was coming to meet her.

She stopped and turned back toward David and Seth who walked several yards behind her, finding it difficult to keep up with her quick pace. "Stop," she told them as they began to approach.

"What's wrong?" David asked as he came up alongside her, Seth trailing behind ever so slightly.

"We will meet them on my terms." She smiled wickedly. "You're with me, brother." She snapped her fingers and pointed to the ground by her feet, signaling for him to approach her. "How good are you at hand-to-hand combat?" she asked David.

"Very," he replied.

"Good." Her smile brightened. "I want you to hide behind those dunes." She pointed off to the south where a cluster of dunes rose from the ground. "Don't move until you know the time is right. I don't think they've seen you yet."

"How would they have seen me?" He laughed.

"Did Seth not tell you? They are led by a seer. He has no doubt seen me, and that caused him to slow down. He doesn't want me to kill the rebels he's leading."

"Then how has he not seen me yet?" he questioned, his eyebrows furrowing.

"Because I haven't let him. Now go and hide. Assess the situation and determine when to come out." She paused. "No need to make it a fair fight—understood?"

"Yes, ma'am." He smiled before he turned and walked to the dunes, lying on his stomach so that he couldn't be seen, while the siblings waited in the open desert.

"They don't deserve to die, Brittany," Seth told her as the four riders finally came into view.

"They would kill me in a heartbeat," she replied. "Who would you rather be dead?"

"None of you need die today," he said. "Let me talk to them—I can stop this."

"I'm not falling for that." She laughed.

"Please, Brittany, listen to me," he pleaded.

"Quiet, brother, or I will—"

"You'll what? You'll kill me? You know you can't do that—Marcus needs me alive."

"Quiet," she growled. "I have no problem with disobeying his orders."

His golden eyes pierced into her, knowing that she would never back down. This was Brittany—the strongest woman he'd ever known. If she wasn't his sister, he would allow the rebels to destroy her black heart, but he couldn't bear to be the one to order his sister's death.

They stood silently for several minutes, waiting for the oncoming riders to arrive. He was just able to determine that there were three men and a woman, the woman looking hopelessly out of place, while the men's stern faces said they were ready for whatever was coming. Seth let out a heavy sigh as their features came into full view, and their horses came to a halt in front of him.

"Give up your prisoner, witch," the dark-skinned male on the far left said, his horse becoming restless when it saw Brittany's eyes—it seemed she had this effect on everyone and everything.

"You've nothing of better value to trade me," she replied. "I think not." She took hold of Seth's arm and pulled him in front of her so that she was almost completely shielded from anything they might throw at her, her head peeking up over her brother's shoulder.

"We have you outnumbered," the man said. "Give him to us."

The wicked smile returned to Brittany's face as her white eyes scanned over the four riders. "I don't even know your names," she said. "I am Brittany, and I'm sure you know my brother, Seth."

"I am Robert," the man replied as he dismounted and stepped closer to them, his tall frame towering over the both of them. "Now give me your prisoner."

"He's not my prisoner." She shrugged.

"Give him to us," one of the other men said as he dismounted and stood beside Robert.

"Ryan, leave this between us," Robert told him harshly.

"Ryan Roux?" Brittany asked. "The strong man? Did you really think that brute strength would help you here, Robert?" She paused. "You cannot stop me."

<hr />

Jameson lay in bed, his arms wrapped around Reem's sleeping form. Since the events of the night before, he wasn't sure that he wanted to fall asleep. He'd told her that he wouldn't let her vision come true, but truthfully, he wondered if he would even be able to stop it from happening. Like Suri had said, none of Reem's visions had been wrong thus far—a thought that haunted him to his very core.

He kissed her forehead as she slept, wondering if these would be the last days he got to spend with his wife. Would he even see his child born? The fear of leaving Reem alone to raise their child cause tears to form in his eyes. Would they be all right without him there to protect them? Who would act as the child's father? Would Reem remarry? For that matter, would she even survive? They didn't know enough about the Purist technology that bound them together, and it was entirely possible that she would die shortly after he did.

"Don't worry," she whispered, startling him. "Like you said, we won't let it happen."

"I didn't know you were awake," he whispered back.

"Sorry." She smiled slightly. "I usually don't listen to your thoughts, but when we're alone, it's hard not to."

"I don't mind." He smiled back. "I just don't like to talk about that."

"I know," she whispered. "I don't either."

"I won't leave you alone." He shook his head slowly.

"No, you'll just leave me with Suri and Nicholas." She laughed. "Sorry—I didn't mean that."

"No, it's fine." He laughed gravely. "I won't let that happen either."

"Why aren't you asleep yet?" she asked.

"I'm not sure I want to be asleep yet," he replied. "What if we won't be together much longer?"

"I won't let you die, Jameson," she replied. "I'll stay with you—if anything happens, I'll be able to heal you."

"And what if something happens to you too?" he asked. "You would have to heal yourself before you could heal me, and by that time, you might be exhausted." He paused. "What if there's no way to change what you saw?"

"I don't want to start thinking that way. Our baby is already nervous enough—he doesn't need to worry about if you're going to die." She paused, smiling brightly. "I think his gifts are starting to develop."

"Really?" he asked, completely astonished. "So soon?"

"Yes, I've started gaining other abilities again, but I can tell they're not coming from me."

"What gifts?"

"He's a healer, and he's telepathic." She smiled back. "He may also be able to give and take gifts, but I don't know for sure yet."

"What do you mean?" His brows furrowed.

"I think he copied the gifts from me—they're both ones that I have, obviously. I think he may have used his gifts to copy my gifts to himself, trying to protect himself." Her smile brightened as she pulled her body closer to his.

"Does he communicate with you?" he asked.

"Sometimes," she replied, burying her face in his chest. "Mostly, I just talk to him. He doesn't know how to talk yet, remember?" She laughed.

"What do you say to him then?" He laughed lightly.

"I sing to him, tell him I love him, things like that." She yawned.

"I'm sorry, I'm keeping you up." He tightened his arms around her.

"Yes, you are." She laughed lightly. "Good night, Jameson," she whispered.

"Good night." He paused. "Reem?"

"Yes?"

"I love you—more than you could possibly know."

Pulse

David watched patiently as the four riders approached, two of them dismounting shortly after they arrived. So far, it seemed Brittany didn't require any assistance—using her brother as a shield was a good trick that would likely keep her out of harm's way. There wasn't a snowball's chance in hell that they would harm their precious little Prophet. He couldn't help but smile at the height distance between the dark-skinned man and Seth and Brittany. Both the siblings were approximately five and a half feet tall, but when compared to the almost seven feet of the man in front of them, they looked more like dwarfs.

He rose slightly to get a better view of the other two—the two who'd stayed on their horses. The man was average in both height and weight, his skin pale as the moon and his hair an unsightly and untamed shade of orange. The woman next to him, however, was anything but average. Her skin was fair, matching her long blonde hair and bluest blue eyes. She looked completely out of place among the three men whose faces were hardened at the sight of their witch—she was naïve, but still afraid. She didn't seem to know why she was here, or for that matter, where here was.

David couldn't seem to take his eyes off the stunning young beauty, even as her head turned toward him and their eyes locked. Her brilliant blue eyes widened at the sight of his warlike appearance.

This was it—he'd made a mistake. There was no turning back now. He kept his eyes locked on her, willing her to stay silent as he rose from behind the dune and started his approach.

Just then, two things happened. One, the woman let out an ear-piercing scream—one that wasn't stopping anytime soon—and two, everyone—himself included—stopped what they were doing to cover their ears, unsuspecting of what would happen mere seconds later.

Kari had seen him. She didn't know what had caused her to look toward the dunes, but she had—and she had seen the man lying in wait there. Their eyes locked as he rose and started walking toward her, and she did what only came natural—she screamed.

But this wasn't a normal, natural scream. The sound was almost mechanical, as though it were coming from a high-pitched machine rather than issuing from her lips. Everyone around her had stopped to cover their ears, Edwin staring at her in shock—not even she knew that she could do this.

It was then that she felt a surge of power building up in her veins. The surge was so powerful that it hurt, burning into her very core. She wanted it out, wanted to make the pain go away, so she opened her palms and willed it to leave—that was when it happened.

She felt the electric pulse as it exited her body and saw it as it passed through Edwin, Ryan, Robert, and Seth, leaving them all standing virtually unharmed while both the witch and her friend fell to the ground, either dead or unconscious. She turned back and forth between the two on the ground, her frantic scream still ushering from her mouth. Suddenly, she felt fingers clamp down on her mouth and cut her scream short. She turned back and saw Robert's confusion-covered face, his eyes staring into hers.

"How did you do that?" he asked.

"I guess that answers the question—she's Advanced," Edwin said before she could open her mouth to respond.

"She's gifted," Robert whispered as he backed away slowly.

Seth had watched in a panic as his sister had fallen to the ground, knowing the entire time what was coming. He was helpless to go to her until Robert had quieted the girl who screamed at the top of her lungs.

Once the screaming stopped, he'd dropped to his knees beside his sister, checking her body for a pulse. She was alive. He could now see her steady breathing as her chest rose and fell. He pulled her into his lap and cradled her head gently. He knew now that there was no way for him to make her see his side of things. He kissed her forehead lightly and laid her gently on the warm sand. He couldn't kill her, and he couldn't bear to see her imprisoned, so this was his only option.

He stood and turned toward the others who had begun to talk among themselves—he hadn't noticed them while he was concentrating on his sister.

"Excuse me," he said, attempting to cut into the conversation, but somehow continuing to be ignored. "Excuse me," slightly louder this time, though they continued in their conversation. He cleared his throat and stepped into the center of the group and spoke once more. "Excuse me, but shouldn't we be on our way?" he asked. "We don't know how long they'll be asleep."

"You're right," Robert replied. "Do you have a horse?"

"My sister doesn't like them." Seth laughed.

Robert nodded and turned to Edwin. "Kari will ride with you." He turned back to Seth. "You'll take her horse."

"Thank you," Seth replied.

"Should we take these two with us?" Ryan asked as he checked David's vitals.

"No, leave them here," Seth replied. "We can't carry the dead weight the whole way."

Ryan nodded and mounted his horse, while Robert helped Kari off her horse and onto Edwin's. He then led Kari's horse to Seth and handed him the reins. "We'll head west a few miles and find out where the others are. I told them to move quickly, so chances are we'll meet up with them easily."

Seth nodded and turned to his horse, mounting at the same time as Robert. Right away, Robert kicked his horse and galloped away, not waiting for the others to follow.

<hr />

Reem stood on the upper balcony of the tower—the highest point in the city—and watched the warriors of her army as they trained in different areas of the city, the sound of their battle cries almost reaching her. Her feet carried her around the balcony, all the way around the tower, until she stood in front of the staircase once again and had seen all of the people in the city.

She'd addressed the people early this morning, and they'd cheered for the chance to war against Marcus Admiri. They were ready now, ready to fight for their freedom, ready to die for what they believed in. They would give Marcus Admiri a run for his money. He would be here in three weeks, and by then, they would be completely organized and trained to kill.

She had seen them fighting in her vision, seen them filled with pride and courage, seen many die the same day as Jameson. She'd saved many in her vision, and then her husband had been brought to her side, and she could do nothing for him. She couldn't let her vision come true, but she didn't know how to change it.

She turned around and leaned her back against the rail as she dropped her head into her hands. Her head had been throbbing for hours now, and so far, nothing Nicholas had given her was helping. Her fingers gently massaged her temples, and she closed her eyes. For some reason, her healing powers were doing nothing for the headache.

"Still not helping?" Nicholas's voice interrupted her thoughts. "Do you want me to get you something else?"

"No, that's alright," she replied, lifting her head to look him in the eye. "Thank you." She smiled.

"You sure you're okay?" he asked as he stepped closer and placed his hand on her shoulder.

"No, I'm not." She laughed lightly, wincing at the pain it brought with it. "But I'll be fine. Thank you, Nicholas."

"Sorry I couldn't do more. I just don't want to give you something that could hurt him."

"I understand." She nodded. "I'm sure it'll go away soon."

He nodded. "I'm sure it will."

"Do you need something?" she asked, changing the subject.

"Suri wanted to talk to you." He shrugged. "She doesn't like it up here."

"Tell her I'll be down in a few minutes." She smiled back, imagining her sister's frightened face a few days earlier when she'd finally gone up to the upper levels of the tower. Clearly, Suri was meant to live on the ground floor.

"I will." He smiled back before he turned and walked back down the stairs.

Reem turned back to look out over the city, watching as the rain clouds that they'd thus far avoided started to roll in from the west. It seemed they wouldn't be living in sun much longer—yet another thing that lined up perfectly with her visions.

She sighed and turned to walk down the stairs after Nicholas, hearing him speaking with Suri in the main chamber below. Slowly, she started to walk down the steps, careful not to let herself fall as she did so—the stairs were steep, and she wouldn't be the first if she were to fall down them face-first.

As she reached the bottom of the steps, Suri appeared and took her by the hand, leading her down the hall and into one of the empty bedrooms. Inside were a large bed and two small tables on either side, with a closet each to the right and left. Suri led her inside and sat her down on the bed, looking seriously into her eyes as she paced back and forth.

"What's wrong, Suri?" Reem asked, smiling brightly.

"Don't play like you don't know." Suri smiled back. "I know you've been reading my mind since Nicholas said I wanted to see you."

"You want to know why I haven't started to prepare the baby's room yet." Reem nodded.

"Exactly." She paused, stopping directly in front of Reem as she stared into her eyes. "So?"

"So what?"

"So why haven't you started to prepare the room yet?" She laughed, taking a seat next to her sister on the mattress.

"I haven't started it because I wouldn't even know what to do with it in the first place, and I'm not sure I want my baby in a different room from mine—at least for the first few months," Reem replied.

322

"Well, I think you need to start," Suri told her. "You may not want to have the baby in a different room—which I completely understand, by the way—but in a few months, you will. And when you have the baby, it'll be even harder for you to find the time to prepare the room." She paused.

"Suri, I really don't have enough time." She shook her head. "I'm their leader, and I have to prepare them for the army's arrival. I don't have enough time to decide what things need to be put in the room right now."

"Well, then I'll do it." Suri shrugged. "It shouldn't be too much work, and I can have the room ready by the time he's born." She smiled brightly.

"Alright, go ahead." Reem smiled back. "It'll keep you off my back for a few months." She winked. "Now Jameson and I need to go down and check on the progress of the warriors. Do you know where he is?" she asked as she stood to her feet.

"I think he's in your room still," Suri answered, stepping out of the way so that Reem could leave the room.

"Thank you." Reem laughed as she left Suri in the baby's room and walked to her own bedroom, opening the door quietly to see Jameson sitting on the edge of the bed, facing away from her. His elbows were rested on his knees, and his head had dropped into his hands. His mind swam with worries and concerns, too engrossed in thought to hear her as she entered the room.

She walked to his side and looked down at his face, only now noticing the tears that ran down his cheeks. His eyes were closed, but she could imagine the pain that would be in his eyes had they been open.

Slowly, carefully, she sat on the bed next to him and leaned her head against his shoulder, wrapping her arms around his waist gently. *"I'm so sorry I told you,"* she whispered in his mind.

"Don't be," he whispered. "I needed to know."

"I hate seeing you like this." She dropped to her knees in front of him and moved his hands away from his face, running her fingers through his hair and wiping the tears from his face, while his hands moved to her waist.

"Don't worry about me." He smiled as his eyes opened to look into her eyes. "Like we said, we won't let it happen."

"We keep saying that, but neither of us really believes that, do we?" she asked, tears forming in her eyes. "You really shouldn't cry in front of a pregnant woman."

He pulled her closer to himself and wrapped his arms tighter around her frame. "I'm sorry," he whispered in her ear as her arms wound around him.

"We can't focus on this right now, Jameson," she whispered. "Our army is preparing, and we need to make sure that they'll be prepared enough to combat Admiri. They're not used to fighting their own."

He nodded. "I know."

"I don't want to lose you, Jameson," she replied as she pulled away to look him in the eye. "But if we don't win this fight, we will all die. Every last one of them will die."

"Then we'd better win." He smiled slightly. "I'll worry about myself. You worry about your people." He nodded.

"I'll worry about all of you," she whispered.

"That's what makes you a leader." He smiled. "You'd never wish for any of them to die."

⁂

Seth rode quietly behind the others, unsure of whether he'd made the right decision. He knew there was nothing he could do to change Brittany's mind, but he wished that he could have left things better between them. She would be angry about what had happened, and it was entirely possible that Marcus would punish her for not getting his way. Since Reem had run from the city, he'd been disappointed by both of his favorite soldiers, and he likely wouldn't take it very well. Now one of them no longer had his gifts, and the other had been bested by her younger brother.

His body ached from the long ride, and his horse looked as though it was about to collapse under the strain of running such a long distance. Robert had insisted that they ride hard and fast, presumably due to another vision. Though he had paranoid tendencies, Seth knew for a fact that Robert was completely loyal to the rebellion and that he would do whatever it took to get them all through safely.

He couldn't help but smile at the pair who rode directly in front of him. Edwin was holding the reins firmly at the request of Kari, but the man looked as though he'd grown up around the creatures. If he had to guess, Seth would say that she'd never ridden before a few days ago at most. She looked as though she wanted to be asleep, but her fear of the animal beneath her was keeping her from it. Her frail arms were wrapped around Edwin's waist, firmly holding herself in place.

Robert and Ryan, on the other hand, both rode silently and firmly, their faces stern and their bodies poised atop the horses. They rode side by side, and Seth could tell just by looking at them that this was not the first time they'd ridden together. He'd chosen them because of how close they were and the way that they worked together. Ryan seemed to have a calming effect on his friend, an effect that helped him with the visions. Robert's mind worked in mysterious ways, and he couldn't always find the information he was looking for, but Ryan could always help him through it.

Somehow, with Edwin and Kari, they worked even better. Robert and Ryan were both trained to fight, though Ryan's gifts were more suited for fighting than Robert's. If all didn't go well, Kari would be their siren, and Edwin would be there to heal whoever was injured if things turned from bad to worse—which wasn't likely considering Kari's second set of gifts. He would have to suggest that the four of them work together in the future—assuming they all survived, that is.

Seth kicked his horse and sped up to ride between Ryan and Robert, who both turned toward him as he did so. "Anything new?" he asked.

"No, sir," Robert replied. "Haven't been able to see anything since I saw us meeting up a few miles ahead."

"How far?"

"Four miles—shouldn't take too much longer at this pace." He nodded, turning toward the sun that was starting to dip below the horizon.

"Then perhaps we should slow down," Seth suggested. "The horses won't be able to take much more of this, and it's getting close to nightfall. At the worst, we'll reach them when they stop to rest."

"My horse could ride at this pace for three days and still continue," Ryan replied.

"They can live without the both of you for a few more hours," Seth said sternly. "We don't need to ride this hard."

Robert nodded slowly and began to slow his pace, holding up his fist to signal to Edwin that they were slowing. Soon Edwin rode next to him, Kari finally asleep and leaning against his back.

"What's wrong?" he asked.

"Seth believes it would be best to slow down for the horses' sake," Robert replied.

Edwin nodded. "How far off are the others?"

"A few miles." He paused. "But Seth is right, we don't want to run them too hard."

"Who is she, Robert?" Seth asked.

"Honestly, I don't know." He shrugged. "We found her a short distance outside the city, unconscious. Edwin healed her, and we decided the best thing to do would be to take her to the savior. She's a mystery, that one." He smiled slightly.

"And she's Advanced?"

"Yes, though she didn't know it before earlier today," Edwin replied.

"Are you sure?" Seth asked, observing the girl. "She seemed like she knew exactly what she was doing."

"I don't believe she did. She was scared and alone when we found her, Seth." He paused. "We saved her life."

"That doesn't mean that she isn't lying to you."

"I know that, but still." Edwin paused again, sighing loudly. "I believe her."

"Why? Because she's beautiful?" Seth asked, tilting his head to the side slightly.

"No," Robert replied, his tone effectively ending the conversation.

Storm

David's eyes slowly blinked open, confusion clouding his memory as he sat up on the desert floor. He was lying facedown on the ground, his hair and nostrils filled with the tiny grains that surrounded him. For the life of him, he couldn't remember what had happened. His last memory was of the woman screaming so loudly that he thought his eardrums might burst—but that was early afternoon, and it had to be midnight or later by now.

His eyes were heavy as he tried to look around, his vision inhibited by both the darkness around him and his eyelids that kept closing under heavy strain. It was a full moon tonight, but thick clouds blanketed the sky, blocking out the moon and all the stars with it. The wind picked up and blew a gust of sand into his eyes and mouth, and he blinked against the pain.

Why was his head throbbing?

Just then, the clouds parted just enough to shed some light on his surroundings. Several feet away from him, Brittany's unconscious form lay almost completely covered in sand. He'd almost forgotten about her. Both of her legs, half her torso, and her left arm were covered in sand, and the wind continued to blow more and more sand atop her body.

He slowly stood and walked to her side, dropping to his knees in his attempt to unbury her. He could just make out the steady rise and fall of her chest. Before he could begin to remove the sand, the clouds shifted once more, blocking his light. He cursed under his breath as he fought to dig her free without the use of light.

Why wasn't she waking up?

He'd thought that she would have woken up shortly after he did—if not before. Something was definitely wrong. His hands slid over her body to her neck, feeling for a pulse.

Had his mind been playing tricks on him? Was she really alive?

The wind picked up again and threw David away from her before he could find her pulse. If a sandstorm was coming, they'd be sitting ducks out here. Two people alone could never survive such a storm—it was unheard of.

He fought to move back to her side, yelling in pain when a gust of wind knocked him back to the ground, the sharp grains of sand cutting at his face. It seemed that each attempt he made to move closer to her was pushing him farther away. He was quickly running out of energy and finally dropped to his belly in the sand, slowly crawling across the desert floor in the direction he thought Brittany's body was located.

The clouds parted once more and allowed him to see a few feet ahead, but he didn't see her. He must've gotten turned around by the wind and sand. He carefully rose to his knees to look around. He turned first to his right and then to his left, finally spotting her almost fifteen feet away—how did he get so far away?

He dropped back to his belly and crawled toward her, seeing the sand covering part of her face. If he didn't get to her soon, she would die of suffocation from the sand in her mouth and nose. Several minutes later, he reached her. Soon he had the majority of her body uncovered, and the wind continued to blow more and more sand at them, slicing their skin open with their sharp edges.

He could feel the cuts on his skin, could feel them getting deeper and deeper as the wind blew harder and harder, and knew that he had to get out of here. He had to get somewhere away from this wind, but he knew the nearest city was Purist—and three miles away.

Slowly, carefully, he rose from the ground and hoisted her onto his shoulders, careful not to fall when the wind continued to whip at his face. The extra weight would drain his energy even faster than it had when he was on the ground, but he knew that this was the only way. He had to get her to safety.

This must have been what the rebels had been running from—the seer must have seen the storm in a vision and known that they would have to go full speed to avoid it.

He still didn't understand how this could have happened—how both of them could have been made unconscious so quickly—but right now, it didn't matter. The only thing that mattered was getting out of the sandstorm and getting to the Purist settlement. Of course, he didn't know how he would get inside the settlement once he got there, but he would take things one step at a time. In his experience, that was the best way to do things—one step at a time.

❧❧◉❧❧

They slowly rode through the maze of sleeping travelers, wary not to allow the horses to step on their sleeping figures. They'd attempted to go the long way around them, but it turned out they hadn't gone far enough. Robert led them, with Ryan following close behind and Edwin to his right, followed by Seth bringing up the rear. So far, only a few of the people they'd passed had woken up—a good thing since Edwin had almost trampled a few of them.

Suddenly, another of the people woke up, this time in a much angrier mood than the last few. He screamed in rage at Robert as he passed, and Ryan quietly slipped off his horse and punched the man in the jaw, ordering that he quiet down. After that, Robert slid off his horse and led it through the people, finding that it was easier to avoid the people when he had to step through them himself. Edwin then followed suit, leaving Kari fast asleep on the horse while Seth continued to ride, knowing that the chances that the horses would step on the people was slim to none at best—they had no intention of harming anyone.

When they finally reached the front of the group where Terrence stood guard, Robert and Ryan placed a stake in the ground and tied their horses to it, knowing that they would need the rest after such a long day. Edwin helped Kari off the horse and laid her on the ground where she soon fell back asleep and he lay down next to her. Seth dismounted and tied his horse to the stake, joining Robert and Ryan where they stood speaking with Terrence—the man Ryan had found to lead the group.

Robert introduced them quickly before they began to discuss what had happened. "Did you run into any trouble?" he asked Terrence.

"No, sir, no trouble," the man replied. "Actually, the entire trip was completely uneventful. The people don't want to travel at the same pace tomorrow though—I was thinking we might let them sleep a little longer before we ride."

Robert nodded slowly. "I agree. We'll leave when the horses are well rested—ten hours at least."

"Thank you, sir," Terrence replied.

"Get some rest," he told him. "I'll take watch."

Terrence nodded and walked away through the people, far enough away that Robert couldn't see where he'd gone.

"Seemed like a good man," Seth told him. "Where's the storm?"

"Right behind us," Robert replied, stroking his chin with his hand. "It turned back toward us. I don't know how I didn't see it before a few minutes ago, but it's approximately fifteen hours away from our current position. Shouldn't take longer than three hours to reach the docks though."

"Are you sure that's enough time to board the boats?"

"It'll have to do. The horses can't make it that far without rest," Robert said, shaking his head. "We don't have much of a choice."

"We'll be fine," Seth added. "The storm is fifteen hours away—we'll rest for ten and be there three hours after that. We have plenty of time."

Ryan nodded slowly and walked back toward the caravan, lying down near Edwin and Kari where he quickly fell asleep.

"Do you really think we'll have enough time?" Robert asked.

"I don't know," Seth replied.

Marcus paced in his quarters, his mind swimming with the possibilities of the next few days. He wouldn't be sending his army until after he'd spoken with Seth Green, but at this rate, it seemed it would be another week before he got to speak to the man. He needed to instill as much fear into them as they had tried to instill in him—something that could take some time, but in this instance, he was willing to be patient.

Brittany and her ward had fallen off the map, and the only thing he was now sure of was that the three of them were somewhere in the middle of the desert. They should have arrived in the city early this morning by his calculations, but it was now midday, and he'd neither seen nor heard from them. It wasn't like Brittany to take so long when she had clear orders.

If he didn't know Brittany as well as he liked to think he did, he would have already sent out a search party to find them. Unfortunately, if he did send the search party and they were found safely, the woman would likely hold it over his head for years to come. She already held enough over him as it was, and he couldn't afford to give her any more.

He sped his pacing, smiling at the memory of Lana telling him that his pacing would wear a hole in the floor. She'd even gotten him to stop pacing completely before he'd met David. That man would one day wear a hold in the floor—he was sure of it.

God, he missed that woman. She could brighten his day even after every scientist he worked with told him what a fool he was. She was perfect in every way. He'd given her the treatment early on—when they thought they'd gotten all of the kinks worked—and she'd developed one of the most fascinating of all the gifts. She'd been given the ability to travel through time. Unfortunately, that gift was unstable and caused her body to shut down after a short period of time. She'd died in his arms seven weeks after she was given the treatment, and they used her death to fix the treatment, making sure that no one else would be killed by an unstable mutation of their genes. Six months later, they'd given the treatment to the public, but Marcus had never gotten over the fact that his love had been the one to die to make all of this possible.

Reem watched as the members of her army practiced their sparring, surprising her with how quickly they'd learned to work together despite the singles matches going on. No one section of the army wanted to lose to the other, and they continued to help each other in the confines of the rules placed on them. She smiled as Nicholas attempted to spar with some of the other civilian types, falling on his back quickly from a thrust to his stomach from the soldier he fought. She'd ordered that the civilians should at least learn the basics of sparring, seeing as if Marcus's army made it into the city, they would be their last line of defense. She needed them all to be in fighting shape—however, it seemed that over a quarter of the people weren't military capable and only a small number of those had gifts that would aid those who fought. Some would be able to help ferry weapons to their troops, and others would be able to heal the wounded. But those were few and far between, and it seemed that many of them had no desire to fight at all.

Jameson was of a mind to send those who didn't want to fight to Mettirna, but Reem didn't want to discount anyone. She had a feeling that when they realized the full gravity of the situation, they would come around. None of them wanted to die at the hand of Marcus Admiri—or his army—and she didn't blame them.

She continued to walk around the fighters, making pointers to those who fell and congratulating those who won. They were almost ready—and Marcus still wouldn't be here for two weeks. Reem was optimistic that they would survive this war, that they might even be able to win it. Marcus didn't have the one thing that they did: a severe loyalty and desire to be free. These people would fight to the death for what they believed in, and Marcus's warriors would only fight until he was dead. If their leader was gone, they would stop the fight. That was what kept her going.

If they could find a way to kill Marcus, there would be no need to fight. His armies would stand down, and they would be free. Right now, it was the only way out that she could find, the only way to end this war.

Jameson followed a few yards behind her, trying to give her space as much as he was trying to avoid the conversation about taking up his training once more. Reem had been training with Nicholas once a day, usually in the evenings; but so far, Jameson had been avoiding it. He didn't want to leave Reem's side in the fight, which meant that he wouldn't be very close to the battle, but she still wouldn't want him to have no way to protect himself. She knew that he would put her life before his, that he would die before he would let anyone get to her, and that she was a better fighter than he was.

He couldn't bring himself to watch her fight in his place, and he didn't know what he would do if he were to lose her. She was carrying his child. How could he live without them?

He paused a moment, watching a few of the fighters sparring in the field before Nicholas walked up behind him, breathing heavily after a long sparring session. "What's wrong?" he asked.

"Nothing," Jameson whispered, shaking his head slowly.

"Doesn't sound like nothing."

Jameson turned to face him, his eyes betraying his confliction. "I don't know if we can win this," he admitted.

"Nor do I." Nicholas shrugged. "But I have faith that we will give Marcus Admiri pause."

Jameson smiled slightly at Nicholas's choice of words. "Pause doesn't mean that we'll survive."

"I never said it did. I just said maybe it'll make him think a bit before the army comes."

"When'd you get so optimistic?" he asked, his eyebrows furrowing.

"I honestly don't know." He laughed.

"What are we talking about?" Reem asked as she walked back to join them.

"Nothing of importance," Jameson replied, trying to hide the truth from her.

"Don't lie to me, Jameson." She paused, stopping by his side and staring up into his eyes. "You really don't think we can win?" she asked.

He shook his head, ashamed to say the words aloud.

She took his hand in hers, linking their fingers tightly. "Look around you, Jameson. These are some of the best fighters in the world. The Purists have sent word. They are sending a few thousand to join us in the battle, and they should be arriving within the week. Seth will be returning soon, and together, we will be able to make sure that the entire army is prepared. There is always hope that we can win this—and besides, I've come up with a new plan." She winked.

"What plan would that be?" he asked.

"We'll be discussing it when Seth returns. I'd like his input on my idea." She smiled brightly, knowing how much he hated her not telling him.

"Tell me, Reem," he ordered.

"I will." She laughed, reaching up to kiss his cheek lightly. "But not now."

He smiled at her, shaking his head over her antics. "I can't stay mad at you."

"I know." She smiled. "C'mon, let's go home. I need rest." She turned and started walking away, keeping Jameson in tow.

"Are you alright?" he asked. "Do you need me to carry you?"

"I'm fine." She smiled. "Just getting a little tired. We're not far from home though."

He nodded. "As long as you're alright."

"I'm fine, Jameson," she said, tilting her head slightly as her smiling eyes stared straight into his. "I promise. I'm fine."

Together, they walked back to the tower, leaving Nicholas to return to his sparring session. Slowly, they ascended the staircase into the central chamber, Reem almost completely exhausted from the amount of walking she'd done. She'd left the tower early this morning and had been on her feet most of the day before now, but she knew she couldn't keep it up much longer. She didn't want the people thinking that she was weak, but she was sure that if she'd stayed out any longer, they would have witnessed her collapsing under the strain. Besides, it was almost time for Nicholas to give her another dose of medication. She could feel when the pain was about to hit her now, which made it easier to determine when to administer the medication.

When they were almost halfway up the stairs, Jameson lifted her off the ground, seeing how much she was struggling with it. He carried her up the steps and into the main chamber, carefully setting her down once they were inside.

"You don't have to hide your pain from me, Reem," he told her as he set her down. "I wish you would tell me."

"I just don't like to let on."

"I know." He smiled. "I'm getting better at figuring it out."

She smiled slightly as she walked toward their bedroom, carefully cradling her stomach with her hands. Her pregnancy was starting to become obvious—her belly was stretching at her shirt, and he guessed she would soon start wearing his instead.

He couldn't help but smile at how beautiful she looked—even now covered in dust from the sparring sessions. Her walk was starting to turn into more of a waddle than a walk, and he couldn't help but laugh when she shot him an angry glare at thinking that.

"I do not waddle," she snapped, trying to hold back a bout of laughter.

Jameson walked up behind her and wrapped his arms around her waist, resting them gently on her stomach and feeling for the child's heartbeat with his gifts. "You look beautiful," he whispered in her ear.

She turned to face him, her blushing face smiling brightly up into his green eyes. "I doubt that." She laughed lightly.

"If you'd like a second opinion, I'm sure Nicholas would agree." He winked. "He still likes you, you know."

"I know." She paused. "But we don't want to put ideas in his head."

Jameson averted his eyes, still trying to avoid the conversation that loomed overhead.

"Which reminds me," she continued, "isn't it about time that you got back to your sparring lessons too?"

"That would require me spending a lot more time away from you, so no." He smiled brightly.

"Jameson, please." Her eyes rolled. "You need training just as much as any one of them."

"We don't know if I'll even make it through the next few weeks as it is. I'd rather be spending as much time with you as possible before then if you don't mind," he argued.

"But what if the thing that kills you is the fact that you don't have any sparring training and don't know how to defend yourself?" she asked.

"Then something must have happened to my gifts, because I can always at least teleport a few feet into the distance without much trouble."

"Jameson, don't be like that. You know as well as I do that you need the training almost as much as Nicholas does." She paused. "Do you really want him to be a better fighter than you?"

Bête Noire

"How's my favorite patient?" Nicholas smiled as he came up the steps behind Reem and Jameson. "I was told I could take the rest of the day off," he added when he noticed their confused glances.

"We'll likely need you in the infirmary more than we'll need you on the battlefield." She winked.

"Speaking of which, where are we setting up the infirmary?" he asked.

"I'm thinking that we'll station it near here—the center of the city. By the time the fighting starts, we should have the majority of the city populated, so it would make sense to put it near the center. We'll have all of our healers kept there, along with whoever has any medical training, though I doubt there will be anyone who has as much experience as you." She smiled brightly. "What do you think about being our head medic?"

His eyes widened at the thought, and Reem couldn't help but laugh at his expression. "You really are the best we have in the city, Nicholas."

"I'm not so sure about that." He shrugged. "I don't have any gifts that help me."

"You've done wonders for Reem, what with the baby on the way," Jameson added.

"I only did what any healer would have done—only without as much success as one of them would have had." He laughed nervously.

"Don't doubt yourself," Reem chided. "You're a wonderful doctor."

"Thank you." He smiled slightly.

"Jameson, there's someone here to see you," Reem whispered, evidently reading the thoughts of someone who approached. "They're on the steps now."

"I'll be right back," Jameson replied, kissing her temple lightly before exiting the room.

"Nicholas, you know if you asked him he would give you a healing gift, don't you?" Reem asked.

"I'm not so sure," he replied.

"We both have the highest respect for you and your work," she said, placing her hand lightly on his shoulder.

"But is that something that I really want? Do I want to be a healer? I only just found out that I was Advanced in the first place." He shook his head.

"That's for you to decide." She smiled. "But I know my husband, and I know he would be happy to give you the gifts you seek. He feels more indebted to you than you know."

"I've done nothing that should make him indebted to me." He shrugged.

"You've been helping me, haven't you?" She winked.

"I've done nothing that I wouldn't do for anyone else."

"We both know that's not true." Her smile brightened. "I know you still care about me, Nicholas. It's not hard to see—even without my gifts."

His eyes dropped to the ground at their feet, shame filling his expression as he did so. "I take it she told you about him," he whispered.

"Alexander, yes." She nodded slightly, dropping her hand from his shoulder to rest on her stomach once more. "What did she tell you?"

"She said she'd spent a lot of time with the teleporter and that he would be back in a few days," he replied. "I wasn't sure that I wanted to hear the rest."

"She loves you, Nicholas." She paused. "She really does."

"Five days ago, I would have agreed with you. Now I'm not so sure." He shook his head.

"She loves you, Nicholas. Believe me." She placed her hand on his cheek, lifting his face so that he looked her in the eye.

"But is that what I really want?" he asked, his eyes staring straight into hers.

"That's for you to decide." She smiled, removing her hand from his face as he reached up to take it in his. "Don't give Jameson a reason to hate you again." She laughed lightly.

His eyes fell to the ground once again, and Reem tilted her head to the side. "She loves you."

"Thank you, Reem," he whispered, his eyes meeting hers once again.

Jameson reappeared in the chamber, walking up to Reem and taking her hand in his. "Sorry I took so long." He smiled.

"It gave me and Nicholas the time to catch up a bit." She smiled back.

"Not that you two don't see each other enough." He laughed lightly. "You should get some rest."

"He's right," Nicholas added. "You've been overworking yourself a lot lately. Take a few hours off—a day even. It would do you good."

"Thank you, Nicholas. Sometimes she needs a friendly reminder of that." He winked.

"I'll take a few hours—no more. We have work to do," Reem replied.

"No, *we* have work to do," Nicholas said. "I'll get started with the medical center, and Jameson can oversee the warriors and their tactics. Take the day off, Reem. As your doctor, I insist."

"Fine." She smiled slightly. "I'll take the day off, spend some time with Suri, hm?" Her eyebrows rose. "Where is my sister?"

"Last I checked she was in what will soon be the baby's room," he replied. "She would love your opinion on everything." He laughed.

"Thank you." She turned and walked down the hall toward her bedroom with Jameson following closely behind.

"Do you need me to stay with you?" Jameson asked.

"No, I'll be fine." She smiled. "I'm just going to get some sleep for now."

"Alright." He nodded. "I won't be far away—don't worry. I can do most everything from the tower, so if you need anything, I can be here."

"I'm fine, Jameson." She laughed, reaching up to kiss his lips gently. "I just need some sleep."

"Sleep well, Mrs. Willow," he whispered as he pulled her into an embrace. "I'll come check on you in a few hours."

Seth rode silently behind Robert, knowing that the man was still searching for any visions about what would happen once they boarded the ships at the docks. Robert would no longer be in charge after they reached the shore. His job was only to ferry the people between Admiri and the docks, and once there, he and Ryan would return to Admiri. Seth had placed the two of them in charge for a reason, and he knew that he still needed them ferrying the people.

They'd been riding for just over two hours now, and Seth could almost smell the ocean ahead of them. Once they arrived, they would be rushed, trying to get everyone aboard the vessels that awaited them. Many of the people were getting anxious—they could tell from Robert's demeanor that something was wrong, but none of them had a clue of what was coming. They fully understood Robert's urgency, knew that he was a seer and only had their best interests at heart, yet many of them were beginning to question why they'd wanted to join the rebellion in the first place.

Directly ahead of him rode Robert and Ryan, with Kari and Edwin to their right. The couple still rode together, talking loudly between themselves about what it would be like to cross the ocean—apparently, Kari had never been on a boat before—while Robert and Ryan whispered quietly. If he had to guess, Seth would say that Robert had just had another vision, but he couldn't even venture a guess as to what it might be. The seriousness of his face and his low tone sounded as though he'd just seen something bad, so Seth kicked his horse to ride beside the seer.

"What did you see?" he asked quietly.

"Admiri is sending his army soon," Robert replied evenly, his eyes conveying the fear he harbored for the people he now led.

"When?" Seth asked.

"Less than two weeks." He paused. "Will you have time to train them all?"

"The Purists are already fully trained, as are the majority of the others," Seth replied. "We can win this, Robert. We will win this."

Robert nodded slowly, contemplating Seth's response. "Do you need Ryan and myself to return with you?" he asked.

"It might be beneficial, yes." Seth nodded.

"I look forward to it." He smiled.

Seth smiled slightly, still deep in thought as he considered Robert's vision. The fact that Admiri would be sending his army sooner changed things. They were running out of time. He had to warn Reem.

Reem stood on the balcony, watching the clouds cover the stars in the sky as rain started to sprinkle down across the city. So far, they'd been lucky—clouds had passed over the city, but no storms had come—and now it looked as though their luck was changing. Raindrops fell from the sky, landing lightly on the rooftops and running down to the ground. She took in a deep breath and smiled brightly—the scent of rain was intoxicating.

"How are you feeling today?" Nicholas asked as he joined her on the balcony.

"Much better than yesterday," she replied, smiling as she turned to face him. "Though I'm not sure if it was the medicine or my gifts that did it."

"Either way, I'm glad you're feeling better." He smiled.

"And how are things with you and my sister?" she asked, her eyebrows rising slightly.

He shook his head in response, shrugging his shoulders. "I don't know," he whispered.

"Did she tell you what she's thinking about this?"

"I was hoping that maybe you could tell me," he said, his eyes dropping to the ground for a moment before meeting hers again. "Please?"

"I can't go prying into her mind just so you can find out what she's thinking about you." She shook her head. "She's my sister."

"Reem, please. You know she'll lie to me if I ask her." He turned to lean his back against the banister.

"I don't know, Nicholas," she replied, cringing at the thought of prying into Suri's mind.

"Just tell me this, Reem, does she love him?" he asked, his eyes piercing into hers.

She nodded slightly and closed her eyes, reaching out to her sister's mind as she searched for the answer to his question. When her eyes reopened, she couldn't bring herself to look him in the eye.

"She does, doesn't she?" he asked, tears forming in his eyes. "More than she loves me?"

She turned to look at him. "Even she doesn't know that." She paused. "I'm sorry."

"And when will he be here?"

"We're expecting them to be here in three days at the most," she replied. "What are you thinking?"

""Maybe I should just leave." His eyes dropped to the ground at their feet.

"No, Nicholas, we need you," she pleaded, placing her hand on his shoulder. "Give her time. She'll remember how much she loves you."

"But do I even want that?" he asked, lifting his eyes to look at her once more. "What if she's not the one that I'm supposed to be in love with?"

"And what if she is?" she replied, her eyes piercing into his.

"I'm not so sure," he replied, leaning forward to kiss her lips passionately, his arms wrapping around her body. He was shocked to find that instead of pushing him away, her arms wound around his neck and her fingers ran through his hair as her lips moved against his.

Reem's eyes snapped open, and she quickly sat up, remembering where she was. It was all a dream—just a dream—it wasn't a vision. It couldn't have been a vision—could it?

Her breathing was heavy as she nervously ran her fingers through her hair, her hands shaking with the small motion.

Beside her, Jameson slept soundly, and his light snoring sounded like music to her ears. Thank goodness he hadn't woken up. He would want to know exactly what she'd seen, and she couldn't lie to him. Besides, she wasn't even sure that it was a vision.

It couldn't have been a vision. She would never kiss Nicholas! Jameson was her husband, and she loved him with all of her heart—and soon they would be having a baby. She would never do that to Jameson—she couldn't stand to hurt him like that. She loved him more than life itself. She slowly lay back down, facing away from him as tears started to run down her cheeks.

It was just a dream.

Just a dream.

"What's wrong?" he whispered, barely loud enough for her to hear as he wrapped his arms around her, pulling her back to his chest and resting his hands on her belly.

"How long have you been awake?" she asked nervously.

"Long enough," he whispered, kissing her temple lightly. "Another vision?" he asked.

"No, just a dream," she whispered. "Go back to sleep."

"Talk to me, Reem," he replied.

"It was just a dream." She paused. "But I think there might be a storm coming."

"Are you sure it was a dream?" he asked.

She shook her head. "I hope it was."

"What did you see, Reem?" He paused. "Tell me."

"I don't think you want to know," she replied, tears forming in her eyes once again.

"Tell me," he whispered, tightening his arms around her protectively.

"There was a storm." She paused, not sure what to say. "I was on the balcony . . . with Nicholas."

"Did he hurt you?"

"No, no—of course not. Nothing like that," she defended.

He paused, letting a beat pass between them. "Did he kiss you?—will he kiss you?"

"Not just that," she replied, ashamed of what she'd seen in her mind's eye.

"You didn't stop him," he whispered, pulling away from her to lie on his back.

"It was just a dream," she said as she turned to face him. "I would never do that, Jameson. I love you. You." She took his hand in hers and kissed it gently, running the fingers of her other hand through his hair.

"So you're just dreaming about kissing him then?" he asked, his tear-filled eyes turning to look into hers.

"It won't happen, Jameson," she told him. "I love you, Jameson. There is nothing between Nicholas and me—my sister is in love with him, not me."

"I don't want the two of you around each other so much anymore," he whispered.

"Okay," she replied. "But you have to remember that he is the new head physician—I won't be able to avoid him, Jameson."

"Just make sure I'm around." He paused. "I don't want to lose you, Reem." He turned to face her, cupping her face in his hands.

"I'm not going anywhere," she promised.

Windblown

David's eyes snapped open when he realized the wind was no longer attacking him. He sat up, realizing instantly that he was no longer outside, and that there were two men staring at him. He tried to move his legs off the side of the bed, cringing when he noticed the cuts that covered his body.

"What's happening?" he asked as he looked at his arms, hands, and torso—all of which were also sliced open by the sand. "Where is she?"

"We found you outside the city," one of the men replied. "I brought you here."

"Where is here?"

"The camp, of course," the other said. "Is something wrong with your memory?"

"Oh," David replied. "The camp. Of course." He nodded. "Of course."

"Why were you out there?" the first man asked. "We've been confined to our homes for days because of the storm—what were you thinking?"

"Where is she?—the woman I was with," he asked, cringing as his hands balled into fists.

"She's here, don't worry," the first man replied as he approached David and gestured for him to lie back down on the bed. "She's in much the same condition as you, except that she's still unconscious."

"Honestly we didn't expect you to wake so soon," the other added. "My sister is attending to her—don't worry."

"I need to see her," David replied, trying to move without screaming at the pain in his joints.

"No, you need to rest. The doctor will be here soon," the first man said. "What's your name?" he asked. "I am Halaq, and this is Malachi."

"David," he replied, fighting against Halaq as he pushed him back against the mattress.

"The doctor is with your friend now. He'll be here in a moment," Malachi said. "What were you doing out there?"

"We came from the docks—we didn't know about the storm until it was too late. There was nothing I could do." He breathed heavily as the warmth of the room started to penetrate his wounds, the pain building inside his body.

"And you were coming to the settlement?" Malachi asked.

"Of course," David whispered. "Where else would we be going? We're not welcome in the city of the Advanced." He moaned, closing his eyes tightly.

"How do you feel?" Halaq asked as he dabbed at David's forehead with a wet cloth. "Can I get you anything, my friend?"

"I'm fine," he said through his teeth.

"Go check on the woman," Halaq ordered. "Bring the doctor as soon as possible."

"Yes, sir," Malachi replied before he ran from the room.

"I know who you are, David Sanders," Halaq whispered in his ear as soon as Malachi left, "and I know who it is you travel with." He paused. "Make no mistake, I will not allow you to complete whatever task you were sent to perform."

"The task is complete," David snarled as he opened his eyes to look at Halaq. "Who are you that you know my name?"

"If you do not already know, then you will never know," Halaq replied.

Seth hurriedly ushered people onto the boats, trying to be as quick and organized as Reem would be in a situation such as this. He had no doubt that Reem would have already gotten everyone aboard in the time it had taken him to get as far as he had—which admittedly wasn't very far at all. It was times like this when he wished that he was still at Reem's side, but he'd done what he needed to do. He'd gone with his sister in the hopes of turning her against Marcus Admiri.

They were approximately halfway loaded up, and he could already see the storm in the distance—it was quickly approaching. Robert had seen it hitting shortly after they'd finished boarding, but he wasn't sure if that would actually happen. His visions were subjective: they only worked as long as everything went the exact same way that he'd seen. Seth could only hope that things would go as Robert had seen. There was nothing else he could do but continue to usher the people onto the seven ships.

Ryan approached him from behind and tapped his shoulder lightly. "I'll take over."

"You sure?" Seth asked. "I'm doing fine."

"Yeah, Robert wants to see you," he replied. "He wants a progress report."

Seth nodded his response and turned toward the docks where Robert stood, counting the people as they boarded the fourth ship. "The first three can leave— we'll be out of here in an hour at most," he said.

"I was thinking the same," Robert replied. "If any of us are going to be caught in the storm, I'd rather it wasn't all of us." He nodded. "How many more?"

"About half, I'd say." Seth shrugged. "We're trying to pick things up, but it's slow going."

"Is there any way we can speed things up?" he asked.

"I'll see what we can do. People are unwilling to leave so much behind, especially since they don't know for sure what's going on."

"Maybe we should tell them—that would guarantee their speed." He smiled.

"I don't know that I'd want to scare them all into boarding the ships." Seth laughed back. "I'll see what I can do to speed it up."

⁂

Halaq walked into the next room where Malachi waited with his sister and the Purist doctor beside Brittany—the witch of Admiri. What the two spies were doing here, he didn't know, but he did know that he would not allow them to harm the people that he'd come to know as his family.

He'd been sent here by Seth months ago, and since his arrival, he'd befriended many of the Purists. They knew his secret, and in line with the alliance between the rebellion and the Purists, they accepted him. He hadn't expected Marcus to send spies or assassins to the settlement—after all, Marcus didn't see them as much of a threat.

He walked to Brittany's side, surprised that he could still recognize her considering the amount of lacerations on her body from the sandstorm. "How is she?" he asked the doctor.

"She's alive," he replied. "That's the best I can do for now. I have no idea why she's still unconscious."

"The man is awake. His name's David," Malachi added. "He seems to be in a great deal of pain."

"I'll get to him as soon as I finish up here," the doctor replied. "I need to make a medicine for them, but we'll have to wait until the storm passes."

"We should be through the worst of it within the next few hours," Malachi's sister replied.

"Thank you, Hanna." Halaq smiled. "Let me know when she wakes."

"I will." Hanna smiled as Halaq exited the room, walking back into the room where David awaited.

"David Sanders," Halaq said as he entered the room, enjoying the pain that the man now felt. It seemed fitting, somehow.

"Who are you?" David asked.

"As I said, if you don't know now, you never will."

"Are you saying you're going to kill me?" David asked through his teeth.

"I'm saying that my identity will remain unknown to you and your witch," he replied. "Whether you die or not will be determined by the doctor and his skillfulness. But if you ask me, you're going to live."

"And then what will you do with me?" he asked as he turned toward Halaq, taking in his appearance for the first time. His hair fell past his shoulders, surprisingly dark despite his ivory white skin; and his face was hard and stern, though lined from laughter. It seemed this man was an oxymoron in every sense of the word.

"I will fulfill my orders at that point—we shall see." Halaq smiled.

"Where's the doctor?" he asked.

"He'll be here as soon as he's done with the witch." He paused. "How long has she been unconscious?"

"That's none of your business."

"In her current state, it seems unlikely that the cause was the storm. She doesn't have any blows to the head, nothing." He moved to David's side, leaning his back against the wall beside the bed. "So what happened to her?"

"I'm not telling you anything," David replied. "So you might as well leave me to die."

"As I said, David, you're not going to die."

"Then kill me," he spat.

"Doctor, thank you for coming." Halaq smiled as the doctor walked into the room.

"Of course," the doctor replied, walking to David's bedside and kneeling to inspect the wounds. "Can you tell me your name, sir?"

"I'll leave you alone," Halaq whispered before he left to join Malachi in the witch's room.

"David. My name is David."

"Good. What can you tell me about where you were before you woke up?" His hands moved professionally over David's wounds, putting a salve on the worst of them.

"I was in the desert—I'm not sure where."

"And what were you doing there?"

"Is this really relevant?" David asked, his eyes finally opening to look into the doctor's hazel eyes. "What does it matter where I was before I got here?"

"I only want to know if there was any damage to your memory." The doctor smiled. "But gauging by your reaction, I assume there is no problem there. Halaq said you wouldn't be very forthcoming."

"What are you putting on me?"

"One of our salves—don't tell me you haven't seen it before? It's one of the most popular for deep cuts," he replied. "It will help your body to heal faster naturally."

David closed his eyes once again. "Leave me alone."

"Once I'm finished." He paused. "My name's Stephen, by the way, and I have been a doctor since I was eleven, so you have nothing to fear. I will help you heal."

"Please, leave me."

"I can't do that. Several of your cuts are severe." He paused, picking up David's broken wrist and inspecting it. "And it looks like your wrist is broken. I'll have to get you a cast for this—and I'm sorry, but it could take a few hours before I can get you one. The storm is preventing me from reaching the majority of my supplies. We should be able to move you in the morning, but until then, I'll have to find something to set your wrist."

"Then get on with it," he snapped.

⚬⚬⚬

Reem watched from the balcony as the clouds blotted out the stars and rain started sprinkling down from the sky, unable to shake the feeling that what she'd seen must have been a vision and yet also unable to turn and walk away. She knew Nicholas would be coming along in a moment, but she also knew that Jameson was just around the corner and that as soon as he heard Nicholas's voice, he would be on the balcony with them.

"How are you feeling today?" Nicholas asked as he joined her on the balcony overlooking the city.

"Much better than yesterday," she replied, smiling nervously as she turned to face him. "Though I'm not sure if it was the medicine or my gifts that did it."

"Either way, I'm glad you're feeling better." He smiled.

"As am I," Jameson added as he walked up to Reem and brushed her hair away from her face. "How are you this evening, Nicholas?" he asked.

"I'm well enough." Nicholas shrugged. "I was actually hoping that I could speak with Reem for a moment if you don't mind."

"Go right ahead." Jameson smiled. "Anything you wish to say to my wife can be said in front of me."

"What's wrong, Nicholas?" Reem asked, quickly throwing Jameson a glare before turning toward her friend.

"I was hoping that you could tell me what's going on in Suri's mind these days." He smiled and shrugged.

"Nicholas, she's my sister. I can't go prying into her mind just so you can know how she feels." She laughed lightly, remembering where this conversation had led in her vision.

"Reem, please, just tell me this: does she love him?"

"She does."

He leaned his back against the banister, running his fingers through his hair as his mind spun with the new information. "More than she loves me?"

343

"Even she doesn't know that, Nicholas. I'm sorry." She paused. "Just give her time. She'll remember how much she loves you."

"And what if she's not the one I'm supposed to be in love with?" he thought.

"Nicholas, don't. I won't stop him from hurting you if you try anything," she replied. *"Jameson, I think we should go."*

"Your dream?" he thought, his brows furrowing.

She nodded slightly, and he took her hand in his. "If you don't mind, Nicholas, my wife and I would like to be alone for a while. If you're uncomfortable staying in the same room as Suri, feel free to take one of the other rooms." He smiled as he led Reem away from the balcony and down the hall into their bedroom. "Safe to say you had another vision?" he asked as she sat on the bed and dropped her head into her hands.

She slowly nodded, afraid to look him in the eye. "I'm sorry, Jameson," she whispered.

"It never happened," he replied seriously. "Reem, look at me." He sat next to her and kissed her temple lightly. When her head turned to look him in the eye, he continued, "Do you realize what this means, Reem?" he asked, smiling slightly.

"That I'm a terrible wife," she replied, tears snaking down her cheek as she turned away once again.

"No, Reem—it means that not all of your visions come true," he replied. "You're not a terrible wife, because it never happened—because your visions don't have to happen." Her head turned back toward his, still not believing that he was okay with all of this as she stared into his loving eyes. "I love you Reem, and I'm not going anywhere—even if something happens with Nicholas."

"Nothing's going to happen," she replied. "I promise."

"I know." He smiled slightly.

⁕⧼⊙⧽⁕

David quietly opened his eyes and gazed around, making sure no one was in the room with him before he sat up and attempted once more to move his legs off the bed and stand on his aching feet. His whole body cried out in pain as he moved, and he realized that this might not be the best of all ideas—but it was the only one he had. As he put all of his weight onto his wounded legs, his knees started to buckle; and he fell back onto the bed, clutching his broken wrist against his chest. This was going to be more difficult than he thought, but he had to see Brittany—he didn't know if she was awake yet or not, but he had to make sure that she was alive. Marcus would never forgive him if she died here.

"I told you to stay in bed," the doctor said as he walked into the room, staring down at his hands where he held the supplies that had just arrived. "I have what I need to cast your arm."

"I don't want your help," David replied. "I'd like to leave as soon as possible."

"And where would you go?" Halaq asked. "The nearest city is Admiri, and we all know how they treat Purists there."

"Is she awake yet?"

"Not yet, no, but she should wake up any time now," the doctor replied. "Now let me see to your wrist."

"No—I told you, I don't want your help," he snapped. "We're leaving as soon as she wakes."

"I don't see that happening," Halaq replied. "That woman will not go easily." He walked up to the doctor and gestured toward the door. "Give us a moment, will you?"

"Of course, my friend." The doctor smiled before walking out of the room.

"Whatever you think you know about her David, you do not. She is not who you think she is," Halaq said. "I've known her for a very long time, and she would never show you who she really is of her own accord."

"Then I will leave now, and I will leave her to you," David replied as he shakily stood to his feet, using the wall to balance himself.

"The doctor would prefer setting your wrist before you go."

"I do not need a doctor, and you know it."

"No, in fact, I was under the impression that Reem Willow turned you into a human," Halaq replied, winking at David's shocked expression. "Word travels fast, my friend." He shrugged. "Marcus Admiri will not give you the healing you desire." He laughed.

"He has no reason not to."

"You've seen what Marcus has done to others who turned human, so what makes you think he won't do the same to you?" he questioned. "You think he'll just let you go when he finds out?"

"He has no reason to fear me." David glared.

"No, but he has every reason to hate you. He hates anything that isn't Advanced." He paused. "Tell me, did Reem take away your gifts permanently?" When David didn't reply, he stroked his chin with his hand. "I thought she might do something like that. She knows you're not to be trusted."

"Who are you?" David asked angrily.

"Haven't we been over this already?" He laughed. "If you don't already know, you will never know. I'm sure I told you that already."

"Tell me!" he demanded.

"I have no reason to." He shrugged. "I have nothing to fear from you."

"If you think that, then you are a fool," David replied as he started to walk toward the door, hugging the wall to keep himself upright.

"You can't even stand under your own power, David. How do you expect to get to Admiri?"

"Well, you're not stopping me." David laughed.

"I don't have to," Halaq replied. "You won't make it out of the settlement with those injuries."

Departure

Marcus watched from his balcony as his army prepared to leave for Athena—he'd made the decision to send them only hours ago, and they were already at least halfway prepared. The journey would be long, and they would be going by foot until they reached the docks, but he was confident that they could reach the rebellion within the week. Of course, the rebels likely already knew the exact time that his army would be arriving, but that wouldn't stop him from packing a few surprises under his sleeves.

He'd already planted a spy of his own within their ranks—though the little one wouldn't live to see daylight if his army won the war. The spy wouldn't be needed unless his army failed, but he needed the assurance that even if they did, he would hold the ace in this game of cards.

Originally, the sandstorm would have put them off schedule, but they weren't called Advanced for nothing. He had one of his men redirect the storm toward the ocean where it would quickly dissipate, making their task slightly easier. This was just one of the many tricks he had. His man could—and was—causing a massive storm to move over Athena to prevent them from training their army until Marcus's army was upon them. They would have no idea what was coming until it hit them—even he didn't know which tactics he would choose for certain.

He smiled wickedly as he watched them, fully aware that many of his men would likely switch sides when they saw their savior impregnated, but he knew that he would continue to have the numbers and that there was little to no chance that he would lose this fight. The only fight he'd ever lost in his life was to the Humans, and even then, they had sustained many casualties.

His army would be leaving before the day was done, and he knew there was no greater army in the world.

Reem watched from the balcony as the rain slowed to a halt under the power of one of her soldiers, and she smiled brightly as the sun once again started to shine down on them.

She saw as her soldiers took the storm's halt in stride, continuing their training just as they had in the rain. It was like she'd taught Nicholas all those weeks ago: if one can fight in the sun but not in the rain, then one shouldn't even be fighting at all. It was important that they were able to continue their training no matter the weather, but it did help to have their own personal weatherman around to keep things in a cool and dry climate. She wanted to do everything possible to make this fight easier on her army and harder on Marcus's.

They'd set up a perimeter two miles around the outside of Athena so they would know when Marcus arrived, even if it was at an unexpected time and from an unexpected angle. They were leaving no side of the city unguarded, as the majority of the city was now inhabited by her people, and soon there would be no room for them to invite more newcomers into the city until they had the time to build onto it.

"Excuse me, ma'am," one of the guards said as he approached her, "a messenger to see you."

"Send him in," Reem replied as she turned to face the guard.

He smiled and nodded before he turned to retrieve the messenger from the staircase outside the main chamber. When he returned, a young blonde-haired Purist child stood next to him, obviously trying to remember the message that he'd come to deliver.

Reem dropped to her knees, bringing herself to eye level with the boy as she smiled brightly into his nervous green eyes—eyes that reminded her of Jameson's. "What have you come to tell me?" she asked.

"I was sent here by Hera of Mettirna," he replied, his voice high and innocent.

"And what did she want you to say?" Her eyebrows rose slightly.

"She wanted me to say"—he paused, trying to remember her exact words—"that her father sent word that Mitchal Sanders negotiated the aid of several members of the Mettirnian army."

"And when will they be arriving?"

"She said"—he furrowed his eyebrows and wrinkled his nose as he thought—"they should be arriving within the next few days." He paused. "I think."

"Thank you." She laughed lightly. "What's your name?"

"Simon," he replied. "My mommy said that I needed to be useful, so I'm a messenger." He smiled proudly.

"So you are." She smiled back. "Was this your first message?"

He nodded, his smile brightening. "Yes, Mrs. Willow."

"Call me Reem." She reached out her hand and ruffled his hair lightly. "Now go back to work—and don't forget to tell Hera that you delivered her message."

He nodded again before he turned and ran through the main chamber and back down the steps.

The guard reached out his hands to help her get to her feet, and she gladly accepted the help before she returned to the balcony to watch her people. If it was true that Mettirna had sent part of their army to aid in the fight, then it was possible that this fight could actually be won. This would be the first time that both Purist and Advanced fought side by side, and she intended to make it a battle to remember.

"Who was that?" Jameson smiled as he teleported into the main chamber, watching as Simon ran down the steps.

"A messenger." Reem smiled back as he walked up and took her hand in his. "Hera sent him to tell me that some of the warriors from Mettirna will be joining us after all—though I'm sure it's not officially sanctioned by the Superiors." She laughed lightly.

"How many?" he asked.

She shrugged. "We'll find out when they get here, which could be any day now."

"So soon?" His eyebrows furrowed as they watched the warriors preparing the city for the oncoming battle.

"Marcus is preparing his army as we speak." She nodded. "We'll be ready for him."

He nodded back. "Yes, we will."

"How was your afternoon?" she asked as she turned to look him in the eye.

"It went well." He smiled. "More practice with hand-to-hand combat."

"I asked that you be fully trained in that area." She paused. "I think there may be more hand-to-hand than anyone realizes."

"What do you mean?" he asked, his brow furrowing.

"I can jam all of their weapons, remember?" She laughed.

"The only way to end this is to kill Marcus Admiri," he replied.

"I know. That's what I need to talk to Seth about." She nodded. "I think I have a way to do just that. If he's out of the way, his followers will stop fighting. Without his direction, they are lost, because without his direction, the other Superiors would start picking each other off one by one for control of the army."

"As long as we're on the same page then." He laughed lightly. "These should be an interesting few days." He ran his fingers through his hair as he considered what was about to happen.

"Don't worry, Jameson." She smiled, placing her hand on his shoulder. "We can win this. Don't forget we have several thousand soldiers on their way here to help us."

"How large is our army compared to theirs?"

"Honestly, not very." She shook her head. "But I'm trying to remain optimistic about this." She smiled brightly. "Besides, I have a feeling that many of them will change sides when they see me."

"I'm not following." His head shook as he shrugged.

"I'm pregnant, Jameson." She laughed. "Almost everyone considered me the savior of the Advanced, and some of them are still questioning whether or not Marcus was right in naming me a traitor. When they see me like this, they are bound to change sides and join us."

"Reem, I don't want you anywhere near that battlefield." His eyes pierced into hers. "I don't want our child anywhere close to the fighting."

"It's the only option we have right now." Her eyes pleaded with his. "I am certain that at least twenty percent of his army would join us, and that alone would make it an even fight."

"It's not happening." He shook his head. "You're staying here where it's safe."

"It won't be safe anywhere," she said. "You know that as well as I do."

"No, Reem." He shook his head as his bright green eyes pierced into her. "No."

"Jameson, you're being unreasonable," she said, immediately regretting her choice of words.

"Then do what you like, Reem." He paused. "You always do." He teleported away, leaving her standing alone on the balcony with tears forming in her eyes.

"I don't want to be disturbed," she told the guard as she walked through the main chamber and down the hall into the baby's room, opening the door and stepping inside. The room was void of people—exactly what she was looking for—and almost ready for the baby's arrival. Suri had decorated it beautifully. She'd placed a rocking chair in one corner and a crib under the window with a changing table next to it. She'd even found some baby clothes and packed them into a small dresser and started knitting a blanket for the little one.

Reem closed the door and took a seat in the rocking chair, crying softly as she rocked back and forth, back and forth, trying to keep the baby calm. She had a feeling that the time was coming sooner than anyone had expected—especially if her stress levels didn't go down. She soon fell asleep to the soft motion of rocking, the tears drying on her cheeks.

When she woke to the gentle motion of someone lifting her into his arms, she kept her eyes shut as he carried her off to her bed, placing her carefully onto the mattress and gently brushing her hair away from her face.

"Sleep well, Reem," Nicholas whispered.

Her eyes snapped open and stared into his brown eyes—not the bright green eyes she'd been expecting. "Nicholas?" she asked, her eyebrows furrowing. "Where's Jameson?"

"I don't know." He shrugged. "I thought you'd be more comfortable here." He paused, noticing the confused look on her face. "I hope that was okay."

"No—I mean, thank you, Nicholas." She smiled crookedly as she sat up.

"If you don't mind me asking, what happened?" he asked.

"Jameson and I just had a fight, that's all." She shook her head. "I said some things I didn't mean, and he teleported." She paused. "He's not far away—I mean, the baby's fine, so he can't be far away—but I don't know where he went."

"Would you like me to go find him for you?"

"No, that's alright. He'll come back when he's ready." She nodded as if she was trying to convince herself as much as him. "Thank you, Nicholas."

He smiled slightly as he stood to his feet. "I'll leave you alone. You should get some rest." He walked out of the room, closing the door behind him.

"Jameson, please come back," she pleaded.

Alexander

Reem cried herself to sleep, still unsure of where Jameson had gone, and worried about the vision she'd seen of herself and Nicholas. What if it could still come true? Jameson wasn't here to help her if anything went wrong. All night long, she dreamt of their first few months together, their marriage, and the day she'd discovered she was pregnant. Ever since they arrived in Athena, their relationship hadn't been the same. He'd tried to be understanding, tried to be patient, and she'd done her best to make him feel as though he was as important to her as the rebellion, but it still wasn't the same. And now with her having the vision about herself and Nicholas and knowing that if she showed herself during the battle their chances of winning would be higher—though the chances of her death would also be higher—was making the whole thing that much harder. She didn't know what to do, so she only cried herself to sleep, wishing that Jameson would come back to her, wishing that they had never come here, wishing that she could go back to the time when they lived in the caves together—when they were happy.

She knew this line of thought was hurting her child as much as it was hurting her, but there was nothing she could do. She couldn't help but think about him, couldn't help but think about the look on his face when he'd told her to do what she wanted—since that was what she always did anyway. The tears streamed down her face as she slept, and she hardly noticed the pain until it woke her from her sound sleep and she cried out, waking up everyone else in the building.

A moment after he heard her shriek, Nicholas barged into her bedroom with Suri at his side. "What's wrong?" he asked as he rushed to her side, completely professional as he laid his hands on her waist.

"The baby is coming," she whispered.

"So soon?" Suri gasped as she hurried to help Nicholas at her side.

"Where's Jameson?" Reem asked. "Where is he?"

"Suri, you need to find Jameson," Nicholas ordered. "I know what to do. I'll help her."

Suri nodded and ran out of the room, hurriedly searching for her sister's husband. "Jameson!" she yelled as she ran up the stairs toward the upper balcony, her fingers gripping tightly to the rail as she faced her fear.

She found him there, sitting on the edge of the balcony with his feet dangling over the side and his head in his hands. He didn't even notice her arrival until she reached the top of the steps and stumbled to his side.

"Jameson, you need to come with me."

"I'm not going anywhere," he replied solemnly as he shook his head.

"Jameson, you don't understand," she said as she laid her trembling hand on his shoulder. "It's Reem." She paused. "She's having the baby."

"What?" His head jerked toward her, shock and confusion on his face. "She's still months from her due date."

"It's coming now," she replied. "You need to come with me—she needs you."

He nodded and stood quickly before teleporting downstairs into his bedroom. He found Reem screaming in agony on the bed as Nicholas checked the baby's progress.

"Reem," he whispered as he knelt by her side, taking her hand in his.

"Where were you?" she screamed as her hand clamped onto his.

"Doesn't matter—how are you?" He leaned in to kiss her forehead lightly.

"She's doing well," Nicholas replied as his eyes met Reem's. "It's almost time for you to start pushing."

⚜

Halaq laughed as he approached David, crawling in the sand a few meters outside the settlement. "Did I not tell you that you wouldn't make it far out of the settlement?" He hooked his arms under David's and hauled him to his feet, carrying him all the way back into the building he'd come out of. "Now if you'll please stay here and let the doctor help you," he said as he laid him down on the bed.

"Take me to Admiri," he ordered. "You don't want me here any more than I want to be here."

"I'm afraid I can't do that." He laughed. "For one thing, the doctor wants you to stay here. And for another, your witch wants to see you."

"She's awake?" he asked.

"She woke up a few moments before I brought you back inside. She's quite insistent that she see you right away, though I have no idea why."

"Take me to her then," he ordered.

"You really should stop ordering me around." Halaq laughed. "Besides, a few moments ago, you wouldn't have wanted my help in getting to the next room." He gestured off to his right where Brittany's room was located.

David grunted and slowly stood, using the wall to keep himself steady as he eased past Halaq and into her room, finally coming to a rest next to her bed.

"What took you so long?" she asked bitterly as he sat.

"What do you mean what took me so long? I'm hurt worse than you are!" he snapped back, holding up his broken wrist as proof.

"That's nothing!" she scoffed, sitting up easily. "I'm sure you've had worse—I know I have." Her eyes rolled at his grimace.

"In the past, I've had a healer on hand to fix these things for me," he whispered under his breath, just loud enough for her to hear.

"Well, we don't have a healer now, so you'll just have to deal with it," she replied. "How did we get here?"

"They didn't tell you?" His eyebrows furrowed as she shook her head. "When I woke in the desert, the sandstorm was almost on us, so I made an executive decision to bring you here since it was a few miles closer than the city." He shrugged, wincing with the pain of the small movement.

"That was an idiotic decision at best," she replied, keeping her voice low. "Did you not think that they would keep us hostage once we arrived? I'm Marcus's mistress, David—most everyone knows he wouldn't just leave me here to die."

"At the moment, I was only thinking about the best way to get through the day," he replied. "You could be more thankful for me saving your life—I could've just left you out there to die."

"You know what Marcus would do to you if you'd done that."

"And we both know that there is no place for me in that city anymore." He stood, once again using the wall for support. "I am no longer Advanced—Marcus would have killed me when he saw me, whether I'd left you behind or not."

"Finally, he sees the light." She smiled slightly. "I was surprised to see how enthusiastic you were about returning to the city. You know what Marcus does to people like you."

"People like me?"

"People who fail their tasks—and fail them so monumentally that they lose their gifts in the process." She laughed. "He wouldn't have just killed you, David. He would have tortured you until you begged him to kill you, and then he would have hung you out to dry."

Slowly and carefully, David made his way back into his own room, trying to ignore the remark that he knew in his heart was true. He'd known it all along, known that there was no possible way that Marcus would have allowed him back inside the city unscathed, but he'd fooled himself into believing that his friend wouldn't be capable of doing such things to him.

He made his way to his bed and slowly lay down, trying his best not to glare as Halaq tried not to laugh at his misery. "Will you please just leave me alone?" he asked.

"I could, yes," Halaq replied. "But you're not exactly the most trustworthy person in the world."

"I can't go anywhere," David whispered. "Why don't you go see to the witch? She's quite pleasant today."

"You're right. I should go bind her to the mattress so she can't get in any trouble." He sighed. "Alright, I'll leave you alone—but the doctor should be here in a few moments to set your wrist." He left, walking into Brittany's room.

⚜

Suri paced outside the tower, having left after Reem had started the process of giving birth. Honestly, the whole thing was more than she could handle. She knew Nicholas would be taking good care of her sister, but she still didn't know if the baby would survive. It was still months before the child was supposed to be born, and in the past, any premature child had slim chances at survival. She hated to think what that would do to her sister.

Jameson was with his wife now, and that was all that mattered at the moment. Without him, Reem would be lost—though she'd never want anyone to know it. She always wanted his approval on everything that was going on in the city, even though he had no idea of the workings of politics.

Suri smiled slightly as she paced, thinking of the look of anger that must have been on Reem's face when Jameson teleported to her side. She was likely wondering why he'd ever put her through this.

"Suri?" a familiar voice whispered from behind her, his deep male voice causing her smile to brighten as she turned to look him in the eye.

"Alexander." She smiled as she stepped forward to embrace him. "How are you here so soon?" she asked. "We weren't expecting any of you for another few days at least."

"I couldn't wait to see you," he admitted as he tightened his arms around her. "I teleported into the city an hour ago."

"Then what took you so long to get here?" She laughed lightly as she reached up to kiss his cheek.

"I guess I'm just an idiot," he whispered, tilting her chin up to kiss her lips gently. "I should've been here days ago." He laughed as she pulled away.

"I missed you," she whispered, smiling into his hazel eyes.

"I missed you too," he replied as he leaned in to kiss her forehead. "What are you doing out here?"

"My sister's having her baby." She paused. "I guess I don't have the stomach for these things." She shrugged, laughing at the amused smirk on his face.

"I don't think I would've stayed either," he whispered, running his fingers through her hair. "I missed you." He smiled. "I don't think I've ever missed anyone this much before."

She reached up and brought her lips to his, kissing him passionately before she pulled away to gaze into his eyes once more. "Come on"—she took his hand—"come inside." She led him up the stairs and into the main chamber, her eyes widening when she heard Reem's scream. "Let's go upstairs—there's a balcony on the roof."

He nodded as she quickly led him up yet another set of stairs onto the upper balcony where she'd found Jameson only moments before, her hand still gripping the railing, though not as tightly when she felt Alexander's hand on the small of her back.

"Sorry about that." She winced. "I forgot how loud she was."

"I don't think I blame her." He shrugged.

"I know I don't." She laughed nervously, turning to look out at the city. "It's beautiful at night, isn't it?"

He silently brushed her hair back behind her ear, his eyes staring straight into hers. "I don't know if I'd say beautiful." He whispered.

⚜

"Reem, meet your new baby girl," Nicholas whispered as he wrapped the child in a cloth and handed her to her mother. "She seems completely healthy, considering how early the birth was."

"Thank you," Reem whispered, tears streaming down her face as she stared at the tiny silver-eyed baby she held in her arms. "She's perfect."

"What's her name?" Nicholas asked.

Reem turned to look up at Jameson, nodding for him to answer Nicholas's question. "Her name's Eliza," he said, kneeling beside his wife. "Eliza Miriam Willow."

"I'll leave the three of you alone," Nicholas whispered as he turned and exited the room. "Let me know if you need anything. Your healing gift should have you up and about soon, I would think." He closed the door behind him and walked out to the main chamber, leaning against the wall and taking a seat on the cold marble floor. He dropped his head into his hands, ashamed that the whole time he'd been helping Reem, he'd been wishing that it was his child and not Jameson's.

"Nicholas," Suri whispered as she descended the staircase from the balcony. "I hadn't expected you to be out here so soon." She paused, waiting for him to respond.

When he continued to stare at the floor, she added, "How's the little one?"

"She's fine," Nicholas whispered.

"They had a girl?" she asked, smiling brightly as she walked closer to him.

"Yes," he replied, lifting his head so that he could look her in the eye. "Eliza Miriam."

"How is she?"

"Reem or Eliza?"

"Both." She smiled.

"Reem's doing fine. Her healing gifts should have done their job by now, and Eliza is well as far as I can tell too. She's surprisingly healthy for her age." He nodded slightly, looking back down at the ground. "Where did you go?"

"I . . ." She paused, unsure of what to tell him. She brushed her hair back behind her ear as she turned to the sound of footsteps on the staircase behind her. "I have someone you should meet," she whispered.

Nicholas reluctantly lifted his head once more as the man descended the staircase, taking Suri by the hand. He was tall with hazel eyes and dark short-cropped hair, his perfectly white teeth smiling brightly as he stared at Suri who sheepishly turned back toward Nicholas.

"Nick, I'd like you to meet Alexander." She smiled as she led the man closer to Nicholas.

"The teleporter, I take it?" Nicholas nodded, refusing to meet the man's eyes.

Alexander nodded his response as they approached Nicholas, his friendly smile completely sincere. "Class three."

"Nice to meet you," Nicholas said. "I'd stand, but well, I don't want to." He laughed.

"Nick is our chief physician," Suri clarified.

"Oh, of course," Alexander replied. "I don't blame you."

"Will Reem be taking any visitors?" Suri asked, her eyebrows rising slightly in wonder.

"I'm not sure." He shook his head. "Try knocking." He winked. "I'll be here if you need me."

"Thank you, Nicholas." She smiled sincerely as she led Alexander down the hall toward Reem and Jameson's room. She gently knocked on the door, and a moment later, Jameson appeared in the doorway, his smile bright and cheerful.

"She's sleeping," he whispered.

"Which one?" She smiled back.

"Reem, but Eliza doesn't look too far off." He laughed lightly. "You can come in if you'd like." He opened the door the rest of the way, gesturing for them to enter the room. "I take it you're the Alexander?"

"And you would be Jameson, class seven teleporter," Alexander replied.

"I'm not so sure about class seven, but Jameson I am." His smile brightened as he firmly shook Alexander's hand.

"It is an honor to meet you."

Jameson ignored his comment and walked to the bed, gently taking Eliza from Reem's sleeping arms and carrying her to Suri. "Eliza, meet your aunt, Suri," he whispered as he handed her the child.

Suri carefully took Eliza from his arms and took a seat on the edge of the bed, smiling brightly at the tiny baby in her arms. She had a full head of curly brown hair and gleaming silver eyes that Suri couldn't help but awe at.

"Jameson?" Reem moaned as she woke.

"I'm here, Reem," he replied, walking to her side and kissing her forehead. "How are you feeling?" he asked.

"I'm fine," she whispered. "Where's Eliza?"

"Right here," Suri replied.

"Oh, Suri, you're back." She smiled, obviously still half asleep.

Suri stood and walked to Jameson, carefully handing Eliza to him. "We'll leave you alone—she needs the sleep." She laughed.

"Thank you," he whispered back. "We'll see you in the morning." He turned toward Alexander. "It was nice to meet you."

"And you," he replied, taking Suri by the hand as he led her out of the room, closing the door behind them.

"So I'm staying a few blocks away from here if you'd like to join me," he told her as they walked back down the hallway toward the main chamber.

"Why don't you just stay here with me?" she asked, stepping in front of him and running her fingers through his hair. "I don't want to be so far away if my sister needs me."

He smiled back, wrapping his arms around her back. "Which room is yours?"

"We're standing next to it." She laughed lightly before he teleported them just inside the door.

"Mm . . . I missed you," he whispered as her arms tightened around his neck.

"Good thing you don't have to go anywhere then." She leaned in and kissed his neck lightly before pulling away and taking a seat on the bed.

"I'm never leaving you again." He smiled and shook his head slowly as he approached her and kissed her lips passionately.

Secrets

Reem woke to the sound of Eliza's crying and rolled over in bed to see Jameson pacing with their daughter in his arms, trying to calm her down. He looked like he'd been around children his entire life, like he knew exactly what he was doing, though she knew he'd only been around children when he was a child himself. She couldn't help but smile at the look on his face when Eliza finally stopped crying and he sat on the edge of the bed, still unaware that Reem was awake.

She sat up and ran her fingers through his hair. "How is she?"

"You're awake." He smiled. "I don't know how you didn't wake up earlier than that."

"How long has she been crying?" she asked, her eyes full of worry.

"Only a little over an hour, don't worry," he replied, leaning in to kiss her forehead lightly. "How are you feeling?"

"My gifts had me good as new hours ago."

"Good." He smiled. "Alexander is here, by the way."

"Suri's Alexander? Already?" she asked, sitting up to lean against the wall while Jameson handed Eliza to her. "He teleported in early?"

"So it would seem." He nodded. "And, Reem, she seems happy."

"Yes, she does." Her eyes unfocused as she used her gifts to read Suri's thoughts. "She's with him now actually."

"He seems like a good man," he added. "And he seems to care for her as much as she cares for him." He paused, stroking Eliza's head with his hand. "How's Nicholas doing with all this?"

"Not well." Her head shook slowly.

"I love her eyes," he whispered as he stroked the top of Eliza's head. "They remind me of yours."

"She's beautiful," she said. "More beautiful than I'd pictured her." She smiled brightly as she lifted her eyes to look into Jameson's.

"I love you." He smiled brightly. "Both of you." He leaned in to kiss the top of Eliza's head before turning to Reem and kissing her lips. "I'm so sorry I left you alone last night."

"Don't be," she whispered. She lifted her hand to stroke his cheek gently. "I'm sorry I wouldn't listen to you." She paused. "Though I'm not sure my idea would work anymore anyway—there's no real way to prove that I gave birth to her anymore."

"Reem, she looks just like you." He shook his head. "That's all the proof anyone should need."

"But I'm afraid that wouldn't be enough for many of them." She shrugged. "I'll stay and help Nicholas in the hospital."

"Is that what you really want?" he asked, staring intently into her eyes.

She smiled slightly. "I can't leave her."

"I can stay with her." He paused. "They need you more than they need me."

"But she needs her mother."

"I understand." He smiled. "You're a good mother, Reem."

"I hope I will be," she whispered.

"You already are, my love." His smile brightened. "You're the perfect mother."

"Thank you." Her eyes lifted to gaze into his, and she leaned forward to kiss his lips. "I love you." She paused. "Nicholas is coming. He wants to check on her."

Jameson nodded and walked to the door, opening it to find Nicholas with his fist in midair, ready to knock on the now-open door. "Hello, Nicholas." He smiled.

"Reem knew I was coming, didn't she?" Nicholas laughed. "Can I then assume she knows I'm here to check on Eliza?"

Jameson nodded and gestured for him to enter the room, stepping aside to make space for him to pass by. "As far as I can tell, they're both fine."

"I'll be the judge of that," he replied as he knelt by the bedside and took Eliza from Reem's arms. "Mind if I take her to the nursery?" he asked.

Reem nodded. "I'll meet you there in a moment."

"Thank you." He smiled as he carried the little one out of the room, letting Jameson close the door behind him.

Reem threw her legs off the side of the bed and slowly stood, walking up behind Jameson and wrapping her arms around his waist. She reached up to run her fingers through his hair while he turned around to face her, lifting her off the ground to bring her lips to his.

Suri slowly ran her fingers up Alexander's arm to his bare chest, her eyes staring straight into his. They stood inside the bedroom, Suri wearing her favorite green sundress and Alexander wearing only a pair of jeans.

"I'm glad you're here," she whispered.

"So am I," he whispered back.

"I'm going to go check on my niece." She paused. "Then we can do whatever you'd like." She smiled brightly as she kissed him. "I'll be back."

"I'll miss you." He smiled.

"I'll miss you too." She laughed lightly before exiting the room and walking down to the nursery where she assumed Eliza and Reem would be. She walked inside to find Nicholas cradling Eliza in his lap while he rocked in the chair she'd found. "Nicholas," she said, "I didn't expect to see you here." The corners of her mouth turned up slightly.

"Hello, Suri," he replied, not looking up from the child in his arms. "How are you?"

"I'm fine." She paused, stepping closer to him. "How is she?"

"Surprisingly healthy, though she's still weaker than most newborns. I think her gifts are helping. She seems to have developed Reem's healing gift as well as a few others."

"May I?" she asked, holding her arms out.

"Of course." He stood and carefully handed Eliza to her. "Reem should be here in a moment if you'd like to see her."

"I would." She smiled. "And, Nicholas, I'm sorry about yesterday. I didn't mean to surprise you like that. I know you weren't looking forward to—"

"No, I should've guessed he'd be here sooner." He shrugged. "What is it with Kahrins and teleporters?" He laughed.

"That's not why—"

"No fighting while Eliza's in the room," Reem cut her off as she stepped inside. "How is she, Nicholas?" she asked, smiling as Eliza's silver eyes opened.

"She's fine." He smiled back.

"Thank you." She turned to look at him. "I'd like to speak with both of you about what's going on with Alexander as soon as you have a chance." She paused, looking to Suri. "I'd just prefer that Eliza wasn't in the room at the time—I have a feeling there could be raised voices." She laughed lightly. "When can the three of us have a chat?"

"I actually have a full day planned," Nicholas replied. "I'm working on getting the hospital set up, and I need to go with Angel to the nearest Purist settlement for some medical supplies."

"Why don't you have Alexander take you?" Suri asked. "He can teleport farther than Angel."

"No, I was actually looking forward to going with Angel, but thank you," he replied.

"And what's your excuse, Suri?" Reem asked.

"I'm spending the day with Alexander since Nicholas doesn't want to," she replied. "Unless you need me here to help with Eliza or anything."

"No, that's fine." She smiled. "When will you be back—both of you?"

"I should be back before nightfall," Nicholas replied.

"Same here, I would think." Suri nodded.

"Alright, then we'll talk this evening." Reem took Eliza from Suri's arms. "And it's not a suggestion. You'd both better be there. Meeting room at eight."

"Of course." Nicholas nodded slowly. "I'd better be on my way if you don't mind."

"Go." She smiled. "You don't want to be late now, do you?" She winked before he turned and exited the room, his legs moving at a much faster pace than usual.

"I'd like to meet him, Suri."

Suri smiled. "I know you'll like him, Reem."

"I'm sure I will." Her smile brightened. "Are you going to go get him, or do I have to keep hinting?" She laughed.

Suri laughed, her face flushing slightly. "We'll meet you here in a moment." She turned and walked out of the room, reappearing a moment later with Alexander holding her hand. "Reem, meet Alexander." She smiled brightly. "Alexander, this is my sister."

"The savior, of course." Alexander smiled as he shook her hand.

"I prefer Reem actually." She smiled. "It's good to meet you. Suri's told me much about you."

"And I you." He dipped his head. "May I?" he asked, holding his arms out toward Eliza.

"I don't see why not." She shrugged, handing him Eliza and resting her hand on his arm, knowing that he couldn't teleport her child anywhere without taking her along provided that her hand was in contact with him.

He knowingly nodded toward her hand as his arms gently cradled her child, and he stared in wonder toward her glimmering silver eyes. "Silver?" he asked, his eyes glancing up toward Reem before looking back at Eliza.

"Jameson thinks she got that from me." She nodded, her eyes starting to shine brightly with silver light. "I've always had silver in my eyes." The corners of her mouth turned up slightly before her eyes stopped shining.

"They're beautiful," he whispered.

"Hers or mine?" She laughed.

"Both actually." He looked up at Suri. "Yours remind me of Suri's." Suri blushed slightly as he reached out to stroke her cheek. "She's the most beautiful thing I've ever seen."

"Marcus," Lana whispered, reaching out to wake him from a deep sleep. "Marcus, wake up."

He moaned and rolled over, his eyes widening when he saw her standing by his bedside. "Lana?" His brows furrowed. "Is that you?" His eyes took in the sight of her light blonde hair falling around her face like a sheet of gold, her kind brown eyes that stared into his.

"Do you remember what advancement I received?" she asked, sitting down on the bed beside him.

"You traveled through time," he whispered. "Lana, your advancement killed you."

"I know, Marcus. I know everything that happened." She smiled slightly. "You've already told me everything."

"When?"

"In the future." She paused. "And now there's something I need to tell you."

"What is it?" he asked, sitting up and leaning against his headboard.

"You need to call the army back."

"Lana, I'm doing this for you—for us. This is what we always wanted." He laughed. "I sent them there to end the rebellion, end all the doubt in my people's minds." He paused. "I can't turn back now." He reached out his hand to touch her face, surprised when she moved away.

"I never wanted this, Marcus." Her head shook. "I never wanted you to rule them by fear."

"What are you talking about?" He laughed. "This is what we wanted, Lana."

"Marcus, you can't do this—you're not going to win this fight," she replied, her eyes filling with tears.

He laughed. "There's no way for me to lose."

"Yes, Marcus, there is." She tilted her head to the side. "She is better than you, smarter than you. She knows everything, or she will as soon as I'm able to speak with her."

"I can't let you do that, Lana." His face turned hard as he stared into her loving eyes. "I won't let you."

"What are you going to do, Marcus? Are you going to kill me?" She laughed. "You deserve to die more than I, and if you keep on this path, you will. Her husband will not show you any mercy if you try to kill her."

He reached out and grasped her arm firmly only seconds before she disappeared from his side, traveling in time once again. He had no way to know where she'd gone or if he would ever see her again, but now he wished he'd spent those precious moments better than he already had. Seeing her face again, he remembered how much he loved her. He'd guessed that he would see her again after she'd died, but he'd had no way to know when or where—though now he knew he would see her at least once more. At least once more.

Lana appeared in the middle of the woods near Athena, her mind completely set on her mission—telling Reem and her husband about Marcus. She hated to turn on her love, but she'd seen what he'd done, and she couldn't let that slip by. She had to change what she'd seen in the future—she couldn't let him win this war. If he won, he would kill that poor, defenseless child, and she couldn't bear to see that happen again.

She cleared her mind and ran as fast as her feet would take her toward the city, knowing that if she didn't get there soon, she would shift again—and once she shifted, there would be no way to know when she would return to this time again.

Hours later, she finally arrived in the city, taking her time as she snuck through the city's outer walls and toward the central tower, knowing that most of them would be too busy training to notice one person sneaking inside. When she reached the tower, however, she had to speak to the guards in order to get inside. They sent a messenger in to find out if she was expected, and a few moments later, they allowed her into the main chamber.

"May I help you?" Jameson asked as he walked into the chamber.

"My name is Lana, and I have things that I must say to your wife—things concerning Marcus Admiri," she replied.

"Anything you have to say to my wife can be said to me." He nodded, relaxing against the wall.

"I must speak to her, Jameson." She paused, stepping closer to him. "Please."

"It's alright, Jameson. I'll speak with her," Reem said as she walked out of the hallway and into the chamber alongside her husband.

He nodded and took her hand in his as they walked into the meeting room with Lana right behind them. "Have a seat," he told the woman as Reem took her place at the head of the table, with Jameson standing behind her.

Lana did as she was asked, sitting across Reem before she spoke. "My name is Lana, and I am a time-shifter." She paused. "I was the first on which the Advancing treatment was successful—though not completely. My advancements will soon kill me."

"How do you know that?" Reem asked.

"Because I shifted to the future on more than one occasion." She smiled slightly. "But we don't have much time for me to explain. My advancements are unstable. I will soon shift again."

"Then you'd better say what you came to." Reem nodded, waiting for her to continue.

"Marcus Admiri is not who you think he is," she said. "For one, he is not Advanced. He uses another short-term treatment to make himself appear Advanced and appear as though he has not aged since the treatment was given to the public. In fact, he does age at a rapid rate, and only his treatment is keeping him alive. If he is not allowed to take it, he would die within days at most."

"How is that even—"

"Please, Jameson, let me finish," Lana continued, cutting him off. "He engineered the treatment he gave to the public so that it wouldn't allow for them to develop more than one advancement, but the truth is, by now, the public should be dead. His treatment doesn't work." She paused, taking a breath. "It never has.

The people in Admiri and Mettirna were given a second treatment somewhat recently—in their water supply—that effectively is like giving them an antidote for the original treatment. It doesn't work the same anymore, but it should've taken half a century for the effects to be seen. On a side note, that could have something to do with your development of other gifts, Reem."

Reem's eyebrows furrowing slightly as she considered everything Lana had told her. "Why are you telling us all of this?"

"Because Marcus Admiri is my husband, and I hate what he's done to the world. I hate everything that he'd done to all of you, and I hate him," she replied, her eyes full of hatred for the man she once loved.

"Your husband?" Reem whispered. "I didn't know Marcus could love anyone."

"I should have known that he couldn't." Lana laughed lightly. "You knew about his treatment, correct?" she asked.

"Yes, I believe that's why he accused me of treason." She nodded slowly. "He didn't want his secret getting out."

"I don't blame him." Lana laughed. "But that's not all he's hiding from you." She shook her head. "He has impregnated a young Advanced woman who will be arriving with the new recruits in a few days—her name is Kari, and she was born for the sole purpose of bearing him a child. Her mother was human, her father Advanced. When Marcus met her, he knew she could be useful. He kept her in a locked room in his palace and recently decided that the time was right for Kari to be of use to him. He is still human, as you know, so the process did work. As far as I know, you are the only couple of Advanced to bear a child on your own." She paused. "But what you need to know is, the child must survive. She will bear him a son, and his son needs to live. Together, his son and your daughter will be the ones to save us all." She paused. "I'm afraid that's all I can say on the matter, but I felt it best that you know who he is. You should also know that you cannot force the two of them to be friends. Your Eliza will be very . . . headstrong." She laughed lightly, leaning back in the chair. "You have a beautiful daughter."

"Thank you," Reem replied. "I envy you for seeing her grown up before I do." She laughed.

"She will love you, Reem, never forget that." She smiled brightly. "She will also need your help with her gifts. They are overwhelming to her even now."

"I will." She nodded.

"I have one more thing I need to tell you," Lana said, leaning across the table toward them. "If you remember nothing else that I've told you, remember this, Marcus—" she whispered as she disappeared, leaving Jameson and Reem alone in the room.

"Do you know what she was going to say?" Jameson asked.

"No," she whispered. "I couldn't read any of her thoughts." She stood and exited the room, quickly making her way back to the nursery where Eliza slept.

Choice

Reem sat in the meeting room, waiting for Nicholas and Suri to arrive. The tension between them was going to cause problems, and until they got it settled, she didn't know if she could have them both living in the tower. To make matters worse, she didn't know which one she would pick to stay with her. Eliza needed Nicholas on hand in case anything happened, but Suri was her sister.

She leaned her elbows on the table and dropped her head into her hands, shaking her head back and forth. There had to be something she could do for them, but at the moment, she couldn't think of anything that wouldn't make matters worse. Her gifts were on the fritz ever since she'd given birth, so she couldn't communicate properly with them short of actually talking to them, and it was causing more problems than she would've thought.

"Sorry I'm late." Suri smiled sheepishly as she ran into the room. "I was—"

"I know." Reem laughed, cutting her off. "You didn't happen to see Nicholas on your way in, did you?" Her eyebrows rose slightly.

"No, I didn't." She shrugged. "Sorry." She took her seat to Reem's right, leaning back in her chair. "He's later than I am." She laughed nervously.

"I may have to send Jameson to find him." Reem sighed seconds before Nicholas appeared in the doorway with Angel at his side. "Nicholas, Angel, it's good to see you." She smiled.

"I just came to drop him off." Angel shrugged, smiling brightly before vanishing into thin air.

"Sorry." Nicholas shrugged. "I wasn't trying to be so late."

Reem smiled. "It's fine, really."

"I'm sure you don't mean that." He winked as he sat across the table from Suri, trying his hardest not to look her in the eye. "So let's get on with it."

"Nicholas, stop acting like this," Suri ordered. "I told you about this upfront—you said you didn't care, remember?"

"You blindsided me!" he snapped. "You told me you'd had an affair with someone, not that you were in love with someone."

"I told you that I cared for him as much as I care for you. What more did you want, Nicholas?" She leaned across the table, her eyes staring straight into his, though he refused to look at her.

"Stop," Reem ordered, using her gifts to slap each of them on the back of the head. "This is exactly why I had you meet me here. You need to get past this—quickly, I might add." She paused, glancing quickly between the two of them. "I'm not going to be the one to try and fix this for you. I'm only the mediator, but I do want you to at least try and fix your friendship before Marcus's army gets here. He will stop at nothing to make sure that everyone in this building is killed before the war is over, and I need to be sure that we are strong. If you two have a problem, then we all have a problem." She paused, leaning back in her chair before standing to her feet. "Fix it. I'll be right outside." She walked out of the room and closed the door, taking a seat on the floor next to it.

"She's actually going to make us stay in here, isn't she?" Nicholas huffed.

"Of course she is," Suri replied. "She doesn't have a choice." She sighed. "Will you please look at me?"

He turned his head to look into her eyes, his eyes piercing into her. "There's nothing to fix."

"Then why won't you look at me?" she asked, her eyebrows rising slightly as she crossed her arms over her chest.

"Do you love me, Suri?" he asked, leaning forward in his chair. "Or do you love him?"

"I . . . ," she whispered, unsure of what to say. "I love both of you—is that so hard to believe?"

"You can't love both of us." He shook his head. "I can't have you love me some days and him others, don't you understand that?"

"But I do," she replied, tears forming in her eyes. "I can't help it."

"Then maybe you shouldn't be with either of us until you can decide who you want," he replied, raising his voice slightly.

"Nick, please! I don't want to do this to either of you—I love both of you!" she shouted back, standing to her feet as she did so. "What do you want me to tell you? You want me to say that I'll love you forever and that I'll leave Alexander for you?" She paused. "That's not going to happen. I can't stop loving him just because you think that I should be with you."

"Suri, I love you," he whispered as he stood and walked to her side, stroking her hair gently. "Why can't you see that anymore?" he asked, leaning in to lightly kiss her lips.

"I don't know." She shook her head, backing away from him. "It's just not the same anymore."

"Please, Suri," he replied, approaching her once again and wrapping his arms around her waist. "I don't want to be without you." He kissed her forehead. "I love you," he whispered in her ear. "I love you so much."

"Nicholas, please stop," she whispered back. "I need time to think." She lifted her hands to his chest and pushed him away. "Please, Nick, please." Tears streamed down her cheeks, and he lifted his hand to brush them away from her face. "No, Nick." She shook her head, wiping the tears away herself. "I can't do this right now." She moved away from him, walking toward the door.

"You're not leaving until you fix this," Reem shouted through the door, causing Suri to turn around and plop down into a chair.

"I know you love me as much as I love you—I know it," Nicholas said, kneeling by her side and running his fingers through her hair. "I know you love me."

"And you know I love him too," she whispered as he kissed her neck. "I don't know what else to tell you." She shrugged, pushing him away once again.

"Suri, think about this," Reem whispered in her mind. *"How well do you know each of them? How do you know one of them isn't going to hurt you?"*

"That's more of a question for you to answer, Reem," Suri thought, closing her eyes while she communicated with her sister.

"They both love you," Reem replied. *"That's all I can tell you—but I know you love one of them more than the other. Tell him the truth, Suri. Please. He deserves that much at least."*

Suri nodded, not knowing what to say or think anymore when she suddenly felt Nicholas's lips against hers and his arms wrapped around her back. "Nicholas, stop!" she shouted, pushing him away for the third time, this time knocking him several feet away from her. "I love him, Nicholas. Him." She paused. "I love you both, but I love him more. I'm sorry." She stood and started walking back toward the door, this time being stopped by Reem's gifts.

"Fix. This," Reem ordered. *"Don't make me come in there."*

Nicholas stood there, stunned by what he'd just heard. She couldn't love Alexander more than she loved him—she couldn't. He stepped back and leaned against the wall, running his fingers through his hair as he did so.

"Nicholas, please look at me," she whispered, placing her hand on his shoulder.

"I should've known you'd love the teleporter more than the man who can hide himself." He shrugged, lifting his eyes to look into hers. "Don't worry, I don't blame you—and I don't hate you." He pushed her hand off his shoulder and walked toward the door, opening it before Reem could stop him. "I'm not going to be a problem, I promise." He smiled. "I'll be spending most of my time in the new hospital anyway."

Reem nodded and stood, her eyes staring straight into his. "I'm sorry. You needed to know."

"I know," he replied, shrugging once more. "Thank you for making me listen." The corners of his mouth turned up slightly before Reem reached up to kiss his cheek lightly.

"I'm sorry, Nicholas," she whispered before she turned and walked back to the nursery where Jameson waited for her.

"I hated doing that to him," Suri whispered as she cradled Eliza in her arms, trying to get her to stop crying.

"He needed to know," Reem replied, massaging her temples lightly while trying to tune out the sound of Eliza's crying. "We're keeping everyone up," she whispered to herself.

"But did he have to find out like that?" she asked as she walked across the room.

"He needed to find out, and you weren't going to tell him on your own free will, so yes." Reem smiled as she took Eliza from Suri's arms.

"I would've told him eventually." She shrugged.

"He had to find out before something bad happened," she replied, sighing loudly when Eliza finally stopped crying.

"Oh thank all that is good and pure in the world." Suri laughed lightly as Reem placed Eliza in her crib, wrapping her tightly in a blanket before taking a seat on the floor. "I know I shouldn't have led him on for so long," she added as she sat beside her sister.

"No, you shouldn't have, but I suppose the damage has been done," she replied, keeping her voice low in an attempt to let Eliza sleep.

"Go get some sleep," Suri whispered. "I'll keep an eye on her."

"Thank you." Reem smiled. "If you need me, I'll be right down the hall."

"I'll be fine, don't worry." Suri smiled as Reem made her way out the door and down the hall.

She quietly opened the bedroom door, surprised to find Jameson standing in front of the window, looking out over the city. Slowly, she walked to him and wrapped her arms around his waist, reaching up to kiss his cheek. "What're you doing up?" she whispered.

"Couldn't sleep," he whispered, smiling as he turned to look her in the eye. "I missed having you next to me."

"I love you." She laughed lightly, pulling his lips to hers.

He wound his arms around her waist and lifted her off the ground, his lips moving passionately against hers as he carried her to the bed, carefully setting her down as she pulled her lips away from his. "You should get some rest," he whispered, kneeling by the bedside, "you're exhausted."

"Do you always have to be like this?" She laughed, pulling him onto the bed beside her while she wrapped her legs around his waist.

Suri reached out and gently stroked Eliza's forehead, gasping when she was jolted into a vision. She saw the army standing on their doorstep, saw the small group that Marcus sent in first asking for them to surrender, saw as Superior Seamus approached Reem in the central chamber, saw as he slapped her face and knocked her to the ground.

Her eyes widened as the vision cleared, and her breathing picked up its pace as she remembered everything she'd just seen. Eliza had shared a vision with her—like she'd shared visions with Reem while she was in her womb. The child's gifts were already fully developed, and Reem had said that they were putting great strain on the little one even though she barely used them. Suri only wished that there was some way that this vision wouldn't come true, some way to save Reem from being beaten to death by the man to whom she'd been promised by Marcus Admiri.

Suri lifted Eliza out of the crib and walked down the hall toward Reem's bedroom. She knocked quietly, not wanting to wake Jameson, but needing to speak with Reem as soon as possible.

A moment later, Reem appeared in the doorway dressed only in a robe—she should've known. Reem's tired eyes stared into Suri's, waiting for her to explain why she'd come.

"Eliza showed me something," Suri blurted out, not knowing what else to say. "She showed me a vision, Reem."

"What did you see?" Reem asked, suddenly very serious as she reached out and took Eliza from her arms, turning and leaving her in Jameson's capable arms before taking hold of Suri's arm and leading her to the end of the hall. "What did you see?" she repeated.

"I saw you," Suri replied. "I saw the day the army arrived." Her eyes dropped to the ground at her feet.

"What happened?"

"Marcus sent a smaller squad in to ask for our surrender, led by Superior Seamus." Her eyes lifted to look Reem in the eye once more. "I saw him beat you, Reem."

"It won't happen." Reem's entire body quivered nervously. "It can't happen." She lifted her hand to her mouth as she gasped, realizing the full scale of what Suri had seen. "He sent Seamus?"

Suri nodded, unsure of what to say. "It was Seamus—I'm sure of it."

"Promise me you won't tell this to Jameson," she whispered, reaching out to place her hands on her sister's shoulders. "Let me tell him myself."

"Are you sure, Reem?" she asked. "Wouldn't it be easier if I told him?"

"No, I'll tell him." Reem nodded. "I don't want him to worry any more than he has to."

"You're not going to tell him." She shook her head.

"I don't think it'll do any good for him to know." She paced in the small amount of space at the end of the hall. "I don't want him to worry about me."

"He's your husband! He deserves to know what you do." She told her sister. "I'm telling him whether you want me to or not, Reem. I will tell him."

"What else did you see, Suri?" she asked.

"Nothing. Just that."

"Are you sure?"

"Positive. All I know is, no one around seemed to be able to move. It looked like one of their gifts was keeping us from helping you—and I don't know how. It doesn't make any sense." She ran her fingers through her hair nervously.

"No, no, it makes sense." Reem nodded. "We'll have to thoroughly scan their gifts before we let them in the city. I don't want to take any chances."

"What are we going to do, Reem?"

⚜︎

Seth watched as the people began to go ashore from the boat, slowly making their way back onto dry land. Soon they would all be on the short journey to Athena. It would take them less than two days by foot—surprising since it took so much longer by teleport—and then they would begin their training with those in the city. It seemed they had even less time than they'd thought to prepare themselves for the arrival of Marcus's army.

He ushered the last of them off the boat only a few hours after they'd started, wishing that those he'd left behind could have been fast enough to board the ship in the first place. He'd hated leaving them behind, but there was nothing he could have done to save them.

He walked down the ramp and onto the dock where he met Robert, sternly staring him down. "What happened, Seth?" he asked.

"I'm sorry," Seth replied. "There was nothing I could do. The storm was on us—we all would have died if I hadn't left them behind. They knew the risks when they signed on. I believe that there is still a chance that they made it off the docks—there were many boats still there when we weighed anchor."

"Then why couldn't you have waited for them to board our ship?" he asked, his eyebrows rising in anger.

"I had to choose between them and the whole—and they sided with me. They knew that if they delayed us any longer, we would all be dead in the heat of the storm. Look at our ship, Robert. Had we stayed, the storm would have destroyed us all." He paused. "It is finished—what is done is done. Consider the future instead of the past, my friend." He turned and walked down the dock and onto the shore, effectively ending the conversation.

A few moments later, they were on their way once again, walking as quickly as they could through the woods outside Athena until they reached the city's outer walls, where they waited to be met by Reem Kahrin herself.

Void

Reem smiled brightly as she approached Seth outside the city's outer wall. She'd known he'd be arriving on this day, and honestly, she hadn't thought it would be so good to see his smiling face until he was standing right in front of her.

"Seth, it's good to see you," she said as she embraced him. "I don't know how you got away from her, but I'm glad that you did." She laughed, pulling away to look him in the eye once again, like a sister would look into the eyes of her long lost brother.

"It's good to see you as well, Reem." He smiled. "We left Brittany in the very capable hands of David Sanders, but I don't know what's become of them." He shrugged.

"You'll see her again, Seth," she replied. "Come, you'll want to meet the latest addition to my family."

"You had your child then, I take it?" he asked, his eyebrows furrowing slightly.

"I did." She smiled. "It's a long story, but she's doing well for her age. It seems her gifts are both helping and hindering her."

Together, they walked back into the city, leaving Suri and Alexander to meet all of the newcomers, along with two of the other telepaths.

When they reached the tower, they found Jameson standing at the top of the steps, holding Eliza in his arms while he walked across the span of the staircase. They walked up to meet him, Seth smiling brightly at the sight of the child in his arms.

"Seth Green, meet Eliza Miriam Willow," Jameson whispered, handing the baby to him.

"She's beautiful," Seth whispered, cradling her in his arms.

"You might want to keep moving," Jameson suggested. "She likes the motion."

Seth nodded and started pacing along the staircase, mimicking Jameson's earlier behavior. "What are her gifts?" he asked as he handed her to her mother.

"She has Jameson's gift—she can at least give gifts, that is," Reem replied. "She has visions. She's a healer and somewhat telekinetic and telepathic. It seems that she tried to mimic both of our gift sets." She smiled.

"That's amazing." Seth shook his head slowly. "She has your eyes, Reem."

"Or at least the silver in them." Reem laughed lightly. "I think she may have a gift similar to the one I have with my eyes, but I don't know for sure yet. She's still trying everything out, and she still doesn't really know what to do with any of them."

"She'll learn." Seth smiled. "And she has the best teachers in the world to show her how."

Before Reem could reply, Suri appeared at the bottom of the steps with Alexander holding her hand. She ran up the steps, leaving Alexander to teleport back to the outer regions to interview the newcomers. "I thought you might need me to watch her for a while," Suri said as she reached the top of the steps. "I know you have a lot on your plate right now."

"Thank you," Reem replied, handing Eliza to her. "I do have some things I need to discuss with Seth at the moment."

"I'll take her to the nursery." Suri smiled before walking past them.

"You have more news?" Seth asked, smiling brightly.

"Yes, as a matter of fact, I do." She nodded. "Was there a young woman with you on your journey—Kari?"

"How did you know that?" he asked, his face shocked and confused. "They found her half dead in the desert, and Robert couldn't find it within himself to leave her behind."

"That's her." She nodded. "Is she pregnant?"

"I don't know." He shrugged. "She's not showing if she is."

"I believe she is carrying Marcus Admiri's child," she replied.

"Meeting room?" Jameson suggested, gesturing inside.

Seth and Reem both nodded and walked inside, Reem taking her seat on one side of the table with Jameson to her right and Seth across from her.

"How is this possible?" Seth asked. "She doesn't even know who Marcus is." He paused. "I've questioned her myself. She doesn't know anything."

"That's because Marcus didn't want her to know anything," Reem replied. "And because Marcus isn't Advanced himself."

"How is that possible?" Seth asked, his eyes widening in shock.

"I didn't know myself until yesterday," she replied. "I mean, I knew that he wasn't Advanced, but I didn't know how."

"How did you find out?" .

"Lana—she was the first person given the treatment successfully, and she was married to Marcus—she came here and told me what she could."

"How? If she's with Marcus, there's no way he would let her come here." He shook his head.

"She's dead, Seth. Her gift was time-shifting, and in the past, she shifted here to tell me what she could about Marcus." She paused. "Apparently, on Marcus, the treatment wasn't entirely successful."

David sighed loudly as Halaq once again entered the room, smiling brightly as he leaned against the wall across from him. "Back so soon?" he asked. "I let the doctor set my arm." He lifted his cast wrist for Halaq to see. "So are you going to let me stay here or not?"

"You can stay here as long as you'd like, but you'll have to stay with me. The priests don't want you out in their settlement without a guard." He shrugged.

"How long until I'm healed?"

"You should be able to walk around in a few days. Most of your wounds have scabbed by now." He smiled. "I'll show you the settlement when the doctor thinks you're ready."

He sat up and leaned against the wall, wincing against the pain of the pressure on his wounds. "I don't have anywhere to go."

"I'm sorry about that," Halaq said. "I know what it's like to be forced to leave your home."

"I highly doubt that—and I wasn't forced to leave, just not welcome back there," he snapped.

"David, I saved you from the storm, I've had a doctor do his best to heal your wounds, and I've even treated your witch. What more do you want from me?" He laughed. "There's not much more I can offer besides a home of your own in this settlement." He stepped forward, looking David squarely in the eye. "The priests aren't keen on the idea of you leaving, so you'll have to make do with what you can. Here."

"I don't belong here."

"You don't belong anywhere." He laughed lightly.

"Who are you, Halaq?" His questioning eyes pierced into Halaq's.

He shrugged. "I'm surprised Marcus didn't warn you about me."

"Are you Advanced?" he asked, furrowing his eyebrows.

"I am." He nodded. "But I'm not telling you what my gifts are."

"You're Void, aren't you?" he asked, his face conveying the recognition in his mind. "You were one of the first—one of the first three who took the treatment."

"I'm afraid you are mistaken, my friend." He laughed lightly.

"No, you're Void." David shook his head. "I know it."

He shrugged. "Tell me, who is this Void you speak of?"

"No one knows what his name really is. They just know that he is against Marcus Admiri, and that his advancements are unstable." .

"And what are his advancements?"

"He can create nothing, I suppose you could say. He can kill someone by making their body void of air or water—that's why they call him Void."

"Interesting." He nodded slowly, walking back to the wall and leaning against it as he slid to the ground. "I've never heard of anyone developing a gift like that."

"The story goes that Marcus changed the treatment so that no one else would develop unstable advancements," David replied. "And as far as I know, Void was the only one of the three who survived."

"Who were the others?" Halaq asked.

"One was Marcus's good friend Lana, and the other was a man named Sullivan. Lana developed a time-shifting gift that eventually drained her energy too much for her body to survive it, and Sullivan's gift never fully developed. The story goes that Sullivan's gift caused his appearance to mutate, and his cells couldn't take the strain." He paused. "How is it that you've never heard this story before?"

"I never said I hadn't." He smiled. "I only implied that I hadn't."

"Why?"

"I wanted to know how accurate the stories were."

"You are Void." He nodded slowly, amazement clear on his face as Halaq stood to his feet and approached him once again.

"Perhaps," Halaq replied, leaning down to look David in the eye. "It's probably best that we keep this information between us. The Purists don't know."

David nodded, unsure of what to say at this new turn of events. He should have known right away that this man was Void. Marcus had only spoken of him a few times, but he still should have known. The man was a legend. "So how much of the story did I get right?" he asked finally.

"Some." He smiled.

"What'd I get wrong?"

"Lana was Marcus's wife, and she suffered multiple organ failure during a time-shift. Marcus watched her die." He paused. "What do the stories say about me?"

"They say that you've never been inside an Advanced city and that you've sworn to stop Marcus yourself," David replied, swallowing at the prospect of the man in front of him being able to kill him with a single thought. "They say that you're gifts are so unstable that you can rarely use them."

"You're sources are incorrect," Halaq replied. "My gifts are unstable, yes, but that only means that I have to be more careful around Sensors." He paused. "And I've not sworn to stop him. I've sworn to kill him." He laughed lightly, standing back to his feet. "Marcus is not who any of you think, and after I expose him, I intend to end his life for good."

Reem stood on the balcony with Jameson at her side, waiting for Seth to return with Robert, Ryan, and Kari. She leaned against the banister, facing the main chamber while Jameson looked out over the city, holding her hand in his.

"What are you thinking?" he asked as he turned to lean his hip against the banister and gently run his fingers through her hair.

"I'm thinking that I know Lana said that we need this child to live, but I don't want him anywhere near my baby," she replied, the corners of her mouth turning up slightly as she turned her head to look him in the eye.

"I don't want him near Eliza either, but what good could come of Lana lying to us? She had no reason to." He shrugged.

"I want to believe her. I really do. But when it comes to Eliza, I'm not sure that I want to," she whispered. "What if he hurts her?"

"Then we have to believe that we'll raise her to know what to do if that happens," he replied, pulling her into his arms. "Lana may have been Admiri's wife, but she saw the evil in him, and she saw that he had to be stopped. Eliza and Kari's son will both be a part of stopping him, Reem—and I don't think we have the right to prevent that from happening."

"I know." She nodded, burying her face in his chest.

"So what are we going to do then?" he asked, pushing her away so he could look her in the eye.

"We talk to her." She shrugged. "We find out as much about her as we can— find out if she knows anything that we can use—and we take care of her. After being in Marcus's care for so long, I'm afraid the poor girl might be in disrepair." She laughed lightly as she reached up to kiss his lips.

He smiled, running his fingers through her hair once more before turning to see Seth walk through the main chamber toward them.

"They're waiting in the meeting room," Seth announced.

"We'll be there in a moment," Reem replied, motioning for him to join the others.

Seth nodded slowly and smiled before he turned and walked into the meeting room, while Reem once again brought her lips to Jameson's, kissing him passionately. A moment later, they stepped through the meeting room doors, finding Robert, Ryan, and Seth seated on one side of the table, with Kari and a red-headed man seated on the opposite side, leaving the throne chair and the seat to its right open. As Reem and Jameson took their seats, Seth stood and introduced everyone, sitting back down when he was finished. "Now that the introductions are complete, let's get down to business." He smiled.

"Thank you, Seth." Reem smiled back, turning to Robert. "Now, you said that you have vital information for me."

"I do," Robert replied. "I had a vision." He paused, leaning forward over the table. "Marcus Admiri has sent his army. We should expect them to be here within the next week."

"I know." Reem nodded. "I had a similar vision a week or so ago—we've been preparing ever since." She paused. "Thank you though, Robert. If not for my daughter, the information would have been invaluable." She nodded seriously. "Is there anything else?"

"It was my understanding that as of yet, I was the only seer in the rebellion."

"As I said, I recently gave birth to my daughter. And before that happened, she shared her visions with me. My daughter is similar to you, Robert." She smiled once more.

"I wasn't aware that you were pregnant," he replied, his eyebrows furrowing. "How is that possible? I mean, assuming Jameson is the father."

"I am," Jameson cut in.

Reem smiled and took Jameson's hand. "As far as we know, it isn't possible." She shrugged. "But it happened, and I'm perfectly fine with that." Her smile brightened.

"That's amazing." Robert's eyes widened.

"In any case, since you already know what we came to tell you, we should be on our way," Ryan added, standing to his feet.

"He's right," Robert replied, following as Ryan started to exit the room. "We should be helping everyone get settled in."

Edwin and Kari nodded and started to follow as well when Reem replied, "Go right ahead." She paused. "But, Kari, I'd like you to stay for a while if you don't mind."

"Of course," Kari replied, taking her seat once more.

"Would you like me to stay with you?" Edwin whispered in her ear.

She smiled. "They seem like nice people. I'll come find you when we're done."

Edwin nodded quickly and left the room, following behind Ryan and Robert.

"What did you want me to stay for?" Kari asked.

"Would you give us a moment?" Reem asked, gesturing for both Jameson and Seth to leave the room. As soon as they were gone, she continued, "There's something you should know."

Children

Brittany struggled to free herself from her bonds, screaming in frustration when Halaq entered and laughed at the futility of her efforts. "Let. Me. Go," she ordered, turning to look him in the eye.

"I'm afraid that's not going to happen." He smiled back, walking up to wipe the sweat-covered hair off her face. "I see why Marcus likes you," he whispered.

"Do you?" she snapped, her white eyes widening. "And how would you know what he likes?"

"I've known him longer than you have, witch," he replied, stroking her cheek with the back of his hand. "And I'll kill him before you see him again."

"Do not make the mistake of thinking I do not know who you are," she whispered. "You've haunted his sleep for years, Void."

"So you do remember me." He smiled, taking a seat beside her on the mattress. "It's good to see you again, Brittany."

"How could I forget the face of my enemy?" she snapped, leaning up as high as she could to spit on his face.

"As I said, it's good to see you again." He reached up and wiped her saliva off his face, smiling once again before he stood and walked out the door. "How's my favorite patient?" he asked David as he leaned against the wall across the man.

"Not so patient," David replied, sitting up and throwing his legs off the side of the bed. "I'd like to try and walk around if you don't mind."

"Of course," Halaq replied, walking to his side and helping him get to his feet. "How are you feeling?" he asked as he strung his friend's arm over his shoulders, helping him to walk around the room.

"Not too much pain," David said, trying not to wince at the movements of his joints. "Nothing I can't handle at least."

"Good—that means the doctor did his job well." He smiled. "You up for a journey?"

"Where to?" David asked, his eyebrows furrowing slightly.

"The city of Admiri," Halaq replied. "Marcus has sent his army to Athena—he'll be left unguarded in the city."

"You want me to help you kill him?" David asked, unable to hide his shock at the thought.

"I can't do it myself." He shook his head. "I'll need your help, David."

"What did you do to Brittany?" he asked, changing the subject. "I heard her scream."

"I did nothing to her—today at least." He shrugged as he helped David back down onto the bed.

"And in the past?" David asked, taking his seat and rubbing his aching joints.

"Nothing that concerns you," Halaq replied. "I'll find someone else." He stood back to his feet, walking toward the door.

"No, wait," David said, stopping Halaq in his tracks. "I'll help you. I just need more time."

"We don't have much time," Halaq replied as he turned to face David once again. "Marcus will only be alone in the city for two weeks at most—I can give you one."

"I'll be good to go by then." David nodded. "If I don't help you kill him, he'll kill me," he whispered.

"You're right—he will." Halaq nodded.

"Halaq!" Brittany yelled. "Halaq, you insolent fool, get back here!"

"I'll be right back." Halaq laughed as he exited the room, once again taking his seat on the edge of Brittany's mattress. "How can I help you?" he asked.

"Untie me," she ordered.

"No." He laughed lightly. "I have no reason to trust you, witch."

"You have no reason to trust him either," she spat.

"More so than you," he replied. "Why did you call me in here?"

"Why are you keeping me here?" she asked, turning to face the wall instead of looking him in the eye.

"I don't have much choice." He shook his head. "If I let you go, you wouldn't exactly leave without killing me first. I know you, Brittany."

"I'll leave peacefully." She smiled, running her knee up his spine.

"You never stop trying, do you?" He laughed as her freed arm swung through the air, landing in his hand inches away from his face. "Nice try though." She grunted as he moved to swing one leg to the other side of her body, binding her arm to the bed once again. "Not that it wouldn't be fun to have another completely volatile relationship with you, my dear, but I have more important things on my mind." He brushed her hair away from her face before standing to his feet and exiting the room, leaving her alone once again.

"I really should post a guard in her room," he said as he joined David. "Somehow, she managed to get her arm free."

David laughed. "She's very . . . resourceful."

"I'm pregnant," Kari exclaimed, pacing along her newly acquired quarters in the city while Edwin stood by and watched, confused by the entire ordeal.

"How?" he asked. "Better yet, who?"

"I don't know!" she replied, dropping her head into her hands. "I never saw his face . . ."

"So you knew you were pregnant?" he asked, his eyebrows furrowing.

"No!" she snapped. "And if I didn't know I was pregnant, how did she know?"

"Her gifts enable her to know things like this, Kari," he replied. "I told you she would be able to give you answers—I never said they would be answers that you would want to hear."

"Well, now what am I supposed to do?" she asked. "I'm pregnant!"

"Kari, Kari, you'll be fine," he comforted, reaching out and taking her hands in his. "I'll help you through this. I promise."

"I don't want a baby," she whispered, shaking her head slowly. "I finally have a life of my own. I don't want a baby to complicate things."

"It'll be fine," he repeated. "I promise you, everything will be fine."

"I don't want this," she whispered, moving away from him. "I think I need to take a walk." She left the room, leaving him standing there wishing that he could have done more for her.

"I think I'm in love with you, Kari," he whispered, knowing that she couldn't hear him but wishing that she could. He didn't know how she'd take it—she'd either say she felt the same or she'd run away screaming, and he couldn't take the chance that the latter would be more likely.

Kari walked quickly through the city, not knowing where she was going but not caring either way. She knew Edwin was only trying to help, but he was making things worse. She didn't even want to think about what was going on, much less talk about it with a man she'd barely met. She didn't know why she trusted him so much, but there was something about him that made her want to trust him. She closed her eyes as she walked, not caring if she ran into anyone or anything until finally she did run into someone—Robert.

"Kari. You should watch where you're going." He laughed lightly.

"Sorry," she replied sheepishly, unable to meet his eyes with hers.

"Are you alright?" he asked, concern edging his voice when he noticed the nervous look on her face.

"I don't know," she replied, still not meeting his eyes.

"What's wrong?" he asked as he took her hand and led her off the road. "What happened?"

"I'm pregnant," she whispered, a tear snaking down her cheek. "Reem told me a few moments ago. I'm not sure how she knew."

"I hadn't even thought of that," he whispered under his breath, pulling her into his arms. "I'm so sorry, Kari." He kissed the top of her head.

"I don't know what to do," she whispered into his chest.

"We'll get you through this, honey," he said like a father to his broken child, wishing that there was something he could do for the young girl he held in his arms. "I'll help you through this."

She stayed there, in his arms, until suddenly, she found herself trusting Robert even more than she'd trusted Edwin, found herself thinking that maybe this was about more than trust. This man clearly cared for her even more than Edwin—he'd been holding her for almost an hour already, without even saying a word. She wished that she knew what to say, wished that she could help him as much as he was helping her without even saying a word. He occasionally kissed the top of her head, not saying anything, just reassuring her that he was here for her and that he would continue to be here for her.

She didn't even notice when the sun started to dip below the horizon, continuing to cry into his chest rather than pay attention to the world around her. She suddenly found Robert lifting her into his arms, carrying her back to her home in the dark of the night. He brought her inside and set her on the bed carefully, pulling away to look her in the eye. "Do you need me to find someone to stay with you?" he asked.

"No, no, I'll be fine," she whispered, trying to smile through the tears as he kissed her forehead and walked toward the door. "Thank you."

He turned and smiled at her before he exited the room, closing the door behind him.

Why was her heart aching even more now that he was gone?

"How is she?" Edwin asked Robert as he stepped out of Kari's home.

"As well as could be expected." He shrugged, leaning against the wall beside his friend. "You care for her, don't you?"

"I do," Edwin whispered back.

"So go to her," Robert told him. "She needs someone to be with her."

"Why didn't you stay with her?" Edwin asked. "She seemed like she wanted you to."

"I know I no longer work for the Superiors, but I intend to be true to my oath. I will not fall in love as long as I live," he replied, shaking his head slowly. "I could never allow anything to happen between myself and anyone." He shrugged. "You should go to her, Edwin." He paused, placing his hand on the man's shoulder. "She shouldn't be alone tonight."

Edwin nodded his response, walking to the door and knocking quietly while Robert made his way back to his own home.

Reem sat in the nursery, cradling Eliza in her arms as she rocked in the rocking chair. She couldn't help but smile at the shining silver eyes of the baby in her arms, couldn't help but worry about the boy growing in young Kari's body, the boy that would be instrumental to the future.

Eliza started closing her eyes in search of sleep, and Reem found herself wishing that she could continue to stare into her baby's silver eyes. She was the most beautiful thing that Reem had ever seen in her life—she couldn't even believe that her baby was already in her arms. If it wasn't for her gifts, Eliza would not have lasted even this long.

"I never thought I'd have a family again after I was put in the camps," Jameson mused as he stepped through the nursery door.

"And now that you have one?" she asked, smiling as she turned to look him in the eye.

"Now I don't even miss them." He smiled back. "There's nothing I need other than the two of you." He walked to her side and took a seat on the floor, leaning his back against the wall.

"I love you, Jameson," she whispered, reaching out to run her fingers through his hair.

"I love you too," he said. "Both of you."

She smiled as she held up Eliza and whispered, "I love you, Daddy."

"I love you too, baby," he whispered, taking her from Reem's arms and cradling her in his lap. "I love you more than anything in the world—other than your mother." He turned to Reem and winked.

"What're you doing here? I thought you were sleeping," she asked.

"Couldn't sleep." He shrugged. "I missed both of you."

"We missed you too." She smiled as Eliza started crying. Reem stood and gestured for Jameson to sit in the rocking chair, knowing that she would calm down if she was rocking.

He sat down and rocked Eliza gently, holding her in one arm, while Reem sat on his lap and leaned her head on his shoulder. He wrapped his arm around her waist and pulled Eliza close to his chest, and soon both his girls were asleep in his arms as he rocked back and forth, back and forth.

He was happier than he'd been in days—his beautiful wife and gorgeous baby girl both safe in his arms. Reem's soft snoring was music to his ears, the soft whisper of her dreams in his mind causing him to smile. Whenever she was having a good dream, she tended to project it into his mind, and it always made him smile to know that his wife loved him so much that she even wanted to share her dreams with him.

A few moments later, he found himself joined by Nicholas who walked in the door to check on Reem and Eliza. "Sorry," he whispered, "Reem wanted me to have a look at her tonight so I didn't have to take time out of my day tomorrow." He shrugged. "I'll come back in the morning."

"No, no, it's fine. I should take Reem to our room anyway." He held Eliza out for Nicholas to take and lifted Reem into his arms once the little one was in

Nicholas's possession. "I'll be right back," he whispered as he carried Reem out the door.

When he returned, he found Nicholas gently laying Eliza back in her crib after finishing his examination. "She's fine," he whispered before Jameson could open his mouth to ask. "She's just as healthy as she was the last time I checked on her." He laughed lightly.

"Thank you, Nicholas," Jameson whispered.

"Of course." Nicholas smiled as they walked out of the room.

"How is the hospital coming along?" he asked as they entered the main chamber.

"Quite well actually." His smile brightened. "It seems that many of the Purists that arrived have training in medicine, and we already had quite a few healers. It shouldn't be long before we're ready."

"Good." Jameson smiled back. "I hope everything works out well for you there."

"As do I." He paused. "And I hope that everything works out well for the three of you. It would be a shame to do all of this and not win the war." He laughed lightly.

"It would indeed." Jameson laughed. "I'll see you at training tomorrow."

"Should be interesting," Nicholas replied as he walked down the steps and out of the building, leaving Jameson to return to Reem.

He quietly entered the room and lay down beside her, trying his best not to wake her from her deep sleep when her eyes suddenly snapped open. "Jameson?" she whispered.

"What's wrong?" he asked, wrapping his arms around her waist.

"Just a dream." She shook her head, settling into his arms.

"You sure?" He smiled as he pulled her closer into his chest.

"Yes, I'm sure this time." She laughed lightly. "It didn't even make any sense."

"Neither did the last one." He joked.

"This one had two of you."

"And this is a change from the usual?" He laughed.

"Very much so." She laughed, reaching up to touch her lips to his before settling back into his chest. "Get some sleep," she whispered. "You have a big day tomorrow."

"Ah yes, the wonders of hand-to-hand training." He smiled, kissing the top of her head before closing his eyes in an attempt to find sleep.

Lavender

Marcus stood on his balcony, waiting for news that his army had docked at the Athena port. He'd estimated that they would be arriving at the docks in a few hours—near midmorning, their time—and would then send in the small squad he'd assembled before they actually declared war against the rebels. He'd sent Superior Seamus to head the squad, knowing that this would be the last person Reem would want to see. She'd been promised to Seamus years ago, and he'd even amended her oath so that Seamus could be with her. He'd known that the man had hurt her, known and looked the other way when he heard her screams.

As soon as she saw the man, she was likely to kill him—an act that would be taken as an act of war—and his army would be ordered to destroy them all. The squad would be teleporting in on the pretense of creating peace between them, but they were there to assess the threat that the rebels posed. If he never heard from any of them again, he would assume that the threat was great, and he would send reinforcements as soon as possible—only half of his army had gone, after all.

Now he had only to wait until he received news of the goings-on across the ocean, and he would be ready to enact whatever plan he saw fit. These people followed him blindly, and he would use that blindness to his advantage. He would use them all until either they died or he did.

"Hello, Marcus," a man whispered from behind him. "It's good to see you again."

"Phillip," Marcus acknowledged, turning to face him. "Or should I call you Halaq?"

"Whichever you prefer." He shrugged, leaning against the wall between Marcus's quarters and the balcony on which he stood, staring down at the ground. "Though I hear they call me Void these days."

"And what do they call me?"

"They call you a human." He lifted his head to look Marcus in the eye. "They should never have called you Advanced, my friend."

"You are not my friend," Marcus replied, quickly walking through the doorway into his quarters, followed closely by Halaq.

"Don't bother calling for security—I've dispatched them all already," Halaq said. "And I won't kill you, Marcus. Not yet anyway." He smiled brightly. "Your time has not yet come."

"And why would you think that?" Marcus asked. "Lana seems to think that my time is running out—and she would know better than most."

"So you have seen her," Halaq whispered. "She came to me too, you know." He paused, leaning against the wall beside the door while Marcus sat on his throne. "She told me you didn't believe her."

"I have no reason to believe her," Marcus snapped. "She betrayed me."

"She loved you, my friend. It was you who betrayed her." He stepped toward his old friend, a fire burning in his eyes. "Your actions forced her to take desperate measures."

"I did nothing." Marcus shook his head.

"Exactly—you did nothing." He stepped up to the throne and pointed his finger in Marcus's face. "You stood by and did nothing while Sullivan died from unstable mutations. You stood by and watched while the scientists told you that the treatment was unsuccessful—you drove her to this."

"You lie," he spat.

"I am telling you the truth, and you know it." He stepped away, walking back to the doorway. "You were my friend, Marcus. How could you have let this happen?"

"You are not my friend!" Marcus shouted, standing up from his throne and approaching Halaq. "You took my wife in your bed! You stole the only thing I ever loved!"

"And you drove her to it," Halaq replied evenly, unflinching as Marcus's angry form approached him. "Is that why you took her from me?" he asked after Marcus threw him to the ground in anger. "Is that why you blinded Brittany? Because you couldn't stand what happened between myself and Lana?"

"You have no right to come into my home and accuse me of these things," he replied, trying to slow his breathing to a more natural rate. "And I did more than blind her—I turned her into what she is today," he whispered, reaching down and wrapping his hand around Halaq's throat. "I gave her the advancements she has—I've done things to her that you would never dream of doing."

"I know what you did to her," Halaq whispered, staring into Marcus's eyes while he clamped his hands around his windpipes. "You turned her against me, and now I will do the same to you." He kicked out with his right leg, knocking Marcus away from him seconds before the guard opened the door, allowing him to escape before Marcus could speak a word.

Soon Halaq was back in his home with the Purists, sitting at Brittany's bedside, watching as she breathed in and out, in and out. He continually found himself wishing that he could go back in time, that he could avoid the night he'd spent with Lana. Had he not allowed her into his room that night, the future might have been different for everyone else. That one night seemed to have changed so much of the future, and he wished he could have taken it back—if only so that he could see Brittany's smiling lavender eyes once more.

He reached out and touched her forehead, wishing that she wasn't so repulsed by him. When she was awake, she would snarl at his touch and spit on his face, all because Marcus Admiri couldn't stand the one night that Halaq wished he could erase from memory.

"I'm so sorry, Phillip," Lana whispered as she stepped into the room. "I should've known this would happen."

"Yes, you should have," Halaq replied. "And please don't call me that, Lana."

"Of course," she said as she approached him, placing her hand on his shoulder. "You were only helping me, Halaq. I didn't know he would react this way, I swear."

"As you said, you should have known." He paused, turning to look her in the eye. "And I should never have let it happen."

"You love her, don't you?" she asked, tears forming in her eyes when she realized the full scale of what had happened. "I'm so sorry," she repeated. "I will fix this, Phillip. I promise you I will fix this." Her voice was hard and sure as she shifted.

<hr/>

Edwin woke to the sound of a knock on the door. He'd spent the night in Kari's home, sleeping on the floor while she tossed and turned on the bed. He knew she was having a hard time with this whole thing, but he didn't know what else he could do but simply be there for her.

He stood and walked to the door, allowing Kari to sleep after the night she'd had. He opened it and stepped outside, closing the door behind him.

"How is she?" Robert asked.

"She's . . . sleeping," he replied, not knowing what else to say. "She had a rough time last night."

"I know," he whispered. "Thanks for looking after her."

"You don't have to thank me." He smiled. "I care about her. I don't want to see her all alone."

"Does she feel the same about you?" he asked as the two of them leaned against the wall the way they had the night before.

"I honestly don't know." He shrugged. "At this point, I wouldn't blame her if she hated everyone she'd ever met."

"I know what you mean." Robert laughed, leaning his head against the wall. "I was told to send you to the underground—Reem's physician is expecting to see every healer down there within the hour to discuss their duties in the war."

"I didn't think we would be preparing for war so soon after arriving." He ran his fingers through his hair nervously. "Honestly, I'm not sure I'm ready for all this."

"You will be," Robert replied. "Just make sure you're there—you're one of the best healers I've met." He smiled as he walked toward the central tower. He'd applied to be one of Reem's guards, and Jameson had requested to see him as soon as possible.

He quickly made his way up the steps and into the meeting room, finding Jameson standing in the far right corner looking up at the sky. "You asked to see me?" Robert asked as he stepped inside.

"Yes." Jameson smiled, shifting his eyes to stare into Robert's. "I hear you want to help protect my wife."

"I think I would be very beneficial to the guards here, yes," he replied. "I can see the future after all, and I know that would help."

"That it would." Jameson nodded. "I'm assigning you to be on her personal detail—as long as she's away from me, I want you and two others with her. I've assigned her previous guard's, Peter and Stephen, to join you."

"Thank you, sir." He dipped his head.

"Just keep her safe, Robert," Jameson replied. "You start first thing in the morning."

"I'll be here." He nodded.

"Make sure that you are," he ordered, walking out of the room to join Reem on the balcony.

Robert hadn't thought that he would be placed on the savior's personal detail. Truth be told, he'd already had a vision, and that was why he'd applied for the position. He knew that someone was coming for her and that he would kill her in an instant if he was allowed to do so.

He stepped out of the meeting room and made his way back down the steps, waving toward Edwin who was on his way to the underground hospital. He made his way back toward Kari's home, unable to stop worrying about the poor girl since the night before.

He reached out and knocked lightly on the door, surprised when Kari answered almost immediately, opening the door and gesturing for him to come inside.

"I just wanted to check on you." He smiled as he stepped through the doorway.

"I'm fine," she whispered, "well, better than yesterday anyway."

"Good." His smile brightened.

"Thank you—for last night." She smiled sheepishly. "I didn't want to be alone."

"Are you going to tell me what the dream was about, or do I have to ask?" Jameson laughed lightly as he wrapped his arms tighter around Reem's waist.

They stood on the balcony as they did every night at this time, watching as the fires slowly started to go out, leaving only the watchtowers slightly lit.

"Hmm," she said, "you'll have to ask."

"Alright then"—he paused, turning her around to face him—"what did you dream about?"

She smiled as she only could, lighting up his life in an instant before reaching up to kiss his lips. "I dreamt that I was taken to see Marcus and that you were with me." She paused, running her fingers through his hair. "They were interrogating us, and they killed you to try to break me."

"I thought you said there were two of me," he mused, his eyebrows furrowing.

"I'm getting there." She laughed. "After they took your body out of the room, you came back inside, this time acting like you had no idea what had just happened—like you hadn't seen me in days." She shrugged, pulling herself closer to him. "It was just a dream. It doesn't even make sense."

"No, I suppose it doesn't." He laughed. "You should get some rest—you have a big day tomorrow."

"Right." She sighed, pushing away from him slightly. "I have to greet the newcomers from Mettirna tomorrow."

"They might like to get to know the person they're fighting for." He smiled. "At any rate, I won't be able to spend the day here anyway, so it's good you have something to occupy your time."

"Of course, because having a child doesn't take up any of my time at all." She laughed, releasing all but his hand as they walked down the hallway toward their bedroom. "How was your training this afternoon?" she asked.

"It went as well as was to be expected." His smile brightened. "I suppose I use my gifts as more of a crutch than I thought." He shrugged, opening the bedroom door for her to enter ahead of him. "I think even Nicholas could beat me if I didn't have the energy to teleport."

"You could give yourself a gift that helped with that, you know." She winked.

"That's cheating, remember?" He laughed, wrapping his arms around her once more as they fell onto the bed. "I assigned Robert to your protection detail by the way."

"The seer?" she asked, furrowing her eyebrows. "What for?"

"For one, he wanted the job"—he paused—"and for another, he's a seer. He'll be better able to keep you out of the way of danger."

"Peter and Stephen will still be with me, right?"

"Of course." He smiled, running his fingers through her hair. "I don't think they'd leave if I told them to."

She shrugged. "They've been guarding me for years."

"Which is why I know they'll be good at it. No one even got close to you while they were with you."

Taken

Reem carried Eliza out to the balcony, Peter, Stephen, and Robert following closely behind. She leaned her back against the banister as she cradled Eliza in her arms, smiling brightly when she opened her silver eyes. "You know you don't have to keep such a watchful eye on me when I'm in the tower," she told the men. "I live here."

"Jameson said we're supposed to keep an eye on you as long as you're not in your bedroom or the nursery," Peter replied.

"Alright then." She smiled. "Why don't you go have a look around or something?"

"Trying to get rid of me again?" He laughed. "I'll take Stephen with me."

"Thank you, Peter." Her smile brightened as the two men left the balcony, checking the perimeter for anything out of the ordinary.

"I take it you know I need to talk to you," Robert said as he moved to stand beside her.

"I do." She nodded.

"I had a vision." He paused, his eyes dropping to the ground. "I think they're coming for you. Today."

"I know," she whispered. "Eliza showed me the same. I'll need you to take her to my sister if they take me."

"Are you sure you want me doing that? I mean, they've been working for you for years."

"Both you and Eliza are seers. I want her with that protection." She nodded. "They're coming soon."

"I know," he whispered. "They should be here within the hour, I'd say."

"And I'll be here to meet them."

"What about Jameson?" he asked, his eyes finally meeting hers.

"He should be back by then."

"Your orders?"

"Don't let them take my baby," she replied, her voice low and angered. "And don't let them separate Jameson and I."

"Of course, the links." He nodded. "I won't let that happen."

"Won't let what happen?" Peter asked as he and Stephen approached once again, stopping just off the balcony.

"Robert had a vision," Reem replied, "and it seems a small group of soldiers is coming to take me to Admiri."

"We'll make sure that doesn't happen," Stephen replied, his hand moving to the weapon at his side. "When?"

"Soon," Robert said. "Very soon."

"Robert, take her to the nursery," Reem whispered, handing Eliza to him. "I don't want her near here when they arrive."

Robert nodded and walked down the hall, cradling Eliza against his chest until he arrived just outside the nursery. "Jameson, when did you get back?" he asked.

"Reem told me they were coming," Jameson replied, gesturing for Robert to enter the nursery.

He nodded, taking Eliza into the room while Jameson walked down the hall to join Reem and the others on the balcony.

"I thought you were training today," Reem whispered as she took his hand.

"I didn't want to leave you alone with all this going on," he whispered back. "When should they be arriving?"

"Any moment now by my calculations," Robert replied as he rejoined them.

Jameson nodded and started to lead Reem into the meeting room when a group of soldiers teleported into the center of the main chamber, seven men standing in a circular formation around the one man Reem wished she would never see again. Superior Seamus snapped his fingers, and the seven aimed their weapons at Peter, Stephen, and Robert, ordering them to stand down.

"Do as they say," Reem whispered, dropping to her knees with her hands on her head.

"Reem, we—"

"No, Peter. Do as they say," she cut him off, pulling Jameson to his knees at her side.

The guards did as she said, dropping to their knees in front of her while the soldiers disarmed them and threw their weapons to the opposite side of the room.

"It seems the rebellion has done well for you," Seamus whispered as he approached Reem.

"Don't touch her," Jameson snapped as Seamus placed his hand under Reem's chin.

"And you do not speak to me in that manner," Seamus replied, his eyes flicking up to one of the soldiers, who then rammed the butt of his weapon into the back of Jameson's head. "Bind him—he'll have to come with us too."

"Don't hurt him, Seamus," Reem begged as she started to stand.

Seamus hit the side of her face with the back of his hand, knocking her back to the ground. "I'll do with both of you as I please." He paused, leaning down to whisper in her ear. "You belong to me."

"I belong to no one," she snapped, using her gifts to throw Seamus across the room.

"Shoot her," Seamus ordered as he stood and wiped the blood from his mouth.

Jameson walked up the steps into the tower, surprised to find the three guards he'd assigned to Reem knocked out on the floor. "What happened?" he shouted.

"How?" Robert whispered as Jameson knelt by his side. "How are you here?"

"I was in training," Jameson whispered. "Where else would I be?"

"You were here," Robert replied. "You were with Reem when they took her."

"You let them take her?" he shouted. "How could you have let this happen?"

"Jameson, if you're here, then who's with Reem?" he asked, ignoring Jameson's question.

Jameson dropped to his seat, shocked at the sudden realization of what had happened. "Suri," he whispered. "Suri is with Reem."

"She's a shape-shifter?"

"Robert, this is important." Jameson paused. "When did they leave?"

"I don't know," he whispered back.

Suddenly, Jameson teleported into the nursery, quickly gathering Eliza into his arms before teleporting into the underground where Nicholas was preparing the hospital. "Nicholas," he whispered, trying not to wake the child in his arms. "Nicholas, I need you to take care of her for a few days."

"What's going on?" Nicholas asked as he took Eliza from Jameson's arms. "Where's Reem?"

"They have her, Nicholas. I'm going to get her back."

"How long ago?" he asked, glancing between Jameson's eyes and the link on his wrist.

"I don't know," he replied nervously. "Just take care of her."

"Shouldn't Suri be the one doing this?"

"She's with Reem, Nicholas. Just take care of my daughter," he snapped.

"I'll send someone after you," Nicholas replied. "Alexander will want to help Suri."

"Thank you," Jameson whispered before disappearing from his side.

Nicholas took the child back to the central tower, finding Alexander standing on the steps outside. "What's going on?" Alexander asked as Nicholas approached. "Where is everyone?"

"They've taken Reem," Nicholas replied as he made his way up the steps. "Suri's with her, and Jameson's gone to save them."

"Where are they taking her?"

"Admiri's my guess." He shrugged, turning to look Alexander in the eyes as they reached the top of the steps. "I need you to put a team together and go after them. You won't be able to catch up at this point, but you can try. Jameson will need you."

Alexander nodded and teleported away, leaving Nicholas alone at the top of the staircase. He took Eliza to the nursery and laid her down in her crib, doing his best to keep her asleep. He leaned his back against the wall, unsure of what to do now that everyone was gone. He closed his eyes and tried his best not to scream out in frustration, knowing that the sound would wake the baby girl who slept in the crib.

He felt like he'd been there for hours when Seth walked in, concern and confusion written on his face when he found Nicholas instead of Reem standing beside the crib. "They've taken her, haven't they?" he asked as he approached.

Nicholas opened his eyes, almost ashamed of the tears that filled them as he looked down at Eliza. "Yes," he whispered.

"And Jameson?"

"He's gone after them."

"That's not right—they wouldn't have taken one without the other," Seth replied as he stood next to Nicholas beside the crib. "They know the links would kill both of them if they did."

"They took Suri. I'm assuming she took Jameson's form," he whispered.

"She gave Jameson a fighting chance," Seth replied, placing his hand on Nicholas's shoulder. "We'll get them back. I'm assuming you sent someone after them?"

"Of course," Nicholas replied. "Alexander."

"Good." He nodded slowly. "Good."

"If they don't come back, she won't have any parents," Nicholas whispered as they stared at Eliza's sleeping form.

"We won't let that happen," Seth replied. "Reem and Jameson are the most capable people I know. They're not leaving their daughter."

Nicholas nodded, unable to speak another word as Eliza's silver eyes opened to look at the two of them. He reached down and stroked her forehead lightly, wishing that she would let him see a glimpse of the future.

"Anything?" Seth whispered.

"Nothing."

"Damn."

Halaq waited at David's bedside while the man walked around the room, testing his joints. They'd been discussing their plan to take out Marcus when David decided it was time to test his limbs again.

"Feeling better, I see," Brittany mocked from the other room as he passed by her doorway. "What's he got you doing for him, David?"

"Nothing that concerns you," David replied evenly before walking back to his bed. "Go back to sleep."

"I much prefer staying awake and watching you limp your way around the room," she snapped. "Why am I not allowed to walk around?"

"Because you would kill me in an instant," Halaq replied.

"What makes you think that?" she asked sweetly.

"Don't try that on me, darling." He laughed. "I'm too good for all that."

"Oh, I know how good you are," she whispered as she struggled to free herself once again.

Halaq stood and walked to the doorway, smiling as she continued her struggle. "It's not going to work, you know." He laughed.

"You'd like to think that, wouldn't you?" She turned to face him, her white eyes staring blankly toward him as he winked.

"Can you see me?" he asked curiously as he approached her. "I haven't seen you since you were blinded."

"My gifts let me see your gifts."

"Then how do you see anything else?" His eyebrows furrowed.

"I have my ways." She laughed lightly. "I have no reason to tell you of them."

"Well, if you don't want to tell me that, then maybe you can tell me about Marcus's personal quarters." He shrugged.

"You only want to kill him," she snapped.

"If that's what it takes, then yes, I will kill him," he replied evenly. "He has done nothing but evil since he took power."

"Do not speak of him like that." She turned to look at the ceiling once again. "He is a great man, and he will come to save me."

Halaq shook his head slowly, almost ashamed that he'd once been in love with the woman who so deeply believed in Marcus Admiri's fight. "He will not do anything that would jeopardize his leadership, Brittany." He paused. "If he were to come for you, he would be doing something that he's never done for anyone else in his inner circle—they would see it as weakness."

"You lie," she spat.

He sighed. "Just know that Marcus Admiri is not coming for you. You will spend the rest of your days here unless you tell me what I want to know."

"Then what do you want to know?" she asked, mocking him with her tone.

"What is the best way to get inside Marcus's personal quarters?"

"The balcony," she whispered, ashamed that she'd answered his question. "The easiest way to get inside is through the balcony."

"Thank you." He smiled before rejoining David in the other room. "We'll be entering through the balcony." He laughed lightly.

"I had a feeling." David smiled back. "When will we be heading out?"

"Tomorrow if you're feeling up to it." Halaq shrugged. "The day after if that works better."

"Either one should be fine," David said.

"We'll see how tomorrow looks then."

David nodded slowly as he walked back to his mattress, slowly easing down to his seat before lying back on his side. "I'm sorry I wasn't able to help on your previous trip," he whispered as he settled in on the mattress.

"I did fine by myself," Halaq replied, "but that was mostly reconnaissance. For this trip I'll need at least one more person on guard duty—plus I hear they've doubled the security in the tower since I was there last. I've a feeling Marcus is up to something."

"He usually is." David nodded. "Should be interesting trying to remove him from the equation."

"True"—Halaq nodded—"but it can be done easily enough."

Inara

Reem woke to find her hands bound behind her back and her gifts completely inactive as she sat up in the darkness. "Jameson?" she whispered. "Jameson, are you there?"

"I'm here," he whispered from a few feet away. "Where are we?"

"You're in Admiri," Seamus replied as he opened the door to the room, allowing the firelight to enter and blind the couple bound on the floor. "Reem, Marcus would like to see you now." He smiled.

"And then what? Then you get to take me back to your bed?" she snapped. "I'm not coming with you, Seamus." She fumbled to stand to her feet, trying her hardest to force her gifts to function.

"Your gifts won't work," Seamus replied, ignoring her comment. "We have a shield who can prevent each of you from using your gifts." He stepped closer to Reem. "I thought it would be best, considering the strength of your skill set."

"Don't touch her!" Jameson shouted as Seamus ran his fingers through her hair.

"I will do with her as I please," Seamus snapped. "She belongs to me."

Without the use of her gifts, Reem suddenly forgot how to fight as Seamus placed his hands on her hips, pulling her closer to him. She could feel the rough hairs of his unshaven face as he moved closer to her, feel his breath on her neck and his hands making their way up her shirt when Jameson kicked in his knee, knocking the man to the ground. She ran to Jameson's side, remembering what it felt like to fight without the use of her gifts when she was stunned to her knees.

"You shouldn't have done that," Seamus said as he stood to his feet, smoothing his black hair over his head. "Now I'll have to take you in by force."

Another man—apparently one with a gift able to knock both Reem and Jameson to the ground without much energy—joined Seamus and helped him to hoist Reem to her feet.

"This is Carey. He's quite useful when it comes to dealing with rebels." Seamus laughed as the man hoisted Reem over his shoulders and carried her out of the room. "I promise I will hurt her," he told Jameson as he exited the room.

As soon as the door closed, Jameson cried out in anger and frustration, not knowing what to do now that they were separated. There was no way for Reem to know his thoughts now, no way for them to communicate over distances, no way to save her if he was trapped in this room.

Seamus walked up the steps from the basement, Carey following closely behind as they entered the main chamber of the central tower of Admiri. He ordered Carey to keep Reem restrained while he entered the meeting room, finding the Great Superior and Superior Inara there waiting for him. As he entered, Marcus took his seat in his throne and Inara stood directly behind him, waiting for him to speak.

"What took you so long?" Inara asked, her voice hard and stern as she took her seat to Marcus's right. She'd worked hard to get to where she was today—the only female of the original seven Superiors. She pushed her black cherry-colored hair behind her ears as she sat, her eyes staring intently into Seamus's. She wore tight black pants and a fitted black top, carrying only a single pistol and knife, both sheathed to her thighs.

"I'm sorry," Seamus replied as he sat to Marcus's left. "She wasn't very thrilled about joining us."

"I told you not to touch her, Seamus," Marcus replied, realizing what must have happened. "Until she has confessed, I do not want her harmed."

"I can get a confession out of her," Inara said seductively, placing her hand on Marcus's. "After all, she's just a girl." She shrugged. "I can have your confession in less than a day."

"I don't think we'll have to resort to that." Marcus smiled as he pulled his hand out from under hers. "We need her alive so that we can make an example out of her."

"What are your plans, my lord?" Seamus asked.

"Once we have our confession, we will take her back to her rebellion and execute her. They will surrender when they see their leader killed before their eyes."

"Why, Marcus, I do believe you've been learning from me." Inara winked.

"It's possible, yes." Marcus smiled. "Bring her in."

A moment later, Carey walked in, pulling Reem along beside him. He unceremoniously shoved her into a chair before bowing and exiting the room. "You know this won't work, Marcus," she snapped.

"You don't even know what my plans are," Marcus said, laughing.

"I know enough." She paused. "I know that you would not have brought me here if you didn't know for sure that your army is completely under your control, and I know that you wouldn't have kept me alive if you didn't need me for something. I also know that if you kill me, they will kill you." Her eyes burned into his.

"Do you honestly believe that?" Inara mocked. "They would bow to us if we were to murder you." She smiled brightly. "They would have no reason to rebel if it wasn't for you."

"We have something that you don't, Marcus," Reem continued, ignoring Inara's remark.

"Your love is weakness, foolish child," Inara snapped.

"Love is stronger than you know," Reem replied coolly. "So what is it that you need from me?"

"I need nothing from you," Marcus said, averting his eyes from hers.

"You want me to confess to killing the Athenians, don't you?" she asked.

"As he said, we need nothing from you," Inara replied as she stood back to her feet and started walking around the table. "Honestly, I don't know how you survived so long," she whispered under her breath as she passed by Reem's chair.

"Are you even a Superior, Seamus? Or are you just here for show?" Reem asked, turning to look Seamus in the eye. "You haven't said a word since I got here."

"I am as much a Superior as Inara," he replied hastily.

"Are you saying that I am not a Superior?" Inara snapped as she approached him from behind.

"It's not as though you have any gifts that make you Superior," he whispered.

"I could make you kill yourself," she whispered in his ear before running her tongue up his neck. "Do it, Seamus. Kill yourself." Her seductive voice seeped into his soul, forcing him to pull his knife from its sheath on his thigh. "Through the heart." He lifted the knife and pointed it at his chest, piercing through the skin and killing himself in a matter of seconds.

"Inara," Marcus said, watching as Seamus's blood poured out onto the floor.

"He was weak, my lord," she replied seriously as she approached Reem once again, squatting at her side. "All he wanted was this one. All he could think about was when you'd ordered this whore into his bed."

"Do not kill another of my men in my presence again, Inara," he warned.

"Of course, my lord." She turned toward him and smiled seductively before turning back to Reem. "He was more her man than yours, my lord."

"I am aware of that."

"I'm starting to think that you're her pet, Marcus," Reem said, her eyes piercing into Marcus's.

"Why would you think that?" Inara asked. "I do nothing that my lord would not approve of."

"And yet it seems you have just expressly disobeyed his orders," Reem replied. "If anyone else had killed a Superior, Marcus would have them skinned alive. So what is it about you?"

"She speaks lies, my lord. I do not see why we are even speaking to her in this manner—she does not deserve our attention." She stood once again and walked up behind Marcus, running her fingers through his hair. "We should send her back into the dungeon until she decides to be more forthcoming."

"See that it is done," Marcus replied. "I'll see you in my quarters when you are ready to talk," he told Reem as he stood and exited the room.

Inara slowly walked back to Reem, placing her finger under her chin. "Stand up," she whispered.

Reem obeyed, finding it virtually impossible not to do as Inara had said. The woman whispered in her ear and told her to go back to the dungeon, so she did, with Inara at her side, unable to do anything other than what Inara had ordered.

She firmly pushed Reem into the dungeon, laughing lightly when Jameson rushed toward the door. "Stop," she whispered, surprised when he didn't obey. She slammed the door shut seconds before he reached her, laughing again when she remembered her gifts wouldn't work down here.

"Jameson," Reem whispered, "I think things may be different than even Lana knew."

Marcus sat on his throne, surprised at Reem's audacity in saying that Inara had been pulling the strings all along. The woman hadn't even been around him until a year ago. He'd moved her from Athena a few months before he'd sent Reem to kill the Athenians. Inara merely had gifts that aided her in her way of life. She wouldn't dare to use her gifts on a man as powerful as him—he would kill her in an instant if she did.

He didn't really need the confession from Reem—not here anyway. He needed to break her. He needed her to believe that there was nothing she could do to save the people in her rebellion. He needed her thinking that they were all dead. He wanted her broken and bleeding on his floor, begging him to kill her. She didn't deserve to be alive. She deserved worse than to die at his hands—she deserved to die in the cruelest way he knew of. She deserved to die Lana's death.

His hands balled into fists as he thought of Lana and how she'd betrayed him. He'd given her everything, and as soon as she'd seen what he'd done for her in the future, she'd gone to Phillip. This whole matter with Reem was so similar—he'd loved her like a daughter, and she'd betrayed his trust. He'd had no choice but to order her into committing treason.

Now he knew that if he didn't kill the girl he'd once thought of as a daughter, either she or her husband would come to kill him. He highly doubted that Phillip would follow through on his threats, but he knew that Jameson always kept his promises. He would kill Marcus—so long as Reem didn't do it first.

"Sir, Inara to see you," the guard said as he entered Marcus's quarters.

"Let her in."

"That husband of hers is quite the fighter," she announced as she walked inside.

"Leave us," Marcus told the guard. "You forgot that you can't use your gifts downstairs, didn't you?" He laughed lightly.

"Not long enough for either of them to escape," she defended.

"I'm sure," he replied. "I can't see you allowing anyone to escape your grasp."

"What are your orders concerning them, my lord?"

"If she has not confessed in twenty-four hours, kill the man. Once he's dead, we can remove the links safely," he ordered.

She smiled seductively. "You're certain that the links won't kill her when we kill him?"

"Of course I'm certain!" he shouted, his anger-filled eyes piercing into hers.

"Sorry, my lord. I didn't mean to imply that you didn't know." She dipped her head.

They stood there several moments, she unsure of what to do and he unsure of whether or not to give her the order. "I need you to do something for me, Inara," he whispered finally.

"Anything, my lord," she whispered, lifting her head to look him in the eye once again.

"I need you to put together a team to retrieve Brittany Green from the Purist camp," he ordered. "I want her back inside Admiri in three days. Do you understand?"

"My lord, are you certain that's wise? The people may see it as weakness if the team were to fail," she replied.

"I am aware of that, Inara. You have only to be certain that the team does not fail." He paused. "If they fail, I will simply tell the people that you sent the team of your own accord."

"Yes, my lord." She dipped her head once again before turning and exiting the room.

<hr />

"I've received word that Marcus has sent Superior Inara to retrieve your witch," Halaq announced as he stepped into David's room, finding the man walking around the room, testing his joints once again.

"I thought you told her he wouldn't send anyone for her," David replied.

"I didn't think he would." Halaq shrugged. "It would've been smarter to let her die here." He laughed lightly as he took a seat on the edge of David's mattress.

"Why would he send someone for her?" he whispered under his breath.

"Honestly, I don't know." He paused. "But this means we may have to postpone our plans to take out Marcus. I think we should wait until after they've made their attempt to reach the witch."

"We can't afford to let them get to her," he replied. "She knows too much already."

"That she does!" Brittany yelled. "She knows all of your plans—you can't let them get to her!"

Halaq stood, walked to her doorway, and leaned against the frame. "Stop talking about yourself in the third person, witch," he ordered.

"Stop ordering me around, fool," she snapped.

"I will do as I please in my home."

"Phillip," Lana's familiar feminine voice whispered from behind him in David's room. "Phillip, I need to speak with you."

Halaq turned toward her, shaking his head at David when the man opened his mouth to ask a question. He walked up to Lana and took her by the arm, leading her into one of the side rooms of his home. "What is it?" he snapped.

"Phillip, I know you're mad at me. And honestly, I don't blame you for that, but I think I know what he did to her," she whispered. "I think he's drugged her."

"If he drugged her, she would be going through withdrawals by now," he replied as he started to walk away from her.

She reached out and clamped her hand down on his shirt collar, preventing him from going far before she replied, "Not if it was something he'd designed to last long enough for her to perform tasks for him."

He turned back toward her, his angry eyes burning as they stared into hers. "And what do you propose I do about it?"

"I can develop a cure for it," she said, her sure eyes flitting around the room.

"Lana, you can't even stay in one time frame for more than a few moments at a time. How would you have the time to develop an antidote?"

"I'm going to die soon, remember?"

"What does that have to do with anything?" he asked impatiently.

"Once I die, I'll start over," she whispered.

"What?"

"After this body is dead, a younger version of me is going to come visit you. She has the ability to create a cure, the same as I do. I'll show up here in a few hours at most—I'll be here for a day." She paused. "That will have to be enough time to develop an antidote."

Halaq nodded, unsure of what to say. "This younger version of you, when did she shift into this time?"

Her eyes filled with tears as she nodded slowly, knowing what he was thinking. "She won't know as much as I do, but she'll know enough to help Brittany."

"Lana"—he paused—"is she the version of you that shifted right after . . ." He stepped back and ran his fingers through his hair, not knowing how to finish the question.

"Yes," she whispered, lowering her eyes to the ground.

"Lana, I don't know if I can—"

"You have to," she cut him off, her hands clutching at her chest.

"What's happening?" David asked as he stepped in the room.

She shrieked in pain, her hands reaching toward Halaq and clutching the air as she fell to the ground seconds before she shifted back to her original timeline.

"She's dead," Halaq whispered. "She'll be back in an hour or so."

"What?"

Antidote

Halaq stood just outside his home, contemplating Lana's recent departure and waiting for the doctor to arrive with supplies, when he heard the shriek he'd been waiting for. He turned and ran back inside to find Lana standing naked in front of him, pausing midstride while she ran for the door. He held out his arms as she ran forward, stopping her in her tracks. "Lana—Lana, it's me," he whispered in her ear.

"Phillip?" she whispered, confusion edging her voice as he pulled his shirt off over his head and draped it over her naked body. "What's going on?" she asked when she noticed the scars on his chest and abdomen.

"You were just with me—remember?" he asked, testing her memory.

"I shifted," she whispered when she realized what must have happened. "When is it?"

"The future." He nodded slowly. "And I need your help."

"Halaq? What's going on?" David asked as he walked up to them.

"David, this is Lana," Halaq replied, smiling slightly at her confusion. "Stay here," he whispered in her ear, "I'll go find you some clothes."

"Thank you," she whispered back, holding out her hand toward David. "It's good to meet you." She smiled sheepishly, tugging at the bottom of her shirt.

"Didn't we already meet?" He tilted his head to the side.

She shrugged. "My life doesn't exactly travel in a straight line."

"I see." He smiled brightly as Halaq returned carrying a pair of his jeans and another tee shirt.

"Sorry if they don't fit. It's all I have," he said as he handed Lana the jeans and pulled the shirt over his scarred chest.

"They'll do fine." She smiled as she dressed. "I'll be shifting back soon enough, right?"

"In a day or so." He shrugged. "Or at least, that's what you told us in your future."

"You said you needed my help," she said as she walked up and took his hand in hers. "What do you need me for?"

"I'm afraid your husband has drugged a friend of mine," Halaq replied. "You said earlier that you should be able to develop an antidote in a day or less with the supplies our doctor has."

"And when will your doctor be here?" Her eyebrows rose inquisitively.

"He should be arriving any moment." He smiled. "You're sure you don't mind helping me?"

"Phillip, you know I'd do anything to help you." She smiled back.

"Then I'll take you to your patient." He led her into Brittany's room, his face growing grave when he found her struggling to be free of her restraints.

"She's a woman," Lana whispered under her breath.

He nodded. "You don't mind, do you? I need a cure for whatever he's done to her."

"No, I'll help her. My husband is not who he once was," she whispered as she approached the girl struggling on the mattress. "Let me know when the doctor arrives."

"Of course." He dipped his head before he turned and exited the room, leaving her alone with her patient as he joined David.

"Who is she?" David whispered.

"An old friend—nothing more," he whispered.

"A very old friend if she refers to you as Phillip," he mused. "She's Marcus's wife?"

Halaq nodded slowly, ashamed to tell his newfound friend the tale of what had happened between him and Lana. "A very old friend," he whispered.

"If I'm going to be working with you, it would be best that I know and understand what's going on here," David replied, unsure of how to ask Halaq what was going on.

"It's a very long story, David," Halaq replied.

"And we have all day," he countered.

"After she gets to work." He nodded. "The doctor should be here soon."

"I was told this was the home of Halaq," a man said as he pushed the curtain door away from its frame, "and I need to speak with him."

"Who are you?" Halaq asked.

"My name is Alexander—I was sent here by the Prophet, Seth," he replied. "I have come to rescue the savior and her sister."

"I was not aware that Reem had been taken captive."

"They've kept quite the secret then, haven't they?" His eyebrows rose. "I have two men with me that will help in the rescue."

"And what of Jameson Willow?" David asked.

"He is already inside the city as far as I know. He left before the three of us."

"I'm afraid we won't be able to mount this rescue for another day at least," Halaq replied. "They are planning to come and take the witch from us, and I will not allow that to happen."

"You have the witch in your possession?"

"I do"—he nodded—"and she is being treated by one of our best people."

"Treated for what illness?" Robert asked as he stepped in the doorway behind Alexander.

"She has been drugged by Admiri," Halaq replied, "but soon she will be healed."

"It seems you have quite the party going on in here." The doctor laughed as he walked inside. "I take it the patient is still in the back room?"

"Go right in, Doctor," Halaq gestured for him to enter Brittany's room. "Give Lana whatever she needs to heal her," he whispered.

"Of course," the doctor replied.

"Give them a day at most to heal her, and then we will mount our rescue," Halaq told Alexander. "For now, if you and your men would guard the door, it would be appreciated."

Alexander dipped his head and took Robert by the collar, dragging him outside to do as he was told. "Obey your orders," he told the man as they exited.

"I still want to know what's going on," David said when he was sure the others couldn't hear his remark.

Halaq nodded. "And I will tell you—now, if you'd like."

"Thank you," he replied.

"You know that I was one of the original four tested, and you know that Lana was married to Marcus"—he paused—"what you don't know is that when she shifted for the first time, she saw what he did to this world, and she hated what she saw. After that, she vowed that she would change the future—and she has. She and Marcus separated, and she lived with me for a time. In fact, when she shifts back may very well be the time that she moves out of my home."

"So she was naked because . . ."

"Yes," Halaq replied. "I should never have let it happen, but it happened. When she shifted here, she realized that I wasn't as in love with her as she was with me, so she left."

"And how does Brittany fit into all this?"

"Two days before Brittany and I were to be married, Marcus took her from me. He changed her into what she is today. He blinded her, drugged her, and trained her to be the mindless witch you know." He sighed. "He took her from me, the same as he believed I took Lana from him."

"Seth said it was an explosion that changed her eyes."

"It was." Halaq nodded. "I was with her at the time—I shielded her body with mine, actually. If not for Marcus, I would be dead. He took both of us to his palace, healed us, and let me go. I didn't see her again until very recently."

"Does she remember what happened?"

"No, she doesn't remember anything before the day of the Crash. I believe he wiped her memory, but I have no way to know what he really did." Tears formed in his eyes as he remembered everything about that day. "Marcus kept me alive so that I could see what he'd done to her—so that I could live to hate him as much as he hated me."

"I can bring her back to you," Lana whispered as she walked up to him. "As far as I can tell, the drug is already starting to wear off. I can give her something that will speed the process."

"I'm sorry, Lana," he whispered back as he brushed her hair behind her ear. "I didn't mean to cause you so much pain."

"It's my fault as much as anyone's." She shrugged. "I want you to be happy, Phillip."

"And I you."

"But we both know I'll never be happy." She sighed. "The least I can do is heal her for you."

"Thank you," he whispered as he pulled her into his arms, holding her tightly against him as her arms wrapped around his waist.

⁂

Reem rocked back and forth on the floor of her cell, keeping an eye and an ear out, while Jameson slept on the ground in front of her. For once in his life, he slept lightly, waking up from every tiny noise rather than snoring on through them.

Something didn't seem right, but she couldn't put her finger on it. She'd blocked out everything in the outside world, giving her body over to meditation while she searched for a way to get around the shield. She'd been testing the fences for over an hour now without much success, and still she continued to test them. She needed to find a way out—needed to know that they wouldn't be trapped down here until they died.

It had been almost sixteen hours since they'd seen or heard from anyone, and the silence was unnerving. She could hear the sounds of the others in their cells, hear as they cried out for someone to kill them just so they would finally be free. Apparently, there weren't many left in the dungeons, but those that were here seemed as though they'd been in their cells for years. It didn't seem like Marcus to allow these people to go on living after he'd sentenced them. She'd always known him as someone who would rather kill his enemies than allow them to live in pain.

She fell to her side as she realized that she and Jameson would likely be left down here at the same mercy as the people who screamed out their pain at the world. Tears streamed down her cheeks as she thought of Eliza who'd been left to live with her aunt because her mother and father wanted a chance at Marcus Admiri. She should have known better—of course Marcus would have some way to prevent them from using their gifts while they were in his custody. It made perfect sense.

She wished with all her heart that she would be able to see her baby girl again.

Control

It had been almost twenty hours now, only four more before Inara would go to the cell and kill the man. Inara knew Reem would never confess the way Marcus wanted her to, and the thought of killing Jameson with her own hands made her smile every time she thought about it. At the moment, Marcus was eating out of the palm of her hand, but she didn't know how long that would last. The man could change his mind in a moment, and as long as she wasn't with him, he was free to do whatever he wanted. The only problem was that he spent the majority of his time alone in his personal chambers, and if she asked to be able to help him in the decision making, she knew he would likely kill her.

She stood outside the dungeon door now, listening intently for the sound of Reem and Jameson deciding whether or not to confess for the sake of their daughter. She wished she could go to Athena and kill the little witch before either of her parents could be freed, but she knew it would be impossible to do so without alerting Marcus of her departure.

She could hear the sounds of screaming issuing from the other side of the door and knew for a fact that none of those sounds came from Reem and Jameson's cell. According to Sharon, the shield, they were doing nothing but resting, but she had a feeling they were doing more than Sharon knew.

Four more hours until Jameson Willow would die at her hands. She couldn't wait to put a bullet through his forehead.

Of course, she would rather that he suffered more than he would with a bullet in his skull; but she knew that if she drew out the process, Reem would have more time to find a way to kill her. The woman was nothing if not brilliant when it came to finding loopholes in people's gifts. As long as Sheila kept them from using their gifts, Inara would be fine. But once Sheila lost her concentration, she had no doubt that Reem would kill them all if only to protect her husband and baby girl.

For now, it was time she prepared the soldiers to retrieve Marcus's mistress—though she still thought it was unintelligent on Marcus's part to send a team for someone who could so easily be left to die.

"I've got it." Lana smiled as she stepped out of Halaq's home and into the sunlit street where everyone waited to hear the news about Brittany.

"So soon?" Halaq smiled back as he approached her in the doorway. "How is she?"

"She's well." She paused. "It'll be a few hours before the drug completely wears off, but she's doing well for the moment."

"Thank you." His smile brightened.

"Go see her, Phillip." She nodded slowly, her smile fading from her face. "I think it'll help."

"With what?" he asked, furrowing his brows slightly.

"If her memories are still there, she'll need to see you to remember."

"Thank you," he whispered. He kissed her forehead before he walked inside to where Brittany was, still bound to her mattress. He walked into the room and knelt beside her, his eyes filling with tears when he saw pain written on her face. Even now when she wanted nothing to do with him, he hated to see her in pain. She didn't deserve to be in pain.

Her eyes snapped open as he placed his hand on her shoulder, and her mouth opened in a grimace. "What are you doing to me?" she asked.

He shook his head slowly. "I'm helping you," he whispered.

"I will tell you nothing," she snarled.

"I'm not asking you to." He winked. "How do you feel?"

"How do I look like I feel?" she screamed, closing her eyes while she writhed in pain. "What have you done to me?" her voice echoed through the building.

"I can give her something for the pain if you'd like," Lana whispered as she walked in the room. "But it'll take longer for the drug to wear off if I do."

"She can take it." He nodded. "I know she can."

"What drug?" Brittany yelled. "What do you want from me?" Tears streamed down her face as the pain increased. "Why are you doing this, Halaq?"

"I think we're getting somewhere." He smiled at Lana. "She hasn't said my name like that in a while—it's usually a curse." He laughed lightly.

"Though technically, she isn't calling you by your name yet." Lana smiled back as she walked up behind him and dabbed a cold cloth on Brittany's forehead.

"Get away from me!" Brittany snarled as Lana wiped the sweat off her face. Lana held her hands up in defense and stepped away as Halaq stood back up and walked to the adjacent wall, leaning his back against it while he watched Brittany writhe in pain.

Lana walked up and stood directly in front of him, her eyes staring fondly into his. "What do you see in her?" she whispered as she wrapped her arms around his neck.

He shook his head slowly as he pried her arms off his neck. "No, Lana," he whispered. "I'm sorry."

"I loved you, Phillip," she snapped. "The least you can do is tell me what you see in her."

"Don't be like this, Lana." He sighed before kissing her forehead and walking into the next room.

"Phillip," she replied as she followed him, "please talk to me." She took him by the hand and prevented him from going outside. "Please."

"What do you want from me?" he asked, crossing his arms over his chest.

"I want to know how you could be making love to me one minute, and the next thing I know, the only thing you'll do to me is kiss my forehead and tell me how much you appreciate my medicinal skills," she replied, crossing her arms as well as they faced off.

"A lot has changed since then," he whispered as his eyes dropped to the ground. "I am truly sorry that it happened this way, but it happened."

"That's not an answer, Phillip," she snapped.

"Lana, please. As I said, things have changed since then. When you get back to our timeline, you move out of my home—and I'm guessing that's because you found out about Brittany and myself."

She reached up and brought her lips to his, pulling her body as close to his as she could until he pushed her away. "Don't tell me you didn't love me too," she whispered, tears forming in her eyes.

"No, don't think that," he whispered back, placing his hand on her cheek. "I did love you, Lana. I did. But things changed. You left me, and I moved on."

"When am I shifting back?" she asked.

"I don't know." He shook his head. "But I need you to focus on Brittany until you do."

She nodded and walked back into Brittany's room as the woman screamed in pain once again.

"We've got company," Robert announced as he barged into the room. "A team of soldiers have come for her."

"How many?" Halaq asked.

"Too many."

"I knew living on the outskirts was a bad idea."

It was time. Inara stood outside Marcus's chambers, waiting for him to give her the order. The guard opened the door and stepped outside, his grim look conveying his orders before he even looked her in the eye. "Do it," he told her.

She nodded and walked away from him, quickly making her way back down to the dungeon. She opened the door and hurried down the steps, taking her pistol from its holster on her thigh as she did so. "Open it," she ordered the guard who stood outside the cell.

"Yes, ma'am," he replied, unlocking the door as quickly as his shaky fingers would allow before he gestured for her to enter. "Do you require my assistance?"

"Not this time." She winked as she stepped past him.

Inside, Reem and Jameson both stood and stared at her as she entered the room, Jameson to her left and Reem to her right. Her smile brightened as she sensed the urgency in them.

"What do you want?" Jameson asked.

"Are you ready to give Marcus what he wants?" Inara asked as she stepped closer to Reem. She shook her head gravely as Inara lifted her pistol and pointed it between Jameson's eyes. "And now?"

"No," she whispered.

"Good." Inara smiled wickedly as she pulled the trigger, her smile growing larger as Jameson's dead body slumped to the ground, void of life. "Perhaps that will be the incentive you need to give Marcus what he wants."

"You shouldn't have done that," Reem whispered, tears streaming down her face as Inara walked behind her and attempted to remove the Locks from her wrists. "They won't come off—not if he's dead nor if he were alive."

"Take her to the Great One," Inara ordered the guard as she pushed Reem out of the cell.

Reem struggled free and turned back to look at Jameson's dead body one more time before they dragged her up the stairs, a gasp issuing from her mouth when she realized the body on the ground of the cell was morphing into another form entirely. "Suri?" she whispered.

"Reem, no!" Jameson shouted, teleporting in front of her.

Reem let go of her control over her gifts, her willingness to fight them suddenly gone with the death of her sister. It was not supposed to go this way. Jameson had the healing gift that would have prevented that bullet from killing him—Suri was not supposed to be here! "You let her die!" she screamed as her hands balled into fists on his chest. "You killed her!" she shrieked, turning to Inara with the full force of her gifts.

"Stop!" Inara shouted, causing both Reem and Jameson to stop in their tracks. "You will harm neither me nor my lord," she ordered, her eyes piercing into Reem's.

Reem snarled as she struggled against the control that Inara held over her. "I will not rest until you are dead," she swore as she used her gifts to lift herself off the ground and propel up the steps. "Don't follow me," she warned as she slammed the door shut and locked it.

"What have you done?" Jameson shouted as he approached Inara, his eyes burning with anger as he stepped closer to her.

"I have done only as my lord has ordered of me," she whispered back, her eyes burning back into his. "You will not harm me or my lord."

"No, I will not," he whispered, "but I know someone who will." He teleported away, leaving her trapped in the dungeon with a dozen screaming voices in the cells around her.

Jameson appeared just outside Marcus's chambers, surprised to find that Marcus had been left alive in the main chamber though every last one of his guards was killed—their heads snapped off their bodies under the full force of Reem's telekinesis. He tried to step closer to the Superior, tried to make his way past the blocks that Inara had placed in his mind, but it was of no use. There was nothing he could do to harm the man who'd threatened to kill his wife.

"Do it then," Marcus spat, holding out his arms to show that he was ready to die.

"You're not mine to destroy," Jameson replied angrily as he teleported away, knowing that Reem would be on her way back to the rebellion.

Halaq helped Brittany off the mattress, keeping her arms bound behind her as he threw her over his shoulder and carried her out the back of the house. They'd left Alexander and his men to take care of the soldiers who'd come for her, and now the two of them snuck out the back way with David and Lana following closely behind. He knew Lana would be shifting again any moment, but he didn't want her caught in a cross fire before she had a chance to finish living her life. There were still things that she had to do, and if she died here, the world would change drastically.

They snuck around the edge of the settlement, and Halaq set Brittany back to her feet. "Can you walk from here?" he asked.

"I'm not going anywhere with you," she snapped, opening her mouth to scream to the soldiers when David covered her mouth with a strip of cloth, tying it behind her head.

"I think we'll have to carry her," he told Halaq.

"The drug isn't wearing off as quickly as I'd hoped. The length of her withdrawals will probably be proportionate to the length of time she was on the drug," Lana whispered.

"Which means this could take a while," David replied. "She's been on it for years if I'm understanding correctly."

Halaq nodded slowly, his eyes glancing back and forth between the two of them. "Lana, I want you to stay here. You'll be shifting back to our timeline before long—it'll be safer if you're not out in the open." He paused. "David and I will make our way to Admiri. I have unfinished business there."

Return

Alexander took hold of Robert's arm and teleported to where Ryan stood on the other side of the building, knowing that there was no way they could get past the soldiers they fought. He placed his hand on Ryan's shoulder and teleported again, landing them in the middle of the desert a short way outside of Admiri. The sun was just beginning to set as they landed, and the three men collapsed on the ground from exhaustion.

"Thank you," Ryan whispered, his breathing uneven and heavy.

"I'm afraid not all of us were so lucky," Alexander replied, gesturing toward Robert.

Ryan gasped and crawled to Robert's side, placing his hands on the bullet holes in his chest to stop the bleeding. "I won't let you die," he whispered as Robert's anguished eyes stared up into his.

"Ryan," Robert gasped, "Ryan, you"—he grunted in pain—"you can't save me this time."

"No—NO!" Ryan screamed as Robert's eyes rolled back in his head. He turned toward Alexander, his eyes filling with tears. "Teleport us into the city—NOW!" he ordered.

"I can't, Ryan," Alexander whispered back. "I can't."

"Do it!" he screamed. "Do it! He needs a healer!"

Alexander crawled to his side, obviously drained of energy. "I can't, Ryan. I'm sorry," he whispered, his hands moving to check Robert's pulse. "He's already gone."

"No!" Ryan cried, his head dropping in sadness as he pulled Robert's dead body into his lap. "No—you can't be gone!" he shouted. "You can't!"

"I'm sorry, Ryan. I'm sorry," Alexander whispered, falling back to the ground as his exhaustion took hold.

"No." Ryan shook his head slowly, tears streaming down his face at the loss of his best friend. "You weren't meant to die this way—none of us were meant to die this way. You saw that in your visions, you know that," he cried, running his blood-covered hands through his hair.

Halaq trailed David by only a few feet, Brittany's weight not slowing him down any more than he'd expected. They'd been hiking for well over three hours, and the sun had already fallen beneath the horizon. By now, Lana would be back in her own timeline, moving out of his home while he was trapped here, trying to save the future from the fate that she'd seen on her first shift. She'd seen Marcus ruling the entire planet by fear, seen how badly he treated his people, and worst of all, she saw that she was not at his side. As far as he knew, she had succeeded in stopping it already, so long as he and David made it to Admiri before dawn and were able to complete their mission. It was time for Marcus Admiri to die.

"Do you need me to carry her?" David asked, turning back toward Halaq as he walked. "I'm strong enough to carry her until you get your strength back."

"I haven't lost any strength," Halaq whispered back. "Besides, I don't want to wake her." She'd been asleep for the better part of an hour now, and he could only hope that when she woke, the drug would have completely worn off. According to Lana, it would've worn off on its own in a few months, but she'd given Brittany something to speed the process. If all went according to plan on Lana's part, the drug should wear off by the time they reached the city. "How far to Admiri?" he asked.

"A few more miles, I'd guess." David shrugged, slowing his pace to walk beside Halaq. "We should be able to reach it before dawn."

"Good." He smiled. "Then let's pick up the pace." He moved his feet as quickly as they would take him, knowing that the sooner they reached the city, the better. They would need to find out where Reem and Jameson were being kept and then determine what needed to be done. At this rate, it seemed that it would take them a few days before they would be able to kill Admiri.

"What do you think happened to the others?" David asked as they walked side by side through the cold desert sand.

"I can only hope that they were able to teleport out of there in time. It's possible that they're already at the city—in which case, our job just got a lot easier." His smile brightened.

"How so?" David's eyebrows furrowed.

"If they're already there, then they can rescue the savior and her husband while we deal with Admiri," Halaq replied.

David nodded slowly, unsure of what to say as they continued on their trek. It seemed that Halaq was keeping more from him, but he wasn't sure he wanted to know everything that was going on inside that man's mind. They'd been hiking for hours already, and this was the first they'd spoken—he had to be thinking about something, but David was too worried that the legendary Void would kill him before he could ask what was going on.

"Do the Purists know who you are?" he asked.

"They know that I am Halaq and that I prefer not to use my gifts." He shrugged. "That is all they needed to know."

"So does anyone other than myself, Lana, and Marcus know who you really are?" he asked, unable to control his curiosity.

"Brittany knows, and Seth figured it out. I believe that's it." Halaq laughed lightly. "Any other questions you'd like me to answer for you?"

David laughed nervously. "Sorry, I didn't mean to pry."

"No, I don't mind." Halaq smiled. "I know you have questions, David."

"Alright"—he paused, taking a deep breath—"what are you hiding from me?"

"Put me down, jackass," Brittany moaned before Halaq could open his mouth to respond, her legs kicking out as she struggled in his hold. "Put. Me. Down."

"That's the Brittany I know and love," Halaq whispered under his breath. "Hold up a moment, David." David smiled slightly and nodded as Halaq set Brittany back down on her feet. "How do you feel?"

"Thank you," she whispered, tears forming in her eyes the moment she made eye contact with Halaq. "I'm so sorry." Her head tilted toward the ground, too ashamed to look up at him.

"David, meet Brittany Green, the second smartest person in the world." Halaq smiled as he cut her bonds and took her hand in his.

"You developed the same gift as your brother?" David questioned, tilting his head to the side.

Brittany nodded slowly before responding. "Marcus prevented me from using it."

"Lana seemed to think that the gifts you later acquired would be gone as soon as the drug wore off," Halaq replied. "I'd like to think she was right."

"I can still sense you—both of you—but my hunting abilities seem to be gone."

"So you can remember everything then?" David asked. "I mean, from before and after what happened with Marcus."

"Yes, I remember everything I did," she whispered. "I'm sorry, David."

"For what?" He laughed lightly.

"For almost killing you." She bit her lip lightly. "We should get moving—we don't want to arrive after the sun comes up."

"Are you alright to walk?" Halaq asked, placing his hand under her chin and tilting her head up toward his. "Or do I need to carry you again?"

"I can walk on my own, you jackass." She winked. "I can see better than you at night, and if anything, I should be carrying you."

"That's my girl." He smiled brightly. "Do as the lady said, David—get moving." He gestured for David to lead the way, waiting for him to start walking away before he leaned down to kiss Brittany's lips.

"Admiri's mine," she whispered angrily as they started following after David.

"I think I hold as much stake in his death as you." He laughed.

⁂

Jameson stood at the Athena port, watching the sky to see if Reem had made it back yet. He knew she would pass by here at some point, but he didn't know if she had already arrived in the city. With her gifts out of control, even he didn't know for certain what she would do. Most likely, she would attempt to destroy Marcus's army and exhaust herself in the process—he only hoped that the process wouldn't kill her along the way.

He stayed there until he could stay no longer. He teleported, landing on the upper balcony of the tower where he could look out on the entire city. Seeing nothing, he ran down the steps to find Seth standing in the central chamber.

"Jameson?" Seth said, his eyebrows furrowing. "What are you doing here?"

"Is she here yet?" he asked.

"Who?"

"Good—she will be soon." He nodded slowly, his breathing uneven and heavy as he walked around in a circle, unsure of what to do while he waited. "How is my daughter?"

"She's fine," Seth replied, taking hold of Jameson's arm and preventing him from continuing to pace. "What's going on?"

He shook his head slowly. "I only know that Reem's gifts are no longer under her control." He paused, his eyes growing grave. "Inara murdered Suri. It wasn't supposed to happen this way."

"What *was* supposed to happen, Jameson?" Seth's eyes pierced into his.

"I gave myself a healing gift a few days ago. Suri wasn't supposed to go with Reem—I was. Suri saw them coming in a vision." He ran his fingers through his hair nervously. "Inara was supposed to kill me—not literally of course. We knew that Marcus would want me dead, but the healing gift would have prevented that from happening. Suri didn't know about our plan." He shook his head. "I suppose she thought she was helping."

"You should have told me about this," Seth replied.

"We didn't want to endanger anyone but ourselves. Reem couldn't live with herself if something happened to any of you," he whispered. "But now her lack of control could kill her. Her gifts were always too strong for her—even with the control that I gave her. When she saw what was supposed to be my dead body lying there . . . she completely lost control, Seth"—tears formed in his eyes—"and I don't know how to help her."

"We'll find a way." Seth nodded slowly. "I won't let her die."

"Neither will I," he whispered. "Where is Eliza?"

"In the nursery with Nicholas." He gestured toward the hallway.

Jameson nodded and hurried down the hall, needing to hold his child in his arms again before he was forced to watch his wife kill herself. He knew there was nothing he could do for Reem at this point—she would attempt to destroy all that Marcus had built up against them, or she would die trying. He'd seen the look in her eyes when she'd propelled herself away from him, seen the look of fear when she realized she'd lost control; and he knew as well as she that once that control was gone, there would be no way to get it back. Reem would die to avenge her sister, and there was nothing anyone could do to stop it.

He hurriedly stepped through the doorway, surprising Nicholas as he did so. "Is she asleep?" he whispered, seeing his daughter in Nicholas's arms.

"Almost," Nicholas whispered back, his eyebrows furrowing at the look of urgency on Jameson's face. "How long have you been back?"

"Not long." He stepped closer and took Eliza from his arms. "Thank you for caring for her."

"Where are Reem and Suri?" Nicholas asked, ignoring Jameson's statement. "Are they alright?"

"Reem will be here soon," Jameson whispered, smiling gravely as Eliza opened her eyes.

"And Suri is with her?" he asked, worry and fear written on his face.

"I'm sorry, Nicholas." He shook his head. "I did all I could."

"And yet Reem still lives?" he shouted, causing Eliza to cry. "Why is it that the woman I love dies while yours lives, Jameson? Why?"

"Quiet, Nicholas!" Jameson snapped, rocking back and forth as he tried to calm the child in his arms. "Reem will die along with her before long, don't worry."

"What?" he whispered, stepping back in shock. "She what?"

"She lost control, Nicholas. You of all people know what that means," he whispered back. "She's going to kill herself."

"We won't let that happen, Jameson," he replied. "She doesn't deserve to die like that."

"And how exactly do you expect to prevent it?" Jameson asked.

"We'll find a way." He nodded slowly.

"There is no way to save her!" he whispered harshly, still trying to calm Eliza.

Death

Alexander sat up in the dim morning light, his body aching from near exhaustion. Beside him, Ryan stared wordlessly at the makeshift grave he'd made for his friend. He hated to see the man in such despair, hated to think that he had caused that despair, but he knew that there was nothing he could have done. There was nothing to be done.

He turned toward the desert, away from the scene beside him. Just ahead stood David, Halaq, and the witch of Admiri, all approaching at a heady pace. He quickly stood and walked toward them, needing to get away from the man who mourned on the desert floor.

"It is good to see you again, Halaq," he said as he approached them.

"And you." Halaq smiled. "I take it you're well?"

"I am, yes"—he nodded—"but I'm afraid Robert was not so lucky. He took a bullet to the chest when we were making our way out of the settlement."

"We will mourn his loss." Halaq dipped his head.

Alexander's eyebrows furrowed as he noticed the witch's fingers entwined with Halaq's. "What did I miss?" he asked, tilting his head toward their hands as his eyes stared into Halaq's.

"Nothing of great importance," Halaq replied. "She's with me—that is all you need to know."

He nodded, turning away from them. "When will we make our move on the city?"

"As soon as we are rested," Brittany replied. "There is not much time to waste."

Alexander turned back and leaned in to whisper in Halaq's ear, "Are you sure we can trust her? She's Admiri's witch."

"As I said, she's with me," Halaq said. "We'll rest for an hour, and then we make our move on the tower. Can you teleport us in?"

"Yes, sir." Alexander nodded. "I'm not sure how willing Ryan will be though," he added, turning to look at the man who still knelt beside his friends' grave. "He's suffered a great loss."

"We'll leave him behind if need be," Brittany replied.

"Let's hope it doesn't come to that," Halaq added, releasing Brittany's hand and stepping closer to the outer wall of the city as he spoke. "For now, it's time we get some rest." He leaned back against the wall and slid down to the ground, motioning for Brittany to join him.

She smiled brightly and walked up beside him, easing down to the ground and leaning her head on his shoulder. "Can I ask you a question?" she whispered.

"Of course," he replied, turning to kiss the top of her head as he linked his fingers with hers.

"Why do they call you Halaq?" She paused.

"I needed a new name after Marcus let me go." He shrugged, lying down in the sand. "Halaq was as good as any."

"Knowing you, there has to be a reason." She laughed lightly as she pulled his head into her lap. "So what is it?"

"You really don't remember, do you?" He smiled up into her white eyes. "You chose it."

"I don't remember ever calling you Halaq." Her eyebrows furrowed as she shook her head.

"Remember the day before you lost your sight?" he asked, reaching up to stroke her cheek. "I know it was a long time ago, but I'm sure you can remember."

She smiled and closed her eyes as the memory came back to her. "Marcus was always barely a step behind us, so we decided to change our names. We wanted names that no one would recognize . . . I decided that your name should be Halaq, and you said mine should be Rachelle," she whispered, running her fingers through his hair as she spoke.

"I still think we should go by those names as long as we're outside of Athena," he replied. "It's still not safe."

"As soon as Marcus is dead, it will be safe," she replied. "And I will kill him, Phillip. I will."

"He's mine to kill," he whispered.

"I think we should cross that bridge when we come to it," Alexander replied as he and David approached them.

"What's our plan once we enter the tower?" Ryan asked as he joined them, his face hard and stern in his new resolve.

Alexander teleported into the main chamber, his eyes scanning the room. The others stood around him in a circle, facing away with their weapons pointed outward toward the group of new soldiers that were arriving. Before anyone could react to their arrival, they started shooting, taking out anyone that wasn't familiar.

Soon they were the only ones left in the room, and Halaq gave the signal for them to split up.

Alexander then tapped Ryan's shoulder and signaled for him to lead the way to the dungeon where Reem and Suri were likely being held. Ryan then took point, scanning side to side, up and down, as he made his way down the staircase with Alexander and David behind him.

At the bottom of the steps, they found the dungeon door, locked tight with no guard holding the key. Ryan turned and nodded to the others before reeling back and sending his fist into the door, knocking it to the ground in a single blow.

"What took you so long, you fools?" a female voice shouted from inside the dungeon. "I've been trapped down here for hours because of your stupidity!"

"It's Inara," Ryan whispered to the others before Alexander stepped through the door, aiming his weapon directly at her as she approached.

"Kneel before your Superior," she said, assuming that they were reinforcements that Marcus had ordered.

"I kneel before no one," Alexander replied, stepping closer and pressing the barrel of his pistol between her eyes. "Where is Reem Kahrin?"

"You won't harm me, rebel scum," she spat, slapping his gun out of her face. "I will tell you nothing."

Alexander turned away from her, unable to point his weapon toward her anymore. He looked toward the open cell, shocked when he saw Suri's body lying on the ground. In his anger, he found the strength to lift his weapon once again, pointing it straight between Inara's eyes.

"Drop your weapon, teleporter," she ordered, smiling when his fingers released the weapon and let it fall to the ground.

"What are you waiting for?" he whispered. "Kill me."

"I have no quarrel with you," she replied. "None of you will harm myself or my lord," she added as she stepped past them and walked up the steps to the main chamber.

⚜

Brittany and Halaq waited outside Marcus's chambers, listening as he ordered his guards to protect him from whatever awaited outside. He had obviously heard the raucous in the main chamber and likely knew what was coming for him. They'd been waiting only a few moments when they'd heard him ordering his men to guard certain parts of the room—making their job much easier.

Halaq picked up a gun off the floor next to one of the dead recruits, following Brittany's example, before they both burst into Marcus's chambers, open firing on anything that moved, focusing on the areas where they knew Marcus's guards would be. In less than a minute, all of the new guards were dead around him as he sat in his throne.

"Miss me?" Brittany asked as she drew a knife from a sheath on her side and threw it at him, embedding it in the wooden chair beside his head. "You know my aim is better than that. I could have killed you with a thought all these years, Marcus."

"You don't want to kill me, Brittany," he replied evenly.

"Yes, I do," she whispered. "You couldn't handle the fact that your wife didn't love you anymore, so you drugged me and forced me into your bed!" she shouted as she stepped closer to him. "I have always wanted you dead! Even when I lay beside you, I wished that you would die."

Marcus shouted as he stood and took the knife from his throne, quickly reaching out and twisting Brittany around, holding the knife against her throat while Halaq stared on from a distance, pointing his weapon toward the both of them.

"You know that won't stop me, Marcus," Halaq said, dropping his weapon as he stepped forward, his eyes turning black as he made his approach. "I need no weapon," he whispered.

"Your advancements are unstable, Phillip. You can't kill me," Marcus snapped. "You would die if you tried."

"Try me," he whispered, stepping closer as his black eyes pierced into Marcus's. "You healed me, remember?"

Marcus's eyes widened as Halaq siphoned the air from his body. He released his hold on the knife, and Brittany snagged it from the air before it could hit the ground, swinging around to stab him in the chest. "Goodbye, Marcus," she whispered in his ear as she wrenched the knife around and pulled it from his bleeding wound.

Halaq stepped up to them and took the knife from Brittany's hands, letting it fall to the ground beside Marcus's dead body. "It is done then," he whispered.

"My lord?" Inara whispered as she stepped into the room. "What have you done?" She ran to Marcus's side, pushing the couple out of her way. "Leave us," she ordered.

Halaq and Brittany left the room, unable to disobey Inara's direct order. They walked into the main chamber where they found David and Ryan whispering to each other while Alexander ascended the staircase with Suri's body in his arms.

"This is Reem's sister?" Halaq asked.

"Yes," Alexander whispered. "This is Suri Kahrin."

"We should take her to her sister," Brittany whispered as she walked up to Alexander. "She deserves a decent burial." She reached out her hand and closed Suri's eyes.

"Is it done?" David asked, gesturing toward Marcus's chambers.

"It is." Halaq nodded. "We should be on our way before Inara decides to kill us."

Alexander nodded slowly and everyone placed their hands on his shoulders before he teleported them out of the city.

As they teleported out, Inara stepped back into the main chamber, screaming out her frustration that she had let them go. She'd wanted Marcus dead, yes, but not until after the failure at Athena. She needed the people to see how weak Marcus was before she took control over the Advanced. If they thought that she was the weak one, they would never follow her. She deserved to be followed, but they needed to see that for themselves. They needed to see Marcus fail before they would follow her.

Lana quietly passed Inara in the main chamber, hoping that she wasn't too late. Inara hadn't seen her when she entered the room, and hopefully, she wouldn't notice her until it was time to shift again. She passed by all of the bodies that lay on the ground, thankful that she hadn't been here to see the carnage. Many had been shot through the heart or head, but more still had been ripped apart under some unknown force. She didn't know what could have caused this much damage, but it certainly wasn't Halaq and the men who followed him. None of them had abilities that would make them capable of crushing a man's head and ripping it from his body. Ryan had the strength to do so, yes, but he had not the heart. He was not a killer.

She walked inside Marcus's chambers, searching for the body that she knew would be among the many dead. His guards lay dead all around the room, shot through the heart by Halaq and through the head by his lover—she knew their signatures well by now. She gasped when she finally saw him, the blood starting to dry on the gaping wound in his chest. It looked as though someone had stabbed him and twisted the blade while it was still in his body—she'd never wanted him to feel so much pain in death. She ran to his side and wiped his hair from his forehead, checking his body for signs of life.

"Marcus," she whispered as she pulled his dying body into her lap. "Marcus, wake up."

His eyes slowly opened to look into hers with happiness she hadn't seen on his face since before they'd started their work on the treatment. "Lana, is that you?" he whispered, coughing up blood as he spoke.

"Don't speak, Marcus," she replied. "I'm here now."

"I'm not ready to die."

"You weren't supposed to live this long." She laughed lightly. "But I'll see you in heaven, my love."

"You know I don't believe in heaven." He shook his head slowly.

"And you know I never believed that." She smiled. "I didn't betray you, Marcus. I helped you. I saw the future, and I changed the future." She paused. "I saved you, Marcus. This is a pleasant death compared to the one I saw before."

"I don't want to die," he whispered, a tear finding its way down his cheek.

"I'm already dead, remember?" she whispered, crying along with him. "I'll be right there for you when you die—I promise. I'm already there, waiting for you to join me." Her tears came full force as Marcus's head slumped back lifelessly.

"Get away from him," Inara ordered as she stepped back into the room. "Stand aside!"

Lana wiped the tears off her face as she stood and stepped away from Marcus's dead body, turning to look into Inara's enraged eyes. "It's not what you think," she whispered.

"It's exactly what I think," Inara snapped. "Pick up that knife." She gestured to the knife that lay beside Marcus's body. "Stab your heart."

"No." Lana shook her head. "It's time to go," she whispered as she reached for the blade, disappearing before she could wrap her fingers around the handle.

Inara screamed in frustration as a new wave of soldiers entered the tower, ready to protect Marcus Admiri. "You fools!" she screamed as three of the men entered Marcus's quarters. "Had you been here sooner, perhaps he wouldn't have died!" She paused. "Check the area—make sure none of them are left in the city."

"Yes, ma'am," the soldiers replied as they exited the room, leaving her alone with the bodies of Marcus and his personal guard. At least the fool of a leader was dead, and hopefully, she would be able to pick up the pieces to save her empire.

She was their Great Superior now.

She smiled wickedly when she saw Marcus's body at her feet, his dead eyes still betraying his only fear—death. The man had cheated his way out of dying for too long. It was only luck that he was dead now. Lucky for him too—she would have dragged the process out, killing him slowly over a period of days rather than minutes. He had no right to have lived so long when he himself was not even Advanced. He was a fraud and a trickster, and he was lucky to be dead at the hand of his wife than at the hand of his under Superior.

Leader

Reem stood atop the watchtower, waiting for Marcus's army to begin their approach. She knew they would be coming any moment now. She had only to wait until they did. She'd arrived just moments before, and she doubted that anyone had seen her arrival. Had anyone seen her, Jameson would have been standing on the top of this tower alongside her, begging her to let him help her regain control.

The truth was, she didn't want to regain control of her gifts. She loved letting go of all the power that ran through her veins. It was a liberating feeling, being able to let loose the gifts that had her bound for so long. Yes, Jameson had helped her in using less concentration to control her gifts, but it still required almost constant concentration not to allow them to take control of her body.

When she'd seen Suri's body lying dead on the ground instead of Jameson's, she'd finally had enough. In her grief, she let go, and the rage that coursed through her veins began to consume her. Why had Suri been there in the first place? Did she think that Reem had not told her husband and developed a plan to combat her vision? She should not have been so rash in her decision making—now she was dead for the mistake.

She could feel the rage growing as she remembered seeing her sister's body lying lifeless on the ground of that cell, morphed from what had once been Jameson's form. She could scarcely believe that her sister was dead. She wasn't supposed to die that way—she wasn't even supposed to have left Athena. She should have been taking care of Eliza, not trying to prove a point about not keeping secrets.

Reem let her anger continue to grow, though she knew that it was draining what little energy she had left. She would need to conserve it if she was going to kill all of Admiri's army, but at the moment, she didn't care. All she wanted was the power to bring her sister back from the grave—a power that had only been heard of in myths.

There was nothing to be done for Suri, but Reem would have her revenge nonetheless.

Jameson paced the length of the nursery, cradling Eliza in his arms as he fed her from one of the bottles Suri had found. He hated to think that he would be caring for the little one on his own for the rest of her life.

He'd been back in the city for over twelve hours now and still had seen no signs of Reem. He knew that she would be arriving within minutes—if she hadn't already arrived. He had no doubt that Reem could have arrived under the radar, knowing that he would be looking for her by now. She knew that he would have returned to the city faster than she possibly could have, and she knew that he would try to stop her from destroying Admiri's army. He had to believe that she still had enough sense to hide from him, because that would mean that she had enough sense to listen when he tried to talk her out of killing herself.

He didn't want to raise Eliza on his own—and Eliza didn't deserve to grow up motherless.

"We've just received word," Seth said as he entered the room. "Admiri's army is on its way."

"Which means if Reem isn't here already, she soon will be," Jameson replied, setting Eliza down in her crib. "Have there been any sightings?"

"Not as of yet, no. But we didn't think we should alert the people about the situation, so she could have slipped in under the radar," he replied, nodding slowly. "I'll send out a team to search for her."

Jameson smiled slightly. "If she is here, I think I know where she'll be."

"Where? I'll send a team to support you."

"No, I only have one person I need," he whispered. "Find Nicholas. Tell him to meet me here as soon as possible."

"Jameson, he's running the hospital," Seth replied. "I don't know how soon he'll be able to—"

"Then I'll go get him." He shrugged.

"No, don't waste your energy." Seth held his hands up in defense. "I'll tell him to meet you."

Jameson nodded as Seth left the room, quickly making his way to the makeshift underground hospital where Nicholas was preparing for war.

Alexander carefully wrapped the soft fabric around Suri's lifeless form, knowing that she would be receiving her funeral once they reached Athena. He hoped that they would have time to grieve for her before the fighting started.

By now, Inara had likely taken control of Admiri's army and ordered them to go ahead on the attack. The only trouble with leaving her alive was that now she was the sole Superior, and her word was the final word. Some people had said that this was like choosing the lesser of two evils, but Alexander wasn't so sure that was the case. He'd spoken with her long enough in the city, and he knew that she could hold her own.

That woman was even more of a witch than Brittany—who seemed to be a completely different person than she was a few days ago. Even now she was laughing and smiling as she spoke with Halaq and David in the next room—something that the witch of Admiri would never do. The rumors had it that Brittany had never once truly smiled in her time as Admiri's servant. She was well known to have the coldest of hearts and to have been the most ruthless killer known to man, but now he wasn't so sure that the rumors weren't intended for Inara.

Tears slipped past his cheek as he started to cover Suri's face with the cloth. He wished that he could have seen her smiling eyes just one last time before she'd died—no, he wished that he had gotten there sooner or that Jameson and Reem would have kept her alive. It wasn't her time to die.

He gently laid her head back on the table and set the cloth down next to it, not wanting to cover the beautiful face that slept peacefully in front of him. He ran his fingers through his hair as the tears flowed full force, not caring who was listening as he wept for Suri Kahrin.

"Are you alright?" Brittany whispered as she stepped into the room.

He shook his head, unable to reply as he wept.

"Go sit down," she whispered, lightly placing her hand on his shoulder. "I'll finish here."

"Thank you," he whispered back, stepping back to lean against the wall while Brittany gently lifted Suri's head off the table and started wrapping the cloth around it.

Once she finished, she joined Alexander beside the wall, staring at the body that lay on the table before them. "She was a beautiful woman," she whispered. "I'm sorry for your loss."

He nodded slowly, not knowing how to respond to her words. "She was perfect," he replied.

"How long had you known her?" she asked.

"A few months," he replied. "We met on the Admiri port." He smiled as he remembered watching Suri on the docks, searching for a boat willing to take her across to the Athena port. "I helped her get to Athena before I made my way up to Old Canada."

"And you fell in love?" She smiled.

"Something like that, yes." He laughed lightly. "We grew very close to each other during that short time, but I fell in love before she did."

"Well, I'd like to think that the sister of Reem Kahrin wouldn't give her heart away so quickly," she whispered. "But she chose a great man."

"I'm not so sure." He shook his head.

"No one could have known what would happen over that time, Alexander, believe me," she replied. "Marcus Admiri changed his mind more times than he blinked."

"I'd heard he had a very one-track mind," he replied.

"That's what he would have everyone believe," she said. "But I knew him better than most."

"What happened to you? If you don't mind me asking," he asked, turning to look her in the eye.

"It's a long story." She shook her head. "One better told when we don't have a war brewing."

He nodded. "I can teleport us all to the docks, but we'll have to wait a few hours there before we make our way across."

"If you need to stay here longer, the Purists don't seem to mind." She smiled. "Halaq doesn't mind either."

"If we stayed here another day, I could teleport us straight across the ocean"—he paused—"but I don't know that I want to stare at her body for that long."

"I understand." She nodded. "Whatever you decide, we will follow you."

"Thank you, Brittany." The corners of his mouth turned up slightly.

"I'll leave you alone," she whispered as he turned back toward Suri's lifeless form. "You'll need to make a decision soon." She paused, turning back toward him. "I thought you'd like to know—Ryan's decided to stay behind. He says he has unfinished business in the city, and he'll meet us in Athena in a few weeks."

He nodded slowly as she exited the room, almost wishing that she hadn't left him alone.

She walked back to the front of Halaq's home where he and David stood watching the sunset. Quietly, she stepped up behind Halaq and wrapped her arms around his waist, bringing her lips to the back of his neck. "Miss me?" she whispered.

"Desperately." He laughed lightly as he pulled her into his arms.

"Alexander's deciding how he wants to do this," she said loud enough for both David and Halaq to hear. "He says we have two options: we either stay here another day and teleport across the ocean from here, or we teleport to the docks and wait a few hours there before going on."

"And he doesn't want to spend more time with the body than necessary." David nodded. "I don't blame him."

"Neither do I," Halaq whispered.

Brittany closed her eyes and leaned her head on Halaq's shoulder, breathing into his neck. "I can't imagine going through that," she whispered.

"Unfortunately, I can," he whispered back, tightening his arms around her.

Inara waited in her new chambers—the chambers of the Great Superior—for her new guard to introduce her to the people. It was time that she told them of the changes she was making in the way of life in the city. The people would do as she wanted, and no one would leave without her express invitation to do so.

For now, the people needed to know that she was not as weak as they thought. When she'd moved here from Athena, it was under the guise that she had issues with authority, and she needed to prove that she had no trouble with any such things. She needed to show them that she was the Superior that they needed—the Superior that would win the war against the rebels.

She slowly paced along the balcony doorway, waiting for the guards to finish assembling the people and prepare them for her speech. She knew exactly what she wanted to say, knew exactly how to make it seem like she was the better Superior; yet for some reason, she was still concerned of the outcome of her first speech.

Of course, she could use her gifts to make them follow her; but for some reason, that seemed like cheating. Besides that, the moment they were out of her sight, they would be better able to find the loophole in her gifts—and she couldn't have that. They needed to see that she was strong without the use of her gifts.

"It's time," the guard whispered through the door. "They're waiting for you."

She took a deep breath and stepped outside, her face stern and serious as she addressed her people. "I am your Great Superior," she shouted. "I am the one you worship—the one you obey." The people stood on silently, still not convinced. "Marcus Admiri was weak! He sent a team to the Purist settlement to retrieve his beloved mistress, the witch, Brittany Green. This was his downfall. The team failed, and his mistress returned and killed him in his throne." Her eyes burned into theirs. "He was too weak to save himself from her—too weak to prevent her from destroying all that he worked so hard to build!" She paused for effect, lifting her hands in triumph. "I am the only survivor of the attack on the tower. I am stronger than your old Superiors. I survived when none else could do so! I drove the rebels out of the tower and prevented them from killing any more of our people! I saved your lives from the rebel scum who would destroy all that you have without a thought!" Her voice echoed through the throngs of people that stood before her. "I am your Superior, and I will bring us to victory against the rebels!"

The people cheered as she ended her speech, resting her hands on the banister of the balcony. She could see that she had their support as many of them shouted their full allegiance to her and her alone. She was their Great Superior now—and she would bring them to victory.

"My lady," her guard whispered as he fell to his knees beside her, "I will follow you and you alone."

She placed her hand on top of his dipped head as she watched the throngs of people following his example, falling to their knees in reverence as she looked on. She smiled wickedly as she watched them, knowing that she now had their complete support and devotion. There was no one on this earth that could prevent her from destroying the rebels and all that they stood for. This world belonged to her now, and she would do with it as she would.

Injection

Reem waited patiently atop the tower while the army slowly made their approach on Athena. She wished that Marcus would come here himself so that she could slaughter him, but she knew he would stay holed up in his city where he thought he was safe. She let out a heavy sigh as she watched his army, knowing that her chances to kill him herself were now at a bare minimum.

Suri deserved to be avenged—she hadn't deserved to die in the first place. Had she just resisted her impulses and stayed in Athena, she would be alive right now. Their plan would have allowed for everyone to live.

The army was just starting to make their final approach now, and her army was ready. She'd looked all around her and seen the best of her army readying themselves from the moment that the Admirians were in range. She'd watched them train for days before this, and she knew that they were ready for anything that Admiri threw at them. After all, they had the advantage. They were on their home soil, they knew the lay of the land, and they had the Humans on their side.

They'd kept their alliance with the Humans secret from even the people in Athena, just in case they had a spy who was relaying information to Admiri. Even now as the Admirians made their approach, the Humans were behind them to take them out from the rear. Admiri's army was surrounded, and they didn't even know it—that is, so long as the Humans kept their word. She had a sneaking feeling that some of them weren't so keen on fighting on the side of the Purists and the rebelling Advanced. After all, they hadn't given the Humans much of anything to form the alliance—only the promise that any information they gained on the treatment would be given directly to the Human scientists.

"Reem, you don't have to do this," Jameson said as he climbed to the top of the tower behind her. "You don't want to do this."

She stood and turned to face him, her face hard as stone as she stared into his tear-filled eyes. "Leave me alone, Jameson," she ordered.

He shook his head. "I know you won't hurt me." He shrugged, reaching out to take her hand in his.

She pulled her hand away, shifting her weight as she slid off the roof, keeping herself upright with the help of her gifts. "You have no right to stop me," she snapped.

"I'm your husband," he replied. "I have every right to stop you."

"Stay away from me!" she shrieked as he stepped closer to the edge of the roof.

⁂

Alexander lifted Suri's limp form off the table, slowly making his way back into the front room where the others were preparing their things. He decided that it made more sense to teleport to the docks and wait until he was fully able to cross the ocean rather than risk teleporting all the way across in one jump.

Inside, he found Brittany and Halaq holding hands as they leaned against the outside wall while David crouched down in the doorway. "You're sure this is what you want?" Brittany asked as he stepped into the room. "We can wait here a few more hours if you'd rather."

"No." He shook his head. "We should go now. It's safer this way."

"Alright then," Halaq said, "we should be on our way."

"Yes, sir," Alexander said, nodding. "I'm ready when you are."

Brittany stepped closer to Alexander, still holding on to Halaq's hand as she placed her free hand on Alexander's shoulder. "David?"

"Of course," David replied, standing to his feet and approaching the teleporter. He cautiously placed his hand beside Brittany's only seconds before they teleported, landing on the beach near the Admiri port. "Beautiful day," he whispered, noting the clear sunny sky and thundering waves.

"How long until we can move on?" Halaq asked, earning himself a spiteful glare from Brittany. "What?" he asked her, shrugging his shoulders.

"A few hours—twelve at most," Alexander replied, dropping to his knees to gently place Suri's body on the ground in front of him. "I'm sorry I cannot return you to your sister sooner, my love," he whispered, tears snaking their way down his cheeks.

"Give him time," Brittany whispered to the others.

David nodded and slowly made his way up the beach, wanting to be alone, while Alexander grieved and the couple spoke of things that no one else could possibly understand. He'd known that none of them were the same as they were before they'd left—after all, they already had to bury one of their own, and another had stayed behind in the settlement with a plan to kill as many people as he could in Admiri before being caught.

Brittany pulled Halaq's arm and led him down the beach in the opposite direction, knowing that he would want to be alone just as much as Alexander. Once she found a suitable spot, she dropped to her seat in the sand, pulling Halaq down beside her. "I don't know what more can be done for him until we reach the city," she whispered.

"Have you ever thought that he might just need the time alone?" Halaq asked, smiling as he turned to wink at her.

"I've seen it in his eyes. He doesn't want to be alone," she whispered. "He wants to have her back in his arms, even if he has to be dead for that to happen."

"You think he's suicidal?" His eyebrows rose.

"Not yet, no." She shook her head. "But if he continues down the road he's on, he soon will be." She turned to look toward the ocean waves. "I don't want to see that happen to him."

"Neither do I," he whispered as he coiled his arms around her and pulled her into his lap.

"Right now, I think the only one who can help him is Suri's sister." She shrugged, leaning her head against his chest. "Until we reach the city, there's not much to be done."

"We'll be there soon."

"I hope it's soon enough," she whispered, rubbing her side lightly.

"Are you alright?" he asked, taking her hands in his. "Are you in pain?"

"Nothing I can't handle." She smiled slightly. "Don't worry about me."

"What's wrong?" he asked as she turned away from him. "Tell me, Brittany."

"I thought my name was Rachelle," she said, laughing.

"Don't change the subject," he ordered, reaching out to turn her face back toward his. "Tell me what's wrong."

"It's nothing, Phillip," she whispered. "I would tell you if it was serious."

"Tell me anyway," he replied.

"I have a couple of broken ribs—nothing that a healer couldn't fix," she replied quickly, nervously turning away from him again.

"Is that all?" he asked. "Please, Brittany. Talk to me."

"It's nothing, I promise."

"You're lying," he whispered as he moved to kneel in front of her. "Tell me," he ordered, staring into her white eyes. "Tell me."

Her eyes filled with tears as she lifted her shirt to show him her abdomen, the injection site red and inflamed. "I don't know what it is," she whispered.

"Lay back," he ordered, reaching out to touch the injection site. "When did this happen?"

She closed her eyes, wincing in pain as his fingers brushed over the wound. "It was Marcus," she replied. "I didn't notice it until after we were in the Purist settlement."

"Damn it!" he shouted, standing up and kicking the sand at his feet. "Damn you, Marcus Admiri!"

"Phillip, Phillip, please," she whispered. "Calm down. I'll be fine." She carefully stood to her feet beside him, taking his hands in hers. "We'll reach Athena soon, and I'll get a healer," she told him. "I'll be fine."

"What's wrong?" David asked as he slowly approached them.

"Not now, David," Halaq snapped, his eyes momentarily shifting toward his.

"I'm sorry for that," Brittany said as she turned to face David. "Halaq is clearly overreacting." She paused, feeling Halaq's hands on her waist, lifting her shirt for David to see what Marcus had done.

"Marcus injected her with something," Halaq told him. "We don't know what it is, and we don't know how long it will take for it to finish the job."

"I can teleport her to the city in an hour," Alexander replied as he joined them. "I can't take all of us across, but I can at least get her to a healer."

"No, I can wait," Brittany replied. "I don't need you to take me ahead of the others."

"Thank you, Alexander," Halaq said, ignoring Brittany's comment. "David and I can take a boat across the ocean and meet you in Athena in a few days."

"And what about Suri?" Brittany asked, searching for a way to change the current course of events. "The body won't last long enough for you to take a boat across."

Alexander shrugged. "It's living people that are the challenge. It won't be difficult to take her along."

"Thank you," Halaq repeated as he firmly wrapped his arms around Brittany. "I am indebted to you."

"I'm not going," Brittany replied as she struggled to free herself from his grasp. "I won't go without you, Phillip."

"Yes, you will," he whispered in her ear. "For me, Brittany. Please."

"No, I won't go without you," she whispered. "You can't force me."

"Give us a moment," Halaq told the others.

"You have an hour." Alexander nodded as he and David made their way back up the beach away from the couple.

"Brittany, I can't sit here all night wondering if you will survive or not," he said as he stared into her eyes. "I need you to go with Alexander."

"I will not go with him," she replied.

"Reem, I beg you, come back," Jameson whispered, holding out his hand toward her.

"Why should I?" she snapped. "You did nothing for my sister—how should I know that you'll do any better for me?" Her dark eyes stared into his, and he almost didn't recognize her under the control of her gifts, bound to do their will.

"You are my wife," he replied. "I would never do anything to hurt you, Reem." He reached out his hand to her, and she drifted farther out into the open air. He could see the strain of using her gifts written on her face, but he could do nothing to help her until she came back to him.

"Stay away from me!" she shrieked once again. "You are not the man I married."

"Then who am I?" he asked, keeping his voice low and even so as not to startle her.

"My husband would have at least tried to save my sister!" she yelled, her eyes turning silver in her anger. "My husband would not have stood by and allowed her to die!"

"I had no choice, Reem. By the time I realized what happened, she was already dead," he said, continuing to stare straight into her eyes though she threatened to take his gifts away.

"Liar!" she shouted, using her gifts to knock him farther away from her. "Stay away from me."

"Reem, please! You don't want to do this!" he shouted as rain began to pour from the sky. "Think of your daughter if nothing else."

"She is not my daughter," she whispered, her hatred and fear clear on her face as she turned away from him toward the army that approached.

"How can you think that?" he asked, watching as Admiri's army made their approach. "You gave birth to her, Reem!" he shouted.

"You killed my sister!" she shouted at the top of her lungs.

Jameson moved to respond when her gifts started to tear apart the army that stood before them. He watched as the soldiers one by one began to fall to the ground, their bodies crushed under the force of her gifts. "No! Don't do this, Reem!" he shouted.

"Don't try and stop me, Jameson," she whispered. "I don't know what I might do."

<hr>

Nicholas stood inside the watchtower, listening as Jameson tried to talk Reem down. He didn't know why Jameson had asked him to wait here, but he knew that Jameson wouldn't have asked him unless it was completely necessary. Even now he could hear them arguing on the roof, and he could see Reem's feet hovering in midair.

He turned to look out at the approaching army when they suddenly began to fall to the ground under the supreme force of Reem's power. He knew that she was one of the most powerful Advanced that ever existed, but even she had limits that should have prevented her from killing them. He could hear Jameson urging her to come back to him, hear her cursing the day she met him, hear everything they said to each other, and knew that his part would come soon.

Soon Reem's gifts would get the better of her, and she would plummet to her death—unless Jameson could manage to coax her back onto the roof. The only problem seemed to be that Reem's gifts had complete control over her body and mind, preventing her from seeing reason. The Reem he knew would never curse the day she met her husband—she was completely and utterly in love with him, and she would do nothing to hurt him.

"Oh, Reem," he whispered as he watched the army fall to the ground before him, knowing that her body would soon collapse under the strain. "Why are you doing this?" he breathed as he leaned over the balcony to get a better look at what was going on above him.

He watched for several long minutes, his eyes glancing back and forth between the collapsing soldiers and the feet dangling above him, until suddenly, the feet were gone. He watched helplessly as Reem was falling in front of him; and he reached his arms out to grab on to her shirt, only to watch as she continued to fall through the air.

Rescue

Brittany lay on the sandy shore of the beach, her body covered in sweat, though the wind made the area quite cool. Her breathing was labored, and her fever was high, likely due to the injection Marcus had given her, though she didn't know for sure.

"You're leaving," Halaq ordered as he wiped her brow with a small cloth. "I don't care if you think you can make it. Alexander can have you in Athena in minutes, and that's where the healers are. You're not leaving me again."

"Please, Phillip," she whispered between breaths. "Please don't make me leave you."

"I'm not," he replied. "I'll meet you in a few days. David already found a boat to take us across—we can leave as soon as we're ready." He kissed her forehead lightly. "Please do this. For me."

"I don't want to leave without you." She shook her head slowly, reaching her hand out to stroke his cheek. "I won't."

"Brittany, I need you to go with Alexander," he whispered. "You're not going to last much longer without a healer."

"No." She shook her head. "Please, Phillip." She closed her eyes, unable to stay conscious any longer.

Halaq picked her up in his arms, carrying her to where Alexander waited beside Suri's body. He carefully set her down beside the man and nodded that she was ready to go. "She's asleep," he whispered. "She can't protest when she's unconscious."

"You're sure about this?" Alexander laughed lightly. "She doesn't want to go without you."

"Just take her—I need to know that she's going to be alright," he replied, anxiously running his fingers through his hair. "Go."

Alexander nodded and teleported, taking Brittany and Suri with him. When he landed, he was near the underground in Athena, rain immediately drenching all of their bodies. "I need a healer!" he shouted, lifting Brittany's body off the ground. "She needs medical attention!"

"What's happened?" Edwin asked as he approached them from the underground hospital. "My name is Edwin. I'm a healer. Who is she?" he asked as he led Alexander down into the hospital.

"Her name is Brittany Green—the Prophet's sister—and she was injected in her abdomen with some unknown toxin by Marcus Admiri," Alexander replied as he laid her body on one of the beds. "Can you help her?"

"I'll do everything I can." He smiled.

"Thank you," Alexander replied, stepping back to allow him to do his work.

Edwin lifted up Brittany's shirt to see the injection site, placing his hand on the wound as he sent his healing powers from his body into hers.

⁂

Halaq paced the width of the small boat, hating not knowing what was happening to Brittany. He knew Alexander would have gotten her there as quickly as he possibly could, and he knew that by now she was probably in the capable hands of a healer, but he still couldn't help but wonder what was happening to her.

All this because Marcus Admiri couldn't stand the fact that his wife had shared a bed with him. It wasn't as though Halaq had lured her into his bed. Marcus and Lana weren't even living with each other at the time—had it been possible, she would have divorced him—but he still hated Halaq for allowing that one night to happen.

If there was one night of his life that he could take away, it would be that night. If he hadn't allowed Lana to enter his room that night, none of this would have happened to the woman he truly loved.

"She's going to be fine," David said as Halaq passed him on the deck.

"I know, I know," Halaq replied, "but I can't help wondering if anything went wrong."

"If you were going to be like this, then maybe we should've just waited on the beach for Alexander to be able to take all of us to Athena." David laughed lightly. "Sit down."

"I can't sit down!" he snapped. "The last I saw, she was dying."

"By now, she's already in Athena, and there's a healer attending to her," David replied calmly. "She's going to be fine."

He smiled slightly. "I finally got her back, and already, she might be leaving me." He dropped his head into his hands as he settled to the floor.

"You're not going to lose her, my friend," he said. "She's with a healer—I haven't seen anything they could not heal."

"You're right," he said, sighing. "You're right. Thank you."

"You're welcome," he replied. "You should get some rest."

"I'll try," he whispered before standing up and walking down into the lower level.

"She'll be fine," David whispered to himself, remembering the pure beauty he'd found the first time he'd seen her face. He knew that he didn't have a chance with her—after all, she and Halaq had been in love for years—but he didn't want to see her die at the hands of Marcus Admiri.

He hoped that she would be all right, if only for Halaq's sake. It had taken him two hours to get Halaq downstairs—though he was likely still pacing. He needed rest, but the image of Brittany's frail form teleporting away with Alexander was the only thing on his mind, and it was preventing Halaq from getting the sleep he needed.

In two days, they would reach the Athena port; and from there, it would take a few hours to reach the city. Hopefully, once they reached the docks, Halaq would be less concerned and more excited about seeing her again. Brittany was in good hands by now, and soon she'd be healed and waiting for him to return to her side.

Soon David found himself pacing across the deck, deep in thought as he walked. It had been many days since he'd had the desire to pace as he once did, and he found it comforting to return to his old habits as he waited on the boat.

"Maybe you should be the one getting some rest." Halaq laughed lightly as he stepped back onto the deck. "Why the pacing?"

"I find it comforting," David replied. "My brother meditates, and I pace."

"I was unaware that you had a brother," he said as he leaned against the railing.

"His name's Mitchal." He smiled. "He was a part of the rebellion in Athena last I knew. I haven't seen him since I left there with Brittany."

"I'm sure you're looking forward to seeing him again," Halaq replied.

"Last I saw him, I told him he was dead to me."

"Then he'll be glad that you do not think that any longer," he said as he stood and placed his hand on David's shoulder, stopping him from continuing to pace along the deck. "You need rest as much as I do, my friend," he added when he saw the dark circles under David's eyes.

David laughed. "The sun will be down soon. I'll try and sleep once it's night."

Halaq nodded and took a seat on the deck, leaning against the railing. "I think I'll stay awake awhile longer."

✦✦✦

"Reem!" Jameson shouted as her eyes rolled back in her head and her body began to fall to the ground. He watched as Nicholas reached for her falling body and saw as his fingers barely missed her arm.

He teleported down just below where he'd last seen her, wrapping his arms around her unconscious body as quickly as he could before he teleported up into the tower where Nicholas awaited them. "Help her!" he shouted, clutching his leg in pain.

434

"Are you alright?" Nicholas asked as he ran back up the stairs toward them. "What happened?"

"I caught her before she hit the ground, but she's still overexhausted," Jameson replied. "We had a hard landing—you should check her for broken bones."

"Why?" Nicholas asked before he turned to see Jameson's broken right leg. "You need a healer as much as she does," he added.

"Help her!" he snapped. "Can you get her to the hospital yourself?"

"I don't think we should move her yet." He shook his head. "Get a healer up here, get yourself healed, and then come back and help me," he ordered as he checked Reem's body for signs of trauma.

"I can't go that far away from her for long," Jameson replied. "The hospital is on the other side of the city."

"I know," Nicholas snapped. "Just get down there and get yourself healed."

"How is she?" he asked, ignoring the order.

"She might have broken ribs. I can't tell yet. But she's extremely exhausted, and I think her gifts are still trying to destroy that army."

"I'll get help." Jameson nodded, teleporting to the hospital where he appeared on one of the beds, trying not to scream in pain from the movement of his leg. "I need two healers!" he shouted as he appeared.

"What happened?" one of the healers asked as he approached Jameson. "How did you break this?"

"I fell," Jameson replied, gritting his teeth against the pain. "Reem's in trouble—she's with Nicholas in one of the towers."

"We need to heal your leg before we can take you back there," the man replied. "Now tell me exactly what happened."

"Alexander!" Jameson shouted as he noticed the man standing a few beds down from him. "I need you to take a healer to Reem and Nicholas," he said as Alexander approached him. "They're in the farthest watchtower—Reem won't last much longer without a healer."

"Of course," Alexander replied, taking the hand of one of the healers and teleporting away.

He landed at the bottom of the tower and led the man up the steps to where he heard Nicholas talking to Reem. "What happened?" he asked as he and the healer reached the top of the steps.

"She has at least one broken rib, and she's extremely exhausted—enough to kill her," Nicholas replied. "Help me," he ordered the healer.

Inara waited in the main chamber for her guards to be assembled. She'd called for them to arrive as soon as possible so that they could escort her to Mettirna—it was time that the rebels lost some of their allies.

Her plan was to speak with the Superiors in Mettirna and convince them that they had made a mistake in siding with the rebels. Her gifts would be instrumental in gaining their trust and bringing them back to her side, and she had no doubt that after they spent even twenty minutes with her, they would be ready to rejoin the fight against the rebellion.

She knew that they were known to be tired and weary of war, but she needed them to be on her side. Without the Mettirnians support, the rebels wouldn't have enough allies to hold their own against her. At the moment, their allies consisted of the Purists and Mettirnians, along with some sort of agreement they currently held with the Humans around Athena—literally everyone, except for those who followed her.

But soon the Mettirnians would break their alliance with the rebels, and whatever few of them wanted to be part of this war would go to Athena, making Athena stand on its own without a place for their people to go if it was overrun. Their agreement with the Humans was strained at best, making it pointless for her to even worry about, but the alliance they held with the Purists would likely stay strong. There wasn't much she could do beyond breaking the alliance between Mettirna and Athena, but that one bold move would be a backbreaker for the rebels.

"How long?" she asked the guards. "We need to leave as soon as possible."

"Not long, my lady," her head guard, Daniel, replied. "We're just discussing the landing sites for the teleporters, and we'll be on our way."

"I want to be in Mettirna as soon as possible," she snapped.

"We will try our best, my lady." He dipped his head in reverence. "We have enough teleporters to get us there before the Athenians even know we've left."

"Good. See to it that I have enough protection from the Humans."

"We have as many men as can safely be teleported across the ocean, my lady," he replied. "I will not let anything happen to you."

"Thank you, Daniel." She smiled seductively. "Let me know when you are ready to leave."

"Of course, my lady." He took her hand and kissed it gently.

"Get to work," she snapped, pulling her hand away from him. He dipped his head once again and walked away from her as she turned and reentered Marcus's old chambers, stepping out onto the balcony, where she could look out on the people of the city. She was surprised how well they'd taken the recent shift in power, but then again, she knew that if any of them had trouble with her lead, they would simply leave for the rebellion. That was her one problem—the rebels continued to steal from her city, taking her most prized warriors for themselves.

Her new guard was promising, however. It seemed he was quite taken with her—she didn't even have to use her gifts on him at all. He appeared to be entirely under her control without her having to force him. In fact, if it was up to him, she had no doubt that he would rule underneath her, but it was possible that his desire to rule was the only reason that he was so taken. She was bending the world to her will, and if she decided that he was worthy to rule at her side, then he would—if not, he would continue to be her guard until he died in the service.

She smiled wickedly as she heard him stepping up behind her. It was time for them to leave. Mettirna had no idea what was in store for them—and neither did the rebels.

⚹🕉⚹

Edwin placed his hand on Brittany's abdomen for the third time, trying his hardest to draw out the poison that coursed through her veins. It seemed that this particular injection was almost impossible to remove with the gifts of a healer. He'd been attempting to heal her for hours now, but to no avail. He'd barely been able to remove what small amount of poison that he had, and by now he had no doubt that this particular poison was meant to be difficult for a healer to remove.

He knew that it would take more power than what he had coursing through his veins to heal her, but he also knew that a battle was brewing right outside the city walls, and they could spare no more healers on this one woman. On the bright side, their head physician wasn't a healer but a doctor of medicine and would hopefully know what to do for the woman who writhed in front of him.

A few beds down, Jameson lay waiting for the healer beside him to finish his work so that he could return to Reem. The trouble was that his ankle had been broken along with his leg, plus a few minor cuts that the healer felt compelled to fix—with Jameson being husband to their leader, it seemed like the right thing to him. So Edwin stood and walked to Jameson's side, gesturing for the healer to allow him to finish the work on Jameson.

"I'm sorry about him," Edwin whispered as Jameson stared up at him. "He means well, but he's not used to using his gifts so frequently—plus he wants to impress you," he said, laughing. "I can have you healed in a few moments."

"Thank you, Edwin," Jameson replied, letting out a sigh of relief. "I was worried I was going to have to teleport away while he was still trying to heal me."

"As I said, he means well." He laughed lightly, placing his hands on Jameson's leg. "It seems he's already finished here. You have a concussion though. You should sit up."

Jameson did as he was told, propping himself up on his elbows. "You can heal that, right?"

"It'll only take a moment." Edwin smiled, moving his hands to the top of Jameson's head, allowing his gifts to flow through his fingertips and into the man's body. "There," he whispered as he finished. "Apart from a few minor wounds, you're as good as new."

"Thank you." Jameson smiled brightly.

"Go get back to your wife." Edwin smiled back only seconds before Jameson teleported away.

Healer

Nicholas lifted Reem's head off the ground, resting it gently on his lap, while the healer attempted to help her cope with her exhaustion. He couldn't help but think that they were too late. Her body was beginning to shut down, and he didn't know what more could be done without Jameson's help.

Alexander had been pacing along the balcony the entire time, apparently concerned for both her and whomever he'd brought to the hospital in the first place. He didn't know what had happened, but he knew it wasn't good.

"Why don't you go see when Jameson will be here?" he asked.

"I believe he intended me to stay with you until he arrived," Alexander snapped.

"Well, then why don't you help us?"

"I don't know what to do." He shrugged.

"Actually, you're right—keep pacing." Nicholas nodded.

"How is she?" Jameson asked as he appeared on the balcony beside Alexander. "How is she, Nicholas?" he snapped, rushing to Reem's side.

"She's not well," Nicholas replied. "Are you well enough to give her more control? I think if she had the ability to rein in her gifts, we might be able to pull her out of this."

"I can try." He nodded. "Other than being exhausted, how is she?" he asked as he took Reem's hand in his, transferring more control into her veins through his palm.

"I've healed her ribs," the healer replied. "There wasn't much more that I could do for her—I can't cure her exhaustion."

"What can you do, Nicholas?" Jameson asked.

"I'm not going to lie, Jameson. If she can't control her gifts, she's not going to make it."

"Reem, listen to me," Jameson whispered, lifting her head off Nicholas's lap and propping her up against him. "You need to get your gifts back under your control," he continued. "Eliza needs you. I need you, Reem." Tears started to form in his eyes as he leaned in and kissed the top of her head. "You can't leave me like this," he whispered.

"Reem," Nicholas whispered, taking both of her hands in his while Jameson continued to cradle her in his arms. "I need you to take control of your gifts."

"Help me," she moaned, writhing in Jameson's arms. "Help me."

"Here," Jameson whispered as he transferred more control from his body into hers. "Can we move her?" he asked, looking up into his friend's eyes.

"I don't want to risk physically moving her, but if you're strong enough, you could teleport her to the hospital." Nicholas nodded. "I can have Alexander take me after you."

Jameson nodded silently before he teleported away.

"Alexander?" Nicholas whispered.

"No, I don't mind teleporting you back," Alexander replied as he stepped closer to Nicholas, placing his hand on the man's shoulder before he teleported back down into the hospital.

"Nicholas, I'm glad you're back," Edwin said, pulling Nicholas toward another patient before he could go to Reem's side. "She's been poisoned—by Marcus," he said gravely.

"I assume you've tried using your gifts to heal her?" Nicholas asked condescendingly.

"Of course I have," Edwin snapped. "It's not responding to my gifts"—he paused—"and I was hoping that you would have some sort of medication that would help."

"I'll see what I can do," Nicholas said, nodding. "Go tend to Reem."

"Yes, sir," Edwin replied. He walked toward where Reem lay with Jameson kneeling beside her. "What's wrong?" he asked.

"She's severely exhausted," Jameson replied.

"No other physical injuries?"

"We had a healer tend to her."

"How is she?" Alexander asked as he walked up behind Edwin and tapped his shoulder lightly. "Brittany—how is she?" he asked again when Edwin stared blankly toward him.

"Talk to Nicholas," Edwin replied. "I've been ordered to care for Reem."

"Thank you," Alexander replied, dipping his head slightly before he turned and walked to Brittany's side, taking her hand as he knelt at her bedside. "You're going to be fine," he whispered in her ear. "I promised Halaq that I wouldn't let anything happen to you, and I intend to keep that promise."

"Brittany?" A voice came from the stairwell behind Alexander.

Alexander turned toward the stairwell to see Seth rushing toward them, his eyes locked on the wound on her abdomen. "What happened?" he asked angrily.

"She was injected with something a few days ago," Alexander replied. "I brought her here ahead of the others to have her treated."

"Where did you find her?" he asked as he ran his fingers through her hair. "The last I saw her was in the middle of the desert."

"She was with Halaq in the Purist settlement," he replied.

"Who did this to her?" Seth whispered back as he took Brittany's other hand in his.

"Admiri," he breathed, unable to look Seth in the eyes.

"Why would he harm her?" he asked, confusion clear on his face as he examined her wound.

"She's . . . different," he whispered. "I don't know what happened, but she's not the witch of Admiri anymore. Though I'm not sure they got it right when they called her that in the first place."

"What do you mean?" His eyebrows furrowed.

"Inara's the real witch of Admiri." He shook his head. "I don't know how anyone could have ever called this woman his witch—not after she killed him."

"She killed him?" Seth asked, shifting his eyes to stare into Alexander's. "She killed Marcus Admiri?"

"That's what Halaq said, yes." He nodded.

"So then the rumors are true," he whispered, leaning back on his heels as he ran his fingers through his hair. "Inara has taken control of Admiri."

"I would assume so." Alexander nodded.

"How long has she been here? Why didn't anyone inform me?" he asked angrily.

"Only a few hours," he replied. "I didn't know where you were, or I would have told you myself."

"Let me through," Nicholas said, pushing Alexander away from Brittany's body. "Do you have any idea what she was injected with?"

"No, I'm sorry," Alexander said. "Can you help her?"

"I can try," he replied.

"You can't let her die, Nicholas," Seth whispered. "Please—she's my sister."

"I know who she is," Nicholas replied. "I will do my best to help her, but right now I need you both to give us some space. I'm expecting more wounded to be arriving within the hour—the war has started on the eastern front."

"So soon?" Seth whispered.

"I've seen it myself," Alexander replied.

"Have the Humans kept their word?"

"I don't know." Alexander shrugged.

"Nicholas!" Jameson screamed as Reem's body started to convulse on the bed. "Nicholas, help me!" he yelled.

Nicholas rushed to Reem's side, taking his medicine bag with him. "Reem," he whispered, "Reem, can you hear me?"

"What's happening?" Jameson asked.

Nicholas took a syringe from his bag and injected its contents into her thigh, finally letting out a heavy breath when her body stopped convulsing and her breathing returned to normal. "I think she's getting better," he whispered. "It seems these two both need more conventional methods of healing."

"What do you mean?" Jameson asked, his eyes flicking across the room to where Seth knelt at Brittany's side before they returned to Nicholas.

"That was another one of the medications developed in the settlement," he replied. "At this point, I can only hope that it's helping to treat the symptoms. As for Brittany, her illness seems to be one that was made to fight off the effects of the healing gift, making my job a little more difficult."

"Can you help her?" Seth asked, not looking away from Brittany's unconscious form.

"As I said, I'll do my best," Nicholas replied as he rejoined Seth. "I'm going to give her something to help with the pain. From there, I'll try to develop something for whatever Marcus gave her."

"Alright." Seth nodded slowly as Nicholas injected the contents of another syringe into Brittany's lower arm. "Why isn't she responding to healing?"

"Because Marcus is smarter than any of us thought," Nicholas replied, keeping his eyes on Brittany rather than meeting Seth's probing gaze.

"If you don't heal her, Halaq is going to kill me," Alexander whispered.

"Then why don't you give me some space and let me do my work?" Nicholas snapped. "Actually," he added, standing up to look Alexander in the eye, "you could take the healers to their designated areas in the city if you're looking for something to do."

"You're angry with me, aren't you?" he asked, suddenly realizing what was going on. "You think her death was my fault."

"Take the healers to the people, Alexander. They need to be ready for the wounded," he replied, pointing toward the staircase. "They're on the surface already."

"If you want me out of your way, then out of your way I'll be." He turned and walked up the stairs to join the healers on the surface.

"Where am I?" Brittany moaned, her eyes opening slowly. "Seth?" she whispered.

"It's alright, Brittany," Seth whispered, taking both of her hands in his. "I'm here."

"Where is he?" she asked as she started to sit up.

"No, no, no, lay back," Nicholas said, pushing her back down on the mattress. "I'm a doctor—I'm trying to help you."

"Where is Phillip?" she asked, her eyes wide with confusion and fear. "What's going on?"

"Alexander brought you here a few hours ago," Nicholas replied. "You were injected with something, remember? I'm trying to find a way to remove the poison from your system."

"Phillip?" Seth whispered.

"He sent me with Alexander?" she asked, ripping her hands away from Seth as she once again tried to sit up.

"Relax, Brittany," Seth ordered, pushing her back down onto the bed. "He'll be here, I promise you."

"You're in no position to promise me anything!" she snapped, tears beginning to fill her eyes.

"Can you sedate her or something?" Seth whispered to Nicholas.

"You're sure you want that?" Nicholas replied.

"She's not going to calm down unless you sedate her." He shook his head.

Nicholas nodded while Brittany continued to struggle in Seth's grasp. He found a sedative in his bag and filled a syringe with the liquid, taking Brittany's arm and cleaning the inside of her elbow before he injected the contents into her bloodstream. "Count backward from one hundred," he whispered.

"Let me go!" she shrieked, struggling even harder before the sedative finally took hold of her system. "Why are you doing this?" she whispered as she fell fast asleep.

"Thank you," Seth whispered. "Do you know how to treat her yet?"

"Had we gotten her here sooner, we could have tried sucking out the poison. But by now, we're just going to have to find something to combat it. I have a few different treatments I can try," he replied.

"Just don't let her die."

"Give me some time." He nodded slowly.

Seth brushed Brittany's hair away from her forehead, while Nicholas rummaged through his bags for the medicine. "What happened to Reem?" he asked, noticing for the first time the severe concern and worry written on Jameson's face.

Jameson knelt at Reem's bedside, unsure of what to do for her, while Edwin continually checked her vital signs and reassured him that everything would be fine. He couldn't help but think that these were the last hours he would spend with his wife.

"She appears to be getting stronger," Edwin whispered. "Has she woken at all?"

"Not since before I brought her here," Jameson replied. "Even then, I wasn't sure she was actually awake and not simply moaning in her sleep."

He nodded slowly. "How long has she been in this state?"

"She's been exhausted for several hours, but she collapsed only a few minutes before I brought her here," he replied. "Is that good or bad?"

"Neither," he whispered. "It would have been better if she hadn't been exhausted," he said. "But we'll do the best we can."

Alexander made quick work of the task Nicholas had set before him, and now it was time for him to do what he'd come to do. He took Suri's body from the house where he'd left it and brought her to the tower where the heroes of the city were burned after their deaths. Suri had every right to be given a funeral of the heroes.

The room was set apart from the rest of the tower, set off to the north side of the building. Inside was a marble funeral pyre decorated in the writing of old and covered with the ashes of those who were remembered before her. Along the wall were placed several bundles of wood and bottles of oil prepared for the funeral processes seen in this room. The room was lit by five torches arranged all around the pyre, ready to be used in the funeral.

He placed her body on the pyre and surrounded it with bundles of wood before he lifted a bottle of oil and ceremoniously poured it over her body and the wood that surrounded it. He removed the cloth from her face and leaned in to kiss her forehead one last time before he retrieved a torch and threw it on the fire, falling to his knees as he screamed in pain and anger at his loss.

He watched as her body burned before him, tears streaming down his face. He hated that he had to give her the ceremony on his own, but he knew that neither Reem nor Jameson would be able to perform it until it was too late. Her body was decaying, and the ceremony had to be done now.

As he watched the fire consume Suri's body, he allowed himself to slump to the ground, fully consumed by his own sadness and grief.

Awakening

Nicholas slowly injected the contents of yet another syringe into Reem's thigh, glad that she'd made it through the night. Her condition seemed to be cycling through deterioration and recuperation, and the drugs were only helping on a short-term basis. All he could do was hope that she would be able to take control of her gifts so that he could actually get his work done.

Brittany, on the other hand, was beginning to show signs of improvement. The swelling in her abdomen was starting to go down, and the redness was fading slightly. Her breathing was starting to return to normal, but he knew she wasn't out of the woods yet. He'd been treating her with multiple medicines they'd developed in the settlement, and it seemed that they were at least helping with her symptoms. He didn't know if the poison was leaving her system yet or not, but he hoped that he was helping instead of making things worse.

The only trouble was that in his line of work, things could go from good to bad very quickly.

"How is she, Nicholas?" Jameson asked as he returned to Reem's bedside with Eliza cradled in his arms.

"Better at the moment," he replied. "How's the little one?"

"She misses her mother," he whispered. "Has she woken up at all?"

"No, not yet. But she does appear to be having some sort of vivid dream—her eyes are moving rapidly," he said, gesturing toward her closed eyelids. "I'm doing everything I can, but she still hasn't fully taken control of her gifts."

"She will," Jameson said, nodding slowly as he stared at Reem's unconscious form. "Thank you, Nicholas. I know this has been hard for you as well."

"You two are the closest thing I have to a family. I don't want to lose you."

"You won't," he replied. "She's going to make it through this."

He smiled slightly. "I just have to help her get there."

"And Brittany?" Jameson asked as Seth descended the staircase and entered the room. He'd left during the night to check on the status of their army, seeing as the three people that made up the majority of the government had been in the hospital since shortly after the war had started.

"I've been giving her a poison treatment that I developed in the settlement, and she seems like she's getting better. But with poisons like this, you don't know until the patient either dies or is physically able to walk away," Nicholas replied. "But I'm feeling optimistic today." He smiled brightly.

"I'll keep an eye on her," he whispered back. "Go check on Brittany."

Nicholas nodded slowly and walked toward where Seth now sat on the floor beside Brittany's bed. "She appears to be getting better," he said as he dropped to one knee at Brittany's side. "But she's not out of the woods yet."

"The swelling's gone down," Seth replied, nodding hopefully.

"It appears that her deterioration has slowed as well, but I don't know enough about the poison to accurately tell you if she's going to make it or not," he said, his tone completely businesslike as he checked her heart rate and blood pressure.

"Do you think I'll miss anything if I oversee things for a few more hours?" he asked, his eyes staring up at Nicholas.

"I think I'll be able to handle it," Nicholas said, nodding. "If you don't mind, I'd like to know how the other healers are doing."

"I'll send someone to find out," he replied. "Let me know if her condition changes. I'll post a messenger outside for you," he added as he stood back to his feet.

"Of course," Nicholas said, gesturing toward the exit. "You know, Jameson, you could join Seth in overseeing everything," he added loudly as Seth disappeared up the ladder.

"She's the one who should be overseeing everything—not me," he whispered.

"Reem seemed to think that you were up to the task," he added.

"Do you really think she's going to make it?"

"I'll do everything I can to make sure she does." At that, they were silent, Jameson leaning against the wall beside Reem, with Eliza crying in his arms and Nicholas shuffling through his bag for Reem's medication.

"I'm going to walk with her. Let me know if anything changes," Jameson whispered as he carried Eliza up the steps.

A few moments later, Nicholas found what he was looking for and returned to Reem's side, lifting her arm to clean it, when he realized her eyes were open and staring into his. "Reem," he whispered, shock edging his voice.

"Nicholas," she whispered back, smiling slightly.

"You're awake." His eyes widened, as her smile faded completely.

"Did I hurt anyone?" she asked, seemingly unaware of what had previously happened. "Are Jameson and Eliza alright?"

"As far as I know, you didn't hurt anyone who didn't have it coming," he replied as he cleared his mind and proceeded to clean the inside of her elbow. "Sorry if this hurts," he added as he injected the syringe's contents into her bloodstream.

"What was that?" she asked flatly as her eyes flickered around the room, surveying her surroundings.

"Just something to help your body cope," he replied. "Jameson's on the surface. Would you like me to get him for you?"

She nodded slightly, her face an image of shock and confusion as she continued to survey her surroundings. "Please," she whispered.

"I'll be right back," he replied. "You'll be alright for a moment?"

"Yes," she whispered, her eyes turning toward the exit before he finally made his way up to the surface.

A few moments later, he returned with the crying Eliza in his arms and Jameson at his side. "She woke up a few moments after you left," Nicholas said as they descended the staircase.

Jameson smiled as he knelt at her bedside. "How do you feel?" he asked as he took her hand in his, surprised when her fingers remained limp in his grasp.

"What happened?" she asked blankly, her eyes staring into his.

"What's the last thing you remember?" he asked.

"Suri," she whispered, as her eyes filled with tears. "Inara killed her."

"I know, I know," he whispered as he leaned in to kiss her forehead. "I was there"—he paused—"and you lost control of your gifts."

"Is that why I can't move?" she asked.

"You can't move?" Nicholas asked as he sat beside her. "You moved your head a moment ago. Can you do anything more than that?"

"I can move my shoulders a little," she whispered as her eyes shifted toward his. "What's happening to me?"

"You severely exhausted yourself, Reem," he replied. "It's possible that this is your body's way of forcing you to get some rest." He paused, handing Eliza back to her father. "I haven't had a patient wake up after that much exhaustion before. I don't know what to expect here."

"Can you give her something to help?" Jameson asked, his eyes shifting back and forth between Reem and Nicholas.

"Chances are she'll regain control of her body in a few days to a few weeks. I think we should continue to treat the preexisting symptoms until we know more."

Jameson opened his mouth to respond, when Reem cut him off. "I trust him, Jameson," she whispered.

"I've already given her the medication, so I suggest that we simply wait and see how she's feeling when it's time for the next dose," Nicholas replied. "Two hours or so."

"Are you sure about this?" Jameson asked as he brushed Reem's hair away from her face.

"No, I'm not," he replied honestly.

"So you have no idea what you're doing?" he asked.

"I'm doing my best," Nicholas replied. "I think it's best that we wait and see how she feels in a few hours."

"Listen to him," Reem whispered.

"Give us a moment, Nicholas," Jameson ordered.

"Of course." He nodded slightly as he stood and walked back to Brittany, taking a seat on the mattress beside her.

"How's my baby?" Reem smiled nervously as Jameson set Eliza beside her.

"Better than her mother, I'm afraid," Jameson whispered. "You don't remember anything that happened?" he asked as he moved to sit beside her.

"I remember thinking I didn't want you to find me, but I don't know why." She shook her head slightly. "You have no idea how strange this feels."

He leaned in to kiss her forehead, his eyes filled with sadness as he stared down at her. "I'm so sorry."

"It's not your fault, Jameson," she replied. "None of this is your fault. I shouldn't have lost control like that."

"You have more power than anyone I've ever met." He smiled slightly and reached out to stroke her cheek as his eyes stared into hers. "I should have been able to help you when it happened—I shouldn't have let it happen."

"I'm the one who should have been more careful," she whispered. "Stop blaming yourself." She paused, turning to kiss his hand. "Who's Nicholas treating?" she asked when she noticed him pacing across the room.

"Seth's sister," he replied. "Alexander brought her here—apparently, Marcus injected her with some form of poison while she and Halaq were dispatching him."

"They found a way to cure her?" she asked, her eyes lighting up.

"Apparently so." He smiled.

"Why doesn't he have a healer work on her?"

"They've tried—Marcus seems to have developed this particular poison to combat the healers' gifts," he replied. "You should be getting rest, Reem."

"I don't have a choice but to rest," she said, laughing quietly. "I just want to know what I missed while I was . . . out of control."

"Can you feel anything?" he asked, sliding his hand down to her waist. "Or are you just immobile?"

"I can feel you." She blushed as his hand moved to her hip. "I just can't move."

"I love you," he whispered, moving his hand to run his fingers through her hair.

"Jameson?" she whispered.

"What do you need?" he asked.

"Kiss me." She smiled as he leaned down to kiss her lips. "I love you too," she whispered as he moved to kiss her forehead.

"I heard you were awake." Seth smiled brightly as he climbed down the ladder. "How is the mighty Reem Kahrin?"

"Other than being unable to move, she seems alright," Nicholas answered from beside Brittany. "I'd like to limit visiting hours, but I don't think she'd appreciate it." He laughed.

"It's good to see you awake," Seth said, ignoring Nicholas's comments as he walked to her bedside. "How are you feeling?"

"Confused, tired, immobile," she said.

"She should be resting—not talking up a storm," Nicholas said as he joined them. "I'm alright with Jameson staying here—so long as you don't disturb her sleep—but Seth and Eliza should go," he ordered in his most professional tone of voice.

"Why Eliza?" Reem asked.

"If she starts crying, she's going to make your stress greater," Nicholas replied. "Seth, would you mind taking her to the nursery? Peter knows how to take care of her."

"Of course." Seth smiled as Jameson lifted Eliza off the mattress and handed her to him. "She's sleeping—I can handle that." He laughed lightly as he walked back up the steps. "I'll make sure no one else bothers you."

"Thank you, Seth," Nicholas replied loudly as Seth disappeared up the ladder. "Now then, give her some space. She needs to sleep," he told Jameson.

Reem smiled slightly as Jameson lifted his hands in defeat and settled onto the floor beside her bed. "I hope you don't mind if I get some sleep myself," he said.

"Not at all," Nicholas replied as he rejoined Brittany.

"But if you snore, I'll have Nicholas hit you."

Life

Two weeks later . . .

Reem sat up in bed, finally able to move her arms and upper torso enough that she could sit comfortably on the mattress. On the floor beside her, Jameson slept soundly, his surprisingly light snoring like music to her ears as she watched Nicholas and Halaq hover over Brittany's still-unconscious form. She could see the concern and care in Nicholas's eyes as he attempted to treat her and the devotion written on Halaq's face as he held her hand.

Brittany had woken a few times since they'd last sedated her, but Nicholas had determined it was safer to keep her sedated during the remainder of her treatment—the last time she woke, she almost killed her brother with her bare hands. It seemed that whatever Marcus had given her was determined to hold on until it had no choice but to give up and die—in some ways, it was similar to a life-form in that it wanted to live on inside her. Reem couldn't help but think that maybe her healing gifts would be able to save Brittany, that maybe that was all it would take, but she knew that she was in no condition to heal anyone until she was rested enough to at least stand on her own two feet.

She'd been out of the hospital a few times over the past week, though the entire time she'd been in either Jameson's or Seth's arms. She'd developed the ability to move her arms a few days after she woke, but full torso mobility hadn't come until two days ago. On the brightest side of all, she was now down to one dose of medication every four to five hours, something that her arms greatly appreciated. She sighed quietly as she tried to remember what it felt like to stand on her own power—to no avail. There was no comparison to the actual feeling of standing on her own feet, and she wished that she could feel the sensation once more.

"Are you alright?" Nicholas asked, his gaze shifting toward her at the sound of her sigh. "Do you need me to get you anything?"

"No, I'm fine." She smiled, wishing that he could grant her the ability to use her legs once again.

Her smile soon faded as Nicholas turned back to Brittany, his eyes fixed on the wound on her abdomen. The swelling had gone down a fair deal as far as she could tell, but something was still worrying him. She didn't know what it was, but she guessed that until she got her legs back, she would be powerless to help him.

Jameson's snore started to pick up in volume, and Nicholas once again shifted his gaze toward her. "Can you wake him up or something?" he asked. He laughed lightly when she reached out and flicked Jameson's forehead, causing him to slam his head into the wall behind it.

"Ow . . . ," Jameson moaned as he rubbed the back of his head. "How loud was I?" He laughed.

"Loud enough for Nicholas to lose his concentration," Reem replied, running her fingers through his hair. "Though it doesn't take much to do that."

"Did you get any sleep?" he asked as he moved to sit beside her on the mattress. "You look even more exhausted than yesterday."

"I'm fine, Jameson," she replied. "I promise."

"Why is it that you'll tell Nicholas if something's wrong, but you won't tell me?" he asked, reaching out to push her hair behind her ear. "Shouldn't it be the other way around?"

"I don't want you to worry," she whispered. "But really, Jameson, I'm fine. I just need to get out of this place for a while."

"Do you want me to take you to the surface?"

"No, no—I mean, I need to get out of here on my own feet." She smiled.

"That could take a while." He smiled back, leaning in to kiss her forehead. "But I can take you outside for a few hours if you'd like."

She nodded slowly, her smile growing brighter as he placed one arm behind her back and the other under her legs to lift her off the mattress. "You don't mind, do you, Nicholas?" she asked as Jameson picked her up.

"Fine by me—just have her back before I need to give her the medication," Nicholas replied.

"Will do," Jameson said as he teleported to the surface, smiling brightly when Reem wrapped her arms around his neck. "Where to, my love?" he asked as they landed.

"Anywhere that isn't here." She laughed.

"Let's go see Eliza." He smiled back. "I think she misses seeing her mother." He paused as he started walking. "Walk or teleport?"

"Walk," she replied before leaning in to kiss his cheek lightly. "So long as it doesn't start raining," she added when she noticed the dark clouds above their heads.

"What, you don't want to get wet?" He laughed as he picked up his pace.

"Not especially." She leaned her head on his shoulder as he carried her. "Have you heard anything from Seth—about the war?" she asked.

"They've suffered more casualties than we have," he replied. "We've got Alexander and Angel running teams outside to attack them from behind, but

Seth seems to think they're catching on. The forests are making it difficult to tell who's who."

"What about the Humans?" she questioned, her eyebrows furrowing slightly.

"So far, they haven't shown up. Seth thinks that they decided it wasn't worth it—they want to be Advanced, so they don't want to side with them," he replied.

"I should've known," she whispered as they started up the stairs. "They still believe they're fighting for Marcus."

"It seems that way, yes," he replied. "They're fighting like they always do—fighting hard and to the death. Seth says they've suffered at least twice the casualties that we have—but we are on home soil. We know the lay of the land better than they do, and we know how they fight."

"And they have no idea what to expect from us." She smiled as they stepped into the main chamber, laughing when she saw the raindrops start to fall to the ground outside. "Good timing," she whispered in his ear.

"Eliza will be happy to see you," he whispered back as he stepped into the nursery, carrying Reem across to the crib. "Can you sit up on your own, or should I take you to one of the bedrooms?"

"I think I can sit in the chair." She nodded.

He smiled as he carried her to the chair and gently eased her down, carefully placing her in a position where she could sit up on her own. "Comfortable?" he asked.

"Very," she replied.

He nodded and walked to the crib, peering down at his smiling baby girl before he gently lifted her and took her to Reem. "Hi, Mommy," he whispered, smiling brightly as Reem took Eliza into her arms.

"Hi, baby." Reem smiled. "Did you miss me?"

"Not as much as I did," he whispered as he kissed her forehead.

"I love you," she said, smiling up at him.

⁂

Halaq knelt beside Brittany's frail form, holding tightly on to her hand while Nicholas injected his medicine into her abdomen near the original injection site. They'd been treating her for two weeks already, feeding her through a tube since it wasn't safe to keep her awake. The last time she'd woken, she'd tried to kill Seth; and since then, they'd been keeping her fully sedated. Occasionally, her eyes would open, but she wasn't the same person he'd sent here with Alexander. She wasn't even the witch of Admiri—she was no one, nothing, an empty shell lying on the mattress in front of him.

"She's getting better," Nicholas whispered. "At least, she's getting stronger."

"What if she doesn't get better?" Halaq whispered, unwilling to look away from Brittany. "The last time she woke up, I didn't even recognize her voice,

Nicholas. She wasn't the same person—what if she won't be the same person again?"

"She will be," Nicholas replied. "She is getting better. Her breathing is getting steadier, and her heart rate is returning to normal." He paused, standing to his feet to return the syringe to his bag. "If I had to guess, she'll be up and about by the end of the week—sooner more likely."

"So soon?" he asked, finally shifting his gaze toward Nicholas. "She doesn't look like she's getting any better."

"That's because you're not a doctor," Nicholas said, laughing lightly. "I, on the other hand, am." He paused as he returned to Brittany's side, taking a seat across Halaq. "Would you like me to wake her up? The sedatives should be wearing off soon."

"Do you think that's a good idea?" His eyes widened.

"It can't hurt," he said, shrugging. "You want to know if she's actually getting better, and having her awake might be the best way for you to do that. The last time she was fully awake was a week ago. By now she should be able to control herself," he said.

"If you're sure." Halaq nodded.

"Shouldn't take too long. I didn't give her the last dose," Nicholas said, smiling. "You can try waking her up yourself if you'd like."

Halaq nodded again and reached out his hand to stroke Brittany's cheek. "Brittany," he whispered, "wake up." He ran his fingers through her hair, trying his best to gently wake her. He smiled brightly as her eyes started to flutter open. "Welcome back," he whispered.

"Where am I?" she groaned, trying to sit up.

"No, no, relax," Nicholas whispered. "Don't try to move."

"Who are you?" she asked, her eyes snapping open nervously.

"My name's Nicholas. I'm a doctor," he replied. "You tried to kill me once."

She groaned. "I've tried to kill a lot of people—most of them are dead now."

"So I've heard." He laughed lightly. "How do you feel?"

"Like I've been injected with poison," she muttered. "How long have I been here?"

"Just over two weeks," Halaq replied. "How do you feel compared with how you felt before Alexander brought you here?"

"Better, I think," she said.

"You're still running a fever, but not as high as before," Nicholas added. "I still don't want you to go anywhere for a couple of weeks, but I think you should be feeling one hundred percent soon."

"Thank you." Her eyes brightened.

"I'll be right back," he replied as he stood and made his way to the staircase, where rain continued to pour through the opening in the ceiling. "There's someone else who will want to see you."

"I'm sorry I made you leave," Halaq whispered. "I know you hated it."

"You were right," she whispered back, linking her fingers with his.

"It's good to see you awake again," Seth beamed as he climbed down into the room, followed by Nicholas, both of them soaked with rainwater.

"Seth," she said, "it's good to see you as well."

"I take it you're not going to try and kill me this time." He laughed as he knelt beside her.

"I'll try not to." She winked.

Before Seth could open his mouth to respond, Jameson teleported inside the hospital with Reem in his arms, smiling brightly when he noticed Seth and Nicholas covered in rainwater. "Miss us?" he asked.

"Not nearly as much as you'd think," Nicholas joked.

"Glad to see you're awake." Reem smiled toward Brittany. "We were worried about you."

"Were you poisoned too?" she asked as Jameson gently laid Reem down on her mattress, propping her up with a few pillows.

"No, I had exhaustion problems," Reem replied. "At the moment, it looks like it'll be a few weeks before I'm able to stand again."

"At least you'll have some company." She smiled brightly.

Six months later . . .

Kari screamed in pain, making both Reem and Jameson cringe as they waited outside her home. Edwin had rushed into the tower in the middle of the night, pulling Nicholas out of bed on the pretense that Kari's water had broken. Once the sun had come up, Reem and Jameson hurried over to Kari's home to make sure everything was all right.

Now they were outside waiting for Nicholas to finish delivering the child. It seemed that Kari was having a much harder time with this than Reem had all those months ago, and Reem was just glad that Edwin was inside to help her along with Nicholas.

"How is she?" Brittany asked as she and Halaq joined them outside Kari's home.

"I don't know much yet," Reem replied. "From what I can tell, the baby will be here in a few moments"—she paused—"but I don't know if Kari's going to make it or not. Her heartbeat is very weak."

"Should we go inside?" Brittany asked.

"Nicholas prefers to work alone," Reem said. "Besides, he has Edwin to help him."

Inside, Nicholas lifted the crying baby into his arms. "It's a boy," he whispered. "Do you have a name picked out?"

"Shane," Kari whispered. "His name is Shane." Her breathing was labored by her erratic heartbeat, the life draining from her veins even as Edwin attempted to heal her. "Don't," she whispered, reaching up to knock his hands away from her. "Take care of him," she ordered.

"I'm not going to let you die," Edwin replied, taking her hand in his as he once again attempted to heal her.

Nicholas set Shane in the crib a few feet away from the bed before he returned to Kari's side and took her other hand, checking for a pulse. "Don't do this," he whispered angrily.

"She can't be dead," Edwin breathed, dropping her hand as he stepped back, tears forming in his eyes. "I promised him I wouldn't let anything happen to her."

"I'm sorry," Nicholas whispered as he stepped away. "I can't bring her back when she doesn't want to live." He shook his head, holding his hands up in defense when Edwin approached him angrily. "You know as well as I do that she didn't want to have this baby and that she certainly didn't want to raise it herself. She didn't want to live with that responsibility, Edwin," he shouted before the man locked his hands around his neck. "You know you won't kill me."

Edwin screamed in anger as he released Nicholas, turning to punch the wall before he walked out of the house as quickly as he could, passing the others outside before they could even speak a word.

"What happened?" Reem asked as she walked inside to find Nicholas rubbing his throat, the baby shrieking in its crib, and Kari's limp form on her bed.

"She's gone," he whispered as he dropped to his knees onto the ground.

"Who's this little guy?" Brittany smiled brightly as she lifted the baby out of the crib. "Shh shh shh shh shh," she whispered. "It's okay, baby, it's okay." She bounced the baby in her arms, trying to quiet his cries.

"He'll need a mother," Nicholas said. "I know Kari wanted Edwin to take care of him, but I don't think he'll do it."

Reem walked to Nicholas's side and placed her hand on his shoulder, closing her eyes as she checked his body for wounds and healed the bruises that were beginning to form around his neck. "We'll find him a family," she whispered.

Brittany's smile brightened as she turned to Halaq, waiting for him to shrug his shoulders before she turned back to Nicholas. "We'll take care of him," she said. "Did she name him?"

"Shane." Nicholas nodded. "His name is Shane."